THE FU MANCHU OMNIBUS

VOLUME 3

THE AUTHOR

Sax Rohmer was the pen name of Arthur Sarsfield Ward, who was born in Birmingham in 1866 of Irish parents. For many years he lived in New York. He worked as a journalist on Fleet Street before he made his name as the creator of the Dr Fu Manchu thrillers.
He died in 1959.

THE
FU MANCHU
OMNIBUS

VOLUME 3

Sax Rohmer

THE TRAIL OF FU MANCHU

PRESIDENT FU MANCHU

RE-ENTER DR FU MANCHU

This omnibus edition first published in Great Britain in 1998 by
Allison & Busby Ltd
114 New Cavendish Street
London W1M 7FD

Reprinted 2000

The Trail of Fu Manchu first published in the USA in 1934
by PF Collier & Son Corporation
by special arrangement with
Doubleday, Doran & Company, Inc.
President Fu Manchu first published in Great Britain in 1936
by Cassell & Company Ltd.
Re-enter Dr Fu Manchu first published in Great Britain in 1957
by Herbert Jenkins Ltd.

A catalogue record for this book is available from the
British Library

ISBN 0 74900 227 1

Designed and typeset by N-J Design Associates
Romsey, Hampshire
Printed and bound in Great Britain by
Mackays of Chatham plc

THE TRAIL OF
FU MANCHU

CONTENTS

Ch. 1 The Great Fog
Ch. 2 The Porcelain Venus
Ch. 3 Sterling's story
Ch. 4 Pietro Ambroso's Studio
Ch. 5 P.C. Ireland Is Uneasy
Ch. 6 Dr. Norton's Patient
Ch. 7 Lash Marks
Ch. 8 Fog in High Places
Ch. 9 The Tomb of the Demurases
Ch. 10 The Mark of Kali
Ch. 11 Sam Pak of Limehouse
Ch. 12 London River
Ch. 13 A Tongue of Fire
Ch. 14 At Sam Pak's
Ch. 15 A Lighted Window
Ch. 16 A Burning Ghat
Ch. 17 The Game Flies West
Ch. 18 "I Belong to China"
Ch. 19 Rowan House
Ch. 20 Gold
Ch. 21 Gallaho and Sterling Set out
Ch. 22 Gallaho Runs
Ch. 32 Fleurette
Ch. 24 The Lacquer Room
Ch. 25 Curari
Ch. 26 Dr. Fu Manchu
Ch. 27 The Pit and the Furnace
Ch. 28 Tunnel Below Water
Ch. 29 At The Blue Anchor
Ch. 30 The Hunchback
Ch. 31 The Si-Fan
Ch. 32 Iron Doors

Ch. 33 Daughter of the Manchus
Ch. 34 More Iron Doors
Ch. 35 The Furnace
Ch. 36 Dim Roaring
Ch. 37 Chinese Justice
Ch. 38 The Blue Light
Ch. 39 The Lotus Gate
Ch. 40 A Fight to the Death
Ch. 41 The Last Bus
Ch. 42 Nayland Smith Refuses
Ch. 43 Catastrophe
Ch. 44 At Scotland Yard
Ch. 45 The Match Seller
Ch. 46 Gallaho Explores
Ch. 47 The Waterspout
Ch. 48 Gallaho Brings up the Rear
Ch. 49 Waiting
Ch. 50 The Night Watchman
Ch. 51 Night Watchman's Story
Ch. 52 "I Am Calling You"
Ch. 53 Powers of Dr. Fu Manchu
Ch. 54 Gallaho Explores Further
Ch. 55 Mimosa
Ch. 56 Ibrahim
Ch. 57 A Call for Petrie
Ch. 58 John Ki
Ch. 59 Limehouse
Ch. 60 Dr. Petrie's Patient
Ch. 61 The Crosslands' Flat
Ch. 62 Companion Crossland
Ch. 63 A Lacquer Cabinet

Chapter 1

THE GREAT FOG

"WHO'S THERE?"

P.C. Ireland raised his red lantern, staring with smarting eyes through moving wreaths of yellow mist. Visibility was nil. This was the great fog of 1934—the worst in memory.

No one replied—there was no sound.

The constable shook himself, and settled the lantern down at his feet, flapped his arms in an endeavour to restore circulation. This chilliness was not wholly physical. Something funny was going on—something he didn't like. He stood quite still again, listening.

Three times he had heard that sound resembling nothing so much as the hard breathing of some animal. Quite close to him in the fog—some furtive thing that crept by stealthily. . . . And now, he heard it again.

"Who's there?" he challenged, snatching up the red lamp.

None answered. The sound ceased—if it had ever existed.

Traffic had been brought to a standstill some hours before; pedestrians there were none. King fog held the city of London in bondage. The silence was appalling. P.C. Ireland felt as though he was enveloped in a wet blanket from head to feet.

"I'll go and have another look," he muttered.

He began to grope his way up a short, semicircular drive to the door of a house. He had no idea what danger threatened Professor Ambroso, but he knew that he would be in for a bad time from the inspector if any one entered or left the professor's house unchallenged. . . .

His foot struck the bottom of the three steps which led up to the door. Ireland mounted slowly; but not until his red lamp was almost touching the woodwork, could he detect the fact that the door was closed. He stood there awhile listening, but could hear nothing. He groped his way back to his post at the gate.

The police 'phone box was not fifty yards away; he would have welcomed any excuse to call up the station; to establish

1

contact with another human being—to be where there was some light other than the dim red glow of his lantern, which, sometimes when he set it down, resembled, seen through the moving clouds of mist, the baleful eyes of a monster glaring up at him.

He regained the gate and put the lantern down. He wondered when, if ever, he would be relieved. Discipline was all very well, but on occasions like this damned fog, when men who ought to have been in bed were turned out, a quiet smoke was the next best thing to a drink.

He groped under his oilskin cape for the packet, took out a cigarette and lighted it. He felt for the coping beside the gate and sat down. The fog appeared to be getting denser. Then in a flash he was on his feet again.

"*Who's there?*" he shouted.

Stooping, he snatched up the red lantern and began to grope his way towards the other end of the semicircular drive.

"I can see you!" he cried, slightly reassured by the sound of his own voice—"don't try any funny business with *me!*"

He bumped into the half-open gate, and pulled up, listening. Silence. He had retained his cigarette, and now he replaced it between his lips. It was the blasted fog, of course, that was getting on his nerves. He was beginning to imagine things. It wouldn't do at all. But he sincerely wished that Waterlow would come along to relieve him, knowing in his heart of hearts that Waterlow hadn't one chance in a thousand of finding the point.

"Stick there till you're relieved," had been the inspector's order.

"All-night job for me," Ireland murmured, sadly.

What was the matter with this old bloke, Ambroso? He leaned against the gate and reflected. It was something about a valuable statue that somebody wanted to pinch, or something. Ireland found it difficult to imagine why anyone should want to steal a statue. The silence was profound—uncanny. To one used to the bombilation of London, even in the suburbs, it seemed unnatural. He had more than half smoked his cigarette when—there it was again!

Heavy breathing and a vague shuffling sound.

Ireland dropped his cigarette and snatched up his lantern.

2

He made a surprising spring in the direction of the sound.

"Come here, damn you!" he shouted. "What the hell's the game?"

And this time he had a glimpse of—something!

It rather shook him. It might have been a crouching man, or it might have been an animal. It was very dim, just touched by the outer glow of his lantern. But Ireland was no weakling. He made another surprising leap, one powerful hand outstretched. The queer shape sprang aside and was lost again in the fog.

"What the hell is it?" Ireland muttered.

Aware again of that unaccountable chill, he peered around him holding the lantern up. He had lost his bearings. Where the devil was the house? He made a rapid calculation, turned about and began to walk slowly forward. He walked for some time in this manner, till his outstretched hand touched a railing. He had crossed to the verge of the Common.

He was on the wrong side of the road.

His back to the railings, he set out again. He estimated that he was half-way across, when:

"Help!" came a thin, muffled scream—the voice of a woman. "For God's sake help me!"

The cry came from right ahead. P.C. Ireland moved more rapidly, grinding his teeth together. He had not been wrong—there *was* something funny going on. It might be murder. And, his heart beating fast, and all his training urging "*hurry—hurry!*" he could only crawl along. By sheer good luck he bumped into the half open gate of the semicircular drive.

Evidently that cry had come from the house.

He moved forward more confidently—he was familiar with the route. Presently, a dim light glowed through the wet blanket of the fog. The door was open.

Ireland stumbled up the steps and found himself in a large lobby, brightly lighted. Fog streamed in behind him like the fetid breath of some monstrous dragon. There were pictures and statuettes; thick carpet on the floor; rugs and a wide staircase leading upwards. It was very warm. A coal fire had burned low in an open grate on one side of the lobby.

"Hello there!" he shouted. "I'm a police officer. Who called?"

There was no answer.

"Hi!" Ireland yelled at the top of his voice. "Is there anyone at home?"

He stood still, listening. A piece of coal dropped from the fire onto the tiled hearth. Ireland started. The house was silent—as silent as the fog-bound streets outside, and great waves of clammy mist were pouring in at the open door.

The constable put down his red lantern on a little coffee table, and then he began to look about him apprehensively. Then he walked to the foot of the stairs and trumpeted through cupped hands:

"Is there anyone there?"

Silence.

He was uncertain of his duty. Furthermore, this brightly lighted but apparently empty house was even more perturbing than the silence of the Common. A telephone stood on a ledge, not a yard from the coffee table. Ireland took up the instrument.

A momentary pause, during which he kept glancing apprehensively about him, and then:

"Wandsworth police station—urgent!" he said. "Police calling."

4

CHAPTER 2

THE PORCELAIN VENUS

THAT PHENOMENAL FOG which over a great part of Europe heralded and ushered in the New Year, was responsible for many
things that were strange and many that were horrible.
Amongst the latter the wreck of the Paris-Strasbourg express
and the tragic crash of an Imperial Airways liner. The triumphant fog demon was responsible, also, for the present
predicament of P.C. Ireland.

A big car belonging to the Flying Squad of Scotland Yard,
and provided with special fog lights, stood outside
Wandsworth police station. And in the divisional-inspector's
office a conversation was taking place which, could P.C.
Ireland have heard it, would have made that intelligent officer realize the importance of his solitary vigil.

Divisional-inspector Watford was a grey-haired, distinguished looking man of military bearing. He sat behind a
large desk looking alternately from one to the other of his two
visitors. Of these, one, Chief-inspector Gallaho, of the C.I.D.,
was well known to every officer in the Metropolitan police
force. A thick-set, clean-shaven man, of florid colouring and
truculent expression, buttoned up in a blue overcoat and
wearing a rather wide-brimmed bowler hat. He stood, resting
one elbow upon the mantelpiece and watching the man who
had come with him from Scotland Yard.

The latter, tall, lean, and of that dully dark complexion
which tells of long residence in the tropics, wore a leather
overcoat over a very shabby tweed suit. He was hatless, and
his close-cropped, crisply waving grey hair excited the envy of
the district inspector. His own hair was of that colour but had
been deserting him for many years. The man in the leather
overcoat was smoking a pipe, and restlessly walking up and
down the office floor.

The divisional inspector was somewhat awed by his second
visitor, who was none other than ex-Assistant Commissioner
Sir Denis Nayland Smith. Something very big was afoot.

Suddenly pulling up in front of the desk, Sir Denis took his pipe from between his teeth, and:

"Did you ever hear of Dr. Fu Manchu?" he jerked, fixing his keen eyes upon Watford.

"Certainly, sir," said the latter, looking up in a startled way. "My predecessor in this division was actually concerned in the case, I believe, a number of years ago. For my own part"—he smiled slightly—"I have always regarded him as a sort of name—what you might term a trade-mark."

"Trade-mark?" echoed Nayland Smith. "What do you mean? That there's no such person?"

"Something of the kind, sir. I mean, isn't Fu Manchu really the name for a sort of political organization, like the Mafia—or the Black Hand?"

Nayland Smith laughed shortly, and glanced at the man from Scotland Yard.

"He is chief of such an organization," he replied, "but the organization itself has another name. There is a Dr. Fu Manchu—and Dr. Fu Manchu *is* in London. That's why I'm here to-night."

The inspector stared hard for a moment, and then:

"Indeed, sir!" he murmured. "And may I take it that there's some connection between this Fu Manchu and Professor Ambroso?"

"I don't know," Nayland Smith snapped, "but I intend to find out to-night. What can you tell me about the professor? He lives in your area."

"He does, sir." The inspector nodded. "He has a large house and studio on the North Side of the Common. We have had orders for several days to afford him special protection."

Nayland Smith nodded, replacing his pipe between his teeth.

"Personally, I've never seen him, and I've never seen any of his work. He's a bit outside my province. But I understand that although he's an Italian by birth, he is a naturalized British subject. What he wants protection for, is beyond me. In fact, I should be glad to know, if anyone can tell me."

Sir Denis glanced at the Scotland Yard man.

"Bring the inspector up-to-date," he directed; "he's evidently rather in the dark."

Watford, resting his arms on the table, stared at the celebrated detective, enquiringly.

"Well, it's like this," Gallaho began in a low, rumbling voice. "If it means anything to you, I'll begin by admitting that it means nothing to me. Professor Ambrose has been abroad for some time supervising the making of a new kind of statue at the Sèvres works, outside Paris. It's a life-sized figure, I understand, and more or less life coloured. Since the matter was brought to my notice, I have been looking up newspaper reports and it appears that the thing has created a bit of a sensation in artistic circles. Well, the professor took it down to an international exhibition held in Nice. This exhibition closed a week ago, and the figure, which is called 'The Sleeping Venus', was brought back to Paris, and from Paris to London."

"Did the professor come along too?"

"Yes. And in Paris he asked for police protection."

"What for?"

"Don't ask me—I'm asking you. The French sent a man down to Boulogne on the train in which the thing was transported—then we took over on this side. There's a man on duty outside his house now, isn't there?"

"Yes. And the fog's so dense it's impossible to relieve him."

Nayland Smith had begun to walk up and down again; but now:

"He can be relieved when the other car arrives," he jerked, glancing back over his shoulder. "I should have pushed straight on, but there is someone I am anxious to interrogate. I have arranged for him to be brought here."

That the speaker was in a state of high nervous tension none could have failed to recognize. He was a man oppressed by the cloud of some dreadful doubt.

"That's the story," Gallaho added. "The professor and his statue arrived by Golden Arrow on Friday evening, just as the fog was beginning. He had two assistants, or workmen—foreigners, anyway, with him—and he had hired a small lorry. A plain-clothes man covered the proceedings, and the case containing the statue arrived at the professor's house about nine o'clock on Friday night, I understand." Then, unconsciously he echoed the ideas of Police Constable Ireland. "What the devil anybody wants to steal a statue for, is beyond me."

"It's so far beyond me," Nayland Smith said rapidly, "that I am here to-night to inspect that work of art."

Watford's expression was pathetically blank.

"It doesn't seem to mean anything," he confessed.

"No", said Gallaho, grimly, "it doesn't. It will seem to mean less when I tell you that we had a wire from the Italian police this evening—advising us that Professor Ambroso had been seen in the garden of his villa in Capri yesterday morning."

"What?"

"Sort that out," growled Gallaho. "It looks as though we've been giving protection to the wrong man, doesn't it?"

"Good Lord!" Watford's face registered the blankest bewilderment. "Is it your idea, sir——?" he turned to Nayland Smith—"I mean, you don't think that Professor Ambroso——"

"Well," growled Gallaho—"go ahead."

"No, of course, if he's been seen alive! Good Lord!" But again he turned to Sir Denis, who was pacing more and more rapidly up and down the floor. "Where does Fu Manchu come in?"

"That's a long story," Smith replied, "and until I have interviewed the professor, or the person posing as the professor, I cannot be certain that he comes in at all."

There was a rap on the door, and a uniformed constable came in.

"The other car has arrived, sir," he reported to Watford, "and there's a Mr. Preston here, asking for Sir Denis Nayland Smith."

"Show him in," said Watford.

A few moments later a young man came into the office bringing with him a whiff of the fog outside. He wore a heavy tweed overcoat and white muffler, and carried a soft hat. He had a fresh-coloured face and light blue, twinkling eyes—very humorous and good-natured. He sneezed several times, and smiled apologetically.

"My name is Nayland Smith," said Sir Denis. "Won't you please sit down?"

"Thank you, sir," and Preston sat down. "It's a devil of a night to bring a bloke out, but I've no doubt it's very important."

"It is," Nayland Smith snapped. "I will detain you no longer than possible."

Gallaho turned in his slow fashion and fixed his observant eyes upon the newcomer. Divisional-inspector Watford watched Nayland Smith.

"I understand that you were on duty," the latter continued, "at Victoria on Friday when the Paris-London service known as the Golden Arrow, arrived?"

"I was, sir."

"It is customary on this service to inspect baggage at Victoria?"

"It is."

"One of the passengers was Professor Pietro Ambroso, accompanied by two servants or workmen, and having with him a large case or crate containing a statue. Did you open this case?"

"I did." Preston's merry eyes twinkled. He sneezed, blew his nose and smiled apologetically. "There was a detective on special duty who had travelled across with the professor, and who seemed anxious to get the job over. He suggested that examination was unnecessary. "But—" he grinned—"I wanted to peep at the statue. The professor was inclined to be peevish, but——"

"Describe the professor," snapped Nayland Smith.

Preston stared in surprise for a moment, and then:

"He's a tall old man, very stooped, with a white beard and moustache. Wears pince-nez, a funny black, continental cape coat, and a wide-brimmed black hat. He speaks with a slight Italian accent, and he's very frightening."

"Admirable thumb-nail sketch," Nayland Smith commented, his penetrating stare fixed almost feverishly upon the speaker. "Thank God for a man who can see straight. Do you remember the colour of his eyes?"

Preston shook his head, suppressing a sneeze.

"He seemed half blind. He peered, keeping his eyes nearly closed."

"Good. Go on. Statue."

Preston released the pent-up sneeze. Then, grinning in his cheerful way:

"It was the devil of a game getting the lid off," he went on.

"But I roped off a corner to keep the curious away, and had the thing opened. Whew!" he whistled. "I got a shock. The figure was packed in on a sort of rest—and there was a second glass lid. I had the shock of my life!"

"Why?" growled Gallaho.

"Well, I'd read about the 'Sleeping Venus' in the papers. But I wasn't quite prepared for what I saw. Really—it's uncanny, and if I may say so, a bit shocking."

"In what way?" jerked Nayland Smith.

"Well, it's the figure of a beautiful girl, asleep. It isn't shiny, as I expected, hearing that it was made of porcelain—it looks just like a living woman. And it's coloured, to represent nature. I mean, finger nails and toe-nails and everything. By gosh!"

"Sounds worth seeing," growled Gallaho.

Nayland Smith dived into some capacious pocket within the leather overcoat, and produced a large mounted photograph. He set it upright on the inspector's desk, right under the lamp. Preston stood up and Gallaho approached the table. Wisps of fog floated about the room, competing for supremacy with the tobacco smoke from Nayland Smith's briar. The photograph was that of a nude statue, such as Preston had described; an exquisite figure relaxed, as if in sleep.

"Do you recognize it?" jerked Nayland Smith.

Preston bent forward, peering closely.

"Yes," he said, "That's her—I mean, that's it. At least, I think so." He peered closer yet. "Damn it! I'm not so sure."

"What difference do you notice?" Nayland Smith asked, eagerly.

"Well . . ." Preston hesitated. "I suppose it was the colouring that did it. But the statue was far more beautiful than this photograph."

There came a rap on the door, and the uniformed constable came in.

"The third car has arrived, sir," he reported to Watford, "and a Mr. Alan Sterling is here."

CHAPTER 3

STERLING'S STORY

ALAN STERLING burst into the room. He was a lean young man, marked by an intense virility. His features were too irregular to be termed handsome, but he had steadfast Scottish eyes, and one would have said that tenacity of purpose was his chief virtue. His skin was very tanned, and one might have mistaken him for a young Army officer. His topcoat flying open revealing a much-worn flannel suit, and, a soft hat held in hand, he was a man wrought-up to the verge of endurance. His haggard eyes turned from face to face. Then he saw Sir Denis, and sprang forward:

"Sir Denis!" he said, "Sir Denis——" and despite his Scottish name, a keen observer might have deduced from his intonation that Sterling was a citizen of the United States. "For God's sake, tell me you have some news? Something— anything! I'm going mad!"

Nayland Smith grasped Sterling's hand, and put his left arm around his shoulders.

"I am glad you're here," he said, quietly. "There is news, of a sort."

"Thank God!"

"Its value remains to be tested."

"You think she's alive? You don't think——?

"I am *sure* she's alive, Sterling."

The three men in the room watched silently, and sympathetically. Gallaho, alone, seemed to comprehend the inner significance of Sterling's wild words.

"I must leave you for a moment," Nayland Smith went on. "This is Divisional-inspector Watford, and Chief Detective-inspector Gallaho, of Scotland Yard. Give them any information in your possession. I shall not be many minutes." He turned to Preston. "If you will give me five minutes' conversation before you go," he said "I shall be indebted."

He went out with Preston. Sterling dropped into the chair which the latter had vacated, and ran his fingers through his disordered hair, looking from Gallaho to Watford.

"You must think I am mad," he apologized. "But I've been through hell—just real hell!"

Gallaho nodded, slowly.

"I know something about it, sir," he said, "and I can sympathize.

"But you don't know Fu Manchu!" Sterling replied, wildly. "He's a fiend—a demon—he bears a charmed life."

"He must," said Watford, watching the speaker. "It's a good many years since he first came on the books, sir, and if as I understand he's still going strong—he must be a bit of a superman."

"He's the Devil's agent on earth," said Sterling, bitterly. "I would give ten years of my life and any happiness that may be in store for me, to see that man dead!"

The door opened, and Nayland Smith came in.

"Give me the details quickly, Sterling," he directed. "Action is what you want—and action is what I'm going to offer you."

"Good enough, Sir Denis." Sterling nodded. He was twisting his soft hat between his hands. It became apparent from moment to moment, how dangerously over-wrought he was. "Really—there's absolutely nothing to tell you."

"I disagree," said Nayland Smith, quietly. "Odd facts pop up, if one reviews what seemed at the time to be meaningless. We have two very experienced police officers here and since they are now concerned in the case, I should be indebted if you would outline the facts of your unhappy experience."

"Good enough. From the time you saw me off in Paris?"

"Yes." Nayland Smith glanced at Watford and Gellaho. "Mr. Sterling," he explained, "is engaged to the daughter of an old mutual friend, Dr. Petrie. Fleurette—that is her name—spent a great part of her life in the household of that Dr. Fu Manchu, whom you, Inspector Watford, seem disposed to regard as a myth."

"Funny business in the south of France, some months ago," Gallaho growled. "The French press hushed it up, but we've got all the dope at the Yard."

"Sir Denis and I," Sterling continued, "went to Paris with Dr. Petrie and his daughter, my fiancée. They were returning to Egypt—Dr. Petrie's home is in Cairo. Sir Denis was com-

12

pelled to hurry back to London, but I went on to Marseilles and saw them off in the *Oxfordshire* of the Bibby Line."

"I only have the barest outline of the facts, sir," Gallaho interrupted. "But may I ask if you went on board?"

"I was one of the last visitors to leave."

"Then I take it, sir, you waved to the young lady as the ship was pulling out?"

"No," Sterling replied, "I didn't, as a matter of fact, Inspector. I left her in the cabin. She was very disturbed."

"I quite understand."

"Dr. Petrie was on the promenade deck as the ship pulled out, but Fleurette, I suppose, was in her cabin."

"The point I was trying to get at, sir, was this," Gallaho persisted, doggedly, whilst Nayland Smith, an appreciative look in his grey eyes, watched him. "How long elapsed between your saying good-bye to the young lady in her cabin, and the time the ship pulled out?"

"Not more than five minutes. I talked to the doctor—her father—on the deck, and actually left at the last moment."

"Fleurette asked you to leave her?" jerked Nayland Smith.

"Yes. She was terribly keyed-up. She thought it would be easier if we said good-bye in the cabin. I rejoined her father on deck, and—"

"One moment, sir," Galllaho's growling voice interrupted again. "Which side of the deck were you on? The seaward side, or the land side."

"The seaward side."

"Then you have no idea who went ashore in the course of the next five minutes?"

"No. I am afraid I haven't, sir."

"That's all right, sir. Go ahead."

"I watched the *Oxfordshire* leave," Sterling went on, "hoping that Fleurette would appear; but she didn't. Then I went back to the hotel, had some lunch, and picked up the Riviera Express in the afternoon, returning to Paris. I was hoping for a message at the Hotel Meurice but there was none."

"Did Petrie know you were staying at the Meurice?"

"No, but Fleurette did."

"Where did you stay on the way out?"

"At the Chatham—a favourite pub of Petrie's"

"Quite. Go on."

"I dined, and spent the evening with some friends who lived in Paris, and when I returned to my hotel, there was still no message. I left for London this morning, or rather—since it's well after midnight—yesterday morning. A radio message was waiting for me at Boulogne. It had been despatched on the *Oxfordshire* . . ." Sterling paused, running his fingers through his hair. . . . "It just told me that Fleurette was not on board; urged me to get in touch with you, Sir Denis, and finally said the doctor was hoping to be transferred to an incoming ship."

"A chapter of misadventures," Nayland Smith murmured. "You see, we were both inaccessible, temporarily. I have later news, however. Petrie has effected the transference. He has been put on to a Dutch liner, due into Marseilles to-night."

The telephone bell rang. Inspector Watford took up the instrument on his table and:

"Yes," he said, listened for a moment, and then: "Put him through to me here."

He glanced at Nayland Smith.

"The constable on duty outside Professor Ambroso's house," he reported, a note of excitement discernible in his voice.

Some more moments of silence followed during which all watched the man at the desk. Smith smoked furiously. Sterling, haggard under his tan, glanced from face to face almost feverishly. Chief Detective-inspector Gallaho removed his bowler, which fitted very tightly, and replaced it at a slightly different angle. Then:

"Hello, yes—officer in charge speaking. What's that? . . ." The vague percussion of a distant vocie manifested itself. "You say you are in the house? Hold on a moment."

"The officer on duty heard a cry for help," he explained; "found his way through the fog to the house; the door was open, and he is now in the lobby. The house is deserted, he reports."

"We are too late!" It was Nayland Smith's voice. "He has tricked me again! Tell your man to stand by, Inspector. Gather up all the men available and pack them into the second car. Come on, Gallaho. Sterling, you join us!"

CHAPTER 4

PIETRO AMBROSO'S STUDIO

EVEN THE POWERFUL SEARCHLIGHTS attached to the Flying Squad car failed to penetrate that phenomenal fog for more than a few yards. Progress was slow. To any vehicle not so equipped it would have been impossible. A constable familiar with the districts walked ahead, carrying a red lantern. A powerful beam from the leading car was directed upon this lantern, and so the journey went on.

P.C. Ireland in the lobby of Professor Ambroso's house learned the lesson that silence and solitude can be more terrifying than the wildest riot. His instructions had been to close the door but to remain in the lobby. This he had done.

When he found himself alone in that house of mystery, the strangest promptings assailed his brain. He was not an imaginative man, but sheer common sense told him that something uncommonly horrible had taken place in the house of Professor Ambroso that night.

The fire was burning low in the grate. There were some wooden logs in an iron basket, and Ireland tossed two on the embers without quite knowing why he took that liberty. Red tape bound him. Furtively he watched the stairs which disappeared in shadows, above. He was a man of action; his instinct prompted him to explore this silent house. He had no authority to do so. His mere presence in the lobby—since he could not swear that the cry actually had come from the house—was a transgression. But in this, at least, he was covered; the divisional inspector had told him to stay there. How did they hope to reach him, he argued. They would probably get lost on the way.

Now that the fog was shut out, he began to miss it. The silence which seemed to speak and in which there were strange shapes, had been awful, out there, on the verge of the Common, but the silence of this lighted lobby was even more oppressive.

Always he watched the stair.

Mystery brooded on the dim landing, but no sound broke the stillness. He began to study his immediate surroundings. There were some very strange statuettes in the lobby—queer busts, and oddly distorted figures. The paintings, too, were of a sort to which he was unused. The entire appointments of the place came within the category which P.C. Ireland mentally condemned under the heading of "Chelsea".

One of the logs which he had placed upon the fire, and which had just begun to ignite, fell into the hearth. He started, as though a shot had been fired.

"Damn!" he muttered, "this place is properly getting on my nerves."

He rescued the log and tossed it back into place. A cigarette was indicated. He could get rid of it very quickly, if the inspector turned up in person, which he doubted. He discarded his oilskin cape, and produced a little yellow packet, selecting and lighting a cigarette almost lovingly. There was company in a cigarette when a man felt lonely and queer. Always, he watched the stair.

He had finished his cigarette and reluctantly tossed the stub into the fire which now was burning merrily, when the sharp note of a bell brought him to his feet at a bound. It was the door-bell. P.C. Ireland ran forward and threw the door open.

A man in a leather overcoat, a grey-haired man, with piercing steely-blue eyes, stood staring at him.

"Constable Ireland?" he rapped.

There was unmistakable authority about the new arrival, and:

"Yes, sir," Ireland replied.

Nayland Smith walked into the lobby, followed by Inspector Gallaho, a figure familiar to every officer in the force. There was a third man, a young, very haggard looking man. But Ireland barely noticed him. The presence of Gallaho told him that in some way which might prove to be profitable to himself, he had become involved in a case of major importance. Fog swept into the lobby. He stood to attention, recognizing several familiar faces, of brother constables, peering in out of the darkness.

"You heard a cry for help?" Nayland Smith went on. His

mode of speech reminded the constable of a distant machine gun. "You were then at the gate, I take it?"

"No, sir."

"Why not?" growled Gallaho.

"There was someone moving about in the fog, sir. When I challenged him, he didn't answer—he just disappeared. At last, I got a glimpse of him, or it, or whatever it was."

"What do you mean by 'it'?" Gallaho demanded. "If you saw something—you can describe it."

"Well, sir, it might have been a man crouching down on his hands and knees—you know what the fog is like—"

"You mean," said Nayland Smith, "that you endeavoured to capture this thing—or person—who declined to answer your challenge?"

"Thank you, sir; yes, that's what I mean."

"Did you touch him or it?" Gallaho demanded.

"No, sir. But I lost my bearings trying to grab him. I found myself nearly on the other side of the road by the Common, when I heard the cry."

"Describe this cry," snapped Nayland Smith.

"It was a woman's voice, sir; very dim through the fog. And the words were 'Help! For God's sake help me!' I thought it came from this house. I groped my way back, and when I reached the door, found it open. I've been here in the lobby, ever since."

"You say it was a woman's voice," Sterling broke in. "Did it sound like a young woman or an old woman?"

"Judging from what I could make out through the fog, sir, I should say, a young woman."

Sterling clutched his hair distractedly. He felt that madness was not far off.

Gallaho turned to Sir Denis.

"It's up to you, sir. Do you want the house searched? According to regulations, we are not entitled to do it."

His tone was ironical.

"Search it from cellar to attic," snapped Nayland Smith. "Post a man at each end of the drive and split the others up."

"Good enough, sir." Gallaho returned to the open doorway. "How many of you have got lanterns—torches are no good in this blasted fog."

17

"Two," came a muffled voice, "and Ireland has a third."

"The two men with lanterns are to stand at the ends of the drive. Anybody coming out—get him. Jump to it. The rest of you, come in."

Four constables came crowding into the lobby.

"Isn't there a garage?" snapped Nayland Smith.

"Yes, sir," Ireland replied. "It opens on to the left side of the drive-in. But nothing has gone out of it tonight."

"Have you any idea where the studio is?"

"Yes, sir. I've been on day duty here. It's behind the garage—but probably, there's a way through from the house."

"Join me, Sterling," said Nayland Smith. "Gallaho, allot a man to each of the four floors. Close the door again, and post a man in charge here, in the lobby."

"Very good, sir."

"Come with me, Ireland. You say the studio lies in this direction?"

"Yes, sir."

"Come on, Sterling."

They crossed the lobby, approaching a door on the left of the ascending staircase. Chief Detective-inspector Gallaho was re-adjusting his bowler. Police constables were noisily clattering upstairs, their torches flashing as they ran. The door proved to open on to a narrow corridor.

"Find the switch," snapped Nayland Smith.

Ireland found it. And in the new illumination, queer paintings assailed their senses from the walls. There was a door at the further end of the passage. They opened it and found themselves in some dark, lofty place.

"There's a switch, somewhere," Nayland Smith muttered.

"I've found it, sir."

The studio of Pietro Ambroso became illuminated.

To one not familiar with the Modern Art movement it must have resembled a nightmare. Those familiar with the phases of the celebrated sculptor could have explained that his mode of expression, which, for a time—indeed, for many years—had conformed to the school with which the name of Epstein is associated, had, latterly, swung back to the early Greek tradition—the photographic simplicity of Praxiteles. All sorts of figures and groups surrounded the investigators. That

18

deplorable untidiness which seems to be inseparable from genius characterised the studio.

There were one or two earlier examples of ceramic experiments—strange figures in porcelain resembling primitive goddesses. But Nayland Smith's entire attention was focussed upon a long, narrow box, very stoutly built, which lay upon the floor. In form, it bore an unpleasant resemblance to a coffin. Its lid was propped against the wall near by, and a sheet of plate glass, obviously designed to fit inside the crate, lay upon the floor. Quantities of cotton wool were scattered about. Nayland Smith bent and peered at the receptacle.

"This is the thing described by Preston," he said.

"Look——" He pointed. "There are the rests which he mentioned—not unlike those used in ancient Egypt for the repose of the mummy."

He stared all around the studio.

"I know what you're thinking, Sir Denis," said Sterling, hoarsely.

"Where is the porcelain Venus?"

There was a momentary silence, and then:

"That Customs officer," came Gallaho's growling voice—he had just come in—"didn't seem to be quite sure that what he saw *was* the porcelain Venus."

"I quite agree, Inspector," said Nayland Smith.

His manner, his voice, indicated intense nervous tension. From an inner pocket he extracted a leather case, and from the leather case, a lens. He bent, peering down into the crate designed to contain the celebrated work of art.

Gallaho watched him silently, respectfully. Sterling, fists clenched, knew that sanity itself depended upon what Nayland Smith should find. Sir Denis completed his examination of the box and then turned his attention to the wooden rests designed to support the figure. This quest, also, seemed to yield no result. Dim voices sounded about the house. The search party was busy. Demon Fog had penetrated to the studio. He could be seen moving in sinister coils about the electric lights. Finally, Sir Denis addressed himself to the cotton-wool packing, and suddenly:

"Ah!" he cried. "By God! I was right. Sterling! I was right. . . ."

"What, Sir Denis? For heaven's sake, tell me, what is it you have found?"

Nayland Smith moved to a bench littered with fragments of plaster, wire frames and other odds and ends, and laid something tenderly down immediately under an overhanging light.

"A wavy, Titian red hair," he said, in a low voice. "Study it closely, Sterling. You know the colour and texture of Fleurette's hair better than I do."

"Sir Denis . . ."

Sterling was electrified.

"Don't despair, Sterling. I suggest that the beautiful figure which Preston saw in his crate, was not constructed at the Sèvres factory to the design of Professor Ambrose, but was . . . Fleurette."

CHAPTER 5

P.C. IRELAND IS UNEASY

"THIS BLASTED FOG is blotting everything out again," said Nayland Smith irritably: "already I can't see the river. By dusk it will be as bad as ever."

He turned from the window and stared across the room in the direction of a leather couch upon which his visitor was extended. Alan Sterling, his keen, tanned face very haggard, summoned up a smile.

A log fire burned in the open hearth. Red leather was the predominant note in the furniture, and there were some fine, strong oil paintings on the wall. The big lofty room was under-furnished, but homely and habitable. One might have supposed its appointments to have been dictated by somebody long resident in the East, and therefore used to scanty furniture. Some of the paintings were of Eastern subjects, and there was some good jade on top of a bookcase which seemed to be filled with works of a medico-legal character, with a sprinkling of Orientalism.

"You know, Sir Denis," said Alan Sterling, sitting upright, "you are like a tonic to me. I am keen enough about my own job, which happens to be botany; but if I may say so, for an ex-Assistant Commissioner of Metropolitan Police to select a residence right in Whitehall—next door, as it were, to Scotland Yard—indicates an even greater keenness."

Nayland Smith glanced swiftly at the speaker. He knew the tension under which Sterling was labouring; how good it was to distract his mind from those torturing queries:—Where is she? Is she alive, or dead?

"You are quite right," he replied, quietly. "I have been through the sort of fires which are burning you now Sterling, and I have always found that work was the best ointment for the burns. It was fate, I suppose, that made me an officer of Indian police. The gods—whoever the gods may be—had selected me as an opponent for——"

"Dr. Fu Manchu," said Sterling.

21

He brushed his hair back from his forehead: it was a gesture of distraction, almost of despair. Nayland Smith crossed to the buffet and from a tobacco jar which stood there, began to load his briar.

"Dr. Fu Manchu. Yes. I know I have failed, Sterling, because the man still lives. But *he* has failed, too; because, thank God I have succeeded in checking him, step by step."

"I know you have, Sir Denis. No other man in the world could have done what you have done."

"That's open to question." Nayland Smith stuffed broad cut mixture into the cracked bowl; "but the point is that if I can't throw him—I can hold him." He struck a match. "He's here, Sterling. He's here, in London."

Alan Sterling clenched his fists and Nayland Smith watched him, as he lighted his pipe. Passivity threatened Sterling, that Eastern resignation with which Smith was all too familiar. It must be combated: he must revivify the man; awaken the fiery spirit which he had good reason to know burned in him.

"Let's review the facts," he went on, briskly, his pipe now well alight. He began to walk up and down the Persian carpet. "You will find, Sterling, that they are not as unfavourable as they seem. To arrange them in some sort of order: (*a*)" —he raised a lean forefinger—"Dr. Fu Manchu, hunted by the police of Europe, succeeds in reaching England disguised as Professor Ambrose. You and I know that he is an illusionist unrivalled since the death of the late Harry Houdini. Very well; (*b*)"—he raised his second finger—"Fleurette Petrie, incidentally, your fiancée, was smuggled off the *Oxfordshire* by means of some trick which we may never solve, and taken to Nice: (*c*)"—he raised his third finger—"doubtless in that state of trance which Dr. Fu Manchu is able to induce, she travelled from Nice to London as the 'Sleeping Venus' of Professor Ambroso, and duly arrived at the house on the North Side of the Common."

"She is dead," Sterling groaned. "They have killed her."

"I emphatically deny that she is dead," snapped Nayland Smith. "Definitely, she was not dead last night,"

"What do you mean, Sir Denis?"

A pathetic light of hope had sprung into the haggard eyes of Sterling.

"A dead girl—foully murdered—her spirit silently appealing to a stolid London policeman."

"But the appeal was not silent. Ireland heard the cry for help."

"Exactly—therefore the girl was not dead."

Alan Sterling, his hands clutching his knees, watched the speaker as, of old, supplicants might have watched the Cumæn Oracle.

"It's an old move of the master schemer; I recognize it. Whilst he holds Fleurette, he holds the winning card. His own safety is bound up in hers. Don't you see that? Let us proceed to (d)." He held up his little finger: "Pietro Ambroso is either a dupe or an accomplice of Fu Manchu—it doesn't matter much one way or the other. But the desertion of his entire household is significant. We have the evidence of P.C. Ireland—an excellent officer—that no car approached or left the house prior to the time of our arrival. Consider this fact. It has extraordinary significance."

"I am trying to think," Sterling murmured.

"Keep on trying, and see if your thoughts run parallel with mine. Look at the blasted fog!"—he jerked his arm towards the window. "There's going to be another blanket to-night. Have you grasped what I mean?"

"Not entirely."

"They can't have taken her far, Sterling. Ireland and his opposite number have been on that point all night and all day."

"My God!" Sterling sprang up, his eyes shining. "You're right, Sir Denis. I see what you mean."

"Dr. Fu Manchu, for the second time in his career, is on the run. You don't know, Sterling, but I have clipped his wings pretty severely. I have cut him off from many of his associates. I am getting very near to the heart of the mystery. He is financially embarrassed. He's a hunted man. Fleurette is his last hope. Don't imagine for one moment that she is dead. Dead—she would be useless; alive, she's a triumph for the doctor."

A muffled bell rang. Nayland Smith crossed to a side table and took up a telephone.

"Yes," he said; "put him through to me, please."

He turned around to Sterling.

"Police constable Waterlow," he said, "on duty outside Professor Ambroso's house. Hello!—yes?" He spoke into the mouthpiece. "Here . . ."

Police constable Waterlow proved to be speaking from a call-box somewhere in Brixton.

"After P.C. Ireland relieved me, sir, and I went off duty, I began thinking. I don't know if I should have reported it—my orders were a bit vague-like. But talking it over with the missis, I came to the conclusion that you ought to know, sir. Divisional-inspector Watford gave me permission to speak to you, and gave me your number."

"Carry on, Constable. I'm all attention."

Well, sir, the inspector didn't seem to think there was anything in it. But he said that you might like to know. There was a funeral next door to Professor Ambroso's house this afternoon——"

"What!"

From a ground-floor flat, sir, in the next house. I can't tell you much about it, because I don't know. But it was a Miss Demuras—has been living there for about a month, I understand. I never thought of mentioning it to Ireland when he took over from me, but my missis says, 'This is a murder case, and here's a funeral next door: ring up the inspector.' I did it, and he said he had instructions to put me straight through to you."

"Who was in charge of the funeral, Constable?"

Alan Sterling sprang to his feet; fists clenched, quivering, he stood watching Nayland Smith at the telephone.

"The London Necropolis Company, sir."

"At what time did it take place?"

"At four o'clock this afternoon."

"Were there any followers?"

"Only one, sir. A foreign gentleman."

"You don't know who was attending the patient?"

"Yes, sir; as it happens, I do. A Dr. Norton, who lives on South Side. He was my own doctor, sir, when I lived in Clapham."

"Thanks, Constable. I wish you had reported this earlier. But it's not your fault."

Nayland Smith turned to Sterling.

"Don't look like that," he pleaded. "It may mean nothing or it may be a red herring. But whilst I pick up one or two things that I want in the other room, get Gallaho at Scotland Yard, and ask him to join us here with a fast car."

CHAPTER 6

DR. NORTON'S PATIENT

DR. NORTON was surprised, somewhat annoyed and obviously perturbed by the invasion of Sir Denis Nayland Smith, Chief-inspector Gallaho and Alan Sterling. His consultations were finished, and he had hastily changed into evening kit. Clearly, he had a dinner appointment. He was a man approaching middle age, of sanguine complexion—West Country, as Nayland Smith recognized at a glance, and clever without being brilliant.

As his three visitors were shown into the upstairs study and made themselves known to Dr. Norton, Nayland Smith's behaviour was somewhat peculiar. Watched by the others, he walked around the room inspecting the bookcases, the pictures, and even the window, smiling in a manner that was almost sad.

"This is the first time I have had the pleasure of meeting you, Sir Denis," said Dr. Norton, "but we have a mutual friend."

"I know," Nayland Smith turned and stared at him. "You bought this practice from Petrie."

"I've stuck it ever since, although it isn't particularly profitable."

Nayland Smith nodded and glanced at Gallaho. The celebrated detective-inspector, on this occasion, had removed his bowler, revealing a close-cropped head, and greying, dark hair.

"You must have observed, Inspector, during your great experience of human life, that things move in circles."

"I have often noticed it, sir."

"Many years have elapsed, and much history has been made since Dr. Fu Manchu first visited England. But it was in this very room—" he turned to Dr. Norton—"that the Mandarin Fu Manchu made his second attempt on my life."

"What!"

Dr. Norton could not conceal his astonishment. "I know

26

something, but very little, from Petrie, of the queer matters to which you refer, Sir Denis, but I hadn't recognized——"

"You hadn't recognized the existence of the circle," snapped Nayland Smith. "No, I suppose we have to live many lives before we do. It's a law, but it always strikes me as odd when I come in contact with it. It was here, in this very room, that Petrie, from whom you bought this practice, came to an understanding with the beautiful woman who is now his wife. It was here that Dr. Fu Manchu endeavoured to remove me by means of the Zayat Kiss. Ah——" he looked about him, and then pulled his pipe and his pouch from the pocket of his tweed jacket. "The circle narrows, I begin to hope again."

Dr. Norton's interest in his dinner engagement was evidently weakening. The magnetic personality of Nayland Smith was beginning to dominate.

"Of course, Sir Denis, one has heard of Fu Manchu. I haven't seen Petrie since he settled in Cairo; but odd things crop up in the Press from time to time. Am I to understand that you gentlemen have called this evening with regard to this mythical monster?"

"That's it," said Gallaho; "the circle to which Sir Denis referred has roped you in now. Doctor."

"I am afraid I don't understand."

"Naturally," rapped Nayland Smith.

"May I suggest whiskies and soda," said the physician. "It doesn't run to cocktails."

"It's a suggestion," Gallaho replied, "that doesn't leave me unmoved."

Dr. Norton dispensed drinks for his unexpected visitors, and then:

"My recognition of the fact," said Nayland Smith, "that fate had brought me back to Petrie's old quarters, with their many associations, rather took me off the track. The point of our visit is this, Doctor——" He fixed his penetrating eyes upon their host: "You have been attending a Miss Demuras, who lived on the North Side of the Common——"

"Yes." Dr. Norton visibly started. "I regret to say that she died yesterday, and was buried to-day."

"Without recourse to your case-book," Nayland Smith went on, "what roughly were the symptoms which led to her end?"

27

Dr. Norton passed his hand over his face, and then brushed his fair moustache. He was considering his reply, but finally:

"It was a case of pernicious anaemia," he replied. "Miss Demuras had resided in the tropics. She was practically alone in the world, except for a brother—with whom she requested me to communicate, and who appeared in time to take charge of the funeral arrangements."

"Pernicious anaemia," Nayland Smith murmured. "It's a rather obscure thing, isn't it, Doctor?"

"As its name implies, and I have used its popular name, it is—pernicious. It's difficult to combat. She was in an advanced stage when I first attended her."

"She occupied a ground-floor flat?"

"Yes."

"Had she any personal servants?"

"No; it was a service flat."

"I see. When did she actually die, doctor?"

"Just before dawn yesterday. A popular hour for death, Sir Denis."

"I know. There was a nurse in attendance, of course."

"Yes. A very experienced woman from the local Institute."

"She called you, I take it, to the patient, fearing that she was in extremis?"

"Yes. It was a painful surprise. I hadn't expected it . . ."

"Quite. But her sudden death was consistent with her symptoms?"

"Undoubtedly. It happens that way in certain cases."

"Had you taken any other opinion?"

"Yes. I called in Havelock Wade only last week."

Gallaho was following the conversation eagerly, his sullen-looking eyes turning from speaker to speaker. Sterling, sitting in an armchair, had abandoned hope of mastering his intense anxiety. He didn't know, and couldn't grasp, what this inquiry portended. But wholly, horribly, his mind was filled with the idea that Fleurette was dead and had been buried.

"Forgive me if I seem to pry into professional secrets," Nayland Smith went on; "but would you mind describing your late patient.

"Not at all," Dr, Norton replied. He began again to brush his moustache. His expression, Nayland Smith decided, was that of an unhappy man. "She was, I think, a Eurasian. I don't know very much of the East; I have never been there. But she was some kind of half-caste—there was Eastern blood in her. Her skin was of a curiously dull, ivory colour. I may as well say, Sir Denis, that she was a woman of great beauty. This uniform ivory hue of her skin was fascinating. To what extent this characteristic was due to heredity, and to what extent to her ailment, I never entirely determined. . . ."

CHAPTER 7

LASH MARKS

"I QUITE UNDERSTAND, Sir Denis," Dr. Norton said. "Please regard any information I can give you as yours. I venture to believe you are wrong in supposing that Miss Demuras was an associate of this group, to which you refer, but I am entirely at your disposal. I will admit here and now, that I was growing infatuated with my patient. Her death, which I had not anticipated, was a severe blow."

Nayland Smith walked up and down, tugging at the lobe of his ear, glancing at the titles of the books, staring about the room; then:

"I suggest that Miss Demuras's eyes were long, narrow and very beautiful?"

"Very beautiful."

"Of a most unusual green colour, at times glittering like emeralds?"

"It occurs to me that you were acquainted with her?" said Dr. Norton, staring hard at the speaker.

"It occurs to me," Nayland Smith replied grimly, glancing at Alan Sterling, "that both Mr. Sterling and I from time to time have come in contact with Miss Demuras! Do you agree, Sterling?"

The young American botanist fixed a pathetically eager gaze upon the face of Nayland Smith; it was taut, grim, a fighting glint in deep-set eyes.

"My God! The net's closing in on us again!" he whispered. "You seem to have an extra sense, Sir Denis, where this man and his people are concerned. It's uncanny . . . but it may be a coincidence."

Inspector Gallaho had resumed his favourite pose. He was leaning on the mantleshelf, moving his thin-lipped mouth as if chewing phantom gum. He was out of his depth, but nothing in his expression revealed the fact.

"I suggest that Miss Demuras was tall, and very slender?" Nayland Smith continued. "She had exquisite hands, slender-fingered and indolent—patrician hands with long, narrow, almond nails, highly varnished?"

"You are right. I see you knew her."

"Her voice was very soothing—almost hypnotic?"

Dr. Norton started violently, and stood up.

"This is either clairvoyance," he declared, "or you knew her better than I knew her. The implication is that Demuras is not her real name. Don't tell me that she was a criminal. . . ."

"There still remains a margin of doubt," said Nayland Smith, rapidly. He suddenly turned and stared at Sterling. "I have just recalled something that you told me—something that you witnessed in Ste. Claire de la Roche. . . . When the Chinese punish, they punish severely. There's just a chance."

He twisted about again, facing Dr. Norton. But the latter had construed the meaning of his words. His sanguine colour had ebbed; he was become pale.

"Ah!" cried Nayland Smith. "I see that you understand me!"

Norton nodded, and dropped back into his chair.

"There is no further room for doubt," he acknowledged. "Whoever my patient was, clearly you knew her. Throughout the time that I attended her, nearly two weeks, she defiantly declined to permit me to make a detailed examination. By which I mean that she objected to exposing her shoulders. In this she was adamant. My curiosity was keenly aroused. She had no other physical reticences. Indeed her mode of dress and her carriage, might almost be described as provocative. But she would never permit me to apply my stethoscope to her back. By means of a trick, as I frankly confess, and which need not be described, I succeeded in obtaining a glimpse of her bare shoulders. She was unaware of this. . . ."

He paused, looking from face to face. He was beginning to regain his naturally fresh colour. He was beginning to realize that his beautiful patient had not been what she seemed.

"There were great weals on her delicate skin—healed, but the scars were still visible. At some time, and not so long ago, she had been lashed—mercilessly lashed."

He clenched his fists, staring up at Nayland Smith.

The latter nodded, and resumed his restless promenade of the carpet; then:

"Do you understand, Sterling?" he snapped.

Sterling was up—his restlessness was feverish.

"I understand that Fah Lo Suee is dead—that she died alone, in that flat."

"Dead!"

"Sir Denis!" Dr. Norton stood up. "I have been frank with you: be equally frank with me. Who was this woman?"

"I don't know her real name," Nayland Smith replied. "but she is known as Fah Lo Suee. She is the daughter of Dr. Fu Manchu."

"What!"

"And it was he, her father, who exercising his parental prerogative left the scars to which you refer."

"My God!" groaned Dr. Norton—"the fiend!—the merciless fiend! A delicate, tenderly nurtured woman!—and an ailing woman at that!"

"Possibly," snapped Nayland Smith. "Delicately nurtured—yes. I am anxious, doctor, to protect your professional reputation. Your certificate was given in good faith. There is no man on the Register who would not have done the same in the circumstances. Of this I assure you. But——" he paused—"I must have a glimpse of the body of your patient."

"Why?"

"I think it can be arranged, sir," growled Gallaho. "I put a few inquiries through this evening after Mr. Sterling 'phoned me at the Yard, and I found that the deceased lady has been buried in a family vault in the old part of the Catholic Cemetery."

"That is correct," Dr. Norton interrupted. "Her only surviving relative, a brother, Manoel Demuras, with whom she had requested the nurse to get into communication, came from Lisbon, as I understand, and the somewhat hurried funeral was due to his time being limited."

"Can you describe this man?" snapped Nayland Smith.

"His ugliness was almost as noticeable as his sister's beauty. The yellow streak was very marked."

"You mean he might almost have passed for a Chinaman?"

"Not a Chinaman. . . ." Dr. Norton stroked his moustache and stared up at the ceiling. "But perhaps a native of Burma—or at least, as I should picture a native of Burma to look."

"There was Eastern blood of some sort in the Demurases," growled Gallaho. "They settled in London nearly a century ago, and at one time had a very big business as importers of Madeira wine. The firm has been extinct for twenty years. But there's a family vault in the old Catholic Cemetery, and that's where the body lies."

"I see."

And thereupon Nayland Smith did a singular thing. . . .

Crossing the room, he jerked a curtain aside, and threw up the window!

All watched him in mute astonishment. Waves of fog crept in, like the tentacles of some shadowy octopus. He was staring down in the direction of the street. He turned, reclosed the window and readjusted the curtain.

"Forgive me, Doctor," he said, smiling; and that rare smile, breaking through the grim mask, almost resembled the smile of an embarrassed schoolboy. "A liberty, I admit. But I had a sudden idea—and I was right."

"What?" growled Gallaho, ceasing the chewing operation, and shooting out his jaw.

"We've been followed. Somebody is watching the house. . . ."

CHAPTER 8

FOG IN HIGH PLACES

THAT PHENOMENAL FOG was getting its grip upon London again when the party set out. But in the specially equipped car, fair headway was made. At the mysterious, deserted house of Professor Ambrose, Gallaho and Sterling were dropped. The detective had certain important inquiries to make there relative to the accessibility of the adjoining ground-floor flat from the studio of Pietro Ambroso. Nayland Smith went on alone.

He had established contact by telephone from Dr. Norton's house with the man he was going to see. He knew this man, his lack of imagination, his oblique views of life. He knew that the task before him was no easy one. But he had attempted and achieved tasks that were harder.

The slow progress of the car was all but unendurable. Nayland Smith snapped his fingers irritably, peering out first from one window, then from another. In the brightly lighted West End streets better going was made, and at last the car pulled up before a gloomy, stone-porched house a few paces from Berkeley Square.

In a coldly forbidding library, a man sat behind a vast writing-table. Its appointments were frigidly correct. His white tie, for he was in evening dress, was a miracle of correctness. He did not stand up as Sir Denis was shown in by a butler whose proper occupation was that of an undertaker.

"Ah! Smith." He nodded and pointed to an armchair.

"Just in time." He glanced at a large marble clock. "I only have five minutes."

Nayland Smith's nod was equally curt.

"Good evening, Sir Harold," he returned, and sat down in the hard, leather-covered chair.

Sir Denis Nayland Smith's relations with His Majesty's Secretary for Home Affairs had never been cordial. Indeed it is doubtful if Sir Harold Sims, in the whole course of his life, had ever known either friendship or love. Nayland Smith, staring at the melancholy face with its habitual expression of

34

shocked surprise, thought that Sir Harold's scanty hair bore
a certain resemblance to red tape chopped up. From a pocket
of his tweed suit, Nayland Smith took out several documents,
opened them, glanced at them, and then, standing up, placed
them on the large, green blotting pad before Sir Harold Sims.

"You know," said the latter, adjusting a pair of spectacles,
and glancing down at the papers, "your methods have always
been too fantastic for me, Smith. I mean, they were when you
were associated with the Criminal Investigation Department.
This thing, which you are asking me to do, is irregular—
wholly irregular."

Nayland Smith returned to the armchair. A man of vision
and dynamic energy, he always experienced, in the proximity
of Sir Harold Sims, an all but unconquerable urge to pick up
His Majesty's Secretary and to shake him until his teeth rattled.

"There are times, Sir Harold," he said, quietly, "when one
can afford to dispense with formalities. In this case, your consent is necessary; hence my intrusion."

"You know—" Sims was scanning the documents suspiciously—"this bugbear of yours, this obsession with the person known as Fu Manchu, has created a lot of unpleasant
feeling."

This was no more than a statement of fact. Sir Denis's
retirement from the Metropolitan Police had coincided fairly
closely with the appointment of Sir Harold to the portfolio
which he still held.

"You may term it an obsession if you like—perhaps it is.
But you are fully aware, Sir Harold, of the extent of my
authority. I am not alone in this obsession. The most dangerous man living in the world to-day is here, in England, and
likely to slip through our fingers. Any delay is dangerous."

Sir Harold nodded, setting one document aside and beginning to read another.

"I shall be bothered by the Roman Catholic authorities," he
murmured; "you know how troublesome they can be. If you
could give me two or three days, in order that the matter
might be regularised. . . ."

"It is to-night, or never," snapped Nayland Smith, suddenly
standing up.

"Really. . . ."

Sir Harold began to shake his head again.

"It is perhaps unfair of me to remind you that I can bring pressure to bear."

Sir Harold looked up.

"You are not suggesting that you would bother the Prime Minister with this trivial but complicated affair?" he asked pathetically.

I am suggesting nothing. I only ask for your signature. I should not be here if the matter were as trivial as you suppose."

"Really—really, Smith. . . ."

The light-blue eyes peering through spectacle lens were caught and arrested by the gaze of eyes deep-set, steely and penetrating. Sir Harold hated this man's driving power—hated his hectoring manner, the force of a personality which brooked no denial. . . .

Five minutes later the police car was stealing through a mist, yellow, stifling, which closed in remorselessly, throttling London.

CHAPTER 9

THE TOMB OF THE DEMURASES

"You are sure there is no other means of access to the cemetery?"

"Quite, sir."

The quavering voice of the old attendant was in harmony with his venerable but wretched appearance. He seemed to belong to the clammy mist; to the phantom monuments which peered through it. He might have been an exhalation from one of the ancient tombs. His straggling grey beard, his watery, nearly sightless eyes, his rusty black garb. A mental vision of Fleurette appeared before Alan Sterling—young, tall, divinely vigorous, an exquisite figure of health and beauty; yet perhaps she lay here, stricken down inscrutably in the bloom and fullness of spring, whilst such shadowy, unhappy beings as this old mortuary keeper survived, sadly watching each fallen bud returning to earth, our common mother, who gives us life, in whose arms we sleep.

"I've got men at both gates, sir," Gallaho growled, "and two more patrolling. Anybody suspicious, they have orders to hold. A rather queer thing has been reported: may have no bearing on the case, but——"

"What?" Nayland Smith asked.

"A small head-stone has been stolen!"

"A small head-stone?"

"Yes, Sir Denis. From a child's grave. Seems a useless sort of theft, doesn't it?"

"Possibly not!" he snapped. "I'm glad you mentioned this, Inspector."

He nodded to the old man.

A dim light shone out from the door of the lodge. It was difficult to imagine the domestic life of this strange creature whose home was amongst sepulchres; all but impossible to believe that he knew anything of human happiness; that joy had ever visited that ghastly habitation.

"Mr. Roberts?"

A young man wearing a dark, waisted overcoat an a muffler conceived in Eton colours, stepped languidly forward out of veiling mists. He wore a soft black hat of most fashionable shape; his small, aristocratic features registered intense boredom. From a pocket of his overcoat he produced a number of documents, and handed them to the old man, gingerly, as if offering a fish to a seal.

"Everything is in order," he said; "you need not trouble to look them over."

"There's no need to waste time," growled Gallaho. "Let's have the key." He raised his voice. "Dorchester!" he shouted.

A uniformed constable appeared, carrying a leather bag, as:

"I suppose it's all right," quivered the old mortuary keeper, looking down blindly at the papers in his hand. "But I shall have to enter it all up, you know."

"You can do that while we're on the job," said Gallaho. "The keys."

When, presently, led by a constable carrying a red lantern they proceeded in silence along a narrow path around which ghostly monuments clustered, it might have been noted, save that the light was poor, that Mr. Roberts, Sir Harold Sims' representative, looked unusually pale. To the left they turned, along another avenue of tombs, and then to the right again, presently penetrating to the oldest part of the cemetery. Grey and awesome, fronted by sentinel cypress trees, ill-nourished and drooping, a building resembling a small chapel loomed out of the fog. There was a little grassy forecourt fronted by iron railings, and a stained glass window right and left of a massive teak door intricately studded with iron nails. A constable in plain clothes was standing there.

"This is the Demuras vault, sir," he reported.

The company pulled up and stood for a moment looking at the building. Despite the chill of the night, Alan Sterling became aware of the fact that perspiration was trickling down his ribs. He glanced at Gallaho who held a bunch of keys in his hand, one separated from the others. The pugnacious face of the detective registered no emotion whatever. Nayland Smith turned to the plain clothes officer, and:

"There may be someone hiding among the monuments," he said, sharply. "You have seen nothing?"

"No, sir."

"If you see or hear anything, while we are inside—sing out, and do your best to make a capture."

"Very good, sir; you can leave it to me."

"Go ahead, Gallaho."

Gallaho opened the little gate, which was not locked, and advanced up three steps to the massive teak door. He inserted the key in the lock and turned it. It was very stiff; it creaked dismally, but responded—and the detective pushed the door open. . . .

When at last the party stood in the vault of the Demuras, dimly lighted by two police lamps and a red lantern, the fog had entered behind them, touching every man with phantom fingers. The dweller amongst the tombs arrived, belated, coming down the stone steps pantingly, and seeming a fitting occupant of this ghastly place.

"I understand," snapped Nayland Smith, "that this is the one we want." He pointed, then turned to Mr. Roberts. "Is it quite in accordance with the wishes of the Home Office that I should open this shell?"

Mr. Roberts drew a handkerchief from an inner pocket and delicately wiped his forehead. He had removed his black hat.

"Quite all right, Sir Denis. This is really rather distressing."

"I am sorry, but much is at stake."

Constable Dorchester came forward. He had discarded his helmet, revealing a closely cropped head of brilliantly red and vigorously upstanding hair. His hazel eyes glittered excitedly.

"Shall I start, sir?"

"Yes, carry on . . ."

Inspector Gallaho, twirling his wide-brimmed bowler in stubby muscular hands, chewed phantom gum. The old sexton stood at the foot of the steps in an attitude which might have been that of prayer. Alan Sterling turned aside, looking anywhere but at the new and brightly polished sarcophagus which had been removed from its niche and which might contain . . .

A cracked bell in the mortuary chapel dimly chimed the hour.

"Do you mind if I wait outside?" said Mr. Roberts. "The fog

seems to be settling in this place. It's following us in—look—it's coming down the steps in waves."

"Quite alright," growled Gallaho; "everything is in order, sir."

Mr. Roberts ascended the steps, brushing almost hastily past the ancient warden who stood head bowed, at their foot.

The squeak of the screws was harrowing. Long trailers of mist wavered fantastically in the dim opening. Generations of Demurases seemed to stir in their happy vineyards and to look down upon the intruders. It was a desecration of their peace—Nayland Smith knew it. By what means, he was unable to guess, but by some means, Dr. Fu Manchu had secured access to this mausoleum.

"Do you mind lending me a hand, sir?"

Constable Dorchester, the handyman of the party, addressed Alan Sterling. The latter turned, clenched his teeth, and:

"O.K." he replied. "How can I help?"

"Just get hold of that end, sir, and ease it a bit. I'll get hold of this."

"Right."

Nayland Smith seemed to be listening for sounds from above. The watcher of the dead, hands clasped, was apparently praying. Chief-inspector Gallaho, from time to time, jerked out words of advice, and then resumed his phantom chewing.

The lid was removed. Sterling dropped back, raising his arms to his eyes.

"Steady!" rapped Nayland Smith. "Keep your grip, Sterling."

"May God forgive them, whoever they were," came the sepulchral voice of the old sexton.

The leaden shell had been sawn open and its top removed. . . .

"Who lies there?" Sterling whispered: "who is it?"

None answered. Complete silence claimed the tomb of the Demurases, until:

"*Look!*" said Nayland Smith . . .

CHAPTER 10

THE MARK OF KALI

"SHALL I LOCK THE DOOR?" Inspector Gallaho inquired, jangling the keys.

Nayland Smith had been last to leave the tomb of the Demurases. That great fog which with brief intervals was destined to prevail for many days, already had claimed this city of the dead. They were a phantom company enveloped in a mist which might have been smoke of the Ultimate Valley. Alan Sterling was restraining an intense excitement.

Mr. Roberts, the Home Office representative, loomed up out of darkness.

"I understand that the shell was empty, Sir Denis?"

Nayland Smith came down the three steps.

"Not empty" he replied. "It was weighted with a head-stone stolen from near by!"

The old guardian of sepulchres stood by the open door. Bewilderment had lent that grey and sorrowful face a haunted expression, which might have belonged to the spirit of some early Demuras disturbed in the mausoleum.

Thereupon, Nayland Smith did a very odd thing. He stooped and began to remove his shoes!

"I say, Sir Denis——"

An upraised hand checked Alan Sterling at those first few words.

"Shut up, Sterling!" Sir Denis snapped. "Listen, everybody." He discarded his leather coat. "I am going back down there."

"Alone?" Gallaho asked.

"Yes."

"Good God!"

"As soon as I've slipped in, partly close the door. Sing out in a loud voice, 'Here are the keys, Sir Denis', or anything you like to convey the idea that I am with you. Understand?"

"Yes," Gallaho answered gruffly. "But if you suspect there's anybody hidden there, it's rather a mad move, isn't it, sir?"

"I can think of no other. Don't really lock the door," said

Nayland Smith in a low voice. "Turn the key, but leave the door slightly ajar——"

"Very good, sir."

Soft-footed, Nayland Smith re-entered the tomb, turned and signalled with his hand. Gallaho began to close the heavy teak door.

"This is ghastly," Mr. Roberts muttered. "What does he expect to find?"

Gallaho rettled the keys, and:

"Shall I lock up, Sir Denis?" he said in his deep, gruff voice, paused a moment, and then: "Very good, sir. You go ahead; I'll follow."

He shot the lock noisily. The door was not more than an inch ajar.

"Silence!" he whispered. "Everybody stand by."

Beyond that ghostly door, guarded by sentinel cypresses, Nayland Smith was creeping down the stone steps, silently, stealthily. Gallaho had played his part well. All too familiar with red tape, Smith knew that short of sand-bagging the man from the Home Office, to have attempted to disturb the repose of another Demuras would have resulted in an adjournment of the investigation. Alone, and uninterrupted, he must convince himself that that queer impression of something which lived and moved in an ancient shell in a stone niche, must be confirmed or disproved by himself alone.

He reached the vault without having made a sound. His feet were chilled by the stone paving. Imagination charged the fog-laden atmosphere with odours of mortal decay. The darkness was intense. Looking up the steps down which he had come, no more than a vague blur indicated the presence of the stained glass windows. On hands and knees he moved cautiously, right, and then crouched down against the wall and directly beneath the niche which contained the mortal remains of Isobel Demuras—or so the inscription stated.

Complete silence prevailed for fully a minute. He could detect no repetition of that furtive movement which he had heard, or imagined he had heard. Turning slowly and cautiously, he looked up . . .

He saw a thing which for a moment touched him with awe. The stone recess above had become vaguely illuminated, as if some spiritual light were thrown out from the shell of Isobel Demuras!

There came a vague shuffling—the same which he had detected when, last to leave, he had paused for a moment at the foot of the steps. Then . . . a ray of light shot across the vault, touching the further wall, where it rested upon a brass plate. The inscription upon this he remembered to have read: here lay Tristan Demuras, founder of the English branch of the family.

The noise above became louder. To it was added a squeaking sound. The ray disappeared from the opposite wall, but the niche above became more brightly illuminated. Nayland Smith on hands and knees crept to the corner of the vault. He had not vacated his former position more than three seconds when light poured down upon the pavement. He was just outside its radius.

The light disappeared; complete darkness fell. There came a renewed and a louder creaking, then a soft thud upon the floor beside him.

In that instant Nayland Smith sprang. . . .

"Gallaho!" he shouted. "Sterling!"

The teak door was opened with a crash. Gallaho shining his torch ahead of him came cluttering down the steps, Sterling close behind.

"The light . . . here, Gallaho—quick!" Nayland Smith spoke hoarsely. "Get his knife!"

"My God!"

Sterling sprang forward.

A lithe yellow man, his eyes on fire with venomous hatred, was struggling in Nayland Smith's grasp! Sir Denis had him by the throat, but with his left hand he clutched the man's lean, muscular wrist. A knife, having a short, curved blade, was grasped in the sinewy fingers. For all Nayland Smith's efforts, its point was creeping nearer and nearer, driven by the maniacal strength which animated the tigerish body. The left arm of the yellow man was thrown around his captor, seeking to drag him down upon the quivering blade . . .

Gallaho twisted the weapon from the man's grasp, and Nayland Smith stood up, breathing heavily. Two constables had joined them now, their lamps reinforcing the illumination.

"Who's got bracelets?" growled Gallaho.

None of the party had handcuffs, but Constable Dorchester, of the spiky red hair, grabbed the prisoner and ran him up the steps.

Outside, held by Dorchester and another, his back against the teak door, he grinned fiendishly, but uttered no word whilst Nayland Smith resumed his shoes and put on his leather overcoat. Gallaho shone the light of a torch on to the face of the captive.

The man wore a soft shirt and no tie; a cheap flannel suit; his ankles were bare, and his lean feet were encased in rubber-soled shoes. His teeth gleamed in that fixed grin of hatred; his sunken eyes held a reddish smouldering fire. Disordered oily black hair hung down over his forehead. He was panting and wet with perspiration.

Nayland Smith raised the damp hair from the man's brow, revealing a small mark upon parchment-like skin.

"The mark of Kali," he said. "I thought so . . . One of the Doctor's religious assassins."

"What ever is the meaning of all this?" Mr. Roberts demanded in a high, quavering voice.

Nayland Smith turned in the speaker's direction, so that from Sterling's point of view, the keen, angular profile was clearly visible against the light of a lamp held by one of the constables.

"It means," Sir Denis began . . .

Something hummed like a giant insect past Sterling's ear, missed Nayland Smith by less than an inch as he sprang back, fists clenched, glittered evilly in the lantern light, and . . . the man whose brow was branded with the mark of Kali gurgled, and became limp in the grip of his two big captors.

A bloody foam appeared upon his lips.

He was pinned to the door by a long, narrow-bladed knife, which had completely pierced his throat and had penetrated nearly an inch into the teak against which he stood!

CHAPTER 11

SAM PAK OF LIMEHOUSE

NAYLAND SMITH walked up and down his study in Whitehall. Heavy blue curtains were drawn before the windows. Alan Sterling from the depths of an armchair watched him gloomily.

"I am satisfied that the other shells in that vault were occupied by deceased Demurases," said Sir Denis. "How long the group has had access to that mausoleum, is something we are unlikely ever to know. But doubtless it has served other purposes in the past. The supposed sarcophagus of Isobel Demuras, as I showed you, was no more than a trick box or hiding-place, having a spy-hole by means of which one concealed there could watch what was going on below. It is certain that I have been covered closely for some days past. We were followed to Dr. Norton's house this evening, and later I was followed to the Home Secretary's. To make assurance doubly sure, the Doctor planted a spy in the mausoleum."

He paused, knocking out his pipe in the hearth.

"That knife was meant for me, Sterling," he said grimly, "and Dr. Fu Manchu's thugs rarely miss."

"It was an act of Providence—the protection of heaven!"

"I agree. The reign of the Mandarin Fu Manchu is drawing to a close. The omens are against him. He smuggled Fleurette from Ambroso's studio to the cemetery. The device seems elaborate; but consider the difficulty of transporting an insensible girl!"

Sterling jumped up, a lean but athletic figure, clenching and unclenching his sunburned hands.

"Insensible—yes!" he groaned. "How do we know she isn't—dead. . . ."

"Because all the evidence points the other way. Dr. Fu Manchu is a good gambler; he would never throw away an ace. Consider the sheer brilliance of his asking police protection for Professor Ambroso—that is, for himself!"

"He had not anticipated that it would be continued in London."

"Possibly not."

He pressed a bell. A tall, gaunt manservant came in. A leathery quality in his complexion indicated that he had known tropical suns; his face was expressionless as that of a Sioux brave; his small eyes conveyed nothing.

"Set out a cold buffet in the dining-room, Fay," Nayland Smith directed.

Fay, seeming to divine by means of some extra sense that this completed his instructions, slightly inclined his close-cropped head and went out as silently as he had come in.

The telephone bell rang. Sir Denis took up the instrument, and:

"Yes," he said; "please show him up at once." He replaced the receiver. "Gallaho is downstairs. I hope this means that the deceased thug has been identified."

Sterling's restlessness was feverish.

"This waiting," he muttered, "is damnably trying."

Nayland Smith unscrewed the top of a tobacco jar.

"Get out your pipe," he snapped. "We'll have a drink when Gallaho arrives. You don't have to be jumpy—there's work ahead, and I'm counting on you."

Sterling nodded, clenched his white teeth, and plunged into a pocket of his suit for his pipe. At which moment, a bell rang. Sir Denis opened the door, crossed the lobby and faced Chief detective-inspector Gallaho at the very moment that the silent Fay admitted him. He could not wait for the Scotland Yard man to cross the threshold, but:

"Who was he?" he snapped; "do you know?"

"Got his history, sir, such as it is."

"Good."

The fog had penetrated to the lift-shaft of the building; wisps floated out on the landing and aleady were penetrating the lobby. When the inspector had come in:

"Have you had any dinner?" snapped Nayland Smith.

"No, sir. I haven't had time to think about eating."

"I thought not. There's a cold buffet in the dining-room, as I gather we may be late to-night. Am I right?"

"Quite probably, sir."

"Excellent."

Sterling had charged his pipe from the tobacco jar, and now

Nayland Smith pulled out a tangle of broad-cut mixture and began stuffing it into the hot bowl of his own cracked briar.

"Help yourself to whisky and soda, Inspector," he said; "it's on the side table there. Please go ahead."

Gallaho nodded, took a glass and helped himself to a modest drink, then:

"The dead man has been identified by Detective-sergeant Pether, of K Division," he went on. "What Pether doesn't know about the Asiatics isn't worth knowing. Can I help you, sir?" indicating the decanter.

"Thanks, Inspector—and one for Mr. Sterling while you're there."

Gallaho, officiating as butler, continued:

"His real nationality, Pether doesn't know, but he's probably Burmese. He always passed for a lascar at Sam Pak's——"

"Sam Pak's?" rapped Nayland Smith.

"You're a bit out of touch with Limehouse, sir," said Gallaho, handing a tumbler to Sir Denis and one to Sterling. "But Sam Pak's is a small restaurant frequented by seamen from ships docking in the river. It's generally known that opium and hashish can be got there. But as its use seems to be confined to the Asiatics, we have never moved. There have been no complaints. Well—" he took a sip of his whisky and soda—"It seems that the dead man was known as 'Charlie'—apparently he had no other name; and sometimes he used to act as a waiter for Sam Pak."

"Highly important," murmured Nayland Smith, beginning to walk up and down. "A very strong link. Gallaho. The doctor's on the run. His available servants are few, and he's back in his old haunts. Very significant. Could you give me a brief character sketch of this Sam Pak?"

"I can try, sir. Pether knows him better than I do, but I didn't bother to bring him along. Let me see . . ." He chewed imaginary gum, staring up at the ceiling, then: "Sam Pak is a small, old, very wrinkled Chinaman. He might be any age up to, say, a hundred. He has a voice like a tin whistle, and speaks pidgin English."

"Stop!" snapped Nayland Smith. "Detective-sergeant Fletcher of K Division retired some years ago didn't he?"

"He did, sir," Gallaho replied, rather startled. "He's

landlord of the George and Dragon in Commercial Road. I happen to know him well."

"Get through to the George and Dragon," Nayland Smith directed. "Find out if Fletcher is home, and if so ask him to come on the line."

"Very good, sir. . . . Now?"

"You might as well; I want to think. You can use the telephone in the lobby."

"Very good, sir."

Inspector Gallaho went out, carrying his tumbler, and:

"You know," said Nayland Smith, turning and staring at Sterling, "I have an idea that I know Sam Pak. I believe he is a certain John Ki, who disappeared from Chinatown some years ago. He was one of Fu Manchu's people, Sterling. I should like to be sure."

Sterling had lighted his pipe and had dropped back into the big armchair, but his mood was far from restful. He sat there, clutching the arms, watching Sir Denis pacing up and down the carpet. Suddenly:

"On your word of honour, Sir Denis," he said, "do you think she's alive?"

Nayland Smith turned and fixed an unflinching gaze upon the speaker.

"On my word of honour," he replied, "I do."

"Thank God!" Sterling murmured. "You're a rock of refuge!"

"He's well on the run," Sir Denis continued, grimly, the cold grey-blue eyes alight with suppressed excitement. "He has doubled back to his riverside haunts. He's finding it difficult to raise funds. The police of Europe are on his tail. He's a cornered rat, and dangerous. The Mandarin Prince has become the common criminal. I wonder if it's to be his fate, Sterling, that having threatened the safety of nations, he is to fall. That would be poetic justice, indeed. In the past, he has shown them scant mercy."

Sterling watched the speaker fascinatedly. He radiated vitality; the force within him vibrated through one's nerves. Only a man who had known Dr. Fu Manchu, as Sterling knew him, could have doubted that the Chinaman's fate was sealed. But knowing, and appreciating, the genius of the great Eastern physician, Sterling, with optimism crying out for recognition in his heart, was forced to admit that the betting was even. Sir Denis Nayland Smith would have been an impossible adversary for any normal man to pit himself against, but Dr. Fu Manchu was *not* a normal man. He was a superman, Satan materialized, and one equipped with knowledge which few had ever achieved: a cold, dominating intellect, untrammelled by fleshly ties, a great mind unbound by laws of man.

The silence which fell was only broken by faint ringings of a telephone bell and the distant rumbling of the voice of Inspector Gallaho. Nayland Smith walked up and down. Sterling smoked, and clutched the arms of the chair. Then, Gallaho, still carrying his glass which now was empty, returned.

"I've found him, sir," he reported, "and by great good luck, got him on the 'phone."

CHAPTER 12

LONDON RIVER

A CONSTABLE PATROLLING the Embankment pulled up and stared suspiciously at a pair of dangerous-looking loafers, possibly sailors, of a type rarely seen in the Westminster area; very dark-skinned fellows wearing greasy caps and smoking cigarettes. To that lurching walk that belongs to the sea, a certain furtive quality seemed to have been added. Some of these foreign sailormen had other jobs when they were ashore, and the officer didn't like the way in which this pair kept staring up towards a certain lighted window in a block of expensive residential flats.

A strong westerly breeze had sprung up, driving banks of fog before it, so that in certain areas, temporarily, the night was clear enough. Such a lucidity prevailed now in this part of Westminster. The face of Big Ben was clearly visible, no great distance away, and the many lighted windows of New Scotland Yard. But whereas most of the windows in the block of flats were shaded, that one which seemed to interest the pair of watchers, a large, bay window, had neither curtains nor blinds drawn.

From time to time a man, apparently tall and thin, who might have been in evening dress, appeared in this window. One would have supposed that he was pacing up and down the room to which it belonged. He was smoking a pipe.

Yes, the officer was certain, it was this window or this man, or both, that the loafers were watching. He determined upon action. Quickly retracing his steps:

"What are you two up to?" He demanded, gruffly.

The shorter of the pair started and turned. He had deep-set, very bright eyes, and a truculence of manner which the constable regarded as suspicious. His companion grasped his arm, and:

"Lêltak sa'îda," he said.

The officer could not be expected to know that the man had wished him good-night in Arabic.

The pair moved off slouchingly.

"Don't hang about here," the constable continued, following them up. "Get a move on."

"Khatrâk!" replied the taller man.

The constable watched them lurching away, unaware that the word meant "good-bye". They did not loiter again, but went on their way. The officer, retracing his steps, glanced up at the lighted window. The tall man smoking a pipe became visible for a moment, then turned and disappeared.

As the two foreign sailormen whose language was presumably Arabic proceeded on their way:—

"Comedy interlude with policeman?" snapped the taller. "Do you think Fay looks the part?"

"I should never have suspected it wasn't you up there, Sir Denis," the other replied. "But, except the constable, did you notice anyone watching?"

"Yes."

"What?"

"A man apparently asleep on the stone steps nearly opposite my window, with a tray of matches on the pavement before him."

"Good God! Are you sure?"

"Quite sure."

"Then we've thrown them off this time?"

"I think so, Sterling. We must be careful how we join Gallaho and Forester. This is a case where a return of the fog would be welcome. Is there anyone behind?"

Sterling glanced back.

"No, not near enough to count."

"Good. This way, then."

He gripped Sterling suddenly, pulling him aside.

"Duck under here! Now, over the wall!"

A moment later they stood at the foot of some stone steps. A dinghy lay there, occupied by one rower, a man who wore the uniform of the River Police. As the pair appeared:

"Careful how you come aboard, sir," he said; "those lower steps are very slimy."

However, they embarked without accident, and ten minutes later were inside the dingy little office of the River Police depot. Chief Detective-inspector Gallaho was leaning against

51

the mantelpiece chewing phantom gum, his bowler worn at that angle made famous by Earl Beatty in the Navy. Forester, a thick-set man who looked more like a Mercantile skipper than a police officer, stood up as the hang-dog couple entered.

"Do you think you've covered your tracks, sir?" he asked, addressing Sir Denis.

"I hope so," snapped the latter. "But anyway, we have to go on now. Too much valuable time has been wasted already."

Big Ben chimed the hour. A high pall of fog still overhung the city, and the booming notes of the big clock seemed to come from almost directly overhead.

"Eleven o'clock. Is it fairly clear down-river, Inspector?"

"It was clearing when I came up, sir," Forester replied. "A lot of shipping is on the move, now. Some of them have been locked up for twenty-four hours. But I'm told it's still very thick in the Channel."

"Sam Pak's I take it, does not close early?"

Inspector Forester laughed.

"To the best of my knowledge it never closes," he replied. "Cigarettes and drinks, of a sort, can be had there all night by anyone in the know."

"Habitual law-breakers?" Nayland Smith suggested.

Exactly, sir. But he's a safety-valve."

"I quite understand. No news from Fletcher?"

"No, sir. I have been expecting it for the last half-hour."

Nayland Smith glanced at a gun-metal watch strapped to his wrist, and:

"I'll give him five minutes," he said, rapidly. "Then, we'll start. The fog may develop at any moment if this breeze drops. You can arrange for any news to be passed down?"

"Certainly, sir."

At which moment, the 'phone bell rang.

"Hello!" the Inspector's voice was eager. "Yes, speaking. He's here—hold on." He turned. "Fletcher on the line, sir."

Nayland Smith took the instrument from the Inspector's hand, and:

"Hello, that you, Fletcher?" he asked.

"Fletcher speaking, sir, and it's like old times to hear your voice. I've been out of touch with Limehouse for some years, but I was really glad of to-night's job. I dropped into this man's place to buy a packet of cigarettes, and managed to stay long enough to get a glimpse of the old boy."

"Well?"

"You're right, sir. It's John Ki, formerly keeper of the *Joy Shop*, now known as Sam Pak."

"Good." Nayland Smith's eyes shone like burnished steel in the mulatto mask of his face. "You didn't arouse his suspicions, of course?"

"Certainly not, sir. I didn't even speak to him—and he couldn't be expected to remember me."

"Good enough, Fletcher. You can go home now. I'll get in touch with you to-morrow."

He replaced the receiver and turned.

"That seems to clinch it," growled Gallaho. "With any luck we ought to make a capture to-night."

Nayland Smith was walking up and down the linoleum covered floor, twitching at the lobe of his left ear.

"Give me some brief idea of your arrangements, Gallaho," he snapped.

"Well . . ." Gallaho closed one eye and cocked the other in the direction of the ceiling: "Inspector Forester, here, has got a cutter tucked away within easy call, with a crew of six. They're watching the place from the river side. Nobody can get out that way. I sent eight men, picked them myself, who are used to this sort of work. You won't see a sign of them when you arrive, but they'll see you, sir."

"Anybody inside?" snapped Nayland Smith.

"Yes," said Gallaho, grinning. "Detective-sergeant Murphy. Fast asleep in the 'club-room'. He's the most wonderful 'drunk' in the C.I.D."

"Good. It's time we started."

CHAPTER 13

A TONGUE OF FIRE

THE PORT OF LONDON had suddenly come to life. A big liner, fog-bound for a day and a night, was bellowing her warning to all whom it might concern as she crept slowly from her dock into the stream. Tugs towing strings of barges congested the waterway. The shipping area was a blaze of light, humming with human activity. That narrow stretch of waterfront behind which lies the ever-dwindling area of Chinatown, alone seemed to remain undisturbed under these new conditions.

Here, a lazy tide lapped muddily at ancient piles upholding pier and wharf and other crazy structures of a sort long since condemned and demolished in more up-to-date districts. The River Police launch lay just outside a moored barge. From this point of vantage the look-out had a nearly unobstructed view of a sort of wooden excrescence which jutted out from a neighbouring building.

It overhung a patch of mud, covered at high tide, into which it seemed to threaten at any moment to fall. It boasted two windows: one looking straight across the river to the Surrey bank and the other facing up-stream. There was a light in this latter window, and the River Police were watching it, curiously.

From time to time a bent figure moved past it—a queer, shuffling figure. For fully ten minutes, however, this figure had not re-appeared.

Each warning of the big steamer reached them more faintly. One of the police crew, who had been a ship's steward, shivered slightly; picturing the warmly lighted cabins, the well-ordered life on board the out-going liner; sniffed in imagination the hot, desert air of Egypt; glimpsed the palm groves of Colombo, and wondered why he had ever joined the police. A tow-boat passed very close to them, creating a temporary swell in which they rocked and rolled violently. The breeze carried some of her smoke across their bows, making them blink and cough. When, suddenly:

"There it is again," muttered the ex-steward.

"What are you talking about?" growled the officer in charge, heartily fed-up with this monotonous duty.

"That blue light, Sergeant."

"What blue light?"

"Nearly over the roof of Sam Pak's. It's the fourth time I've seen it."

"I can't see anything."

"No. It's just gone again."

"You're a bit barmy, aren't you?"

"I've seen it too, Sergeant," came another voice. "Not tonight for the first time, either."

"What?"

"I first saw it early last week. I was with the four o'clock boat. It sort of dances in the air, high up over the roof."

"That's right," said the other man.

"Something like a gasworks," the sergeant suggested facetiously.

"That's it, Sergeant, only not so bright, and it doesn't stay long. Just comes and goes."

The tide lapped and sucked and whispered all around them. The deep voice of the liner moaned down-stream. Metal crashed on metal in the dockyard, and the glare of a million lights created the illusion of a tent stretched overhead; for that high pall still floated above London, angrily, as if waiting to settle again at the first opportunity.

A bent figure moved slowly past the lighted window.

"Tell me if you see it again," said the sergeant.

Silence fell upon the watchers . . .

"Hello!—who's this?" the sergeant growled.

The creaking of oars proclaimed itself, growing ever nearer. Hidden in shadows, the River Police watched the approach of a small rowboat. The rower had all the appearance of a typical waterman. He had two passengers.

"What's this?" muttered the sergeant. "I believe he's making for Sam Pak's . . . *Ssh!* Quiet!"

The crew of six watched eagerly; any break in the monotony of their duty was welcome. The sergeant's prediction was fulfilled. The boat was pulled in close to rotting piles which at some time had supported a sort of jetty. At the margin of mud and shingle, the two passengers disembarked, making a perilous way along slippery wooden girders until they reached the sloping strand. The crunch of their heavy boots was clearly audible; and as the boatman pulled away, the two mounted a wooden stair and disappeared into a dark opening.

"H'm!" said the sergeant. "Of course, they may not be going to Sam's. People are often ferried across here. It's a short cut to the 'bus route. Hello!"

He stood suddenly upright in the bows of the launch, and might have been seen staring upward at a point high above the roof of Sam Pak's establishment.

"There you are, Sergeant . . . that's what I meant!"

A curious, blue light played there against the pall above. At one moment it resembled a serpent's tongue, or rather, the fiery tongue of a dragon; then it would change and become a number of little, darting tongues; suddenly, it disappeared altogether.

"Well—I'm damned!" said the sergeant. "That's a very queer thing. Where the devil can it come from?"

Chapter 14

AT SAM PAK'S

THE EXTERIOR of Sam Pak's presented the appearance of a small and unattractive Chinese restaurant, where also provisions might be purchased and taken away.

As one entered, there was a counter on the left; the air was informed with an odour of Bombay duck and other Chinese delicacies. Tea might be purchased or drunk on the establishment, for there were two or three cane-topped tables on the other side of the shop. Although midnight had come and gone, lights were still burning in this shop, and a very fat woman of incalculable nationality was playing some variety of patience behind the counter, and smoking cigarettes continuously.

A curious, spicy smell, mingling with that of the provisions indicated that joss-sticks might be purchased here; rice, also, and various kinds of cold eatables, suitable for immediate consumption. Excepting the fat lady, there was no one else in the shop at the moment that Nayland Smith and Sterling entered.

They had been well schooled by a detective attached to K Division, and Nayland Smith, taking the lead, leaned on the counter, and:

"Cigarette please, Lucky Strike," he said, his accent and intonation that of one not very familiar with English.

The lady behind the counter hesitated for a moment, and then put another card in place. Laying down those which she still held in her hand, she reached back, abstracted a packet of the desired cigarettes from a shelf, and tossed it down before the customer, without so much as glancing at him.

He laid a ten shilling note near to her hand.

"Damn thirsty," he continued; "got a good drink?"

Piercing black eyes were raised instantaneously. Both men recognized that at that moment they were being submitted to a scrutiny as searching as an X ray examination. Those gimlet eyes were lowered again. The woman took the note, dropping it into a wooden bowl, and from the bowl extracted silver change.

"Who says you get a drink here?" she muttered.

"All sailors know Sam Pak keeps good beer," Nayland Smith replied rapidly, in that Shanghai vernacular which sometimes passes for Chinese.

The woman smiled; her entire expression changed. She looked up, replying in English.

"How you know Chinese?" she asked.

"Live for ten years in Shanghai."

"You want beer or whisky?"

"Beer."

The woman pushed a little paper pad forward across the counter, and handed the speaker a pencil.

The paper was headed "Sailors' Club."

"Please, your name here," she said; then, glancing at Sterling, "your friend too."

Nayland Smith shrugged his shoulders as if helplessly, and then, laboriously traced out some characters to which no expert alive could possibly have attached any significance or meaning.

"Name of ship, please, here."

A stubby finger, with a very dirty nail, rested upon a dotted line on the form. They had come prepared for this, and Nayland Smith wrote, using block letters in the wrong place "*s.s. Pelican*".

"Now you, please."

The beady eyes were fixed on Sterling. He wrote what looked like "John Lubba" and put two pencil dots under Smith's inscription—*s.s. Pelican.*

"One shilling each," said the woman, extracting a two shilling piece from the change and dropping the coin into the wooden bowl. "You members now for one week."

She pressed a bell-button which stood upon the counter near to her hand, and a door at the end of the little shop was opened.

Nayland Smith, carefully counting his change, replaced it in a pocket of his greasy trousers, and turned as a very slender Chinese boy who walked with so marked a stoop as to appear deformed, came into the shop. He wore an ill-fitting suit and a red muffler, but, incongruously, a small, black Chinese cap upon his head. Perhaps, however, the most singular item of his make-up, and that which first struck one's attention, was an eye-patch which obscured his left eye, lending his small, pale yellow features a strangely sinister appearance. To this odd figure the stout receptionist, tearing off the form from the top of the block, passed the credentials of the two new members, saying rapidly in Chinese:

"For the files."

Sterling did not understand, but Nayland Smith did; and he was satisfied. They were accepted.

The one-eyed Chinese boy signalled that they should follow, and they proceeded along a short, narrow passage to the "club". This was a fair-sized room, the atmosphere of which was all but suffocating. Ventilation there was none. A velvet-covered divan, indescribably greasy and filthy, ran along the whole of one wall, tables being set before it at intervals. At the farther end of the place was a bar, and, on the left, cheap wicker chairs and tables. The centre of the floor was moderately clear. It was uncarpeted and some pretence had been made, at some time, to polish the deal planks.

The company present was not without interest.

At a side table, two Chinamen were playing Mah jong, a game harmless enough, but interdict in Limehouse. At another table, a party, one of whom was a white girl, played fan-tan, also illegal in the Chinese quarter. The players spoke little, being absorbed in their games.

Although the fog had cleared from the streets of Limehouse and from the river, one might have supposed that this stuffy room had succeeded in capturing a considerable section of it. Visibility was poor. Tobacco smoke predominated in the "club", but with it other scents were mingled. Half a dozen nondescripts were drinking and talking—mostly, they drank beer. One visitor seated alone at the end of the divan, elbows resting on the table before him, glared sullenly into space. He had a shock of dark hair, and his complexion was carrot-coloured. His prominent nose was particularly eloquent.

"Gimme another drink, Sam," he kept demanding. "Gimme another drink, Sam."

Save for two chairs set before the table upon which the thirsty man rested his elbows, there was no visible accommodation in the "Sailors' Club".

"Go ahead!" Nayland Smith whispered in Sterling's ear. "Grab those two chairs."

No one took the slightest notice of their entrance, and walking towards the bar, they seated themselves in the two vacant chairs. The one-eyed boy stood by for orders.

"Two pints beer," said Nayland Smith in his queer broken English.

The boy went to the bar to give the order. And the barman to whom he gave it was quite easily the outstanding personality in the room. He was a small Chinaman, resembling nothing so much as an animated mummy. His chin nearly met his nose, for apparently he was quite toothless; and there was not an inch of his skin, nor a visible part of his bald head, which was not intricately traced with wrinkles. His eyes, owing to the puckering of the skin, were almost invisible, and his hands when they appeared from behind the counter resembled the talons of some large bird.

"Gimme another drink, Sam," hiccupped the man on the divan. "Never mind those blokes—gi' *me* another drink."

One elbow slipped and his head fell right forward on the table.

"O.K. sir," came a low whisper. "Detective-sergeant Murphy. Something funny going on here to-night, sir."

Nayland Smith turned to the aged being behind the bar.

"Give him another drink," he said rapidly in Chinese. "Charge me. He is better asleep than awake."

The incredible features of Sam Pak drew themselves up in a ghastly contortion which may have been a smile.

"It is good," he whistled in Chinese—"a sleeping fool may pass for a wise man."

The one-eyed boy was bending over the counter, placing the mugs on a tray. Sterling watched, and suddenly:

"Sir Denis," he whispered—"look! That isn't a boy's figure."

"Gimme a drink," blurted Murphy; then, in a whisper: "It isn't a boy, sir—it's a *girl* . . ."

CHAPTER 15

A LIGHTED WINDOW

FORESTER of the River Police had taken charge of the party covering Sam Pak's from the Thames. His presence, which was unexpected, had infused a new spirit into the enterprise. The fact that he was accompanied by the celebrated Inspector Gallaho of the C.I.D., caused a tense but respectful silence to fall upon the party. Everyone knew now that some very important case lay behind this monotonous duty.

A sort of rumour hitherto submerged, now ran magically from man to man, the presence of the famous detective lending it wings.

"It' s the Fu Manchu business—I told you so. . ."

"He's been dead for years. . . ."

"If you ever have the bad luck to meet him, you'll . . ."

"Silence on board!" said Forester, in a low but authoritative voice. "This isn't a picnic: you're on duty. Listen—isn't one of you an able-bodied seaman?"

The ex-steward spoke up.

"I was an A.B., sir, before I became a steward."

"You're the man I want. You see that lighted window—the one that belongs to Sam Pak's?"

"Yes, sir."

"It isn't more than three feet below the roof and there's plenty of foothold. Do you think you could climb it?"

There was a moment of silence, and then:

"To the roof, sir?"

"Yes."

"I could try. There wouldn't be much risk if the tide was in, but I'm not so sure of the mud."

"How do you feel about it?"

"I'll take a chance."

"Good man," growled Gallaho. "Inspector Forester has brought a rope ladder. We want you to carry a line up to make the ladder fast. The idea is to get a look in at that lighted window. Bear it in mind. But for the love of Mike, don't make any row. We are taking chances."

Merton, the ex-sailor, rather thought that *he* was the member of the party who was taking chances. He was endeavouring to find suitable words in which to express this idea, when:

"That's a good man, Inspector," snapped a voice from the barge. "Always keep your eye on a man who volunteers for dangerous duty."

Merton looked up as two men who resembled Portuguese deck-hands dropped from the barge into the tail of the cutter. But the speaker's voice held an unmistakable note. Rumour had spoken truly.

The presence of Inspector Gallaho had started tongues wagging; here was someone vastly senior to Gallaho, and masquerading in disguise. The attitude of the famous C.I.D. detective was sufficient evidence of the seniority of the last speaker.

The River Police craft was eased alongside the rotting piles which supported that excrescence of Sam Pak's restaurant. Merton swarmed up without great difficulty towards a point just below the lighted window. Here he paused, making signs to the crew below.

"Push out," snapped Nayland Smith in a low voice.

The little craft was eased away, and Merton, carrying the line, proceeded to the second and more difficult stage of his journey, watched breathlessly by every man aboard the River Police launch. Twice he faltered, and, once, seemed to have lost his hold. But at last a sort of sympathetic murmur ran around the watching party.

He had reached the roof of the wooden structure. He waved, and began to haul in the line attached to the rope ladder.

A stooping figure passed behind the lighted window. . .

Merton, in response to signals from Gallaho, moved further left, so that when the ladder was hauled up it just cleared the window. Some delay followed whilst Merton, disappearing from the view of those below, sought some suitable stanchion to which safely to lash the ladder. This accomplished, he gave the signal that all was fast, and:

"As soon as I'm on the ladder," said Nayland Smith, "get back to cover. The routine, as arranged, holds good."

He began to climb . . . and presently he could look in at the lighted window.

CHAPTER 16

A BURNING GHAT

A WOMAN attired in scanty underwear was pulling on high-heeled, jade green shoes. She was seated on a cheap dilapidated wooden chair. Depended upon a hanger on the wall behind this chair, was a green frock, which Nayland Smith guessed to be probably a creation of Worth. A dressing-table of a kind which can only be found in the second-hand stores appeared at one end of the small rectangular room. It was set before a window, and this was the window of the wooden superstructure which looked out towards the Surrey bank of the Thames. A flannel suit, a pair of shoes, a muffler, and a Chinese cap, lay upon the floor.

Fascinated and unashamed, Nayland Smith watched the toilet of the woman who squeezed tiny feet into tiny jade green shoes.

She stood up, walked to the mirror, and smeared her face with cream from a glass jar which once had contained potted meat. The features of the one-eyed Chinese waiter became obliterated.

The classic features of Fah Lo Suee, daughter of Dr. Fu Manchu, revealed themselves!

Fah Lo Suee, having cleansed her skin, hurriedly carried the one chair to the dressing-table, and seating herself before a libellous mirror, set to work artistically to make up as a beautiful woman; for that she was.a beautiful woman Nayland Smith had never been able to deny.

Silently, cautiously, he began to descend. The River Police craft was pulled up beneath him. Forester and a member of the crew hung on to the end of the ladder as Nayland Smith came aboard.

"Put me ashore," he snapped. "Gallaho! Sterling! Then stand by for Merton."

Sterling grabbed the speaker's arm. His grip was violent in its intensity.

"Sir Denis!" he said—"for God's sake tell me—who is up there? What did you see?"

Nayland Smith turned. They were alongside the barge, across the deck of which they had come, and by the same route were returning.

"Your old friend Fah Lo Suee! When I gave the sign to Murphy and came out, I thought you had recognized her, too. I was interested in the fact that she seemed to have a base somewhere upstairs."

"Fah Lo Suee," Sterling muttered. "Good heavens! now that you point it out, of course, I realize it *was* Fah Lo Suee."

"The Doctor is using her remorselessly: every hour of her day is fully occupied. Late though it is, she has some other duty to perform. She must be followed, Sterling."

They were crossing the deck of the barge, Gallaho at their heels, his bowler hat jammed on at a rakish angle, when:

"*Look!*" said Nayland Smith.

With one hand he grabbed the C.I.D. man, with the other he grasped the arm of Sterling.

A wavering blue light, a witch light, an elfin thing, danced against the fog mantle over the house of Sam Pak.

"Good Lord!" Gallaho muttered. "I heard of it for the first time to-night, but I'm damned if I can make out what it is."

All watched in silence for a while. Suddenly, the mystic light disappeared.

"It looks like something out of hell," said Gallaho.

"Very possibly it is," Nayland Smith jerked. He turned to Sterling. "Did you notice anything curious about the air of the Sailors' Club?"

"It had the usual fuggy atmosphere of places of that kind."

"Certainly it had, but did anything in the temperature strike you?"

"Temperature . . .?"

"Exactly."

"Now, that you mention it, it was certainly very hot."

"Exactly."

"Now that you mention it, it was certainly very hot."

"Undoubtedly it was, and twice as hot at the bar end as at the other."

"Maybe it's central heated," said Gallaho. "I'll ask Murphy about it."

"Nothing of the kind," snapped Nayland Smith. He was

still staring up at that spot above the roof of Sam Pak's where the queer, spirituous flame had appeared. "Certain sects in India burn their dead on burning ghats. Were you ever in India, Gallaho?"

"No sir. But whatever do you mean?"

"You would know what I meant if you had ever seen a burning ghat at night. . . ."

CHAPTER 17

THE GAME FLIES WEST

"Whichever way the dame comes out," said Gallaho, "she's got to pass this corner to get on to the main road. It's a pound to a penny there's another way out into that yard which adjoins the restaurant, and I'm told that a car is sometimes garaged there. It may be there to-night."

"Evidently it is," said Nayland Smith. "Listen."

Gallaho ceased speaking and he and Sterling listened intently. Someone had started a car at no great distance away.

"Quick!" snapped Nayland Smith. "Your man's standing by?"

"Yes."

"I'll wait here. I want to see who is in the car. Directly it has passed, pick me up. . . ."

Gallaho and Sterling set off down a side-turning. In a narrow opening between a deserted warehouse and the adjoining building, the Flying Squad car was hidden, all lights out. They had no more than reached it, when the car from the yard beside Sam Pak's passed the head of the street.

The Scotland Yard driver pulled out smartly. On the corner he checked and Nayland Smith jumped in.

"Fah Lo Suee!" he said simply.

Sam Pak's remained under cover. Anyone leaving would be shadowed to his destination, but Smith's instructions were urgent upon the point that the suspicions of the old Chinaman must not be aroused. . .

Deserted Commercial Road East reached, the police car drew up closer to the quarry—for at one point a curtain of fog threatened to descend again. Beyond, however, it became clearer.

"What car is it, Gallaho?" Nayland Smith asked. "I can't quite make out."

"It's a Morris, sir, and they're making it shift a bit." Nayland Smith laughed shortly.

"Once, it would have been at least a Delage," he murmured.

66

Silence fell again as they proceeded along one of the most depressing thoroughfares in Europe. Occasional lorries bound dockward constituted practically the only traffic: pedestrians were very few indeed. The occasional figure of a policeman wearing his waterproof cape brought the reflection to Sterling's mind that the duties of the Metropolitan Police force would not appeal to every man. Entering the City boundaries, the driver pulled up much closer to the pursued car. By the Mansion House the fog had disappeared altogether. Sterling glanced aside at Sir Denis. The bright light of a street lamp was shining in. He started, then laughed aloud. Shadow came again.

"What is it?" snapped Sir Denis.

"I had forgotten what you looked like," Sterling explained , "and your appearance was rather a shock."

"Anyone seeing us," growled Gallaho, "would take it for granted that I had one of you chained to each wrist."

He turned to Sir Denis. "I don't quite understand, sir, why you have handed the Limehouse end of the inquiry over to Forester. You have got definite evidence that it's the base of this Fu Manchu. Why not raid it? There's every excuse, if ever we want to do it. It's only necessary to find a single opium pipe on the premises!"

"I know," Nayland Smith replied, speaking unusually slowly. "But in dealing with Dr. Fu Manchu, I have found it necessary to follow certain instincts. These may be the result of an intimate knowledge of the Doctor's methods. But having been inside Sam Pak's to-night, I am prepared to assert with complete confidence that Dr. Fu Manchu is not there. I think it highly probable that his beautiful and talented daughter is leading us to him now, however."

"Oh, I see," Gallaho growled. "You don't think by any chance that this fly dame spotted you through your disguise, and is making a getaway?"

"I don't think so. But it is a possibility, nevertheless."

"I mean," the detective went on doggedly. "it isn't clear to me what she was doing down there, unless her job was that of a lookout. You tell me she's very much the lady, so that her idea of fun wouldn't be serving beer to drunken sailormen?"

"Quite," murmured Nayland Smith.

After which staccato remark he fell into a reverie which he did not break until the great bell of St. Paul's boomed out from high above their heads.

"Two o'clock," he murmured, and peered ahead. "Hello! Fleet Street. The game flies West, Gallaho."

The Street of Ink was filled with nocturnal activity, in contrast to the deserted City thoroughfares along which, hitherto, their route had lain. Into the Strand, across Trafalgar Square and on to Piccadilly, the hunt led; then the Morris turned into Bond Street, and Gallaho broke a long silence.

"I've just remembered," he remarked, "that they've got an extension at the Ambassadors' Club to-night. Funny if that's where she's going."

"H'm!" and Nayland Smith, glancing aside at Sterling, as the light from the window of a picture dealer's shone into the car. "We sha'n't be able to obtain admittance!"

"Just what I was thinking," growled Gallaho. "Yes—look, sir! That is where she's going!"

The Morris pulled up before the door of the club, and a commissionaire assisted a slender, fur-wrapped figure to alight. Fah Lo Suee, her jade coloured shoes queerly reflected upon the wet pavement, her gossamer frock concealed beneath a white wrap, went in at the lighted doorway.

"I can soon find out who she's with and what she's up to," growled Gallaho. "You two gentlemen had better stay out of sight."

He stepped out and proceeded in the direction of the club.

By the entrance he paused for a moment as another car pulled up and the be-medalled commissionaire sprang forward to the door. A distinguished looking gentleman who might have been a diplomat, who affected a grey, pointed beard and who wore a monocle, stepped out hurriedly, discarded a French cape and, tossing it back into the car, nodded to the commissionaire and went in. He vibrated nervous energy.

"H'm!" muttered Gallaho, watching the long, fawn and silver car disappearing in the direction of Bruton Street. "Sir Bertram Morgan!"

The last arrival was the newly appointed governor of the Bank of England.

Gallaho was about to turn to the commissionaire, with whom he was acquainted, when, following from the tail of his eye the slim, debonaire figure of the banker, he saw a slender woman dressed in jade green rise from a settee in the lobby and advance with extended hand to meet Sir Bertram.

In the brief glimpse which he had of her, Gallaho recognized the fact that she was the woman they had followed from Limehouse—according to Sir Denis Nayland Smith, the daughter of Dr. Fu Manchu. She was exotically beautiful. The strange pair disappeared.

Gallaho changed his mind.

"Good evening, sir," said the commissionaire, and was about to salute; then grinned broadly and nodded instead.

"Good," said Gallaho. "I am glad you remembered. Never salute a plain clothes officer."

"No, sir."

"Good night."

"Good night, sir."

Gallaho walked on as though his presence there had been merely accidental. Within his limitations he was an artist. It was no uncommon thing for the tracker to be tracked; keen eyes might be watching his every movement.

He crossed to Grafton Street, stood on the corner for a while, and looked back. Accustomed to the ways of spies, he was satisfied that no one was on his trail. He retraced his steps—but on the other side of Bond Street.

CHAPTER 18

"I BELONG TO CHINA"

SIR BERTRAM MORGAN was deeply intrigued with Madame
Ingomar. He had met her three years before at the villa of a
mutual friend in Cairo. Anglo-Egyptian society is not exactly
Bohemian, and Sir Bertram, at first, had been surprised to
find an obvious, if beautiful, half-caste a guest at this somewhat exclusive establishment.

She was, it appeared, the widow of a physician. But this
alone was not enough. And noting the patrician elegance,
almost disdain, which characterized the beautiful widow, Sir
Bertram had not been surprised to learn later, that on her
father's side there was royal Manchu blood.

An experienced man of the world is the adventuress's easi-
est quarry. Sir Bertram, a widower of almost illimitable
means, naturally knew much of women; he thought there was
no design whose pattern he had not met with at some time.
He distrusted Madame Ingomar. But she attracted him in a
way that was almost frightening.

They met again on the Riviera a year later.

Discreetly, and as if telling an Oriental fairy tale, she had
spoken of the existence of an hereditary secret in her family,
smilingly pointing out that the widow of a brilliant, but penniless physician, could not otherwise dress as she dressed.

Other explanations occurred to Sir Bertram at the time,
but just when he had been sharpening his wits to deal with
this dazzling cocotte, she had disappeared.

It seemed to be a habit of hers.

Now, she was in London. They had met accidentally, or
apparently accidentally, and he, anxious to test her,
because she was so desirable, had challenged the claims
which she had made in France. The challenge, lightly, had
been accepted.

The life of Madame Ingomar was a fascinating mystery.
Her appointment at a fashionable dance club, made for two
o'clock in the morning, was odd. Sir Bertram was in the

toils—he knew it; he was prepared to believe that royal blood of China ran in this woman's veins; prepared to believe that she was really the widow of a distinguished physician; but he had no means of testing these claims. One, however—the hereditary secret—he *could* test: it came within his special province. And to-night she had offered him an opportunity.

"My dear Madame Ingomar," he said, and kissed her hand, for his courtly manners were famous throughout Europe. "This is indeed a very great privilege."

The maître d'hôtel led the way to that table which was always reserved for Sir Bertram whenever he required it. Madame Ingomar declined supper, but drank a glass of wine.

Sir Bertram having draped her white fur wrap across the back of her chair, ivory shoulders and perfectly modelled arms were revealed by a gossamer green frock. She smoked almost continuously, not as other women of his acquaintance smoked, but, and it seemed almost a custom of a bygone generation, using a long jade holder.

Her hands were exquisite, her exotic indolence conjured up visions of vanished empires. She talked brilliantly, and Sir Bertram, watching her, decided she was quite the most attractive woman he had ever known. He sighed. He was uncertain of her; and he had reached an age, and a position in the world, when the worst thing that could befall him would be to become laughable.

Madame Ingomar caught his glance, smiled, and held it. Her long, narrow eyes, were brilliantly green. He had never seen such eyes. This was their second meeting since her appearance in London and he had noticed as a man who took an interest in women, that whereas most of those upon the dance floor wore dresses which exposed their backs, in some cases to the waist, Madame Ingomar's frock was of a different pattern.

She had an uncanny trick—it disturbed him—of answering one's unspoken thoughts; and:

"My frock is not quite the mode," she murmured smilingly—her voice had the most soothing quality of any voice to which he had ever listened—"you wonder why?"

"Really, my dear Madame Ingomar, you embarrass me. Your dress is completely charming—everything about you is perfect."

She placed her cigarette-holder in an ash-tray, glancing swiftly about the room.

"I do not live the sheltered life of other women," she said tensely; "perhaps you would understand me better if you knew something of the things I have suffered."

"Whatever do you mean?"

She smiled again, and taking a cigarette from Sir Bertram's open case, fitted it to the jade holder.

"I belong to China," she murmured, lowering her dark lashes, "and in China, women are treated as . . . women."

This was the kind of conversation which at once intrigued and irritated Sir Bertram. It was her hints at some strange, Oriental background into which from time to time she was absorbed, which first had thrown a noose about his interest. But always . . . he doubted.

That she had Chinese blood in her, none could deny. But that she belonged in any other sense to the Far East he was not prepared to admit. These odd references to a mode of life divorced from all ideals of Western culture, were part and parcel with that fabulous story of the hereditary secret.

As Sir Bertram lighted her cigarette. Madame Ingomar glanced up.

Those wonderful eyes held him.

"You have always mistaken me for an adventuress," she said. And the music of her voice, because it was pitched in so curious a key, reached him over the strains of the dance band. "In one way you are right, in another you are very wrong. To-night, I hope to convert you."

Believe me, I require no conversion; I am your most devoted friend."

She touched his hand lightly; her long, slender fingers, with extravagantly varnished nails, communicated to Sir Bertram a current of secret understanding which seemed to pulse through his veins, his nerves, and to reach his brain.

He was in love with this Eurasian witch. Every line and curve of her body, every wave of her dark hair, her voice, the perfume of her personality, intoxicated him.

Silently, he mocked himself:—There is no fool like an old fool.

"You are neither old nor a fool," she said, and slipped slender fingers into his grasp. "You are a clever man whom I admire, very, very much."

He squeezed those patrician fingers almost cruelly, carried away by the magnetism of this woman's intense femininity; so that for fully half a minute the uncanny character of those words did not dawn upon him.

Then, it came crashingly. He drew his hand away—and stared at her.

"Why did you say that?" he asked. He was more than startled; he was frightened. "I did not speak."

"You spoke to *me*," she said, softly. "You understand me a little bit, and so I can hear you—sometimes."

"Good God!"

Madame Ingomar laughed. Her laughter, Sir Bertram thought, was the most deliciously musical which had ever fallen upon his ears.

"In the East," she said, "when we are interested, we know how to get in touch."

He watched her in silence. She had turned her glance away, lolling back in her chair, so that she seemed to emerge like an ivory goddess from the mass of white fur, for she had drawn her wrap about her shoulders. She was watching the dancers, and Sir Bertram saw her as an Oriental empress, watching, almost superciliously, a performance organized for her personal entertainment.

Suddenly, she glanced aside at him.

"I promised that to-night I would prove my words," she said, slowly. "If you wish it, we will go."

Sir Bertram started. She had called him back from a reverie in which he had been a guest at a strange Eastern banquet.

"I am very happy, here, with you," he replied. "But what you wish is what I desire to do."

"Let us go, then. My father has consented to see you."

For anyone to "consent" to see the great Sir Bertram Morgan was a novelty in that gentleman's life. Yet, oddly enough, the phrase did not strike him as insolent, or even curious. One of the greatest powers in the world of finance, he accepted this mysterious summons.

CHAPTER 19

ROWAN HOUSE

SIR BERTRAM'S fawn and silver Rolls, familiar in many of the capitals of Europe, was brought up to the door of the club, and the courtly financier handed his beautiful companion to her seat.

"I warn you, Sir Bertram, we have some distance to go."

"How far?"

"Fourteen or fifteen miles into Surrey."

"The journey will pass very quickly with you."

"If you will tell your man to go to Sutton By-pass I will direct him when we get there how to find Rowan House."

"Rowan House? Is that where you are going?"

"It's a very old house—a sort of survival. It came on the market some years ago. It was once the property of Sir Lionel Barton, the famous explorer."

"Barton?" Sir Bertram got in beside Madame Ingomar, having given rapid instructions to the chauffeur. "I have met Barton—a madman, but brilliant. He nearly brought about a rising a year or two ago, in Afghanistan, or somewhere, by stealing the ornaments from a prophet's tomb. Is that the man you mean?"

The car started smoothly on its way.

"Yes," said Madame Ingomar, leaning back upon the cushions and glancing in the speaker's direction. "It is the same man. The house was very cheap, but in many ways suitable."

Madame Ingomar turned her head again, staring straight before her, and Sir Bertram, studying that cameo-like profile, groped for some dim memory which it conjured up. Bending forward he pulled down the front blind.

"The lights of approaching cars are so dazzling," he said. "That is more restful."

"Thank you, yes," she murmured. . . .

The big Rolls, all but silently, quite effortlessly, was devouring mile after mile of London highway. The Flying Squad car, close behind, at times was fully extended by the driver to keep

74

track of the quarry. Chief detective-inspector Gallaho had twice removed his hat since they had left Bond Street, on each occasion replacing it at a slightly different angle, which betokened intense excitement, Sterling was silent, as was Nayland Smith. . . .

Madame Ingomar touched Sir Bertram's hand. He raised her fingers to his lips and kissed them rapturously.

"Please, please," she pleaded. "I will not allow you to make love to me, while you doubt me so much. If I did, I should feel like a courtesan."

Sir Bertram drew back, watching her. She dropped her wrap and turned away from him, glancing back over her right shoulder.

"You are a man of honour," she said, the gaze of those magnetic eyes fixed upon him suddenly, overpoweringly. "I need your assistance; but you will never understand me until you know something of the dangers of my life."

She slipped her shoulders free of the green frock. Sir Bertram suppressed an exclamation.

That ivory back was wealed with the marks of a lash!

He stared fascinatedly, fists clenched. With a graceful, almost indolent movement of her slender arms Madame Ingomar readjusted her dress, pulled her fur wrap about her, and lay back in the corner, watching him under lowered lashes.

"What fiend did that to you?" he muttered. "What devil incarnate could deface that ivory skin?"

He was bending over her, one knee upon the floor of the car, a supplicant, literally at her feet. But she stared straight before her. When he seized her hands, they lay listless in his grasp.

"Tell me!"—the hoarseness of his own voice surprised him: "I want to know—I must know."

"It would be useless," she replied, her tones so low that he could only just catch the words. "In this you *cannot* assist me. But—" she looked down at him, twining her fingers in his—"I wanted you to know that what I have told you of my life is not a lie."

Sir Bertram kissed her hands, kissed her arms, and quite intoxicated by the beauty of this maddening, incomprehensible woman, would have kissed her lips, but a slender hand, two of the fingers jewelled, intervened between his lips and hers.

Gently, she thwarted him, for her half-closed eyes were not unkind.

"Please . . . not yet," she said. "I have told you that you make me feel like a wanton."

Sir Bertram recovered himself. Seated, staring straight ahead, his teeth very tightly clenched, he tried to analyse his emotions.

Was he in the toils of the most talented adventuress who had ever crossed his path? Did these waves of insane passion which from time to time swept him away, mean that where Madame Ingomar was concerned, self-control had gone? If she was what she claimed to be, what were his intentions about her?

He taxed himself—was he prepared to marry her?

Beside him, she remained silent. He was conscious of the strangest urges. Not since his Oxford days had he experienced anything resembling these. Undeterred by that gentle rebuff, he wanted to grasp Madame Ingomar in his arms and silence her protests with kisses. He wanted to demand, as a lover's right, the real explanation of those marks upon her shoulders. He wanted to kill the man who had caused them, and it was his recognition of this homicidal desire which checked, in a measure, the tumult of his brain.

Was it possible, that he, at his age, holding his place in the world, could be driven quite mad by a woman? He wrenched his head aside and looked at her.

She lay back against the cushions. Through half-closed eyes she stared before her abstractedly, and Sir Bertram captured that fugitive memory.

It was the profile of Queen Nefertiti, that exquisite mystery whose portrait by an unknown artist has been the subject of so much dispute.

Deserted streets offered no obstacles to the chauffeur. The outskirts of London reached, the police car behind had greater difficulty in keeping Sir Bertram's Rolls in sight.

"I can't make this out at all," growled Gallaho. "Where the devil is she going?"

"I haven't been in this neighbourhood for some time,"

snapped Nayland Smith. "But it brings back curious memories. It was in an ancient house in a sort of back-water near Sutton, that I first met Sir Lionel Barton."

"The explorer?"

"Yes. He inherited a queer old place somewhere in this neighbourhood. It was the scene of very strange happenings at the beginning of the Fu Manchu case. And . . . by heaven, as I live, that is just the direction we are heading now!"

In the leading car, the blind having been raised again, Madame Ingomar was giving instructions to the chauffeur. And presently, so guided, the Rolls turned into a darkly shadowed avenue which in summer must have been a veritable tunnel. At the end of it, through the temporary clearness of the night, one saw Rowan House, a long, squat building, hemmed in by trees and shrubs.

When presently Sir Bertram found himself in the entrance hall, he recognized the hand of the brilliant, but eccentric explorer and archeologist who had been the former owner of Rowan House. The place was a miniature Assyrian hall, and the present occupier had not disturbed this scheme. Animal skins and one or two exotic rugs alone disturbed the expanse of polished floor; and in the opening hung curtains of some queerly figured material which resembled that represented in ancient wall paintings.

The exterior of the house, Sir Bertram had noted, presented an unpleasantly damp and clammy appearance. And now as he stood looking about him, but glancing from time to time at the Oriental servant who had opened the door, he became aware at once of a curious perfume, almost like that of incense, yet having an overpowering quality about it which gave him the impression that Rowan House was not exactly a healthy abode.

Madame Ingomar was speaking rapidly to the butler who had admitted them, a squat Burman, dressed in white, and possessing an incredible width of shoulder. They spoke in a language which Sir Bertram did not understand.

CHAPTER 20

GOLD

THE ROOM TO WHICH Madame Ingomar presently conducted Sir Bertram was astonishing in many respects.

"I will tell my father you are here," she said—and he found himself alone.

From the lacquer armchair in which he sat, Sir Bertram surveyed his surroundings. He saw a room Orientally elegant, having entrances closed with sliding doors. Two shaded lanterns swung from the ceiling, illuminating the room warmly, and a number of brightly coloured cushions were strewn about the floor. There were tapestries in which red and gold ran riot, so that one lost the head of a dragon and failed to recover it again in endeavouring to trace his tail. Rich carpets and cushioned divans; a number of handsome cabinets containing fine pottery, a battalion of books in unfamiliar bindings arranged upon shelves which, conforming to the scheme of the room, were of dull red lacquer.

At the end remote from that where Sir Bertram sat, in a deep tiled hearth, a small chemical furnace threw its red glow into the room. On a shelf just above this furnace there was a row of jars which contained preserved lizards, snakes and other small reptiles; there was a large table, apparently of Italian workmanship, magnificently inlaid, upon which were some open faded volumes and a number of scientific instruments.

One of the lacquer doors slid noiselessly open and a man came in. Sir Bertram hesitated for a moment and then stood up.

The newcomer was a singularly tall Chinaman who wore a plain yellow robe which accentuated the gaunt lines of his figure. A black cap surmounted by a bead crowned his massive skull. Introductions were superfluous: Sir Bertram Morgan knew that he stood in the presence of the Marquis Chang Hu.

The man radiated authority. He was impressive to a degree exceeding Sir Bertram's experience. Perhaps the similarity of the profile of Madame Ingomar to that of the long-dead, beautiful Egyptian queen subconsciously prompted the image, but Sir Bertram thought, as others had thought before him, that the aged, ageless, majestic face of the man in the yellow robe resembled the face of the Pharaoh Seti I whose power, unexercised for four thousand years, may still be felt by anyone who bends over the glass case in Cairo which contains the mummy of that mighty king.

"You are welcome, Sir Bertram." The tall Chinaman advanced, bowing formally. "Please be seated. I honour my daughter for arranging this interview.

"It is a pleasure to me, too, sir."

Sir Bertram spoke sincerely. He was used to nobilities and to the off-shoots of imperial trees, but this survivor of the royal Manchus was a Prince indeed.

He wondered what he was doing in England. Knowing something of the situation in China, he wondered if the charming and promising adventure with Madame Ingomar had been no more than a lead-up to this; an attempt to enlist him in some hopeless campaign, financially to readjust the hopeless muddle which had taken the place of the once great Chinese Empire.

The Marquis Chang Hu seated himself behind the Italian table and Sir Betram dropped back into his armchair. He had never heard a voice quite like that of Chang Hu. It was harsh, but imperious. He spoke perfect English. Long after this strange interview, Sir Bertram recognized that the impressiveness of the Marquis's lightest words was due to one peculiarity:— Sir Bertram was old enough to have heard John Henry Newman speak; and in the diction of this majestic Chinaman he recognized later, the unalloyed beauty of our language as the poet-cardinal had spoken it.

"It is not my wish, Sir Bertram," said his strange host, "to detain you any longer than is necessary."

Sir Bertram's chair was set very near to the big table, and Chang Hu, bending courteously across that glittering expanse, placed an ingot of metal in his visitor's hand.

"You will have observed that I have some small facilities here. If you wish to make any tests, I shall be happy to assist you."

Sir Bertram glanced at the ingot and then looked up. He closed his eyes swiftly. He had met a glance unlike any he had ever known. The eyes of Madame Ingomar were fascinating, hypnotic; the eyes of the Marquis, her father, held a power which was shattering.

Looking down again at the ingot in his hand:

"In the case of a man of my experience," he replied, "tests are unnecessary. This is pure gold."

CHAPTER 21

GALLAHO AND STERLING SET OUT

"STOP! SNAPPED NAYLAND SMITH through the speaking tube. "Back into the lane we have just passed on the right."

The driver of the C.I.D. car checked immediately, stopped and reversed. There was no trace of fog on this outskirt of London. The night was limpidly clear. The big car was backed into the narrow lane which Nayland Smith had indicated.

"Good," growled Gallaho; "but what's the next move, sir?"

"It's almost certain," said Sterling excitedly, "that this is Dr. Fu Manchu's new base. It's almost certain . . . that Fleurette is here."

"Go easy." Sir Denis grasped his shoulder. "We must think. A mistake, now, would be fatal."

"I am wondering," said Gallaho, "what madness brought Sir Bertram Morgan here to-night?"

"The madness," Smith replied, "which has brought many men to disaster . . . a woman."

"Yes," Gallaho admitted; "she's a good looker. But I should have thought he was getting past it."

"Sir Denis . . ." Sterling's voice trembled. "We're wasting time."

They tumbled out of the car. They had sponged the make-up from their faces, but were still in the matter of dress, two rough-looking citizens. Smith stood there in the dusk of that silent by-way, tugging at the lobe of his left ear; then:

"I am wondering" he murmured. "Including the driver, Gallaho, we are only a party of four. . . ."

"What have you got in mind, sir?"

"I have this in mind. I propose to raid Rowan House."

"While Sir Bertram Morgan is there?"

"Yes. Unless he comes out very soon."

"You think . . . ?"

"I think nothing. I know. Dr. Fu Manchu is in that house! If Sir Bertram Morgan is in danger or not I cannot say, but the man we want is there. I take it you have the warrant in your pocket, Inspector?"

Chief detective-inspector Gallaho coughed loudly.

"You may take it that I have, sir," he replied.

Nayland Smith grasped his arm in the darkness.

"I didn't mean what you're thinking, Inspector," he said, "but we are so tied by red tape that any absurd formality overlooked might mean the wreck of the case."

Gallaho replied almost apologetically.

"Thank you, sir; I entirely agree with you. Perhaps I was rather forgetting the fact that you have suffered from red tape as much as I have. But I take it you mean, sir, that we may meet with opposition."

Sterling, clenching and unclenching his fists, was walking up and down in a fever of excitement, and:

"Sir Denis!" he exclaimed, "why are we delaying? Surely, with a woman's life at stake . . . ?"

"Listen, Sterling," snapped Sir Denis. "I understand and sympathize—but I'm in charge of this party, and you belong to it."

"I am sorry," said Sterling hoarsely.

The driver of the car, seated at the wheel, was watching the trio expectantly, and then:

"Listen, Gallaho," said Nayland Smith, rapidly: "how far are we from a call-box?"

"I'm afraid I don't know, sir. This is rather outside my area. Do you know?" addressing his question to the driver.

"No, sir. The last one we passed was at the crossroads."

"Drive back," Nayland Smith instructed. "It's your job to put a call through to local headquarters."

"Very good, sir."

"I want a raid squad here within twenty minutes. When you know where to go, drive there to pick 'em up."

"Very good, sir."

Silently and smoothly the big car moved out of the lane.

"In moments of excitement," said Nayland Smith, "I am afraid I relapse into Indian police terms, Do you think your man can manage it, Gallaho?"

"Certainly, sir." Gallaho replied. "The Flying Squad's pretty efficient. We shall have all the men you want inside twenty minutes."

"My fault," said Nayland Smith, "not to have had a radio car."

"They're all on duty, sir."

"One could have been recalled. We had time."

"What now, sir?"

"We must look for vulnerable points, and keep well under cover. I don't want Sir Bertram's driver to see us. I trust nobody where Dr. Fu Manchu is concerned. Come on!"

He led the way towards the tree-shadowed drive of Rowan House. Their cautious footsteps seemed loudly to disturb the damp silence of the avenue, but they pressed on till the lights of Sir Bertram's Rolls, drawn up before the porch of the squat residence, brought them to a halt.

"Sterling!" Nayland Smith's voice was low, but urgent. "Through the shrubbery here, and right around that wing on the left. You are looking for a way in, preferably a French window, of course. But any point where an entrance can be made quickly. If you meet anybody, tackle him, and then sing out. Are you armed?"

"Yes; it's become a habit since I met Dr. Fu Manchu."

"Good. Walk right around the house until you meet Gallaho, then return by the more convenient route, and this point is to be our meeting place. And now, you, Gallaho, stick to the shadow of that lawn, there, and work around the right of the house till you meet Sterling. I am going to direct my attention to obtaining a glimpse of Sir Bertram's chauffeur. His appearance and behaviour will tell me much. We meet here in five minutes."

Gallaho and Sterling set out.

CHAPTER 22

GALLAHO RUNS

CHIEF DETECTIVE INSPECTOR GALLAHO started his voyage of exploration under conditions rather more difficult than those which confronted Sterling.

The west wing of the house was closely invested by shrubbery; and although there were a number of windows, some of which were lighted, it was impossible to approach near enough to take advantage of any chink in the curtains. Some of the shrubs, which were of varieties unfamiliar to the inspector, remained in full leaf, others displayed flowers; and there was a damp, sweet, but slightly miasmatic smell about the place.

He remembered that the house had belonged for some years to the eccentric explorer, archeologist and author, Sir Lionel Barton. No doubt this freak vegetation had been imported by him. Gallaho, who was no floriculturist, did not quite approve of shrubs which flowered in mid-winter.

Pressing on, walking on wet grass, he presently reached a gate in a wall which threatened to terminate his journey. He tried the gate—it was unlocked; he opened it. It communicated with a paved yard. Out-buildings indicated that this had formerly been the stables of Rowan House.

Gallaho stood still, looking about him suspiciously.

He was satisfied that no horses were kept; the place was very silent. In the windows of the main building visible from where he stood, no light showed. This was not surprising at such an hour in the morning. The domestic staff might be expected to have retired. It was the sort of place, however, in which an experienced man expected to meet a watch-dog.

Gallaho, holding the door ajar, assured himself that there was no dog, before proceeding across the yard. He examined doors and windows, and came out presently into a neglected garden. He pulled up to take his bearings.

From somewhere a long way off came the wail of a train whistle; and . . . was that a muffled crash?

He had made a half-circuit of the house, which was not large. Sterling should have met him at about this point.

Gallaho stood still, listening.

Except for that vague murmuring which makes London audible for twenty miles beyond the city's boundaries, the night was still.

It was very queer.

Gallaho had noted that all windows in the domestic quarters were fastened. The ideal point of entrance had not presented itself. He pushed on. What had become of Sterling?

Weed-grown flower beds bordered the wall of the house. There was nothing of interest to tempt him to approach nearer.

Suddenly, he stopped, fists clenched.

Somewhere—somewhere inside the house, he thought . . . a woman had screamed!

He began to run. He ran in the direction of an out-jutting wing. It was very dark here, but Gallaho found gravel beneath his feet. He raced around the abutment and found himself staring at a French window.

There was no light in the room to which it belonged. Gallaho could see that heavy curtains were drawn. But there was no indication that the interior was illuminated. Nevertheless—from that room the cry might well have come.

He ran forward.

His first discovery was a dramatic one. A glass pane immediately above the lock had been shattered!

The absence of Sterling was now becoming inexplicable. Gallaho could only suppose that he had made some discovery which he had felt to be of such importance as to justify his returning and reporting to Sir Denis. Otherwise, palpably they must have met some considerable time before this.

Gallaho slipped his hand through the opening in the glass, encountering velvet draperies, groped about and found the lock.

There was no key in it.

Yet there was something very sinister about this broken window—that dim scream.

Searching his memory, he seemed to recall that at one point in his fruitless journey, just after he had crossed the stable yard, at about the same time that a distant train whistle had disturbed the silence, he had imagined that he heard a muffled crash. Here, perhaps, was the explanation.

But where was Sterling?

He ran on to the corner of this wing of the house; and now, through close growing but leafless trees, could see the tunnel-like drive along which they had come. Sterling was not in sight, nor could he see Sir Denis. . . .

CHAPTER 23

FLEURETTE

ALAN STERLING was fully alive to the selfishness of his own motives. Nayland Smith was working for the welfare of humanity, striving to defend what we call Civilization from the menace which Dr. Fu Manchu represented. Gallaho officially assisted him. But he, Sterling, hard though he might fight to thrust personal interest into the background, to seek the same goal, knew in his heart that his present objective was the rescue of Fleurette—if she lived—from the clutches of the Chinese doctor.

Through long days and all but unendurable hours of sleepless nights, since the message of Dr. Petrie, her father, had reached him, he had known this yearning for the truth, dreadful though it might be. Was she dead or alive? If alive, to what condition of mindless slavery—to what living death—had she been subjected by the brilliant devilish master of her destiny?

He forced his way through damp shrubbery; thorny bushes obstructing his path. He was anxious to avoid making any unnecessary noise. Frequently he glanced towards the porch of Rowan House before which the long, lithe outlines of Sir Bertram's Rolls glittered dimly in reflected light. The headlamps had been turned off, but the sleek body was clearly visible.

Scratches were not to be avoided. At last he was clear of the shrubbery, and found himself upon the damp soil of a flowerbed. He ploughed forward, aiming for a dimly seen path, reached it and felt hard gravel beneath his feet. He was now out of sight from the porch. Glancing back swiftly, he crossed the path and found himself in shelter from the point of view of anyone watching from the front of the house.

He became aware of an oppressive, sickly sweet perfume. He saw a long, dead wall upon which some kind of creeper grew, despite the wintry season, bearing small yellow flowers. Heavy of limb, it climbed almost to the eaves of this wing of Rowan House.

One dark window he saw, high above his head, marked it, but knew that it could only be reached by means of a ladder. He pressed on.

In all directions vegetation hemmed the place in; until, through a chink in heavy curtains drawn behind a French window having small leaded panes, a spear of light shot across the damp gravel path, revealing many weeds, and was lost in shadowy shrubbery. Sterling crept forward cautiously, step by step, until at last he could peer into the room to which this French window belonged.

He found himself looking into a sort of small library. At first, all that he could see was shelf upon shelf laden with faded, well-worn volumes. Cautiously, he moved nearer to the pane, and now was able to enlarge his field of vision.

Intensely he was excited, so excited that he distrusted himself. He was breathing rapidly.

He saw more bookshelves, and, craning his neck still further, saw a floor plainly carpeted. There was little furniture in the place. He could not see the source of the illumination: he could see books, books, books: one or two Oriental ornaments; a coffee table with an open volume upon it; and a number of cushions.

A shadow fell across the carpet.

Sterling watched intently, fists clenched.

The shadow grew more dense, shortened—and then the person who occasioned it walked slowly into view, head lowered in the act of reading a small, very faded-looking volume.

It was Fleurette—*his* Fleurette! Petrie's daughter!

Sterling experienced a wave of exultation which swept everything else from his mind. Nayland Smith's instructions were forgotten—the chief purpose of the expedition, the apprehension of Dr. Fu Manchu, was forgotten . . . Fleurette was alive—only a few panes of glass separated them.

And how beautiful she was!

The hidden light, gleaming upon her wonderful hair, made it glow and shimmer in living loveliness. She was so slender—so divinely graceful; that rarest creation of nature, as the Chinese doctor had once declared, a perfect woman.

He rapped urgently upon the window.

Fleurette turned. The book dropped from her hand. Her eyes, opened widely, were fixed upon the gap in the curtains.

Sterling's heart was beating wildly as he pressed his face upon the glass. Surely in the light shining out from the room she could see him?

But she stood motionless, startled, gazing, but giving no sign.

"Fleurette!" Sterling spoke in a low voice, yet loudly enough for the girl in the room to hear him. "It's Alan. Open the window, darling—open the window!"

But she gave no sign.

"Fleurette! Can you hear me? It's Alan. Open the window."

He had found the handle. The strangeness of his reception by this girl who only a few days before had lain trembling in his arms because three or four weeks of separation pended, was damping that glad exultation, chilling the hot blood dancing through his veins.

The window was locked, as he had assumed it would be. He could see the key inside.

"Fleurette, darling! For God's sake open the window. Let me in. Don't you understand? It's Alan! It's Alan!"

Fleurette shook her head, and turning, walked across the room.

Surely she had recognized him? In spite of his rough dress, could Fleurette, his Fleurette, *fail* to recognize him?

Pressing his face against the glass, Sterling, astounded, saw her take up a pencil and a writing-block from a dimly seen bureau. He could endure no more. Premature action might jeopardize the success of Nayland Smith's plans, but there were definite limits to Sterling's powers of endurance. These had been reached.

Stepping back a pace he raised his right foot, and crashed the heel of his shoe through the small leaded pane of glass just above the lock of the French window.

He had expected an echoing crash; in point of fact the sound made was staccato and oddly muffled. He paused for a second to listen . . . Somewhere in the distance a train whistle shrieked.

Thrusting his hand through the jagged opening, he turned the key, pushed the French window open and stepped into the room. Three swift strides and he had Fleurette in his arms.

She had turned at the crash of his entrance—eyes widely opened, and a look of fear upon her beautiful face.

"My darling, my darling!"—he crushed her against him and kissed her breathlessly. "What has happened? Where have you been? Above all, why didn't you open the window?"

Fleurette's eyes seemed to be looking through him—beyond him—at some far distant object. She made a grimace of pain— good God! Of *contempt*. Leaning back, continuing to look not at him, but through him, and wrenching one arm free, she brushed it across her lips as if something loathsome had touched them!

Sterling released her.

He had read of one's heart growing cold, but was not aware that such a phenomenon could actually occur. Where there had been mystery—there was mystery no more. Fleurette's love for him was dead. Something had killed it.

With a tiny handkerchief she was wiping her lips, watching him, watching him all the time. There was absolute silence in the room, and absolute silence outside. He found time to wonder if Gallaho had heard the crash, if those inside the house had heard it.

But this thought was a mere undercurrent.

All of him that was real, all of him that lived, was concentrated upon Fleurette. And now, looking him up and down, with a glance of such scornful anger as he had never sustained in his life from man or woman:

"You are just a common blackguard, then?" she said, in that musical voice which he adored, and yet again raised the fragment of cambric to her lips. "I hate you for this."

"Fleurette, darling!"

His own voice was flat and toneless.

"If you ever had a right to call me Fleurette, you have that right no longer."

Her scorn was like a lash. Alan Sterling writhed under it. But although she stared straightly at him, he could not arrest that strange, far-away gaze. She turned suddenly, and walked towards the bureau. Over her shoulder:

"Get out!" she said. "I am going to call the servants, but I will give you this chance."

"Fleurette, dear!" he extended his arms distractedly. "My darling! What has happened? what wrong have I done?"

He followed her, but she turned and waved him away, fiercely.

"Leave me alone!" she cried, her eyes flashing murderously. "If you touch me again, you will regret it."

She picked up a pencil and began to write.

Sterling, quivering in muscle and nerve, stood close beside her. Whoever had interfered between himself and Fleurette, upon one point he was determined. She should not remain here, in this house. Explanations could come later. But he proposed to pick her up, regardless of protests, and carry her out to the police car. Slowly he moved nearer, making up his mind just how he should seize her. There was a silk-shaded lamp on the bureau and in its light he was able quite clearly to read the words which Fleurette was writing upon the pad.

As he read, he stood stock still, touched by a sort of supernatural horror. This is what he read:-

"Alan darling. If you touch me I shall try to kill you. If I speak to you I shall tell you I hate you. But I can write my real thoughts. Save me, darling! Save me! . . ."

Came a flash of inspiration—Alan Sterling understood.

Fleurette was the victim of some devilish device of the Chinese physician. He had induced in her either by drugs or suggestion, a complete revulsion of feeling in regard to those she had formerly loved. But because of some subtlety of the human brain which he had over-looked, although, as in some cases of amnesia, she could not express her real thoughts in words, she could express them in *writing!*

"My darling!"

Sterling bent forward and tore the page from the writing-block.

Whereupon Fleurette turned, her face contorted.

"Don't touch me! I detest you!"—she glared at him venomously; "I detest you!"

Sterling stooped, threw his left arm around her waist and his right under her knees. He lifted her. She screamed wildly and struck at him.

He forced her head down upon his shoulder to stifle her cries, and carried her towards the open window. . . .

CHAPTER 24

THE LACQUER ROOM

GALLAHO by now very breathless pulled up, watching the porch of Rowan House.

The front door was open; this dimly, he could divine; but there seemed to be no light in the entrance hall.

The head lamps of Sir Bertram's Rolls gleamed dimly but the inside lights were turned off. Evidently, Sir Bertram was leaving—after a very brief visit.

Why was there no light in the entrance hall?

Gallaho's bewilderment was growing by leaps and bounds. To the problems of the scream, the broken window and Sterling's absence now was added that of Sir Denis's disappearance. Gallaho's own inclination, for he was a man of forthright action, was to run up the drive quite openly to the porch, and to demand to see the occupier of the house.

But Sir Denis was in charge to-night. He could not act without his authority, and his last instruction had been:

"Do nothing, until I give the word."

Between them, Gallaho thought bitterly, they were likely to make a mess of things.

A muted bang told him that the door of Sir Bertram's car had been closed. Who had entered it he didn't know. Suddenly the head lights cleaved a lane through darkness, illuminating the gravel drive, depicting trees of elfin shapes in silhouette, goblin trees. The entrance to Rowan House was transformed magically into a haunted forest.

The Rolls moved off, turned, and entered the drive. Gallaho darted half right into the shrubbery, crouched down, and watched. . . .

Someone was seated beside the chauffeur. The fleeting impression which Gallaho derived conveyed to his mind the idea of a native servant of some kind. This surely meant that Sir Bertram was not returning home, but was proceeding elsewhere?

And there was no means of following! The Flying Squad car

was presumably at the local police station, picking up a party of men to raid Rowan House!

The Rolls purred swiftly by. Of its occupants, Gallaho had never a glimpse. But as it passed he sprang to his feet and stepped out on to the drive.

"Where in hell has everybody got to?" he growled.

The door of the house was open. He could see the black gap which it made in the dingy grey frontage of the pillared porch. Something very strange was happening here—had already happened; and now:

"Gallaho!" came a distant voice, "Gallaho!"

It was Nayland Smith!

"Where are you, sir?" Gallaho shouted.

He raced towards the porch of the house from which the cry had seemed to come, throwing precaution to the winds now, for there was urgency in Nayland Smith's voice.

And as he reached the steps he saw him. . . .

Sir Denis was standing in the open doorway, the lobby behind him in darkness.

"He's slipped us, I think, Gallaho. We're too late. But my main concern at the moment is not with him. . . . show a light here. I am looking for the switch."

Gallaho's torch flashed in the darkness of that strange Assyrian hall.

"There it is, sir."

The lights were switched on. It was a queer looking place, of pillars and bas-reliefs, a freak of the former eccentric owner of Rowan House. There was no sound. They might have been alone in the building.

"What the devil has become of Mr. Sterling?"

Gallaho's face looked very lined and grim. "And I thought I heard a woman scream."

"I *did* hear a woman scream," snapped Smith. "I started around the house in the direction you had taken. Did you notice a door in a sort of archway which opens into the stable yard?"

"Yes, it was locked."

"Not when I reached it," Smith replied grimly. "I went in, venturing to use my torch. It communicated with an absolute-ly unfurnished passage, which I followed, and found myself here, looking out of the open front door—just as Sir Bertram's car disappeared down the drive. Ssh! What's that?"

From somewhere within the recesses of the silent house, a faint sound of movement had come. . . .

Slowly and with extreme caution, in order not to rattle the rings, Inspector Gallaho drew aside a curiously patterned curtain which hung in one of the square openings of the Assyrian hall. It was from behind this curtain that the slight sound had come.

A thickly carpeted passage appeared, dimly lighted. There was a door at the further end immediately facing them and one to the right. That at the further end—apparently a sliding door-was ajar . . . and light shone out from the room beyond.

Nayland Smith exchanged a significant glance with the detective, and the two tip-toed along the corridor. Their footsteps made next to no sound upon the thick carpet. Outside the door, both paused, listening.

In the room beyond, someone was walking up and down, restlessly, ceaselessly.

Gallaho displayed an automatic in his open palm. Smith nodded, and drew the door open.

He found himself in a fairly large room which was a combination of a library and a laboratory. It was a type of room with which he had become familiar during the long years that he had battled with Dr. Fu Manchu. There were preserved snakes and reptiles in jars upon a high shelf. Many queer looking volumes in orderly rows appeared behind a big table upon which, in addition to evidences of literary activity, there was a certain amount of chemical paraphernalia. Lacquer was the dominant note.

At the moment of Nayland Smith's entrance, the man who had been promenading the room turned, startled, and stared at the intuders.

It was Sir Bertram Morgan, Governor of the Bank of England.

"Well I'm damned!"—the growling words came from Gallaho.

"Sir Bertram!" Nayland Smith exclaimed.

Sir Bertram Morgan experienced a not unnatural difficulty in recognizing Smith, whom he had met socially, in his present attire; but at last:

"Sir Denis Nayland Smith, I believe?" he replied.

The financier had quite recovered his poise. He was a man of remarkably cool nerve. "The Marquis Chang Hu did not inform me that I should have the pleasure of meeting you here to-night."

Gallaho exchanged glances with Sir Denis and then stood by the open door, listening—listening for the Scotland Yard car and the raiding party. Sir Denis twitched at the lobe of his ear, staring all about him, and then:

"I fear, Sir Bertram," he said, "that you have been decoyed here under false pretences.

"Decoyed . . . ?"

Sir Bertram assumed his well-known expression which has appeared in so many Press photographs, his bushy eyebrows slightly raised in the centre.

"I said 'decoyed' advisedly. You came with a woman. She is half Chinese. By what name you know her I cannot say. I have known her by several."

"Indeed! You probably refer to Madame Ingomar?"

Nayland Smith smiled, but without mirth.

"Fah Lo Suee's invention is failing her," he murmured; "that was the name in which she crept into the good graces of Sir Lionel Barton in Egypt three years ago. However, all this is beside the point. You have taken a very grave risk, Sir Bertram."

The banker, unused to that brusque mode of address which characterised Nayland Smith in moments of tension, stared rather coldly.

"Your meaning is not clear to me," he replied. "I was invited to this house to discuss what I may term a purely professional matter with the Marquis Chang Hu."

"Chang Hu? Will you describe Chang Hu?"

Sir Bertram was becoming definitely offended with Nayland Smith, largley because the latter's force was beating him down.

"A tall, distinguished Chinese aristocrat," he replied quietly.

"Correct. He is tall, he is distinguished, and he is an aristocrat. Pray proceed."

"A member of a former Royal House of China."

"Correct. He is."

"A man, roughly, sixty years of age."

"Say a hundred and sixty," snapped Nayland Smith, "and you may be rather nearer the mark! However, I quite understand, Sir Bertram. May I ask you briefly to outline what occurred?"

"Certainly." Sir Bertram leaned against a bookcase which contained works exclusively Chinese in character. "I met the marquis by appointment. His daughter, Madame Ingomar, had informed me (frankly, I didn't believe her) that her father, an advanced student of mineralogy, had perfected a system for the transmutation of gold. I know something of gold . . ."

"You *should*," Nayland Smith murmured.

But his smile was so disarming—it was that delightfully ingenious smile which so rarely relieved the ruggedness of his features—that no man seeing it could have held antagonism.

Sir Bertram was mollified. He smiled in return.

"To-night," he went on impressively, and pointed to the big table, "an ingot of gold was offered to me by the Marquis Chang Hu, together with the assurance that he was prepared to supply any quantity up to three hundred-weights in the course of the next few weeks!"

"What!"

"Sst!"

Gallaho at the open door had raised his hand in warning. "Listen!"

The purr of an approaching car became audible.

"It's Markham with the police," said Gallaho.

He ran out.

Nayland Smith was staring curiously at Sir Bertram.

"It was pure gold?"

"Pure gold."

"He claimed to be able to make gold," murmured Smith. "I wonder . . . I wonder. May I ask, Sir Bertram, how the interview terminated?"

"Certainly. Madame Ingomar, my host's daughter, called out from somewhere in the house. The door was closed, and her cry was somewhat indistinct, but her father, naturally, was disturbed."

"Naturally."

"He excused himself and went to see what had occurred, begging me to remain here."

"He took the ingot of gold?"

"Apparently he did."

"He closed the door behind him?"

"He did. I opened it recently, beginning to wonder what had become of the marquis."

"It may surprise you to learn, Sir Bertram," said Nayland Smith quietly, "that only three or at the outside four of the rooms in Rowan House are furnished."

"What!"

"It was a plot. But by a miracle the plotters have been tricked. I regret to say that this is not the worst. I don't know all the truth, yet, but when the police arrive, I hope to learn it."

Detective-inspector Gallaho appeared in the open doorway, Sir Bertram's chauffeur at his heels.

"Preston!" Sir Bertram exclaimed—"what's this?"

"A very nasty business, sir, if I may say so," the man replied.

He was an obvious ex-Service man, clean limbed and of decent mentality. His hazel eyes were very angry and his fists clenched.

"Tell me," Sir Bertram directed, tersely.

"Well, sir," Preston went on, looking from face to face. "that Burmese butler who opened the door when we arrived, you remember, came out about ten minutes ago, and I naturally thought you were leaving. As I went up to him in the dark he jabbed a pistol in my ribs, and invited me to jump to the wheel. I am sorry, sir, but I did it. . . ."

"Don't blame you," growled Gallaho.

"Several people got into the car, sir. I had an impression that one was *carried* in. Then, the coloured swine beside me gave the order to go."

"Where did you go to?" asked Nayland Smith.

"To an old mews not three miles from here, sir, where I was told to pull up—and I pulled up. This blasted Burman sat with his gun in my ribs the whole time that the party in the car were getting out. But I had my eye on the reflector and I think there were two women and two men."

"Any idea of their appearance?" Smith demanded.

"Not the slightest, sir. It was very dark. I'm not sure, even, of their number. But one of the men was very sick, the others seemed to drag him out of the car."

The roar of the powerful engine of the Flying Squad proclaimed itself; voices were heard.

"Here they are!" said Gallaho.

"Quick!" Sir Denis directed Preston: "What happened then?"

"The Burman jumped off, keeping me under cover. He told me to drive back. I couldn't think of anything else to do, sir."

Uniformed police were pouring into Rowan House.

CHAPTER 25

CURARI

"NOTHING HERE!" declared Nayland Smith.

They had searched every foot of the deserted mews.

"A sort of cache?" suggested Sir Bertram Morgan, who had accompanied them, now keenly interested in their quest. "No doubt they kept a car here."

"There's evidence that they did," said Gallaho. "And we'll know more about it to-morrow. But in the meantime," he turned to Sir Denis, "what's the next move, sir?"

Rowan House had proved to be a mere shell, a mockery: the greater part of it unfurnished. The library in Rowan House in which Dr. Fu Manchu had received Sir Bertram, and the corridor leading to it from the Assyrian hall, were the only properly furnished parts of the place. There was a small writing-room on the other side of the house, the glass in the French window of which had been smashed, containing a number of bookshelves, a bureau and one or two other odds and ends. But with the exception of fragmentary belongings of the former tenant, the eccentric Lionel Barton, the place was unfurnished from floor to attic—nor was there a soul in it, although the police had searched it foot by foot.

The property had been sold by Sir Lionel Barton, but the last tenant had left nearly a year before. The books and some of the ornaments in the two furnished rooms, unreadable volumes in Sanskrit, Chinese and Persian, had been left behind by the out-going tenant as they had been left behind by Sir Lionel. The Chinese library, with its sliding doors and lacquer fittings, had been a feature of Rowan House during the time that Barton had occupied it. The place had been baited for the evening; a mouse-trap. The caretaker had vanished.

"They've got Sterling!" groaned Nayland Smith. "God knows why they've taken him—but they've got him!"

Sir Bertram was now keenly interested, tuned up for the hunt; his sentiments in regard to Madame Ingomar had undergone a definite change, yet he knew in his heart,

99

although he could not doubt the assurance of the ex-Assistant Commissioner, that if she beckoned to him again—he would follow. . . .

He wondered how far he would go, to what extent he would fall under the influence of those magnetic eyes, that compelling voice. He shuddered. Perhaps he had had a nearer escape than he realized. But the gold had been . . . *gold*.

The raiding party returned to the depot in the Yard car, and Sir Denis and Chief detective-inspector Gallaho accepted a lift home in Sir Bertram Morgan's Rolls.

Fog met them in the London suburbs . . .

It was at some hour not far removed from that when dawn should have been breaking over London, that Nayland Smith prepared a whisky and soda for Gallaho and passing it to him raised his glass silently.

"I know sir," said Gallaho; "it's been a very bad show for us to-night."

"A bad show all along," snapped Sir Denis.

"Cramped, trammelled, cut off from his resources, Fu Manchu is *still powerful*. First, he gets Petrie's daughter, a wonderful hostage, by one of the most amazing tricks in my experience. He smuggles her into England. And now . . ."

"That's the devil of it, sir."

"The devil indeed. He's got Sterling."

"Dead or alive?"

"Since he is a friend and a first-class type of man (I have worked with him in the past) I prefer to think, Inspector—alive. I doubt if Dr. Fu Manchu would burden himself with—"

"A corpse?"

"A corpse, yes."

Nayland Smith's gaze became abstracted, and plucking at his ear, he crossed the room and pulled a heavy curtain aside, gazing out upon the foggy Embankment.

There came a rap on the door.

"Come in!"

Fey entered, despite the approach of dawn, immaculate and unperturbed. Nayland Smith was still holding the heavy curtain aside, and:

"Have you noticed the window, sir?" Fey asked.

"No."

Nayland Smith turned, and examined the window.

"By gad!" he rapped.

There was a neat, but slightly jagged hole an inch in circumference in one of the panes! He closed the curtains, and faced Fey. Gallaho, glass in hand, was staring from man to man.

"While I was walking up and down sir." Fey went on coolly, "as you told me to do, earlier to-night, or rather, last night, sir, *this* came through the window—missed me by no more than an inch."

He handed a small feathered dart to Nayland Smith.

The latter stepped to a lamp and examined it closely.

"Gallaho", he said, "I should say that this thing had been fired from an air gun. But examine the point."

The Scotland Yard man came forward, eagerly bending over the table.

"It seems to be covered in gum."

"I won't say *curari*, but a very brief analysis will settle the point. The cornered rat is showing his teeth . . . and they are poisoned teeth."

CHAPTER 26

DR. FU MANCHU

ALAN STERLING looked around the cellar in which he lay.

It was brick-paved; its roof was formed by half an arch. There was a very stout looking door in the corner opposite that in which he found himself. An unshaded electric bulb hung on a piece of flexible cable from the roof. He could trace the cable down the sloping brickwork to a roughly hollowed gap through which it disappeared.

There was no furniture of any kind in the cellar, but the place was singularly hot, and it seemed to be informed by a ceaseless buzzing which, however, presently he identified with his own skull.

He had an agonizing headache. Raising his hand, he found a great lump immediately above his left ear.

The first idea which flashed through his bemused mind was a message of thanksgiving. He must have had a very narrow escape from death. Then came memories—chaotic, torturing.

He had had Fleurette in his arms: then, something had happened.

What had happened?

It was beyond him. He could recall nothing but the fact that she had screamed unnaturally, that he had struggled with her. Then there was a gap, and now . . . where was this place in which he found himself? Where had he been when he had struggled with Fleurette?

He clutched his throbbing skull, trying to force thought. Memories began to return to him in fragments; then, as a complete story.

He tried to stand up. The effort was too much for his strength. He dropped back again upon the stone pavement. By God! He had had a devil of a whack! Gingerly he touched the swelling on his skull, leaning back against the wall and still trying to think.

Fleurette was alive—thank God for that! But in some way, she had changed towards him. He was not quite clear about it. But for this he must be thankful: that she, whom he had thought was dead—was alive. The minor difficulty, no doubt, would resolve itself.

Nayland Smith! Of course! He had been with Nayland Smith! . . . And Gallaho? What had become of Gallaho?

Above all—where was he? Where was this unfurnished cellar located? He made another attempt to stand up; but it was not entirely successful. He was anxious to find out if that heavy door was locked, or bolted. But the journey, one of four paces, was too much for him.

He sank down on to the floor again, leaning back against the wall. The throbbing in his head was all but unendurable, and the heat was stifling—unless, like the buzzing, due to internal conditions.

Separate now from that buzzing, which he knew to belong to his injured skull, Sterling became aware of a muted roaring sound. It was somewhere beneath his feet. It was uncanny; when first he accepted the reality of its existence, he was dismayed; for what could it be? From where could it come?

He was about to make a third attempt to stand up, when the heavy door opened.

A very tall, gaunt man stood in the opening, looking at him. He wore a long, white linen coat, linen trousers, and white rubber-soled shoes. The coat, tunic fashion, was buttoned to his neck—a lean, sinewy neck supporting a head which might have been that of Dante.

The brow was even finer than the traditional portraits of Shakespeare, crowned with scanty, neutral coloured hair. The face of the white-clad man was a wonderful face, and might once have been beautiful. It was that of a man of indeterminable age, heavily lined, but lighted by a pair of such long, narrow, brilliant green eyes that one's thoughts flashed to Satan—Lucifer, Son of the Morning: an angel, but a fallen angel. His slender hands, with long, polished nails, were clasped before him. Although no trace of expression crossed that extraordinary face, perhaps a close observer watching the green eyes might have said that the man motionless in the doorway was surprised.

Alan Sterling succeeded in his third attempt to stand up. He was very unsteady, but by means of supporting himself against the wall with his left hand, he succeeded in remaining upright.

So standing, he faced Dr. Fu Manchu.

"The fact that you are alive—" the words came sibilantly from thin lips which scarcely seemed to move—"surprises me."

Sterling stared at the speaker. Every instinct in his mind, his body, his soul, prompted: "Kill him! Kill him!" But Sterling knew something of Dr. Fu Manchu, and he knew that he must temporize.

"I am surprised, too," he said.

His voice shook, and he hated his weakness.

The green eyes watched him hypnotically. Sterling, leaning against the wall, wrenched his gaze away.

"It is not my custom," the harsh voice continued, "to employ coarse methods. You were, to put it bluntly, bludgeoned in Rowan House. Your constitution, Alan Sterling, must resemble that of a weazel. I had intended to incinerate your body. I am not displeased to find that life survives."

"Nor am I," said Sterling, calculating his chances of a swift spring, and a blow over the heart of this Chinese fiend whom he knew to be of incalculable age; then a hook to that angular jaw—and a way to freedom would be open.

With the instinct of a boxer he had been watching the green eyes whilst these thoughts had flashed through his mind, and now:

"You could not strike me over the heart," said Dr. Fu Manchu; "I am trained in more subtle arts than the crudities of boxing have ever appreciated. As to your second blow aimed, I believe, at my jaw, this would not occur—you would be disabled."

For a moment, a long moment, Alan Sterling hesitated; in fact, until the uncanny quality of these words had penetrated to his brain. Then he realized, as others had realized before him, that Dr. Fu Manchu had been reading his thoughts. He stood quite still; he was recovering from the effects of the assault which had terminated his memories of Rowan House, and now was capable of standing unsupported.

"There is a monastery in Thibet," the cold voice proceeded; "it is called Rachë Churân. Those who have studied under the masters of Rachë Churân have nothing to fear from Western violence. Forget your projects. Rejoice only that you live—if you value life."

CHAPTER 27

THE PIT AND THE FURNACE

ALAN STERLING stood upon a wooden platform, clutching a rusty iron rail and looking down upon a scene which reminded him of nothing so much as an illustration of Dante's *Inferno*.

Dim figures, inhuman, strangely muffled like animated Egyptian mummies, moved far below. Sometimes they were revealed when the door of some kind of furnace was opened, to disappear again like phantom forms of a nightmare, when the door was closed. A stifling heat rose from the pit.

"The simile of a mummy has occurred to you," said the voice of Dr. Fu Manchu out of the darkness, that strange voice which stressed gutturals and lent to sibilants a quality rarely heard in the voice of an English speaker. "You are ignorant of Ancient Egyptian ritual, or other images would occur to you. In point of fact, these workers are protected against the poisonous fumes generated at certain points in the experiment now taking place below. These gases do not reach us here. They are consumed by a simple process and dispersed by means of a ventilation shaft. Pray continue to descend."

Sterling, clutching the rusty iron rail, went down more wooden steps.

To some degree he was regaining mastery of himself, but his brain failed to suggest any plan of action other than to accept the orders of the uncanny being into whose power, once again, he had fallen. Something which Nayland Smith had said, long, long ago—he was quite unable to recall when— came buzzing through his brain like a sort of refrain:

"Behind a house which we have passed a hundred times, over a hill which we have looked at every morning for months together, on the roof of a building in which we have lived, beneath a pavement upon which we walk daily, there are secret things which we don't even suspect. Dr. Fu Manchu has made it his business to seek out these secret things. . . ."

Here was the theory demonstrated! He was in a trap: he

hadn't the remotest idea where he was. This ghastly place might be anywhere within a fifty mile radius of the house in Surrey. He must wait for a suitable opening; try to plan ahead. He went on down the steps; the heat grew greater and greater. Dr. Fu Manchu followed him.

"Stop!" the harsh voice directed.

And Sterling stopped.

One thing there was which gave him power to control his emotion, which gave him strength to temporize, patience to wait: Fleurette was alive!

Some wizardry of the Chinese physician had perverted her outlook. He, Sterling, had seen such cases before in households belonging to Dr. Fu Manchu. The man's knowledge was stupendous—he could play upon the strongest personality as a musician plays upon an instrument in an orchestra.

"You will presently observe something phenomenal." The high voice continued, "something which has not occurred for several centuries. The mating of the elements. At the moment of transmutation, the fumes to which I have referred escape to a certain extent from the furnace."

Sterling paused, looking down into the hot darkness.

"My facilities here are limited," Dr. Fu Manchu continued, "and I am using primitive methods. I am cut off from my once great resources—to a certain extent by the activities of your *friend*—" he stressed the word, speaking it upon a very high note—"Sir Denis Nayland Smith. But it is possible to light a fire by rubbing two pieces of wood together, if your burning glass is absent or if one has no matches. The work is about to complete itself——" his voice rose to a key which Sterling had thought, before, indicated that Nayland Smith was right when he had declared Dr. Fu Manchu to be a brilliant madman. "Note the fires of union!"

The heat of the place as they descended nearer and nearer to the furnace was becoming almost unendurable. But now came a loud and vicious crackling, the clang of metal, and the furnace door was thrown open.

A blaze of light from the white-hot fire poured across the floor below. Mummy-like figures moved in it to approach that miniature hell, now extending instruments resembling long narrow tongs.

106

From the white heat of the furnace they grabbed what looked like a ball of light, and lowered it to the floor.

The furnace doors were reclosed by two more mummy-like figures which appeared out of the shadows.

The scene became more and more fantastic. The incandescent globe was shattered. Where it had been, Sterling saw a number of objects resembling streaks of molten metal; their glow grew dim and more dim.

"This work," said Dr. Fu Manchu, "will engage your attention in the immediate future. You have grossly interfered with my plans in the past, and I might justly and perhaps wisely, kill you. Unfortunately, I am short of labour at the moment, and you are a physically strong man——"

"You mean," asked Sterling, "that you are going to make me work down in that hell?"

"I fear it must be so——" the speaker's voice was very sibilant. "Continue to the base of the stairs."

And Sterling, descending, found himself at the bottom of the huge black shaft. The furnace was closed—the Inferno dimly lighted. Not one of the mummy-wrapped figures was to be seen. But the heat——

A tunnel sloped away on his right. Far down it, a solitary lantern appeared, as if to indicate its clammy extent—for, as he could see, this tunnel dripped with moisture and its floor was flooded in places. A grateful coolness was perceptible at the entrance to this unwholesome looking burrow.

"You will observe," said Dr. Fu Manchu—who invariably spole as if addressing a class of students—"that the temperature is lower here than on the stairs. We are actually a hundred and twenty feet below the surface. . . . We will return."

The authority behind Dr. Fu Manchu's orders had a quality which created awe, without making for resentment. Sterling had expereinced in the past this imposition of the Chinaman's gigantic will. The power of Fu Manchu's commands lay in his acceptance of the fact that they would never be questioned.

He passed the Chinaman, stepped on to the narrow stair, and clutching the iron rail proceeded upwards.

"It may interest you to learn," came the harsh voice from

behind him, "that human flesh is excellent fuel in relation to this particular experiment. . . ."

Sterling made no reply . . . the implication was one he did not care to dwell upon. He remembered that Dr. Fu Manchu had said, "I had intended to incinerate your body."

These stairs with their rusty hand-rails, seemed all but interminable. Descent had been bad enough, but this return journey, following on the spectacle below, was worse. Vague gleams from the pit fitfully lighted the darkness. From behind, Dr. Fu Manchu directed a light upon the crude wooden steps. . . .

Sterling found himself back again in a curiously high, narrow, brick corridor which led to the vault in which he had first awakened. He had just passed a low door, deep sunken in brickwork, when:

"Stop," the imperious voice directed.

There came a sound of rapping on the door—that of a bolt shot free—a faint creaking.

"Step back a pace, lower your head, and go in."

Sterling obeyed. He knew that the alternative was suicide. This place, he began to realize, in addition to its heat, had a vague but ghastly charnel-house odour. . . .

He went ahead along a narrow passage; someone who had opened the door stood aside to allow him to pass. He found himself in a small, square, brick chamber illuminated by one unshaded bulb hanging on a length of cable. He heard the outer door being bolted.

There was a camp bed, a chair and a table on which stood a glass and a bottle of water. This square brick chamber had never been designed for habitation; he was in the bowels of some uncompleted engineering plant. . . .

The man who had admitted him—who had stood aside when he had entered—appeared now in the doorway—a huge negro with a pock-scarred face.

For one breathless moment Alan Sterling stared, not daring to believe what he saw—then:

"Ali Oke!" he whispered.

The expression on the black face of the man so oddly named defied definition—but it resolved itself into a grin. Ali Oke raised a finger to his lips in warning—and closed the heavy door. Sterling heard the sound of a bolt being shot. . . .

Ali Oke! It was all but incredible!

Ali-called "Oke" because this term was his equivalent for "I understand" or "very good, sir"—had been Sterling's right-hand man on his Uganda expedition! He found it hard to believe that the faithful Ali, pride of the American Mission School, could be a servant of Dr. Fu Manchu. . . .

Complete silence. Even that queer dim roaring had ceased. . . .

Yet—Sterling reflected—better men than Ali Oke had slaved for the Chinese doctor. He stared at the massive wooden door. A faint, sibilant sound drew his gaze floorward.

A piece of paper was being pushed under the door!

Sterling stooped and snatched it up. It was a fragment from the margin of a newspaper, and on it in child-like handwriting was written in pencil:—

Not speak. Somebody listen. Write something. Can send somebody. Ali.

CHAPTER 28

TUNNEL BELOW WATER

INVESTIGATIONS IN SURREY brought some curious points to light

It was late in the afternoon when Gallaho came to Sir Denis's apartment to make his report. To be on duty for twenty-four hours was no novelty to the C.I.D. man, but he was compelled to admit to himself that he felt extremely tired. Sir Denis, who wore a dressing-gown, but who was fully dressed beneath, simply radiated vitality. He was smoking furiously, and his blue-grey eyes were as keen as if, after a long and dreamless sleep, he had emerged fresh from his bath.

Gallaho, who guessed Sir Denis to be ten years his senior—as a matter of fact, he was wrong—found a constant source of amazement in Nayland Smith's energy.

He reported that the mews to which Sir Bertram Morgan's car had been driven was known to have accommodated a Ford lorry belonging to a local contractor.

Nayland Smith laughed shortly, pacing up and down the carpet.

"When it comes to making important engagements in an unoccupied house, but one with which in the past—and he never forgets anything—the Doctor has been familiar; when, above all, he condescends to travel in a decorator's lorry . . ."

He laughed again, and this time it was a joyous, boyish laugh, which magically lifted the years and showed him to be a young man.

"It's all very funny," Gallaho agreed, "especially as Sir Bertram, according to his own statement, examined an ingot of pure gold which this Chinese magician offered to sell to him!"

Nayland Smith turned, and stared at the speaker.

"Have you ever realized the difficulty of selling gold, assuming you had any—I mean, in bulk?"

Gallaho scratched his upstanding hair, closed one eye, and cocked the other one up at the ceiling.

"I suppose it would be difficult, in bulk," he admitted;

110

"especially if the gold merchant was forced to operate under cover."

"I assure you it would," said Nayland Smith. "No further clues from Rowan House, I suppose?"

"Nothing. It's amazing. But it accounts for an appointment at half-past two in the morning. They just dressed the lobby and two rooms of the house like preparing a stage-set for a one-night show."

"Obviously they did, Gallaho—and it is amazing, as you say. I remember the place very well; I was there on many occasions during the time Sir Lionel Barton occupied it. I remember, particularly, the Chinese Room, with its sliding doors and lacquer appointments. Those decorations which were not Barton relics—I refer to the preserved snakes, the chemical furnace, and so forth—were imported for Sir Bertram Morgan's benefit."

"That's where the Ford lorry came in!"

Nayland Smith dashed his right fist into his left palm.

"Right! You're right! That's where the lorry came in! The missing caretaker?"

"He's just described by local tradesmen as 'an old foreigner'——"

"Someone employed by, or bought by, Fu Manchu. We shall never trace him."

Gallaho chewed invisible gum.

"Funny business," he muttered.

"Rowan House has known even more sinister happenings in the past. However, I will look it over myself—some time today if possible. What about the lorry?"

"I have seen the former owner" Gallaho pulled out a book and consulted some notes. "He sold it on the fourteenth instant. The purchase price was thirty pounds. The purchaser he describes as 'a foreign bloke.' I may say, sir—" looking up at Sir Denis—"said contractor isn't too intelligent; but I gather that the 'foreign bloke' was some kind of Asiatic. It was up to the purchaser to remove the lorry at his convenience."

"How was the payment made?"

"Thirty one-pound notes."

"Very curious," murmured Sir Denis. "Very , very curious. I am wondering what the real object could be in the purchase

111

of this lorry. Its use last night was an emergency measure. I think we may take that for granted. Have you traced it?"

"No, sir. Not yet."

"Has any constable reported having seen it?"

"No one."

"What about the Morris out of the yard in Limehouse?"

"I have a short report about that," Gallaho growled, consulting his notes. "It's the property of Sam Pak, as we surmised, and various birds belonging to his queer aviary seem to drive it from time to time. My own idea is that he uses it to send drunks home. But it's for hire, and according to Murphy, who has been on the job down there, it was hired last night, or rather, early in the morning, by a lady who had dined on board a steamer lying in West India Dock."

"You have the name of the steamer, no doubt?"

"Murphy got it."

"Did any lady dine on board?"

"The ship mentioned in my notes, sir," Gallaho replied ill-humouredly, "pulled out when the fog lifted. We have no means of confirming."

"I see," snapped Nayland Smith, his briar bubbling and crackling as he smoked furiously. "But the driver?"

"A man called Ah Chuk—he's a licensed driver; he's been checked up—who hangs about Sam Pak's when he's out of a job. His usual work is that of a stevedore."

"Has anyone seen this man?"

"Yes—Murphy. He says, and Sam Pak confirms it, that he took the car down to the gates of West India Dock and picked up a lady who was in evening dress. He drove her to the Ambassadors' Club——" Gallaho was reading from his notes—"dropped her there and returned to Limehouse."

"Where is the car now?"

"Back in the yard."

Nayland Smith walked up and down for some time, and then:

"A ridiculous, but a cunning story," he remarked. "However, Ah Chuk will probably come into our net. Anything of interest in the reports of the men who trailed customers leaving Sam Pak's?

"Well——" Gallaho's growl grew deeper—"those that left

were just the usual sort. Funny thing, though, is, that some of the customers you reported seeing inside didn't leave at all!"

"What!"

"Murphy reported seven people, six men and a woman in the 'Sailors' Club'. Only three—two men and the woman—had come out at seven o'clock this morning!"

"Very odd," Nayland Smith murmured.

"There are two things," said Gallaho, "that particularly worry me, sir."

He closed his note-book.

"What are they?"

"That funny light, which I had heard of but never seen; and . . . Mr. Sterling."

He stared almost reproachfully at Sir Denis. The latter turned, smiling slightly.

"I can see that you are worrying," he said. "and quite rightly. He is a splendid fellow—and he was very unhapppy. But an individual described by the hall-porter as a loafer, left this note for me an hour ago."

He crossed to the writing-table, took up an envelope and handed it to Chief detective-inspector Gallaho. The latter stared at it critically. It was an envelope of poor quality, of a kind which can be bought in packets of a dozen at any cheap stationer's and upon it in what looked like a child's handwriting, appeared:—

> *Nayland Smith*
>   *No 7 Westminster Court*
>   *Whitehall*

The inscription was in pencil. Gallaho extracted the contents—a small sheet of thin paper torn from a pocket-book. Upon this, also in pencil, the following message appeared:

> To:—*Nayland Smith*
>   *N 7 Westminster Court*
>   *Whitehall.*
> *In hands of Fu Manchu. In some place where there is a deep pit, a furnace, and a tunnel below water. I know no more. Do your best.*
>   *Alan Sterling.*

By the same hand which had addressed the envelope, one significant word had been added below the signature:

Limehouse

Gallaho stared across at Sir Denis. Sunshine had temporarily conquered the fog. The room was cheerful and bright. Gallaho found himself looking at a puncture in one of the windows, through which quite recently a message of death had come but had missed its target.

"Is this Mr. Sterling's writing?"

"Yes." Nayland Smith's eyes were very bright. "What do we know about *tunnels*, Gallaho?"

CHAPTER 29

AT THE BLUE ANCHOR

THE MAN with the claret coloured nose was becoming quarrelsome. His unshaven friend who wore a tweed cap with the brim pulled right down over his eyes, was drunk also, but in a more amiable way.

John Bates, the landlord of the Blue Anchor, shirt-sleeved behind the bar, watched the pair inquiringly. The man with the claret nose came in at longish intervals, and was usually more or less drunk. Bates supposed that he was a hand in one of the coasting steamers which sailed from a near-by dock. His friend was a stranger, nor did he look like a sailor.

The Blue Anchor had only just opened and there were no other customers in the private bar, which was decorated with sporting prints and a number of Oriental curiosities which might have indicated that the landlord, or some member of his family, had travelled extensively in the East. John observed with satisfaction that the phenomenal fog which had lifted during the day, promised to return with the coming of dusk.

From long experience of dockland trade, John had learned that fog was good for business. He lighted a cigarette, leaning on the bar and listening to the conversation of the singular pair.

"I bet you half a quid as it was above Wapping."

The claret nosed man was the speaker, and he emphasized his words by banging his fist upon the table before him. John Bates was certain now that he was a sailor and that he had a pay-roll in his pocket. The other man stolidly shook his head.

"You're wrong, Dick," he declared, thickly. "It was somewhere near Limehouse Basin."

"Wapping."

"Limehouse."

"Look here." Claret Nose rose unsteadily to his feet, and approached the bar. "I'm goin' to ask you to act as judge between me and this bloke here. See what I mean, guv'nor?"

John Bates nodded stolidly.

"It's a bet for half a quid."

Bates liked bets; they always led up to rounds of drinks, and:

"Put your money on the counter," he directed; "I'll hold the stakes."

Claret Nose banged down a ten shilling note and turning:

"Cover that!" he shouted, truculently.

The othe man, who proved to be tall and thin when he stood up, extracted a note from some inner pocket and placed it upon that laid down by the challenger.

"Right." John Bates inverted a tumbler upon the two notes. "Now, what's the bet about?"

"It's like this," said the red-nosed man—"we was talkin' about tunnels——"

"Tunnels?"

"Tunnels is what I said. We talked about the Blackwall Tunnel, the Rotherhithe Tunnel and all sorts of bloody tunnels——"

"What for?" John Bates inquired.

"We just felt like talkin' about tunnels. Then we got to one what was started about fifty years ago and never finished. A footpath, it was, to go under the Thames from somewhere near Wapping Old Stairs——"

"Limehouse."

The lean man, bright eyes peering out from beneath the brim of his remarkably large tweed cap, had imparted a note of challenge to the word.

"I don't know what you're talking about," said Bates. "I never heard of such a tunnel."

"Fifty years ago, everybody'd heard about it."

"I wasn't here fifty years ago."

"I thought you knew all there was to know about this part o' the world"

"I know a lot but I don't know that. The Old Man would know."

"Well ask the Old Man."

"He's upstairs, having a lay down." Bates turned to a grinning boy who now stood at his elbow. "Keep an eye on that money, Billy," he instructed. "I sha'n't be a minute."

He raised the flap of the bar, came through, and went upstairs.

"While we're waitin'," said Claret Nose, "another couple o' pints wouldn't do no harm."

"Right," the other agreed, and nodded to the boy. "The loser pays, so——" pointing to the notes beneath the inverted tumbler, "you take it out of one of those."

John Bates returned inside three minutes from his interview with the invisible Old Man. He was grinning broadly, and carrying a cloth-bound book.

"Which of you said Limehouse?" he demanded.

"I did," growled the man in the tweed cap.

Bates, stepping in between the two, raised the tumbler, and returned a ten shilling note to the last speaker. "The drinks are on you," he said, addressing the other. "I'll have a small whisky and soda."

"Ho!" said the red nosed one, "you will, will you? You will when you tell me where the bloody tunnel *was*, and prove it wasn't Wapping."

John Bates opened what proved to be a scrapbook, placing it upon the counter. He pointed to a drawing above which the words "Daily Graphic June 5, 1885" appeared. There were paragraphs from other papers pasted on the same page.

"There you are, my lad. What the Old Man doesn't know about this district, nobody can tell him. Never mind about closing one eye, George——" addressing Claret Nose; "I don't think you could read it even then. It boils down to this: There was a project in 1885 to build a footpath from where we stand now, to the Surrey bank. A shaft was sunk and the tunnel was commenced. Then the scheme collapsed, so the Old Man tells me."

"Ho!" said the loser, staring truculently at the grinning boy behind the bar. "A small whisky and soda for the guv'nor, and take it out of that——" pointing to the note.

"What did they do with this 'ere shaft?" growled the man in the tweed cap.

"The Old Man doesn't know," Bates replied. Everybody about here, except him, has forgotten all about it. But if you're in any doubt, I can tell you something else. He told me to tell you."

"What's that?"

The voice of the man in the tweed cap exhibited an unexpected interest, and John Bates glanced at him sharply; then:

"You know the old wharf?" he jerked his thumb over his shoulder, "which has been up for sale for years—sort of Chinese restaurant backs right on to it."

"I know it," growled the red-nosed man.

"Well, the one and only ventilation shaft of this tunnel comes out there, so the Old Man says; in fact, it must run right up through the building, or at the side of it."

"Ho!" said the man in the tweed cap. "Have another drink."

CHAPTER 30

THE HUNCHBACK

NAYLAND SMITH, wearing his long-peaked, large, check cap, and Detective-sergeant Murphy, very red of nose but no longer drunk, stood upon a narrow patch of shingle. That mysterious mist which had claimed London for so many days in succession had already masked the Surrey bank. They were staring up at the roof of that strange excrescence belonging to Sam Pak's restaurant.

"The ventilation shaft which Bates referred to," said Sir Denis, "is at the back of the bar, for a bet. It accounts for the heat at that end of the room.

"Why *heat*, sir?"

"It is probably regarded as an old flue," Nayland Smith went on, apparently not having heard his query, "and it very likely terminates in that big square chimney stack up yonder."

"It's above there that the light is seen."

"I know, hence my deduction that that is where the ventilation shaft comes out. Unofficial channels, Sergeant, often yield more rapid information than official ones."

"I know, sir."

"It was a brain wave to apply to the Blue Anchor for information respecting the site of this abandoned tunnel of fifty years ago. It is significant that no other authority, including Scotland Yard, could supply the desired data."

"But what's your theory, sir? I am quite in the dark."

"It wasn't a theory, it was a mere surmise until last night, when Sir Bertram Morgan told me that Dr. Fu Manchu had shown him an ingot of pure gold. I linked this with the phantom light which so many people have seen above the restaurant of Sam Pak; then my rough surmise became a theory."

"I see, sir," said Sergeant Murphy respectfully: as a matter of fact, he was quite out of his depth.

"There is no sign of the light to-night."

"No," snapped Nayland Smith, "and there's no sign of Forester's party."

A stooping figure passed the lighted window in the wooden outbuilding which abutted upon Sam Pak's.

"They are on the down-stream side of the place, sir. Inspector Forester thought they might have been spotted, and so to-night, he has changed his tactics."

"Good enough. I hadn't been notified of this."

They scrambled up the muddy shingle, climbed a ladder, and entered a little shadowy alley. A figure showed for a moment in misty darkness.

"Gallaho!" Nayland Smith challenged.

"O. K. sir. Everything's ready."

"Has the light been seen to-night?"

"Yes. Two hours ago; it hasn't appeared since."

"From my memories of Sam Pak, formerly known as John Ki," said Smith rapidly, "he sleeps as lightly as a stoat. He may appear to be ignorant of the fact that his premises are being covered by the police, but appearances, in the case of an aged and cunning sinner of this kind, are very deceptive. To penetrate a second time to the Sailor's Club, is rather like walking into the lions' den."

"I have heard a lot about Chinese cunning," growled Gallaho, "and I have seen something of what this Dr. Fu Manchu can do. But you ought to know, sir, that the C.I.D. can put up a pretty sound show. I don't think for a moment that there's anything suspected inside there."

"In any event," said Nayland Smith, significantly, "don't waste time if I give you the signal. Several lives are at stake."

Two minutes later, he lurched into the Chinese delicatessen store of Sam Pak, Murphy close behind him. His make-up was identical with that which he had worn on his previous visit; but whereas in the Blue Anchor he had spoken Cockney, he now assumed that queer broken English of which he had a complete mastery.

The very stout lady was playing patience behind the counter. She did not look up. There was no one else in the shop.

Fourth wife of the venerable Sam Pak, sometime known as John Ki, she had borne him two sons, bringing the grand total to Sam's credit up to eighteen. She knew something, but by no means all, of the life of her aged husband. He was an influential member of his Tong. He had secret dealings with great people; there was some queer business in the cellar, below the Sailor's Club; and the Sailor's Club, although it showed a legitimate profit, was really a meeting place for some secret Society of which she knew nothing, and cared less. Sam treated her well—his affairs were his own.

"Lucky Strike, please," said Nayland Smith; "club price."

Mrs. Sam Pak looked up sharply, recognized the new member, grinned at the old and drunken one, and nodded.

"Get them inside," she said—and focussed her attention upon her cards.

Nayland Smith nodded, and walked to the door which led to the "club". He opened it, went along the narrow passage, and presently entered the club room, Murphy following.

The place presented much of its usual appearance. One of those games disallowed in Chinatown was being played. A fan-tan party occupied a table on the left. Two nondescript sailormen were throwing dice. Old Sam Pak sat behind the bar, apparently dead.

Nayland Smith and Murphy dropped down on to the dirty settee, half-way up the right-hand side of the room. From the withered lips of Sam Pak a faint whistle emitted.

A hunchback Chinese boy with a patch over his eye appeared from the doorway on the left of the bar and approached the new arrivals.

"Beer!" said Murphy, in a loud, thick voice, assuming his usual rôle of a hard drinker.

The visible eye of the waiter opened widely. It was a long narrow eye, brilliantly green, and dark-lashed. Automatically, as it seemed, the waiter bent over the table and swabbed it with a dirty duster.

"Sir Denis," came the soothing voice of Fah Lo Suee, "you are in danger.

"Blimey," muttered Murphy, "we're spotted!"

"Thank you," Nayland Smith replied in a low tone. "I rather suspected it."

"It is useless to attempt anything to-night. You would find nothing." She continued to swab the table. "I will join you if you say so. I mean it."

"I could never trust you."

"My life has been hell, since something you know about. I

121

am sincere—I don't wish *his* death . . . but I must get away."

"I wonder . . ."

Old Sam Pak whistled again, this time more shrilly. One of the fan-tan players deserted the party, and crossed to the door which communicated with the shop.

"Oh God!" whispered Fah Lo Suee. "He knows! If I can save *you*, will you save *me*?"

"Yes!" snapped Nayland Smith.

CHAPTER 31

THE SI-FAN

"HANDS UP!"

Nayland Smith was on his feet, covering the room.

He had noted that the door which now barred the way out to the shop and to the street was a heavy iron door of that kind which at one time gave so much exercise to the police of New York's Chinatown. The man who had closed the door, turned, and, back to it, slowly raised his hands. He was a short, incredibly thick-set Burman, built like a gorilla, with long arms and a span of shoulder which told of formidable strength.

The other men at the fan-tan table also obeyed the order. Fah Lo Suee, following a moment's hesitation, caught a swift side-glance from Smith and raised her hands.

Murphy, pistol ready, slipped behind Sir Denis and made for the Burman.

The bowl of a heavy bronze incense-burner stood upon the counter where it was used as a paper-weight and a receptacle for small change. At this moment, the aged Sam Pak—snatching it up with a lighning movement incredible in a man of his years—hurled the heavy bowl with unerring aim.

It struck Nayland Smith on the right temple.

He dropped his automatic, staggered, and fell forward over the table.

Sergeant Murphy came about in a flash, a police whistle between his teeth. Stupefaction claimed him for a moment as he saw Sir Denis lying apparently dead across the table . . . for no more than a moment; but this was long enough for the baboon-like Burman who guarded the door.

In two leaps worthy of the jungle beast he so closely resembled, the man hurled himself across the room, sprang upon the detective's shoulders, and, herculean hands locked about his neck, brought him to the floor!

Too late to turn to meet the attack, Murphy had sensed the man's approach. At the very moment that the Burman made his second spring, the detective pulled the trigger.

The sound of the shot was curiously muffled in that airless, sealed-up place. The bullet crashed through the woodwork of the bar, and into a wall beyond, missing old Sam Pak by a matter of inches. But that veteran, motionless in his chair, never stirred.

As the pistol dropped from Murphy's grasp, the Burman, kneeling on his back, lifted one hand to the detective's jaw, and began to twist his head sideways—slowly.

"No!" Fah Lo Suee whispered—"*No!*"

The wrinkled yellow lips of Sam Pak moved slightly.

"It is for the Master to decide," he said, in that seaport bastard Chinese which evidently the Burman understood.

Fah Lo Suee, wrenching the patch from her eye and the cap from her head, turned blazing eyes upon the old Chinaman.

"Are you mad?" she said, rapidly in Chinese. "Are you mad? This place is surrounded by police!"

"I obey the orders, lady."

"Whose orders?"

"Mine."

A curtain on the left of the bar was drawn aside—and Dr. Fu Manchu came in . . .

The Orientals in the room who were not already on their feet, stood up; even old Sam Pak rose from his chair. The Burmese strangler, resting his right foot upon Murphy's neck, rose to confront the Master. A queer hush descended where a scene of violence had been. All saluted the Chinese doctor, using the peculiar salutation of the Si-Fan, that far-flung secret society which Nayland Smith had spent so many years of life in endeavouring to destroy.

Dr. Fu Manchu wore Chinese indoor dress, and a mandarin's cap was set upon his high skull. His eyes were half closed, but his evil, wonderful face exhibited no expression whatever.

Nevertheless, he was watching Fah Lo Suee.

A muffled scream in a woman's voice, doubtless that of Mrs Sam Pak, broke this sudden silence. There were loud cries; the flat wailing of a police whistle; and then a resounding crash.

The wooden door of the Sailors' Club had been broken down . . . but the iron door now confronted the raiding party.

Dr. Fu Manchu turned slowly, holding the curtain aside.

"Let them all be brought down," he directed.

CHAPTER 32

IRON DOORS

INSPECTOR GALLAHO heard the sound of the shot—but very dimly. Later he was to know why it had sounded so dim. At the time he did not understand, and wondered where the shot had been fired. It was not the prearranged signal, but it was good enough.

He was leaning out of a window above a shuttered-up shop. The room to which it belonged, a dingy bedroom, had recently been leased by a respectable man of the sea. The landlady who owned the shop, a little general store, had been given tickets for the second house at the Palladium, as her well-behaved lodger was unable to use them that evening. It was unlikely that she would be back until considerably after midnight.

The room was full of plain-clothes police.

"Jump to it, Trench," growled Gallaho. "That was a shot!"

The door behind him was thrown open. Heavy footsteps clattered down the stairs. He waited at the window, watching.

He saw Detective-officer Trench come out from the door below and dash across to the entrance to Sam Pak's restaurant, two men close behind him. He waited until the rest of the party had set out for their appointed posts; then himself descended.

There was a smell of paraffin and cheese on the staircase which he found definitely unpleasant. In the open door-way he paused for a moment, readjusting his bowler. A woman's scream came from Sam Pak's shop. Something about it did not sound English. There was a sudden scuffling—a crash—another crash. On the river bank a police whistle wailed.

Gallaho crossed and walked in.

Mrs. Sam Pak, her gross features curiously leaden in hue, sat in a state of semi-collapse upon a chair before one of the small tables. Trench and another man were breaking down the door at the other end of the shop; the third detective guarded the woman.

"What is this?" she demanded. "Are you bandits? By what right do you break up my place?"

"We are police officers," growled Gallaho, "as you have already been informed. I have a warrant to search your premises."

The third man turned.

"She locked the door and hid the key the moment we came in, Inspector."

"You know the penalty, don't you?" said Gallaho.

Mrs. Sam Pak watched him sullenly.

"There is nothing in my house," she said; "you have no right to search it."

The lock gave with a splintering crash—but the door refused to open more than a few inches.

"Hello!" said Trench, breathing heavily. "What's this?"

"Let *me* have a look," said Gallaho.

As he stepped forward, torch in hand, the third man advanced also, but:

"Close the shop door, and pull the blinds down," Gallaho directed, tersely.

He reached the broken door which refused to open fully, and shot the light of his torch through the aperture, then:

"K Division has been blind to this dive," he growled. "They've got an *iron door!*"

"Whew!" whistled Trench.

The four men stared at each other; then, their joint gazes were focussed upon Mrs. Sam Pak, seated, ungainly but indomitable, upon a small chair which threatened to collapse beneath her great bulk.

"You are under arrest," said Gallaho, "for obstructing the police in the execution of their duty."

There came the roar of a powerful motor. The Scotland Yard car concealed not far away, had arrived.

"Open the door," Gallaho directed, "and take her out."

The woman, breathing heavily and pressing one hand over her heart, went out without protest.

"What now, Inspector?"

"We've got to find another way in. Make contact with Forester. That sailor man of his is on the job again to-night. We shall have to go up the ladder and in at the back window."

"Very good, Inspector."

At any hour in any London street, whatever the weather conditions, a crowd assembles magically at the first sign of trouble. A sort of drizzling rain descended through the mist which overhung Limehouse. Few pedestrians had been abroad when that muffled shot had sounded at Sam Pak's. But now an interested group, eight or ten strong, formed a semicircle before the door as the man detailed to get in touch with the River Police came out and ran rapidly along the street.

As he disappeared in the mist, Gallaho opened the door and stepped out on to the wet pavement. Two police constables came up at the double.

"Clear these people away," Gallaho directed. "I'm in charge here, and I don't want loafers."

At that the two constables got busy with the well-known formula "Move on, there." The reluctant ones were gently shoved, and by that combination of persuasion and force which is one of the highest assets of the Metropolitan Police, the immediate neighbourhood was cleared of unofficial spectators. Windows had been opened, and heads craned curiously from them. The police car had pulled up half a block away, but now the officer in charge of the party came forward.

"What's the trouble, sir?" he asked, saluting Gallaho. "Can't we get through?"

"Iron door," growled the Inspector.

"That means the finish of Sam Pak."

"I know it does—and I'm wondering why it's worth it."

Forester of the River Police, handling the matter in accordance with his own ideas, had already sent Merton up with a line, and the rope-ladder was attached fully ten minutes before the signal reached him.

The shot in the Sailors' Club he did not hear. A tugboat was passing at the time and the noise of its passage entirely drowned that of the muffled shot. But he heard the whistle.

Regardless on this occasion of attracting attention the River Police craft was pushed as near as possible to the overhanging superstructure. Forester got on to the ladder, and began to climb. He turned.

"Nobody else until I give the word!" he shouted.

He reached the lighted window and looked in. He saw a dismal kind of bedroom, with a cheap iron bedstead in one corner, a dressing-table by the further window on his right, a chair, a number of odds and ends suggesting occupancy by a woman, and very little else. He crashed a heavy sea-boot through the glass, bent perilously, found that the window was unlatched, and raised it an inch or two with the heel of his boot. Then, descending a rung, he raised it fully, reached over the ledge and drew himself into the room.

He stood for a moment listening. There was not a sound.

He leaned out of the window.

"Come on!" he shouted.

Forester turned left, running along the room in the direction of a half-open door, and found himself upon a staircase, uncarpeted. Not waiting for the party, he went clattering down.

The room above had been lighted by an unshaded electric bulb, and there was a similar crude light upon the stair. But, reaching its foot and jerking a curtain aside, a curtain of some kind of rough patterned material, Forester saw darkness ahead of him.

Voices and bumping sounds indicated that his men were tumbling into the room above.

Forester shot the light of a torch into a place resembling a small restaurant. He stood, he discovered, at the end of a fairly well-stocked bar; dirty plush-covered seats ran along the wall on his left; there were a number of tables and chairs. Some of the tables were upset, and there was a faint tang,, perceptible above the fugg of the place, which told him that it was here the shot had been fired.

Footsteps sounded upon the stairs behind him.

But Forester continued to direct the light of his torch steadily upon a door immediately ahead. It was an iron door of the kind one meets with in strong-rooms.

Forester whistled softly and walked forward.

"Hullo, Chief, where are you?" called a voice.

"O.K. Try to find a switch and light this place up."

The door, Forester saw at a glance, was one which locked automatically on being closed. Furthermore, a huge steel bolt had been shot into place. He withdrew the bolt, ignoring the scurrying footsteps of his men seeking the light control. Presently, one of them found it and the place became illuminated.

Forester pulled back the catch and hauled the door into the niche which it normally occupied, safe from the view of any casual visitor, and only to be discovered by one definitely searching for it.

A dingy corridor, dimly lighted, opened beyond. Forester found himself confronted by a badly damaged wooden door, the lock wrenched out of place and surrounded by jagged splinters, which lolled drunkenly in the opening. He started along the passage.

Another door, but this of a cheap wooden variety, was open at the end, and presently he found himself in Sam Pak's delicatessen store. Only one shaded light was burning, that behind the counter.

"Who's there?" came sharply.

A man was standing in the darkened shop, his hands thrust into the pockets of his overcoat.

"Inspector Forester. Who are you?"

The man drew his hands from his pockets.

"Detective-sergeant Trench, Inspector," he introduced himself; "C.I.D. You got through from the back, then?"

"Yes, we're in. Where's Inspector Gallaho?"

"I'll get him."

CHAPTER 33

DAUGHTER OF THE MANCHUS

NAYLAND SMITH tried to fight his way back to consciousness. He found himself unable to dissociate delirium from reality.

"My love, who has never loved me . . . Perhaps it might never have been, but now, it is too late . . ."

A woman's voice, a soothing, musical voice—and someone was bathing his forehead with Eau de Cologne.

Another blank came . . .

He was lying on a camp bed, in a low, square, brick chamber. His head throbbed agonizingly, but a soft arm pillowed his head, and soothing fingers caressed his brow. He struggled again to recover himself. This was phantasy, a distorted dream.

Where was he?

The act of opening his eyes alone had been an exquisite torture. Now, turning them aside, he experienced new pain. A woman, strangely dressed, knelt beside the bed upon which he lay. Her dark hair was disordered, her long green eyes watched him, piteously, supplicatingly, as the eyes of a mother watching a sick child.

Those long green eyes stirred latent memories, stimulating the dull brain. What woman had he known who possessed those eyes?

She was a strange creature. Her beautifully moulded lips moved as if she spoke, softly. But Nayland Smith could detect no words. Her shoulders were bare; her skin reminded him of ivory. And now, perhaps recognizing some return of understanding , she bent, fixing the gaze of her brilliant eyes upon him.

A moment of semi-lucidity came. He had seen this woman before; this woman with the ivory shoulders and the green eyes. But if a woman, why did she wear coarse grey flannel trousers? . . . She was perhaps half a woman and half a man . . .

Hot lips were crushed to his own, as darkness came again.

"You have never known . . . you would never have known . . . but at least we shall die together . . . Wake, oh, my dear! Wake; for the time is so short, and because I know I have to die, now I can tell you . . ."

Nayland Smith, as if in obedience to those urgent words, fought his way back to full consciousness.

The brick chamber and the camp bed had not been figments of delirium. He actually lay upon such a bed in a square brick chamber. The woman tending him was Fah Lo Suee!

Recognizing the return of full consciousness, she gently withdrew her arm from beneath his head, composedly rearranging the silk straps of a tiny garment which afforded a strange contrast to the wrinkled flannel trousers.

Nayland Smith saw that a grey coat, a complement of the trousers, lay upon the floor near by. There was a bowl of water on a little table beside him, a small bottle and a piece of torn silk saturated with Eau de Cologne.

Fah Lo Suee replaced the coat which was part of the uniform of the one-eyed waiter, and quietly seating herself on the solitary chair which the chamber boasted, watched him coolly and without embarrassment.

Had he heard aright? Had he heard this woman—thinking that she spoke to an unconscious man—profess her love? Had she pressed her lips to his? He was beginning to remember; now clearly recalled all that had happened. Perhaps those later impressions were unreliable, or perhaps—a possibility— it was a deliberate move on the part of this daughter of an evil father. A new plot—but what could its purpose be?

Good God! He was in the power of Dr. Fu Manchu, his life-long enemy!

It was the end! She had said it was the end, unless he had dreamed. He moved his head so that he could see her more clearly. Heavens! Who and what had struck him? His memories afforded no clue to the identity of his assailant. And Sergeant Murphy? What had become of Sergeant Murphy?

Fah Lo Suee watched him under lowered lashes.

Any make-up which she had worn in her role of Chinese waiter, had been removed. He must suppose that those long lashes were naturally dark. But her lips were pale, and now, from the pocket of the dirty flannel jacket, she took out a lip-stick and a mirror which formed the lid of a small round-box. Unaffectedly, she adjusted her appearance to her own satis-faction, delicately rouging her cheeks.

Sir Denis watched her. Slowly he was regaining control of mind and body. Finally, replacing the tiny toilet case, Fah Lo Suee pulled out a yellow packet of cigarettes and bending for-ward, offered one.

A picture of the elegant Madame Ingomar flashed momen-tarily before his mind . . . The long jade holder; those patri-cian cigarettes of the finest yenedji . . .

"Thank you," he said, and was glad to find that his voice was steady.

He took the cigarette, and Fah Lo Suee, placing another between her lips, dropped the packet back into her pocket, producing a lighter which she snapped into life, and lighting both.

Nayland Smith cautiously sat upright. This ghastly brick chamber, which might have been part of a sewer works, swam around him. His head ached mercilessly. His sight, too, was queerly dim. He had been struck upon the temple. He leaned back against the wall in an angle of which the bed was set.

"Fah Lo Suee," he said—"for I know you by no other name: where are we, and why are we here together?

She glanced at him swiftly, and as swiftly looked aside.

"We are in part of the workings of an abandoned Thames tunnel. We are together because . . . we are going to die together."

Nayland Smith was silent for a moment, watching her, and then:

"Is this place below Sam Pak's" he asked.

"Yes."

"Then the raiding party will break through at any moment."

"There are iron doors," Fah Lo Suee replied, tonelessly. "Long before they can force them, we . . ."

She shrugged her shoulders, fixing the gaze of her long, narrow eyes upon him. Nayland Smith met that queer, con-templative gaze.

He realized how rarely in the past, in all his battles with the group surrounding Dr. Fu Manchu, he had looked into the eyes of Fah Lo Suee. How much had he dreamed?—to what extent now were his impressions his own, and to what extent due to the hypnotic power which he knew this woman to possess?

"Fu Manchu's daughter," he said: "Do you hate me as your father hates me?"

Fah Lo Suee closed and opened the slender fingers of her left hand. He watched that hand fascinatedly—thinking of the dirty yellow fingers of the Chinese waiter. His thoughts drew his glance floorwards, for there, near the chair upon which Fah Lo Suee sat, lay two crumpled objects which had puzzled him.

They were painted gloves!—gloves which had concealed the varnished nails and slim, indolent fingers of this daughter of the Manchus.

He glanced up again, and swiftly though Fah Lo Suee lowered her lashes, nevertheless, she had answered his question.

And he was silenced.

"I have loved you since the first day I ever saw you," she replied, quietly.

And, listening to the music of her voice, Nayland Smith understood why so many men had fallen under its spell . . .

"I have had many of those experiences which are ridiculously called 'affairs', but the only man I could ever love, was the only man I could never have. You would never have known, for I should never have told you. I tell you now, because, although we could not live together, we are going to die together."

CHAPTER 34

MORE IRON DOORS

"NO WAY OUT," said Gallaho, flashing his light about a low cellar, which contained stores of various kinds: bottles of wine, casks of beer, and cases of gin and whisky. There were cheeses, too, and even less fragrant delicacies of Chinese origin.

"This way, sir," came a voice from somewhere above. "Here's the way down!"

Gallaho came out of the cellar, and hurried up to a kitchen where Trench was standing before an open cupboard. The shelves of this cupboard contained all kinds of rubbish—tins, old papers, cardboard boxes. But in some way, probably by accident, the Scotland Yard man had discovered a hidden latch, and had swung all these shelves inward, for they constituted a second, masked door.

Hot, stifling air came up out of the darkness beyond.

"This is just below the bar, Inspector, and I noticed how hot it was at the end of the club room."

"What's in there? Be careful."

Gallaho came forward and shot his light into the cavity. A steeply sloping passage with wooden steps was revealed.

"Come on," he growled, and led the way.

Ten steps down there was a bend, Gallaho cautiously rounded it, and saw more steps ahead. It was very hot in this place, a thing for which he was quite unable to account. A brick landing was reached. Some of the brickwork had fallen away, and:

"This is built into an iron framework," came a voice from somewhere behind.

There was a steady tramp of feet upon the stairs.

"Oh!" said Gallaho. "That's funny!" He paused and looked about him. "I wonder if this is anything to do with the tunnel that Sir Denis has been inquiring about?"

"It's been built a long time."

"So I see. Also, it goes down a long way."

The formation of the steps became more crude, the lower they went. They were merely boards roughly attached to cement. Now came a long, straight passage, brick-walled and cement floored. Gallaho led on; but it was so extensive that before he had reached the end, the whole of the party engaged in searching Sam Pak's premises filed along behind him.

"This is a queer go," said someone.

"We must be below Thames level."

Gallaho pulled up with a jerk.

"Thames level or not," he growled, "we've struck it here."

"What is it, Inspector?"

Trench and others came crowding forward; Forester, far behind, was bringing up the rear.

"It's this: another blasted *iron door!* I want to know the history of this place, and I want to know why no report has ever been made upon it. Iron doors in a restaurant—why?"

CHAPTER 35

THE FURNACE

ALAN STERLING had abandoned hope. The message to Nayland
Smith written on a leaf of his pocket-book (for nothing had
been taken from him with the exception of his automatic) and
pushed under the door to Ali, had miscarried, or perhaps it
had never been dispatched.

No duties were allotted to him; no one came near the room.
He was surrounded by an oppressive silence, through which,
from time to time, that muted roaring seemed to vibrate. In
his fall he had smashed his wristwatch and so had no means
of knowing the time.

Hour after hour went by. He was desperately thirsty, but
for a long time resisted his desire to pour out a drink from the
water bottle.

Logic came to his rescue. Since he was completely in the
power of the Chinese doctor, why should the latter trouble to
tamper with the drinking water, when without danger or difficulty he could shoot him down at any time?

And what had become of Ali? Was it possible that he had
been detected, and that he, Sterling, was doomed to be left
locked in this dark brick prison somewhere in the bowels of
the earth, perhaps even under water? So situated, hope of rescue there was none, if those who had placed him there chose
to remain silent.

In short, his life depended upon that note having reached
Sir Denis, and upon his success in tracing the subterranean
tunnel, so vaguely referred to in it.

Hours passed in silence and a great weariness claimed
him. Telling himself over and over again "You must not fall
asleep . . . you must not fall asleep," perhaps by the very
monotony of reiteration, he presently lost all knowledge of his
surroundings.

His awakening was a rude one.

He felt himself seized in a herculean grasp, lifted and then
thrown face downward upon the bed!

Blindly, he began to struggle, but his ankles were grasped and firmly tied, throughout being held in such a manner that he was unable to reverse his position. Then, again, he was lifted by his unseen assailant, lightly as a woman lifts a toy dog, and thrown back upon the bed.

A short, yellow man, stripped to the waist, grasped his arms, clasped them together with a remorseless strength which appalled Sterling, and adroitly tied his wrists with some kind of fine, strong twine.

The man was built like a baboon; his forehead was abnormally low, his arms incredibly long and of a muscularity which Sterling found almost incredible. The upper arms resembled the thighs of an athlete. The man had Crotonean shoulders and amazing chest development. His face was like a yellow mask; his sunken eyes registered no expression.

Sterling's heart sank.

This could only mean one thing. Ali Oke had been detected—his message to Nayland Smith had never reached its destination! Dr. Fu Manchu had changed his mind. Instead of employing him in the subterranean hell, he had determined to kill him . . .

This frightful awakening had temporarily robbed him of the power of speech, but now:

"Who are you?" he demanded, angrily. "Where are you taking me?"

The Burman, ignoring his words, treating him as he might have treated a heavy sack, grasped Sterling by the middle and threw him over his left shoulder. Stooping, he walked out through the open doorway.

As he hung limply across the gigantic shoulder, he could have wept with rage, for his very weakness.

He, a physically powerful man, as normal men go, had no more chance against this deformed monster than a child would have had against himself. Yet, the horrible Burman, with his thick bandy legs, was all of three inches shorter than Sterling!

On to those nightmare stairs which led down into the pit, he was carried. From time to time, fitful gleams of light danced on the iron girders, or sent a red glow up into the darkness. He was being carried to his death: every instinct told him so. . . .

One shaded lamp burned in the pit.

It hung directly in front of the furnace door. From time to time, at bends in the staircase, through eyes clouded by reason of his unnatural position, Sterling observed squat figures firing the furnace. The heat grew greater and greater. The place quivered and roared as white hot flames were whipped up under a forced draught.

The bottom reached, his captor and carrier dropped him unceremoniously upon the concrete floor.

Bruised, dazed, he yet succeeded in rolling over into a position from which he could inspect the shadows surrounding that ring of light in front of the furnace.

Several things became visible which conjured up horrible possibilities.

He saw a number of rough wooden trestles, some six feet in length and eighteen inches wide, laid upon the floor in the circle of light.

What could their purpose be?

Some inert body lay quite near to him. He strained his eyes to peer through the darkness; but beyond the fact that it appeared to be the body of a man, he could make out no details. Two muscular Chinamen stripped to the waist appeared now under the light. One, he thought he recognized, unless he was greatly mistaken—for to Western eyes Chinese faces are very similar—as a man who had formed one of the fan-tan party on the night that he and Nayland Smith had visited the Sailors' Club.

The furnace door crashed open.

Scorching, blinding heat, poured out. Sterling wrenched his head aside. The Chinese stokers, probably professional firemen, fired the furnace, working mechanically and apathetically, although sweat poured down their faces and bodies like rain.

The furnace door was clanged into place again. Sterling lay so near to it that it had been impossible to take more than quick glances about him during the time that the door had been open, for the heat had seared his eyes. Nevertheless he had seen enough to know that his doom was sealed . . . perhaps the doom of all who stood in the path of Dr. Fu Manchu.

The man lying near to him, gagged and bound, was Ali Oke . . .

Alone, this discovery would have been sufficient to dash his last hope. But there was worse.

On the other side of the furnace door and nearly opposite to where he lay, Nayland Smith crouched on one elbow, bound as he was bound. He had glimpsed him searching the place with agonized eyes, as he himself had searched it.

It was the end.

CHAPTER 36

DIM ROARING

"THERE'S ONLY ONE THING to do here," growled Gallaho, banging his fist on the iron door which barred further progress. There's a bit of a cavity—so I suppose the hinges are sunk. A couple of dynamite cartridges will shift something."

"It might shift too much," said Forester, who had pushed his way from the rear, and now stood at the speaker's elbow. "Wouldn't it be better to send for a blow-torch?"

"Do you realize how long it would take to blow through this door?" Gallaho demanded. "Are you forgetting who's inside, and what may be happening?"

"I'm not forgetting. It was just a suggestion. Anyway, it's going to take time to get either."

"The longer we stand talking here, the longer it's going to take."

Gallaho, in common with many men of action, had a tendency to lose his temper when checked by such a barrier as this iron door.

"What do you suggest?"

"May I suggest something, sir?" came a voice.

"Yes, my man, what is it?"

"The Kinloch Explosive Works in Silvertown carry on all night. We could get there and back in half an hour in the Squad car, and probably bring someone with us who understands how to employ explosives on a job of this kind."

"Good man," growled Gallaho. "I'd better come along, as they won't act without authority. Will you take charge, Forester?"

"Certainly. But if I can get hold of a blow-torch by hook or by crook, I'm going to start."

"Good enough. No harm done."

Gallaho adjusted his bowler and set out. He disappeared along the corridor lighted only by the torches of the police. Forester turned to Trench.

"What about getting through to the Yard?" he suggested.

"See if it's possible to get a blow-torch rushed down."

"We can try," Trench agreed. "Leave two men here in case the door happens to open from the other side—and there's a telephone upstairs in the shop."

These dispositions were made, and the remainder of the police tramped up the concrete stairs and the wooden stairs into the premises of Sam Pak.

The shop blinds had been drawn—all lights put out. A constable was on duty on the pavement outside. At the moment that they reached the shop, the roar of the Flying Squad motor proclaimed itself as Gallaho dashed by on his journey to Silvertown.

"Here's the telephone, Inspector," said one of the men.

Forester nodded to Trench.

"This is your department, not mine," he said. "You know who to call up, no doubt."

Trench nodded and stepped behind the counter, taking up the instrument.

He called Scotland Yard and waited.

A tense silence descended upon all the men present until the call was answered.

"Detective-sergeant Trench speaking," he said, and gave a code word in an undertone. "Thanks."

A further interval of silence, and then:

"Oh, is he, Inspector? Oh, I see . . . Yes, I suppose so, if those are the orders."

Trench placed his hand over the mouthpiece and turned.

"The Commissioner is standing by for a report on this job!" he whispered. "It wouldn't surprise me if he turned up——"

"Hello, sir. Yes, speaking from there, now. I'm sorry to report, sir, that Sir Denis has disappeared. We have reason to believe that he's been smuggled into the cellars of this place.

An interval of respectful silence, and then:

"The difficulty is, sir, they've got iron doors, here. I am speaking for Chief detective-inspector Gallaho, sir. He has proceeded in person to Silvertown to try to get an explosive expert to deal with one of the doors below, here. . . . Yes, sir. We thought a blow-torch might do the trick, if it's possible to get one down in time. . . .Very good, sir. Yes, every exit is covered."

He replaced the receiver and turned to Forester.

"The hell of it is," he said, "we don't know what's going on below, there, and we can do nothing! Our only arrest is Mrs. Sam Pak, and I don't believe she knows a thing!"

"*Sst*! . . . what's that?"

All stood silent, waiting for a repetition of the sound, and presently it came—a muffled cry.

"It's one of the men in the passage," said Trench, and ran off, Forester following, his heavy boots making a booming sound upon the wooden floor. They were halfway down the stairs when the man who had called out, met them. His expression indicated excitement.

"Come this way, Inspector," he said, "and listen."

Their torch lights moving eerily upon brick and plaster walls, they proceeded to the end of the long passage. Another man was standing with his ear pressed to the iron door. He signalled, and they all approached, standing silently, listening.

"Do you hear it?"

Forester nodded, grimly.

"What the hell is it?" he muttered.

A dim, but dreadful roaring was perceptible, coming it seemed, from remote deeps beyond the iron door.

CHAPTER 37

CHINESE JUSTICE

STERLING REALIZED as the horror in this hell pit rose ever higher that the company of the shadow was now complete.

Someone else had been borne down those many stairs and thrown like a sack upon the concrete floor. The doors of the furnace were opened again by the Chinese firemen, and again the heat seared his eyes. He tried to take advantage of that white glare; in a measure, he was successful.

Detective-sergeant Murphy had joined the company of the doomed; trussed and helpless he lay beyond Ali Oke.

The sweating Chinamen fed the hungry furnace.

It was the closest reproduction of the traditional hell which he believed could ever have been created. He struggled to his feet: his ankles were bound, his wrists were bound. But in some way to be upright again, though he could not move a step, seemed to reinforce his failing courage. The furnace doors were reclosed.

"Sir Denis!" he shouted, his voice reverberating in that shadow-haunted shaft. "Sergeant Murphy!"

In his extremity he spoke with the accent of the Middle West; indeed, his father's face was before him. He saw the home in which he had been born, Edinburgh University, too, where he had taken his degree; all the happy things of life. And Fleurette! Fleurette! Merciful heaven!—where was Fleurette? He would never see her again!

Murphy answered.

"O.K., sir," he called. "While there's life there's. . . ."

A dull thud, that of a blow, terminated the words.

"Murphy!" Sterling cried again, and was in that state when he recognized hysteria in his own voice, yet fought against it. Sir Denis, he remembered to have noticed in the glare of the furnace, had a bandage over his mouth. "Murphy!"

No answer came—but, in silhouette against the light, the gorilla shape of the Burman appeared.

"You yellow swine!" said Sterling viciously, and bound

143

though he was, launched himself upon the broad, squat figure.

He received a blow upon the mouth which knocked him backwards. He tasted blood; his lips were split.

"If I could meet you in the open, you bandy-legged horror," he shouted, madly, "I'd knock you silly!"

The Burman, who wore heavy shoes, kicked him in the ribs.

Sterling groaned involuntarily. The pain of this last brutality threatened to overcome him. The horrible shadowy place began to swim before his eyes.

His wrists were aching: his hands were numb. Nevertheless he clenched his fists, clenched his teeth. He was writhing with pain; a rib had caved in—he knew it. But his supreme desire was to retain consciousness; to be on the job if any eleventh hour hope should offer.

"Be silent," came a musical voice out of the darkness. Fah Lo Suee!

"My friend, you only add more pains to those that are to come."

Sterling succeeded in conquering himself. His maltreated body had threatened to master his brain. But his brain won.

Above the ever increasing roar of the furnace, a voice reached him:

"I'm here, Sterling, old man—I couldn't speak before."

It was Nayland Smith.

In some way, the shadows of that dim shaft seemed to possess weight—to bear down on one oppressively. From where he lay, Sterling could not see the mouth of the tunnel, but he was oddly conscious of its presence, somewhere beyond the furnace. There was water above, a great quantity of water, probably the River Thames.

This sense of depth, of being buried far below the surface, alone was horrifying; with the accompaniments which surrounded him, plus a split lip and a dislocated rib, it stretched endurance to breaking point.

And then another voice spoke out of the darkness. It was a voice which, once heard, could never be forgotten: the voice of Dr. Fu Manchu.

"Sir Denis Nayland Smith: you are, I believe, acting for the Secret Service. You are a legitimate enemy. Detective-sergeant Murphy: You are attached to the Criminal

144

Investigation Department of Scotland Yard, and therefore entitled to my respect. Mr. Alan Sterling, you have voluntarily thrown yourself into the midst of my affairs, but since your motives are of a kind sometimes termed chivalrous, I shall accord to you also the honours of war."

The strange cold voice ceased for a moment.

Sterling struggled into a crouching position, ignoring the blood dripping from his chin, striving to forget the sharp pain of his injured rib.

"To-night may well be a climax in my war against folly and misrule; but if I triumph to-night, my path will be clear. My chief enemy will no longer obstruct me in my work, nor treachery live in my household. . . ."

That strange, impressive voice ceased—then uttered a short, guttural command.

The squat Burman appeared in the circle of light, dragging by the heels the inert body of Ali.

It now became obvious that the Nubian was bound hand and foot, and that a cloth was tied tightly over his mouth. His eyes seemed to bulge from his skull; his face was wet with the sweat of fear.

The Burman withdrew into the shadows, but appeared again almost immediately swinging a short, curved sword, which he seemed to handle with familiarity.

"This man is a traitor," the guttural voice said softly; "I have held my hand too long."

A swift, hissing word of command; and during some few, dreadful seconds in which Alan Sterling's heart seemed to remain still in his breast, the Burmese executioner obeyed.

Twining the fingers of his left hand into the frizzy, black hair of the Nubian, he jerked him to his feet with a single movement of that long, powerful arm. And, as the man stood there bent forward, swaying—with one mighty, unerring sweep of the scimitar he severed his head from his body!

"My God!" groaned Sergeant Murphy—"my God!"

Unconcernedly, the executioner threw the body on to one of the wooden frames, lashed the trunk and feet with lines which were attached to the woodwork, and stood up, glancing into the darkness in the direction from which the voice of Dr. Fu Manchu had come.

In response to another hissing command, the two Chinese firemen came forward and threw open the furnace door. They raised the head of the framework to which the body was lashed. The Burman seized the other end.

They began to swing it to and fro, chanting in unison: "Hi yah, hi yah, hi yah!" as they swung.

Then, with a final shouted "HI!" they propelled it into the white heart of the furnace.

They were about to close the door, when the Burman checked them—and stooped . . .

CHAPTER 38

THE BLUE LIGHT

"IT'S BY NO MEANS as simple as all that, Inspector," the chemist in charge assured Gallaho. "Before I attempt a mining operation such as you describe, I should like to know what's above and what's below. Also, what's on the other side of this wall that you want me to blow down. You say it's a concrete wall?"

"It appears to be," growled Gallaho, fretfully; technicians were always an infernal nuisance.

"We could probably blast a way through the wall, but I'm wondering what that wall supports. We don't want half Limehouse to fall in on us."

"Well, come and see for yourself; but come provided—for almost anything may be happening to the people we want to rescue."

"I shall certainly come, Inspector. I don't fancy the responsibility, but it's not the kind of thing I want to delegate."

There were further delays whilst mysterious apparatus was assembled, and Gallaho, seated in the office of the chief chemist, tapped his fingers irritably upon the table, glancing from minute to minute at a big clock over the mantelpiece. Messengers were scouring the extensive works in search of an expert with the musical name of Schumann. His attendance, according to Mr. Elliot, the chief chemist, was indispensable.

Gallaho was getting very angry.

Finally, arrangements were completed. Two workmen who seemed to enjoy this break in their night duties carried mysterious boxes, packages and coils of cable. Schumann, who proved to be a taciturn, bearded German, merely nodded and grunted when the chief chemist explained the nature of the project.

At long last, they all climbed into the police car, and set out recklessly for Limehouse. Gallaho sat in front with the driver. He was altogether too irritable for conversation, and at a point in their journey not far from their destination:

"Pull up!" he directed, sharply.

The brakes were applied, and the car promptly brought to a standstill.

Inspector Gallaho stared forward and upward, and now, resting his hand on the driver's shoulder:

"Look!" he said. "What's that? Right over the river bank, in a line with the smokestack?"

The driver looked as directed. And then:

"Good Lord!" he whispered, "what is it?"

There was very little mist in the air, but lowering clouds overhung the river; and there, either in reality or reflected upon them as upon a screen danced that bluish, elfin light; Gallaho knew that it was directly above the roof of Sam Pak's.

"Go ahead!" he growled. . . .

There was not much evidence of activity in the neighbourhood of the restaurant. The night life of Chinatown, such as it is, is a furtive life. A constable was standing on an adjacent corner, but there was little now to indicate that anything unusual had taken place there that evening, except the fact that the store was closed.

One or two customers who had applied there had gone away much puzzled by this circumstance.

No doubt there were watchers behind dark windows.

No doubt the fact was known throughout the Chinese quarter that Sam Pak's had been raided and his wife arrested. But those who shared this secret information kept it very much to themselves, and kept themselves carefully out of sight.

Entering the shop, followed by the technicians with their apparatus:

"Anything new?" Gallaho growled.

Trench was waiting there.

"A most extraordinary roaring sound from somewhere below," he reported; "and the heat at the top end of the room," said Gallaho. "I can't make head nor tail of it." He walked forward. "Yes; the difference is very marked. What the devil can it be?"

"The place to hear the roaring, sir," said another voice, "is at the end of the passage, below, outside the iron door."

"Come on," said Gallaho, and made his way there. "Any report from the river?"

"Yes. That blue light has been seen up over the roof."

"I know . . . I have seen it myself."

CHAPTER 39

THE LOTUS GATE

STARK HORROR coming on top of physical pain all but defeated Alan Sterling. As the furnace doors were reclosed and the three yellow men sweating and half-naked were lost in the shadows outside the ring of light, he thought he heard a groan . . . and he thought that the man who groaned was Nayland Smith.

The gruesome place swam about him; the hard floor seemed to be moving like the deck of a ship.

He ground his teeth together and clenched his fists. He knew that a mighty effort was called for, or he should faint. If this happened he should despise himself; and if he must die, at least let him carry his self-respect to the end.

Nevertheless, it was touch and go. Physical nausea saved him.

He was violently sick.

"The bloody swine!" came out of the darkness which concealed Sergeant Murphy. "By heaven! There's something coming to this lot!"

"There is something coming to all of us, Sergeant Murphy," It was the cold, measured voice of Dr. Fu Manchu which spoke. "To-night, I am destroying some of the weeds which choked my path."

Somewhere in the neighbourhood of the tunnel, the entrance to which Sterling could not see from where he lay, a pump was at work. The roar of the furnace increased in volume. It was like the sustained roar of some unimaginable, ravenous beast.

He took a firm grip upon himself.

He was shaking violently: complete collapse threatened. . . . There was an interval during which the furnace door was opened again, but Sterling resolutely turned his head aside. At the clang of its closing he opened his eyes again.

"Paracelsus," came that strange voice out of the darkness—and, now, with a note of exaltation in it, a note of fanaticism, an oddly rising cadence—"Paracelsus, although in some respects an impostor, yet was the master of many truths; of

149

the making of gold he knew something, but few have understood his dictum 'Vita ignis corpus lignum' (light is the fire, the body the fuel)."

He was silent for a moment. The roar of the furnace increased again in volume.

"The body the fuel . . ." he repeated. "Sir Denis Nayland Smith, Mr. Alan Sterling, Detective-sergeant Murphy. War is merciless, and I regret that you stand in my way. But in order that you shall realize the selflessness of my motives, I wish you, before going to join the shades of your ancestors, to be witnesses of my justice."

He uttered again that short, guttural command.

A figure walked gracefully out of the shadows into the light.

It was his daughter—Fah Lo Suee. She wore a green robe, cut low upon the shoulders, and of so fine a texture that every line of her slender body might be traced in its delicacy. There were jewels on her fingers and she smiled composedly.

Within the ring of light she knelt, and bowed her head in the direction of the unseen speaker.

The Burmese executioner had followed her. He stood behind her, now, looking upward.

"Of all the spies who have penetrated to my councils,"—the voice became more and more sibilant, rising ever upon a higher key—"this woman, my daughter, has been the chief culprit. There is a traitor blood in her, but she has betrayed me for the last time."

Fah Lo Suee knelt motionless, her graceful head lowered.

"One who would do the work to which I have set my hand, must forget mercy in favour of justice. Yet because, though execrable, detestable, you are my daughter, I offer you the Lotus Gate of escape. Do you accept it?"

Fah Lo Suee raised her head. She was still smiling proudly.

"I accept," she said. "I have only loved one man in my life—and I accept on condition that the same gate shall be opened for him."

"I agree to this condition."

The tones of the speaker indicated repressed madness.

Fah Lo Suee extended her slender arms.

"Denis Nayland Smith," she said, and there was tragedy in her musical voice—"until to-night, you never even suspected. I have told you and I am unashamed. You go with me through the gate. Death gives me something that life could never give."

She paused; only the roar of the furnace could be heard. Then, stretching her arms upward, towards the hidden Dr. Fu Manchu:

"I am ready."

"To this I had been blind, yet I might have known—for woman is a lever which a word can bend."

The strange voice, exalted, oracular in mad inspiration, drew nearer in the darkness until Dr. Fu Manchu appeared in the circle of light.

His mask-like face was transfigured, his eyes glittered like jewels. He was a seer, a prophet, a man set above human laws. He carried a small, cut-glass goblet, upheld like a chalice.

"Rise," he commanded.

Fah Lo Suee stood upright.

"You are ready?"

"I am eager. It is my wedding night."

"Here is the desire of your heart . . . and death."

"Good-bye," said Fah Lo Suee, her lips curved in that proud, fearless smile.

She took the glass and drained its contents.

The crystal crashed to the floor. Fah Lo Suee sank down, slowly; her smile became a smile of rapture. She extended herself upon the concrete still wet with the blood of an earlier victim, and opened her arms ecstatically.

"Denis, my dear, my dear!" she whispered. "Hold me close. Then, I shall not be afraid."

Her arms dropped—she lay still . . .

Sterling was past speech; even Murphy was silent, Dr. Fu Manchu turned and paced slowly back into the shadows. As he reached them, he uttered that quick, guttural order.

The Burman stooped, and placed the body of Fah Lo Suee upon one of the wooden racks. The two Chinamen appeared and the furnace door was thrown open.

Sterling had reached cracking point.

He heard an hysterical scream, but was unaware of the fact that he had uttered it. His last recollection of the scene was that of a monotonous chanting:—

"Hi yah, hi yah . . ."

151

CHAPTER 40

A FIGHT TO THE DEATH

DR. PETRIE reached London late at night.

One knowing him, who had met him at Victoria Station, would have noticed that whereas for many years his hair had been streaked with grey, the grey was now liberally streaked with white. He was but recently recovered from an illness which only an iron constitution and a will to live—not for the sake of life itself, but for his wife and newly discovered daughter—had enabled him to survive.

He had advised Nayland Smith of the time of his arrival; but, jumping from the train, for his activity was unimpaired by the stresses which had been imposed upon him, and looking eagerly up and down the platform, he failed to see the tall, gaunt figure of his friend.

This was unlike Smith.

Leaving a porter in charge of his baggage, he pushed rapidly on to the barrier. There was no sign of Nayland Smith, or even of Fey, that strange, taciturn creature who had been in Smith's service in Burma, who had now rejoined him in England.

It was unaccountable; a crown, almost crushing to the anxiety which possessed him.

Fleurette!

He recognized in this moment of loneliness, of disappointment, that he had even dreamed of finding Fleurette there. Smith's last message had held out such a hope. Yet, there was no one here at all!

"Dr. Petrie," came a voice. "Dr. Petrie."

Petrie stared all about him, and then recognized that the speaker was a commissionaire.

"Yes!" he said eagerly; "I am Dr. Petrie."

"Good evening, sir—" the man saluted. "I come from Sir Denis Nayland Smith's flat, sir. My orders are to ask you to proceed there at once."

Hope beckoned again, but anxiety remained.

"Is that all, Sergeant?"

"That is all I was told to say, sir."

"Thank you," said Dr. Petrie, wearily. "Have a drink as you go out, Sergeant."

"Thank you, sir. Good night."

The assembly of his baggage was a tedious business. A man who travelled light himself, on this occasion he was cumbered with many trunks and boxes belonging to Fleurette. He deposited the bulk of them in the cloakroom, and jumping into a taxi, proceeded to Westminster.

Fey admitted him.

Petrie observed with astonishment, for he knew the man for a perfect servant, that a large briar pipe was fuming in an ash-tray in the lobby.

"Good evening, sir." Fey turned to the hall porter. "Leave the baggage to me. Your room is prepared, sir."

"Is Sir Denis at home?"

"No, sir."

Fey took Petrie's hat and coat and Petrie walked through into the cheerful, lofty, sitting-room. He observed that the curtains had not been drawn in the bay window.

A premonition of some new disaster began to creep upon his mind. Fey joined him almost immediately.

"Whisky and soda, sir?"

"Thank you."

Fey prepared one in silence, Petrie watching him; then:

"Where is Sir Denis?" he asked.

Fey handed the doctor his drink upon a silver tray, and then:

"I don't exactly know, sir," he replied; "and with regard to the pipe, sir: as you are aware, I am not unlike Sir Denis in build, and my orders are to keep walking up and down in view of the Embankment, below, smoking a pipe, but not to show my face too much."

Petrie set his glass down.

"Do you mean that he is out on some investigation—and that your job is to pretend that he is at home?"

"Exactly, sir—excuse me."

Fey went out and returned smoking the briar, strolled forward and stared out of the window. The night was damp but not foggy. The sky was overcast. He turned and walked back into the room.

"Is there any news, Fey, of . . . my daughter?"

"Sir Denis is certain that she is in London, sir, and alive."

"Thank God!"

Dr. Petrie finished his whisky and soda at a gulp.

"There's a bit of a mix up, sir, I am sorry to say. Things have been moving very fast. That Chinese devil has got hold of Mr. Sterling."

"What!"

"But he was O. K. this morning; we had a message from him. I am a bit anxious to-night, though, and I'm glad you've arrived, sir."

The unusual volubility of Fey alarmed Dr. Petrie anew.

"Where is Sir Denis?" he asked; "I must get in touch with him."

"He's gone to a place called Sam Pak's, sir, in Limehouse. Somehow, I didn't like the sound of it to-night, sir. This Chinese devil is desperate; it's a fight to the death . . ."

CHAPTER 41

THE LAST BUS

FLEURETTE OPENED HER EYES and looked in the direction where she thought the porthole of her cabin should be.

She closed them again quickly. She saw a small curtained window, but not a porthole. This seemed to be a cottage bedroom, very cleanly and simply furnished. She opened her eyes again.

The room remained as she had first seen it—she was not dreaming.

She clenched her hands tightly and sat up in bed.

Only a few hours before, her brain told her, she had parted from Alan in her cabin on the *Oxfordshire*. She remembered how much that last smile had cost her, that struggle to restrain her tears. She had heard his footsteps on the deck. And then, she had sat down, she remembered quite well, and had poured out a glass of water . . .

And now, what in heaven's name had happened? Where was she? And how had she got here?

It was very silent, this place in which she found herself, until a slight movement in an adjoining room told her that there was someone in there.

The room was lighted by moonlight, and although she could see that there was a lamp on the table beside the bed, she was afraid to switch it on. Throwing off the bedclothes she slipped lightly to the floor.

She realized that she was wearing a suit of pyjamas which did not belong to her. But, staring at a heap of garments in an armchair, she recognized the suit which she had actually been wearing when she had parted from Alan on the ship!

Her head ached slightly, and she knew that she had been dreaming. It was difficult to believe that she was not dreaming, now. She stepped to the window, and gently drawing the curtain aside, looked out.

She saw a little hedge-bordered garden with a smooth patch of grass in the centre of which stood a stone bird bath.

There was a gaunt looking apple tree on the left, leafless now, a weird silhouette against the moon. Over the hedge, she could see the tops of other trees; but apparently the ground fell away there. She was, as she had supposed, in a cottage.

Whose cottage? And how had she got there?

Above all, where was Alan, and where was her father?

Was it possible that she had been seriously, dangerously ill?—that there had been a hiatus of which she knew nothing—that now she was convalescent?

Perhaps that person whose movements she had detected in the next room was a nurse. She retraced her steps, her bare feet making no sound upon the carpet, and looked for evidence to support this theory. There were no medicine bottles or cooling draughts upon the table beside the bed; nothing but a cigarette case—her own—and a box of matches.

A further slight movement in the adjoining room indicated that someone was seated there, reading. Fleurette had heard the rustle of a turned page.

She recognized with gratitude that despite this insane, this inexplicable awakening, she was cool and self-controlled. The theory of serious illness did not hold good. She felt perfectly fit except for that slight headache. She seated herself on the side of the bed, thinking deeply.

Her first impulse, to open the door and demand of whoever was in the next room what it was all about, she conquered. Fleurette had had the advantage of a very singular training. She had been taught to think, and this teaching availed her now. She crossed to the door very quietly, and by minute fractions of an inch began to turn the handle.

The door was locked.

Fleurette nodded.

A louder movement in the next room warned her that someone might be approaching. She slipped back into bed, drawing the clothes up close to her chin, but preparing to peep under her long lashes at anyone who should come in.

A key was quietly turned in the lock and the door opened.

Light shone in from a little sitting-room; Fleurette could see one end of it from where she lay. A newspaper and some illustrated magazines were upon a table beside which an arm-chair was drawn up. Her nostrils were assailed by that stuffy smell which tells of a gas fire. A strange looking old woman came into the bedroom.

She was big and very fat. In the glimpse which Fleurette had of her face in the lamplight, before she crossed the threshold, she saw that this was a puffy, yellow, wrinkled face, decorated by wide rimmed spectacles. The woman wore a costume which might possibly have been that of a hospital nurse. In silence she stood just within the little room, looking down at Fleurette.

To her horror, Fleurette saw that the woman carried a hypodermic syringe in her hand.

"Are you asleep?" she whispered softly.

She spoke in English, but with a strange accent. There was something in the crouching attitude of this huge woman, and something in the tones of her voice so threatening and sinister, that Fleurette clenched her hands beneath the coverlet. She lay quite still.

"Ah hah!" the woman sighed, evidently satisfied.

She returned quietly to the outer room, closing and gently relocking the door.

Fleurette listened intently, and whilst she listened she was thinking hard.

Sounds of subdued movements came from the outer room:—the chinking of glass, that subdued popping sound which indicates that a gas fire has been turned off; then a click—and the streak of light beneath the door vanished. Soft footsteps, evidently the woman wore padded slippers, moved beyond the partition against which Fleurette's bed was set. A door was closed.

Her guardian had gone to bed.

Controlling her impatience only by means of a great effort, Fleurette waited, her ear pressed to the wooden partition.

She could hear the woman moving about in what was evidently an adjoining bedroom, and at last came the creak of a bed, as the heavily built custodian retired. Finally, she heard the click of an extinguished electric light.

Fleurette got up quietly, and began to dress. It did not take her long, but she could find no hat and no shoes. But she found a pair of red bedroom slippers; these would serve her purpose. A handbag, her own, lay on the cheap dressing-table.

Its contents seemed to be undisturbed since she had laid it on the sofa berth in her cabin.

Dropping cigarette case and matches into the bag, Fleurette very quietly drew the curtains aside from the low square window.

It was latched, and the room, though cold, was stuffy. The latch was a difficult problem—it was a very old fitting, much worn and warped. Once, it emitted a terrifying squeak.

Fleurette stopped dead in her operations, and creeping across the room, applied her ear to the wooden partition.

Sonorous snores sounded from the adjoining bedroom.

She raised the window steadily but firmly. To her great surprise it made very little noise. She looked out and saw a neglected flower border immediately below. Then came a moss-grown, paved path leading on the right to a little pergola. This, in turn, communicated with a gate.

Fleurette dropped her bag on to the flower-bed, put on her slippers, and wriggled through the opening. It was not a particularly easy business, but Fleurette was fit and very athletic. She knew that her hands were filthy dirty and her feet muddy, when at last she stood outside; but these things did not matter.

Picking up her bag, she walked quickly around to the gate, opened it, and found herself in a narrow, hedge-bordered lane.

An oak tree overhung it a few paces back on the left—there were other dark buildings ahead. But in none of them did any light show. She looked around her eagerly, sniffing the cold night air, then climbed the opposite bank and saw that where the ground fell away, there were farm buildings, beyond, backed by trees, and beyond these trees, evidently several miles beyond, a searchlight moved regularly. This, she decided, was an aerodrome.

It was utterly, horribly, mysterious, for she should have been far out in the Mediterranean, whereas the very scent of the air told her that she was in England!

In one direction, the lane terminated, beyond the cottage from which she had come, at a gate, with a stile. She decided to proceed the other way. The lane was very roughly paved; and now, banks of cloud suddenly obscured the moon.

She was forced to walk slowly, for trees overhung the way

and it was very dark. She passed two other buildings lying back from the lane on her right, but they showed no signs of life and she pressed on. She came to a wider lane, much better paved, hesitated whether to turn left or right, and finally decided upon right.

From the position of the moon and the darkness in the houses she passed (and these were few,) she realized that it must be late at night, how late, she could only guess.

On the corner of the second lane there was a large house surrounded by a high brick wall; also a post box and an electric lamp standard.

She pulled up, breathing quickly. She had reached a main road.

The lodge of some large residence directly faced her; but, whilst she had been hurrying along, she had been thinking clearly. She heard the sound made by the approach of a heavy vehicle; and presently came the glare of its headlights.

A green motor bus pulled up directly by the lodge gates.

There were very few passengers, but she saw that at least two were alighting. She raced across.

In the light of the standard lamp she read upon the side of the bus: "Reigate—Sutton—London".

She sprang on to the step, the vehicle restarted. The conductor helped her on board.

"Are you going to London?" she asked, breathlessly.

"Yes, miss. This is the last bus."

CHAPTER 42

NAYLAND SMITH REFUSES

IN THE DEPTHS below Sam Pak's the furnace roared hungrily.

Sterling groped his way back through imaginary horrors to the real and greater horror of his actual surroundings.

If he had ever doubted, he knew now what his end was to be. He believed that he was no greater coward than the average man, but just as life with Fleurette had beckoned to him so sweetly, it must end. And what an end!

"Are you all right?" came a shaky whisper from the darkness. It was Sergeant Murphy.

"Yes, thank you, Sergeant."

"We're in hell before our time, sir."

Sterling tried to control his nerves, to concentrate upon one thing to the exlusion of all others. He must not give this fiendish maniac the satisfaction of seeing him quail. If a woman could meet death as Fah Lo Suee had met it, then— by heaven!—it was up to the Middle West to show its mettle!

"Sir Denis Nayland Smith." The tones of that implacable voice fell upon Sterling like a cold douche.

"The hour of our parting has come."

There was a pause; a guttural order.

The sound of a groan from the darkness where Nayland Smith lay, completed the horror of the scene. It was a groan of defeat, of bitter humiliation; then:

"Dr. Fu Manchu," came Smith's voice, and—to Sterling it seemed a miracle—its tone was steady, "order your human baboon to untie my ankles. I prefer to walk to death rather than to be carried. This, I think, I am entitled to ask."

Another order was spoken rapidly. There was a faint scuffling sound—and Nayland Smith walked into the circle of light before the furnace door.

"Oh, my God!" Murphy whispered. "What are they doing up there. Why don't they break through?"

The Burmese executioner followed Sir Denis out of the shadows, and stood at his elbow.

"Because in your long battle with me, Sir Denis," Dr. Fu Manchu continued, stressing now a note of insane exaltation, "you have always observed those rules of clean warfare which, rightly or wrongly, are an English tradition, I respect you. I, too, have traditions to which I have always adhered."

Nayland Smith, his hands behind him, stared up into the darkness which concealed the speaker.

"I bear you no personal animosity; indeed, I admire you. I have won—although my triumph may have come too late; and, therefore, Sir Denis, I offer you the Lotus Gate of escape."

"I thank you, but I decline."

Sterling struggled on to his elbow, watching, and listening.

"He's playing for time, Murphy! Can't we do anything to help him?"

"What can we do?"

"You prefer the sword? The end of the common criminal?"

"I decline that also, if I have any choice."

"You reduce me——" there was repressed frenzy now in the tones of Dr. Fu Manchu—"to the third alternative of . . . the fire."

There followed a moment of silence which Sterling knew that if he lived, he should never forget. Nayland Smith stood in the circle of light, motionless, looking upward. Beside Sterling, Murphy was breathing so heavily that he was almost panting in his suppressed emotion.

"Is there no other alternative?"

"None."

An order was spoken—one sibilant word. The Burman sprang forward. . . .

CHAPTER 43

CATASTROPHE

NOW EVENTS BEGAN to move rapidly to that astounding conclusion which, although it was the result of men's combined efforts, seemed to Sergeant Murphy, a devout Roman Catholic who had begun to pray fervently, to be an intervention by a Higher Power.

Sir Denis Nayland Smith in the course of his long career as a police officer, had studied assiduously whenever the opportunity offered, those branches of practical criminology with which his work had brought him in contact, East and West. He was something of a physician, understanding poisons and antidotes. Lock combinations had no mysteries for him, and there were few locks he could not force if called upon to do so. Knot-tying in all its intricacies, as practised by the late Harry Houdini, he had studied in Rangoon, his professor being a Chinese malefactor who was a master of the art.

When the ape-like Burman had come to tie him up, Smith had recognized at a glance that physical resistance was out of the question. It would have called for three powerful men and trained wrestlers at that to deal with him. His peculiar development warned Smith that the man was an expert in the art of ju-jitsu, which, together with his herculean strength, set him in a class apart.

Fah Lo Suee had gone when the tying took place.

Nayland Smith submitted, feigning weakness. When he saw the narrow twine that was to be used, he anticipated what was coming, and permitting the man to wrench his arms behind his back, he put into practice a trick whereby many illusionists have mystified their audiences; Chinese in origin, but long well-known to professional magicians of the West.

The man tied his thumbs, as well as his wrists.

By means of maintaining a certain muscular stress during this painful operation, the result, though satisfactory to Dr. Fu Manchu's private executioner, was also acceptable to Nayland Smith.

The latter knew that he could withdraw his hands at any moment convenient to him!

The lashings of his ankles was a different matter. Here, he knew himself to be helpless, and recognized expert handiwork.

He had preceded Alan Sterling down the stairs of the shaft, slung sackwise across one incredible shoulder of the Burmese killer . . .

Now, as he stood, his arms apparently tied behind him, but his ankles unlashed, staring up to where Dr. Fu Manchu sat veiled in darkness, he was actually a free man. He held the twine which had confined his wrists tightly clenched in his left hand.

He was calculating his chances—tensing himself for what he must do.

With the exception of his automatic, his personal possessions had not been disturbed; these included a pocket knife. He had opened its most serviceable blade, and held it now concealed in his right hand. He knew but one mode of attack calculated to give him the slightest chance against his scarcely human enemy.

If it failed, his fate could be no worse.

It was not a type of combat which he favoured; but having watched this man performing his ghastly work, he found that his scruples had fled.

As the harsh command was spoken and the monstrous Burman stepped forward, Nayland Smith sprang away, turned—and kicked with all the speed and accuracy of his Rugby forward days! He put every ounce of power in his long, lean body into that murderous kick . . .

The man uttered a roar not unlike the booming of a wounded gorilla—a creature he closely resembled—doubled up, staggered . . . and fell.

A shrill order, maniacal in its ferocity, came out of the darkness above. It was Dr. Fu Manchu speaking in Chinese. The order was:

"Shoot him!—shoot him!"

Smith ducked and darted out of the radius of light into the surrounding shadow where Sterling and Murphy lay. He almost fell over Sterling.

"Quick, quick!" he panted—"your wrists."

"I'm crocked; don't count on me. Untie Murphy."

But Smith cut the twine from Sterling's wrists and ankles.

"Stay where you are until I give the word."

He bent over Sergeant Murphy.

"Ankles first . . . now wrists."

"Thank God!" cried the detective. "At least we'll die fighting!"

There was a flash in the darkness and a bullet spat on the floor close beside the speaker.

"Can you walk, Sterling?"

"Yes."

A second shot, and a second bullet whistled by Nayland Smith's ear. The voice of Dr. Fu Manchu, high-pitched and dreadful, came again, still speaking in Chinese.

"The lights, the lights!" he screamed.

Detective-sergeant Murphy, not too sure of cramped muscles, nevertheless set out through the darkness in the direction from which those stabs of flame had come.

Light suddenly illuminated the pit . . .

Dr. Fu Manchu stood upon the stairs, his clenched fists raised above his head, his face that of one possessed by devils. A wave of madness, blood lust, the ecstasy of sweeping his enemies from his path, ruled him. That great brain rocked upon its aged throne.

Murphy saw a Chinaman stripped to the waist not two paces from him. The man held an automatic: the sudden light had dazed him. Murphy sprang, struck, and fell on top of the gunman, holding down the hand which held the pistol. A second Asiatic, similarly armed, was running forward from the foot of the stairs. The Burmese strangler writhed on the floor before the furnace.

"Kill them! Kill them!" cried the maniacal voice.

Nayland Smith raced forward and threw himself down beside the struggling men—just as another shot cracked out.

The bullet grazed Murphy's shoulder.

He inhaled sibilantly, but hung on to the Chinaman. Smith wrenched the weapon from the man's grasp. He pulled the trigger as he released it, but the bullet went wide—registering with a dull thud upon some iron girder far up the shaft.

The second Chinaman dropped to his knee, took careful aim, and fired again. But he pulled the trigger a decimal point too late.

Nayland Smith had shot him squarely between the eyes.

Dr. Fu Manchu's mania dropped from him like a scarlet cloak discarded. His face became again that composed, satanic mask which concealed alike his genius and his cruelty. He descended three steps.

The place was plunged in darkness.

Fiery gleams from chinks in the furnace door pierced the gloom; one like an abler spear struck upon the contorted face of the Burman, lying now apparently unconscious where he had fallen.

Then came the catastrophe.

A booming explosion shook the place, echoing awesomely from wall to wall of the pit.

"My God!" cried Murphy, grasping his wounded shoulder, "what's that?"

The words were no sooner uttered than, heralded by a terrifying roar, a cataract of water came crashing down the shaft.

"The river's broken through!" cried Sterling.

Above the crash and roar of falling water:

"Head for the stair!" shouted Nayland Smith. "All head for the stair!"

CHAPTER 44

AT SCOTLAND YARD

THE COMMISSIONER of Metropolitan Police stood up as Dr. Petrie was shown into his room at New Scotland Yard.

The Commissioner was a very big man with an amiable and slightly bewildered manner. His room was a miracle of neatness; its hundred and one official appointments each in its correct place. A bowl of violets on his large writing desk struck an unexpected note, but even the violets were neatly arranged. The Commissioner, during a distinguished Army career, had displayed symptoms of something approaching genius as an organizer and administrator. If he lacked anything which the Chief of the Metropolitan Police should possess, it was imagination.

"I'm glad to meet you, Dr. Petrie" he said extending a very large hand. "I know and admire your work and I understand why you asked to see me tonight."

"Thank you," said Petrie. "It was good of you to spare me the time. May I ask for the latest news?"

He dropped into an armchair which the Commissioner indicated, and stared at the latter, curiously. He knew that his words had not been prompted by courtesy. In matters of exact information, the man's brain had the absorbing power of a sponge—and he had the memory of an elephant.

"I was about to call for the last report, Dr. Petrie. Normally, I am not here at this hour. It is the Fu Manchu case which has detained me. Excuse me a moment—I thoroughly understand your anxiety."

He took up one of the several telephones upon the large desk, and:

"Faversham," he said, "bring the latest details of the Fu Manchu case to my room."

He replaced the receiver and turned to Dr. Petrie.

"I am naturally in a state of intense anxiety about my daughter," said Petrie. "But first, tell me—where is Nayland Smith?"

The Commissioner pulled at his moustache and stared down at the blotting-pad before him; then:

"The last report I had left some little doubt upon that point," he replied, finally, fixing penetrating blue eyes upon the visitor. "As to your daughter, Dr. Petrie, in the opinion of Sir Denis she is somewhere in London." He paused, picking a drooping violet from the bowl between a large finger and thumb, snipping off a piece of the stem and replacing it carefully in water. "The theory of the means by which she was brought here is one I do not share—it is too utterly fantastic—; but Sir Denis's record shows that in the past——" he frowned in a puzzled way— "he has accomplished much. At the moment, as you may know, he is very highly empowered; in fact——" he smiled, and it was a kindly smile, "in a way—in regard to this case, I mean he is, in a sense, my senior."

The Commissioner's weakness for parentheses was somewhat bewildering, but Petrie, who grasped his meaning, merely nodded.

"I am very anxious about Sir Denis at the moment," the Commissioner added.

There was a rap on the door, and in response to a gruff "Come in," a youngish man entered, immaculately turned out in morning dress; a somewhat unexpected apparition so long after midnight. He carried a cardboard folder under his arm.

"This is Wing Commander Faversham," the Commissioner explained, staring vaguely at the newcomer, as though he had only just recognized him. "Dr. Petrie's name will be familiar to you, Faversham. This is Dr. Petrie."

Faversham bowed formally, and laid the folder open upon the table. Although the Commissioner's manner seemed to invite familiarity, it was a curious fact that none of his subordinates ever accepted that illusive lead.

"Ah!" said the Commissioner, and adjusting spectacles, bent and read.

"This brings us up to date, Dr. Petrie," he said in a few moments, looking up and removing his glasses. "Sir Denis, and Detective-sergeant Murphy—attached to the Criminal Investigation Department—visited a restaurant in Limehouse to-night, posing as sailormen. Sir Denis——" he added, in parentheses,—"has a gift for make-up. For my own part I don't believe in disguise at any time or in any circumstances. However—Chief detective-inspector Gallaho, one of the best men we have here—you agree with me, Faversham?—"

"Absolutely, sir."

"Chief detective-inspector Gallaho was in charge of raiding operations, assisted by . . ." there was a momentary pause, but the wonderful ,memory functioned . . . "Inspector Forester of the River Police branch."

"So I understand," said Petrie eagerly, "but what happened?"

"The agreed signal was given," said the Commissioner, slowly, "and the party entered the premises. But the suspects had slipped into some underground cellar, and I regret to say—for no such report has ever reached me—that an iron door was encountered."

"An iron door?"

"I was notified by Detective-sergeant Trench, at——" he readjusted his glasses and turned over a page in the folder— "11.49 p.m. Detective-sergeant Trench," he added, laying his glasses upon the blotting-pad, "is attached to the Flying Squad—that Gallaho was proceeding to the Kinloch Works in Silvertown in order to secure expert advice upon the forcing by explosives of this iron door, or of the wall adjoining it."

"You will notice, sir," said Faversham coughing respectfully, "that a party with chemical equipment according to your instructions, left at 12.15."

The Commissioner nodded.

"I have noted this," he replied. "The latest news, then, Dr. Petrie——" he fixed his rather tired looking blue eyes upon the latter—"is this: Sir Denis Nayland Smith, presumably accompanied by Detective-sergeant Murphy is, we must assume, a prisoner in the cellars of this place; and according to a report received not more than ten minutes ago, from Chief detective-inspector Gallaho, experts from the explosive works were about to blast a way through the concrete wall, adjoining the iron door. The party to which wing Commander Faversham refers had not then arrived."

He paused, folded up his spectacles and placed them in a green leather case.

"I am strongly disposed," he said, slowly, "since this is a case of major importance, to proceed to Limehouse myself; unless definite news is received within the next five minutes. Should you care to accompany me, Dr. Petrie?"

CHAPTER 45

THE MATCH SELLER

FEY STARED REFLECTIVELY down from the bay window to where beyond the misty Embankment, the Thames flowed. A small steamer was passing, and Fey found himself calculating how long a time must elapse before that steamer would be traversing Limehouse Reach.

To-night, he was assured, his monotonous duty was also a useless duty. These yellow devils knew that Sir Denis was in Limehouse, but stoically Fey continued to smoke the large briar, and to walk up and down in accordance with orders. Dr. Petrie had set out for Scotland Yard not long before. It was trying, even to so patient a man, to stand so near the edge of the arena and yet be unable to see what was going on.

Fey was worried.

He had not said anything to the doctor, but through glasses from a darkened bedroom window, he had been studying an old match seller whose place of business on the Embankment almost immediately faced these flats.

Sir Denis, before leaving on that mysterious affair which still occupied him, had told Fey to watch this man and to note what he did. The man did nothing for five minutes or so, merely remaining seated against the parapet. Then he stood up.

Since Fey had assumed him to be a cripple, this was a surprise. But almost immediately, the match vendor sat down again.

Fey continued to watch.

One of those derelicts who haunt this riverside thoroughfare came shuffling along, paused for a moment, talking to the man seated on the pavement, and then retraced his steps.

Fey had been wondering, right up to the time of Dr. Petrie's arrival, if this had been a mere coincidence, or if it had been a signal to a second watcher that there was something to report. For the entrance to the mansions was visible from that point, and Fey was disposed to believe that Sir Denis, in

169

spite of his disguise, had been recognized as he went out that way, and that the news of his departure had been passed on.

His theory was confirmed shortly after Dr. Petrie's departure.

At about the time that the doctor would have been walking down the steps, the match seller stood up again . . . and again the derelict shuffled along, spoke to him and disappeared.

The match seller was in his usual position again, now, but Fey from time to time slipped into the adjoining room and inspected him through binoculars. Had orders not forbidden it he would have slipped out and had a closer look at this suspicious character. However, he had discovered something.

The apartment was under close observation—and to-night the enemy was aware that Sir Denis was not at home; aware, furthermore, that Dr. Petrie had been and had gone . . .

Dimly Fey detected the sound made by the opening of the lift gate, and knew from experience that someone was alighting on that floor. He stood still for a moment listening.

The door bell rang.

He went out into the lobby, placing his pipe in an ashtray on a side table, and opened the door.

Fleurette Petrie stood there, her hair wind-blown, her face pale!

He observed that she wore a walking suit with the strange accompaniment of red bedroom slippers. They were combing the slums of Asiatic Limehouse for her, and here she was!

Fey's heart leapt. But his face betrayed no evidence of his joy.

"Oh Fey!" she exclaimed, "thank heaven I have got here!"

"Very pleased to see you, Miss," said Fey composedly.

He stood aside as she entered, noiselessly closing the door. Her excitement, intense but repressed, communicated itself to him. Its effect was to impose upon him an almost supernatural calm.

"Is Sir Denis in, Fey?"

"No, Miss. But your father was here less than twenty minutes ago."

"What!"

Fleurette seized Fey's arm.

"My father! Oh, Fey, were has he gone? He must be in a

frightful state of mind about me. And of course, you had no news for him."

"Very little, but I tried to reassure him."

"But where has he gone, Fey?"

"He rang up the Commissioner, Miss, and then went across to interview him."

"He may still be there. Could you possibly get through for me, Fey?"

"Certainly. I was about to suggest it. But can I get you anything?"

"No, Fey, thank you. I am so anxious to speak to my father."

Fey bowed and went out into the lobby. Fleurette, tingling with excitement, crossed the room and stared out of the bay window down at the misty Embankment. She retraced her steps, and stood by the lobby door, too anxious even to await Fey's report. He had just got through to Scotland Yard, and:

"Sir Denis Nayland Smith's man speaking," he said. "Would you please put me through to the Commissioner's office?"

There was an interval which Fleurette found barely endurable, then:

"Yes, sir. Sir Denis Nayland Smith's man speaking. Dr. Petrie left here recently to call upon the Commissioner, and I have something urgent to report to him."

"Bad luck," said a voice at the other end of the wire; it belonged to Faversham, the immaculate private secretary. "Dr Petrie and the Commissioner proceeded to Limehouse not more than five minutes ago."

"Oh, I'm sorry. Thank you, sir."

"What is it?" Fleurette whispered. "Isn't he there?"

"Just gone out with the Commissioner. But excuse me a moment——" He spoke into the mouthpiece again. "Would it be possible, sir, to reach them at their destination?"

"Yes," Faversham replied. "It's some kind of store. I'll instruct the people downstairs to get in touch with the officer in charge. Do you wish him to give Dr. Petrie any particular message?"

"Yes, if you don't mind, sir," he replied. "Tell Dr. Petrie that his daughter has returned."

"What!" Faversham exclaimed. "Are you sure? Where is she?"

"She's here, sir."

"Good God! I'll get through immediately; this is splendid news!"

"Thank you, sir."

Fey replaced the receiver, and came out of the lobby.

"Excuse me one moment, Miss," he said.

He went into the adjoining room and focussed his glasses upon that spot far below where the itinerant match vendor plied his trade.

The man was standing up—and at the very moment that Fey focussed upon him, he sat down again!

Fey placed the glasses on the table, and returned to the sitting-room.

Fleurette had thrown herself into an armchair and was lighting a cigarette. She felt that she needed something to steady her nerves. The mystery of that hiatus between her parting from Alan on the steamer and her awakening in that little Surrey cottage, was terrifying.

"Excuse me, Miss," said Fey. "But did you by any chance go to the window a moment ago? I mean, just as I went out to the telephone?"

"Yes." Fleurette nodded. "I did. I remember staring down at the Embankment, thinking how desolate it looked."

Fey nodded.

"Why do you ask, Fey?"

"I was only wondering. You see I am sort of responsible for you."

Very thoughtfully, but to Fleurette's great amazement he went out into the lobby, took up a large briar pipe, lighted it, and began with an abstracted air to walk up and down the room. Astonishment silenced her for a moment, and then:

"Fey!" she exclaimed. "Are you mad?"

Fey took the pipe from between his teeth, and: "Sir Denis's orders, Miss," he explained.

172

CHAPTER 46

GALLAHO EXPLORES

A STIFLED BOOM of an explosion snapped the tension which had prevailed in Sam Pak's shop from the moment that the man from Kinloch's had finally been satisfied about the position of the charge, to that when, up there on street level, he had pressed the button.

The time occupied in these methodical preparations had driven Gallaho to the verge of lunacy, and now:

"Come on!" he shouted, making for the head of a descending stairway concealed behind the curtain at the end of the bar. "There's been time for a hundred murders. Let's hope we're not too late!"

The stairway led to a kitchen in which was the ingenious door which in turn communicated with that long underground corridor. The masked door was open now and a length of cable lay along the passage.

"Wait for the fumes to clear," came a voice from behind.

"Fumes be damned!" growled Gallaho; then: "Hell! What's that?"

A black jagged hole appeared in the wall beside the iron door. A bluish acrid vapour showed in the torch-light But at the moment that the party led by Gallaho entered the passage-way, there came from somewhere beyond the iron door a rending crash as if a battering ram had been driven through concrete.

Now, hard upon it, followed an awful sound of rushing waters echoing, roaring down into some unsuspected depth!

Part of the wall above and to the right of the gap collapsed, and water began to spray out into the passage . . . .

"I was afraid of this—did I not warn you?" The voice was Schumann's. "This place is below the tidal level. It is the Thames breaking in!"

"God help them!" groaned Trench, "if they're down there!"

Ignoring the vapour and the drenching spray, Galllaho, shining the ray of his torch ahead, ducked, and peered through the jagged opening.

"Be careful! The whole place may collapse!"

The spectacle before the detective was an awe-inspiring one. Within a foot of his right hand, a smooth torrent of yellowish water poured out of some unseen gap, crashed upon a dim structure of wood and iron beneath, and from thence leapt out into the darkness of an incredible pit.

His iron nerve was momentarily shaken.

The depth indicated by the tumult of that falling water staggered him. Trench entered behind Gallaho.

"Stand clear of the water!" the latter bellowed in his ear. "It would sweep you off like a fly!"

He shone the powerful light downwards. There were wooden stairs in an iron framework. The torrent was breaking upon the first platform below, and thence descending, a great, shimmering, yellow coil, to unknown depths. Others were pushing through, but:

"Stand back!" Gallaho shouted. "There's no more room between the water and the edge!"

Trench pressed his lips to Gallaho's ear.

"This must be the shaft leading down to the tunnel." He yelled. "But no one could pass that platform where the water is falling."

Gallaho turned and pushed the speaker back through the opening into the passage. Startled faces watched them climbing through.

"Forester!" he cried. "Up to the room in the wooden outbuilding. We want all the rope and all the ladder you have!"

"Right!" said Forester, whose usually fresh colouring had quite deserted him, and set off at a run.

Gallaho turned to Trench.

"Did you notice the heat coming up from that place?"

Trench nodded, moistening his dry lips.

"And the smell?"

"I don't like to think about the smell, Inspector," he said unsteadily.

At which moment:

"Inspector Gallaho!" came a cry, "you're wanted on the telephone upstairs."

"What's this?" growled Gallaho and ran off.

It was possible to make oneself heard in the corridor, and:

"I believe that place leads down to hell," said Trench. "If so it will run the Thames dry."

"What's the inspector's idea about a rope ladder, Sergeant?"

"I don't know, unless he thinks he can swing clear of the waterfall to a lower platform. He's a braver man than I am if he is going to try it."

There were muttered questions and doubtful answers; fearful glances cast upward at the roof of the passage. Schumann and the works manager had gone out and around to the river front, to endeavour to locate the spot at which the water was entering the cellars.

And now, came Merton, the ex A.B. trailing a long rope ladder. As he reached the passage way he pulled up, brushing perspiration from his eyes, and:

"Here I say!" he exclaimed, staring at the spray-masked gap beside the iron door. "I'm not going in there for anybody!"

"You haven't been asked to," came Gallaho's growling voice.

All turned as the detective-inspector came along the dimly lighted passage with his curious, lurching walk.

"Any news?" Trench asked.

"The Old Man's on his way down." (The Old Man referred to was the Commissioner of Police.) Dr. Petrie's with him— the girl's father."

"Whew!" whistled Trench.

"The queer thing is, though, that the girl's turned up."

"What!"

"She's at Sir Denis's flat; they had the report at the Yard only a few minutes ago."

He divested himself of his tightly fitting blue overcoat, and, turning to Merton:

"I want you to come through there with me," he said, "because you understand knots and ropes, and I can rely on you. I want you to lash that ladder where I'll show you to lash it."

"But I say, Gallaho!" Forester exclaimed . . .

"Unless, of course," said Gallaho ironically, "you consider, Inspector Forester, that this properly belongs to your province."

Chapter 47

THE WATERSPOUT

STERLING GROPED HIS WAY through darkness in the direction of the foot of the stairs. The roar of falling water was deafening. At one point he was drenched in spray, and hesitated. A small ray shone through the gloom, higherto unbroken except for stabs of yellowish light through chinks in the furnace door. He turned sharply, aware from the pain in his chest that he was fit for little more.

The light came nearer and a grip fastened upon his arm. Close to his ear:

"Around this way—we can't reach the steps direct."

The voice was Nayland Smith's.

A pocket-torch had been amongst the latter's equipment, and now it was invaluable. Using it sparingly, Nayland Smith indicated the edge of a great column of water which was pouring down into the pit, so that anywhere within ten feet of it one was drenched in the spray of its fall. A rushing stream was pouring down the tunnel, the entrance to which they were now passing.

Even as Sterling, horrified as he had never been in his life, stared along that whispering gallery, a distant lantern went out, swept away by the torrent.

Then they turned left; and, stumbling onwards, presently Sterling saw the foot of the wooden steps. But Dr. Fu Manchu was not there.

His lips close to Sterling's ear:

"It's only a matter of minutes," shouted Nayland Smith, "before the water reaches that ghastly furnace. Then . . . we're done!"

Spray drenched them—a sort of mist was rising. The booming of the water was awful. Sterling had been along those rock galleries cut beneath Niagara Falls: he was reminded of them now. This was a rivulet compared with the mighty Horseshoe Fall; but, descending from so great a height and crashing upon concrete so near to where they stood, the effect was at least as dreadful.

Into the inadequate light, penetrating spray and mist, of Nayland Smith's pocket torch there stumbled a strange figure—a drenched, half-drowned figure moving his arms blindly as he groped forward.

It was Murphy!

Suddenly, he saw the light, and sweeping his wet hair back from his forehead, he showed for a moment a white blood-stained face in the ray of the torch.

From that white mask his eyes glared out almost madly.

Nayland Smith turned the light upon his own face, then stepping forward, grasped Murphy's arm.

Far above, a dim light shone through the mist and spray. It revealed that horror-inspiring shaft with its rusty girders, and the skeleton staircase clinging to its walls: this, eerily, vaguely, as a dream within a dream. But it revealed something else:

That ever-increasing cataract descending from some unseen place, sprouted forth remorselessly from one of the upper platforms!

No human being could pass that point. . . .

Nayland Smith staring upward flashed the feeble light of his torch in a rather vain hope that it would be seen by those at the top of the shaft; for that at long last a raiding party had penetrated, he was convinced.

The light above became obscured in ever increasing mist; it disappeared altogether.

Much of that stair which zigzagged from side to side had remained mantled in impenetrable shadow during the few seconds that light had shone through at the head of the pit. If Fu Manchu and those of his servants who remained alive were on the stairs they were invisible.

To one memory Nayland Smith clung tenaciously.

Dr. Fu Manchu at the moment that his killings had been interrupted, had descended three steps and extinguished the lamps. Somewhere, hereabouts, there was a switch.

Suddenly, he came upon it, and reversed it.

There was no result.

The explosion had disconnected the current.

He glanced back ere beginning to climb. Water was creeping up to the first step. Spray and mist obstructed this view of the furnace. He wondered if the Burmese horror, to whom human life meant no more than wood to a circular saw, had triumphed over injury, or if he was doomed to be swallowed in that unnatural tide.

Smith started up the stairs.

He was planning for the imminent catastrophe, nor thinking any further ahead than the moment when the rising water should reach the furnace. He had placed the direction of the fall, and knew that except at one point where the waterspout came perilously near to the stairs, these were navigable to within one stage of the top.

Beyond that point, progress was impossible—and the volume of water was increasing minute by minute.

His feet were wet when he began to mount. The tunnel must be full, now, right to the dead end. It was only a question of time for this forgotten shaft to be filled to its brim.

Sterling was breathing heavily and Sergeant Murphy was giving him some assistance, when Nayland Smith caught up with them on the stairs.

He shouted in Sterling's ear:

"Did that yellow swine crock you?"

Sterling grasped his arm and gripped it strongly, pressing his lips to the speaker's ear.

"It's only my wind," he explained; "otherwise O.K."

Smith who had momentarily snapped his torch on, snapped it off again, nursing the precious light. Fighting against the brain-damning clamour of falling water, he tried to estimate their chances.

He guessed that now the tunnel would be full. The flood would rise in the shaft at least a foot a minute. Failing inspiration on the part of the police, ultimate escape was problematical.

But he was thinking at the moment of that white hot furnace when steam was generated. That one point on the stairs almost touched by the waterspout was the only possible shelter. That an explosion there in the depths might wreck the entire shaft, was a possibility which one could not calculate.

Up they went, and up, until the spray cut off by an iron girder lashed them stingingly. Nayland Smith pressed the switch of his torch.

Sterling had sunk down upon the step—Murphy was supporting him. Smith bent to Murphy's ear.

"Stay where you are!" he shouted

He groped his way upward.

CHAPTER 48

GALLAHO BRINGS UP THE REAR

"Is it fast?" shouted Gallaho.

"It's fast," Merton shouted back, "but you're not going down there!"

Gallaho bent to Merton's ear.

"Mind your own bloody business, my lad," he roared. "If ever I want your advice I shall ask for it."

Chief detective-inspector Gallaho climbed over the hand rail and began to descend the rope ladder, his bowler hat firmly screwed on to his bullet skull. Immediately, he was drenched to the skin.

Steam was rising from the shaft. The touch of the water was icy, numbing. But he knew that unless the ladder was too short he could reach a point of the staircase just below that ever-increasing cataract, and follow it down. He was a man with a clear-cut idea of what duty demanded.

The ladder proved to be of ample length. Gallaho gained the wooden steps, flashed his powerful torch, and saw that he stood near the waterfall thundering down into those unimaginable depths.

A faint light flickered far below.

Gallaho, his torch in his left hand, held well clear of his body, directed its ray towards that spot of light visible through the mist.

At first, what he saw was no more than a moving shadow, then it became concrete; and in the light, haggard, staggering, he saw Sir Denis Nayland Smith!

Gallaho ran down the intervening steps, and as the light showed more and more clearly the lean angular features, the detective saw the ghost of a smile break through their haggardness.

An unfamiliar wave of emotion claimed him. He threw his arm around Sir Denis's shoulder, and, shouting:

"Thank God I've found you, sir!" he said.

Smith bent to his ear.

"Good man!" he replied.

"The others sir?"

Nayland Smith indicated the steps below, and Gallaho lighting the way, the two began to descend. A sheet of water swept the point at which Smith had left Sterling and Sergeant Murphy.

Their situation had become untenable and they had mounted half-way up to the next platform. Smith's chief worry was concerned with Sterling who was obviously in bad shape. But the sight of Gallaho afforded just that stimulus which he required. And the detective, throwing an arm around him to help him upwards, and recognizing that he was nearly spent, had an inspiration.

Bending close to his ear:

"Stick it, sir!" he shouted. "Your friend Miss Petrie is safe and well in Sir Denis's flat!"

That stimulus was magical.

Nevertheless, the rope ladder, now nearly submerged in the ever widening waterspout, taxed Sterling to the limit. Murphy followed up behind. Merton, at the top, when collapse threatened, at the critical moment craned over and hauled Sterling to safety.

Nayland Smith came next—Gallaho truculently having claimed the right to bring up the rear.

He had earned that perilous honour.

The men in the brick passage-way broke into unorthodox cheers; nor did Forester check them.

"All out!" cried Nayland Smith. "Anything may happen when the furnace goes!"

The passage already was an inch deep in water, but they retreated along it, Gallaho and Nayland Smith last of the party.

They had reached the masked door in Sam Pak's kitchen when the furnace exploded. Steam belched out of the corridor as from a huge exhaust. The ancient building shook.

Nayland Smith turned to Gallaho and very solemnly held out his hand.

CHAPTER 49

WAITING

"NOTHING TO REPORT," said Inspector Gallaho.

Nayland Smith nodded and glanced at Alan Sterling seated smoking in the armchair. It was the evening of the sixth day after the subterranean explosion in Chinatown, an explosion which had had several remarkable results.

The top of that forgotten pit leading down to the abandoned tunnel was actually covered, as later investigations showed, by the paved yard which adjoined Sam Pak's restaurant. The ventilation shaft passed right through his premises; and there seemed to be a distinct possibility that the old house as well as the wooden superstructure, were actually part of the abandoned workings, modified and adapted to their later purpose.

A great crack had appeared in one wall of the restaurant. But no other visible damage appeared upon the surface.

Something resembling a phenomenal tide had disturbed Limehouse Reach that night, and was widely reported from crafts upon the river. The shaft with its horrible secrets was filled to within fifteen feet of the top.

Even allowing for secret getaways communicating with adjoining premises, it was reasonable to assume that neither Dr. Fu Manchu nor any of those attached to his service had escaped alive from the fire and flood.

A cordon had been thrown around the entire area with the cooperation of the River Police. Of old Sam Pak and the other Asiatics who had been in the Sailors' Club, nothing had been seen. A house to house search in the yellow light of dawn satisfied Gallaho that they were not concealed in the neighbourhood. Nothing came of these researches to afford a clue to the mystery.

A guarded communication was issued to the newspapers under the Commissioner's direction, to the effect that in forcing a way into suspected premises a buttress had collapsed and an old tunnel working been flooded by the river.

Fleet Street suspected that there was a wonderful story behind this communiqué, but the real story if ever discovered was never published.

Mrs. Sam Pak was let off with a fine and had been covered assiduously ever since. Her movements had afforded no clue to those who watched her. She accepted the disappearance of her aged husband as philosophically as she had accepted his presence. She was permitted to re-open the shop but not the Sailors' Club.

Enquiries at Dovelands Cottage, Lower Kingswood, revealed the fact that the place belonged to a Mrs. Ryatt, who lived in Streatham and who used it in the summer but let it when possible during the winter months.

The place had been vacant for a long time, but had recently been leased by a gentleman whose address proved to be untraceable, for the convalescence of his daughter who had had a nervous breakdown. Mrs. Ryatt had actually visited the cottage on the evening that her new tenant entered into occupation, and reported that the daughter was an uncommonly pretty girl whose manner was very strange; and the nurse in charge was an elderly foreign woman of rather forbidding appearance.

She had been satisfied, however, of the respectability of her tenant and had returned to London.

No trace of the woman described by Mrs. Ryatt and by Fleurette could be found. . . .

Nayland Smith, tugging at the lobe of his ear, walked up and down the room. He glanced several times at a large clock upon the mantelpiece; then:

"I expected no news, Gallaho," he said, rapidly. "Yet——"

"Surely you have no doubts left, sir?"

Sterling stared eagerly at Sir Denis, awaiting his reply.

"Fleurette's manner disturbs me," snapped the latter. "She seems to have inherited from her mother a sort of extra sense where Dr. Fu Manchu is concerned. It is no doubt due, in both cases, to the fact that he has subjected Fleurette—as he subjected Karamanèh—to hypnotic influences at various times."

Sterling moved cautiously in the armchair. He was nursing an injured rib.

"In fact," Smith went on, "I never feel entirely happy about her, when she is not here, actually under my own eyes."

"Dr. Petrie, her father, is with her," Gallaho growled.

"I agree, she could not be in better hands. It's just an instinctive distrust."

"Based upon her queer ideas, sir?" Gallaho went on in a puzzled way.

He had assumed his favourite pose, one elbow resting on the mantelpiece.

"Surely her manner is to be expected in one who has suffered the sort of things that she has suffered. I mean—" he hesitated, seeking for words—"it will naturally take some little time before she gets over the idea that her movements are controlled. Now that I know her history, I think she is simply wonderful."

"You are right, Inspector," said Sterling, warmly. "She *is* wonderful. If you or I had been through what Fleurette has been through I wager we should be stretcher cases."

"You are probably right," said Gallaho.

Nayland Smith, his back to the room, stood staring out of the window. He was thinking of the itinerant match seller, who beyond any shadow of doubt had been a spy of Dr. Fu Manchu. Fey's report of what had happened down there on the Embankment on the night of the destruction of the Thames tunnel, frequently recurred to his mind, but the match seller—like the other mysterious servants of the Chinese doctor—had disappeared; all enquiries had failed to establish his identity.

He was said to have traded there for many years, but there was some difference of opinion on this point between constables patrolling that part of the Embankment. Nayland Smith was inclined to believe that the original vendor had been bought out, or driven out, and that an understudy made up to resemble him had taken his place.

Suddenly turning:

"Switch the lights up, Gallaho, if you don't mind," he said.

The lofty, homely room became brilliantly illuminated.

"Ah!" muttered Gallaho—"this will be the doctor and the young lady."

The faint but familiar sound of the lift gate had arrested his attention. A moment later, Fey opened the outer door. The

184

voice of Fleurette was heard—as she came running in, followed by Dr. Petrie.

She was very lovely, and ignoring Petrie's frown, Sterling struggled to his feet.

"Please sit down, dear!" Fleurette pressed her hands on his shoulders. "No! you must rest."

"But I feel so rottenly guilty."

"I know it's a shame that this big darling has to come pottering around all the shops with me," said Fleurette, laughingly. "But there are so many things I want before we leave for Egypt. The longer we stay the more I shall want! And I don't believe he really minds." She linked her arm in Petrie's and leaned her head upon his shoulder. "Do you?"

"Mind?" he said, and hugged her. "It's a joy to be with you, dear. And although Alan is temporarily crocked, it's only right that you should get out sometimes, after all."

"I suggest cocktails," said Sir Denis, his good humour quite restored; and was about to press a bell when the ringing of a telephone in the lobby arrested him in the act.

"*I* can make cocktails," said Fleurette, gaily. "I'll make you one none of you has ever tasted before, if you'll just wait until I take my hat off."

She ran out. Petrie watched her with gleaming eyes. This miraculous double of his beautiful wife had brought a new happiness into his life, keen as only a joy can be which one has relinquished for ever.

Fey rapped upon the door, and in response to Nayland Smith's snappy "Come in," entered.

"Yes, Fey, what is it?"

"There's a P.C. Ireland on the telephone, sir; he says you know him—and he has something which he believes to be important to tell you."

"Ireland?" Gallaho growled. "That's the constable who was on duty at Professor Ambroso's house on the night the business started."

"A good man," snapped Nayland Smith. "I marked him at the time."

He went out to the lobby.

CHAPTER 50

THE NIGHT WATCHMAN

"STRANGELY LIKE old times, Smith!"

Nayland Smith stared at Petrie. Gallaho, bowler worn at a rakish angle, sat on the seat before them in the Scotland Yard car.

This was one of those nondescript nights which marked the gradual dispersal of the phenomenal fog of 1934. There was a threat in the air that the monster might at any moment return. The car was speeding along beside a Common. Lamps gleamed yellowly where roads crossed it. One could see, through gaunt, unclothed trees, a distant highroad.

"Yes," Smith returned. "Some queer things have happened to us, Petrie, on that Common."

"The queerest thing of all is happening now," Petrie went on. "The inevitable cycle of it is almost appalling. Here we are, after all the years, back again in the same old spot."

"Sir Denis pointed out to me this queer cycle, doctor, which seems to run through our lives," Gallaho said, glancing back over his shoulder. "I've thought about it a lot since. And I can see, now that over and over again it crops up. I suppose Sir Denis has told you that we were actually in your old room early last week?"

"Yes," said Petrie, and stared vaguely from the window.

There came a silent interval.

Sterling had been deposited in his apartment at a hotel in Northumberland Avenue. "You are under my orders, now," Petrie had said, "and I don't want you out on this foul night. I dislike that cough. Lie down when you have had something to eat. I shall of course come and see you when I return. . . ."

The doctor had been loath to leave his daughter at Sir Denis's flat, where they were staying. But recognizing how keenly he wanted to go, Fleurette had insisted. "I have victimized you all the afternoon, dear; I think you deserve an hour off. I shall read until you come back. . . ."

"This may be a wild-goose chase," growled Gallaho

suddenly, "but on the other hand, it may not. We've got to remember the old bloke may have been drunk or he may have been barmy. . . ."

"From what Ireland told me," said Nayland Smith, "I don't think either of those possibilities calls for consideration. Hello! Isn't this where we get out?"

The driver pulled up on a street corner and the three alighted.

This street, lined with small suburban houses, so characteristic of the outlying parts of London, vividly recalled to Petrie the days when he had practised in this very district, and when his patients had inhabited just such houses. There was a considerable stream of traffic and at some points beyond it seemed to be badly congested.

P.C. Ireland was standing in the shadow of a wall which lined the street for twenty yards or so on one side, bordering the garden of a large house situated upon a corner facing the Common.

"Ah, there you are, Constable," Gallaho said gruffly.

"Good evening," said Sir Denis. "All luck comes your way in this case, Constable."

"Yes, sir. It looks like it."

"Repeat," Smith directed tersely, "in your own words, what you told me on the telephone."

"Very good, sir." The man paused for a moment; then:

"There's some cable-laying job going on at the corner of the lane there which cuts across the Common; a big hole in the road and a lot of drain pipes stacked up. When the gang ceased work this evening, and the night watchman came on, I thought there was likely to be a jam with the traffic, and so I stepped across and asked him to put another red lamp on this side to show where drivers should pull out. That's how I got into conversation with him, sir. He's a bit of a character and he said—I'm sticking as nearly as possible to his own words—if all coppers were human, it might be better for some of them. I asked him what he meant by that; but when he told me the story, which I thought it was my duty to report to you——"

"You were quite right," snapped Nayland Smith.

"——I called up the inspector, and he told me to stand-by

as you suggested, sir; there's another man on my beat."

"We'll get the rest of the story from the night watchman," growled Gallaho.

"He's no friend of the Force, Inspector," Ireland nodded. "He might talk more if you said you were newspaper men."

"Bright lad!" growled Gallaho. He turned to Sir Denis. "Will you do the talking, sir?"

Nayland Smith nodded.

"Leave it to me."

The hole in the road with its parapets of gravel and wood blocks protected by an outer defence of red poles from which lanterns were suspended, was certainly obstructing the traffic. But at the moment that the party of three reached it, a temporary clearance had been effected, and the night watchman surveyed an empty street.

His quarters, a sort of tarpaulin cave constructed amidst a mass of large iron piping, housed a plank seat and some other mysterious items of furniture. A fire in a brazier glowed redly in the darkness, and added additional colour to that already possessed by the night watchman.

This peculiar character, who favoured a short grey beard but no moustache—his upper lip appearing to possess a blue tinge in contrast to the redness of his nose—wore the most dilapidated bowler hat which Nayland Smith had ever seen in his life, and this at an angle which startled even Inspector Gallaho. He also wore two overcoats; the outer garment being several inches shorter than the inner.

He was engaged at the moment upon the task of frying bacon in the square lid of a biscuit tin which he manipulated very adroitly with a pair of enormous pincers, obviously designed for some much less delicate task. He looked up as the three men paused, leaning on one of the red poles.

"Upon my word!" Nayland Smith exclaimed, importing a faint trace of Cockney into his accent. "You blokes do get about, don't you?" He turned to Gallaho. "Funny I should see this chap here, to-night. Last week I saw him down in Limehouse."

"Did you, now?" said the watchman, evidently much gratified. "I'll say that's funny; I'll say more, I'll say it's bloody funny!"

He removed the biscuit tin skilfully, and tipped the rashers with their succulent fat on to a cracked enamel plate. He produced a knife and fork and a great chunk of bread. Standing up, he set a kettle on the fire, then sat down again, and, the plate on the plank beside him, began very composedly to eat his supper.

"Yes, it is funny," Nayland Smith went on. "I was down there for my paper on the story of that raid in Chinatown. But all the suspects slipped away. It would be last Saturday night, wouldn't it?"

"It would," said the night watchman, his mouth full of hot bacon. "That would be the night."

He dropped some tea into a tin pot, set it on the ground beside him, and continued stolidly to eat his bacon.

"A night wasted," Nayland Smith mused aloud. "And what a night it was! What ho! The fog."

"It certainly were foggy."

"The blooming coppers had something up their sleeve; they kept it to themselves."

"You're right, mister." He spat out a piece of bacon rind, picked it up, contemplated it critically and then threw it on the fire. "Coppers is a lousy lot!"

"Wish I'd stopped for a chat with you, that night, and a spot over the fire." Nayland Smith leaned across the rail and passed a flask to the night watchman. "Slip a gill in your tea. I'm homeward bound with a couple of pals. I sha'n't need it."

"Blimey!" cried the night watchman, unscrewed the flask and sniffed the contents. "Thanks, mister. This is a bit of all right."

"Those blasted chinks," Sir Denis continued, "slipped out of that place as though they'd been dissolved,"

"How many, guv'nor?"

"Four, I think they were looking for."

Mingled with the sound of whisky trickling into a tin mug, came a muted rumbling which examination of the face of the night watchman might have suggested to an observer to be due to suppressed mirth; then:

"You might have done worse than stop for a chat with me, guv'nor," said the man, re-screwing the flask and returning it to Sir Denis.

189

CHAPTER 51

NIGHT WATCHMAN'S STORY

"IT WAS THIS WAY with me," the night watchman continued, endeavouring to chuckle and eat bacon at the same time, "as I told the young scab of a copper down there what come walkin' by. He says 'you've 'ad one over the eight, haven't you?' he says. See what I mean, mister?"

"I know those young coppers," snapped Nayland Smith, glancing at Gallaho. "They've got no sense."

"Sense!" The night watchman made a strong brew of tea. "What I want to know is: how do they get into the Force? Answer me that: how do they get into the Force? Well, this bloke I'm tellin' you about. . . ."

The dammed up stream of traffic was trickling slowly past the obstruction, under Constable Ireland's direction. Things were going fairly well. But nevertheless it was difficult to hear the speaker, and Nayland Smith and Gallaho bent over the red barrier, listening intently. Petrie craned forward also, his hand resting on Gallaho's shoulder.

"This bloke says to me," the night watchman repeated, "'ad one over the eight, haven't you?" So I didn't say no more to him, except, 'Bloody bad luck to you if you ain't'. That was what I said."

With all the care of a pharmacist preparing a prescription, he added a portion of whisky from the tin cup to a brew of hot tea in a very cracked mug.

"I let him go—it's silly talkin' to coppers. He went away laughin'. But the laugh was mine, if I says so—but the laugh was mine! I'll tell you what I told 'im, mate—I told him what I see."

He swallowed a portion of bread and bacon.

"You're a newspaper man. Well, you'd have got your story all right, if you stopped, like you wanted to do, that night. What a story. Here it is. I work for a firm, if you follow what I mean; I ain't a Council man—that's why I travels so much. Very well. The same firm what done this job 'ere was on the Limehouse job. . . ."

He added sugar and condensed milk from a tired looking tin to the brew in the mug, stirred it with a piece of wood and took an appreciative sip.

"Good 'ealth, mister. Where I'm workin' in Limehouse is on West India Dock Road and not far from the corner of the old Causeway. That's where you see me, if I heard you right."

"That's it," said Smith patiently; " a grand fire you had."

"I'd got some chestnuts," chuckled the night watchman. "I remember as well as if it were an hour ago, and I'd roasted 'em and I was eating 'em. Did you notice me eating 'em?"

"No, he didn't," growled Gallaho; "at least, he never told me he did."

Nayland Smith grasped the speaker's arm.

"Oh, didn't he?" said the night watchman, lifting a tufted eyebrow in the direction of the detective.

"Well, I was. And through the fog there, what did I see? . . ."

He drank from the mug. Rain had begun to fall; the roar of the passing traffic rendered it necessary to bend far over the red pole in order to hear the man's words. He set down his mug and stared truculently from face to face.

"I'm askin' a bloody question," he declared. "What did I see?"

"How the hell do I know, mate?" Gallaho shouted, in the true vernacular, his voice informed by suppressed irritation.

The night watchman chuckled. This was the sort of reaction he understood.

"Course you don't know. That's why I ask' you . . . I see a trap what belongs to the main sewer open from underneath. Get that? It just lifted—and first thing I thought was: an explosion! It wasn't no further from me than"——he hesitated,—"that bus. It was lifted right off. There's nobody about; it's the middle of the night. It was set down very quiet on the pavement, and what did I see then? . . ."

He took another sip from his mug; he had finished the bread and the bacon. Gallaho had sized up his witness, and: "What did you see, mate?" he inquired.

"Here's a story for the newspapers," the watchman chuckled, as Nayland Smith reached across the barrier and offered him a cigarette from a yellow packet. "Thanks, mister—here's a story!"

He succeeded in some mysterious way in lighting the cigarette from the fire in the brazier.

"A Chinaman popped up . . ."

"What!"

"You may well say 'what'! But I'm tellin' you. A Chinaman popped up out of the trap."

"What kind of a Chinaman?"

Nayland Smith was the speaker, but in spite of his eagerness he had not forgotten to retain the accent.

"Looked like a Chinese sailor, as much as I could see of 'im through the fog—not that there was a lot of fog at the time; but there was some—there 'ad been more. He took a look round. I sat quiet by my fire because, as I told that lousy cop what laughed at me, I thought for a minute I was dreamin'. Then he bent down and 'elped another Chinese bloke to come up. The second Chinese bloke was old. He was an old Chinee, he were. . . ."

"What did he wear?" Smith inquired, pulling out a notebook and pencil, casually.

"Ho, ho!" chuckled the watchman. "I thought you'd want to make some notes. He wore a kind of overcoat and a tweed cap. But although I couldn't see his face, I know it was a very funny face—very old and 'aggard, and he were very tall——"

"Very tall?"

"That's what I said—Very tall. Another bloke come up next——"

"Also a Chinaman?"

"Likewise Chinese, wearin' a old jersey and trousers with his 'ead bare. He bent back like the first bloke had done, and 'auled up another Chinese——"

"Not another one," growled Gallaho, acting up to the situation.

"Another one!" the watchman repeated truculently, fixing a ferocious glare upon the speaker, whom instinctively he disliked—"and another old 'un—" challengingly, the glare unmoved from Gallaho—"*and another old 'un! . . .*"

Nayland Smith was apparently making rapid notes; now:

"Was the other old one tall?" he inquired.

"He were not, he was just old."

"Did you notice what he wore?"

"Listen . . ." The night watchman puffed his cigarette and then stood up slowly—"*you're* not suggestin' I'm barmy, are you?"

"You bet I'm not," snapped Nayland Smith cheerfully. "You've given me a grand paragraph."

"Oh, I see. Well, he wore a seedy kind o'suit like I might wear, and an old soft hat."

"What did they do?"

"The two younger chinks put the trap back and stamped it down. Then they all crossed the road behind my 'ut, and that's all I know about it."

"Didn't you see where they went?"

"Listen, mister . . ." The watchman sat down again on his plank seat, refilling his mug from the pot and adding the remainder of the whisky to its contents. "There was nobody about. I ain't as young as I used to be. If you saw chinks—two of 'em tough lookin' specimens—come up put of a sewer . . . see what I mean? Do you know what I done? I pretends to be fast asleep! And now, I'm goin' to ask *you* a question. In the circs,—what would *you* 'ave done?"

"That's sense," growled Gallaho.

"But you reported it to the constable on the beat when he came along?" said Nayland Smith.

"As you say, mister. And he not only give me the bird, he told me I was barmy or blind-oh. It'll be a long time before I gives information to the bloody police again, whatever I sees—whatever I sees."

CHAPTER 52

"I AM CALLING YOU"

FLEURETTE KNEW that Alan must not be out after dusk in this misty weather. He had developed an unpleasant cough as a result of the injuries he had received; but Fleurette had found a faith almost amounting to worship in the wisdom of Dr. Petrie, her father so newly discovered, but already deeply loved.

He had assured her that this distressing symptom would disappear when the lesion was healed.

She had not wanted Alan to go. Her love for him was a strange thing, impossible to analyse. It had come uncalled for, unwanted; she almost resented the way she felt about Alan.

The curious but meaningless peace of her previous life, her fatalistic acceptance of what she believed to be her destiny, had been broken by this love for Alan. He had represented storm; the discovery of her father had represented calm.

She knew, but nevertheless experienced no resentment of the fact, that she had been used as a pawn in the game of the brilliant man who had dominated her life from infancy. Even now, after her father and Sir Denis had opened her eyes, gently, but surely, to the truth—or what they believed to be the truth—about the Prince (for she always thought of him as the Prince) Fleurette remained uncertain.

Sir Denis was wonderful; and her father—her heart beat faster when she thought of her father—he, of course, was simply a darling. In some way which she could not analyse, her allegiance, she knew, was shared between her father and Alan. It was all very new and very confusing. It had not only changed her life; it had changed her mode of thought—her outlook—everything.

Curled up in the big armchair before the fire, Fleurette tried to adjust her perspective in regard to this new life which opened before her.

Was she a traitor to those who had reared her, so tenderly and so wonderfully, in breaking with the code which had almost become part of herself? Was she breaking with all that was true, and plunging into a false world? Her education, probably unique for a woman, had endowed her with a capacity for clear thinking. She knew that her thoughts of Alan Sterling were inspired by infatuation. Would her esteem for his character, although she believed it to be fine, make life worth while when infatuation was over?

In regard to her father, there was no doubt whatever. Her discovery of him had turned her world upside down. She resettled herself in the chair.

The Prince was fighting for her.

That strange hiatus in her life, about which the doctor had been so reticent, meant that he still had power to claim her. Now, they said he was dead.

It was unbelievable.

Fleurette found it impossible to grasp this idea that Dr. Fu Manchu was dead. She had accepted the fact—it had become part of her life—that one day he would dominate a world in which there would be no misunderstanding, no strife, no ugliness; nothing but beauty. To this great ideal she had consecrated herself, until Alan had come.

"Little Flower . . . I am calling you!"

It was *his* voice—speaking in Chinese!

And Fleurette knew that ancient language as well as she knew French and English.

She sat bolt upright in the armchair. She was torn between two worlds. This normal, clean room, with its simple appointments, its neatness, its homeliness—the atmosphere which belonged to Sir Denis, that generous, boyish-hearted man who was her father's trusty friend; and a queer, alluring philosophy, cloying, like the smoke of incense, which belonged to the world from which Nayland Smith had dragged her.

"Little Flower—I am calling you."

Fleurette wrenched her gaze away from the fire.

In the burning logs, the face of Dr. Fu Manchu was forming. She sprang to her feet, and pressed a bell beside the mantelpiece.

There was a rap on the door.

"Come in."

Fey entered. He brought Western reason, coolness, to her racing brain.

"You rang, miss?"

Fleurette spoke rather wildly; and Fey, although his manner did not betray the fact, was studying her with concern.

"You see, Fey, I arranged to wait dinner until my father and Sir Denis came back. As a matter of fact, I am rather hungry."

"Quite, miss. Perhaps a little snack? Some caviar and a glass of wine?"

"Oh, no, Fey. Nothing quiet so fattening. But if you would get me just two tiny egg sandwiches with a layer of cress—you know what I mean—and perhaps, yes, a glass of wine . . ."

"Certainly, miss, in a moment."

Fey went out.

Fleurette pulled the armchair around, so that she did not face the fire. It was a gesture—but a defensive one.

That voice—that voice which could not be denied—"Little Flower I am calling you"—had sounded, she knew, in her subconscious mind only. But *because* she knew this . . . she feared. If she had not known how this voice had reached her, she would have surrendered, and have been conquered. Because she did know, and was not prepared to surrender, she fought.

They thought he was dead . . He was not dead.

She heard Fey at the telephone giving terse orders. She was really hungry. This was not merely part of a formula designed to combat the subconscious call which had reached her; but it would help. She knew that if she wanted Alan, that if in future she wished to live in the same wholesome world to which her father belonged, she must fight—*fight*.

She wandered across to a bookshelf and began to inspect the books. One watching her would have said that she smiled almost tenderly. Nayland Smith's books betrayed the real man.

Those works which were not technical were of a character to have delighted a schoolboy. Particularly Fleurette was intrigued by a hard-bitten copy of *Tom Sawyer Abroad* which had obviously been read and re-read. Despite his great brain and his formidable personality, what a simple soul he was at heart!

Fleurette began to read at random.

". . . But I didn't care much. I am peaceable and don't get

up no rows with people that ain't doing nothing to me. I allowed if the paynims was satisfied I was. We would let it stand at that . . ."

She read other passages, wondering why her education had not included Mark Twain; recognizing by virtue of her training that the great humorist had also been one of the world's great philosophers.

"Your sandwiches, miss."

Fleurette started.

Fey was placing a tray upon a small table set beside the armchair. Removing the silver cover he revealed some delicately cut sandwiches. With a spoon and fork he adroitly placed two upon a plate, removed a half-bottle of wine from an ice-bucket, uncorked it and poured out a glassful.

He set down the glass beside the plate, adjusted the armchair in relation to the fire with careful consideration, bowed slightly, and went out.

The man was so efficient, so completely sane, that no better antidote could have been prescribed in Fleurette's present mood. Mark Twain had begun the cure; Fey had completed it.

She began to eat egg sandwiches with great relish. She knew instinctively that the expedition upon which her father had gone to-night, with Sir Denis and that strange character, Inspector Gallaho, would result in the discovery of the fact that Dr. Fu Manchu had survived the catastrophe in the East End, of which she knew very little, for they had withheld details. She was disposed to believe that Gallaho, alone, had faith in the Prince's death; her father's manner betrayed doubt; Sir Denis had said nothing, but she divined the fact that until he saw Dr. Fu Manchu dead before him he would never believe that that great intellect had ceased to function.

Fleurette ate three sandwiches, drank a glass of wine, and, in a mood of contemplation, found herself staring again into the fire.

"Little Flower, I am calling you."

His voice again!

She sprang up. She knew, for she had been trained to know, that no voice really had sounded in the room. It was her subconscious brain. But . . . this she knew also—it was real—it was urgent.

197

Already she began to see again that glamorous but meaningless life out of which she had climbed, assisted by Alan, as a swimmer clambers out of a tropical sea. She could see it in the fire. There were snow-capped mountains there, melting into palm groves, temples and crowded bazaar streets; a hot smell of decay and perfume—and now, all merged into two long, gleaming eyes.

She watched those eyes fascinatedly; bent closer, falling under their thraldom.

"Little Flower, I am calling. . . ."

Her lips parted. She was about to speak in response to that imperious call, when a sound in the lobby snatched her back to the world of reality.

It was the ringing of the door bell.

Fleurette stood up again and walked towards the book case. She pulled out *Tom Sawyer Abroad*, which she had replaced, and opened it at random. She read, but the words did not register. She could hear Fey crossing the lobby and opening the front door of the apartment. She did not hear any word spoken.

She thought she detected a vague scuffling sound.

Fleurette replaced the book, and stood still, very near to the door communicating with the lobby, listening. The scuffling continued; then came a dull thud.

Silence.

A wave of apprehension swept over her, turning her cold.

"Fey!" she called, and again more urgently, *"Fey!"*

There was no reply.

She ran to the bell beside the mantlepiece, pushed it and actually heard it ringing. She stood still, hands clenched, watching the door.

No one came.

"Fey!" she called again, and heard with surprise the high note upon which she called.

The door opened. The lobby beyond was in darkness.

A tall man was coming in.

But it was not Fey. . . .

CHAPTER 53

POWERS OF DR. FU MANCHU

"I CAN'T MAKE this out!" said Nayland Smith.

He, Dr. Petrie and Inspector Gallaho stood before the door of the apartment. Smith had rung twice and there had been no reply.

Smith stared hard at Petrie.

"You've got the key, sir, no doubt?" Gallaho growled.

"Yes." Nayland Smith drew a bunch of keys from his trouser pocket. "I have the key, but I am wondering where Fey can have gone."

They had called on Sterling, the invalid, in his room at the hotel near by, and they had broken the unpleasant news that unless Mr. Samuel Grimes (such was the night watchman's name) suffered from a singular hallucination, it was almost certain that Dr. Fu Manchu was still alive.

Petrie had attended to his patient, who was of a type difficult to handle; and with a final drink upon which the doctor had frowned severely, they had come away . . . . .

"Dinner for four at eight-thirty was my last order if I remember rightly," said Nayland Smith. "It's just possible, of course——" he placed the key in the lock—"that he may have gone down to the kitchen. But why doesn't Fleurette answer?"

He turned the key and swung the door open.

"Hello!" Gallaho exclaimed, "what's this?"

"My God!" groaned Petrie.

A heavy smell resembling that of mimosa swept out from the lobby to greet them, and . . . the lobby was in darkness!

Nayland Smith sprang forward, groped for the light, stumbled, and fell.

"Smith!"

Petrie rushed in behind him.

"All right!" came in the staccato fashion which characterized Nayland Smith in moments of tension. "I've fallen over . . . somebody."

Inspector Gallaho switched on the light.

199

Sir Denis had jumped up. He was staring down, jaws clenched, at an insensible man who lay upon the carpet.

It was Fey.

Petrie raised his hand to his brow and groaned.

"Smith," he said, in a strangled voice, "Smith! *He* has got her again!"

"Lend me a hand, Gallaho," cried Nayland Smith, savagely. "We'll get him on to the settee in the sitting-room."

The door being thrown open by Petrie, it was warmly lighted. There was no one there.

Out from that lobby which reeked of mimosa, they carried the insensible man, and laid him upon the settee. He was breathing regularly, but heavily; otherwise, there was complete silence in Nayland Smith's apartment.

"Can you do anything, Petrie? You know something about this damnable drug of the Doctor's."

"I can try," said Petrie, quietly, and went out to the room which he occupied.

Sir Denis had accommodation for two guests, or, at a pinch, three. Dr. Petrie and his daughter were his guests now; and Fleurette . . . ?

Inspector Gallaho, who had forgotten to remove his bowler, removed it, not without difficulty, showing a red mark where it had been crushed down upon his bullet head.

"This is a hell of a go," he growled, tossing his hat into an armchair. "It's easy enough to see what's happened, sir. This queer smell is one, I take it, you have met with before?"

"I have," said Sir Denis, grimly.

A powerful anaesthetic?"

"Exactly."

"Very well. Someone rang the bell, and the moment Fey opened the door, sprang on him with a pad saturated in this stuff—and the rest of the story tells itself." He began to chew phantom gum. "She's a lovely girl," he added. "It's enough to make a man burst!"

Dr. Petrie came in carrying a medicine case, and kneeling down, began to examine Fey. Gallaho went out into the lobby.

"The smell of this stuff makes my head swim," he growled.

He was looking for something which might give a clue to the identity of Fey's assailant. Nayland Smith, tugging at the lobe of his ear, was walking up and down before the open fire, watching Petrie at work; afraid to say what he thought, but suffering much of the agony of mind which he knew his old friend to be experiencing at this moment.

Some sandwiches and part of a bottle of champagne were on a table beside an armchair.

There came a strange interruption.

Someone who had a fresh, mezzo-soprano voice, began to sing very quietly in an adjoining room!

She sang in French, and one would have said that the singer was happy.

Dr. Petrie came to his feet at a bound.

"Good God, Smith!" He grasped Sir Denis's arm—"that's *Fleurette!*"

Gallaho came running in from the lobby.

"The young lady's in the flat, sir! What the devil does it mean?"

The song was interrupted from time to time, suggesting that the singer was moving about engaged upon some pleasant task, and singing from sheer lightness of heart. Under Dr. Petrie's tan it was yet possible to detect how pale he had grown.

"*I'll* go, Smith," he said.

He crossed the lobby, entered a short passage and threw a door open; Sir Denis was close behind him.

Fleurette, dressed as they had left her, was amusing herself with hats and frocks and stockings strewn all over the room, and singing lightly from time to time. She was smoking a cigarette.

"Fleurette, darling!" cried Petrie. "Thank God you are safe. Surely you heard us come in?"

Fleurette turned, a cigarette between her fingers, tossing a little green hat on to the coverlet of the bed, and staring in a vaguely puzzled way at the speaker.

There was no recognition in her eyes.

"I am waiting to be called," she said; "I may have to leave at any moment. Please let me get on with my packing."

"Fleurette!" Her father stepped forward and grasped her shoulders. "Fleurette! Look at me. What has happened here to-night?"

Fleurette smiled at him as she might have smiled at a

perfect stranger; then looked past him with a puzzled frown to where Nayland Smith stood in the open doorway, his face very grim, and his eyes gleaming.

"Nothing has happened," she replied. "I don't know you, but it is very kind of you to ask. May I please go on with my packing?"

"She's hysterical," came a growling voice beyond Sir Denis. "Something that has happened here to-night has unbalanced her."

It was Gallaho.

Nayland Smith exchanged a rapid glance with Dr. Petrie. Petrie, his expression indicating that he was exercising a tremendous effort of control, shook his head. He released Fleurette and forced a smile.

"By all means go on, dear," he said. "Let me know if you want anything."

Fleurette looked up at him questioningly.

"You are so nice," she said. "I'm glad you've come, but I don't want anything, thank you."

Petrie signalled to Smith to go out. They returned to the lobby, Petrie leaving the door ajar. And as they entered it, that same singing, uncanny, now, was renewed.

"There's no other way out of this flat except through the front door, here, is there?" asked Petrie.

"No." Sir Denis shook his head. "Except through a window."

Petrie glanced at Nayland Smith; agony peeped out of his eyes.

"I don't think it's likely," he said. "That is not what I fear."

"Doctor," growled Gallaho, "this is a frightful blow. Something so horrible happened here to-night that the poor girl has lost her reason."

"Something horrible—yes," said Petrie, slowly; "but . . . she hasn't lost her reason."

Gallaho stared uncomprehendingly. Nayland Smith turned to him, and:

"If you knew all that I know of the powers of Dr. Fu Manchu," he said, "you would know that not only is he alive, but . . ."

"What, sir?"—for the speaker had paused.

"He has been here to-night. I don't understand." He began to walk up and down feverishly—"I don't understand. . . ."

CHAPTER 54

GALLAHO EXPLORES FURTHER

"Have you been on duty all night?"

Chief detective-inspector Gallaho stood in the hall porter's office. The hall porter, a retired sergeant-major of the Black Watch, rather resented his presence and his manner.

"Certainly; I've been on duty all night."

"I wasn't suggesting you hadn't," growled Gallaho. "I was merely asking a question."

"Well, the answer is: Yes,"

"The answer is 'Yes'. Good. Now I'm going to ask you a few more questions."

The sergeant-major recognized a character at least as truculent as his own; when Gallaho was in difficulties, Gallaho's manner was far from soothing. The hall porter glanced him up and down with disfavour, and turning to a side-table, began to arrange a stack of letters which lay there.

"You might as well know that I'm a police officer," Gallaho went on, "and your answers to the questions I am going to ask you may be required in evidence. So make 'em snappy and to the point."

The porter tuned: he was no longer so sure of himself.

"Has something happened here to-night?" he asked.

"You are the man that should know that," said Gallaho; "so you're the man I've come to. Listen—he leaned on the flap of the half-door; "how many apartments are there on the floor where Sir Denis Nayland Smith lives?"

"Four. Sir Denis's and three others."

"Who are the occupiers of the three others?"

"One is vacant at the moment. Another belongs to Major General Sir Rodney Orme; the third to Mrs. Crossland, the novelist."

"Are these people at home?"

"Neither of them, as a matter of fact. The General is in the south of France, and his flat is shut up; and Mrs. Crossland has been in America for some time."

"I suppose her place is shut up, too?"

203

"No. As a matter of fact, it isn't. But their Egyptian servant lives up there, cleans the rooms and looks after correspondence. He has been with them, I believe, for many years."

"Egyptian servant?"

"Yes, Egyptian servant."

"Is he up there now?"

"I suppose so."

"Have you seen him to-night?"

"No."

"Are there any apartments above that?"

"No; only some storerooms. The lift goes no further than Sir Denis's floor."

"I see." Gallaho chewed invisible gum. "Now, has anybody been up to or down from that floor in the last few hours?"

"No. A gentleman called and asked for the General, but I told him he was abroad."

"So no one has gone up to the top floor, or come down from the top floor during the past few hours?"

"No one."

"People have been moving about on the other floors, of course?"

"Two or three have come down and two or three have gone up. But no one I haven't seen before. I mean they were either residents, friends of residents or tradespeople."

"Quite."

Gallaho turned, and went lounging in the direction of the lift. He paused, however, turned, and:

"Where are the kitchens?" he called; "in the basement?"

"Yes. You have to use the service lift if you want to go down there."

"Where is it?"

"In the passage on the right."

A few minutes later, Gallaho had stepped into a small elevator, controlled by a very pert boy.

"Kitchens," he growled.

"What d'you mean, kitchens?" the boy inquired. "The kitchens is private."

"My lad," said Gallaho—"when a detective-inspector says to you—'kitchens'—do you know what you do?"

"No, sir," the boy replied, suddenly awed.

"You take him there, and you jump to it."

Gallaho presently found himself in a place inhabited by men in high white caps, a hot place informed by savoury smells. His appearance created mild surprise.

"Who's in charge, here?" he demanded, sharply.

"I am a police officer, and I have some questions to ask."

A stout man whose cap was higher and whiter than the others, came forward.

"I hope nothing's wrong, Inspector," he said.

"Something *is* wrong, but it's not your fault. I only want to know one thing. You are of course acquainted with Fey, Sir Denis Nayland Smith's man?"

"Certainly."

"Did he order dinner to be prepared for a party to-night?"

"He didn't. He ordered some sandwiches just before seven o'clock and they were taken up."

"You are sure?"

"Certain."

"Thank you."

Gallaho lounged back to the lift.

The outrage must have taken place shortly after their departure. Otherwise, it was almost certain that Fey would have made arrangements with the chef for dinner. It seemed probable, but not certain, that no stranger had gone up to the top floor, or come down from it. But although the sergeant-major claimed to be acquainted with all those who had visited other floors, Gallaho realized that the evidence on this point was not conclusive, and:

"Have you been on duty all night?" he asked the man running the residents' lift.

"I came on at six o'clock, sir."

"Have you taken any strangers up or down during the evening?"

"Strangers, sir?"

They had reached the top floor, and the man opened the gate, and stood there, considering.

"There were guests came to dinner at number fourteen, and a gentleman I hadn't seen before went up this evening with another resident, but they went out together about half-past seven."

"Nobody else?"

"Nobody at all, sir."

When Sir Denis opened the door to Gallaho, the latter could hear Fleurette singing in the inner room.

CHAPTER 55

MIMOSA

"I'VE ADOPTED somewhat unusual methods, Smith," said Petrie, with the ghost of a smile, glancing up from where he sat beside the unconscious Fey.

"I hope to heaven they succeed," snapped Smith. "He may or may not be able to throw some light upon this business."

"During the time that I was a guest of Dr. Fu Manchu"—— Petrie was obviously talking with the idea of distracting his mind from the sound of that sweet voice singing snatches of songs in an adjoining room—the Doctor was good enough to impart to me some particulars of his preparation, Mimosa 3— probably the most remarkable anaesthetic ever invented by man. He claims for it that there are practically no evil after-effects, and of this you yourself have had evidence in the past. The patient may also be readily revived by those means which you have just seen me adopt."

And even as he spoke the words, Fey raised his drooping eyelids, staring vaguely from face to face.

"How are you, Fey?" said Petrie; "feeling better, I see. Let me help you up. I want you to drink this."

Fey sat up and swallowed the contents of the glass which Petrie held to his lips. Looking about him in a dazed way, he began sniffing.

"Funnily enough," he replied, "I feel practically all right. But I can still smell that awful stuff. Miss Fleurette?" He jumped to his feet, then sat down again. "She is safe, sir? She's safe?"

Fleurette had ceased to sing but could be heard moving about in the inner room.

"She's in her room, Fey," said Nayland Smith, shortly.

Fey's glance wandered to the large clock on the mantel-piece:

"Good God! Sir," he muttered. "I've been asleep for two hours!"

"It's not your fault, Fey," replied Dr. Petrie. "We all

understand. What we are anxious to hear is exactly what happened."

"Yes, sir," Fey replied. "I can understand that——" he paused, listening.

That lighthearted, sweet voice had reached him from the inner room. He glanced at Dr. Petrie:

"Miss Fleurette, sir?"

"Yes, Fey. But please go ahead with your story."

"I'd just made up my menu, sir." He glanced at Nayland Smith, who had begun restlessly to walk up and down the carpet. "I mean, I had worked out a little dinner which I thought would meet with your approval, and gone to the telephone in the lobby to talk to the chef down below. I was just about to take up the instrument when the door bell rang."

"Stop, Fey," snapped Nayland Smith. "Did you hear the lift gate open?"

"No, sir—of that I am positive."

"Go ahead."

"I'm beginning to see the light," growled Gallaho.

"One moment, Fey," Nayland Smith interrupted; "this would be, I take it, some ten to twenty minutes after our departure?"

"Exactly, sir. I thought it might be one of the staff who had come up in the service lift, which can't be heard from here, or old Ibrahim, Mrs. Crossland's butler——"

"You know this man, Ibrahim?" said Gallaho.

"Yes, sir. He's an Egyptian. He's travelled a lot, as I have. He's a funny old chap; we sometimes have a yarn together. Anyway, I opened the door."

He paused. He was a man of orderly mind. He was obviously endeavouring to find words in which exactly to express what had occurred. He went on again.

"There was a tall man standing outside the door, sir. He wore an overcoat with the collar turned up, and a black felt hat with the brim pulled down. The only light in the lobby was the table lamp beside the telephone, so that I couldn't make out his features."

"How tall was this man?" jerked Nayland Smith.

"Well, unusually tall, sir. Taller than yourself."

"I see."

"He held what looked like a camera in his hand, and as I opened the door he just stood there, watching me."

"'Yes?' I said.

"And then without moving his head, which he held down, so that I never had more than a glimpse of his features, he raised this thing and something puffed right out into my face."

"Something?" growled Gallaho. "What sort of thing?"

"Vapour, sir, with a most awful smell of *mimosa*. It blinded me—it staggered me. I fell back into the lobby, gasping for breath. And the tall man followed me in. I collapsed on the carpet where you found me, I suppose. And I remember his bending over me."

"Describe this man's hands," Nayland Smith directed.

"He wore gloves."

"As he bent over you," said Dr. Petrie, eagerly, "just before you became quite unconscious, did you form no impression of his features?"

"Yes, sir, I did. But I may have been dreaming. I thought it was the devil bending over me, sir. He had long, green eyes, that gleamed like emeralds."

"We know, now," said Sir Denis, continuing to walk up and down, "roughly what occurred. But I don't understand. . . . I don't understand."

Fleurette in the inner room sang a bar or two with the happy abandon of a child, and Fey glanced uneasily from Sir Denis to Dr. Petrie.

"What don't you understand, Smith?" the latter asked, sadly.

"Either this deathless fiend, who is harder to kill than an earwig, has employed one of his unique drugs or he has hypnotically dominated Fleurette. Whichever is the true explanation, what is his purpose, Petrie?"

There came a moment of silence. Fleurette, ceasing to sing, might be heard moving about; then:

"I think I see what you mean, Smith," Petrie replied, slowly. "He could have taken her away or he could have——"

"Exactly," snapped Sir Denis. "Why has he left her . . . and in this condition?"

"Who are you talking about, sir?" growled Gallaho.

"Dr. Fu Manchu."

"What! Do you really mean *he* has been here to-night?"

"Beyond any shadow of doubt."

"But what for?"

"That's what we are trying to work out, Gallaho." Nayland Smith was the speaker. "Frankly, it has me beaten."

"There's one line of enquiry," Gallaho replied, "which with your permission I propose to take up without delay."

"What's that?" Petrie asked.

"This tall lad, with the box of poison gas, according to the gentleman with all the medals downstairs, hasn't come into Westminster Mansions to-night, and hasn't gone out. You say yourself, Fey—" he stared at the man, chewing vigorously— "that the lift wasn't used? My conclusion is this, sir." He turned to Nayland Smith: "Dr. Fu Manchu is somewhere in this building."

Smith glanced at Petrie.

"Go and take a look at her," he said. "She's been quiet for some time. I am very anxious."

Petrie nodded, and went out.

"If the evidence of the watchman we interviewed to-night can be relied upon," Sir Denis continued—"and personally, I have no doubt on the point——"

"Nor have I, sir."

"Very well. All the men who were in that place called the Sailors' Club at the time of the tragedy, escaped by some means we don't know about. But, evidently, into a main sewer—"

"*One* seems to have been missing, sir!"

"Yes!—and I'm glad he is!" snapped Nayland Smith viciously. "The Burmese killer evidently met his end there. But that the tall man described by the witness is Dr. Fu Manchu, personally I cannot doubt."

"It certainly looks like it. But how did he get into this building? And where is he hiding?"

Dr. Petrie returned. His eyes were very sorrowful.

"Is she all right?"

He nodded.

"That yellow conjurer has got her under control," he said between clenched teeth. "I know the symptoms. I have suffered them myself. God help us! What are we going to do?"

"What I'm going to do," Gallaho growled, picking up his bowler from the armchair where he had thrown it, "is this: I am going to step along to Mrs. Crossland's flat and have a serious chat with your friend——" he glanced at Fey— "Ibrahim."

CHAPTER 56

IBRAHIM

"I HAVE NEVER MET Mrs. Crossland," said Nayland Smith irritably, "nor her husband. One can live in a block of London flats for years and never know one's neighbours. But I am acquainted with them by sight, and also with their Egyptian servant, Ibrahim."

"What do you think of him, sir?" growled Gallaho.

"Perfectly normal, and probably very trustworthy. But it doesn't follow that he hasn't been for all his life a member of the Si-Fan."

"This Si-Fan business, sir, is beyond me."

"It has proved to be beyond me," said Nayland Smigh, shortly.

Gallaho gave voice to an idea.

"It must be very unpeasant," he said, "to be the unknown husband of a well-known woman."

They reached the door of Mrs. Crossland's flat. Gallaho pressed the bell.

An elderly Egyptian in native dress opened the door. He was a very good Arab type and a highly ornamental servant. He stared uncomprehendingly at Inspector Gallaho, and then bowed to Sir Denis.

"This is Mrs. Crossland's flat, I believe?" said the detective.

"Yes, sir. Mrs. Crossland is abroad."

"A crime has been committed in this building to-night," Gallaho went on, in his threatening way, "and I want to ask you a few questions."

The Egyptian did not give way; he stood squarely in the doorway. It was a type of situation which has defeated many a detective officer. Gallaho knew that his ankles were tied by red tape; that he dared not, if intrusion should prove to have been unjustified, cross the threshold against the will of the man who held it.

Nayland Smith solved the situation.

Stepping past Gallaho, he gently but firmly pushed the Egyptian back, and entered the lobby.

"There are questions I want to ask you, Ibrahim," he said in Arabic, "and I wish my friend to be present." He turned. "Come in, Gallaho."

The lobby of Mrs. Crossland's flat resembled the entrance to a harêm. It was all mûshrabîyeh work and perforated brass lanterns. There were chests of Damascus ware, and slender Persian rugs upon the polished floors. Ibrahim's amiable face changed in expression; his dark eyes glared dangerously.

"You have no right to come into this place," he said in English.

And Nayland Smith, noting that he spoke in English even in this moment of excitement, recognized an unusual character; for *he* had spoken in Arabic.

Gallaho entered behind Sir Denis. He knew that the latter was not trammelled as he was trammelled; that he was strong enough to trample upon regulations.

"Close the door, Gallaho," snapped Sir Denis; and, turning to the Egyptian: "Lead the way in. I want to talk to you."

Ibrahim's expression changed again. He bowed, smiled, and indicating with an outstretched arm an apartment similar in shape to Nayland Smith's sitting-room, led the way.

Gallaho and Sir Denis found themselves in an apartment queerly exotic. The bay window which in Smith's room admitted waves of sunlight, here was obstructed by a mûshrabîyeh screen. Dim light from shaded lanterns illuminated the place. It was all divans and brassware, rugs and cushions; a stage-setting of an Oriental interior. Mrs. Crossland's reputation and financial success rested upon her inaccurate pictures of desert life; of the loves of sheiks and their Western mistresses.

Nayland Smith looked about him.

Ibrahim stood by the door leading into the room in an attitude of humility, eyes lowered. But Sir Denis had sized up the man and knew that the task before them was no easy one.

"You have a Chinese friend, O Ibrahim," he said in Arabic— "a tall, distinguished Chinese friend."

Nothing in Ibrahim's attitude indicated that the words had startled him, but:

"I have no such Chinese friend, effendîm," he replied, persistently speaking in English.

"You belong to the Si-Fan."

"I do not even know what you mean, effendîm."

"Tell me. You may as well speak now——" Sir Denis had abandoned Arabic—"since you will be compelled to speak later if necessary. How long have you been in the service of Mrs. Crossland?"

"For ten years, effendîm."

"And here, in this flat?"

"My lady and gentleman live here for five years."

"I suggest that Mrs. Crossland or her husband has a tall distinguished Chinese friend, who sometime visits here."

"I am not acquainted with such a person, effendîm."

Nayland Smith tugged at his ear, whilst Gallaho watched him anxiously. It was a situation of some delicacy; because, always, there was a possibility that they were wrong.

The sinister visitor with the camera-case might have been working from some other base.

"There are no other resident servants?"

"None, effendîm."

It was an impasse. Failing some more definite clue Nayland Smith recognized the fact that despite his contempt for red tape where a major case was concerned he could not possibly force this perfect servant to give him access to the other rooms of the apartment.

He stood there tugging at his ear, and staring from object to object. The very air was impregnated with pseudo Orientalism. It held a faint tang of ambergris. He wished, now, that Petrie had been with him; for Petrie sometimes had queer intuitions. But of course, it had been impossible to leave Fleurette alone.

He glanced at Gallaho.

The latter took the cue immediately, and:

"A mistake, sir, I suppose?" he growled; and to Ibrahim: "Sorry to have troubled you."

They returned to the lobby: Gallaho had actually gone out into the corridor, when:

"This is a very fine piece, Ibrahim," said Sir Denis.

He stood before an Egyptian sarcophagus half hidden in a recess.

"So I am told, effendîm."

"Has Mrs. Crossland had it long?"

"No, effendîm." At last, the Egyptian's deadly calm was disturbed. "It was bought by Mr. Crossland in Egypt recently. It was delivered less than a week ago."

"Beautiful example of late eighteenth," murmured Nayland Smith. "Shipped through to London, I suppose?"

"Yes, effendîm."

They were bowed out by the Egyptian. The door was closed.

"Call to the Yard the moment we reach my flat!" snapped Nayland Smith. "Have this entire block covered."

"Very good, sir. I was thinking the same thing."

"We weren't wrong—but our hands are tied."

"My idea exactly, sir."

Fey opened the door in response to their ring.

"How is Miss Petrie?" Nayland Smith challenged.

"The doctor is with her, sir."

They went in and Gallaho took up the telephone. Sir Denis walked on into the sitting-room, pacing the carpet restlessly.

Gallaho's gruff voice could be heard as he spoke to someone at Scotland Yard. Presently, Dr. Petrie came in. He shook his head.

"No change, Smith," he reported. "She declines to leave her room. She is packing, methodically, but refuses all assistance. The idea has been implanted upon her mind that a call to leave here is coming shortly. God help us if we can't find the man who imposed that thing upon her!"

"What would it mean?" snapped Smith.

"It would mean, I fear, that she would remain in this condition to the end of her life."

"The poisonous swine! He is very powerful!"

"He has the greatest brain in the world to-day, Smith."

Gallaho completed his directions at the telephone and came into the room. All idea of dinner had been brushed from their minds. There was a moment of awkward silence. Sounds of faint movement reached them: Fleurette was still engaged in her packing.

Then, the telephone bell rang.

There was something in this call coming at that moment which seemed to possess a special significance. All three waited. All three listened to Fey's voice, out in the lobby.

And presently, Fey came in.

He had quite recovered his normal self. There was nothing in his appearance or in his behaviour to suggest that he had passed through an amazing ordeal. He bowed slightly to Dr. Petrie.

"Someone wishes to speak to *you*, sir."

"What name?"

"Dr. Fu Manchu was the name, sir."

CHAPTER 57

A CALL FOR PETRIE

As PETRIE CROSSED the lobby, Nayland Smith turned to Gallaho.

"Do you realize, Inspector," he said, "that the greatest menace to the peace of the world who has come on earth since the days of Attila the Hun, is at the other end of that line?"

"I am beginning to realize that what you say about this man is true, sir." Gallaho replied. "But I think we can trace him by this call."

"Wait and see."

He kept glancing towards the door which communicated with Fleurette's room. There was silence there. He wondered what she was doing. In this, perhaps, the incomprehensible plan of Dr. Fu Manchu reached its culmination. Nayland Smith walked to the lobby door and listened to Petrie's words.

These did not help him much, consisting principally of "yes" and "no". At last, Petrie replaced the receiver, stood up, and faced Smith.

His features were very drawn. Smith recognized how the last year had aged him.

"What am I to do?" he said, speaking almost in a whisper. "What am I to do?"

"Come in here," said Sir Denis quickly. "Gallaho wants to use the line."

Gallaho sprang to the telephone as Dr. Petrie and Nayland Smith walked into the sitting-room. They faced one another, and:

"What are his terms?" said Smith.

Petrie nodded.

"I knew you would understand."

He dropped into an armchair and stared straight before him into the embers of the open fire.

"He wants something," Nayland Smith went on evenly, "and he demands acceptance of his terms, or——" he pointed in the direction of the door beyond which Fleurette's room lay. . . .

Petrie nodded again.

"What am I to do? What am I do to?"

"Give me the facts. Perhaps I can help you."

"It was Dr. Fu Manchu at the end of the line," said Petrie, in a monotonous voice. "Any doubts I may have had, disappeared the moment I heard that peculiar intonation. He apologized for troubling me; his courtesy never fails except in moments of madness——"

"I agree," murmured Nayland Smith.

"He admitted, Smith, that you had made things pretty warm for him, assisted by the English and French police. Access to agents of the Si-Fan in England was denied to him—his financial resources were cut off. Of this he spoke frankly."

"Finally, he reached the point at which he had been aiming. He regretted that it had been necessary to make a clandestine call at this apartment; but Fleurette, the woman he had chosen for his bride" (Petrie spoke in almost a monotone) "had been torn from him. Matters of even greater urgency demanded . . ."

He paused, staring into the heart of the fire.

"Demanded *what?*" Nayland Smith asked, quietly.

He was listening—but no sound came from the room occupied by Fleurette.

"He has an exaggerated idea of my powers as a physician. He is a man of great age—God knows what age; and it appears that he is cut off from a supply of the strange elixir by means of which, alone, he remains alive. His offer is this: I am to bring him certain ingredients which he has named, and assist him in preparing the elixir, which apparently he is unable to prepare alone; or——"

"I fully appreciate the alternative," snapped Nayland Smith. "But one thing I don't quite understand. I am wondering if something else underlies it, why his need of *your* services?"

Perrie smiled unmirthfully.

"It appears that he is in a situation—he frankly admits that he is hunted—where the attendance of any physician attached to his group would be impossible. Also, it appears, the pharmaceutical details require adroit manipulation."

"What does he want you to do?"

Gallaho came in from the lobby.

"That was a Westminster call, sir," he reported. "The caller was in this area. I expect further details later."

"Excellent," murmured Nayland Smith. "Listen to this, Gallaho. Go ahead, Petrie."

"He assured me," Dr. Petrie went on, "and neither you nor I, Smith——" he looked at Sir Denis appealingly—"has ever doubted his word, that Fleurette would remain mentally his slave in the state in which she is, now, unless he chose to restore her to normal life."

"If he said so," said Nayland Smith solemnly, "I don't doubt it."

"Your job is to go, sir," said Gallaho, with a faint show of excitement. "I'll have you covered, and we'll get this yellow devil!"

"Thank you, Inspector." Dr. Petrie smiled wearily. "Where Dr. Fu Manchu is concerned, things are not quite so simple as that. You see, my daughter's sanity is at stake."

"You mean that no one but this Fu Manchu can put her right?"

"That's what I mean, Inspector."

Chief detective-inspector Gallaho picked up his hat, looked at it, and threw it down again. He began to chew invisible gum, glancing from Sir Denis to Dr. Petrie.

"Sir Denis and I know this man," the latter went on; "we know what he can do—what he *has* done. You would be entitled officially to take the steps you have mentioned, Inspector; I can only ask you *not* to take them; to treat what I have told you as a confidence."

"As you say, sir."

"I am ordered to assemble certain drugs; some of them difficult to obtain, but none, I believe, unobtainable. The final ingredient, the indispensable ingredient, is a certain essential oil unknown anywhere in the world except in the laboratory of Dr. Fu Manchu. A small quantity of this still remains in existence."

"Where?" jerked Nayland Smith.

Dr. Petrie did not reply for a few seconds. He bowed his head, resting it in a raised hand; then:

"At a spot which I have given my word not to name." He replied. "I am to go there, and get it. And when I have collected the other items of the prescription, and certain chemical apparatus described to me. I am to join Dr. Fu Manchu."

"Where are you to join him?" Inspector Gallaho asked, hoarsely.

"This I cannot tell you, Inspector. My daughter's life is at stake."

There was another silence, and then:

"He is, then, in extremis?" murmured Nayland Smith.

"He is dying," Dr. Petrie replied. "If I can save him, he will restore Fleurette to me—on the word of Fu Manchu."

Nayland Smith nodded.

"Which in all my knowledge of his execrable life, he has never broken."

CHAPTER 58

JOHN KI

"DON'T WAKE HER," said Dr. Petrie.

He beckoned to the nurse to follow him. Outside in the sitting-room, where misty morning light was just beginning to assert itself, Nayland Smith in pyjamas and dressing-gown was pacing up and down smoking furiously. Petrie was fully dressed, and:

"Hello, Petrie!" said Smith. "You'll crack up if you go on like this."

"She is so beautiful," said the nurse, a dour Scotch woman, but as capable as all London could supply. "She is sleeping like a child. It's a strange case!"

"It is a very strange case." Petrie assured her. "But you fully understand my instructions, nurse, and I know you will carry them out."

"You may count upon that, Doctor."

"Go back to your patient now, and report to Sir Denis, here, if there is any change when she awakens."

"I understand, Doctor."

Nurse Craig went out of the room, and Petrie turned to Nayland Smith. The latter paused in his restless promenade, puffing furiously on a cracked briar, and:

"This job is going to crock you, Petrie," he declared. "Neither you nor I is getting younger; only Dr. Fu Manchu can defy the years. You look like hell, old man. You have been up all night, and now——"

"And now my job begins," said Petrie quietly. "Oh, I know I am stretching myself to the limit, but the stakes are very high, Smith"

Nayland Smith gripped Petrie's shoulder and then began walk up and down again.

Petrie dropped into an armchair, clutching his knees, and staring into the heart of the fire. Fey came in unobtrusively and made the fire up. It had been burning all night, and he, too, had not slept.

"Can I get you anything, sir?"

"Yes," said Nayland Smith, "Dr. Petrie has to go out in an hour. Get bacon and eggs, Fey, and coffee."

"Very good, sir."

Fey went out.

"I haven't slept," rapped Nayland Smith; "couldn't sleep, but at least I have relaxed physically. You," he stared at Petrie, "haven't even undressed.

"No——" Petrie smiled; "but as you may have observed, I have shaved."

"A hit, Petrie. *I* haven't. But I propose to do so immediately. Take my advice. Strip and have a bath before bacon and eggs. You'll feel a new man."

"I believe you are right, Smith."

And when presently, the two, who many years before had set out to combat the menace represented by Dr. Fu Manchu, sat down to breakfast, except for asides to Fey who waited at table, they were strangely silent. But when Fey had withdrawn:

"I don't doubt," said Nayland Smith, "and you *cannot* doubt, that Fleurette would live in a borderland to the end of her days if the man who has set her there does not will it otherwise. We are compromising with a remorseless enemy, Petrie, but in this compromise I am wholly with you. Gallaho is out for the moment. He is the most fearless and the most conscientious officer I have met with in recent years. He will go far. It rests between *us* now, old man, and I suppose it means defeat."

"I suppose it does," said Petrie, dully.

"Naturally, you know where to assemble the drugs and paraphernalia demanded by Dr. Fu Manchu. You have passed your word about the place where the particular ingredient is to be found."

He ceased speaking and glanced at the clock on the mantlepiece.

"I shall have to be going, Smith," said Petrie, wearily. "It is utterly preposterous and utterly horrible. But——"

He stood up.

Nayland Smith grasped his hand.

"It's just Fate," he said. "Dr. Fu Manchu seems to *be* our fate, Petrie."

"You don't blame me for consenting?"

"Petrie, you had no choice."

Dr. Petrie discharged his taxicab at a spot in Vauxhaull Bridge Road where he had been told by Dr. Fu Manchu to discharge it. Carrying the suitcase with which he had set out from Nayland Smith's flat, and which now contained drugs and apparatus which must have surprised any physician who examined them, and which indeed surprised Dr. Petrie, he walked along that dingy thoroughfare until he came to a certain house.

It was a grey and a gloomy house, its door approached by three dirty steps.

Battersea was coming to life.

Battersea is one of London's oddest suburbs—a suburb which produced John Burns, a big man frustrated; Communist to-day, if votes count for anything, encircled in red on the Crimes' Map; yet housing thousands of honest citizens, staunch men and true. A queer district—and just such a district as might harbour an agent of Dr. Fu Manchu.

Laden tramcars went rocking by, bound cityward. There were many pedestrians. Battersea was alert, alive—it was a nest of workers.

But of all this Dr. Petrie was only vaguely conscious: his interest lay far from Battersea.

He went up the three steps and rang the bell.

In response to his ringing, the door, presently, was opened by a very old Chinaman.

Petrie stared at an intricate map of wrinkles which decorated that ape-like face. Memory bridged the years; he knew that this was John Ki, once keeper of the notorious "Joy Shop" in the older Chinatown, and now known as Sam Pak.

A sort of false gaiety claimed him. He had gone over to the enemy, become one with them, and accordingly:

"Good morning, John," he said; "a long time since I saw you."

"Velly much long time before."

The toothless mouth opened in a grin, and old Sam Pak ceremoniously stood aside, bowing his visitor in.

Petrie found himself in a frowsy, evil-smelling passage, the floor covered with worn and cracked linoleum; hideous paper peeling from the walls. There was a room immediately on the left, the door of which was open. He entered, heard the front door close, and the old Chinaman came in behind him.

This was a room which had apparently remained untouched, undecorated and undusted since the days of Queen Victoria. Upon a round mahogany table were wax flowers under a glass case; indescribably filthy horsehair chairs; a carpet through which the floor appeared from point to point; a large print on one wall representing King Edward VII as Prince of Wales, and a brass gas chandelier hanging from the centre of a ceiling of the colour of Thames mud.

Petrie set down his suitcase very carefully on the floor, and turned to Sam Pak.

"What now, John?"

"Waitee, please; go be long yet."

The aged creature went out; and Petrie, staring through indescribably dirty lace curtains upon the prospect outside, saw a Morris car pull up.

It was driven by a man who wore a tweed cap, pulled well down over his eyes, but who almost certainly was an Asiatic . . .

Old Sam Pak, better known to Dr. Petrie as John Ki, returned.

He was carrying a small steel casket. He handled it as though it had been a piece of fragile Ming porcelain, and with one skinny hand indicated the suitcase.

Petrie nodded, and unfastened the case.

A quantity of cotton waste was produced by Sam Pak from somewhere, and wrapped around the steel receptacle; this was then deposited in the case, and the case was closed.

"Key?"

The aged Chinaman extended upon one skinny finger a curiously shaped key attached to a ring.

"Keep—velly particular."

"I understand."

Dr. Petrie took it, placed it in his note-case and returned the note-case to his pocket.

Sam Pak signalled from the window and the driver of the Morris came up the steps.

He carried the suitcase out to the car.

"Very careful, my man!" called Petrie, urgently; and realized that, for the first time in his life, he was interested in the survival of Dr. Fu Manchu.

He was indifferent to his destination. He lay back in the car and dully watched a panorama of sordid streets.

CHAPTER 59

LIMEHOUSE

THAT STRANGE JOURNEY terminated at a small house in Pelling Street, Limehouse.

The driver of the Morris, who might have been Chinese, but who more probably was a half-caste, jumped down and banged on an iron knocker which took the place of a bell.

The door was opened almost immediately, but Petrie was unable to see by whom.

His driver's behaviour during this long and dismal journey had been eccentric. Drizzling rain had taken the place of fog, and the crowded City streets under these conditions would have reduced a Sam Weller to despair. Many byways had been explored for no apparent reason. The driver constantly pulled up, and waited, and watched.

Dr. Petrie understood these manoeuvres.

The man suspected pursuit, and was anxious to throw his pursuers off the track.

Now he signalled to Dr. Petrie to come in. Petrie climbed out of the car and walked into the open door-way.

"The bag?" he said.

"Leave now," the driver replied; "get presently."

"Those are my orders, Dr. Petrie," came in a cultured voice.

And Petrie found that a Japanese gentleman who wore spectacles was smiling at him out of the shadows of the little passage-way.

"If those are your orders, good enough."

The driver went out; the door was closed. And Petrie followed the Japanese to a back room, the appointments of which aroused him from the lethargy into which he was falling.

This might have been a private room in an up-to-date hairdresser's establishment, or it might have been an actor's dressing-room. All the impedimenta of make-up was represented and there was a big winged mirror set right of the window. The prospect was that of a wall beyond which appeared a number of chimneys.

"My name is Ecko Yusaki," said the man who wore the spectacles, " and it is a great privilege to meet you, Dr. Petrie. Will you please sit in the armchair, facing the light.

Petrie sat in the armchair.

"Your interests are not the same as my own," the smooth voice continued, and Mr. Yusaki busied himself with mysterious preparations; "but they are, I imagine, as keen. I am one of the most ancient brotherhood in the world, Dr. Petrie—the Si-Fan." (He made a curious gesture with which Petrie was unpleasantly familiar) "and at last my turn has come to be useful. I am——" he turned displaying a row of large, gleaming teeth—"a specialist in make-up, but recently returned from Hollywood."

"I see," said Petrie. "Regard me as entirely in your hands."

Thereupon, courteously, and with a deft assurance which spoke of the enthusiast, Mr. Yusaki set to work.

Petrie submitted, closing his eyes and thinking of Fleurette, of his wife, of Nayland Smith, of Sterling, of all those caught in the mesh of the dreadful Chinese Doctor.

At last, Mr. Yusaki seemed to be satisfied, and:

"Please glance at this photograph, Dr. Petrie," he said . . . "No! one moment!" he snatched the photograph away . . . "Through these!"

He adjusted tortoise-shell rimmed spectacles over Petrie's ears.

Petrie stared at a photograph nearly life size which the Japanese was holding before him. It was that of a man apparently grey-haired, who wore a moustache and a short pointed beard, and who also wore spectacles; a sad looking man nearer sixty than fifty, but well preserved for his years.

"You see?"

"Yes. Who is it?"

"Please look now in the mirror."

Petrie turned to the big mirror.

"Good God!" he exclaimed. "Good God!"

He saw the original of the photograph—yet the face at which he looked was his own!

Speech failed him for a moment, and then:

"Who am I?" he asked, in a dull voice.

"You are a member of the Si-Fan——" Again the respectful

gesture resembling the Roman Catholic Sign of the Cross—
"who to-day is making a great sacrifice for the Cause. My part
is done, Dr. Petrie—except for a small change of dress; and
the car is waiting. . . ."

CHAPTER 60

DR. PETRIE'S PATIENT

WHEN THE *Queenstown Bay* came to her berth, Dr. Petrie was one of the first visitors aboard.

Shortly after he reached the deck, endeavouring to recall his instructions, an elderly Egyptian, wearing European dress, approached him. The usual scurry characterized the docking of the liner; stewards and porters were rushing about with baggage; visitors were looking for those they had come to meet; cargo was being swung out from the holds; and drizzling rain desended dismally upon the scene.

"Dr. Petrie!"

The man spoke urgently, close to Petrie's ear.

"Yes."

"My name is Ibrahim. Please—your dock check."

Petrie handed the slip to the Egyptian.

"Please wait here. I shall come back."

He moved along the deck, and presently disappeared amongst a group of passengers crowding towards the gangway.

Petrie felt that he was in a dream. Yet he forced himself to play his part in this grotesque pantomime, the very purpose of which he could not comprehend: the sanity of his daughter was at stake.

Ibrahim rejoined him. He handed him a passport.

"Please see that it is in order," he said. "You have to pass the Customs."

Petrie, inured to shock, opened the little book; saw a smaller version of the photograph which Mr. Yusaki had shown him, gummed upon the front page; and learned that he was a Mr. Jacob Edward Crossland, aged fifty-five, of no occupation, and residing at 14, Westminster Mansions!

The extent and the powers of the organization called the Si-Fan were so amazing that he had never succeeded in getting used to them. No society, with the possible exception of the Jesuits, ever had wielded such influence nor had its roots so deeply set in unsuspected quarters.

He could only assume that Mr. Crossland, husband of the well-known woman novelist, was one of these strange brethren: assume, too, that Mr. Crossland would slip ashore as a visitor.

And—what?

Disappear from his place in society? Yusaki had said he was making a great sacrifice for the Cause. It was all very wonderful and very terrifying.

"I have tipped the stewards, effendîm—and your baggage is already in Custom House. Will you please follow me? . . ."

Dr. Petrie walked down the ladder wearing a white rain-coat which he had acquired at the house of Mr. Yusaki, and a grey hat of a colour and style which he detested.

Apparently, Mr. Crossland travelled light. A small cabin-trunk and a suitcase lay upon the Customs bench. The cabin trunk he was requested to open. Ibrahim produced the necessary key, displaying wearing apparel, a toilet case, books and other odds and ends. The two pieces were passed. The porter hired by Ibrahim carried them out towards the dock gates.

"Be careful, please," the Egyptian whispered.

Detective-inspector Gallaho and Sergeant Murphy were standing at the gate!

Nothing quite corresponding to this had ever occurred in Petrie's adventurous life. He had joined the ranks of the law breakers!

He must play his part; so much was at stake. He must deceive his friends, those interested, as he was interested, in apprehending the Chinese physician. If his nerve, or the art of Mr. Yusaki should fail him now—all would be lost!

The critical gaze of Gallaho was fixed upon him for a moment, then immediately transferred to Ibrahim.

Petrie passed the detective, forcing himself not to look in his direction. A taxicab was waiting upon which the pieces of baggage were loaded, under the supervision of Ibrahim. Petrie observed with admiration that his own suitcase had already been placed inside.

He knew now where his course lay, and his amazement rose by leaps and bounds.

The presence of Gallaho at the dock gates was explained. The police were covering the Crossland flat. The man, when he had left that morning, had naturally been followed. He was regarded as a factor so important in the case that Gallaho had covered in person. Gallaho would be disappointed. The cunning of the group surrounding Dr. Fu Manchu exceeded anything in Petrie's experience.

He glanced at the placid, elderly Egyptian seated beside him, and:

"How long have you belonged to the Si-Fan?" he asked, speaking in Arabic.

Ibrahim shrugged his shoulders.

"Sir," he replied in the same language, "it is not possible for me to reply to your questions. Silence is my creed."

"Very sound," Petrie murmured, and gave it up.

His sentiments when he reached Westminster, and was greeted respectfully by the hall porter as Mr. Crossland, were of a kind inexpressible in any language known to man.

Then, as he stepped out of the elevator—Nayland Smith was standing on the landing!

Petrie suppressed an exclamation. One piercing stare of those blue-grey eyes had told him that he was recognized.

But Smith gave no sign, merely bowing and stepping aside as Ibrahim busied himself with the baggage.

Three mintues later, Dr. Petrie stood in the pseudo-Oriental atmosphere of the Crossland flat, and Ibrahim closed the door behind him.

"Please wait a moment."

The Egyptian walked through the harêm-like apartment which opened out of the lobby, and disappeared.

Petrie had time to wonder if the authoress of the celebrated novels of desert love also was a member of the Si-Fan, or if this must be counted a secret of her husband's life which she had never shared. He wondered what part this man normally played in their activities, and doubted the nationality of Crossland.

Surely no man entitled to his name could link himself with a monstrous conspiracy to subject the Western races to domination by the East?

Above all, to what reward did Crossland look which should make good the loss of his place in the world of decent men?

"If you will please come this way, sir."

Ibrahim, who had carried out the precious suitcase, now

returned without it, and stood bowing before Petrie.

Petrie nodded and followed the Egyptian across that shaded room with its mûshrabîyeh windows, and through a doorway beyond, which, in spite of the Oriental camouflage, he recognized to correspond with one in Nayland Smith's apartment.

He found himself in a large bedroom.

The Eastern note persisted. The place, viewed from the doorway, resembled a stage-set designed by one of the more advanced Germans for a scene in Scheherazade. The bed stood upon a dias; its posts were intricately carved and inlaid, and a canopy of cloth of gold overhung its head. A low couch he saw, too, and a long, inlaid table of Damascus work. Upon this table chemical apparatus appeared, striking a strange note in that apartment. He noted that the contents of his suitcase had been added to the other materials upon the table.

And, in the bed, Dr. Fu Manchu lay. . . .

Petrie stared, and stared again, unable to accept the evidence of his own senses.

Less than two months had elapsed since he had seen the Chinese doctor. In those two months, Fu Manchu had aged incredibly.

He was shrunken; his strange, green eyes were buried in his skull; his long hands lying on the silk coverlet resembled the hands of a mummy. The outline of his teeth could be seen beneath drawn lips. To the keen scrutiny of the physician, the truth was apparent.

Dr. Fu Manchu was dying!

" 'O mighty Caesar! Dost thou lie so low?' " came sibilantly through parched lips. "I observe, Dr. Petrie, that this beautiful passage from an otherwise dull play is present in your mind . . . You honour me."

Petrie started, felt his fists clenching. The body of Fu Manchu was in dissolution, but that phenomenal brain had lost none of its power. The man still retained his uncanny capacity for reading one's unspoken thoughts.

"I must harbour what little strength remains to me," the painful whisper continued. "For your daughter's health of mind and body, you need have no fear. I was compelled, since there is still work for me if I can do it, to impose a command upon her. It nearly exhausted my powers, which are dwindling minute by minute."

The whispering voice ceased.

Petrie watched that strange face, but no words came to him. In it he had seen, as others had seen, a likeness to the Pharaoh, Seti I—but the Pharaoh as one imagined him in his prime. Now, the resemblance to the mummy which lies in Cairo was uncanny.

Ideas which his scientific mind rejected as superstitious, danced mentally before him. . . .

What was the real age of this man?

"I have removed the command which I imposed upon her," the whistling voice continued, "because I have accepted your word, as you have always accepted mine. Your daughter, Dr. Petrie, is restored to you as you would wish her to be. I shall never again intrude upon her life in any way."

"Thank you!" said Petrie—and wondered why he spoke so emotionally.

He was thanking this cold-blooded, murderous criminal for promising to refrain from one of his many crimes! Perhaps the secret of his sentiment lay in the fact hat he knew the criminal to be one whose word was inviolable.

"I have taken these steps——" Fu Manchu's voice sank lower—"because with all your great skill, which I respect, your assistance may have come too late."

He paused again. Petrie watched him fascinatedly.

"Sir Denis Nayland Smith has succeeded for the . . . first time in his life in sequestering me from most of those resources upon which normally . . . I can draw. . . . In these circumstances I was compelled to forego one . . . of the periodical treatments upon which my continued . . . vitality depends. . . . I was then cut off from the material. My present condition is outside my experience . . . I cannot say if restoration . . . is possible. . . ."

Complete resignation sounded in the weak voice.

"In the absence of Dr. Yamamata . . . who usually acts for me, but who unfortunately at present is in China . . . there is no other physician known to me who could possibly . . . assist—in any way. I shall be obliged, Dr. Petrie, if you will give the whole of your attention to . . . the written formula which lies . . . upon the table. Any error would be fatal. . . . Only one portion of the essential oil remains in the phial contained in the steel casket. . . ."

He ceased speaking and closed his eyes.

His hands had never moved; it was like listening to a dead man speaking from the grave.

CHAPTER 61

THE CROSSLAND'S FLAT

"DETECTIVE-INSPECTOR GALLAHO, sir," Fey announced.

It was approaching evening when Gallaho called on Nayland Smith; and, entering the lobby, he wrenched his bowler off, threw it on to a chair and walked into the sitting-room.

"Hullo, Gallaho!" said Sir Denis. "A devil of a row going on in the corridor?"

"Yes, sir. The vacant flat has been let—to an Indian Army gentleman, I believe. His stuff is being moved in."

"You've checked up, I see!"

"Well——" Gallaho leaned on the mantelshelf— "I've got a man posted at each of the four exits, and I've sized up the workmen from Staple's depository on the job. Nobody is going to slip out in the confusion—that is, nobody over six feet in height that I don't know!"

"Efficient work, Inspector."

Gallaho stared, chewing invisible gum.

"I have come to a certain conclusion, sir," he declared. "What I do about it depends upon your answer to a question I am going to ask."

"What's the question?" snapped Nayland Smith.

"It's just this, sir: who's in charge of this Fu Manchu case?"

"I am."

"Good enough. That means I am under your orders, definitely."

"Definitely."

"That saves me a lot of trouble," sighed Gallaho, leaning upon the mantelpiece. "Because I have certain theories, and I can't act upon them without your instructions."

He paused, and seemed to be listening.

"I know what you're listening for," said Sir Denis. "But I am very happy to be able to tell you, Gallaho, that Miss Petrie is entirely restored. The nurse installed by Dr. Petrie insists that she shall remain in bed. But there isn't really the slightest occasion for it. Mr. Sterling and the nurse are with her now. She is completely normal."

"That's an amazing thing," growled Gallaho.

Nayland Smith stared past him as if at some very distant object, and then:

"The powers of the mind *are* amazing," he said, quietly. "But this theory of yours, Gallaho?"

"Well, sir, my theory is this: that slimy old Arab. Ibrahim, went out this morning and I followed him. I took Murphy along in case we had to split up. He went to West India Dock, and went on board a liner in from Jamaica. He came ashore again, with his employer, Mr. Crossland."

"I know," Sir Denis interrupted. "I met them here, as they arrived."

"Oh, I see. . . ." Gallaho stared very hard. "Well, in my opinion, there's something funny about it. You see, sir, I had some inquiries made about Mr. Crossland. His wife's in New York. That's certain—I mean the woman who writes books. But Mr. Crossland himself was last heard of in Madeira."

"He might have joined the ship at some port of call."

"He might," Gallaho replied. "In fact, he must have done. But it's very funny. Except the Egyptian, nobody has come out of that flat since we visited it. . . . I'm wondering who's still inside——"

Nayland Smith did not answer for some moments, then:

"You mean, Gallaho," he said, "that you don't think the man who is now presumably in Mr. Crossland's flat, is really Mr. Crossland at all?"

"I suppose I must be mad," growled Gallaho, almost rubbing his elbow into the mantelpiece. "His passport was obviously in order; he was accepted by the servants downstairs here, and he was met by Ibrahim, who took charge of his baggage. I suppose I must be barmy. But there's something about it that isn't right. I can't put my finger on the weak spot—but I wish I had your authority to barge into Mr. Crossland's flat. I think I should find something."

Nayland Smith walked up and down in silence, but at last:

"In my opinion, you are right, Inspector," he replied. "If my opinion is of any value, I regard you as a man brilliantly equipped for his chosen profession."

Detective-inspector Gallaho became definitely embarrassed.

"You apparently don't know the meaning of fear, although you have an active imagination. I owe my life to this singular combination, and this, I shall never forget."

"Thank you, sir."

"The present Commissioner and myself do not see eye to eye, but I don't dispute his brilliance as an organizer. What I mean is this, Gallaho; you have hit the nail on the head."

Gallaho, watching the speaker, was chewing assiduously, and now:

"Am I to understand, sir," he asked, "that you agree with my view of this case?"

"I do."

"You mean you have reason to suppose, as I have reason to suppose, that the proper course, in the interests of justice, would be to secure powers to examine the flat of Mr. Crossland?"

"Exactly."

There was a further interval of silence. Tramcars rocked upon their way, far below. Some vague hint of activity upon the river reached that high apartment.

"I take it, sir, you are officially in charge?"

"I have told you so."

"And you don't wish Mr. Crossland's apartment to be searched?"

"Definitely, I forbid the step."

"Very good, sir."

Gallaho's eyes strayed in the direction of the door which communicated with the room occupied by Fleurette.

"You see," said Nayland Smith, "you are not dealing with a common criminal. You are dealing with the Emperor of Lawbreakers. Dr. Petrie and myself have worked side by side for many years, opposing this man's monstrous plans. I have never succeeded in bringing him to justice. There are reasons why I can do nothing at the moment—nothing whatever. . . ."

He fixed his keen eyes upon Inspector Gallaho.

"I understand, sir. When do I get the O.K.?"

"When Dr. Petrie rejoins us."

CHAPTER 62

COMPANION CROSSLAND

INTO THE ORIENTAL BEDROOM dusk had crept. Long ago Ibrahim had turned the lamps on.

Petrie had lost identity: he was merely a physician battling with the most difficult case ever entrusted to him. He sat beside Dr. Fu Manchu, holding the lean, yellow wrist and registering the pulse; watching the mummy-like face, wondering if he had committed any error, and hoping—yes, hoping—that success would crown his hours of effort!

Under no obligation whatever, for no man who had ever met him had doubted the word of Fu Manchu, he was battling to save the life of this monster, this octopus whose tentacles, stretching out from some place in Asia, touched, it seemed, the races of the world. He was cherishing a plague, fanning into life again an intellect so cold, so exact, that the man in whose body it was set could sacrifice his own flesh and blood in the interests of his giant, impersonal projects.

For one insane moment, the glamour of the Si-Fan swamped common-sense. Petrie found himself questioning his own ideals; challenging standards which he believed to be true. Definitely, the world was awry; perhaps it was possible that this amazing man—for that he was an outstanding genius, none could deny—had a plan to adjust the scheme of things "nearer to the heart's desire".

How could he know?

Weighed in the balance with the mandarin doctor, he was a negligible quantity. Perhaps the redemption of mankind, the readjustment of poise, could only be brought about by a remorseless, steely intellect such as that of Dr. Fu Manchu. Perhaps he was a fool to fight against the Si-Fan . . . Perhaps the Si-Fan was right, and the Western world wrong!

Night had come, and upon its wings had descended again that demon Fog. Wisps streaked the room. . . .

And the night wore on—until ghostly spears of dawn broke through the shaded windows.

Dr. Fu Manchu suddenly opened his eyes.

Their brilliant greeness was oddly filmed; a husky whisper reached Petrie's ears:

"Success!"

He had never believed that he could touch without loathing the person of the Chinese physician, but now, again, he tested his pulse, and as he did so:

"You observe the change?" the weak voice continued. "I have challenged Fate, Dr. Petrie, but again I have won. The crisis is past."

Petrie stated at him in amazement. Not only his pulse, but his voice, indicated a phenomenal return of vitality.

"The life property—which is the sun." said Dr. Fu Manchu, "revivifies swiftly. You are surprised."

The queer film left his eyes. It appeared to the amazed stare of Petrie that the hollows in those yellow cheeks already were filling out. . . .

"Of the Western physicians whom chance has thrown in my path, I have not yet met your peer. You are a modest man, Dr. Petrie. True healers are rare—but you are one of these. If ever you join me it will be voluntarily. From this day onward you have nothing to fear from any plans I may deem necessary to undertake."

The treatment which Dr. Petrie had administered to Fu Manchu was one which, personally, he should have described as imbecile. The B. M. A. would have disowned any physician employing such measures. He had been unable to discover any element of sanity, any trace of unity in the drugs which he had been directed to assemble.

The queer oil, with its faint violet tinge, was the only element in the strange prescription which he could not identify. Yes; it was magic!—something transcending the knowledge of the Western world!

Dr. Fu Manchu was growing younger, hour by hour. . . .

"You are amazed, Dr. Petrie." The harsh voice was beginning to regain its normal quality. "Any physician of Europe or America would be amazed. Perhaps you do not realize, even yet, that the old herbalists were not all mad. There is an essential oil—you have used it to-night—which contains those properties the alchemists sought. It is the other ingredients, and they are simple, which convert it into that elixir vitæ found only once in the Middle Ages."

He sat up!

Petrie started back. Before the Fu Manchu against whom he had fought for so many years, the vital, powerful Fu Manchu, he found himself an enemy. He faced a menace which had all but wrecked his own happiness; which yet might wreck the structure of Western society.

"My compliments, Dr. Petrie. I had not overestimated your accomplishments."

Ten years—twenty years—a hundred years—had been shed by the speaker, as a snake discards its old skin. The man who now sat upright in the bed fixing the gaze of his green eyes upon Dr. Petrie, was a phenomenon; the Phoenix had arisen from its ashes.

A vision of what this might mean to the world crossed Petrie's mind:—a battle-piece red with blood and violence; a ghastly picture of death and destruction.

"You have played your part honourably," said Dr. Fu Manchu. He reached out a long, yellow hand, and pressed a bell. Ibrahim entered—and, realizing the miracle which had taken place, prostrated himself upon the carpet and pronounced a prayer of thanksgiving.

There were sounds of movement in the corridor outside. Vaguely, Petrie recalled that a similar disturbance had occurred during the previous evening—but it had reached him as through a fog.

Ibrahim was followed by a man wearing morning dress—a clean-shaven man whose lined face seemed out of keeping with his jet black hair. At Dr. Petrie—who still wore the make-up imposed by Mr. Yusaki—this man stared amazedly.

"This is Companion Crossland," said Dr. Fu Manchu sibilantly. "His counterfeit presentment intrigues him. Companion Crossland has resigned his place in the world which knew him. I am ready."

He moved towards the door.

"Ibrahim will assist you to resume your normal appearance. I ask for your word that you will remain here until Ibrahim tells you it is time to go."

"I agree."

"Dr. Petrie, I salute you—and bid you farewell. . . ."

CHAPTER 63

A LACQUER CABINET

RELAYS OF DETECTIVES had been on duty all night, watching every exit from the building. Nayland Smith was pacing up and down the sitting-room when Gallaho was announced. He had paced up and down all night. Fleurette, ignoring the orders of the nurse, had joined him. She was curled up in the big armchair. Alan Sterling had 'phoned twice.

"Any news, sir?"

"No."

Gallaho leaned on the mantelshelf.

"It's beginning to occur to me that we may be wrong."

"Always a possibility, Gallaho. . . ."

The detective taking reports from the men on duty, had observed that the remainder of the incoming tenant's furniture was being delivered. A secretary, wearing smart morning dress, had taken charge of operations. One of Staple's large green vans was outside the service entrance; a smaller one was drawn up behind it.

"Those mahogany chairs," the secretary had said as Gallaho had lingered for a moment, "and the large lacquer cabinet are to be brought down again. There is no room for them. Put them on the small van. . . ."

"I mean," Gallaho went on doggedly, "we may have been barking up the wrong tree. There's the possibility . . ."

The door bell had been ringing, but Gallaho had failed to hear it. Fey had opened the front door. And now:

"Darling!" cried Fleurette—

She leapt from the armchair and threw herself into her father's arms. . . .

For Dr. Petrie had walked in!

Fleurette broke down completely.

She was still crying like a little child, but crying happily, when a small covered van which had left the building some ten minutes before was pulled up in a builder's yard in Chelsea.

A man wearing a morning suit and a soft black hat got down from his place beside the driver and ran around to the rear of the van. Its load consisted of a set of mahogany chairs and a tall blue lacquer Japanese cabinet.

Climbing into the van, he opened the door of this Cabinet. Dr. Fu Manchu stepped out.

"Companion Crossland," he said, "you have earned merit—"

PRESIDENT
FU MANCHU

CONTENTS

CHAPTER

1. The Abbot of Holy Thorn
2. A Chinese Head
3. Above the Blizzard
4. Mrs. Adair
5. The Special Train
6. At Weaver's Farm
7. Sleepless Underworld
8. The Black Hat
9. The Seven-eyed Goddess
10. James Richet
11. Red Spots
12. Number 81
13. Tangled Clues
14. The Scarlet Brides
15. The Scarlet Brides (concluded)
16. "Bluebeard"
17. The Abbot's Move
18. Mrs. Adair Reappears
19. The Chinese Catacombs
20. The Chinese Catacombs (concluded)
21. Carnegie Hall
22. Moya Adair's Secret
23. Fu Manchu's Water-Gate
24. Siege of Chinatown
25. Siege of Chinatown (concluded)
26. The Silver Box
27. The Stratton Building
28. Paul Salvaletti
29. Green Mirage
30. Plan of Attack
31. Professor Morgenstahl

32. Below Wu King's
33. The Balcony
34. "The Seven"
35. The League of Good Americans
36. The Human Equation
37. The Great Physician
38. Westward
39. The Voice from the Tower
40. "Thunder of Waters"

CHAPTER 1

THE ABBOT OF HOLY THORN

THREE CARS drew up, the leading car abreast of a great bronze door bearing a design representing the beautiful agonized face of the Saviour, a crown of thorns crushed down upon His brow. A man jumped out and ran to this door. Ten men alighted behind him. The wind howled around the tall tower and a carpet of snow was beginning to form upon the ground. Four guards, appearing as if by magic out of white shadows, lined up before the door.

"Stayton!" came sharply. "Stand aside."

One of the guards stepped forward—peered. A tall, slightly built man who had been in the leading car was the speaker. He had a mass of black, untidy hair, and his face, though that of one not yet west of thirty, was grim and square jawed. He was immediately recognized.

"All right, Captain."

The man addressed as captain turned to the party and issued orders in a low tone. The leader, muffled up in a leather, fur-collared topcoat, his face indistinguishable beneath the brim of a soft felt hat already dusted with snow, rang a bell beside the bronze door.

It opened so suddenly that one might have supposed the opener to have been waiting inside for this purpose; a short, elegant young man, almost feminine in the nicety of his attire.

The new arrival stepped in and quickly shut out the storm, closing the bronze door behind him. In a little lobby communicating with a large square room equipped as an up-to-date office, but at this late hour deserted, he stood staring at the person who had admitted him.

A churchlike lamp, hung from a bracket on the wall, now cast its golden light upon the face of the man wearing the leather coat. He had removed his hat, revealing a head of crisp, greying hair. His features were angular to the point of gauntness, and his eyes had the penetrating quality of

247

armoured steel, while his complexion seemed strangely out of keeping with the climate, being sun-baked to a sort of coffee colour.

"Are you James Richet?" he snapped.

The elegant young man inclined his glossy head.

"At your service."

"Lead me to Abbot Donegal. I am expected."

Richet perceptibly hesitated; whereupon, plunging his hand with an irritable, nervous movement into some pocket beneath the leather topcoat, the visitor produced a card and handed it to Richet. One glance he gave at it, bowed again in a manner that was almost Oriental and indicated the open gate of an elevator.

A few moments later:

"Federal Agent 56," Richet announced in his silky tones.

The visitor entered a softly lighted study, the view from its windows indicating that it was situated at the very top of the tall tower. From a chair beside a book-laden desk the sole occupant of the room—who had apparently been staring out at the wintry prospect far below—stood up, turned. Mr. Richet, making his queer bow, retired and closed the door.

Federal Agent 56 unceremoniously cast his wet topcoat upon the floor, dropping his hat on top of it. He was now revealed as a tall, lean man, dressed in a tweed suit which had seen long service. He advanced with outstretched hand to meet the occupant of the study—a slightly built priest, with the keen, ascetic features sometimes met with in men from the south of Ireland and thick, greying hair; a man normally actuated by a healthy sense of humour, but to-night with an oddly haunted expression in his clear eyes.

"Thank God, Father, I see you well."

"Thank God, indeed." He glanced at the card which Richet had laid upon his desk even as he grasped the extended hand. "I am naturally prepared for interference with my work, but this thing . . ."

The newcomer, still holding the priest's hand, stared fixedly, searchingly, into his eyes.

"You don't know it all," he said rapidly.

"This imprisonment——"

"A necessity, believe me. I have covered seven hundred

miles by air since you broke off in the middle of your radio address this evening."

He turned abruptly and began to pace up and down that book-lined room with it sacred pictures and ornaments, these seeming strangely at variance with the large and orderly office below. Pulling a very charred briar pipe from the pocket of his tweed jacket he began to load it from a pouch at least as venerable as the pipe. The Abbot Donegal dropped back into his chair, running his fingers through his hair, and:

"There is one favour I would ask," he said, "before we proceed any further. It is difficult to talk to an anonymous man."

He stared down at the card upon his desk. This card bore the printed words:

FEDERAL AGENT 56

but across the bottom right-hand corner was the signature of the President of the United States.

Federal Agent 56 smiled, a quick, revealing smile which lifted a burden of years from the man.

"I agree," he snapped in his rapid, staccato fashion. "Smith is a not uncommon name. Suppose we say Smith."

The rising blizzard began to howl round the tower as though many wailing demons clamoured for admittance. A veil of snow swept across uncurtained windows, dimming distant light. Dom Patrick Donegal lighted a cigarette; his hands were not entirely steady.

"If you know what really happened to me to-night, Mr. Smith," he said, his rich, orator's voice lowered almost to a murmur, "for heaven's sake tell me. I have been deluged with telephone messages and telegrams, but in accordance with your instructions—or" (he glanced at the restlessly promenading figure) "should I say orders—I have answered none of them."

Smith, pipe alight, paused, staring down at the priest.

"You were brought straight back after your collapse?"

"I was. They would have taken me home, but mysterious instructions from Washington resulted in my being brought here. I came to my senses in the small bedroom which adjoins this study."

"Your last memory being?"

"Of standing before the microphone, my notes in my hand."

"Quite," said Smith, beginning to walk up and down again. "Your words, as I recollect them, were: 'But if the Constitution is to be preserved, if even a hollow shell of Liberty is to remain to us, there is one evil in this country which must be eradicated, torn up by its evil roots, utterly destroyed. . . .' Then came silence, a confusion of voices, and an announcement that you had been seized with a sudden illness. Does your memory, Father, go as far as these words?"

"Not quite," the priest answered wearily, resting his head upon his hand and making a palpable effort to concentrate. "I began to lose my grip of the situation some time earlier in the address. I experienced most singular sensations. I could not co-ordinate my ideas, and the studio in which I was speaking alternately contracted and enlarged. At one moment the ceiling appeared to become black and to be descending upon me. At another, I thought that I stood in the base of an immeasurably lofty tower." His voice grew in power as he spoke, his Irish brogue became more pronounced. "Following these dreadful sensations came an overpowering numbness of mind and body. I remember no more."

"Who attended you?" snapped Smith.

"My own physician, Dr. Reilly."

"No one but Dr. Reilly, your secretary, Mr. Richet, and I suppose the driver of the car in which you returned, came up here?"

"No one, Mr. Smith. Such, I am given to understand, were the explicit and authoritative orders given a few minutes after the occurrence."

Smith stopped on the other side of the desk, staring down at the abbot.

"Your manuscript has not been recovered?" he asked slowly.

"I regret to say, no. Definitely, it was left behind in the studio."

"On the contrary," snapped Smith angrily, "definitely it was not! The place has been searched from wall to wall by those who know their business. No, Father Abbot, your manuscript was not there. I *must* know what it contained—and from what source this missing information came to you."

The ever-rising wind in its fury shook the Tower of the Holy Thorn, shrieking angrily round that lofty room in which two men faced a problem destined in its outcome to affect the whole nation. The priest, a rapid, heavy smoker, lighted another cigarette.

"I cannot make it out," he said—and now a natural habit of authority began to assert itself in his voice—"I cannot make out why you attach such importance to my notes for this speech, nor why my sudden illness, naturally disturbing to myself, should result in this sensational Federal action. Really, my friend"—he leaned back in his chair, staring up at the tanned, eager face of his visitor—"in effect, I am a prisoner here. This, I may say, is intolerable. I await your explanation, Mr. Smith."

Smith bent forward, resting nervous brown hands on the priest's desk and staring intently into those upturned, observant eyes.

"What was the nature of the warning you were about to give the nation?" he demanded. "What is this evil growth which must be uprooted and destroyed?"

These words produced a marked change in the bearing of the Abbot Donegal. They seemed to bring recognition of something he would willingly have forgotten. Again he ran his fingers through his hair, now almost distractedly.

"God help me," he said in a very low voice, "I don't know!"

He suddenly stood up; his glance was wild.

"I cannot remember. My mind is a complete blank upon this subject—upon everything relating to it. I think some lesion must have occurred in my brain. Dr. Reilly, although reticent, holds, I believe, the same opinion."

"Nothing of the kind," snapped Smith; "but that manuscript has to be found! There's life or death in it."

He ceased speaking abruptly and seemed to be listening to the voice of the storm. Then, ignoring the priest, he suddenly sprang across the room and threw the door wide open.

Mr. Richet stood bowing on the threshold.

CHAPTER 2

CHINESE HEAD

IN AN APARTMENT having a curiously painted ceiling (one might have imagined it to be situated in the crest of a minaret) a strange figure was seated at a long, narrow table. Light, amber light, came through four near-Gothic windows set so high that only a giant could have looked out of them. The man, whose age might have been anything from sixty to seventy—he had a luxurious growth of snow-white hair—was heavily built, wearing a dilapidated woollen dressing-gown; and his long sensitive fingers were nicotine-stained, since he continuously smoked Egyptian cigarettes. An open tin of those stood near his hand, and he lighted one from the stump of another—smoking, smoking, incessantly smoking.

Upon the table before him were seven telephones, one or other of them almost always in action. When two purred into life simultaneously, the smoker would place one to his right ear, the other to his left. He never replied to incoming messages, nor did he make notes.

In the brief intervals he pursued what one might have supposed to be his real calling. Upon a large wooden pedestal was set a block of modelling clay, and beside the pedestal lay implements of the modeller's art. This singular old man, the amazing frontal development of his splendid skull indicating great mathematical powers, worked patiently upon a life-sized head of an imposing but sinister Chinaman.

In one of those rare intervals he was working delicately upon the high, imperious nose of the clay head, when a muffled bell sounded and the amber light disappeared from the four Gothic windows, plunging the room into complete darkness.

For a moment there was no sound; the tip of a burning cigarette glowed in the darkness. Then a voice spoke, an unforgettable voice, by which gutturals were oddly stressed but every word was given its precise syllabic value.

"Have you a later report," said this voice, "from Base 8?"

The man at the long table replied, speaking with German intonations.

"The man known as Federal Agent 56 arrived at broadcasting station twenty minutes after midnight. Police still searching there. Report just to hand from Number 38 states that this agent, accompanied by Captain Mark Hepburn, U.S. Army Medical Corps, assigned to Detached Officers' List, and a party of nine men arrived Tower of the Holy Thorn at twelve-thirty-two, relieving federals already on duty. Agent 56 last reported in conference with Abbot Donegal. The whole area closely covered. No further news in this report."

"The Number responsible for the manuscript?"

"Has not yet reported."

"The last report from Numbers covering Weaver's Farm?"

"Received at 11.07. Dr. Orwin Prescott is still in retirement there. No change has been made in his plans regarding the debate at Carnegie Hall. This report from Number 35."

The muffled bell rang. Amber light appeared again in the windows; and the sculptor returned lovingly to his task of modelling a Chinaman's head.

CHAPTER 3

ABOVE THE BLIZZARD

IN Dom Patrick Donegal's study at the top of the Tower of the Holy Thorn, James Richet faced Federal Officer 56. Some of his silky sauvity seemed to have deserted him.

"I quite understand your—unexpected—appearance, Mr. Richet," said Smith, staring coldly at the secretary. "You have greatly assisted us. Let me check what you have told me. You believe (the abbot unfortunately having no memory of the episode) that certain material for the latter part of his address was provided early on Saturday morning during a private interview in this room between the Father and Dr. Orwin Prescott?"

"I believe so although I was not actually present."

There was something furtive in Richet's manner; a nervous tremor in his voice.

"Dr. Prescott, as a candidate for the Presidency, no doubt had political reasons for not divulging these facts himself." Smith turned to Abbot Donegal. "It has always been your custom, Father, to prepare your sermons and speeches in this room, the material being looked up by Mr. Richet?"

"That is so."

"The situation becomes plainer." He turned to Richet. "I think we may assume," he went on, "that the latter part of the address, the part which was never delivered, was in Dom Patrick's own handwriting. You yourself, I understand, typed out the earlier pages."

"I did. I have shown you a duplicate."

"Quite," snapped Smith; "the final paragraph ends with the words 'torn up by its evil roots, utterly destroyed.'"

"There was no more. The abbot informed me that he intended to finish the notes later. In fact, he did so. For when I accompanied him to the broadcasting station he said that his notes were complete."

"And after his—seizure?"

"I returned almost immediately to the studio. But the manuscript was not on the desk."

"Thank you. That is perfectly clear. We need detain you no longer."

The secretary, whose forehead glistened with nervous perspiration, went out, closing the door silently behind him. Abbot Donegal looked up almost pathetically at Smith.

"I never thought," said he, "I should live to find myself so helpless. Can you imagine that I remember nothing whatever of Dr. Prescott's calling upon me? Except for that vague, awful moment when I faced the microphone and realized that my mental powers were deserting me, I have no recollection of anything that happened for some forty-eight hours before! Yet it seems that Prescott was here and that he gave me vital information. What can it have been? Great heavens"—he stood up, agitatedly—"*what* can it have been? Do you really believe that I am a victim, not of a failure in my health, but of an attempt to suppress this information?"

"Not an attempt, Father," snapped Smith, "a success! You are lucky to be alive!"

"But who can have done this thing, and how did he do it?"

"The first question I can answer; the second I might answer if I could recover the missing manuscript. Probably it's destroyed. We have a thousand-to-one chance. We are indebted to a phone call, which fortunately came through direct to you, for knowledge of Dr. Prescott's whereabouts."

"Why do you say 'which fortunately came through'? You surely have no doubts about Richet?"

"How long with you?" snapped Smith.

"Nearly a year."

"Nationality?"

"American."

"I mean pedigree."

"That I cannot tell you."

"There's colour somewhere. I can't place its exact shade. But one thing is clear: Dr. Prescott is in great danger. So are you."

The abbot arrested Smith's restless promenade, laying a hand upon his shoulder.

"There is only one other candidate in the running for dictatorship, Mr. Smith—Harvey Bragg. Yet I find hard to believe that he . . . You are not accusing *Harvey Bragg*?"

"Harvey Bragg!" Smith laughed shortly. "Popularly known as 'Bluebeard,' I believe? My dear Dom Patrick, Harvey Bragg is a small pawn in a big game."

"Yet—he may be President, or Dictator."

Smith turned, staring in his piercing way into the priest's eyes.

"He almost certainly *will* be Dictator!"

Only the mad howling of the blizzard disturbed a silence which fell upon those words—"He almost certainly *will* be Dictator."

Then the priest whose burning rhetoric, like that of Peter the Hermit, had roused a nation, found voice; he spoke in very low tones:

"Why do you say he certainly will be Dictator?"

"I said *almost* certainly. His war-cry 'America for every man—every man for America' is flashing like a fiery cross through the country. Do you realize that in office Harvey Bragg has made remarkable promises?"

"He has carried them out! He controls enormous funds."

"He does! Have you any suspicion, Father, of the source of those funds?"

For one fleeting moment a haunted look came into the abbot's eyes. A furtive memory had presented itself, only to elude him.

"None," he replied wearily; "but his following to-day is greater than mine. Just as a priest and with no personal pretensions, I have tried—God knows I have tried—to keep the people sane and clean. Machinery has made men mad. As machines reach nearer and nearer to the province of miracles, as Science mounts higher and higher—so Man sinks lower and lower. On the day that Machinery reaches up to the stars, Man, spiritually, will have sunk back to the primeval jungle."

He dropped into his chair.

Smith, resting a lean, nervous hand upon the desk, leaned across it, staring into the speaker's face.

"Harvey Bragg is a true product of his age," he said tensely—"and he is backed by one man! I have followed this man from Europe to Asia, from Asia to South America, from South to North. The resources of three European Powers and of the United States have been employed to head that man off. But he is here! In the political disruption of the country he sees his supreme opportunity."

"His name, Mr. Smith?"

"In your own interests, Father, I suggest it might be better that you don't know—yet."

Abbot Donegal challenged the steely eyes, read sincerity there, and nodded."

"I accept your suggestion, Mr. Smith. In the Church we are trained to recognize tacit understandings. You are not a private investigator instructed by the President, nor is 'Mr. Smith' your proper title. But I think we understand one another. . . . And you tell me that this man, whoever he may be, is backing Harvey Bragg?"

"I have only one thing to tell you: Stay up here at the top of your tower until you hear from *me!*"

"Remain a prisoner?"

Patrick Donegal stood up, suddenly aggressive, truculent.

"A prisoner, yes. I speak, Father, with respect and authority."

"You may speak, Mr. Smith, with the authority of Congress, of the President in person, but my first duty is to God; my second to the State. I take the eight o'clock Mass in the morning."

For a moment their glances met and challenged; then:

"There may be times, Father, when you have a duty even higher than this," said Smith crisply.

"You cannot induce me, my friend, to close my eyes to a plain obligation. I do not doubt your sincerity. I have never met a man more honest or more capable. I cannot doubt my own danger. But in this matter I have made my choice."

For a moment longer Federal Agent 56 stared at the priest, his lean face very grim. Then, suddenly stooping, he picked up his leather topcoat and his hat from the floor and shot out his hand.

"Good night, Father Abbot," he snapped. "Don't ring. I should like to *walk* down, although that will take some time. Since you refuse my advice, I leave you in good hands."

"In the hands of God, Mr. Smith, as we all are."

Outside on the street, beyond the great bronze door with its figure of the thorn-tortured head, King Blizzard held high revel. Snow was spat into the suffering face when the door was opened, as though powers of evil ruled that night, pouring contumely, contempt, upon the gentle Teacher. Captain Mark Hepburn, U.S.M.C., was standing there. He had one glimpse of the olive face of James Richet, who ushered the visitors out, heard his silky "Good night, Mr. Smith"; then the bronze door was closed, and the wind shrieked in mocking laughter around the Tower of the Holy Thorn.

Dimly through the spate of snow watchful men might be seen.

"Listen, Hepburn," snapped Smith, "get this address: Weaver's Farm, Winton, Connecticut. Phone that Dr. Orwin Prescott is not to step outside for one moment until I arrive. Arrange that we get there—fast. Have the place protected. Flying hopeless to-night. Special train to Cleveland. Side anything in our way. Have a plane standing by. Advise the pilot to look up emergency landings within easy radius of Weaver's Farm. If blizzard continues, arrange for special to run through to Buffalo. Advise Buffalo."

"Leave it to me."

"Cover the man James Richet. I want hourly reports sent to headquarters. This priest's life is valuable. See that he's protected day and night. Have this place covered from now on. Grab anybody—*anybody*—that comes out to-night."

"And where are you going, Chief?"

"I am going to glance over Dom Patrick's home quarters. Meet me at the station. . . ."

CHAPTER 4

MRS. ADAIR

MARK HEPBURN drove back through a rising blizzard. The powers of his newly accredited chief, known to him simply as "Federal Agent 56," were peculiarly impressive.

Arrangements—"by order of Federal Agent 56"—had been made without a hitch. These had included sidetracking the Twentieth Century Limited and the dispatch of an army plane from Dayton to meet the special train.

Dimly he realized that issues greater than the fate of the Presidency were involved. This strange, imperious man, with his irritable, snappy manner, did not come under the jurisdiction of the U.S. Department of Justice; he was not even an American citizen. Yet he was highly empowered by the government. In some way the thing was international. Also, Hepburn liked and respected Federal Agent 56.

And the affection of Mark Hepburn was a thing hard to win. Three generations of Quaker ancestors form a stiff background; and not even a poetic strain which Mark had inherited from a half-Celtic mother could enable him to forget it. His only rebellion—a slender volume of verse in the university days, "Green Lilies"—he had lived to repent. Medicine had called him (he was by nature a healer); then army work, with its promise of fresh fields; and now, the Secret Service, where in this crisis he knew he could be of use.

For in the bitter campaign to secure control of the country there had been more than one case of poisoning; and toxicology was Mark Hepburn's special province. Furthermore, his military experience made him valuable.

Around the Tower of the Holy Thorn the blizzard wrapped itself like a shroud. Only the windows at the very top showed any light. The tortured bronze door remained closed.

Stayton stepped forward out of a white mist as Hepburn sprang from his car.

"Anything to report, Stayton? I have only ten minutes."

"Not a soul has come out, Captain, and there doesn't seem

to be anybody about in the neighbourhood."

"Good enough. You will be relieved at daylight. Make your own arrangements."

Hepburn moved off into the storm. Something in the wild howling of the wind, some message reaching him perhaps from those lighted windows at the top of the tower, seemed to be prompting his subconscious mind. He had done his job beyond reproach. Nevertheless, all was not well.

One foot on the running board of the car, he paused, staring up to where that high light glimmered through snow. He turned back and walked in the direction of the tower. Almost immediately he was challenged by a watchful agent, was recognized, and passed on. He found himself beside a wall of the building remote from the bronze door. Here there was no exit and he went unchallenged. He stood still, staring about him, his fur coat-collar turned up about his ears, the wind frolicking with his untidy wet black hair.

A slight sound came, only just audible above the shrieking of the blizzard, the opening of a window. . . . He crouched close against the wall.

"All clear. Good luck. . . ."

James Richet!

Then someone dropped, falling lightly in the snow almost beside him. The window closed. Hepburn reached out a long sinewy arm, grabbed and held his captive . . . and found himself looking down into the most beautiful eyes he had ever seen!

His prisoner was a girl, little above medium height, but slender, so that she appeared much taller. She was muffled up in a mink coat as a protection against that fierce wind; a Basque beret was crushed down upon curls which reminded him of polished mahogany. A leather satchel hung from one wrist, and she was so terrified that Hepburn could feel her heart beating as he held her in his bear-like grip.

He realized that he was staring dumbly into those uplifted deep-blue eyes, that he was wondering if he had ever seen such long, curling lashes . . . when *duty*, *duty*—that slogan of Quaker ancestors—called him sharply. He slightly relaxed his hold, but offered no chance of escape.

"I see," he said, and his dry, rather toneless voice revealed no emotion whatever. "This is interesting. Who are you and where are you going?"

His tones were coldly remorseless. His arm was like a band of steel. Rebellion died and fear grew in the captive. Now she was trembling. But he was forced to admire her courage, for when she replied she looked at him unflinchingly.

"My name is Adair—Mrs. Adair—and I belong to the staff of the Abbot Donegal. I have been working late, and although I know there is some absurd order for no one to leave, I simply must go. It's ridiculous, and I won't submit to it. I insist upon being allowed to go home."

"Where is your home?"

"That can be no business of yours!" flared the prisoner, her eyes now flashing furiously. "If you like, call the abbot. He will vouch for what I say."

Mark Hepburn's square chin protruded from the upturned collar of his coat; his deep-set eyes never faltered in their regard.

"That can come later if necessary," he said; "but first——"

"But first, I shall freeze to death," said the girl indignantly.

"But first, what have you got in the satchel?"

"Private papers of Abbot Donegal's. I am working on them at home."

"In that case, give them to me."

"I won't! You have no right whatever to interfere with me. I have asked you to get in touch with the abbot."

Without relaxing his grip on his prisoner, Hepburn suddenly snatched the satchel, pulling the loop down over her little gloved hand and thrusting the satchel under his arm.

"I don't want to be harsh," he said, "but my job at the moment is more important than yours. This will be returned to you in an hour or less. Lieutenant Johnson will drive you home."

He began to lead her towards the spot where he knew the Secret Service cars were parked. He had determined to raise a minor hell with the said Lieutenant Johnson for omitting to post a man at this point, for as chief of staff to Federal Agent 56 he was personally responsible. He was by no means sure of himself. The girl embraced by his arm was the first really disturbing element which had ever crashed into his Puritan life;

261

she was too lovely to be real: the teaching of long-ago ancestors prompted that she was an instrument of the devil.

Reluctantly she submitted; for ten, twelve, fifteen paces.
Then suddenly resisted, dragging at his arm.

"Please, please for God's sake, listen to me!"

He pulled up. They were alone in that blinding blizzard,
although ten or twelve men were posted at points around the
Tower of the Holy Thorn. A freak of the storm cast an awning
of snow from the lighted windows, down to the spot upon
which they stood, and in that dim reflected light Mark
Hepburn saw the bewitching face uplifted to him.

She was smiling, this Mrs. Adair who belonged to Abbot
Donegal's staff; a tremulous, pathetic smile, a smile which in
happier hours had been one of exquisite but surely innocent
coquetry. Now it told of bravely hidden tears.

Despite all his stoicism, Mark Hepburn's heart pulsed more
rapidly. Some men, he thought, many, maybe, had worshipped those lips, dreamed of that beckoning smile . . . perhaps lost everything for it.

This woman was a revelation; to Mark Hepburn, a discovery. He was suspicious of the Irish. For this reason he had
never wholly believed in the sincerity of Patrick Donegal. And
Mrs. Adair was enveloped in that mystical halo which haunts
yet protects the Celts. He did not believe in this mysticism,
but he was not immune from its insidious charm. He hated
hurting her, he found himself thinking of her as a beautiful,
helpless moth torn by the wind from some green dell where
fairies still hid in the bushes and the four-leaved shamrock
grew.

He felt suddenly glad about, and not ashamed of, "Green
Lilies". Mrs. Adair, for one magical moment, had enabled him
to recapture that long-lost mood. It was very odd, out there in
the blizzard, with his radical distrust of pretty women and of
all that belonged to Rome. . . .

It was this last thought—Rome—that steadied him. Here
was some black plot against the Constitution. . . .

"I don't ask you, I *entreat* you to give me my papers and let
me go my own way. I promise, faithfully, if you will tell me
where to find you, that I will see you to-morrow and explain
anything you want to know."

Hepburn did not look at her. His Quaker ancestors rallied around him. He squared his grim jaw.

"Lieutenant Johnson will drive you home," he said coldly, "and will bring you your satchel immediately I am satisfied that its contents are what you say they are."

II

In the amber-lighted room, where the man with that wonderful mathematical brow sat at work upon the bust of a sinister Chinaman, one of the seven telephones buzzed. He laid down the modelling tool with which he had been working and took up the instrument. He listened.

"This is Number 12," said a woman's voice, "speaking from Base 8. In accordance with orders I managed to escape from the Tower of the Holy Thorn. Unfortunately I was captured by a federal agent—name unknown—at the moment that I reached the ground. I was taken under escort of a Lieutenant Johnson towards an address which I invented at random. A Z-car was covering me. Heavy snow gave me a chance. I managed to spring out and get to the Z-car. I regret that the federal agent secured the satchel containing the manuscript. There's nothing more to report. Standing by here awaiting orders."

The sculptor replaced the receiver and resumed his task. Twice again he was interrupted, listening to a report from California and to another from New York. He made no notes. He never replied. He merely went on with his seemingless endless task; for he was eternally smearing out the work which he had done, now an ear, now a curve of the brow, and patiently remodelling.

A bell rang, the light went out, and in the darkness that unforgettable, guttural voice spoke:

"Give me the latest report of Harvey Bragg's reception at the Hollywood Bowl."

"Last report received," the Teutonic voice replied, and a cigarette glowed in the darkness, "one hour and seventeen minutes ago. Pacific Coast time: twelve minutes after ten. Audience of twenty thousand people, as earlier reported. Harvey Bragg's slogan, 'America for every man—every man

263

for America' was received without enthusiasm. His assurance, hitherto substantiated, that any reputable citizen who is destitute has only to apply to his office to secure immediate employment, went well. Report of end of speech not yet to hand. No other news from Hollywood Bowl. Report sent in by Number 49."

A moment of silence followed, silence so complete that the crackling of burning tobacco in an Egyptian cigarette might have been heard.

"The report of Number 12—" he glanced at an electric clock upon the table—"at 2.05 a.m."

"Whereupon, word for word, this man of phenomenal memory repeated the message received from Base 8 exactly as it had been delivered.

A dim bell rang and the room became lighted again. The sculptor picked up a modelling tool.

CHAPTER 5

THE SPECIAL TRAIN

THE SPECIAL train bored its way through mists of snow.

"They won't attempt to wreck us, Hepburn!" Federal Officer 56 smiled grimly and tapped the satchel which had belonged to Mrs. Adair. "*This* is our safeguard. But there may be an attempt of some other kind."

In the solitary car Smith sat facing Hepburn. Seven of the party which had taken command of the Tower of the Holy Thorn were distributed in chairs about them. Some smoked and were silent; others talked; others again neither smoked nor talked, but glanced furtively in the direction of Captain Hepburn and his mysterious superior.

"You have done a first-class job, Hepburn," said Smith. "I tricked the man Richet (who is some kind of half-caste) into an admission that this"—he tapped the satchel—"was material supplied by Dr. Prescott."

"I ordered Richet's arrest before I left."

"Good man."

The train roared through the night and Smith leaned forward, resting his hand upon Hepburn's shoulder.

"The enemy knows that Dr. Prescott has found out the truth! How Dr. Prescott found out we have got to learn. Clearly he is a brilliant man. I'm afraid, Hepburn—I am afraid—"

He gripped Hepburn's shoulder and his grip was like that of a vice.

"You have read this thing . . . and the part which is in Father Donegal's handwriting tells the story. How he was prevented from broadcasting that story I begin to suspect. Note this particularly, Hepburn: I observed that Dom Patrick, when looking over the typescript brought in by James Richet, moistened the tip of his thumb in turning over the pages. A habit. The point seems significant?"

"Not to me," Hepburn confessed, staring rather haggardly at the speaker.

"Ah! Think it over," said Smith; then: "I know why you are downcast. You lost the woman—but you got what we were really looking for. Here's the story of an outside organization aiming to secure control of the country. Don't worry about Mrs. Adair; it's only a question of time. We'll get her."

Mark Hepburn turned his head aside.

The contents of the satchel had proved to be the completed text of Abbot Donegal's address, the last five pages revealed a plot which, if carried out, would place the United States under the domination of some shadowy being, unnamed, who apparently controlled inexhaustible supplies not only of capital but of men!

Following this revelation, his new chief, "Federal Officer 56," had given him his entire confidence. He had suspected, but now he knew, that a world drama was being fought out in the United States. A simple soul at heart, he was temporarily dazzled by recognition of the fact that he had been appointed chief of the staff in an international crisis to Sir Denis Nayland Smith, Ex-Commissioner of Scotland Yard, created a baronet for his services not only to the British Empire but to the world.

And in a moment of weakness he had let the woman go who might be a link, an irreplaceable link, between their task and this thing which aimed to place the United States under alien domination!

In that hour of disillusionment he felt a double traitor, for this man, Nayland Smith, was so dead straight. . . .

An atmosphere of impending harm hovered over the party. Mark Hepburn was not alone in having seen the venomous blizzard spitting snow unto that bronze Face. Among the seven who accompanied them were members of the ancient faith upheld sturdily by the hand of Abbot Donegal; and these, particularly—touched, he told himself, by medieval superstition—doubted and wondered as they were blindly carried through the stormy night. They were ignorant of what underlay it all, and ignorance breeds fear. They knew that they were merely a bodyguard for Captain Hepburn and Federal Officer 56.

Suddenly, appallingly, brakes were applied, all but throwing the nine men out of their chairs. Nayland Smith came to his feet at a bound, clutching the side of the car.

"Hepburn!" he cried, "go forward with two men. This train can slow down but it must not stop!"

Mark Hepburn ran forward along the car, touching two of the seven on their shoulders as he passed. They followed him out. A flare spluttered through snowy mist, clearly visible from the off-side windows.

"Switch off the lights!"

The order came in a high-pitched, irritable voice.

A trainman appeared and the car was plunged in darkness. A second flare broke through the veil of snow. Federal Officer 56 was crouching by a window looking out, and now:

"Do you see!" he cried, and grabbed the arm of a man who was peering out beside him. "Do you see!"

As the train regained momentum, presumably under the urge of Hepburn, a group of men armed with machine guns became clearly visible beside the tracks.

The special was whirling through the night again when Hepburn came back. He was smiling his low smile. Federal Agent 56 turned and stood up.

"This train won't stop," said Hepburn, "until we make Cleveland."

CHAPTER 6

AT WEAVER'S FARM

"WHAT'S THIS?" muttered Nayland Smith hoarsely.

The car was pulled up. They were in sight of the woods skirting Weaver's Farm. Night had fallen, and although the violence of the storm had abated there was a great eerie darkness over the snow-covered landscape.

Parties of men carrying torches and hurricane lanterns moved like shadows through the trees!

Smith sprang out on to a faintly discernible track, Mark Hepburn close behind him. They began to run towards the woods, and presently a man who peered about among the silvered bushes turned.

"What has happened?" Smith demanded breathlessly.

The man, whose bearing suggested military training, hesitated, holding a hurricane lamp aloft and staring hard at the speaker. But something in Smith's authoritative manner brought a change of expression.

"We are federal agents," said Mark Hepburn. "What's going on here?"

"Dr. Orwin Prescott has disappeared!"

Nayland Smith clutched Hepburn's shoulder: Mark could feel how his fingers quivered.

"My God, Hepburn," he whispered, "we are too late!"

Clenching his fists, he turned and began to race back to the car. Mark Hepburn exchanged a few words with the man to whom they had spoken and then doubled after Nayland Smith.

They had been compelled by the violence of the blizzard to proceed by rail to Buffalo; the military plane had been forced down by heavy snow twenty miles from the landing place selected. At Buffalo they had had further bad news from Liuetenant Johsnon.

Crowning the daring getaway of Mrs. Adair, James Richet, whose arrest had been ordered by Mark Hepburn, had vanished. . . .

268

And now they were ploughing a way along the drive which led up to Weaver's Farm, a white frame house with green shutters, sitting far back from the road. A survival of Colonial New England, it had stood there , outpost of the white man's progress in days when the red man still hunted the woods and lakes, trading beads for venison and maple sugar. Successive generations had modernized it so that to-day it was a twentieth-century home equipped from cellar to garret with every possible domestic convenience.

The door was wide open; and in the vestibule, with its old prints and atmosphere of culture, a tall, singularly thin man stood on the mat talking to a little white-haired old lady. He held a very wide-brimmed hat in his hand and constantly stamped snow from his boots. His face was gloomily officious. Members of the domestic staff might dimly be seen peering down from an upper landing. Unrest, fear, reigned in this normally peaceful household.

The white-haired lady started nervously as Mark Hepburn stepped forward.

"I am Captain Hepburn," he said. "I think you are expecting me. Is this Miss Lakin?"

"I am glad you are here, Captain Hepburn," said the little lady, with a frightened smile. She held out a small, plump, but delicate hand. "I am Elsie Frayne, Sarah Lakin's friend and companion."

"I am afraid," Hepburn replied, "we come too late. This is Federal Officer Smith. We have met with every kind of obstacle on our way."

"Miss Frayne," rapped Smith in his staccato fashion, "I must put a call through immediately. Where is the telephone?"

Miss Frayne, suddenly quite at ease with these strange invaders out of the night, smiled wanly.

"I regret to say, Mr. Smith, that our telephone was cut off some hours ago."

"Ah!" murmured Smith, and began tugging at the lobe of left ear, a habit which Hepburn had come to recognize as evidence of intense concentration. "That explains a lot." He stared about him, his disturbing glance finally focusing upon the face of the thin man.

"Who are you?" he snapped abruptly.

"I'm Deputy Sheriff Black," was the prompt but gloomy answer. "I have had orders to protect Weaver's Farm."

"I know it. They were my orders—and a pretty mess you've made of it."

The local officer bristled indignantly. He resented the irritable, peremptory manners of this "G" man; in fact Deputy Sheriff Black had never been in favour of Federal interference with county matters.

"A man can only do his duty, Mr. Smith," he answered angrily, "and I have done mine. Dr. Prescott slipped out some time after dusk this evening. Nobody saw him go. Nobody knows why he went or where he went. I may add that although I may be responsible, there are federal men on this job as well, and not one of them knows any more than I know."

"Where is Miss Lakin?"

"Out with a search party down at the lake."

"Sarah has such courage," murmured Miss Frayne. "I wouldn't go outside the house to-night for anything in the world."

Mark Hepburn turned to her.

"Is there any indication," he asked, "that Dr. Prescott went that way?"

"Mr. Walsh, a federal agent who arrived here two hours ago, discovered tracks leading in the direction of the lake."

"John Walsh is our man," said Hepburn, turning to Smith. "Do you want to make any inquiries here, or shall we head for the lake?"

Nayland Smith was staring abstractedly at Miss Frayne, and now;

"At what time, exactly," he asked, "was your telephone disconnected?"

"At five minutes after three," Deputy Sheriff Black's sombre tones interpolated. "There are men trying to trace the break."

"Who last saw Dr. Prescott?"

"Sarah," Miss Frayne replied—"that is, so far as we know."

"Where was he and what was he doing?"

"He was in the library writing letters."

"Were these letters posted?"

"No, Mr. Smith, they are still on the desk."

"Was it dark at this time?"

"Yes. Dr. Prescott—he is Miss Lakin's cousin, you know—had lighted the reading lamp, so Sarah told me."

"It was alight when I arrived," growled Deputy Sheriff Black.

"When did you arrive?" Smith asked.

"Twenty minutes after it was suspected Dr. Prescott had left the house."

"Where were you prior to that time?"

"Out in the road. I had been taking reports from the men on duty."

"Has anyone touched those letters since they were written?"

"No one, Mr. Smith," the gentle voice of Miss Frayne replied.

Nayland Smith turned to Deputy Sheriff Black.

"See that no one enters the library," he snapped, "until I return. I want to look over the room in which Dr. Prescott slept."

Deputy Sheriff Black nodded tersely and crossed the vestibule.

But even as Nayland Smith turned towards the stair, a deep feminine voice came out of the night beyond the entrance doors, which had not been closed. The remorseless wind was threatening to rise again, howling wanly through the woods like a phantom wolf pack. Flakes of fine snow flutterd in.

"He has been kidnapped, Mr. Walsh—because of what he knew. His tracks end on the shore of the lake. It's frozen over . . . . but there are no more tracks."

And now the speaker came in, followed by two men carrying lanterns; a tall, imperious woman with iron-grey hair, aristocratic features, and deep-set flashing eyes. She paused, looking about her with a slow smile of inquiry. One of the two men saluted Hepburn.

"My name is Smith," said Federal Officer 56, "and this is Captain Hepburn. You are Miss Lakin, Dr. Orwin Prescott's cousin? It was my business, Miss Lakin, to protect him. I fear I have failed."

"I fear it also," she replied, watching him steadily with her fine grave eyes. "Orwin has gone. They have him. He came here for a rest and security. He always came here before any important public engagement. Very soon now at Carnegie Hall is the debate with Harvey Bragg." (She was very impressive, this grande dame of Old America.) "He had learned something, Mr. Smith—heaven knows I wish I had shared his knowledge—which would have sent Bluebeard back forever to the pinewoods."

"He had!" snapped Smith grimly.

He reached out a long, leather-clad arm and gripped Miss Lakin's shoulder. For a moment she was startled—this man's electric gestures were disturbing—then, meeting that penetrating stare, she smiled with sudden confidence.

"Don't despair, Miss Lakin. All is not lost. Others know what Dr. Prescott knew——"

At which moment somewhere a telephone bell rang!

"They've mended the line," came the gloomy voice of Deputy Sheriff Black, raised now on a note of excitement.

He appeared at a door on the right of the vestibule.

"All incoming calls are covered," snapped Smith "as you were advised?"

"Yes."

"Who is calling?"

"I don't know," the deputy sheriff replied, "but it's someone asking for *Sir Denis Nayland Smith*."

He looked in bewilderment from face to face. Nayland Smith stared at Miss Lakin, smiled grimly and walked into a long, low library, a book-lined room with a great log fire burning at one end of it. The receiver of a telephone which stood upon a table near the fire was detached from the rest.

Someone closed the outer door, and a sudden silence came in that cosy room where the logs cracked. Sarah Lakin stood at the threshold, watching with calm, grave eyes. Mark Hepburn stared in over her shoulder.

"Yes," snapped Smith; "who is speaking?"

There was a momentary silence.

"Is it necessary, Sir Denis, for me to introduce myself?"

"Quite unnecessary, Dr. Fu Manchu! But it is strangely unlike you to show your hand so early in the game. You are

272

outside familiar territory. So am I. But this time, Doctor, by God we shall break you."

"I trust not, Sir Denis; so much is at stake: the fate of this nation, perhaps of the world—and there are bunglers who fail to appreciate my purpose. Dr. Orwin Prescott, for instance, has been very ill-advised."

Nayland Smith turned his head towards the door, nodding significantly to Mark Hepburn; some trick of the shaded lights made his lean, tanned face look very drawn , very tired.

"Since you have a certain manuscript in your possession, I assume it to be only a question of time for you to learn why the voice of the Holy Thorn became suddenly silent. In the Father's interests and in the interests of Dr. Prescott, I advise you to consider carefully your next step, Sir Denis——"

Nayland Smith's heart pulsed a fraction faster—Orwin Prescott was not dead!

"The abbot's eloquence is difficult to restrain-and I respect courage. But some day I may cry, in the words of your English King—Henry the Second, was it not?—'Will no one rid me of this turbulent priest . . .' My cry would be answered—nor should I feel called upon to walk, a barefooted penitent, to pray at the Father Abbot's tomb beside his Tower of the Holy Thorn."

Nayland Smith made no reply. He sat there, motionless, listening.

"We enter upon the last phase, Sir Denis . . ."

The guttural voice ceased.

Smith replaced the receiver, sprang up, turned.

"That was a cut-in on the line," he snapped. "Quick, Hepburn! The nearest phone in the neighbourhood: Check up that call if you can."

"Right." Mark Hepburn, his jaw grimly squared, buttoned up his coat.

Sarah Lakin watched Nayland Smith fascinatedly.

"Hell-for-leather, Hepburn! At any cost you *must* get through to Abbot Donegal to-night. Dr. Fu Manchu warns only *once*. . . ."

CHAPTER 7

SLEEPLESS UNDERWORLD

MARK HEPBURN replaced a tiny phial of a very rare re-agent on a shelf above his head and, turning, stooped and peered through a microscope at something resembling a fragment of gummy paper. For a while he studied this object and then stood upright, stretching his white-clad arms—he wore an overall—and yawning wearily. The small room in which he worked was fitted up as a laboratory. Save for a remote booming noise as of distant thunder, it was silent.

Hepburn lighted a cigarette and stared out of the closed window. The boom as of distant thunder was explained: it was caused by the ceaseless traffic in miles of busy streets.

Below him spread a night prospect of a large area of New York City. Half-right, framed by the window, the tallest building in the world reared its dizzy head to flying storm clouds. Here was a splash of red light; there, a blur of green. A train moved along its track far away to the left. Thousands of windows made illuminated geometrical patterns in the darkness. To-night there was a damp mist, so that the flambeau upheld by the distant Statue of Liberty was not visible.

A slight sound in the little laboratory on the fortieth floor of the Regal-Athenian Tower brought Hepburn around in a flash.

He found himself looking into the dark, eager face of Nayland Smith.

"Good Lord, Sir Denis! You move like a cat——"

"I used my key. . . ."

"You startled me."

"Have you got it, Hepburn—have you got it?"

"Yes."

"What?" Nayland Smith's lean face, framed in the upturned fur collar of his topcoat, lighted enthusiastically. "First-class job. What is it?"

"I don't know what it is—that is to say I don't know from what source it's obtained. But it's a concoction used by certain tribes on the Upper Amazon, and I happened to remember that the Academy of Medicine had a specimen and borrowed it. The preparation on the MS., the envelopes and the stamps gives identical reaction. A lot of study has been devoted to this stuff, which has remarkable properties. But nobody has yet succeeded in tracing it to its origin."

"It is called *kaapi*?"

"It is."

"I might have known!" snapped Nayland Smith. "He has used it before with notable results. But I must congratulate you. Hepburn: imagination is so rarely allied with exact scientific knowledge."

He peeled off the heavy topcoat and tossed it on a chair. Hepburn stared and smiled in his slow fashion.

Nayland Smith was dressed in police uniform!

"I was followed to headquarters," said Smith, detecting the smile. "I can assure you I was not followed back. I left my cap (which didn't fit me) in the police car. Bought the coat—quite useful in this weather—at a big store with several entrances, and returned here in a taxicab."

Mark Hepburn leaned back on a glass-topped table which formed one of the appointments of the extemporized laboratory, staring in an abstracted way at Federal Officer 56.

"They must know you are here," he said, in his slow dry way.

"Undoubtedly! They know I am here. But it is to their advantage to see that I don't remain here."

Hepburn stared a while longer and then nodded.

"You think they would come right out into the open like that?"

Nayland Smith shot out his left arm, gripping the speaker's shoulder.

"Listen. You can hardly have forgotten the machine-gun party on the track when an attempt was made to hold up the special train? This evening I went out by a private entrance kindly placed at my disposal by the management. As I passed the corner of Forty-eighth Street, a car packed with gunmen was close behind me!"

"What!"

"The taxicab in which I was driving belonged to a group known as the Lotus Cabs. . . ."

"I know it. One of the biggest corporations of its kind in the States."

"It may be nothing to do with them, Hepburn. But the driver was in the pay of the other side."

"You are sure?"

"I am quite sure. I opened the door, which is in front of the Lotus Cabs, as you may remember, and crouched down beside the wheel. I said to the man: 'Drive like the devil! I am a federal agent and traffic rules don't apply at the moment.'"

"What did he do?"

"He pretended to obey but deliberately tried to stall me! In a jam, the gunmen close behind, I jumped out, wriggled clear of the pack, cut through to Sixth Avenue and chartered another cab."

He paused and drew a long breath. Pulling out the time-worn tobacco-pouch he began to load his briar.

"This ink-shop of yours is somewhat oppressive," he said. "Let's go into the sitting-room."

He walked out to a larger room adjoining, Hepburn following. Over his shoulder:

"Both you and I have got to disappear!" he snapped.

As he spoke he turned, pipe and pouch in hand. Hepburn met the glance of piercing steely eyes and knew that Nayland Smith did not speak lightly.

"The biggest prize which any man ever played for is at stake—the control of the United States of America. To his existing organization—the extent of which even I can only surmise—Dr. Fu Manchu has added the most highly efficient underworld which civilization has yet produced."

Nayland Smith, his pipe charged, automatically made to drop the pouch back into his coat pocket, was hampered by the uniform, and tossed the pouch irritably on to a chair. He took a box of matches from the marble mantelpiece and lighted his briar. Surrounded now by clouds of smoke he turned, staring at Hepburn.

"You are rounding up your Public Enemies," he went on, in his snappy, staccato fashion; "but the groups which they controlled remain in existence. Those underground murder gangs are still operative, only awaiting the hand of a master. That master is here . . . and he has assumed control. Our lives

Hepburn"—he snapped his fingers—"are not worth that! But let us review the position.

He began to walk up and down, smoking furiously.

"The manuscript of Abbot Donegal's uncompleted address was saturated with a preparation which you have identified, although its exact composition is unknown to you. His habit, of wetting his thumb in turning over the pages (noted by a spy, almost certainly that James Richet, the secretary who has escaped us) resulted in his poisoning himself before he reached those revelations which Dr. Fu Manchu regarded as untimely. The abbot may or may not recover his memory of those pages, but in is own intersts, and I think in the interests of this country, he has been bound to silence for a time. He is off the air. So much is clear, Hepburn?"

"Perfectly clear."

"The gum of those stamps and envelopes, reserved for Dr. Prescott's use at Weaver's Farm, had been similarly treated. Prescott seems to have left he house and proceeded in the direction of the lake. He was, of course, under the influence of the drug. He was carried, as our later investigations proved, around the bank to the north end of the lake, and from there to the road, where a car was waiting. Latest reports regarding this car should reach headquarters to-night. It was, as suspected, undoubtedly proceeding in the direction of New York."

"We have no clue to the person who tampered with the stationery at Weaver's Farm," Hepburn's monotonous voice broke in.

"At the moment, none."

Nayland Smith moved restlessly in the direction of one of the windows.

"Somewhere below there," he went on, shooting out a pointing forefinger, "somewhere among those millions of lights, perhaps in sight from this very spot—Orwin Prescott is hidden!"

"I think you are right," said Mark Hepburn, quietly.

"I am all but certain! New York, and not Washington, would be Dr. Fu Manchu's selection as a base. He has been operating here, through chosen agents, for some months past. Others are flocking to him. I had news from Scotland Yard only this morning of one formidable old ruffian who has slipped though their nets for the twentieth time and is believed to be here. And Prescott will have been brought to the Doctor's headquarters. God knows what ordeal faces him—what choice he will be called upon to make! It is possible even that he may be given no choice!"

Nayland Smith clenched his fists and shook them desperately in the direction of the myriad of dancing lights of New York City.

"Look!" he cried. "Do you see? The mist has lifted. There is the Statue of Liberty! Do you realize, Hepburn"—he turned, a man all but imperturbable moved now by the immensity of his task—"do you realize what that figure will become if we fail?"

The wild light died from his eyes. He replaced his pipe and audibly gripped the stem between his small, even white teeth.

"We are not going to fail, Sir Denis," Hepburn replied in dry unmusical tones.

"Thank you," snapped Nayland Smith, and gripped his shoulder. "Dr. Fu Manchu being a Chinaman, in which quarter of the city should you think it most unlikely he would establish a base?"

"Chinatown."

Nayland Smith laughed gleefully.

"That is exactly how *he* will argue."

II

In a small room, amber lighted through high windows, a man worked patiently upon a clay model of a Chinese head. A distant bell sounded, and the room became plunged in darkness. Only the glowing end of a cigarette showed through this darkness. A high-pitched guttural voice spoke.

"Give me the latest report from the number responsible for covering Federal Officer 56 in New York."

"Only one other report to hand," the modeller replied immediately; "received at eight forty-five. Federal Officer 56 is occupying an apartment in the Regal-Athenian Tower. Federal Officer Captain Mark Hepburn is also located there, and engaged upon chemical experiments. A few minutes after eight o'clock, Federal Officer 56 left by a service door and engaged one of the Lotus cabs. The driver notified the Number covering Lexington exits. A protection car was instructed, but 56 gave them the slip on the corner of Forty-eighth and reached Centre Street at eight thirty-five. Report concluded as follows: 'Presume he is still at police headquarters as no notification that he has left is to hand.' "

Following a few moments of silence:

"Inform me," the guttural voice continued, "directly any report is received from Number 38, now proceeding from Cleveland to New York City."

The distant bell rang again and amber light prevailed once more in the small, domed room. The white-haired intellectual sculptor blinked slightly as though this sudden illumination hurt his eyes. Then, taking up tortoise-shell rimmed spectacles which he had laid down at the moment that the light had become extinguished, he dropped the stump of an Egyptian cigarette in an ash tray, having ignited another from the burning end. Taking up a modelling tool he returned to his eternal task.

CHAPTER 8

THE BLACK HAT

A LOTUS cab, conspicuous by reason of its cream body-work and pink line, drew up at the corner of Mulberry and Bayard Streets. The passenger got out; a small man, very graceful of movement, dark, sleek, wearing a grey waterproof overcoat and a soft black hat. He stood for a moment beside the driver as he paid his fare, glancing back along the route they had followed.

His fare paid, he crossed Pell Street and began to walk east.

The driver turned his cab, but then made a detour, crossing Mott Street. He pulled up before Wu King's Bar and went in. He came out again inside three minutes and drove away.

Meanwhile, the man in the black hat continued to walk east. A trickle of rain was falling, and a bleak wind searched the Chinese quarter. He increased his pace. Bright lights shone out from stores and restaurants, but the inclement weather had driven the Asiatic population under cover. In those pedestrians who passed him in the drizzle the man in the black hat seemed to take no interest whatever. He walked on with an easy, swinging stride as one confident that no harm would come to him in Chinatown.

When he passed an open door, to his nostrils came a whiff of that queer commingling of incense and spice which distinguishes the quarter. The Chinaman is a law-abiding citizen. His laws may be different from those of the Western world, but to his own codes he conforms religiously. Only a country cousin on a sight-seeing expedition could have detected anything mysterious about the streets through which the man in the black hat hurried. Even Deputy Inspector Gregory of the branch accountable for the good behaviour of Chinatown had observed nothing mysterious in his patrol of the public resorts and private byways.

Except for a curious hush when he had stopped in at Wu King's Bar for a chat with the genial proprietor and a look around for a certain Celestial there was nothing in the slightest degree suspicious in the behaviour of the people of the Asiatic quarter. This impression of a hush which had fallen at the moment of his entrance he had been unable to confirm—it might have been imaginary. In any event Wu King's was the headquarters of the Hip Sing Tong, and if it meant anything it probably meant a brewing disturbance between rival Chinese societies.

He was still considering the impression which this hush, real or imaginary, had made upon his mind when, turning a corner, he all but bumped into the man with the black hat.

The black hat was lowered against the keen wind: the detective, wind behind him, was walking very upright. Then, in a flash, the black-hatted man had gone. Momentarily the idea crossed the detective's mind that he had not seen the man's face—it might have been the face of a Chinaman, and he was anxious to meet a certain Chinaman.

He turned for a moment, looking back.

The man in the black hat had disappeared.

It was a particularly foul night, and Gregory had more than carried out his instructions. He trudged on through the icy drizzle to make his report. Secret orders had been received from headquarters calling upon all officers to look out for a very old Chinaman known in London as Sam Pak, and now believed to be posing as a residing alien. His description was vividly etched upon the detective's mind. The man in the black hat could not possibly fill the part, for this Sam Pak was very old. What this very old man could be wanted for was not clear to the deputy inspector. Nevertheless, that momentary instinct would have served him well had he obeyed it. . . .

The man whose features he had failed to see turned the first corner behind the police officer. When Gregory looked back the man was watching. Seeing Gregory walk on, he pursued his way. This led him past the corner occupied by Wu King's Bar and right to the end of the block. Here the man in the black hat paused in shelter of a dark doorway, lighting a cigarette and shielding the light with an upraised hand. He then consulted a type-written sheet which he drew from his raincoat pocket. Evidently satisfied that he had not misunderstood his instructions, he replaced the lighter and glanced

281

swiftly right and left along the street. This inspection assured him that none of the few pedestrians in sight was Gregory (whom he had recognized for a police officer). He groped along the wall on his right, found and pressed a bell.

Then again he looked cautiously. Only one traveller, a small, furtive Asiatic figure, was approaching in his direction. A slight sound told the man in the black hat that a door had opened. He turned, stepped forward and paused, seeking now with his left hand. He found a switch and depressed it. He heard the door close behind him. A moment more he waited, then fumbling again in the darkness, he discovered a second switch, and the light sprang up in the narrow passage in which he stood. The door which had opened to admit him was now shut. Another closed door was at the end of the passage. There was a bell-push beside it. He pressed the bell seven times—slowly . . .

II

Deputy Inspector Gregory had not quite reached the end of the block, when heading towards him through the mist and rain he saw a tall, gaunt figure, that of a Salvation Army captain, grey moustached and bespectacled. He would have passed on, for the presence of Salvation Army officials in unlikely quarters and the most inclement weather was a sight familiar enough. But the tall man pulled up directly in his path and:

"Excuse me if I am wrong," he said, speaking slowly and harshly, "but I think you are a police officer?"

Gregory glanced the speaker over and nodded.

"That's right," he replied. "What can I do for you?"

"I am looking," the harsh voice continued, "for a defaulter, a wayward brother who has fallen into sin. I saw him not five minutes ago, but lost him on the corner of Pell Street. As you were coming from that direction it is possible that you passed him."

"What's he like to look at?"

"He is a small man wearing a grey topcoat and a black soft hat. It is not our intention to charge him with his offence, but it is my duty to endeavour to overtake him."

"He passed me less than two minutes ago," Gregory replied sharply. "What's he listed for?"

"Converting money to his own uses; but no soul is beyond redemption."

The harsh, gloomy voice held that queer note of exaltation which Inspector Gregory had heard so often without being able to determine whether it indicated genuine piety or affection.

"I'll step back with you," he said tersely. "I know the corner he went round, and I know who lives in every house on that street. We'd better hurry!"

He turned and hurried back against the biting wind, the tall Salvation Army officer striding along beside him silently. They came to the corner on which Wu King's Bar was situated— the resort which Gregory had so recently visited; turning around it, they were temporarily sheltered from the icy blast.

"He may have gone into Wu's," said Gregory, as they looked along a deserted street, at one or two points of which lights shone out on the rain-drenched sidewalk. "Just stay here, and I'll check up."

He pushed open the door of the restaurant. To the nostrils of the Salvation Army official who stood outside was wafted a breath of that characteristic odour which belongs to every Chinatown in the world. In less than a minute the detective was out again.

"Not been in Wu's," he reported. "He must have gone in somewhere farther along, otherwise there wouldn't be any object in going that way; unless he's out for a walk. There's no other joint open back there. Do you know of any connections he has in this quarter?"

"Probably many," the harsh voice replied, and there was sadness in the tone. "He's attached to our Chinatown branch. I'm obliged to you but will trouble you no further, except to ask that if ever you see this man, you will detain him."

Gregory nodded, turned, and started off.

"No trouble," he said. "Hope you find the guy."

The Salvation Army official walked to the end of the street, gloomily scrutinizing closed doors to right and left, seeming to note the names over the shops, the numbers, the Chinese signs. Then turning to the right again at the end of the block, he walked on through the rain for a considerable distance and finally entered an elevated railroad station. . . .

Salvation Army delegates from all over the United States were assembled in New York that week, and a group of the senior officials had been accommodated at the Regal-Athenian Hotel. Therefore, no one in the vast marble-pillared lobby of that palatial establishment was surprised to see the tall and gloomy captain walk in. No confrère was visible in the public rooms through which he passed: the last had retired fully an hour earlier. Entering a tower elevator:

"Thirty-three," he announced gloomily.

He stepped out on the thirty-third floor, where two deputies from neighbouring States were sharing an apartment. He did not go to their apartment, however. He opened a door at the end of the long carpeted corridor and began to mount a stair. He met no one on his way, but at the fortieth floor he opened a door and peered out into another deserted carpeted corridor. . . .

Captain Mark Hepburn, pacing restlessly from room to room of the suite at the top of the tower, sometimes looking out of the window at rain-drenched New York below him, sometimes listening to the whine of the elevator, and sometimes exchanging glances with the equally restless Fey, Nayland Smith's man, who also wandered disconsolately about, suddenly paused in the little vestibule. He had heard quick footsteps.

A moment later the door opened, and a gloomy Salvation Army captain entered.

"Thank God! Sir Denis," said Hepburn and tried to repress the emotion he felt. "I was getting really worried."

The Salvation Army captain removed his cap, his spectacles, and, very gingerly, his grey moustache, revealed the gaunt, eager features of Nayland Smith.

"Thanks, Hepburn," he snapped. "I am sorry to have bothered you. But I was right."

"What!"

Fey appeared silently, his stoic face a mask.

"A whisky and soda, sir?" he suggested.

"Thanks, Fey; a stiff one."

A triumphant light danced in Smith's steely eyes, and:

"It looks as though you had some news," said Hepburn.

"I have." Nayland Smith extracted pipe and pouch from the pocket of his uniform jacket. "My guess was right—a pure guess, Hepburn, no more; but I was right. Can you imagine whom I saw down there in Chinatown to-night?"

"Not——"

"No—my luck didn't go as far as that. But just as I was turning out of Mott Street, right in the light from a restaurant, I saw our friend James Richet—the Abbot Donegal's ex-secretary!"

"Richet?"

"Exactly; one of the key men. Luck was with me. Then, suddenly, it turned. Of all the unimaginable things, Hepburn . . a real Salvation Army officer came up to me! Following a brief conversation he challenged me to establish my identity, and I was forced to do so."

He pulled back the top of his tunic, revealing the gold badge of a federal agent.

"A clumsy business, Hepburn. But what could I do? In the meantime I had lost my man. I met a detective officer as I went racing round the corner. He was unmistakable. I know a policeman, to whatever country he belongs, a quarter of a mile away. He had passed my man and did his best. I have memorized all the possible places into which he may have gone. But one thing is established, Hepburn—Dr. Fu Manchu has a Chinatown base. . . ."

CHAPTER 9

THE SEVEN-EYED GODDESS

JAMES RICHET, known to the organization of which he was a member as Number 38, stepped though a doorway—the fifth he had counted—and knew he must be below sea level. This door immediately closed behind him.

He found himself in a lobby with stone-faced walls. A silk-shaded lantern hung from an iron bracket. Immediately facing him was another arched doorway, curtained. Above the curtain-rod glowed a dim semi-circle of light. This place smelled like a joss house. The only other item of furniture was a narrow cushioned divan, and upon this a very old Chinaman was squatting. He wore a garment resembling a blue smock; he crouched forward on the divan, his veinous, claw-like hands resting upon his knees. He was a man of incalculable age: an intricate network of wrinkles mapped the whole of his face. His eyes were mere slits in the yellow skin. He might have been a chryselephantine statue, wrought by the cunning hands of a Chinese master.

A movement ever so slight of the bowed head indicated to Richet that the man on the divan was looking at him. He raised the left lapel of his topcoat. A small badge, apparently made of gold and ivory, not unlike one of the chips used at the Monte Carlo gaming tables, was revealed. It bore the number 38.

"James Richet," he said.

One of the talon hands moved back to the wall—and in some place beyond a bell rang, dimly. A clawish finger indicated the curtained doorway. James Richet crossed the lobby, drew the curtain aside and entered.

The night out of which he had come was wet and icily cold, but the moisture which he wiped now from his forehead was not entirely due to the rain. He had removed his hat and stood looking about him. This was a rectangular apartment, also stone-faced; the floor was of polished stone upon which several rugs were spread. There were seven doors, two in each of the long walls, two in that ahead of him, and the one by which he had entered. Above each of them, on an iron bracket, a lantern was hung, shaded with amber silk. All the openings were draped, and the drapery of each was of a different colour. There were cushioned seats all around the walls, set between the seven openings.

There was no other furniture except a huge square block of black granite, set in the centre of the stone floor and supporting a grotesque figure which only an ultra-modern sculptor could have produced: a goddess possessing seven green eyes, so that one of her eyes watched each of the openings. There was the same perfume in the place as of stale incense, but nevertheless unlike the more characteristic odour of Chinatown. The place was silent, very silent. In contrast to the bitter weather prevailing up above, its seemed to be tropically hot. There was no one visible.

Richet looked about him uneasily. Then, as if the proximity even of the mummy-like Chinaman in the lobby afforded some sense of human companionship, he sat down just right of the opening by which he had entered, placing his black hat upon the cushion beside him.

He tried to think. This place was a miracle of cunning— Chinese cunning. As one descended from the secret street door (and this alone, was difficult to find) a second, masked door gave access to a considerable room. He realized that a police raid would almost certainly end there. Yet there were three more hidden doors—probably steel—and three short flights of stone steps before one reached this temple of the seven-eyed goddess. These doors had been opened from beyond as he had descended.

No sound came from the lobby. Richet slightly changed his position. A green eye seemed to be watching him. But it proved to be impossible to escape the regard of one of those seven eyes; and, viewed from any point, the grotesque idol displayed some feminine line, some strange semblance of distorted womanhood. . . .

James Richet was a qualified attorney, and had practised for several years in Los Angeles. The yellow streak in his pedigree—his maternal grandmother had been a Kanaka— formed a check to his social ambition. Perhaps it was an operative factor in his selection of an easier and more direct path to wealth than the legitimate practice of his profession had offered him. He had become the legal adviser to one of the big beer barons. Later, the underworlds of Chicago and New York held no secrets from him. . . .

The silence of this strange stone cellar was very oppressive; he avoided looking at the evil figure which dominated it. . . .

His former chiefs, one after another, had been piled up on the rocks of the new administration. Then a fresh tide had come in his affairs, at a time when he began seriously to worry if Federal inquiries would become focussed upon himself. Some new control had seized upon the broken group of which he was a surviving unit. A highly paid post was found for him as legal adviser and secretary to Abbot Donegal. He was notified that special duties would be allotted from time to time. But in spite of all his cunning—for he was more cunning than clever—he had not up to the present moment succeeded in learning the political aims of the person or persons who, as he had realized for a long time, now controlled the vast underworld network which extended from coast to coast of the United States.

Of his former associates he had seen nothing during the time that he was attached to Abbot Donegal's staff at the Shrine of the Holy Thorn. Copies of the abbot's colossal mailing list he had supplied to an address in New York City; advance drafts of all sermons and lectures; and a précis of a certain class of correspondence.

Personal contact between himself and his real employer was made through the medium of Lola Dumas. His last urgent instructions, which had led to the breakdown of Abbot Donegal during a broadcast lecture, had been given to him by Lola . . . . that provocative study in slender curves, creamy skin and ebony-black hair, sombre almond-shaped eyes (deep, dark lakes in which a man's soul was drowned); petulant scornful lips . . . Lola.

Lola! She was supremely desirable, but maddeningly elusive. Together, what could they not do? She knew so many things that he burned to learn; but all that he had gathered from her was that they belonged to an organization governed by a board of seven. . . .

Hot though the place was, he shuddered. Seven! This hell-inspired figure which always watched him had *seven* eyes!

From time to time Lola would appear in the nearby town without warning, occupying the best suite in the best hotel and would summon him to meet her. It was Lola Dumas, on the first day that he had taken up his duties, who had brought him his badge. He had smiled. Later he had ceased to smile. Up to the time that he had fled from the Shrine of the Holy Thorn he had never learned how many other agents of the "Seven" were attached to the staff of the abbot. Two only he had met: Mrs. Adair, and a man who acted as night watchman. Now, shepherded from point to point in accordance with typed instructions headed: "In the event of failure" and received by him on the morning before the fateful broadcast, he was in New York; at last in the headquarters of his mysterious chief!

Something in the atmosphere of this place seemed to shake him. He wondered—and became conscious of nervous perspiration—if his slight deviation from the route laid down in his instructions had escaped notice. . . .

One of the coloured curtains was swept aside and he saw Lola Dumas facing him from the end of the temple of the seven-eyed goddess.

CHAPTER 10

JAMES RICHET

MARK HEPBURN sat at the desk by the telephone, making notes of many incoming calls, issuing instructions in some cases. Nayland Smith, at the big table by the window, worked on material which seemed to demand frequent reference to one of two large maps pinned on the wall before him. Hepburn lighted numberless cigarettes. Nayland Smith was partially hidden behind a screen of pipe smoke.

Despite the lateness of the hour, Fey, the taciturn, might be heard moving about in the kitchenette.

The doorbell rang.

Smith turned in his chair. Hepburn stood up.

As Fey crossed the sitting-room to reach the vestibule:

"Remember orders, Fey!" Smith rapped.

Fey's Sioux-like, leathern features exhibited no expression whatever. He extended a large palm in which a small automatic rested.

"Very good, sir."

He opened the door. Outside stood a man in Regal-Athenian uniform and another who wore a peaked cap.

"He's all right," said the man in uniform. "He is a Western Union messenger. . . ."

When the door was closed again and Fey had returned to his cramped quarters, Nayland Smith read the letter which the man had delivered. He studied it carefully, a second and a third time; then handed it to Hepburn.

"Any comments?"

Mark Hepburn took the letter and read:

WEAVER'S FARM
WINTON, CONN..

DEAR SIR DENIS:

Something so strange has occurred that I feel you should know at once. (I regret to say that my telephone is again out of order.) A man called upon me early this evening who gave the name of Julian Sankey. Before this, he made me promise to tell no one but you what he had to say. He implied that he had information that would enable us to locate Orwin. He was a smallish, dark man, with very spruce lank black hair and the slyly ingratiating manners of an Argentine gigolo. A voice like velvet.

I gave my promise, which seemed to satisfy him, and he then told me that he was a reluctant member of an organization which planned to make Harvey Bragg dictator. He conveyed the idea that he knew the inside of this organization and that he was prepared, on terms, and with guaranteed government protection, to place all his knowledge at our disposal. He assured me that Orwin was a prisoner in New York, and that his (Sankey's) safety being assured by you, he would indicate the exact spot.

I have an address to which to write, and it is evidently urgent. I shall be in New York tomorrow and will call upon you, if I may, at four o'clock.

What do you think we should do?

Very sincerely yours,
SARAH LAKIN.

Mark Hepburn laid the letter down upon the table.

"The description," he said drily, "would fit James Richet as well as any man I know."

Nayland Smith, watching him, smiled triumphantly.

"I am glad to hear you say so." He declared. "You order this man's arrest; he disappears. He is out to save his skin—"

"It may be."

"If it is Richet, then Richet would be a valuable card to hold. It's infuriating, Hepburn, to think that I missed grabbing the fellow to-night! My next regret is that our fair correspondent omits the address at which we can communicate with this 'Julian Sankey.' Does any other point in the letter strike you?"

"Yes," said Hepburn slowly. "It's undated. But my own sister, who is an honour graduate, rarely dates her letters. The other thing is the telephone."

"The telephone is the all-important thing."

Mark Hepburn turned and met the fixed gaze of Nayland

291

Smith's eyes. He nodded.

"I don't like the disconnected telephone, Hepburn. I know the master schemer who is up against us . . . ! I am wondering if this information will ever come to hand . . . ."

II

A man who wore a plain yellow robe, in the loose sleeves of which his hands were concealed, sat at a large lacquered table in a small room. Some quality in the sound which penetrated through three windows, all of them slightly opened, suggested that this room was situated at a great height above a sleepless city.

Two of the walls were almost entirely occupied by bookcases; the lacquer table was set in the angle formed by these books, and upon it, in addition to neatly arranged documents, were a number of queer-looking instruments and appliances.

Also there was a porcelain bowl in which a carved pipe with a tiny bowl rested.

The room was very hot and the air laden with a peculiar aromatic smell. The man in the yellow robe lay back in a carved, padded chair; a black cap resembling a biretta crowned his massive skull. His immobile face resembled one of those ancient masterpieces of ivory mellowed in years of incense; a carving of Gautama Buddha—by one who disbelieved his doctrine. The eyes in this remarkable face had been closed; now, suddenly, they opened. They were green as burnished jade under moonlight.

The man in the yellow robe put a on pair of tinted spectacles and studied a square, illuminated screen which was one of the several unusual appointments of the table. . . . Upon this screen, in miniature, appeared a moving picture of the subterranean room where the seven-eyed goddess sat eternally watching. James Richet was talking to Lola Dumas.

The profound student of humanity seated at the lacquer table was cruelly just. He wished to study this man who, after doing good work, had seen fit to leave his ordered route and to visit the cousin of Orwin Prescott. Steps had been taken to check any possible consequences. But the fate of the one who

292

had made these measures necessary hung now in the balance.

They stood close together, and although their figures appeared distant, but not so perhaps through the lenses of the glasses worn by the Chinaman, their voices sounded quite normal, as though they were speaking in the room in which he sat.

"Lola, I have the game in my hand." Rcihet threw his left arm around the woman's shoulders and drew her to him. "Don't pretend. We're in this thing together."

Lola Dumas' lithe body bent backward as he strove to reach her lips.

"You are quite mad," she said breathlessly. "Because I was amused once, why should you think I am a fool?" She twisted, bent, and broke free, turning and facing him, her dark eyes blazing. "I can play, but when I work, I quit play. You are dreaming, my dear, if you think you can ever get control."

"But I tell you I have the game in my hand!" The man, fists clenched, spoke tensely, passionately. "It is for you to say the word. Why should a newcomer, a stranger, take charge when you and I——"

"You young fool! Do you want to die so young?"

"I tell you, Lola, *I'm* not the fool. I know Kern Adler, the big New York lawyer, is in this. And what I say goes with Kern. I know 'Blondie' Hahn is. And Blondie stands for all the useful boys still at large. I know how to handle Blondie. We're old friends. I have all the Donegal material. No one knows the inside of the Brotherhood of National Equality as I know it. What's more—I know where to go for backing, and I don't need Bragg! Lola . . ."

A slender ivory hand, the fingernails long, pointed and highly burnished, moved across the lacquered table in that distant high room.

Six of the seven lights over curtained openings went out.

"What's this?" muttered Richet. "What do we do now?"

He was inspired by his own vehemence; he felt capable of facing Satan in person.

"Go into the lighted alcove," said the woman coldly. "The President is ready to interview you."

Richet paused, fists still half clenched, stepped towards the light, then glanced back. Lola Dumas had gone. She was lost in the incense-haunted darkness . . . but one green eye of the goddess watched him out of the shadows. He moved forward, swept the curtain aside and found himself in a small, square stone cell, possessing no furniture whatever. The curtain fell back into place with a faint swishing sound. He looked about him, his recent confidence beginning to wane. Then a voice spoke—a high-pitched, guttural voice.

"James Richet, I am displeased with you."

Richet looked right, left, above and below. Then:

"Who is speaking?" he demanded angrily. "These stage illusions are not impressive. Was *I* to blame for what happened? I wish to see you, speak to you face to face."

"An unwise wish, James Richet. Only Numbers one to twelve have that privilege."

Richet's brow was covered with nervous perspiration.

"I want a square deal," he said, striving to be masterful.

"You shall have a square deal," the implacable, guttural voice replied. "You will be given sealed orders by the Number in charge of Base 3. See that you carry out his instructions *to the letter*. . . ."

III

Mark Hepburn sprang up in bed.

"All right, Hepburn!"—it was Nayland Smith's voice. "Sorry to awaken you, but there's a job for us."

The light had been switched on, and Hepburn stared somewhat dazedly at the speaker, then glanced down at his watch. The hour was 3.15 a.m. But Nayland Smith was fully dressed. Now wide awake:

"What is it?" Hepburn asked, impressed by his companion's grim expression and beginning also to dress hastily.

"I don't know—yet. I was called five minutes ago—I had not turned in—by the night messenger. A taxi—perhaps a coincidence, but it happens to be a Lotus taxi—pulled up at the main entrance. The passenger asked the man to step into the lobby and inquire for me——"

"In what name?"

"The title was curiously accurate, Hepburn. It was typed on

294

a slip of paper. The man was told to ask for Federal Agent Ex-Assistant Commissioner Sir Denis Nayland Smith, O.B.E.!"

Hepburn was now roughly dressed. He turned, staring:

"But to everybody except myself and Fey you are plain Mr. Smith!"

"Exactly. That is why I see the hand of Dr. Fu Manchu, who has a ghastly sense of humour, in this. The man proceeded to obey his orders, I gather, but he had not gone three paces when something happened. Let's hurry down. The man is there . . . so is his passenger."

The night manager and a house detective were talking to Fey by the open door of the apartment.

"Queerest thing that ever happened in my experience, gentlemen," said the manager. "I only hope it isn't a false alarm. The string of titles means nothing to me. But you are Mr. Smith and I know you are a Federal agent. This way. The elevator is waiting. If you will follow me I will take you by a shorter route."

Down they went to the street level. Led by the manager they hurried along a service passage, crossed a wide corridor, two empty offices, and came out at the far end of the vast pillared and carpeted main foyer. Except for robot-like workers vacuum cleaning, it was deserted and in semi-darkness. A lofty, shadow-haunted place. Light shone from the open door of the night manager's room. . . .

A man who wore a topcoat over pyjamas was examining a still figure stretched on a sofa. There were three other men in the room, one of them the taxi driver.

Nayland Smith shot a searching glance at the latter's pale, horrified face, as, cap on the back of his head, he stared over the doctor's shoulder, and then, pushing his way forward, he too looked once, and:

"Good God!" he muttered. "Hepburn"—Mark Hepburn was beside him—"what is it? Have you ever met with anything like it?"

There was a momentary silence, grotesquely disturbed by the hum of a distant vacuum cleaner.

The prostrate man, whose torso had been stripped to restore cardiac action, exhibited on his face and neck a number of vivid scarlet spots. They were about an eighth of an inch in diameter and on the dull white skin resembled drops of blood. . . .

"Never."

Mark Hepburn's voice was husky. The doctor looked up. He was a heavily built Teutonic type, his shrewd eyes magnified by powerful spectacles.

"If you are a brother practitioner," he said, "you are welcome. This case is outside my experience."

"When did he actually die?" rapped Nayland Smith.

"He was already dead when I arrived—although I worked over him for ten minutes or more——"

"The scarlet spots!" blurted the taxi driver in a frightened voice—"That's what he called out, 'The scarlet spots'—and then he was down on the sidewalk rolling about and screaming!"

Mark Hepburn glanced at Nayland Smith.

"You were right," he said; "we shall never get that information."

The dead man was James Richet, ex-secretary to Abbot Donegal!

Chapter 11

RED SPOTS

"WHAT IS IT, mister," the taximan whispered, "some new kind of fever?"

"No," said Nayland Smith. "It's a new kind of a *murder!*"

"Why do you say so?" the hotel doctor asked, glancing in a puzzled way at the ghastly object on the sofa.

But Nayland Smith did not reply. Turning to the night manager:

"I want no one at present in the foyer," he said, "to leave without my orders. You"—he pointed to the house detective—"will mount guard over the taxicab outside the main entrance. No one must touch it or enter it. No one must pass along the sidewalk between the taxi and the hotel door. It remains where it stands until further notice. Hepburn"—he turned—"get two patrolmen to take over this duty. Hurry. I need you here."

Mark Hepburn nodded and went out of the night manager's room, followed by the house detective.

"What about anyone living here and coming in late?" asked the night manager, speaking with a rich Tipperary brogue.

"What's your house detective's name?"

"Lawkin."

"Lawkin!" cried Smith, standing in the open door, "any residents are to be directed to some other entrance."

"O.K., sir."

"The use of an office, Mr. Dougherty," Nayland Smith continued, addressing the manager, "on this floor? Can you oblige us?"

"Certainly Mr. Smith. The office next to this."

"Excellent. Have you notified the police?"

"I considered I had met regulations by notifying yourself and Captain Hepburn."

"So you have. I suppose a man is not qualified to hold your job unless he possesses tact." He turned to the taximan. "Will you follow Mr. Dougherty to the office and wait for me there?"

The driver, a man palpably shaken, obeyed Dougherty's curt nod and followed him out, averting his eyes from the sofa. Two men and the doctor remained, one wearing dinner kit, the other a lounge suit. To the former:

"I presume that you are the assistant night manager?" said Nayland Smith.

"That is so. Fisk is my name, sir. This"—indicating the square-jowled wearer of the lounge suit—"is James Harris, assistant house detective."

"Good," rapped Nayland Smith. "Harris—give a hand to Lawkin outside." Harris went out. "And now, Mr. Frisk, will you please notify Mr. Dougherty that I wish to remain alone here with Dr.——?"

"My name is Scheky," said the physician.

"—with Dr. Scheky."

The assistant night manager went out. Nayland Smith and Dr. Scheky were alone with the dead man.

"I have endeavoured to clear this room, Doctor," Smith continued, addressing the burly physician in the topcoat, "without creating unnecessary panic. But do you realize that you and I face risk of the same death"—he pointed—"that *he* died?"

"I had not realized it, Mr. Smith," the physician admitted, glancing down with a changed expression at the bright red blotches on the dead man's skin; "nor do I know why you suspect murder."

"Perhaps you will understand later, Doctor. When Captain Hepburn returns I am sending for certain equipment. If you care to go to your apartment I will have you called when we are ready. . . ."

In an adjoining office, amid cleared desks and closed files, the pale-faced taximan faced Nayland Smith's interrogation.

"I took him up to Times Square. . . . No, I never seen him before. He gave the address 'Regal Athenian, Park entrance.' . . . Sure he seemed all right; nothing wrong with him. When we get here he says: 'Go in to the desk and ask if this man is in the hotel'—and slips me the piece of paper through the window. 'Give 'em the paper'—that was what he said. 'It's a hard name—'

"Sure of that?" rapped Nayland Smith.

"Dead sure. I took the paper and started. . . . There was nobody about. As I moved off, he pulled out of his pocket what looks like a notebook. I guess it's out there now. . . . Next minute I hear his first yell—mister, it was awful! He had the door open in a flash and falls right out on to the sidewalk."

"Where were you? What did you do?"

"I'm half-way up the hotel steps. I started to run back. He's lashing around down there and seems to be tearing his clothes off—"

"Stop. You are quite certain on this point?"

"Sure," the man declared earnestly; "I'm sure certain. He had his topcoat right off and ripped his collar open. . . . He's yelling, 'The scarlet spots!' like I told you. That's what I heard him yell. And he's fighting and twisting like he was wrestling with somebody. . . . Gee!"

The man pulled his cap off and wiped his brow with the back of his hand.

"I run in here. There wasn't a cop in sight. Nobody was in sight. . . . What could I do, mister? I figured he'd gone raving mad. . . . When we got out to him he's lying almost still. Only his hands was twitchin. . . ."

The night manager came into the office.

"All heat turned off on this floor," he reported, "and all doors closed. . . ."

Outside the Regal-Athenian the atmosphere was arctic. Two patrolmen watched Mark Hepburn with an electric torch and a big lens examining every square foot of sidewalk and the carpeted steps leading up to the main entrance. Residents who arrived late were directed to a door around the corner. In reply to questions the invariable answer of the police was:

"Somebody lost something valuable."

The death cab had been run into an empty garage. It had been sealed; and at this very moment two men wearing chemist's masks were pumping it full of a powerful germicidal gas.

Later, assisted by Dr. Scheky—both men dressed as if working in an operating theatre—Hepburn stripped and thoroughly examined the body and the garments of James Richet. The body was then removed, together with a number of objects found in Richet's possession. The night manager's room was sealed, to be fumigated. The main foyer, Nayland Smith ordered, must be closed to the public pending further orders. Dawn was very near when Dr. Scheky said to Hepburn:

"You are not by chance under the impression that this man died of some virulent form of plague?"

Mark Hepburn stared haggardly at the physician. They were dead beat.

"To be perfectly frank, Doctor," he answered, "I don't know of what he died. . . ."

CHAPTER 12

NUMBER 81

IN THAT DOOMED room, amber lighted through curious Gothic windows, the white-haired sculptor sat smoking Egyptian cigarettes and putting the finishing touches to a sinister clay head which one might have assumed to be his life's work. Pinned upon a wooden panel beside the tripod on which the clay was set, was some kind of small coloured picture, part of which had been masked out so that what remained resembled a tiny face surrounded by a margin of white paper.

This the sculptor examined through a powerful magnifying glass, and then lowering the glass, scrutinized the clay. Evidently his work was to attempt to produce a life-sized model of the tiny head pinned to the board.

Seeming to be not wholly satisfied, the sculptor laid down the lens with a sigh and wheeled the clay along to the end of the table. At which moment the amber light went out, the dim bell rang. A high-pitched, imperious, guttural voice spoke.

"The latest report from the Regal-Athenian."

"Received at 5.10 a.m. from Number in charge. Foyer closed to the public by Federal orders. Night manager's office sealed. Taxi in garage on Lexington. The body of the dead man identified as that of James Richet, late secretary to Abbot Donegal, removed at 5 a.m. to police mortuary. Cause of death unknown. Federal Agents Smith and Hepburn in their quarters in the tower. End of report."

Followed some moments of silence, broken only by an occasional faint ticking from an electric clock. Then:

"Fix the recording attachment, Number 81," came an order. You are free for four hours."

Amber light poured again into the room. Number 81 stood up. Opening a cupboard in the telephone table, he attached three plugs to a switchboard contained in the cupboard. One of these connected with the curious electric clock which stood upon the desk; another with a small motor which operated in connection with the telephone; and a third with a kind of dictaphone capable of automatically recording six thousand words or more without change of cylinder.

As he was about to close the cupboard, a dim buzz indicted an incoming message. The faint hum of well-oiled machinery followed; a receiver-rest was lifted as if by invisible fingers, and a gleaming black cylinder began to revolve, the needle-point churning wax from its polished surface as the message was recorded. A tiny aluminium disc dropped into a tray below the electric clock, having stamped upon it the exact time at which the telephone bell had rung.

Number 81, as if his endless duties had become second nature, waited until the cylinder ceased to revolve. The telephone-rest sprang up into its place; from the electric clock came the sound of a faint tick. Number 81 pressed a button on the desk. The cylinder began to revolve again and a voice spoke—that of the man whose report had just been recorded.

"Speaking from Base 3. The Abbot Donegal reported missing. There is reason to believe that he slipped away during the night and may be proceeding to New York to be present at the debate at Carnegie Hall. All Numbers along possible routes have been notified, but no report to hand. Number 44 speaking."

Presumably satisfied that the mechanism was running smoothly Number 81 closed the cupboard and stood up. Thus seen, he was an even bigger man than he had appeared seated; an untidy but an imposing figure. He took up the clay model, lifting it with great care. He slipped a tin of Egyptian cigarettes into a pocket of his dressing-gown and walked towards one of the panels which surrounded the seemingly doorless room.

This he opened by pressing a concealed switch. A descending staircase was revealed. Carrying the clay model as carefully and lovingly as a mother carries her newly-born infant, he descended, closing the door behind him. He went down one flight and entered a small, self-contained apartment. A table littered with books, plans and all sorts of manuscripts stood by an open window. There was a bed in an alcove, and beyond, through an open door, a glimpse might be obtained of a small bathroom. Clearing a space on the littered table, Number 81 set down the clay model. He crossed the room and opened a cupboard. It showed perfectly empty. He raised a telephone from its hook. In German:

"The same as last night," he said harshly; "but the liver sausage was no good. Also, I must have the real German lager. This which you send me is spurious. Hurry, please, I have much to do."

These orders given, he crossed to the table and stared down dully at a large open book which lay there, its margins pencilled with numerous notes in tiny, neat handwriting. The book was "Interstellar Cycles" by Professor Albert Morgenstahl, Europe's greatest physicist and master mathematician, expelled a year earlier from Germany for anti-Nazi tendencies and later reported to be dead.

At this work Number 81 stared for some time, turning the pages over idly and resting a long tobacco-stained finger upon certain of the notes. There was a creaking in the cupboard and a laden wagon occupied its previously vacant space. Upon this wagon a substantial repast was set. Taking out a long-necked bottle of wine and uncorking it, Number 81 filled a glass. This he tasted and then set it down.

He threw open the french windows upon one side of the room, revealing a narrow balcony with a high railing of scrolled ironwork. A weather-beated table stood there, and for a moment Number 81 leaned upon it, gazing down upon a night panorama of the great city below; snow-covered roofs, leaden sky. It was bitterly cold at that great elevation; an icy breeze stirred the mane of white hair.

But, as if immune to climatic conditions, Number 81 bore out the clay head of the majestic Chinaman and set it upon the table. Below him a dome, its veins gilded, every crack and cranny coated with snow, swept down gracefully to a lower parapet. Muffled noises from streets set in deep gullies, reached his ears. He returned for his glass of wine, raised his head to the leaden sky, and:

"To the day of freedom!" he cried. "To the day when we meet face to face." And now his eyes, glaring insanely, were lowered to the clay head—"To the day when we meet face to face; when those wheels in which I am trapped, which seem to move, inexorable as the planets in their courses, are still forever."

He drank deeply, then tossed the remainder of the wine

contemptuously into the face of the modelled head. He dashed the glass on the paving at his feet and, picking up the work to which he had devoted so many hours of care, raised it in both hands high above his head.

His expression mechanical, his teeth bared in a wolfish grin, far out over the dome he hurled it. It fell with a dreadful thud on the leaden covering. It broke, the parts showering down to the parapet, to fall, meaningless fragments, into some street far below....

CHAPTER 13

TANGLED CLUES

IN THE LIGHT of a grey wintry dawn creeping wanly through the windows, Nayland Smith and Mark Hepburn stood looking down at some curious objects set out upon the big corner table. These had been found in Richet's possession.

One was a gold and ivory badge. Hepburn took it up and stared at it curiously. It bore the number 38.

"According to the taximan," said Nayland Smith, "to whom I showed it, these badges simply mean that the wearer is an official of Harvey Bragg's League of Good Americans. It appears that no man is eligible for employment by the Lotus Cab Corporation who is not a member of this league."

"There's more to it than that," Hepburn murmured thoughtfully.

"I agree; but I don't think the man knew it. He admitted that they sometimes had orders from wearers of such badges requiring them to pick up certain passengers at indicated points and to report where they set them down."

"But he denied that he had any such orders last night?"

"He stuck to it grimly. According to his account, the choice of his cab by Richet was a coincidence."

Hepburn laid the badge down.

"There are only two other points of interest," said Nayland Smith, "although we may learn more if we can trace Richet's baggage. These are his notes of Weaver's Farm and of this address, and . . . that."

The object to which he pointed, found upon the floor of the taxi, was certainly an odd thing for a man to carry about. It was a cardboard case made to hold a pack of playing cards . . . but there were no cards!

Several sheets of blank paper had also been found, folded in a manner which seemed to indicate that they had been in the cardboard case. This case, in Smith's opinion, was the object which the driver had mistaken for a notebook.

"Richet was actually holding it in his hand, Hepburn," he

rapped energetically, "at the moment of his attack. The fact is of first-rate importance."

Hepburn, eyes half closed, nodded slowly. The nervous energy of this man surpassed anything in his experience. And as if recognition of his companion's weariness had come to him suddenly, Nayland Smith grasped Hepburn's arm.

"You are asleep already!" he declared, and smiled sympathetically. "Suppose we arrange to meet for ham and eggs at noon. Don't forget, Miss Lakin is due at four o'clock. If you meet her—not a word about Richet."

II

The bell rang, and Fey, his leathery face characteristically expressionless, crossed the vestibule and opened the door. A woman stood there, tall and composed, her iron-grey hair meticulously groomed as it peeped from beneath the brim of a smart but suitable hat. She was wrapped in furs. Beside her stood a man who wore the uniform of the Regal-Athenian Hotel. He exchanged a glance with Fey, nodded, turned and went away.

"Sir Denis is expecting you, madam," said Fey, standing aside.

And as the visitor entered the vestibule, Nayland Smith hurried from the adjoining sitting-room, hand outstretched. His lean brown features exhibited repressed excitement.

"Miss Lakin," he exclaimed, "you are very welcome. I received the letter which you sent by special messenger, but your phone message has intrigued me more than the letter. Please come in and sit down and give me all the details."

The sitting-room in which Miss Lakin found herself possessed several curious features. The windows which occupied nearly the whole of one wall afforded a view of a wide area of New York City. Storm clouds had passed; a wintry sun lighted a prospect which had a sort of uncanny beauty. Upon countless flat roofs far below, upon the heads of gargoyles and other grotesque ornamentations breaking the lines of the more towering buildings, snow rested. The effect was that of a city of ice gnomes magically magnified. Through clear, frosty air the harbour was visible, and one might obtain a glimpse of the distant sea. Above a littered writing-table set near one of the windows, a huge map of the city was fixed upon the wall; the remainder of this wall was occupied by a map, on a much smaller scale, of the whole of the United States. These maps had one character in common: they were studded with hundreds of coloured pins which appeared to have been stuck in at random.

"The room is rather warm, madam," said Fey. "Allow me to take your coat."

The heavy fur coat draped carefully across his arm:

"A cup of tea, madam?" he suggested.

"English tea," snapped Nayland Smith.

"Thank you," said Miss Lakin, smiling faintly; "you tempt me. Yes, I think I should enjoy a cup of tea."

Nayland Smith stood before the mantelpiece, hands behind him. He had that sort of crisp, wavy hair, silvery now at the sides, which always looks in order; he was cleanly shaven, and his dark-skinned face offered no evidence of the fact that he had had only six hours' sleep in the past forty-eight. He wore a very old tweed suit, and what looked like a striped shirt with an attached collar, but which closer scrutiny would have revealed to be a pyjama jacket. As Fey went out:

"Miss Lakin," he continued, and his manner was that of a man feverishly anxious, "you have brought me the letter to which you referred?"

Sarah Lakin took an envelope out of her handbag and handed it to Nayland Smith, watching him with her steady, grave eyes. He took it, glanced at the hand-written address, then crossed to the writing-table.

"I have also," she said, "a note of the place at which we were to communicate with the very unpleasant person who called upon me yesterday."

Nayland Smith turned; his expression was grim.

"I fear," he said rapidly, "that we cannot hope for much help from that quarter." He turned again to the littered table. "Here are three letters written by Orwin Prescott at Weaver's Farm immediately prior to his disappearance. You know why I detained them and what I have discovered?"

Miss Lakin nodded.

"Copies have been sent to the persons to whom the letters were addressed, but I should judge, although I am not a specialist in the subject, that this is in Dr. Prescott's hand-writing?"

"I can assure you that it is, Sir Denis. Intellectually my cousin and I are too closely akin for any deception to be possible. That letter was written by Orwin. Please read it."

A subdued clatter of teacups became audible from the kitchenette to which Fey had retired, as Nayland Smith extracted the letter from the envelope. Sarah Lakin watched Sir Denis intently. He fascinated her. Brief though her acquaintance with him had been, her own fine nature had recognized and welcomed the keen, indomitable spirit of this man, who in an emergency personal and national, had thrown the weight of his trained powers into the scale.

He studied the letter silently, reading it once, twice. He then read it aloud:

"DEAR SARAH,

This is to relieve your anxiety. By this time you will know that I am the victim of a plot; but I have compromised with the enemy, *pax in bello*, and I congratulate you and those associated with you upon the manner in which you have succeeded in restraining the newspapers from reference to the subject of my temporary disappearance. I have instructed Norbert, who will communicate with you. The experience has been unpleasant and even now I am not wholly my own master. Please conduct yourself as though you were ignorant of this misadventure, but have no fears respecting my appearance at Carnegie Hall. I shall be there. I dislike seeming to mystify, but it would be to my best interests if you make no attempt to communicate with me until the night of the debate. It is unnecessary that I should tell you to have courage.

Always affectionately yours,
ORWIN."

"No date," Nayland Smith commented. "No address. A sheet torn from a common type of writing-block. The envelope, also, is of a very ordinary kind, bearing a New York postmark. H'm . . . !"

He dropped letter and envelope upon the desk and, taking up a tobacco pouch, began to load his pipe. Fey entered with a tea tray which he placed upon a small table before Miss Lakin.

"Cream or milk?"

"Milk, and one piece of sugar, thank you."

Except for a certain haggardness visible on the face of Nayland Smith and the strangeness of his attire in one obviously trained to conform to social custom, there was little in the atmosphere of this room high above the turmoil of New York to suggest that remorseless warfare raged about the pair who faced one another across the tea-table.

"I am entirely at a loss what to do, Sir Denis."

As Fey withdrew, the deep voice of Miss Lakin broke the silence; her steady eyes were fixed upon Nayland Smith. He lighted his pipe, paused, looked down at her, and:

"A very foul briar is unusual at tea-time," he snapped, and dropped his pipe in an ash tray. "Please forgive me. I am up against the greatest and perhaps the last problem of my life."

"Sir Denis . . ." Miss Lakin bent forward, took up the charred pipe from the tray and extended it towards him. "Surely you know that I understand. I have lived in a wider world than Connecticut, and I want your advice badly. Please concentrate upon the problem in your own way. What should I do? What do you advise me to do?"

Nayland Smith stared hard at those grave eyes of the speaker; then, pipe in hand, began to walk up and down the room, tugging at the lobe of his left ear. They were forty floors above the streets of New York, and yet the ceaseless bombilation of those amazing thoroughfares reached them through such windows as were open: the hooting of lorry horns, the roar of ten thousand engines, the boom of a distant train rumbling along the rails, the warning siren of a tug-boat on East River. The city was around them, throbbing, living, an entity, a demi-god, claiming them—and as it seemed in this hour, demanding their destruction.

"Is the phrasing characteristic of your cousin's style?" Nayland Smith demanded.

"Yes, broadly."

"I understand. It struck me as somewhat pedantic."

"He has a very scholarly manner, Sir Denis, but as a rule it is not so marked in his intimate letters."

"Ah. . . . Who is Norbert?"

"Maurice Norbert is Orwin's private secretary."

"I see. May I take it, Miss Lakin, that in this fight for domination of the United States your cousin did not actually aim at the Presidency?"

"He did not even desire it, Sir Denis. He is what our newspapers term a hundred-per-cent American, but in the best sense of the phrase. He hoped to break the back of Harvey Bragg's campaign. His aims were identical with those of the Abbot Donegal. His disappearance from the scene at this time would be fatal."

"I agree! But it seems that he is not going to disappear."

"Then do you believe that what he says is true?"

"I am disposed to believe it, Miss Lakin. My advice is to conform strictly to the letter and spirit of his request."

Miss Lakin was watching him intently, then:

"I am afraid I don't agree with you, Sir Denis," she said.

"Why?" He turned and faced her.

"That Orwin was kidnapped we know. Thank God he is alive! Surely he was forced to write this letter by the kidnapers. They are playing for time. Surely you can see that they are playing for time!"

CHAPTER 14

THE SCARLET BRIDES

IN A SMALL, book-lined room, high above New York City, dimly lighted and pervaded by a faint smell of incense, Dr. Fu Manchu, wearing a yellow robe but with no cap crowning his massive skull, sat behind a large lacquered table, his eyes closed. From a little incense burner on one corner of this table a faint spiral of smoke arose-some might have ascribed this to a streak of effeminacy in an otherwise great man, but one who knew the potency of burning perfumes as understood in the ancient Orient would have placed a different construction upon the circumstances. The Delphic Oracle was so inspired; incense cunningly prepared, such as the *khyfi* of the ancient Egyptians, can exalt the subconscious mind. A voice was speaking as though someone stood in the room, although except for the presence of the majestic Chinaman it was empty.

Dr. Fu Manchu pressed a button, the voice ceased, and there was silence in the incense-laden place. For two, three, five minutes the Chinaman sat motionless, his lean, long-fingered hands resting upon the table before him, his eyes closed.

"I am here, Master," said a feeble voice speaking in Chinese.

"Listed carefully," Dr. Fu Manchu replied in the same language. "It is urgent How many of our Scarlet Brides from New Zealand have you in reserve?"

"Fifteen, Master. I sacrificed five in the case of the man James Richet, fearing that some might not survive the cold."

"It is reported that Danger Number One—I hear you hiss, my friend—invariably sleeps with his windows open. Sacrifice ten more of our little friends. See that he does not sleep alone to-night."

"My lord, I have no one who could undertake the work. If I had Ali Khan or Quong Wah, or any one of our old servants. But I have none. What can I do in this uncivilized land to which my lord has exiled me?"

Several moments of silence followed. The long ivory hands

with their incredible nails, beautiful even in their cruelty, rested motionless upon the table, then:

"Await orders," said the imperious, guttural voice.

Another button was depressed and there was silence. The pencil of smoke rising from the incense burner was growing more and more faint. Dr. Fu Manchu opened his eyes, staring straight before him; his eyes were green as emeralds, glittering gems reflecting an inexorable will. His right hand moved to a small switchboard. He inserted a plug, and presently a spot of red light indicted that he was connected.

"Is that 'A' New York?"

"Kern Adler here."

"You know to whom you are speaking?"

"Yes. What can I do for you, President?"

The voice was unctuous but nervous.

"We have not yet met," the imperious tone continued, "but I assume, otherwise I should not have appointed you, that you can command the services of the New York underworld?"

There was a perceptible pause before Kern Alder replied.

"If you would tell me, President, exactly what you want, I should be better able to answer."

"I want the man called Peter Carlo. Find him for me. I will then give you further instructions."

Another pause . . .

"I can find him, President." The nervous voice replied "but only through Blondie Hahn."

"I distrust this man Hahn. You have recommended him, but I have not yet accepted him. I have my reasons. However, speak to him now. You know my wishes. Report to me when they can be carried out."

The red light continued to glow; one yellow finger pressed a small switch with the result that the office of Kern Adler, Attorney, and one of the biggest survivors of the underworld clean-up, seemed to become acoustically translated to the study of Dr. Fu Manchu. Adler could be heard urgently calling a number; and presently he got it.

"Hello, Kern," came a coarse voice; "want the boss, I guess. Hold on; I'll get him." There was an interval during which dim sounds of dance music penetrated to the incense-laden room, then:

312

"Hello, Kern," came in a deep bass; "what's new with you?"

"Listen, Blondie. I'm telling you something. If you want a quiet life you have to fall into line. I mean it. It'll be good for your health to go to work again. Either you come in right now or you stay right out. I want something done to-night—you have got to do it."

"Listen to me, Kern. You've spilled a mouthful. But what you don't seem to know is this: you've been washed up—and you figure you're still afloat. You're stone dead but you won't lie down. Come clean and I'll talk to you. I'm standing all ready on my two big feet. I don't need your protection."

"I want 'Fly' Carlo, and I'm prepared to pay for him. He has to get busy to-night. President's orders——"

"President nothing! But listen—you can have Carlo, when *I* hold the pay roll. That's my terms now and always. What's the figure? Carlo will cost the President (like hell he's the President!) all of two thousand dollars. He can only get him through me. I'm his sole agent and my rake-off is my own pidgin."

"Your terms are ridiculous, Blondie. Talk sense."

"I'm talking sense all right. And I've got something very particular to say to *you*." The deep, gruff voice was menacing "Somebody got busy among my records last night while I was at a party. If I thought it was *you*, I'd steal you away from your girl friends, little man. Next time you wrote a love letter it'd be with a quill from an angel's wing."

At which moment Kern Adler's line became suddenly disconnected.

"Hello there!" Hahn bawled. "You cut me off! What in hell——"

His protests were silenced. A guttural voice came across the wires:

"You have been put through to *me*—the President. . . . Paul Erckmann Hahn—I believe this is your name?—you possess a certain brute force which attracts me. You are crude; but you might possibly be used."

"Used?" Hahn's voice sounded stifled. "Listen——"

"When I speak, it is *you* who must listen. The person 'who got busy among your records,' as you term it, was one of my own agents—in no way connected with Kern Adler. I learned much that I had wished to know about you, Mr. Hahn . . ."

"Is that so?" came a bull-like bellow. "Then listen, pet!—
You're a Chink if I ever heard one. That tells me plenty. I've
been checking up on *you*. The 'G' men are right on your tail,
yellow baby. Centre Street has got your fingerprints, and
Hoover knows your toenails by sight. You're using an old hide-
out in Chinatown, and there's a blue-eyed boy from Britain on
the trail. You're in up to the ears, President. You'll need me
badly to save your scalp. Adler can't do it. He's out of print.
Come up to date and talk terms."

Long ivory fingers remained quite motionless upon the
table. Dr. Fu Manchu's eyes were closed.

"Your remarks impress me," he said softly, sibilantly. "I feel
that you are indispensable to my plans. By all means let us
talk terms. The matter is urgent. . . ."

II

Mark Hepburn tried, and tried in vain, to sleep. The image
of a woman haunted him. He had checked her up as far as
possible. He thought that he had her record fairly complete.

She was the widow of a United States naval officer. Her
husband had been killed in the Philippines three years
before. There was one child of the marriage—a boy. In fact,
the credentials with which she had come to Abbot Donegal
were authentic in every way. A thousand times, day and
night, he had found himself in an imaginary world sweeter
than reality—looking into those deep blue eyes. He found it
impossible to believe that this woman would stoop to anything criminal. He would not entertain the idea despite
damning facts against her.

He wanted to hear evidence for the defence, and he was
fully prepared to take it seriously. In all his investigations he
hoped yet feared to come across her. He wondered if at last he
had fallen in love—and with a worthless woman. Her flight
on that night from the Tower of the Holy Thorn, the fact that
she had been endeavouring to smuggle away the incriminat-
ing manuscript which explained the collapse of Abbot
Donegal; these things required explanation. Yet the official

record of Moya Eileen Adair, as far as he had traced it, indicated that she was a young gentlewoman of unblemished character.

She came from County Wicklow in Ireland; her father, Commander Breon, was still serving with the British navy. She had met her late husband during the visit of an American fleet to Bermuda, where she had been staying with relatives. He was of Irish descent; he, too, was a man of the sea, and they had been married before the American fleet sailed. All this Mark Hepburn had learned in the space of a few days, employing those wonderful resources at his disposal Now, tossing wearily on his bed, he challenged himself. Had he been justified in instructing more than twenty agents, in expending nearly a thousand dollars in radio and cable messages, to secure this information?

The fate of the country was kept spinning in the air by those who juggled with lives. Sane men prayed that the Constitution should stand foursquare; others believed that its remodelling as preached by Dr. Prescott would form the foundations of a new Utopia. Others, more mad, saw in the dictatorship of Harvey Bragg a Golden Age for all. . . . And the Abbot of Holy Thorn held a choir of seven million voices in check awaiting the baton of his rhetoric.

Bribery and corruption gnawed rat-like into the very foundations of the State; murder, insolent, stalked the city streets. . . And he, Mark Hepburn, expended his energies tracing the history of one woman. As he lay tossing upon his pillow the whole-hearted enthusiasm of Sir Denis Nayland Smith became a reproach.

Then suddenly, he sprang upright in bed, repeater in hand. The door of his room had been opened very quietly. . . .

"Hands up!" he rasped. "Quick!"

"Not so loud, Hepburn, not so loud."

It was Nayland Smith.

"Sir Denis!"

Smith was crossing the room in his direction.

"I don't want to arouse Fey," the incisive but guarded tones continued. "He has had a trying day. But it's *our* job, Hepburn. Don't make any noise; just slip along with me to my room. . . . Bring the gun."

In silence, pyjama-clad, barefooted, Hepburn went along the corridor, turning right just before reaching the vestibule. In the room occupied by Nayland Smith the atmosphere was perceptibly cooler. The windows were wide open; heavy curtains were drawn widely apart; a prospect of a million lights gleamed far below; the muted roar of New York's ceaseless traffic rose like rumbling of distant thunder.

"Close the door."

Mark Hepburn closed the door behind him as he entered.

"You will notice," Nayland Smith continued, "that I have not been smoking for some time, although I have been wide awake. I was afraid of the glow from my pipe."

"Why?"

"For this reason, Hepburn. Our brilliant enemy has become a slave to routine. It is now almost a habit with him to test his death-agents upon someone else, and if the result is satisfactory to try them on me . . ."

"I'm not too clear about what you mean——"

"I mean that unless I am greatly mistaken, I am about to be subjected to an attempt upon my life by Dr. Fu Manchu!"

"What! But you are forty storeys up from the street!"

"We shall see. You may remember that I deduced the arrival of certain weapons in the Doctor's armoury from circumstances connected with the death of Richet . . ."

"I remember. But a long night's work was wasted."

"Part of our trade," rapped Nayland Smith dryly. "You will notice, Hepburn—there is ample reflected light—two trunks upon the top of a chest of drawers set against the wall on your left. Climb up and hide yourself behind the trunks—I have placed a chair for the purpose. Your job is to watch the windows but not to be seen——"

"Good God!" Hepburn whispered, and clutched Smith's arm.

"What is it?"

"There's someone in your bed!"

"There's no one in my bed, Hepburn, nor is there any time to waste. This job is life or death. Get to your post."

Mark Hepburn rallied his resources: that shock of discovering the apparent presence of someone in the bed had shaken him. But now he was icily cool again, cool as Nayland

Smith. He climbed on to the chest of drawers, curled up there behind the trunks, although space was limited, in such a manner that he had a view of the windows while remaining invisible from anyone in the room. This achieved:

"Where are you, Sir Denis?" he asked, speaking in a low voice.

"Also entrenched, Hepburn. Do nothing until I give the word. And now listen. . . ."

Mark Hepburn began to listen. Clearly he sensed that the menace came from the windows, although its nature was a mystery to him. He heard the hooting of taxis, the eerie wail which denotes that the Fire Department is out, the concerted whine of motor engines innumerable. Then, more intimately, these sounds becoming a background, he heard something else. . . .

It was a very faint noise but a very curious one; almost it might have been translated as the impact of some night bird, or of a bat, against the stone face of the building. . . .

He listened intently, aware of the fact that his heartbeats had accelerated. He allowed his glance to wander for a moment in quest of Nayland Smith. Presently, accustomed now to the peculiar light of the room, he detected him. He was crouching on a glass-topped bureau, set just right of the window, holding what Hepburn took to be a sawn-off shot-gun in his hand.

Then again Hepburn directed the whole of his attention to the windows.

Clearly outlined against a sullen sky he could see one of New York's tallest buildings. Only three of its many windows showed any light; one at the very top, just beneath the cupola, and two more in the dome itself which crowned the tall, slender structure. Tensed as he was, listening, waiting, for what was to come, the thought flashed through his mind: Who lived in those high, lonely rooms—who was awake there at this hour?

Another curious light was visible from where he lay—a red glow somewhere away to the left towards the river; a constantly changing light of which he could see only the outer halo. Then a moving blur appeared far below, and a rumbling sound told him that a train was passing. . . .

Suddenly, unexpectedly, a sharp silhouette obscured much of this dim nocturne. . . .

Something out of that exotic background belonging to the man who, alone, shared this vigil to-night, had crept up between the distant twinkling lights and Mark Hepburn's view.

Vaguely he realized that the phenomenon was due to the fact that someone, miraculously, had climbed the face of the building, or part of it, and now, as he saw, was supporting himself upon the ledge. There was a moment of tense silence. It was followed by activity on the part of the invader perched perilously outside. A light, yellow-muffled, shone into the room, its searching ray questing around, to rest finally for a moment upon the bed.

Mark Hepburn held his breath; almost, he betrayed his presence.

The appearance of the disordered bed suggested that a sleeper, sheets drawn up right over his head, lay there!

"Dr. Fu Manchu has become a slave of routine"—Nayland Smith's words echoed in Hepburn's mind. "It is almost a habit with him to test his death-agents upon someone else, and if the result is satisfactory to try them on me."

The shadowy silhouette perched upon the window ledge projected some kind of slender telescopic rod into the room. It stretched out towards the bed. . . . Upon it depended what looked like a square box. The rod was withdrawn. The visitor accomplished this with a minimum of noise. Hepburn, his ears attuned for the welcome word of command, watched. An invisible line was wound in, tautened, and jerked.

Suddenly came a loud and insistent hissing, and:

"Shoot!" snapped the voice of Nayland Smith. "Shoot that man, Hepburn!"

III

The shadowy shape at the window had not moved from that constrained, crouching attitude—two enormous hands, which appeared to be black, rested on the window ledge—when Mark Hepburn fired—once, twice. . . . The sinister silhouette

318

disappeared; that strange hissing continued; the muted roar of New York carried on.

Yet, automatic dropped beside him, fist clenched, he listened so intently, so breathlessly, that he heard it. . . .

A dull thud in some courtyard far below.

"Don't move, Hepburn," came Nayland Smith's crisp command. "Don't stir until I give the word!"

An indeterminable odour became perceptible—chemical, nauseating. . . .

"Sir Denis!"

It was the voice of Fey.

"Don't come in, Fey!" cried Nayland Smith. "Don't open the door!"

"Very good, sir."

Only a very keen observer would have recognized the note of emotion in Fey's almost toneless voice.

The hissing noise continued.

"This is terrible!" Hepburn exclaimed. "Sir Denis! What has happened?"

The hissing ceased: Hepburn had identified it now.

"There's a switch on your right," came swiftly. "See if you can reach it, but stay where you are."

Hepburn, altering his position, reached out, found the switch, and depressed it. Lights sprang up. He turned—and saw Nayland Smith poised on top of the bureau. The strange weapon which vaguely he had seen in the darkness proved to be a large syringe fitted with a long nozzle.

The air was heavy with a sickly sweet smell suggesting at once iodine and ether.

He looked towards the bed . . . and would have sworn that a figure lay under the coverlet—a sheet drawn up over its face! On the pillow and beside the place where the sleeper's head seemed to lie rested a small wooden box no more than half the size of those made to contain cigars. One of the narrow sides—that which faced him—was open.

There seemed to be a number of large black spots upon the pillow. . . .

"It's possible," said Nayland Smith, staring across the room, "that I missed the more active. I doubt it. But we must be careful."

Above the muted midnight boom of New York, sounds of disturbance, far below, became audible.

"I'm glad you didn't miss our man, Hepburn!" rapped Nayland Smith, dropping on to the carpeted floor.

"I have been trained to shoot straight," Mark Hepburn replied monotonously.

Nayland Smith nodded.

"He deserved all that came to him. I faked the bed when I heard his approach. . . . Jump into a suit and rejoin me in the sitting-room. We shall be wanted down there at any moment. . . ."

Three minutes later they both stood staring at a row of black insects laid upon a sheet of white paper. The reek of iodine and ether was creeping in from the adjoining bedroom. Fey, at a side table, prepared whiskies imperturbably. He was correctly dressed except for two trifling irregularities: his collar was that of a pyjama jacket, and he wore bedroom slippers.

"This is your province, Hepburn," said Nayland Smith. "These things are outside my experience. But you will note that they are quite dead, with their legs curled up. The preparation I used in the syringe is a simple formula by my old friend Petrie: he found it useful in Egypt. . . . Thank you, Fey."

Mark Hepburn studied the dead insects through a hand-lens. Shrunken up as they were by the merciless spray which had destroyed them, upon their dense black bodies he clearly saw vivid scarlet spots—"Scarlet spots"—the last words spoken by James Richet!

"What are they, Hepburn?"

"I'm not sure. They belong to the genus *Latrodectus*. The malmignatte of Italy is a species, and the American Black Widow spider; but these are larger. Their bite is probably deadly."

"Their bite is certainly deadly!" rapped Nayland Smith. "An attack by two or more evidently results in death within three minutes—also a characteristic vivid scarlet rash. You know, now, what was in the cardboard box which James Richet opened in the taxi-cab! No doubt he had orders to open it at the moment that he reached the hotel. One of the Doctor's jests. I take it they are tropical?"

"Beyond doubt."

"Once exposed to the frosty air, and their deadly work done, they would die. You know, now, why I provided myself with that"—he pointed to the syringe. "I have met other servants of Fu Manchu to whom a stone-faced building was a grand staircase."

"Good God!" Mark Hepburn said hoarsely. "This man is a fiend—a sadistic madman——"

"Or a genius, Hepburn! If you will glance at the receptacle which our late visitor deposited on my pillow, you will notice that it is made from a common cigar box. One side lifts shutterwise: there is a small spring. It was controlled, you see, by this length of fine twine, one end of which still rests on the window ledge. This hook on top was intended to enable the Doctor's servant to lift it into the room on the end of the telescopic rod. The box is lightly lined with hay. You may safely examine it. I have satisfied myself that there is nothing alive inside. . . ."

"This man is the most awful creature who has ever appeared in American history," said Hepburn. "The situation was tough enough, anyway. Where does he get these horrors? He must have agents all over the world."

Nayland Smith began to walk up and down, twitching at the lobe of his ear.

"Undoubtedly he has. In my experience I have never felt called upon to step more warily. Also, I begin to think that my powers are failing me."

"What do you mean?"

"For years, Hepburn, for many years, a palpable fact has escaped me. There is a certain very old Chinaman whose records I have come across in all parts of the world; in London, in Liverpool, in Shanghai, in Port Said, Rangoon and Calcutta. Only now, when he is in New York (and God knows how he got here!), have I realized that this dirty old barkeeper is Dr. Fu Manchu's chief of staff!"

Mark Hepburn stared hard at the speaker, and then:

"This accounts for all the men at work in Chinatown," he said slowly. "The man you mean is Sam Pak?"

"Sam Pak—none other," snapped Nayland Smith. "And the truth respecting this ancient reprobate"—he indicated the

321

writing-table—"reached me in its entirety only a few hours ago. If you could see him you would understand my amazement. He is incredibly old, and—so much for my knowledge of the East—I had always set him down as one step above the mendicant class. Yet, in the days of the empress, he was governor of a great province; in fact, he was Dr. Fu Manchu's political senior! He was one of the first Chinamen to graduate at Cambridge, and he holds a science degree of Heidelberg."

"Yet in your knowledge of him he has worked in slums in Chinatown—been a barkeeper?"

"It might occur in Russia to-morrow, Hepburn There are princes, grand dukes—I am not speaking of gigolos or soi-disant noblemen—spread about the world who, the right man giving the word, would work as scavengers, if called upon, to restore the Tsars."

"That's true enough."

"And so, you see, we have got to find this aged Chinaman. I suspect that he has brought with him an arsenal of these unpleasant weapons which the doctor employs so successfully—Hullo! There's the phone. We are wanted to identify the climber. . . ."

CHAPTER 15

THE SCARLET BRIDES (*concluded*)

OLD SAM PAK was performing his nightly rounds of Base 3. Two Chinese boys were in attendance.

Up above, political warfare raged; the newspapers gave prominence to the Washington situation in preference to love, murder, or divorce. Dr. Orwin Prescott was reported to be "resting up before the battle." Harvey Bragg was well in the news. Other aspirants to political eminence might be found elsewhere: "Bluebeard of the Backwoods" was front-page stuff. America was beginning to take Harvey Bragg seriously.

But in the mysterious silence of Base 3, old Sam Pak held absolute sway. Chinatown can keep its secrets. Only by exercise of a special sense, which comes to life after years of experience in the ways of the Orient, may a Westerner know when something strange is afoot. Sidelong glances; sudden silences; furtive departures as the intruder enters. Police officers in Mott Street area had been reporting such trivial occurrences recently. Those responsible for diagnosing Asiatic symptom had deduced the arrival in New York of a Chinese big-shot.

Their diagnosis was correct. By this time every Chinaman from coast to coast knew that one of the Council of Seven controlling the Si-Fan, most dreaded secret society in the East, had entered America.

Sam Pak pursued his rounds. The place was a cunning maze of passages and stairs; a Chinese rabbit warren. One narrow passage, below the level of the room of the seven-eyed goddess, had a row of six highly-painted coffins ranged along its wall. They lay on their sides. Lids had been removed and plate glass substituted. This ghastly tunnel was vile with the smell of ancient rottenness.

One of Sam Pak's attendant Chinamen switched on a light. The old mandarin, who had known nearly a century of vicissitudes, carried a great bunch of keys. In his progress he had tried door after door. He now tested the small traps set in the sides of the six coffins. In the sudden glare, insidious nocturnal things moved behind glass. . . .

There was a big iron door in the wall; it possessed three locks, all of which proved to be fastened. Here at once was part of that strange arsenal which Nayland Smith suspected to have been imported , and a secret sally-port the existence of which police headquarters would have given much to know about. It communicated with an old subterranean passage which led to the East River. . . .

On a floor above, Sam Pak opened a grille and looked into a neatly appointed bedroom. Dr. Orwin Prescott lay there sleeping. His face was very white.

A dim whirring sound broke the underground silence. Sam Pak handed the bunch of keys to one of the boys and shuffled slowly upstairs to the temple of the green-eyed goddess. It was in semi-darkness; the only light came through the coloured silk curtain draped before one of the stone cubicles.

Sam Pak crossed, drew the curtain aside, and spoke in Chinese:

"I am here, Master."

"You grow old, my friend," the cold, imperious tones of Dr. Fu Manchu replied. "You keep me waiting. I regret that you have refused to accept my offer to arrest your descent to the tomb."

"I prefer to join my ancestors, marquis, when the call reaches me. I fear your wisdom. While I live I am with you body and soul in our great aims. When my hour comes I shall be glad to die."

Silence fell. Old Sam Pak, withered hands tucked in wide sleeves, stooping, waited. . . .

"I will hear your own report on the matter which I entrusted to you."

"You know already, Master, that the man, Peter Carlo, failed. I cannot say what evidence he left behind. But your orders regarding the other, Blondie Hahn, were carried out. He brought the man Carlo to Wu King's Bar, and I interviewed them in the private room. I instructed Carlo, and he set out. I then paid Hahn his price. It was a waste of good money, but I obey. Ah Fu and Chung Chow did the rest . . . there are now only three Scarlet Brides left to us. . . ."

It was an hour after dawn when Nayland Smith and Mark Hepburn stood looking down at two stone slabs upon which two bodies lay.

One of the departed in life had been a small but very muscular Italian with uncommonly large, powerful hands. He presented a spectacle, owing to his many injuries, which must have revolted all but the toughest. There was a sound of dripping water.

"You have prepared your report, Doctor?" said Nayland Smith, addressing a plump, red-faced person who was smiling amiably at the exhibits as though he loved them.

"Certainly, Mr. Smith," the police doctor returned cheerily. "It is quite clear that Number One, here (I call him Number One because he was brought in an hour ahead of the other), died as the result of a fall from a great height——"

"Very great height," rapped Nayland Smith. "Fortieth floor of the Regal Tower."

"So I understand. Remarkable. He has two bullet wounds: one in his right hand and one in his shoulder. These would not have caused death, of course. It was the fall which killed him—quite naturally. I believe he was wearing black silk gloves. An electric torch and a telescopic rod of very bright metal were found near the body."

Nayland Smith turned to a police officer who stood at his elbow.

"I am told, Inspector, that you have now checked up on this man's history: there is no doubt about his identity?"

"None at all," drawled the inspector, who was chewing gum. "He's Peter Carlo, known as 'The Fly'—one of the most expert upper-storey men in New York. He could have climbed the outside of the Statue of Liberty if there'd been anything worth stealing at the top. He always wore a black silk mask and silk gloves. The rod was to reach into rooms he couldn't actually enter. He was so clever he could lift a lady's ring from a dressing-table fifteen feet away!"

"I don't doubt it," muttered Mark Hepburn. "So much for Peter Carlo. And now . . ."

He turned to the second slab.

Upon it lay the body of a huge blond man of Teutonic type. His hands were so swollen that two glittering diamonds which adorned them had become deeply embedded in the puffy fingers. Sodden garments clung to his great frame. Scarlet spots were discernible on both of the hairy hands, and there was a scarlet discolouration on his throat. The glare of his china-blue eyes set in that bloated caricature of what had been a truculently strong face afforded a sight even more dreadful than that of the shattered body of Peter Carlo.

"Brought it from the river just north of Manhattan Bridge ten minutes before you arrived," explained Inspector McGrew, chewing industriously. "May be no connection, but I thought you'd like to see him."

He glanced around, meeting a curiously piercing glance from Federal Agent Smith as he did so. Federal Agent Smith had steely eyes set in a sun-browned face framed, now, in the fur collar of his topcoat; a disconcerting person, in Inspector McGrew's opinion.

"Now, here," explained the smiling police surgeon, "we have a really mysterious case! Although his body was hauled out of East River, he was not drowned——"

"Why do you say so?" Smith demanded.

"It's obvious." The surgeon became enthusiastic and, stepping forward, laid a finger on the bloated, discoloured skin. "Note the vivid scarlet urticarial rash which characterizes the oedema. This man died from some toxic agency: he was thrown into the river. A post-mortem examination will tell us more, but of this much I am sure. And I understand, Inspector"—glancing over his shoulder—"that he, also, is well known to the police?"

"Well known to the police!" echoed Inspector McGrew, "he's well known all over New York. This is Blondie Hahn, one of the big shots of the old days. He was booking agent for 'most all the gunmen that remain in town. These times, I guess he had a monopoly. He ran a downtown restaurant, and although we knew his game, he had strong political protection."

"You are prepared to make your report, Doctor?" said Smith rapidly. "I examined Carlo shortly after he was found. I presume we can now search the person and garments of Hahn."

326

"That's been done already," Inspector McGrew replied. "The stuff is on the table inside."

The grey-blue eyes of Federal Agent Smith glared out from the haggard brown mask of his face. Inspector McGrew was a hard man, but he found himself transfixed by that icy stare.

"Those were not my orders!"

"It had been done before the Federal instructions came through."

"I want to know by whose authority!" The speaker's piercing glance never left McGrew's face. "I won't be interfered with in this way. You are dealing, Inspector, not with the operations of a common, successful crook, but with something bigger, vastly bigger than you even imagine. Any orders you receive from me must be carried out to the letter."

"I'm sorry," said the inspector, an expression he had not used for many years, unless possibly to his wife; "but we didn't know you were interested in Hahn, and the boys just went through with the routine."

"Show me these things."

Inspector McGrew opened a door, and Nayland Smith walked through to an inner room, followed by Hepburn and the inspector. In the doorway he turned, and addressing a grim-looking man in oilskins:

"I understand," he said, "that you were in charge of the boat which recovered the body. I shall want to see you later."

On a large, plain, pine table two sets of exhibits were displayed. The first consisted of a nearly empty packet of Lucky Strike cigarettes, a lighter, a black silk mask, black silk gloves, a quill tooth-pick, three one-dollar bills, and an eight-inch metal baton—which contained fifteen feet of telescopic rods. Smith examined these, the sole possessions found upon Fly Carlo, quickly but carefully. He had seen them already.

"You understand," McGrew explained, "Hahn had only just been brought in—our routine was interrupted."

"Forget your ordinary routine," came rapidly. "From now on *your* routine is *my* routine."

Federal Officer Smith transferred his attention to the second set of exhibits. These were more numerous than interesting. There was a very formidable magazine pistol of German manufacture; a small pear-shaped object easily identified as a

327

hand grenade; a gold cigar-case decorated with a crest; a body-belt, the pockets of which had been emptied of their contents: ten twenty-dollar gold pieces; an aluminium lighter, two silk handkerchiefs; a diamond pin; a bunch of keys; a packet of chewing gum; and a large shagreen wallet, the contents of which had been removed. These were: a number of letters, and a photograph sodden by immersion. There was, lastly, a limp carton which had once contained playing cards, and two thousand dollars in hundred-dollar bills.

"Where was the diamond pin?" snapped Nayland Smith.

"He always wore it in his coat like a badge," Inspector McGrew replied.

"Where were the dollar bills?"

"Right in the card-holder?"

"Can you think of any reason," Smith asked "why a man should carry money in a card-holder?"

"No," the inspector admitted; "I can't."

"Assuming that this money had just been sent to him, can you think of any reason why it should be sent in such a way?"

"No."

Inspector McGrew shook his head blankly, staring in a fascinated way at the speaker.

"Yet the card-holder," Nayland Smith continued, "is the solution of the mystery of Blondie Hahn's death." He turned abruptly—he seemed to move on springs—the man's nervous tension was electrical. "I want all these exhibits to go with me in the car."

He rested his hand on Mark Hepburn's shoulder. Hepburn looked very pale in the grey light.

"Note the two thousand dollars in the card case," he said in a low voice. "There was something else in there as well. Dr. Fu Manchu always settles his debts . . . sometimes with interest. . . ."

CHAPTER 16

"BLUEBEARD"

MOYA ADAIR closed her eyes as those green eyes opened. The man behind the table spoke, in that imperious, high-pitched voice.

"I accept your explanation," he said. "None of us is infallible."

Mrs. Adair raised her lashes and tried to sustain the speaker's regard, but failed, turning her glance aside.

The face of Dr. Fu Manchu sometimes reminded her of a devil mask which hung upon the wall of her father's study in Ireland.

"You serve me admirably. I regret that your service is one of fear. I prefer enthusiasm. You are a beautiful woman; for this reason I have employed you. Men are creatures of wax which white fingers can mould to their will—to my will. For always, Moya Adair, *your* will must be *my* will—or, we shall part. . . ."

The blue eyes were turned swiftly in his direction, and then swiftly away again. Mrs. Adair was perfectly dressed, perfectly groomed and apparently perfectly composed. This awful Chinaman who had taken command of her life held in his grasp all that made life dear to her. Her gloved hand rested motionless upon the chair-arm, but she turned her head aside and bit her lip.

The air of the small, quiet room was heavy with a smell of stale incense.

"I am an old man," the compelling voice continued; "older than your imagination would permit you to believe." Those jade-green eyes were closed again—the speaker seemed to be thinking aloud. "I have been worshipped, I have been scorned; I have been flattered, mocked, betrayed, treated as a charlatan—as a criminal. There are warrants for my arrest in three European countries. Yet, always I have been selfless." He paused. He was so still, so seemingly impassive, that he might have been a carven image. . . .

"My crimes, so termed, have been merely the removal from my path of those who obstructed me. Always I have dreamed of a sane world, yet men have called me mad; of a world in which war should be impossible, disease eliminated, over-population checked, labour found for all willing hands—a world of peace. Save only three, I have found no human soul, of my own race or another, to work wholly for that goal. And now my most implacable enemy is upon me. . . ."

Suddenly the green eyes opened. Long, slender yellow hands with incredibly pointed nails were torn from the sleeves of the yellow robe. Dr. Fu Manchu stood upright, raising those evilly beautiful hands above him. A note of exaltation came into his voice. Mrs. Adair clutched the arms of the chair in which she sat. Never before had her eventful life brought her in touch with inspired fanaticism.

"Gods of my fathers"—pitched so high that strange voice laid a queer stress on sibilants—"masters of the world! Are all my dreams to end in a prison cell, in the death of a common felon?"

For a while he stood upright, arms upraised, then dropped back again into his chair and concealed his hands in the sleeves of his robe.

Moya Adair strove for composure. This man terrified her as no man in her experience ever had had power to do. Instinctively she had realized the dreadful crimes that marked his life. He was coldly remorseless. Now, shaken emotionally by this glimpse of the hidden Fu Manchu, she wondered if she had become subjected to an inspired madman. Or had this eerie master of her destiny achieved a philosophy beyond the reach of her intellectual powers?

When the chinaman spoke again his harsh voice was perfectly cool.

"In the United States I have found a crude, but efficient, organization ready to my hand. Prohibition attracted to this country the trained law-breakers of the world. They had no purpose but that of personal gain. The sanity of President Roosevelt has terminated some of these promising careers. Many spiders are missing, but the webs can be mended. You see, Moya Adair"—the green eyes were fixed upon her, glittering, hypnotically—"although women can never under-

330

stand, were not meant to understand—it is to women that men always look for understanding."

Now she was unable to withdraw her gaze. He had taken control of her—she knew herself helpless. There was magic in those long green eyes; their power was terrible. But something there was also—something she had not looked for—which reconciled her to this control.

"I do not trust you—no woman is to be trusted in a world of men. Yet because I am a man too, and very lonely in this my last battle to crush what the West calls civilization . . . I will admit you one step further into my plans—I have means of watching those who profess to serve me. I know where I can place my trust. . . ."

Mrs. Adair experienced a sensation as though the speaker's eyes had usurped the whole of the small room. She was submerged in a green lake, magnetic, thrilling, absorbing. The strange voice reached her from far away: she was resigned to the thraldom.

"There is no crime except the crime of disobedience to my will. My conception of life transcends the laws of all men living to-day. When I achieve my ambition, those who stand beside me will share my mastery of the world. Of the demagogues battling for power in this troubled country I have selected one as my own. . . ."

Moya Adair emerged from the green lake. Dr. Fu Manchu had closed his eyes. He sat like a craven image of a dead god behind the lacquered table.

"I am sending you," the guttural, imperious voice continued, "to Harvey Bragg." You will act in accordance with instructions."

II

In the large Park Avenue apartment of Emmanuel Dumas, Harvey Bragg was holding one of those receptions which at once scandalized and fascinated his millions of followers when they read about them in the daily newspapers. These orgiastic entertainments which sometimes resembled a burlesque of a Neronian banquet and sometimes a parody of a

331

Hollywood cabaret scene, had marked his triumphal progress from the state which he represented right up to New York.

"Bluebeard of the Backwoods"—as some political writer had dubbed him—Bragg had interested, amused, scandalized and horrified the inhabitants of the South and of the Middle West, and now was preparing to show himself a second Cyrus, master of modern Babylon. New York was the bright orange upon which the greedy eyes were set. New York he would squeeze dry.

Lola Dumas' somewhat equivocal place in his affairs merely served to add glamour to the man's strange reputation. Now, entertaining in her father's home, he demonstrated himself to be that which he believed himself to be—an up-to-date emperor whose wishes transcended all laws.

Lola had been twice married and twice divorced. After each of these divorces she had reverted to her family name, of which she was inordinately proud. Emmanuel Dumas, who had made a colossal fortune in the boom and lost most of it in the slump, claimed, without warranty which any man could recognize, to be descended from the brilliant quadroon who created the Three Musketeers. If a picturesque personality and a shock of frizzy white hair had been acceptable as evidence, then any jury must have granted his claim.

A moral laxity, notable even during the régime of Prohibition, had characterized his scandalous life. In later years, when most of his Wall Street contemporaries had been washed up, the continued prosperity of Emmanuel Dumas became a mystery insoluble. The prurient ascribed it to the association between his beautiful daughter and the flamboyant but eccentric politician who threatened to become the Mussolini of the United States.

The room in which the reception was being held was decorated with a valuable collection of original drawings by Maurice Leloir, representing episodes in the novels of Alexandre Dumas. Rapiers, pistols, muskets adorned the walls. Here was a suit of armour which had once belonged to Louis XIII; there a red hat in a glass case, which, according to an inscription, had been worn by that king's subtle minister, the Cardinal de Richelieu. There were powder boxes, mirrors and jewels, once the property of Anne of Austria. These historical objects, and many others, arrested the glance in every direction.

Lola Dumas wore an emerald-green robe, or rest gown, its gauzy texture scarcely more than veiling her slender body. She was surrounded by a group of enthusiastic journalists. Her father was attired in a sort of velvet smock tied with a loose black bow at his neck. He, also, held court.

As a prominent supporter, and frequently the host, of Harvey Bragg, he had entered upon a new term of notoriety. These two, father and daughter, by virtue of their beauty alone—for Emmanuel Dumas was a strikingly handsome man—must have focussed interest in almost any gathering.

The room was packed from end to end. Prominent society people, who once would have shunned the Dumas' apartment, might be seen in groups admiring the strange ornaments, studying the paintings; eager to attract the attention of this singular man once taboo, but now bathed in a blaze of limelight.

Politicians of all shades of opinion were represented.

The air was heavy with tobacco smoke; the buzz of chatter simian; champagne flowed almost as freely as water from the fountains of Versailles. Many notable people came and went unnoticed from this omnium-gatherum, for the dazzling personalities of the hostess and her father outshone them all. One would have thought that no man and few women could have diverted attention from the glittering pair; yet when, unheralded, Harvey Bragg came striding into the room, instantly the Dumas were forgotten.

All eyes turned in Bragg's direction. Sascha lamps appeared from leather cases in which they had lain ready; a platoon of cameras came into action; notebooks were hastily opened.

Bluebeard Bragg was certainly an arresting figure. His nick-name was double-edged, Bragg's marital record alone would have explained it; the man's intense swarthiness equally might have accounted for the "bluebeard". Slightly above medium height, he was built like an acrobat. The span of his shoulders was enormous: his waist measurement would have pleased many women. Withal, he had that enormous development of thigh and the muscular shapely calves seen in male members of the Russian Ballet. He had , too, the light, springy walk of a boxer; and his truculent, black-brown face, lighted by clear hazel eyes that danced with humour, was crowned by a profusion of straight, gleaming, black hair. Closely though he was shaved—for Harvey Bragg was meticulous in his person—his jaw and chin showed blue through the powder.

"Folks!" he cried—his voice resembled that of a ship's officer bellowing orders through a gale—"I'm real sorry to be late, but Mr. and Miss Dumas will have been taking good care of you, I guess. To tell you the truth, folks, I had a bad hangover . . ."

This admission was greeted by laughter from his followers.

"I've just got up, that's the truth. Knew I was expected to see people; jumped in the bath, shaved and here I am!"

There came a dazzling flash of light. The cameras had secured a record, in characteristic pose and costume, of this ex-lord of the backwoods who aimed at the White House.

He wore a sky-blue bathrobe, and apart from a pair of red slippers, apparently nothing else. But he was Harvey Bragg— Bluebeard; the man who threatened the Constitution, the coming Hitler of the United States. His ugliness—for despite his power and the athletic lines of his figure the man was ugly—dominated that gathering. His circus showman's voice shouted down all opposition. No normal personality could live near him. He was Harvey Bragg. He was "It." He was the omnipresent potential Dictator of America.

Among the group of reporters hanging on Bragg's words was one strange to the others; a newcomer representing New York's smartest weekly. He was tall, taciturn, and slightly built. He had thick, untidy hair, greying over the temples, a stubbly black beard and moustache, and wore spectacles. His wide-brimmed black hat and caped coat spoke of Greenwich Village.

His deep-set eyes had missed nothing, and nobody, of importance in the room. He had made few notes. Now he was watching Bluebeard intently.

"Boys and girls!"—arms raised, Harvey Bragg gave his benediction to everyone present—"I know what you all want to hear. You want to hear what I'm going to say to Orwin Prescott at Carnegie Hall."

He lowered his arms in acknowledgement of the excited buzz followed by silence which greeted this remark.

"I'm going to say just one thing. And this goes, boys"—he included with a sweeping gesture of his left hand the whole of the newspaper men present—"with you as well as with everybody else. I'm going to say just this: Our country, which we all love, is unhappy. We have seen hard times—but we've battled through. We've got sand. We're not dead yet by a long shot. No, sir! But we're alive to the dangers ahead. Are you peddling junk for the Abbot of Holy Thorn or are you selling goods of your own?"

Loud applause followed this, led by Dumas *père et fille*.

"I'm not saying, folks, that Abbot Donegal's stuff is all backfire. I'm saying that second-hand promises are bad debts. I want to hear of anything that Orwin Prescott has promised which Orwin Prescott has done. *I* don't promise things. I *do* things. No decent citizen ever reported for work to a depot of the League of Good Americans who didn't get a job!"

Again he was interrupted by loud applause. . . .

"The man we're all looking for is the man who does things. Very well. Seconds out! The fight starts! On my right: Donegal—Prescott. On my left: Harvey Bragg! America for every man and every man for America!"

Cheers and a deafening clapping of hands rewarded the speaker. Harvey Bragg stood, arms upraised forensically, dominating that gathering excited by his crude oratory. At which moment, even as Sascha lights flashed and cameras clicked:

"A lady to see you, Mr. Bragg," came a discreet whisper.

Harvey Bragg lowered his arms, reluctantly relinquishing that heroic pose, and glanced aside. His confidential secretary, Salvaletti, stood at his elbow. There was an interchange of glances. Reporters surged around them.

"Urgent?" Harvey Bragg whispered.

"Number 12."

Bragg started, but recovered himself.

"Easy-looking?"

"A beauty."

"Excuse me, folks!" Bragg cried, his tremendous voice audible above the excitement, "I'll be right back in two minutes."

Of those who actually overheard this whispered conversation, Lola Dumas was one. She bit her lip, turned, and crossed to a senator from the South who was no friend of Harvey Bragg's. The other was the new reporter. He followed Lola Dumas and presently engaged her in conversation.

More wine was uncorked. Newspaper men always welcomed an assignment to the Dumas' apartment. . . .

Rather more than five minutes had elapsed when Harvey Bragg came back. He was holding the hand of a very pretty young woman whose smart frock did justice to a perfect figure, and whose little French hat displayed mahogany curls to their best advantage.

"Folks!" he roared. "I want you all to know my new secretary." His roving glances sought and found Lola Dumas: he smiled wickedly. "What this little girl doesn't know about the political situation not even Harvey Bragg can tell her. . . ."

III

Although one calling might not have suspected the fact, the whole of the Regal Tower, most expensive and fashionable part of the Regal-Athenian Hotel, was held by police officers and federal agents. Those visitors who applied for accommodation in this section of the hotel were informed that it was full; those who had been in occupation had very courteously been moved elsewhere on the plea of urgent alterations.

From porters at the door in the courtyard to the clerks in the reception desk, the liftman and the bell-boys, there was no man whose uniform did not disguise a detective.

Elaborate precautions had been taken to ensure the privacy of incoming and outgoing telephone calls. No general headquarters ever had been more closely guarded. Armageddon was being waged, but few appreciated the fact. In the past Wellington had crushed Bonaparte's ambition to control Europe, but the great Corsican fought at Waterloo with a blunted sword. Foch and his powerful allies had thrown back Marshal von Hindenburg and the finest military machine in history since the retreat from Moscow broke the Grand Army of Napoleon. But now Nayland Smith, backed by the government of the United States, fought, not for the salvage of the Constitution, not for the peace of the country, but for the future of the world. And the opposing forces were commanded by a mad genius. . . .

Dressed in an old tweed suit, pipe clenched between his teeth, he paced up and down the sitting-room. His powers were all that a field-marshal could have demanded. His chief of staff, Mark Hepburn, was one such as he would have selected. But. . . .

Someone had unlocked the door of the apartment.

Fey appeared in the vestibule as if by magic, his right hand in his coat pocket. Nayland Smith stepped smartly to the left, taking up a position from which he could see the entrance. A tall, pale, bearded man came in, wearing a caped coat and a wide-brimmed black hat. . . .

"Hepburn!" cried Smith, and hurried forward to meet him. "Thank heavens you're back safe. What news?"

Captain Mark Hepburn, U.S.M.C., a parody of his normal self, smiled wryly. His pallor, his greying temples, were artificial, but the beard and moustache were carefully tended natural products, although at the moment chemically improved. The character he was assuming was one which he might be called upon to maintain for a considerable time, in accordance with plan.

"Just left the Bragg reception at the Dumas apartment," he said, removing his glasses and staring rather haggardly at Nayland Smith. "There isn't much to report except that Bragg's confidential secretary, Salvaletti, is pretty obviously the link with Fu Manchu."

"Then Bragg is doubly covered," said Nayland Smith grimly. "Lola Dumas is almost certainly one of Dr. Fu Manchu's agents."

"Yes." Mark Hepburn dropped wearily into an armchair. "But there's some friction in that quarter. A woman was announced just before I left, and Bragg went out to interview her. I managed to pick up some scraps of the conversation between Salvaletti and Bragg, but from the way Lola Dumas watched Bragg, I gathered that their relations were becoming strained."

"Describe Salvaletti," said Nayland Smith succinctly.

Mark Hepburn half closed his eyes. Smith watched him. There was something odd in Hepburn's manner.

"Above medium height, pale, stooping. Light-blue eyes, dark, lank hair, a soft voice and a sickly smile."

"Seen him before?"

"Never! He's a new one on me."

"Probably indigenous to the American underworld," Smith murmured; "therefore I should not know him. You are sure it was a woman who was announced?"

"Positive. Harvey Bragg brought her into the room and displayed her to the company as his new secretary. It's about this woman I want to talk to you. I want your advice. I don't know what to do. It was Mrs. Adair. . . . who escaped, thanks to my negligence, from the Tower of the Holy Thorn. . . ."

CHAPTER 17

THE ABBOT'S MOVE

IN THE GOTHIC dome where most of the life of the Memory Man was passed, lights were extinguished. A red spark marking the tip of a burning Egyptian cigarette glowed in the darkness.

There was a short silence, and then:

"Report," directed the familiar, hated voice, "from Numbers covering Nayland Smith."

"Three have been received since I relayed. Shall I repeat them in detail or summarize their contents?"

"Summarize."

"There is no certain evidence that he has left his base during the last twelve hours. A report from Number 44 suggests that he may have visited the police mortuary. This report is unconfirmed. Two Numbers and eight operatives, with two Z-cars, covering Centre Street. Federal Agent Hepburn not reporting to have moved out from the Regal Tower. This is a summary of the three reports."

Darkness still prevailed.

"The latest report regarding Abbot Donegal."

"Received thirty minutes after that last relayed. A man answering to the abbot's description reported as hiring a car at Elmira. Believed to have arrived there from the West by American Airlines. Posing as Englishman. Wears single eyeglass and carries golfing kit. . . ."

In the tower study, so oddly corresponding in point of elevation with Nayland Smith's headquarters, but which bore an atmosphere of stale incense whereas the apartment high above the Regal-Athenian Hotel was laden with fumes of broad-cut smoking mixture, Dr. Fu Manchu sat behind the lacquer table. There was no one else in the room.

The life of one who aspires to empire—though thousands may await his commands—is a wan and lonely life. Solitude is the mother of inspiration. The Chinaman, these reports from the Memory Man received, sat in his high, carven chair, eyes closed. He was speaking as though to one standing near him. On the little polished switchboard two spots of light glowed; green, and amber.

"Dispatch a party in a Z-car," he directed, his voice unemotional but the gutturals very marked. "Explore all farms, roadhouses and hotels along the route which I have indicated. Abbot Donegal is reported as travelling incognito. He may be posing as an English tourist. If found, he is not to be molested, but he must be detained. Instruct the Number in charge to send in reports from point to point. This is a personal order from the President."

A slender yellow hand with long, pointed nails reached out. The two lights disappeared. Dr. Fu Manchu opened his eyes: their greenness was dimmed. He raised the lid of a silver box which stood upon the table and from it took a small, exquisitely made opium-smoking outfit. He lighted the tiny lamp and inserted a gold bodkin into a container holding the black gum which is born of the white poppy. He had not slept for forty-eight hours. . . .

Almost at the same moment, in a room at the top of the Regal Tower, Mark Hepburn spoke on the telephone. He had had all calls put through to his own room in order that Nayland Smith might not be disturbed; for, at last, Smith was sleeping.

"This Englishman who left Airlines at Elmira," he said in his dry, monotonous voice, "sounds to me like the man we're looking for. The fact that he wears plus fours and a monocle doesn't count, nor the fact that he is travelling with a golf bag. I have learned that Abbot Donegal used a single eye-glass before he took to spectacles. He could probably get along with it quite well except for reading. Also, he's a golfer. The English accent means nothing. Abbot Donegal is a trained orator. Check up on all roadhouses and hotels along possible routes which he might follow if, as you suspect, he left by road from Elmira. Take a radio car so we keep track of you. Report from point to point. If he is definitely identified take no action until you have my instructions. We have contrived to silence the newspapers about his disappearance. But he is probably coming to New York to take Prescott's place at Carnegie Hall—if Prescott fails to arrive. This would ruin our plans. . . . All right—good-bye."

He hung up the receiver.

In the vestibule of a small country hotel two men sat over their coffee before a crackling log fire. Outside, a storm raged. The howling of the wind could be heard in the chimney, and whenever the main door was opened a veil of sleet might be seen in the light shining out from inside. It was a wild night.

The men seated before the fire were an odd couple. One, of slight but wiry build, clean-shaven and fresh coloured, lean-faced, his hair greying, wore a tweed suit with plus fours, thick woollen stockings and brown brogues. A monocle glittered in the firelight as he bent to refill his pipe. His companion, a clergyman equally lean of feature, watched him, blinking his eyes in the way of one shortsighted. A close observer might have noted a physical but not a spiritual resemblance.

"I mean to say," said the man with the monocle, stuffing tobacco into the bowl of his briar, "it's a bad time to see America. I agree; but I couldn't help myself, if you see what I mean. It had to be now or never sort of thing. People have been awfully nice——" he paused to strike a match—"I am the silly ass; nobody else to blame. Thanks to you, I know it would be stupid to push on to-night."

"I am told," said the priest, his gentle voice a contrast to that of the other speaker, "that Colonel Challoner lives some twenty miles from here. For my own part I have no choice."

"What!" The man with the monocle, in the act of lighting his pipe, paused, looking up. "You're pushing on?"

"Duty demands."

"Oh, I see, sir. A sick call, I take it?"

The clergyman watched him silently for a few moments.

"A sick call—yes. . . ."

The outer door opened, admitting a blast of icy air. Three men came in, the last to enter closing the door behind him. They were useful-looking men, thick set and hard.

"In luck at last!" one of them exclaimed.

All three were watching the man with the monocle. One, who was evidently the leader of the party, square-jawed and truculent, raised his hand as if to silence the others, and

341

stepped forward. As he did so the proprietor of the hotel appeared through an inner doorway. The man paused, glanced at him.

"Find some Scotch," he ordered—"real Scotch. Not here—inside, some place. Me and these boys have business to talk over."

The proprietor, a taciturn New Englander, nodded and disappeared. The speaker, not removing his hat, stood staring down at the man with the eye-glass. His companions were looking in the same direction. The focus of attention, pipe between his teeth, gazed at the three in blank astonishment.

"Don't want to intrude——" the leader gave a cursory nod to the clergyman—"real sorry to interrupt; but I must ask *you*——" he placed a compelling hand on the shoulder of the wearer of the monocle—"to step inside for just a minute. Got a couple o' questions."

"What the deuce d'you mean?"

"I'm a government agent, and I'm on urgent business. Just a couple o'questions."

"I never heard such balderdash in my life." The other declared. He turned to the clergyman. "Did you?"

"It will probably save trouble in the long run if you assist the officer."

"Right-oh. I'm obliged for the tip. Very funny and odd. But still. . . ."

Pipe firmly clenched between his teeth, he walked out followed by the leader of the party, the other two members of which bought up the rear. They found themselves in a small back hall from which arose a stair communicating with upper floors. On a table stood a bottle of whisky, glasses and a pitcher of ice water.

"No need to go farther," said the agent; "we're all set here." He stared hard at the man in plus fours. "Listen, Abbot: why the fancy dress?"

"What d'you mean, Abbot?" was the angry reply. "My name's not Abbot, and if it were you'd have a damned cheek to address me in that way!"

"Cut the funny lines. They ain't funny. I'm here on business. What's the name that goes with the eye-window?"

"I'm tempted," said the man addressed, speaking with a

cold anger which his amiably vacant manner would not have led one to anticipate, "to tell you to go to hell." He focussed an icy stare in turn upon each of the three grim faces. "You've stepped off with the wrong foot, my friends."

He plunged to an inside pocket. Instantly three steel barrels covered him. He ignored them, handing a British passport to the leader of the party. There was a minute of ominous silence, during which the man scrutinized the passport and the photograph, comparing the latter with its subject. At last:

"Boys!"—he turned to his satellites—"we're up the wrong gum tree. We've got hold of Captain the Honourable George Fosdyke-Fosdyke of the Grenadier Guards! Schultz, jump to the phone. Notify Base and ask for President's instructions. . ."

Some ten minutes later the Honourable George Fosdyke-Fosdyke found himself in sole possession of the little vestibule. The three federal officers had gone. He had had a glimpse through the driving sleet of a powerful car drawn up before the door. The amiable clergyman had gone. He was alone, mystified, irritated.

"Well, I'm damned!" he said.

At which moment, and while through the howling of the storm the purr of the departing car might still be heard, came the roar of a second even more powerful engine. Again the door was thrown open, and two men came in. Fosdyke-Fosdyke turned and faced them.

"O.K. this time, Chief!" said one, exhibiting a row of glittering teeth.

The other nodded and stepped forward.

"Good evening, Dom Patrick Donegal," he said, and pulled inside a dripping leather overcoat to exhibit a gold badge. "A nice run you've given us!"

"Here! I say!" exclaimed Fosdyke-Fosdyke. "This damn joke is getting stale!"

And in a dilapidated but roadworthy Ford the amiable priest was driving furiously through the storm in the direction of New York: the Abbot of Holy Thorn was one stage further on his self-imposed journey.

CHAPTER 18

MRS. ADAIR REAPPEARS

MOYA ADAIR stepped out of the elevator, crossed the marble lobby of the luxurious apartment house and came out on to Park Avenue. She was muffled up in her mink coat, the little Basque beret which she wore in rough weather crushed tightly upon mahogany-red curls. A high, fiercely cold wind had temporarily driven the clouds away, and a frosty moon looked down from a glittering sky. Moya inhaled delightedly the ice-cold air from the Avenue. It was clean and wholesome in contrast to the smoke-laden atmosphere of the Dumas' apartment.

Her new assignment terrified her. For some reason known only to the President, that awful Chinaman who dominated her life, she had been chosen to supplant Lola Dumas. And she feared the enmity of Lola Dumas second only to that of the President. It was the yellow streak, more marked in her than in her father, which made her terrible; Moya, who had met her several times, had often thought of Lola as a beautiful, evil priestess of Voodoo—a dabbler in strange rites.

She began to walk briskly in the direction of a nearby hotel where, as Miss Eileen Breon, accommodation had been provided for her by the organization to which unwillingly she belonged. She felt as though she had escaped from an ever-present danger.

Harvey Bragg, potential Dictator of America, had accepted her appearance in the spirit in which sultans had formerly welcomed the present of a Circassian slave girl. And she had nowhere to turn for help—unless to the President. Oddly enough, she trusted that majestic but evil man.

The newspapers, in which politics occupied so much space, were nevertheless giving prominence to the mysterious death of James Richet. In her heart of hearts Moya Adair believed that James Richet had been executed by the President's orders. The power of the sinister Chinaman ws terrifying; yet although he held a life dearer than her own in his hands,

Moya's service was not wholly one of fear. He had never called upon her to do anything which her philosophy told her to be despicable. Sometimes in her dreams she thought that he was Satan, fallen son of the morning, but in her very soul she knew that his word was inviolable; that execrable though his deeds appeared to Western eyes, paradoxically he might be trusted to give measure for measure.

Her first instructions in regard to Bragg had related to the forthcoming debate at Carnegie Hall. She had given him certain typed notes, with many of which he had quarrelled furiously. The odd fact had dawned upon her during this first interview that Bragg had never met the President!

"I'll play this bunch of underground stiffs just as long as their funds last out," he had declared. "But you can tell your 'President' that what I need is money, not his orders!"

Moya pointed out that directions received in the past had invariably led to success. Bragg, becoming more and more deeply intrigued, had tried to cross-examine. Failing, he had changed his tactics and made coarsely violent love to her. . . .

She raised her face, as she hurried along, to the healing purity of the moonlight. Salvaletti tactfully had terminated that first hateful interview; but she shrank from Salvaletti as she instinctively shrank from snakes. Since then, the scene had been re-enacted—many times.

She had reached her hotel and was just turning into the doorway when a hand touched her shoulder. . . .

It had come—and, almost, it was welcome!

Since that snowy night outside the Tower of the Holy Thorn, hourly she had expected arrest. She glanced swiftly aside.

A tall, bearded man who wore glasses, a black hat and a caped topcoat stood at her elbow.

"Live here, Mrs. Adair?" he asked drily.

A stream of traffic released at that moment by a changing light almost drowned her reply, in so low a voice did she speak.

"Yes. Who are you, and what do you want?"

Yet even as she spoke she knew that she had heard that monotonous voice before. Under the shadow of his hat brim the man's eyes glistened through the spectacles.

"I want to step inside and have a word with you."

"But I don't know you."

The man pulled the caped coat aside and she saw the glitter of a gold badge. Yes, she had been right—a federal officer! It was finished: she was in the hands of the law, free of that awful President, but. . .

The lobby of the expensively discreet apartment hotel was deserted, for the hour was late. But as they sat down facing each other across a small table, Moya Adair had entirely recovered her composure. She had learned in these last years that she could not afford to be a woman; she blessed the heritage of courage and common sense which was hers. It had saved her from madness, from suicide; from even worse than suicide.

And now the federal agent removed his black hat. She knew him and, in the moment of recognition, wondered why she was glad.

She smiled into the bearded face—and Moya was not ignorant of the fact that her smile was enchanting.

"Am I to consider myself under arrest?" she asked. "Because, if so, I don't expect to have the same luck as last time."

Mark Hepburn removed his black-rimmed spectacles and stared at her steadily. She remembered his deep-set eyes— remembered them as dreamy eyes, the eyes of a poet. Now, they were cold. Her brave flippancy had awakened the Quaker ancestors, those restless Puritan spirits who watched eternally over Mark Hepburn's soul. This was the traditional attitude of a hardened adventuress. When he replied, his voice sounded very harsh.

"Technically, it's my duty to arrest you, Mrs. Adair; but we're not so trammelled by red tape as the police." He was watching her firm, beautifully modelled lips and trying to solve the mystery of how she could give her kisses to Harvey Bragg. "I have been waiting ever since that night at the Tower for a chat with you."

She made no reply.

"An associate of yours on Abbot Donegal's staff was murdered recently, right outside the Regal Hotel. You may have heard of it?"

Moya Adair nodded.

"Yes; but why do you say he was murdered?"

"Because I know who murdered him and so do you: *Dr. Fu Manchu.*"

He laid stress on the name, staring into Moya's eyes. But with those words he had enabled her to speak the truth, unafraid. That he referred to the President she divined; but to all connected with the organization the President's name was unknown, except that on two occasions she had heard him referred to as "the Marquis."

"To the best of my knowledge," she replied quietly, "I have never met anyone called Dr. Fu Manchu."

Mark Hepburn, who had obtained Nyaland Smith's consent to handle this matter in his own way, realized that he had undertaken a task beyond his powers. This woman knew that she was fighting for her freedom—and he could not torture her. He was silent for a while, watching her, then:

"I should hate to think of you," he said, "undergoing a police interrogation, Mrs. Adair. But you must know as well as I know that there's a plot afoot to obtain control of this country. You are in on it: it's my business to be. I can guarantee your safety; you can quit the country if you like. I know where you come from in County Wicklow; I know where your father is at the present time. . . ."

Moya Adair's eyes opened fully for a moment and then quite closed. This man was honest, straight as a die: he offered her freedom, the chance to live her own life again . . . and she could not, dared not, accept what he offered!

"You have no place in murder gangs. You belong in another sphere. I want you to go back to it. I want you to be on the right side, not the wrong. Trust me, and you won't regret it, but try any tricks and you will leave me no alternative."

He ceased speaking, watching Moya's face. She was looking away from him with an unseeing gaze. But he knew because of his sensitively sympathetic character that she understood and was battling with some problem outside his knowledge. The half-lighted lobby was very quiet, so that when a man who had been seated in a chair at the farther end, unsuspected, crossed to the elevator, Mark Hepburn turned sharply, glancing in his direction. Mrs. Adair remained abstracted. At the end of a long silence:

347

"I am going to trust you," she said, and looked at him steadily, "because I know I can. I am glad we have met—for after all there may be a way. Will you believe me if I swear to carry out what I am going to suggest. . .?"

Two minutes later, the man who had gone up in the elevator was speaking on the telephone in his apartment.

"Miss Eileen Breon talking in the lobby with a bearded man wearing spectacles and a black caped topcoat. Time 2.55 a.m. Report from Number 49."

CHAPTER 19

THE CHINESE CATACOMBS

ORWIN PRESCOTT opened his eyes and stared about the small bedroom—at two glass-topped tables, white enamelled walls, at a green-shaded lamp set near an armchair in which a nurse was seated; a very beautiful nurse whose dark eyes were fixed upon him intently.

He did not speak immediately, but lay there watching her and thinking.

Something had happened—at Carnegie Hall. The memory was not clear-cut; but something had happened in the course of his debate with Harvey Bragg. Had over-study, over-anxiety, resulted in a nervous breakdown? This was clearly a clinic in which he found himself.

In this idea he thought he saw a solution of the mental confusion in his mind. He was fascinated by the darkly beautiful face framed in the white nurse's cap. Vaguely, he knew that he had seen the nurse before. He moved slowly, and found to his delight that there seemed to be nothing physically wrong with him. Then he spoke:

"Nurse——" his voice was full, authoritative; he recognized that in brain and body he was unimpaired by whatever had happened—"this is very bewildering. Please tell me where I am."

The nurse stood up and walked to the bed: she was very slender, her movements were graceful.

"You are in the Park House Clinic, Dr. Prescott, and I am happy to say entirely your old self again."

He watched her full lips, sensitive with sympathy.

"I collapsed during the debate?"

She shook her head smilingly.

"What a strange idea, Doctor. But I can understand that that would be upon your mind. Surely you remember walking out from Weaver's Farm, your cousin's home? There was snow on the ground, and you slipped and fell; you were unconscious for a long time. They brought you here. You are under the care

349

of Dr. Sigmund. But all's well, you see."

"I feel as well as I ever did in my life."

"You *are* as well."

She sat down beside the bed and rested a cool hand on his forehead. Her dark eyes when she bent towards him he thought extraordinarily beautiful.

And now Orwin Prescott sat up. There was vigour in his movements.

"Still I don't understand. I assure you I recall whole passages of the debate at Carnegie Hall! I can remember Bragg's triumph, my own ineptitude, my inability to counter his crude thrusts. . ."

"You were dreaming, Doctor; naturally the debate has been on your mind. Don't overtire yourself."

Gently she compelled him to lie down again.

"Then what really occurred?" he challenged.

The nurse smiled again soothingly.

"Nothing has occurred yet: except that we have got you in splendid form for the debate to-night."

"What!"

"The debate at Carnegie Hall takes place tonight, and after a talk with your secretary, Mr. Norbert, who is waiting outside, I am quite sure you will be ready for it."

Orwin Prescott stared at the speaker fixedly. A new, a dreadful idea, had presented itself to him, and:

"Do you assure me," he said—"I beg you will be frank—that the debate has not taken place?"

"I give you my word," she answered, meeting his glance with absolute candour. "There is no mystery about it all except that you have had a vivid dream of the thing upon which your brain has been centred for so long."

"Then I have been here——?"

"Ever since the accident, Doctor." She stood up, crossed, and pressed a bell. "I am sending for Mr. Norbert," she explained. "He is naturally anxious to see you."

But whole phases of the debate seemed to ring in Prescott's ears! He saw himself, he saw Bragg, he saw the vast audience as though a talking picture were being performed inside his brain!

The door opened, and Norbert came in; dark, perfectly

groomed. The neat black moustache suggested a British army officer. He came forward with outstretched hand.

"Dr. Prescott!" he exclaimed, "this is fine." He turned to the nurse. "Nurse Arlen, I must congratulate you. Dr. Sigmund, I know, is delighted."

"Perhaps, Norbert," said Prescott, "now that you are here we can get this straight. There are many points which are quite dark to me. It is all but incredible that I could have lain here——"

"Forget all that, Doctor," Norbert urged, "for the moment. I am told that you are fit to talk shop, and so there is one thing upon which to concentrate—to-night's debate."

"It really is to-night?"

"I understand your bewilderment—but it really is to-night. Imagine our anxiety! It means the biggest check in Bragg's headlong career to the White House. I am going to refresh your memory with all our notes up to the date of the accident at Weaver's Farm. I had left you, you recall, to go to Washington. I have added some later points. Do you feel up to business?"

He turned to the nurse. "Nurse Arlen, you are sure it will not tire him?"

"Dr. Sigmund is confident that it will complete his cure."

Orwin Prescott's glance lingered on the beautiful dark face. Then, again sitting up, he turned to Maurice Norbert. He was conscious of growing enthusiasm, of an intense ardour for his great task.

"Perhaps one day I shall understand," he said, "but at the moment——"

Norbert opened his portfolio.

II

In a small, square, stone-faced room deep in the Chinese Catacombs, old Sam Pak crouched upon a settee placed against a wall. One would have thought, watching the bent motionless figure, that it was that of an embalmed Chinaman. There was little furniture in the room: a long narrow table, with a chair set behind it; upon the table appointments suggesting a medical consultant; upon the floor, two rugs. The arched doorway was closed by scarlet tapestry drapings.

Now these were drawn aside. A tall figure entered, a man who wore a black overcoat with heavy astrakhan collar, and an astrakhan cap upon his head; also, he wore spectacles. As he entered, and he entered quite silently, Sam Pak stood up as if electrified, bowing very low in the Chinese manner. The tall man walked to the chair behind the table and seated himself.

He removed his spectacles. The wonderful lined face which had reminded so many observers of that of Seti I was revealed in its yellow mastery. Dr. Fu Manchu spoke.

"Be seated," he said.

Sam Pak resumed his seat.

"You guarantee," the harsh, guttural voice continued—those brilliant green eyes were fixed inflexibly upon the ancient Chinaman, "the appearance of Dr. Orwin Prescott to-night?"

"You have my word, Marquis."

Three drops of the tincture must be administered ten minutes before he leaves."

"It shall be administered."

"Already, my friend, we are suffering at the hands of the bunglers we are compelled to employ. The pestilential priest Patrick Donegal has slipped through all our nets. Nor is it certain that he is not in the hands of Enemy Number One."

The ancient head of Sam Pak was slowly nodded.

"The appearance of the Abbot at Carnegie Hall," Dr. Fu Manchu continued, "might be fatal to my plans. Yet"—removing heavy gloves he laid two long bony hands upon the table before him—"I remain in uncertainty."

"In war, Master, there is always an element of uncertainty."

"Uncertainty is part of the imperfect plan," Fu Manchu replied sibilantly. "Only the fool is uncertain. But the odds are heavy, my friend. Produce to me the man Herman Grosset, whom you have chosen for to-night's great task."

Sam Pak moved slightly, pressing a bell. The curtain was drawn aside, and a Chinese boy appeared. A few words of rapid instructions and he went out, dropping the curtain behind him.

There was silence in the queer room. Dr. Fu Manchu, eyes half closed, leaned back in his chair. Sam Pak resembled a mummy set upright in ghastly raillery by some lightminded excavator. Then came vigorous footsteps, the curtains were switched aside, and a man strode in.

Above medium height, of tremendously powerful build, dark faced and formidable, Herman Grosset was a man with whom no one would willingly pick a quarrel. He looked about him challengingly, meeting the gaze of those half-closed green eyes with apparent indifference and merely glancing at old Sam Pak. He stepped to the table, staring down at Dr. Fu Manchu.

His movements, his complete sang-froid, something, too, in the dark-brown face, might have reminded a close observer of Harvey Bragg; and indeed, Grosset was a half-brother of the potential dictator of the United States.

"So you are the President?" he said—and his gruff voice held a note of amused self-assurance. "I'm sure glad to meet you, President. There's some saying about 'fools step in . . .' I don't know if it applies to me, but it's kind of funny that you've stayed in the background with Harvey, but asked me to step right into the office."

"The circumstances under which you stepped into the office," came coldly, sibilantly, "are such that if you displease me, you will find it difficult to step out again."

"Oh! I'm supposed to be impressed by the closed auto and the secret journey?" Grosset laughed and banged his fist on the table. "Look!"

With a lightning movement he snatched an automatic from his pocket and covered Dr. Fu Manchu.

"I take big risks because I know how to protect myself. While you're for Harvey, I'm for you. If I thought you'd dare to cross him, you'd start out for your Chinese paradise this very minute. Harvey is going to be President. Harvey is going to be Dictator. Nothing else can set the country to rights. I wouldn't hesitate——" he tapped the gun barrel on the table, watching out of the corner of his eye the old Chinaman on the settee— "I wouldn't hesitate to shoot down any man living that got in his way. When he made me boss of his bodyguard he did the right thing."

Dr. Fu Manchu's long yellow hands with their cruelly pointed nails remained quite motionless. He did not stir a muscle; his eyes were mere green slits in the yellow mask. Then:

"No one doubts your loyalty to Harvey Bragg," he said softly; "That point is not in dispute. It is known that you love him."

"I'd die for him."

The automatic disappeared into the pocket from which it had been taken. Two men stripped to the waist entered so silently that even the movement of the curtain was not audible. They sprang from behind like twin panthers upon Grosset.

"Hell!" he roared, "what's this game!"

He bent his powerful body forward, striving to throw one of his assailants across his shoulder, but realized that he was gripped in a stranglehold.

"You damned yellow double-crosser." he groaned, as his right arm was twisted back to breaking-point.

From behind, an expanding gag was slipped into his gaping mouth. He gurgled, groaned, tried to kick, then collapsed as the pressure of fingers made itself felt, agonizingly, upon his eyeballs. . . .

He had not even seen his assailants when straps were buckled about his legs, and his arms lashed behind him.

Throughout, Dr. Fu Manchu never stirred. But when the man, his eyes fixed in frenzied hate upon the Chinese doctor, was carried, uttering inarticulate sounds, from the room, and the curtain fell behind his bearers:

"It is good, my friend," Fu Manchu said gutturally, addressing the mummy-like figure on the settee, "that you succeeded in bringing me a few expert servants."

"It was well done," old Sam Pak muttered.

"To-night," the precise tones continued, "we put our fortunes to the test. The woman Adair, to whom I have entrusted the tuition of Harvey Bragg, is one I can rely upon; I hold her in my hand. But the man himself, in his bloated arrogance, may fail us. I fear for little else." His eyes became closed; he was thinking aloud. "If Enemy Number One has Abbot Donegal, all approaches to Carnegie Hall must be held against them. This I can arrange. We have little else to fear."

From the material upon the table he delicately charged a hypodermic syringe with a pale-green fluid. Sam Pak watched him with misty eyes, and Dr. Fu Manchu stood up.

"It is unfortunate," he said, but there was a note of scientific enthusiasm in the guttural voice, "that my first important experiment in the use of this interesting drug should involve in success or failure such high issues. Come, my friend; I desire you to be present. . . ."

Across the silent temple of the seven-eyed goddess they went: Fu Manchu with his cat-like walk; old Sam Pak shuffling behind. The place was silent and empty. They descended a stone stair, traversed the corridor lined with six painted coffins, and passed the steel door beyond which a secret passage led to East River.

In a small, cell-like room, lighted by a pendant lamp, Herman Grosset lay strapped to a fixed teak bench. The immobile Chinamen had just completed their task as Dr. Fu Manchu entered, and:

"Go!" he commanded in Chinese.

The men bowed and went out; their muscular bodies were dewy with perspiration. Grosset's skin also gleamed wetly. He had been stripped to the waist; his eyes were starting from his head.

"Remove the gag, my friend," Dr. Fu Manchu directed.

Old Sam Pak stepped forward, bent over Grosset, and with a sudden, amazingly agile movement, wrenched the man's mouth open and plucked out the expanding gag. Grosset turned his head aside and spat disgustedly; then:

"Dirty yellow thugs!" he whispered: he was panting. "You've been bought over! Maybe you think"—his powerful chest expanded hugely—"that if you get Harvey, Orwin Prescott has a chance! I'm telling you this: If any harm comes to Harvey, there'll never be a Dictator in the United States."

"We do not doubt," said Dr. Fu Manchu, "your love for Harvey Bragg."

"No need to doubt it! Looks like I'm dying for him right here and now. I want to tell you this: He's the biggest man this country has known for a whole generation and more. Think that over. I say it."

"You would not consider changing your opinion?"

"I knew it!" Grosset was recovering vigour. "Saw it coming. Listen, you saffron-faced horror! You couldn't buy me for all the gold in Washington. I've lived for Harvey right along . . . I'll die for Harvey."

"Admirable sentiments," Dr. Fu Manchu muttered, and bent over the strapped figure, hypodermic syringe in hand.

"What are you going to do to me?" Grosset shrieked, a sudden note of horror in his voice. "What are you going to do to me? Oh, you filthy yellow swine! If only my hands were free!"

"I'm going to kill you, my friend. I have no future place for you in my plans."

"Well, do it with a gun," the man groaned, "or even a knife if you like. But that thing——"

He uttered a wild, despairing shriek as the needle point was plunged into his flesh. Veins like blue whipcords sprang up on his forehead, on his powerful arms, as he fought to evade the needle point. All was in vain: he groaned and, in the excess of his mental agony, became still.

Dr. Fu Manchu handed the syringe to the old mandarin, who unemotionally had watched the operation. He stooped and applied his ear to the diaphragm of the unconscious man. Then, standing upright, he nodded.

"The second injection two hours before we want him." He looked down at the powerful body strapped to the bench. "You have killed many men in defence of your idol, Grosset," he murmured, apostrophizing the insensible figure. "Seven I have checked, and there are others. You shall end your career in a killing that is really worth while. . . ."

III

Carnegie Hall was packed to saturation point. It was an even bigger audience than Fritz Kreisler could have commanded; an audience equally keen with anticipation, equally tense. The headlong advance made by Harvey Bragg—once regarded as a petty local potentate by serious politicians, now recognized as a national force—had awakened the country to the fact that dictatorship, until latterly a subject for laughter, might, incredible though it seemed, be imminent.

356

The League of Good Americans reputedly numbered fifteen million members upon its roll. That many thousands of the homeless and hopeless had been given employment by Harvey Bragg was an undisputed fact. The counter measures of the old administration, dramatically drastic, had apparently done little to check a growing feverish enthusiasm awakened throughout the country by "Bluebeard."

An ever-expanding section of the public regarded him as a saviour; another and saner element recognised that he was a menace to the Constitution. Dr. Orwin Prescott, scholarly, sincere, had succeeded in driving a wedge between two conflicting bodies—and the gap was widening.

That Orwin Prescott advocated a sane administration, every sensible citizen appreciated. His avowed object was to split the Bragg camp; but there were those who maintained, although he had definitely denied the charge, that secretly he aimed at nomination to the Presidency.

There was a rumour abroad that he would declare himself to-night.

Among the more thoughtful elements he undoubtedly had a large following, and if the weight of the Abbot of Holy Thorn at the eleventh hour should be thrown into the scales, it was obvious to students of the situation that the forces of Orwin Prescott would become as formidable as those of Harvey Bragg.

In the course of the last few hectic months other contestants had been wiped off the political map. Republican voters, recanting their vows of 1932, had rallied to Orwin Prescott. Agriculture stood solid for the old administration, although Ohio had a big Bragg faction. The ghost of a conservative third party had been exercised by Abbot Donegal, a close friend of Prescott.

There was a certain studious mystery about Dr. Orwin Prescott which appealed to a large intellectual class. His periodical retirements from public life, a certain aura of secret studies which surrounded him, and the recent silence of Abbot Donegal, had been interpreted as a piece of strategy, the importance of which might at any moment become manifest. One would have had to search far back in American history for a parallel of the almost hysterical excitement which dominated this packed assembly.

The huge building was entirely in the hands of police and federal agents. Hidden patrols covered the route from the Dumas' apartment on Park Avenue right to the door of the hall by which Harvey Bragg would enter. Up to an hour before the meeting was timed to open, no one knew where Prescott was, or even if he were in the city. The audience, which numbered over three thousand, had been admitted to their seats, every man and woman closely scrutinized by hawk-eyed police officers. The buzz of that human beehive was something all but incredible.

A military band played patriotic music, many numbers being sung in unison by three thousand voices. Suspense was intense; excitement electrical.

Nayland Smith, in an office cut off from the emotional vibrations of that vast gathering, was in constant touch with police headquarters, and with Fey, who sat at the telephone at the top of the Regal Tower. Mark Hepburn, bearded and bespectacled, ranged the building from floor to floor, reporting at intervals in the office which Nayland Smith had made his temporary base.

Outside, limelight turned night into day, and a team of cameramen awaited the arrival of distinguished members of the audience. Thousands who had been disappointed in obtaining admittance thronged the sidewalks; the corner of 57th Street was impassable. Patrolmen, mounted and on foot, kept a way open for arriving cars.

Hepburn walked into the office just as Nayland Smith replaced the telephone. Smith turned, sprang up.

Sarah Lakin, seated in a rest-chair on the other side of the big desk, flashed an earnest query into the bespectacled eyes. Mark Hepburn shook his head and removed his spectacles.

"Almost certainly," he said in his dry, unemotional way, "Abbot Donegal is not in the hall, so far."

Nayland Smith began to walk up and down the room tugging at the lobe of his ear, then:

"And there is no news from the Mott Street area. I am beginning to wonder—I am beginning to doubt."

"I have deferred to your views, Sir Denis," came the grave voice of Miss Lakin, "but I have never disguised my own opinion. In assuming on the strength of a letter, admittedly in his own hand, that Orwin will be here to-night, I think you have taken a false step."

"Maurice Norbert's telephone message this morning seemed to me to justify the steps we have taken." said Hepburn drily.

"I must agree with you there, Captain Hepburn," Miss Lakin admitted; "but I cannot understand why Mr. Norbert failed to visit me or to visit you. It is true that Orwin has a custom of hiding from the eyes of the Press whenever an important engagement is near, but hitherto I have been in his confidence." She stood up. "I know, Sir Denis, that you have done everything which any man could do to trace his whereabouts. But I am afraid." She locked her long, sensitive fingers together. "Somehow, I am very afraid."

A sound of muffled cheering penetrated to the office.

"See who that is, Hepburn," snapped Nayland Smith.

Hepburn ran out. Miss Lakin stared into the grim, brown face of the man pacing up and down the floor. Suddenly he stopped in front of her and rested his hand upon her shoulder.

"You may be right and I may be wrong," he said rapidly. "Nevertheless, I believe that Orwin Prescott will be here to-night."

Mark Hepburn returned.

"The Mayor of New York," he reported laconically. "The big names are beginning to arrive." He glanced at his wrist-watch. "Plenty of time yet."

"In any event," said Nayland Smith, "we have neglected no possible measure. There is only one thing to do—wait."

CHAPTER 20

THE CHINESE CATACOMBS (*concluded*)

ORWIN PRESCOTT dressed himself with more than his usual care. Maurice Norbert had brought his evening clothes and his dressing-case, and in a perfectly appointed bathroom which adjoined the white bedroom, Prescott had bathed, shaved, and then arrayed himself for the great occasion.

The absence of windows in these apartments had been explained by Nurse Arlen. This was a special rest room, usually employed in cases of over-tired nerves and regarded as suitable by Dr. Sigmund, in view of the ordeal which so soon his patient must face. The doctor he had not seen in person; quite satisfied with his progress, the physician—called to a distant patient—had left him in the care of Nurse Arlen. Orwin Prescott would have been quite prepared to remain in her care for a long time. Although he more than suspected the existence of a yellow streak in Nurse Arlen's blood, she was the most fascinating creature with whom he had personally come in contact.

He knew that he was forming an infatuation for this graceful nurse, whose soothing voice had run through all the troubled dreams which had preceded his complete recovery. And now, as he stood looking at himself in the glass, he thought that he had never appeared more keenly capable in the whole of his public life. He studied his fine, almost ascetic features. He was pale, but his pallor added character to the curt, grey military moustache and emphasized the strength of dark eyebrows. His grey hair was brushed immaculately.

The situation he had well in hand. Certainly there were remarkable properties in the prescriptions of Dr. Sigmund. His mental clarity he recognized to be super-normal. He had memorized every fact and every figure prepared for him by Norbert! He seemed to have a sort of pre-vision of all that would happen; his consciousness marched a step ahead of the clock. He knew that to-night no debater in the United States

360

could conquer him. He had nothing to fear from the crude rhetoric of Harvey Bragg.

Satisfied with his appearance, delighted with the issue of this misadventure which might well have wrecked his career, he rang the bell as arranged, and Maurice Norbert came in. He, too, was in evening dress and presented a very smart figure.

"I have arranged, Doctor," he said, "for the car to be ready in twenty minutes. I will set out now to prepare our friends for your arrival, and to see that you are not disturbed in any way until the debate is over. I have never seen you look more fit for the fray."

"Thanks to your selection of a remarkable physician, Norbert, I have never felt more fit."

"It's good to hear you say so. I'll go ahead now; you start in twenty minutes. I will collect the brushes and odds and ends to-morrow. I thought it best to arrange for a car with drawn blinds. The last thing we want is an ovation on the street which might hold you up. You'll be driven right to the entrance, where I shall be waiting for you."

Less than two minutes after Norbert's departure, Nurse Arlen came in.

"I was almost afraid," said Orwin Prescott, "that I was not to see you again before I left."

She stood just by the door, one hand resting on a slender hip, watching him with those long, narrow, dark eyes.

"How could you think I would let so interesting a patient leave without wishing him every good fortune for to-night?"

"Your wishes mean a lot to me. I shall never forget the kindness I have experienced here."

The woman's dark eyes closed for a moment, and when they reopened, their expression had subtly changed.

"That is kind of you," she said. "For my own part I have obeyed orders."

She seated herself beside him on the settee and accepted a cigarette he offered from the full case which Norbert had thoughtfully brought along. Vaguely he was conscious of tension.

"I hope to see you again," he said, lighting her cigarette. "Is that too much to hope?"

"No," she replied laughingly; "there is no reason why I shouldn't see you again, Doctor. But"—she hesitated, glanced at him quickly, and then looked aside—"I have practically given up social life. You would find me very dull company."

"Why should you have given up social life?" Orwin Prescott spoke earnestly. "You are young, you are beautiful. Surely all the world is before you."

"Yes," said Nurse Arlen, "in one sense it is. Perhaps some day I may have a chance to try to explain to you. But now . . ." She stood up. "I have one more duty before you leave for Carnegie Hall—physician's orders."

She crossed to a glass-topped table and, from a little phial which stood there, carefully measured out some drops of a colourless liquid into a graduated glass. She filled it with water from a pitcher and handed it to Orwin Prescott.

"I now perform my last duty," she said. "You are discharged as cured."

She smiled. It was the smile which had haunted his dreams: a full-lipped, caressing smile which he knew he could never forget. He took the glass from her and drained its contents. The liquid was quite tasteless.

Almost immediately, magically, he became aware of a great exhilaration. His mental powers, already keen, were stimulated to a point where it seemed that his heel was set upon the world as on a footstool; that all common clay formed but stepping-stones to a goal undreamed of by any man before him. It was a kind of intoxication never hitherto experienced in his well-ordered life. How long it lasted he was unable to judge, or what of it was real, and what chimerical.

He thought that, carried out of himself, he seized the siren woman in his arms, that almost she surrendered but finally resisted. . . .

Then, sharply, as lightning splits the atmosphere, came sudden and absolute sobriety.

Orwin Prescott stared at Nurse Arlen. She stood a pace away watching him intently.

"That was a heady draught," he said, and his tones were apologetic.

"Perhaps my hand shook," Nurse Arlen replied; her caressing voice was not quite steady. "I think it is time for you to go,

Dr. Prescott. Let me show you the way."

He presently found himself in a small elevator, which Nurse Arlen operated. Stepping out at the end of a narrow corridor, and a door being opened, he entered a covered court-yard where a Cadillac was waiting. The chauffeur, who wore driving-glasses, was yellow skinned—he might have been an Asiatic. He held the door open.

"Good night," said Orwin Prescott, one foot on the step.

He held Nurse Arlen's hand, looking, half afraid, into her dark eyes.

"Good night," she replied—"good luck!"

The windows were shaded. A moment after the door was closed the big car moved off.

II

Dr. Fu Manchu sat in the stone-faced room behind that narrow table whose appointments suggested those of a medical consultant. His long yellow fingers with their pointed nails rested motionless upon the table-top. His eyes were closed. The curtain which draped the opening was drawn aside, and Sam Pak entered: "Sam Pak"—a name which concealed another once honoured in China.

Dr. Fu Manchu did not open his eyes.

"Orwin Prescott is on his way to Carnegie Hall, Master," the old man reported, speaking in Chinese, but not in the Chinese which those of the London police who knew him and who knew something of Eastern languages were accustomed to hear. "The woman did her work, but not too well. I fear there were four and not three drops in the final draught."

"She is a broken reed." The sibilant voice was clearly audible, although the thin-lipped mouth appeared scarcely to move. "She was recommended in high quarters, but her sex vibrations render her dangerous. She is amorous, and she has compassion: it is the negroid stain. Her amours do not concern me. If men are her toys, she must play; but the fibre and reality of her womanhood must belong to *me*. If she betrays me, she shall taste the lingering kiss of death. . . . For this reason I removed her from Harvey Bragg in the crisis, and substituted the woman Adair. You are uncertain respecting the drops?"

The jade-green eyes opened, and a compelling stare fixed itself upon the withered face of Sam Pak.

"I was watching—her hand was not steady; he became intoxicated. By this I judged."

"If she has failed me, she shall suffer." The guttural voice was very harsh. "The latest report regarding this pestilential priest?"

"Number 25, in charge of Z-cars covering Carnegie Hall, reports that the Abbot Donegal has not entered the building."

There was a silence of several moments.

"This can mean only one of two things," came sibilantly. "He is there, disguised, or he is in Federal hands and Enemy Number One may triumph at the last moment."

Old Sam Pak emitted a sound resembling the hiss of a snake.

"Even I begin to doubt if our gods are with us," the high, precise voice of Fu Manchu continued. "What of my boasted powers, of those agents which I alone know how to employ? What of the thousands of servants at my command throughout the world? That Nayland Smith has snapped at my heels—may now at any moment bark outside my door. This brings down my pride like a house of cards. Gods of my fathers"—his voice sank lower and lower—"is it written that I am to fail in the end?"

"Quote not from Moslem fallacies," old Sam Pak wheezed. "Your long contact with the Arabs, Marquis, is responsible for such words."

"Few living men could have sustained the baleful glare of those jade-green eyes now fully opened. But Sam Pak, unmoved by their hypnotism, continued:

"I, too, have some of the wisdom, although only a part of yours. The story of your life is traced by your own hand. This you know: fatalism is folly. I, the nameless, speak because I am near to you and am fearless in your service."

Dr. Fu Manchu stood up; his bony but delicate fingers selected certain objects on the table.

"Without you, my friend," he said softly, "I should indeed be alone in this my last battle, which threatens to become my

364

Waterloo. Let us proceed"—he moved cat-like around the end of the long table—" to the supreme experiment. Failure means entire reconstruction of our plans."

"A wise man can build a high tower upon a foundation of failures," crooned old Sam Pak.

Dr. Fu Manchu, silent-footed, went out into the room haunted by the seven-eyed goddess; crossed it, descended stairs, old Sam Pak following. They passed along the corridor of the six coffins and came to the dungeon where Herman Grosset lay upon a teak bench. The straps had been removed—he seemed to be sleeping peacefully.

One of Sam Pak's Chinamen was on guard. He bowed and withdrew as Dr. Fu Manchu entered. Old Sam Pak crouched beside the recumbent body, his ear pressed to his hairy chest. Awhile he stayed so, and then looked up, nodding.

Dr. Fu Manchu bent over the sleeping man, gazing down intently at the inert muscular body. He signalled to Sam Pak, and the old Chinaman, exhibiting an ape-like strength, dragged Grosset's tousled head aside. With a small needle syringe Dr. Fu Manchu made an injection. He laid the syringe aside and watched the motionless patient. Nearly two minutes elapsed. . . . Then, with an atomizer, Dr. Fu Manchu projected a spray first up the right and then up the left nostril of the unconscious man.

Ten seconds later Grosset suddenly sat upright, gazing wildly ahead. His gaze was caught and held by green compelling eyes, only inches removed from his own. His muscular hands clutched both sides of the bench; he stayed rigid in that pose.

"You understand"—the strange voice was pitched very low: "The word of command is 'Asia'."

"I understand," Grosset replied. "No man shall stop me."

"The word," Fu Manchu intoned monotonously, "is Asia."

"Asia," Grosset echoed.

"Until you hear that word"—the voice seemed to come from the depths of a green lake—"forget, forget all that you have to do."

"I have forgotten."

"But remember . . . remember, when you hear the word 'Asia' . . . "

"Asia."

"Sleep and forget. But remember that the word is *Asia*."

Herman Grosset sank back and immediately became plunged in deep sleep.

Dr. Fu Manchu turned to Sam Pak.

"The rest is with you, my friend," he said.

CHAPTER 21

CARNEGIE HALL

HARVEY BRAGG turned round in the chair set before the carved writing-table in the study of the Dumas' apartment. He was dressed for the meeting destined to take its place in American history. Above the table, in a niche and dominating the room, was a reproduction of the celebrated statue of Bussy d'Ambois. The table itself was an antique piece of great value, once the property of Cardinal Mazarin.

"Listen, Baby, I want to get this right." Harvey Bragg stood up. "I'm all set, but I'm playing a part, and I'm not used to playing any part but the part of Harvey Bragg. Bring me into the party, Eileen. Nobody knows better than you. Lola is a hard case. But I guess you're a regular kid."

Moya Adair, seated at the end of the table, raised her eyes to the speaker.

"What do you want to know?" she asked.

"I want to know"—Bragg came a step nearer, rested his hands on the table, and bent down—"I want to know if I'm being played for a sucker; because if I am, God help the man who figures to put that stuff over on me! I've had dough to burn for long enough—some I could check up and some from this invisible guy, the President. Looks to me like the President's investment is a total loss . . . and I never met a rich guy who went around looking for bum stock. This crazy shareholder is starting to try to run the business for me. Listen, Eileen: I'll step where I'm told, if I know where I'm stepping."

There was a momentary silence broken only by the dim hum of traffic in Park Avenue below.

"You would be a fool," said Moya calmly, "to quarrel with a man who believed in you so implicitly that he is prepared to finance you to the extent of so many million dollars. His object is to make you President of the United Sates. He has selected me to be your secretary because he believes that I have the necessary capacity for the work. I can tell you no more. He is a man of enormous influence and he wishes to remain anonymous. I can't see that you have any cause for quarrel with him."

Harvey Bragg bent lower, peering into the alluring face.

"I've learned up a lot of cues," he said; "cues you have given me. Seems I have to become an actor. And"—he banged his open hand upon the table—"I don't know even at this minute that Orwin Prescott is going to be there!"

"Orwin Prescott will be there!"

"It's big fun, isn't it"—now his face was but inches removed from Moya's—"to know that my secretary is wised up on the latest moves and that I'm a pawn in the game. There's another thing, Eileen. Maybe you know what's become of Herman Grosset? He checked in on nowhere more than an hour back, and I never move out without Herman."

He grasped Moya's shoulders. She turned her head aside.

"You're maybe wiser than you look, pretty. You know where I stand. No President can baulk me now. We've started wrong. Let's forget it. Look at me. I want to tell you something——"

Came a discreet rap on the study door.

"Hell!" growled Harvey Bragg. He released Moya, stood upright and turned:

"Come in."

The door opened, and Salvaletti entered, smiling but apologetic.

"Well!" Bragg challenged.

"It's time we left for Carnegie Hall."

Salvaletti spoke in a light, silvery voice.

"Where's Herman? I want to see him."

Salvaletti slightly inclined his head.

"You have naturally been anxious; so have I. But he is here."

"What!"

"He arrived only a few minutes ago. His explanation of his absence is somewhat . . ." He shrugged.

"What! On the booze, on a night like this?"

"I don't suggest it. But, anyway, he is perfectly all right now."

"Ask him to step right in here," roared Harvey Bragg, his voice booming around the study. "I want a few words with Herman.

"Cutting it rather fine. But if you insist . . ."

"I do insist."

He cursed under his breath as Salvaletti went out, turned, and stared angrily at Moya Adair; her calm aloofness maddened him.

"Something blasted funny going on," he growled. "And I guess, Miss Breon, you know all about it."

"I know no more than you know, Mr. Bragg. I can only ask you in your own interests to remember——"

"The coaching! Sure I'll remember it. I'm in up to the eyebrows. But after to-night, I climb out!"

The door was thrown open, and Herman Grosset burst in. His eyes were wild as he looked from face to face.

"Harvey'" he said hoarsely, "I'm real sorry. You won't believe me, but I've been dead sober all day. I guess it must be blood pressure, or maybe incipient insanity. It's in the family isn't it, Harvey? Listen"—he met the angry glare: "Don't talk yet—give *me* a word. I got a funny phone message more than an hour back. I thought it needed investigation. But hell burn me! That's all I can remember about it!"

"What do you mean?" growled Harvey Brag.

"I mean I don't know what happened from the time I got that message which I can't remember—up to five minutes ago, when I found myself sitting on a chair down in the vestibule feeling darn sleepy and wondering where in hell I'd been."

"You're a drunken sot!" Harvey Bragg bawled. "That's what you are—a drunken sot. You've been soused all afternoon. And this is the damn-fool story you think you can pull on me. Get out to the cars; we're late already."

"I don't like your words," said Herman Grosset truculently. "They ain't just, and they ain't right."

"Right or wrong—get out!" yelled Harvey Bragg. "Get on with your job. I have to get on with mine. . . ."

Two minutes later a trio of powerful cars roared down Park Avenue bound for Carnegie Hall. In the first were four armed bodyguards; in the second Harvey Bragg and Salvaletti; in the third, three more guards and Herman Grosset.

"Bluebeard" was well protected.

In Nayland Smith's temporary office in Carnegie Hall silence , vibrant with unspoken thoughts, had fallen.

Maurice Norbert had just ceased speaking. He stood looking smilingly from face to face. Nayland Smith, seated on the edge of the desk, lean brown hands clutching one upraised knee, watched him unflinchingly. Sarah Lakin's steady grave eyes were fixed upon him also.

Senator Lockly, one of Orwin Prescott's most fervent supporters, had joined the party, and his red, good-humoured face now registered bewilderment and doubt. Nayland Smith broke the silence.

"Your explanation, Mr. Norbeert," he replied, "presents certain curious features into which at the moment we have no opportunity to inquire. We are to understand that Dr. Prescott communicated with you roughly at the same time that he communicated with Miss Lakin, and gave you certain instructions which you carried out. These necessitated your meeting a car at an agreed point and being driven to an unknown destination, where you found Dr. Prescott receiving medical attention under the care of a physician whom you did not meet?"

"Exactly."

Maurice Norbert continued to smile.

"You had been instructed to take a suit-case and other items, and we are to understand that Dr. Prescott has come to some arrangement with those responsible for his disappearance whereby he will be present here, to-night?"

"Exactly," Maurice Norbert repeated.

Sarah Lakin continued fixedly to watch Norbert, but she did not speak. Senator Lockly cleared his throat, and:

"I don't understand," he declared, "why, having found him, you left him. It seems to me there's no guarantee even now that he will arrive."

"One of the curious features," rapped Nayland Smith, standing up and beginning to pace the floor, "to which I referred. . . ." He turned suddenly, facing Norbert. "I don't entirely understand your place in this matter, Mr. Norbert.

And I believe"—glancing aside—" that Miss Lakin shares my doubts."

"I do," Sarah Lakin replied in her deep, calm voice.

"Forgive me"—Norbert bowed to the speaker—"but in this hour of crisis we are naturally overwrought, every one of us. It isn't personal, it's national. These facts will wear a different complexion to-morrow. But accept my assurance, everybody, that Dr. Prescott will be here." He glanced at his wristwatch, "in fact, I must go down to meet him. I beg that you will do as I have asked. Senator, will you join me. He has requested that we shall be with him on the platform."

Senator Lockly looked rather helplessly from Sarah Lakin to Nayland Smith, and then followed Norbet out of the office. As the door shut behind them:

"How long employed by Dr. Prescott?" rapped Nayland Smith.

"Maurice Norbert," Sarah Lakin replied, "has been in my cousin's service for rather more than a year."

"Hepburn has been checking up on him. It has proved difficult, but we expect all the details to-morrow."

At which moment the door was thrown open again, and the Abbot of Holy Thorn, wearing the dress of a simple priest stepped into the office!

The bearded face of Mark Hepburn might have been glimpsed over his left shoulder. Nayland Smith sprang forward.

"Dom Patrick Donegal!" he cried, "Thank God I see you here —and safe!"

Mark Hepburn came in and closed the door.

"My experiences, Mr. Smith," the abbot replied calmly, "on my journey to the city, have convinced me that I have incurred certain dangers." He smiled and gripped the outstretched hand. "But I think I warned you that I am a prisoner hard to hold. It is my plain duty in this crisis, since I am denied the use of the air, to be here in person."

"One of our patrol cars" said Hepburn drily, "picked up the abbot twenty minutes ago and brought him here under escort. I may add . . . that the escort was necessary."

"That is quite true," the priest admitted. "A very tough-looking party in a Cadillac had been following me for several miles. But"—he ceased to smile and assumed by a spiritual gesture the rôle of his Church—"I have achieved my purpose. If I am to consider myself technically under arrest I must nevertheless insist, Mr. Smith, upon one thing. . . . Failing the appearance of my friend Orwin Prescott, *I* shall confront Harvey Bragg to-night."

A sound resembling an approaching storm made itself audible. Mark Hepburn nodded to Nayland Smith and went out. Sarah Lakin stood up, her grave calm ruffled at last. Smith stepped to the doorway and stared along the corridor.

The sound grew louder—it was the cheering of thousands of voices. Dimly the strains of a military band were heard. Mark Hepburn came running back.

"Dr. Prescott is on the platform!" he cried, completely lifted out of himself by the excitement of the moment. "Harvey Bragg has just arrived. . . ."

III

The classic debate which the Moving Finger was writing into American history took place in an atmosphere of tension unequalled in the memory of anyone present. After the event there were many who recalled significant features: as, for instance, that Harvey Bragg used notes, his custom being to speak extemporaneously (if in the mood, for many hours). Also, that he frequently glanced in the direction of his secretary, Salvaletti, who seemed at times to be prompting him.

Hidden from the audience, Dom Patrick Donegal looked on at the worldly duel. And, helpless now to intervene, he realized, as everyone in that vast gathering realized, that Dr. Orwin Prescott was a beaten man.

As oratory, his performance was perhaps the finest in his career; his beautiful voice, his scholarship, put to shame the coarse bellowing and lamentable historical ignorance of his opponent. But in almost every sentence he played into the hands of Harvey Bragg: he fell into traps that a child could have avoided. With dignity, assurance, perfect elocution, he made statements which even the kindest critic must have branded as those of a fool.

At times it seemed that he was conscious of this. More than once he raised his hand to his forehead as if to collect his thoughts, and especially it was noticed that points raised in response to the apparent promptings of Salvaletti resulted in disaster for Dr. Orwin Prescott.

His keenest supporters lost heart. It appeared long before the debate was ended that Harvey Bragg offered the country prosperity. Dr. Prescott had nothing to offer but beautifully phrased sentences.

And the greatest orator in the United States, the Abbot of Holy Thorn, dumbly listened—looked on! While his friend Orwin Prescott, with every word that he uttered, broke down the fine reputation which laboriously and honourably he had built up.

It was the triumph of "Bluebeard."

IV

In that book-lined room high above New York, where sometimes incense was burned, Dr. Fu Manchu sat behind the lacquered table.

The debate at Carnegie Hall was being broadcast from coast to coast. Robed in yellow, his mandarin's cap upon his head, he sat listening. Reflected light from the green-shaded table-lamp enhanced his uncanny resemblance to the Pharaoh Seti I: for the eyes of Dr. Fu Manchu were closed as he listened.

His hands, stretched out upon the table before him, had remained quite motionless as Orwin Prescott became involved more deeply in the net cunningly spread for him by Harvey Bragg. Only at times, when the latter hesitated, fumbled for words, would the long pointed nails tap lightly upon the polished surface.

On three occasions during this memorable debate an amber point came to life on the switchboard.

Without in any way allowing his attention to be distracted, Dr. Fu Manchu listened to reports from the man of miraculous memory. These all related to Numbers detailed to intercept Abbot Donegal. The third and last induced a slight tapping of long nails upon the lacquered surface. It was a report to the effect that a government patrol had rescued the abbot (picked up at last within a few miles of New York) from a Z-car which had been tracking him. . . .

The meeting concluded with wildly unrestrained cheers for Harvey Bragg. In that one hour he had advanced many marches nearer to the White House. Politically he had obliterated the only really formidable opponent who remained in the field. Except for the silent Abbot of Holy Thorn, the future of the United States now lay between the old régime and Harvey Bragg.

Deafening cheers were still ringing throughout Carnegie Hall when Dr. Fu Manchu disconnected. Silence fell in that small book-lined room distant from the scene of conflict. Bony fingers opened the silver box: Fu Manchu sought the inspiration of opium. . . .

Orwin Prescott, bewildered, even now not understanding that he had wiped himself off the political map, that he was committed to fatal statements that he could never recall, dropped down into an armchair in Nayland Smith's office, closed his eyes and buried his face in his hands.

Sarah Lakin crossed and sat beside him. Senator Lockly had disappeared. Nayland Smith glanced at Mark Hepburn, and they went out together. In the corridor:

"Where is Abbot Donegal?" said Nayland Smith.

"In care of Lieutenant Johnson," Hepburn answered drily. "Johnson won't make a second mistake. Abbot Donegal stays until he has your permission to leave."

"Orwin Prescott was either drugged or hypnotized, or both," rapped Nayland Smith. "It's the most damnably cunning thing Fu Manchu has ever done. With one stroke tonight, he has put the game into Harvey Bragg's hands."

"I know." Mark Hepburn ran his fingers through his dishevelled hair. "It was pathetic to listen to, and impossible to watch. Abbot Donegal was just quivering. Sir Denis! This man is a magician! I begin to despair."

Nayland Smith suddenly grabbed his arm as they walked along the corridor.

"Don't despair," he snapped, "yet! There's more to come."

They had begun to descend to the floor below when Harvey

374

Bragg, flushed with triumph, already tasting the sweets of dictatorship, the cheers of that vast gathering echoing in his ears, came out into a small lobby packed with privileged visitors and newspapermen.

His bodyguard, as tough a bunch as any man had ever collected in the United States, followed him in. Paul Salvaletti walked beside him.

"Folks!" Bragg cried, "I know just how you feel." He struck his favourite pose, arms raised. "You're all breathing the air of a new and better America. . . . That's just how I feel! Another obstacle to national happiness is swept away. Folks! There's no plan but my plan. At last we are getting near to the first ideal form of government America has ever known."

"Which any country has ever known," said Salvaletti, his clear, musical voice audible above the uproar. "American, Africa, Europe—or Asia."

As he spoke the word *Asia*, Herman Grosset, hitherto flushed with excitement, suddenly became deathly pale. His eyes glared, foam appeared at the corners of his mouth. With that lightning movement which no man of the bodyguard could equal, he snatched an automatic from his pocket, sprang forward and shot Harvey Bragg twice through the heart. . . .

There was a moment of dazed silence; a sound resembling a moan. Then the faithful bodyguard, one second too late, almost literally made a sieve with their bullets of Herman Grosset.

He died before the man he had assassinated. Riddled with lead, he crashed to the floor of the lobby as Harvey Bragg collapsed in the arms of Salvaletti.

"Herman! My God! *Herman!*" were Bragg's dying words.

CHAPTER 22

MOYA ADAIR'S SECRET

"I AM UNCERTAIN, Hepburn," rapped Nayland Smith, pacing up and down the sitting-room. "I cannot read sense into the crossword puzzle."

"Nor can I," said Mark Hepburn.

Smith stared out at the never familiar prospect. The day was crystal clear; the distant Statue of Liberty visible in sharp detail. Some strange quality in the crisp atmosphere seemed to have drawn it inland, so that it appeared like a miniature of itself. Towering buildings had crept nearer: a wide section of New York City seemed to be looking in at the window.

"That Orwin Prescott should suffer a nervous collapse and entirely lose his memory was something for which I was not unprepared. His deplorable exhibition at Carnegie Hall was the result of some kind of post-hypnotic suggestion, a form of attack of which Dr. Fu Manchu is a master."

Mark Hepburn lighted a cigarette.

"There was a time," he said slowly, "when I thought that the powers which you attributed to this man must be exaggerated. I think now that all you said was an understatement. Sir Denis! He's more than the greatest physician in the world—he's a magician."

"Cut the 'Sir Denis,'" came crisply; "I was born plain Smith. It's time you remembered it."

Mark Hepburn smiled—a rare event in those days: it was the self-conscious smile of a nervous schoolboy—life had never changed it.

"I am glad to hear you say that," he declared awkwardly—"Smith, because I'm proud to know that we are friends. Maybe that sounds silly, but I mean it."

"I appreciate it."

"I can understand," Hepburn went on, "after what you have told me, that it might be possible—although it's quite outside my own medical experience—to drug a man in some way and impose certain instructions upon him to be carried out later. I mean I can believe that this is what happened to Orwin Prescott. It's a tough story, but your experience can provide parallels. Mine can't. We are dealing with a man who seems to be a century ahead of modern knowledge."

"Dismiss Prescott," said Nayland Smith curtly; "he's out of the political arena. But he's in good hands now, and I hope to heaven he recovers from whatever ordeal he has passed through. I am disappointed about the escape of the man Norbert. That was bad staff work, Hepburn, for which I take my full share of responsibility."

"We'll get him yet," said Hepburn harshly, "if we comb every state for him. His getaway had been cunningly planned. I have checked it all up. Nobody is to blame. This thing goes back a year or more. Dr. Fu Manchu must have been working, through agents, long before he arrived in person."

"I know it," rapped Nayland Smith; "I have known it for some time past. But what I don't know and cannot work out is this: Where does the death of Harvey Bragg fit into the Doctor's plans?"

He fixed a penetrating stare upon Hepburn and almost automatically began to load his pipe. . . .

"The man Herman Gorsset was a drunken ruffian; his only redeeming virtue seems to have been his attachment to his half-brother. He was a killer, as your records show. Such a man is like an Alsatian dog—his savagery may be turned upon his master. I wonder . . ." He dropped his pouch back into the pocket of his dressing-gown and lighted a match. . . . "I wonder? . . ."

"So do I," said Mark Hepburn monotonously; "I have been wondering ever since it happened. That this damnable Chinaman was running Harvey Bragg is a fact beyond doubt. It isn't conceivable that Bragg's death should form any part of his plan. If he wanted to turn a blustering demagogue into a hero, he has succeeded. Why"—he paused . . . "Smith! He lay in state right here in New York City! Now his embalmed body is being taken back to his home town. He's a bigger man dead than alive. Fifty per cent of uninformed American opinion to-day thinks that the greatest statesman since Lincoln has been snatched away in the hour of need."

"That's true." Nayland Smith blew a puff of smoke into the air. "As I said a while ago, I cannot read sense into the crossword puzzle. I am tempted to believe that the Doctor's plans have been thwarted."

He began to walk up and down again restlessly.

"Salvaletti's broadcast oration," said Hepburn monotonously, "was quite in the classic manner. In fact it was brilliant, although I don't see its purpose. It has made Harvey Bragg a national martyr."

"Salvaletti is going South by special train," jerked Nayland Smith, "with the embalmed body. There will be emotional scenes at every stop. Have we details regarding this man?"

"They should be to hand any moment now. All we know, so far, is that he's of Italian origin, was trained for the priesthood, left Italy at the age of twenty-three, and became a United States citizen five years ago. He's been with Bragg since early 1934."

"I listened to him, Hepburn. Utterly out of sympathy as I am with the subject of his eloquence, I must confess that I never heard a more moving speech."

"No—it was wonderful. But now—er—Smith, I am worried about this projected expedition of yours."

Nayland Smith paused in his promenade and stared, pipe gripped between his teeth, at Mark Hepburn.

"No more worried than I am regarding yours, Hepburn. You know what Kipling says about a rag and bone and a hank of hair . . ."

"That's hardly fair, Smith. I quite frankly admitted to you that I'm interested in Mrs. Adair. There's something very strange about a woman like that being in the camp of Dr. Fu Manchu."

Nayland Smith paused in front of him, reached out and grasped his shoulder.

"Don't think I'm cynical, Hepburn," he said—"we have all been through the fires—but, be very careful!"

"I just want time to size her up. I think she's better than she seems. I admit I'm soft where she's concerned, but maybe she's straight after all. Give her a chance. We don't know everything."

"I leave her to you, Hepburn. All I say is: be careful. I'd

gamble half of the little I possess to see into the mind of Dr. Fu Manchu at this moment! Is he as baffled as I am?"

He resumed his promenade.

"However . . . we have a heavy day before us. Learn all you can from the woman. I am devoting the whole of my attention to Fu Manchu's Chinatown base."

"I am beginning to think," said Hepburn, with his almost painful honesty, "that this Chinatown base is a myth."

"Don't be too sure," rapped Nayland Smith. "Certainly I saw the late secretary of the Abbot Donegal disappear into a turning not far from Wu King's Bar. Significant, to say the least. I have spent hours, in various disguises, exploring that area and right to the water fronts on either side of it."

"I worry myself silly whenever you delay at——"

"My *own* Chinatown base?" Nayland Smith suggested.

He burst out laughing—and his laughter seemed to lift a load of care from his spirits. . . .

"You should congratulate me, Hepburn. In the character of a hard-drinking deck-hand sacked by the Cunard and trying to dodge the immigration authorities until I find a berth, I have made a marked success with my landlady, Mrs. Mulrooney of Orchard Street! I have every vice from hashish to rum, and I begin to suspect she loves me!"

"What about the rag and bone and a hank of hair?" Hepburn asked impishly.

Nayland Smith stared for a moment, and then laughed even more heartily.

"A hit to you," he admitted; "but frankly, I feel that my inquiries are not futile. The Richet clue admittedly has led nowhere; but my East River investigations are beginning to bear fruit."

He ceased laughing. His lean brown face grew suddenly grim.

"Think of the recovery by the river police of the body of the man Blondie Hahn."

"Well?"

"All the facts suggested to me that he did not die on the water front or even very near to it. I maybe wrong, Hepburn . . . but I think I have found Dr. Fu Manchu's water-gate!"

"What!"

"We shall see. The arrival in New York this morning of the Chinese general, Li Wu Chang, has greatly intrigued me. I have always suspected Li Wu Chang of being one of the Seven."

"Who are the Seven?"

"Nayland Smith snapped his fingers.

"Impossible to go into that now. I have much to do to-day if our plans are to run smoothly to-night. Your post is in Chinatown. We both have plenty to employ us in the interval. Should I miss you, the latest details will be on the desk"—he pointed—"and Fey will be here in constant touch. . . ."

II

Mark Hepburn, from his seat overlooking the pond in Central Park, watched the path from the Scholar's Gate. Presently he saw Moya Adair approaching.

It was a perfect winter's day; the air was like wine, visibility was remarkable. Because his heart leapt his dour training reproached him. He had abandoned the cape, property of an eccentric artist friend, and now his bearded chin stuck out from an upturned fur collar.

On the woman's side this meeting was a move in a fight for freedom. But Mark Hepburn, starkly honest, knew that on his side it was a lover's meeting. It was unfair to Nayland Smith that this important investigation, which might lead to control of a bridge to the enemy's stronghold, should have been left in his hands. Moreover, it was torture to himself. . .

He loved the ease of her walk, the high carriage of her head. There was pedigree in every graceful line. Her existence in this gang of superthugs, who now apparently controlled the whole of the American underworld, was a mystery which baulked his imagination.

She smiled as he stood up to meet her. He allowed the mad idea that they were avowed lovers—that he had a right to take her in his arms and kiss her—to dazzle his brain for one delirious moment. Actually, he said:

"You are very punctual, Mrs. Adair."

She sat down beside him. Her composure, real or assumed,

was baffling. There was a short silence, an uneasy one on Mark Hepburn's side; then:

"I suppose," he said, "the death of Harvey Bragg means a change of plan?"

Moya shook her head.

"For me, no," she replied. "I am continuing my work at Park Avenue. The League of Good Americans is to go on, and Paul Salvaletti has taken charge."

She spoke impersonally, a little wearily.

"But you must regret the death of Harvey Bragg?"

"As a Christian, I do, for I cannot think that he was fit to die. As a man"—she paused for a moment, staring up at the cold, blue sky—"if he had lived, I don't know what I should have done. You see"—she turned to Hepburn—"I had no choice: I had to go to him. But my life there was hell."

Mark Hepburn looked away. He was afraid of her eyes. Nayland Smith's injunction, "Be very careful," seemed to ring in his ears.

"Why did you have to go to him?" he asked.

"Well—although I know how hard this must be for you to understand—Harvey Bragg, although he never knew it, was little more than a cog in a wheel. I am another cog in the same wheel." She smiled, but not happily. "He never really controlled the League of Good Americans, nor the many other organizations of which he was the nominal head."

"Then who does control them?" he questioned harshly.

"When I say that I don't know, I am literally speaking the truth. But there's someone far bigger than Harvey Bragg working behind the scenes. Please believe that I dare not tell you any more now."

Hepburn clenched his fists, plunged deep in the pockets of his topcoat.

"Was Harvey Bragg's murder in accordance with the"—he hesitated—"revolutions of this wheel?"

"I don't know. All I know is that it is not to be allowed to interfere with the carrying on of the objects of the league."

"What are these objects?"

Moya Adair paused for a moment.

"I think, but I am not sure, to introduce a new form of government into the United States. Truly"—she stood up—"it is impossible for me to tell you any more. Mr. Purcell, you made a bargain with me, and our time is very short. When you understand more about my position you will see how hard it is to answer some of your questions."

Mark Hepburn stood up also, and nodded. His middle name (his mother's) was Purcell, and as Purcell he had introduced himself to Mrs. Adair.

"Which way do we go?"

"This way," said Moya, and side by side they walked in the direction of the Sherman equestrian statue. Hepburn was silent, sometimes glancing aside at his equally silent companion. She made no attempt to break this silence until they had passed the end of the bridle path, when:

"Shall we want a taxi?" Hepburn asked.

"Yes, but not a Lotus."

"Why?"

They came out through Scholar's Gate.

"I have my reasons. Look! This one will do."

As the taxi moved off to a Park Avenue address of which he made a careful mental note:

"I understand," said Hepburn drily, "that Harvey Bragg was a director of the Lotus Transport Corporation?"

"He was."

The immensity of the scheme was beginning to dawn upon him. Vehicles belonging to the Lotus Corporation, of one kind or another, ranged practically over the States. All employees belonged to the League of Good Americans: so much he knew. Assuming that they could be used, if necessary, as spies, what a network lay here at command of the master mind! As the countless possibilities presented themselves he turned and stared at Moya Adair. She was watching him earnestly.

"When we arrive at the apartment to which we are going," she said, "I shall have to ask you to play the part of an old friend. Do you mind?"

Mark Hepburn clenched his teeth. Moya's gloved hand rested listlessly upon the seat beside him. He grasped and held it for a moment.

"I sincerely wish I were," he replied.

She smiled; and he thought that her smile, although passionless, was almost affectionate.

"Thank you. I mean, we must address each other by our Christian names. So you have my permission to call me Moya. What am I to call *you?*"

Suddenly that alluring coquetry which had delighted and then repelled him at the Tower of the Holy Thorn made her eyes dance. A little dimple appeared at the left corner of her mouth.

"Mark."

"Thank you," said Moya. "I think very soon you will find yourself christened 'Uncle' Mark."

III

Dr. Fu Manchu pressed a button on his table, and in a domed room where the Memory Man, as a result of many hours of patient toil, had nearly completed another of those majestic clay heads, the making of which alone relieved the tedium of his life, the amber light went out.

"Give me the latest report," came a curt, guttural order, "from the Number in charge of Mott Street patrol."

"To hand at 3.10 p.m. Report as follows: Strength of government agents and police in this area doubled since noon. Access to entrances one and two impossible. A government agent, heavily guarded and so far unidentified, in charge. Indications point to a raid pending. This report from Number 41."

Amber light prevailed again in the Gothic room, and the sculptor, Egyptian cigarette in mouth, proceeded to accentuate the gibbous brow of his subject.

Dr. Fu Manchu, who had produced this change of light by the pressure of a button, sat for a while with closed eyes. The next steps in his campaign had been successfully taken. The next step was by far the most difficult. The atmosphere of that strange study must have been unbreathable by an average man. A greying pencil of smoke arose from an incense burner set upon one corner of the table. Dr. Fu Manchu had his own methods of inducing mental stimulation. Presently he touched a switch, and two points of light appeared. A moment he waited, and then:

"Attend carefully to the orders I am about to give," he directed: he spoke in Chinese.

"A plot is brewing to set the dogs upon us, my friend. Listen with great care. No one is to enter or to leave Base 3 until further instructions are received from me. Doors leading to street entrances are to remain locked. Our visitors to-night will enter by the river-gate. Their safety rests with you. All are important; some are distinguished. I shall keep you informed. . . ."

IV

"That is the reason . . . Mark (I must get used to calling you Mark while you are here), why I am so helpless."

Through uncurtained french windows Mark Hepburn looked out from the penthouse apartment on to a roof garden. The vegetation of the rock plants was scanty at this season; a little fountain was frozen over. But he could imagine that in spring and summer this was a very pleasant spot. In the frosty sunlight a small, curly-haired boy was romping with a nurse, a capable-looking woman nearing middle age. Her habitual expression Hepburn assumed to be grim, but now she was laughing gaily as she played with her little charge.

Her gaiety was nor forced—that of a dutiful employee; it radiated real happiness. With the aid of a pile of cushions set beside the wall the small boy was making strenuous endeavours to stand on his head. His flushed face, every time that he collapsed and looked up at her, reduced the nurse to helpless laughter. He gave it up after a while and sat there grinning.

"God bless us, bairn, you'll bring all the blood to your daft little head if you keep on," she exclaimed, speaking with a marked Scottish accent.

"Is there blood in my head, Goofy?" the boy inquired, wide eyed. "I fought it on'y came up to here"—he indicated his throat.

"Where d'you think it comes from when your nose bleeds?"

"Never fought of that, Goofy."

Mark Hepburn, watching the mop of red-brown curls ruffled by the breeze, the clear blue eyes, the formation of the child's mouth, the roundness of his chin, experienced an unfamiliar sensation of weakness compounded of pity and of swift, intense affection. He turned his head slowly, looking at Moya Adair.

Her lips trembled, but her eyes were happy as she smiled up at him and waited.

"There's no need for me to ask." He said. His harsh voice seemed to have softened slightly. He was recalling the details of Mrs. Adair's record which he had been at such pains to secure. "I should have remembered."

"Yes." She nodded. "My big son. He's just four. . . ."

v

When, presently, Mark Hepburn met Robbie Adair, the boy registered approval save in regard to Hepburn's budding beard. He was a healthy frank young ruffian and took no pains to disguise his distastes. He had a disarmingly cheerful grin.

"I like you, Uncle Mark, all 'cept your whiskers," was his summary.

This dislike of beards, so expressed, produced a shocked protest from Nurse Goff and led to further inquiries by Moya, frowning, although her eyes danced with laughter. Interrogation brought to light the fact that Robbie associated beards and untidy hair with a peculiar form of insanity.

"There's someone I know, up there," he explained, pointing vaguely apparently towards heaven; "his hair blows about in the wind all in a mess like yours. And he's got funny whiskers too. He makes heads. He holds 'em up and then he smashes 'em. So you see, Uncle Mark, he *is* mad."

Robbie grinned.

"Whatever are you talking about, Robbie?" Moya, kneeling on a cushion, threw her arm around the boy's shoulders and glanced up at Mark Hepburn. "Do *you* know what he means?"

Mark shook his head slowly, looking into the beautiful eyes upraised to his, so like, yet so wonderfully different from, the eyes of the boy. He became aware of the fact that he was utterly happy; a kind of happiness he had never known before. And down upon this unlawful joy (for why should *he* be happy in the midst of stress, conflict, murder, black hypocrisy) he clapped the icy hand of a Puritan conscience. Nurse Goff had gone into the apartment, leaving the three together.

Some change in Hepburn's expression made Moya turn

aside. She pressed her cheek against Robbie's curly head.

"We don't know what you mean, dear," she said. "Won't you tell us?

"I mean," said Robbie stoutly, turning and staring into her face from a distance of not more than an inch away. "there's a man who is a man; he has whiskers: and he lives up there!"

"Where exactly do you mean, Robbie?"

She glanced aside at Mark Hepburn. He was watching her intently.

The boy pointed.

"On the very top of that tall tower."

Mark Hepburn stared in the direction which Robbie indicated. The building in question was the Stratton Tower, one of New York's very high buildings, and the same which formed a feature of the landscape as viewed from the apartment he shared with Nayland Smith. He continued to stare in that direction, endeavouring to capture some memory which the sight of the oblisk-like structure topped by a pointed dome sharply outlined against that cold, blue sky, stirred in his mind.

He stood up, walked to the wall surrounding the roof garden and took his bearings. He realized that he stood at a level much below that of the fortieth floor of the Regal Tower, but in point of distance much nearer to the building the boy indicated.

"He always comes out at night. On'y sometimes I's asleep and don't see him."

It was the word "night," which gave Hepburn the clue, captured a furtive memory—a memory of three lighted windows at the top of the Stratton Tower which he had seen and speculated about on the night when, with Nayland Smith, he had waited for the coming of Fly Carlo.

He turned and stared at Robbie with new interest.

"You say he makes heads, young fellow?"

"Yes. I see him up there, making 'em."

"At night?"

"Not always."

"And then you say he smashes them?"

"Yes, he always smashes 'em"

"How does he smash them, dear?" Moya asked, glancing up at the earnest face of Mark Hepburn.

According to the boy's graphic description, this notable

madman hurled them down on to the dome below, where they were shattered into fragments.

Hepburn, conquered again by the picture of the charming mother kneeling with one arm round Robbie's shoulders, stooped and succumbed to the temptation of once again ruffling the boy's curly head.

"You seem to have quite a lot of fun up here, Robbie!" he said.

Later, in the cosy sitting-room delicately feminine in its every appointment, Mark Hepburn sat looking at Moya Adair. She smiled almost timidly.

"I suppose," she said, "it's hard for you to understand, but——"

The door opened, and a curly head was thrust into the room, followed by a grin.

"Don't go, Uncle Mark," Robbie cried, "till I say good-bye."

He disappeared. Mark Hepburn, watching Moya as with mock severity she signalled the boy to run away, wondered if there was anything more beautiful in nature than a young and lovely mother.

"I am glad," he said, and his monotonous voice in some queer way sounded different, "that you have this great interest in your life."

"My only interest," she replied simply. "I go on for him. Otherwise"—she shook her head—"I should not be here now."

"Still I don't understand why you serve this man you call the President."

"Yet the explanation is very simple. Although the guards are not visible, both entrances to this building are watched night and day. Whenever Robbie goes out with his nurse he is covered until they return. He is never allowed to walk on the streets, but is driven to the garden of a house on Long Island. That is his only playground except the one on the roof outside."

"I suppose I am dense," said Mark Hepburn, "but I don't understand!"

"This apartment belongs to the President, although he rarely visits it. Mary Goff is my own servant; she has been in my service since the boy was born. Otherwise—I have no one. For two months Robbie disappeared——"

"He was kidnapped?"

"Yes, he was kidnapped. That was before all this began. Then the President sent for me. I was naturally distracted; I think I should very soon have died. He made me an offer which, I think, any mother would have accepted. I accepted without hesitation. I am allowed to come here, even to bring friends, while I carry out the duties allotted to me. If I failed"—she bit her lip—"I should never see Robbie again."

"But after all," Mark Hepburn exclaimed hotly, "there's a law in the land!"

"You don't know the President." Moya replied. "*I* do. No law could save my boy if he determined to spirit him away. You've promised, and you will keep your promise? You won't attempt to do anything about Robbie without my consent?"

Mark Hepburn watched her silently for a while, and then:

"No," he replied; "but it's a very unpleasant situation. I have exposed you to a dreadful danger. . . . You mean"—he hesitated—"that my visit here to-day will be reported to the President?"

"Certainly, but Robbie is allowed visitors if they are old friends. You seem to know enough of my history to pass for an old friend, I think?"

"Yes," said Mark Hepburn; "you may regard me as an old friend. . . ."

VI

In the room where the Memory Man worked patiently upon his stange piece of modelling, a distant bell rang and the amber light went out.

"Give me the latest report," came the hated, dominating voice, "of the Number in charge of party covering Base 3."

"A report to hand," came an immediate reply in those terse Teutonic tones, "timed 5.15. Police have been further rein-forced. Chinese approaching the areas one, two and three have been interrogated. Government agent in charge not yet identified. Several detectives and federal agents have been in Wu King's Bar since noon. Report ends. From Number 41."

Following a silent interval, during which, in the darkness, the Memory Man lighted a fresh Egyptian cigarette from the stump of the old one:

"The latest report," the voice directed, "from Number covering Eileen Breon."

"Report to hand timed 4.35. A man, bearded, wearing glasses and driving coat with a fur collar, age estimated at thirty-five, arrived in her company at the apartment at 3.29. He remained for an hour; covered on leaving. He proceeded on foot to Grand Central. Operatives covering lost his track in the crowd. Report ends. This is from Number 39."

"Most unsatisfactory. Give me the latest report from the Regal-Athenian."

"Only one to hand, timed 5.10 p.m. Owing to long non-appearances of Federal Agents Hepburn and Smith, Number suggests——"

"Suggestions are not reports," the gutteral voice said harshly. "What's this man's number?"

Following a further brief silence:

"Make the connections, " the harsh voice directed. "You are free for four hours."

Amber light prevailed again. The sculptor, brushing back his mane of white hair with a tragic gesture, adjusted the dictaphone attachment which during his hours of rest took the place of his phenomenal memory. No message came through during the time that he gathered up lovingly the implements of his art, sole solace of the prisoner's life.

Carrying the half-completed clay model, he crossed to the hidden door, opened it, and descended to that untidy apartment which, with the balcony outside, made up his world. He threw wide the french windows and went out.

A setting sun in a cloudless sky fashioned strange red lights and purple shadows upon unimaginable buildings, streaked the distant waters almost reluctantly with a phantom, carmine brush, and painted New York City in aspects new even to the weary eyes of the man who had looked down upon it so often.

Setting the clay upon the table, he returned and took a photographic printing-frame from its place in the window. Removing the print, he immersed it in a glass tray. As the tones grew deeper, it presented itself as an enlargement of that tiny coloured head—the model which eternally he sought to reproduce.

Mark Hepburn, fully alive to the fact that he had been covered from the moment when he had left the apartment where Moya Adair's small son lived—a prisoner—experienced an almost savage delight in throwing his pursuers off the track in the great railway station.

He had detected them—there were two—by the time that he descended the steps. He knew that Moya's happiness, perhaps the life of Robbie, depended upon his maintaining the character of a family friend. Whatever happened, he must not be identified as a federal agent.

Furthermore, at any cost he must combat a growing fear, almost superstitious, of the powers of Dr. Fu Manchu; even a minor triumph over the agents of that sinister, invisible being would help to banish an inferiority complex which threatened to claim him. He succeeded in throwing off his pursuers, very ordinary underworld toughs, without great difficulty.

A covered lorry was waiting at a spot appointed. In it, he donned blue overalls and presently entered a service door of the Regal-Athenian, a peaked cap pulled down over his eyes and carrying a crate upon his shoulders.

The death of Blondie Hahn, demi-god of the underworld, and of Fly Carlo, notorious cat-burglar, had been swamped as news by the assassination of Harvey Bragg. In the railway station, on every news-stand that he had passed, the name Bragg flashed out at him. The man's death had created a greater sensation than his life. Thousands had lined up along the route of his funeral train to pay homage to Harvey Bragg.

Mark Hepburn abandoned the problem of how this atrocity fitted into the schemes of that perverted genius who aimed to secure control of the country. He was keyed up to ultimate tension, insanely happy because he had read kindness in the eyes of Moya Adair; guiltily conscious of the fact that perhaps he had not performed his duty to the government, indeed, did not know where it lay. But now, as Fey, stoic-faced, opened the door of the apartment, he found himself to be doubly eager for the great attempt planned by Nayland Smith to trap some, at least, of these remorseless plotters—it might be even the great chief—in their subterranean lair.

CHAPTER 23

FU MANCHU'S WATER-GATE

"SHUT OFF," snapped Nayland Smith. "Drift on the current."

The purr of the engine ceased.

A million lights looked down through frosty air upon them, lights which from river level seemed to tower up to the vault of the sky. Upon the shores were patches of red light, blue light, and green, reflected upon slowly moving water. Restless lights, like fireflies, darted, mingled, and reappeared again upon the bridges. The lights of a ferry boat crossed smoothly astern: lights of every colour, static and febrile, fairy lights high up in the sky, elfin lights, Jack-o'-lanterns, low down upon the sullen tide. Hugging the shore, the motor launch, silent, drifted in an ebony belt protected from a million remorseless eyes. In the shadows below a city of light they crept onward to their destination.

"I understand"—Nayland Smith's voice came through the darkness from the bows—"that a fourth man has been reported?"

"Correct, Chief," Police Captain Corrigan replied. "He was checked in and reported by flash two minutes ago."

Staccato, warning blasts of tugs, sustained notes of big ships, complemented that pattern painted by the lights: the ceaseless voice of the city framed it. The wind had dropped to a mere easterly breeze; nevertheless it was an intensely cold night.

"There's a ladderway," said Corrigan, "with a trap opening on the dock above."

"And the property belongs to the South Coast Trade Line. . . ."

"That's correct."

The late Harvey Bragg, as Nayland Smith had been at pains to learn, had held a controlling interest in the South Coast Trade Line. . . .

"Here we are," a voice announced.

"No engine," Nayland Smith directed. "Ease her in; there's plenty of hold."

391

The lights of Manhattan were lost in that dusky waterway. Sirens spoke harshly, and a ferry returning from the Brooklyn shore threw amber gleams upon the oily water. A tugboat passed very close to them; her passage set the launch dancing. All lights had been doused when that of an electric torch speared the darkness.

A wooden platform became visible. From it a ladder arose and disappeared into shadow above. The tidal water whispered and lapped eerily as they rode the swell created by the back wash of the tugboat.

"Quiet now!" Nayland Smith spoke urgently. "Lift the spar up and get it across the rail. How many men, Corrigan?"

"Forty-two, Chief."

"I can't see a soul."

"Good work by me!"

Nayland Smith rested his hand upon the shoulder of the man in the bows and mounted to the wooden platform. Another tugboat went by as Corrigan joined him. Her starboard light transformed the launch party below into a crew of demons and gleamed evilly on the barrel of a gun which Corrigan carried.

"It was the same two men who brought the fourth passenger?" Smith asked.

"Can't confirm that until we check up with Eastman, who's in charge above. But the other three were brought down by a pair of Chinks, and one of the Chinks rang a bell—which I guess I can locate: I was watching through binoculars. How many times he rang—except it was more than once—is another story."

"I know how many times he rang, Corrigan. *Seven* times. . . . Find the bell."

"Got my hand on it!"

The spar, raised upon the shoulders of the launch party, now rested on the rail of the platform. Slowly, quietly it was moved forward. Corrigan snapped his fingers as a signal when it all but touched the door.

"We don't know which way it opens," he whispered— "always supposing it *does* open."

The spar separated the two men.

"That doesn't matter. Ring seven times."

Police Captain Corrigan raised his hand to a sunken bell-push and pressed it seven times. Almost immediately the door opened. Beyond was cavernous darkness.

"Go to it, boys!" Corrigan shouted.

Lustily the spar was plunged through the opening. Nayland Smith and Corrigan shot rays of light into the black gap. Somewhere above a whistle blew. There came a rush of hurrying footsteps upon planking, a subdued uproar of excitement.

"Come on, Corrigan!" snapped Nayland Smith.

Corrigan leaped over the spar and followed his leader into black darkness now partly dispersed by the light of two torches. It was a brick tunnel in which they found themselves, illimitable so far as the power of the lights was concerned. Corrigan paused, turned, and:

"This way, boys!" he shouted.

The patter of feet echoed eerily in that narrow passage. Vaguely, against reflection from the river, the spar could be seen jammed across the doorway. Nayland Smith's light was already far ahead.

"Wait for me, Chief!" Corrigan yelled urgently.

The officer in charge of the hidden party which secretly had been assembled for many hours appeared, a silhouette against a background of shimmering water, leading his men as Corrigan sprang along the tunnel behind Nayland Smith.

Five paces Corrigan had taken when Nayland Smith turned.

"Wait for the men, Corrigan," he cried, his snappy instructions echoing weirdly.

Corrigan paused, turned, and looking back. A line of figures, ant-like, streamed in from the river opening. Then:

"My God! what's this?" Corrigan groaned.

Something, something which created a shattering crash, had blotted out the scene. Corrigan turned his light back. Nayland Smith was running to join him.

An iron door, resembling a sluice-gate, had been dropped between them and the river. . . . They were cut off!

CHAPTER 24

SEIGE OF CHINATOWN

THE TEMPLE of the seven-eyed goddess was illuminated by light which shone out from its surrounding alcoves. Since each of these was draped by a curtain of different colour, the effect was very curious. These curtains were slightly drawn aside so that from the point occupied by the seven-eyed idol it would have become apparent that many cells were occupied.

There were shadowy movements depicted upon the curtains. At the sound of a gong these movements ceased.

The brazen note was still humming around the vault-like place when Dr. Fu Manchu came in. He wore his yellow robe, and a mandarin's cap was set upon his high skull. He took his seat at a table near the pedestal of the carved figure. He glanced at some notes which lay there.

"Greeting," he said gutturally.

A confused murmur of voices from his hidden audience responded.

"I may speak in English," he continued, his precise voice giving its exact value to every syllable which he uttered, "for I am informed that this language is common to all of us present to-night. Those of the Seven not here in person are represented by their accredited nominees, approved by the council. But in accordance with our custom whereby only one of all the Seven shall know the other six, it has been necessary, owing to the presence of such nominees, to hold this meeting in the manner arranged."

A murmur which might have been one of assent greeted his words.

"I have succeeded in placing the chief executive we have selected in a position from which no human agency can throw him down. You may take it for granted that he will enjoy the support of the League of Good Americans. The voice of the priest, Patrick Donegal, I have not yet contrived wholly to control. . . . Because of a protective robe which seems to cover him, I regard this priest as the challenge of Rome to our older and deeper philosophy. . . .

"Suitable measures will be taken when the poppy is in flower. There is much more which I wish to say, but it must be temporarily postponed, since I have arranged that we shall all hear our chosen executive speak to-night. He is addressing a critical audience in the assembly hall in which Harvey Bragg formerly ruled as king. This is his second public address since Bragg was removed. It will convince you more completely than any words of mine could do of the wisdom of our selection. I beg for silence: you are now listening to a coast-to-coast broadcast."

So closely had Dr. Fu Manchu timed his words that the announcer had ceased speaking when radio contact was made.

Tremendous uproar rose to an hysterical peak, and then slowly subsided. Paul Salvaletti began to speak a speech destined both by virtue of beauty, phrasing and the perfect oratory of the man to find a permanent place in American forensic literature.

Salvaletti, to be known from that hour as "Silver Tongue," was, as befitted a selection of Dr. Fu Manchu, probably one of the four greatest orators in the world. Trained by the Oratorian fathers and then perfected in a famous dramatic academy of Europe, he spoke seven languages with facility, and he learned the subtle art of mass control as understood by the Eastern adepts in the Tiberan monastery of Rachê Churân. For two years, efficiently but unobtrusively, he had laboured in silence as confidential secretary to Harvey Bragg. He had the absolute confidence of Harvey Bragg. He had a more intimate knowledge of the inner workings of the League of Good Americans, of the Lotus Transport Corporation, and of the other enterprises which had formed the substantial background of the demagogue, than any man living. He understood human nature, but had the enormous advantage over Bragg of a profound culture. He could speak to the South in the language of the South; he could speak to the world in the language of Cicero.

He began, with perfect art, to deliver this modern version of Mark Antony's oration over the body of Caesar. . . .

"What in hell's this?" growled Police Captain Corrigan. "We're jammed!"

The light of his torch and that of Nayland Smith's became concentrated upon the iron door which had fallen behind them. Dimly, very dimly, they could hear the voices of the party outside.

"Hadn't counted on this," muttered Nayland Smith. "But we mustn't get bothered—we must think."

"Looks to me, Chief," said the police officer, "as if the seven rings work automatically, and that after an interval this second door comes down—like as not to make sure that a big party isn't bullying in."

"Something in that Corrigan," Nayland Smith rapped. "Outstanding point is—we are cut off."

"I know it."

They stood still, listening. Shouted orders from somebody who had taken charge became dimly audible. Words reached their ears as mere murmurs. The iron door was not only heavy but fitted perfectly in its grooves.

"Can you hear a sound like water, Chief?" Corrigan said in a low voice.

"Yes."

The ray from Nayland Smith's torch searched the floor, the walls, as far ahead as it could reach, revealing nothing but an apparently endless brick tunnel.

"I kind of fancy," Corrigan went on, "that I've heard there used to be a brook or a stream hereabouts in the old days, and that it was switched into a sewer. You can hear running water?"

"I can," said Nayland Smith.

"I guess we're beside it or over it. Used to run from some place near Columbus Park where there was a pond. . . ."

"We have to suppose," said Nayland Smith quietly, "that so far everything is in order——"

"Except that we're trapped!"

"I mean, if, as you suggest, the river door opens mechanically and this outer door falls at an agreed interval, we shall be quite safe in pushing ahead."

"I should feel safer with forty men behind me."

"So should I. The proper routine would be in all probability to re-close the river door, ring the bell seven times, and continue in this way until the whole party was inside."

"Sounds reasonable—but how do we do it? . . . Hullo! Look at this!"

Corrigan directed the light of his torch downwards; his hand shook with excitement. Discord of shouting voices grew louder. A crack appeared at the bottom of the iron door. Slowly, it was being raised!

"The opening of the outer door drops it automatically in half a minute or less," said Nayland Smith. "Normally it is raised when the door is closed. They must have moved the spar. Contact has been established which raises it again."

"I'm waiting," Corrigan replied grimly, his gaze fixed upon the slowly moving door. "I'm not built like an eel. When I can get out I'll be the first to cheer. . . ."

In the streets of Chinatown a cordon had been drawn around the suspected area. During the course of the day a census had been taken of the inhabitants in the section indicated by Nayland Smith; outgoings and incomings, all had been accounted for. Most of those interrogated were Chinese, and the Chinaman is a law-respecting citizen. Almost any other would have openly resented the siege conditions to which the inhabitants of this section of New York City found themselves subjected on this occasion.

Mark Hepburn with a guard of three men directed operations. He was feverishly anxious, as his deep-set eyes indicated to everyone he approached. His duty was to make sure that none of the invisible members of Dr. Fu Manchu's organization should escape by the street exits which the vigilance of government men and police engaged upon the inquiry had failed to detect. The importance of his duty was great enough to enable him to force into the background the problem of Moya Adair. Apart from his personal interest, she formed an invaluable link, if only he could succeed in reconciling his conscience with his duty, his own interests with those of the State.

The night had grown bitterly cold; high winds had blown themselves away across the Atlantic; the air had that champagne quality which redoubles a man's vigour.

Many streets were barricaded; a sort of curfew had been imposed upon part of Chinatown. Every householder had been made responsible for the members of his household. Restaurants and cafés were scrutinized from cellar to roof, particularly Wu King's Bar. Residents returning to the barricaded area were requested to establish their identity before being admitted. Visitors who did not reside there were escorted to their destinations and carefully checked up.

Mark Hepburn had tackled the situation with his usual efficiency. Pretence had been cast aside. All Chinatown knew that the section was being combed for one of the big shots of the underworld.

And all Chinatown remained in suspense; for now the news had spread through those mysterious channels which defy Occidental detection that other members of the Council of the Seven of the Si-Fan were in the city. The dreaded Black Dragon Society of Japan was no more than an offshoot of the Si-Fan, which embraced in its invisible tentacles practically the whole of the coloured races of the world. No dweller east of Suez or west of it to Istanbul would have gambled a dollar on the life of a man marked down by the Si-Fan.

III

In the cave of the seven-eyed goddess Dr. Fu Manchu sat, eyes closed, long, ivory hands extended upon the table before him, listening to the silver tones of that distant speaker, to the rising excitement of the audience which he addressed; an audience representing but a fraction of that which from coast to coast hung upon his words—words destined to play a strange part in the history of the country. The other listeners, invisible in queer cells which surrounded the central apartment, were equally silent, motionless.

In the seventh of these, that which communicated with a series of iron doors protecting the place from the street above, old Sam Pak crouched mummy-like upon a settee listening with others to that wonderful, inspiring voice speaking in a southern state.

A very faint buzz directly above his head resulted in slitlike eyes being opened in the death mask. Sam Pak turned, glanced up. A tiny disc of blue light showed. Slowly he nodded his shrivelled head and watched this blue light. Two, three, four minutes elapsed—and the blue light still prevailed. Where upon that man of vast knowledge and experience acted. There was something strange here.

The appearance of the blue light was in order, for a seventh representative even now was expected by way of the river-gate. The blue light indicated that the river-gate had been opened by one of the two men on duty who knew its secret. Its persistence indicated that the river-gate had not been re-closed; and this was phenomenal.

But even as Sam Pak stood up and began silently to shuffle in the direction of the door, the blue light flickered, dimmed, flickered again and finally went out.

Something definitely was wrong!

A lesser man would have alarmed the council, but Sam Pak was a great man. Quietly he opened the iron door and ascended the stairs beyond. He opened a second door and mounted higher, switching on lights. Half-way along a stone-faced corridor, stone-paved, he paused beneath a pendant lamp. Reaching up he pulled this pendant.

It dropped, lever fashion, and a section of the seemingly solid wall some five feet high and three feet wide dropped backward like a drawbridge. So perfectly was it fitted, so solid its construction, that he would have been a clever detective indeed who could have found it when it was closed.

Sam Pak, stooping, went into the dark opening. An eerie lapping of moving water had become audible at the moment that the secret door had dropped back. There was a dank, unwholesome smell. He reached for, and found, an iron rail; then from beneath his blue robe he produced a torch and shone its ray ahead.

He stood on a gallery above a deep sewer, an inspection-gallery accessible to, and sometime used by, the sanitary authorities of the city. Into this a way had been struck from the secret warren below Chinatown and another way out at the farther end by the river bank.

He moved slowly along, a crouched, eerie figure in a whispering, evil place.

At a point where the oily waters disappeared beneath an arch, the gallery seemingly ended, and before a stone wall he paused.

His ancient, clawlike hands manipulated some piece of mechanism, and a small box came to light, a box in which a kind of telephone stood. Sam Pak raised the instrument; he listened.

"Chee, chee, chee!" he hissed.

He hung up the telephone, re-closed the box in which it was hidden and began to return along the iron gallery, moving now with extraordinary rapidity for a man of his years. The unexpected, but not the unforeseen, had happened.

The enemy had forced the water-gate.

IV

At the corner of Doyers Street a crowd had gathered beyond the barricade. Those who wished to pass were referred by the police officer on duty to another point, which necessitated a detour. A tall, bearded man, his coat collar turned up and his hat brim pulled down, stood beside a big car, the windows of which were bullet-proof, lurking in shadow and studying the group beyond the barricade. A messenger from local police headquarters made his way to his side.

"Captain Hepburn?"

"Yes. What is it?"

"We seem to have lost contact with the party operating under Federal Officer Smith down on East River."

"No news?"

"Not a thing."

Mark Hepburn experienced a sudden, great dread. The perils of the river-gate, although a large party had been assembled, were unknown—unknown as the resources of the formidable group which Nayland Smith sought to break up. His quick imagination presented a moving picture of things which might have happened. Johnson was perfectly capable of taking charge of routine here on the street; indeed, Johnson had done most of the work, Hepburn merely supervising and taking reports. On the other hand, a dash to the waterfront would be technically to desert his post. He turned to the man beside him.

"Go personally," he directed in his monotonous way; "take a launch if you can't make it on shore. Then hurry right back to me to report just what you have seen."

"All right, Captain."

The man set out.

Mark Hepburn entered the bullet-proof car and gave brief directions to the driver.

Outside Wu King's Bar the car stopped. Mark Hepburn went in, followed by the three men who had accompanied him. The place was almost wholly patronized by Asiatics, except when squads of sightseers were brought there, Wu King's being one of the show places in Chinatown tours.

A buzz of conversation subsided curiously as the party entered. Following Hepburn's lead they walked through the restaurant to the bar at the farther end, glancing keenly at the groups of men and women occupying the tables set in cubicles. Behind the bar Wu King, oily and genial, presided in person, his sly eyes twinkling in a fat, pock-marked face.

"Ah, gen'l'men," he said, rubbing his hands and speaking with an accent which weirdly combined that of the Bowery and Shanghai, "you want some good beer, eh?"

Everyone in the place except Wu King spoke now in a lowered voice; this serpentine hissing created a sinister atmosphere.

"Yes," said Hepburn, "some beer and some news."

"Anything Wu King know, Wu King glad to tell." He pumped up four glasses of creamy lager. "Just say what biting you and Wu King put right, if know enough, which probably not."

Mark Hepburn paid for the beer and nodded to his companions. Leaning against the bar they all directed their attention toward the groups in the little cubicles. There was another room upstairs, and according to the local police, still another above that where fan-tan and other illegal amusements sometimes took place.

"You seem to be pretty busy?" Hepburn said.

"Yes," The Chinaman revealed a row of perfect but discoloured teeth. "Plenty busy. Customers complain funny business outside. You gen'l'men know all about it I guess?"

"My friends here may know. What I want is copy."

"Oh sure! You a newspaperman?"

"You've got it, Wu. I guess you know most of your customers?"

"Know 'em all, mister. All velly old friend. Some plenty money, some go tick, but all velly good friend. Chinaman good friend to each other, or else"—he shrugged his shoulders—"What become of Chinaman?"

"That's true enough. But I'm out for a story." He turned, fixing deep-set eyes upon the fat face of the proprietor. "I'm told that one of *the Seven* is in town. Is that right, Wu?"

Less experienced than Nayland Smith in the ways of the Orient, he looked for some change of expression in the pock-pitted face—and looked in vain. Wu King's immobile features registered nothing whatever.

"The Seven?" he said innocently. "What seven's that, mister?"

V

"I'll say I'm glad to get out," said Corrigan as, assisted by willing helpers, he crawled under the partly raised door. "I don't like the looks of that tunnel."

From out of the echoing hollow under the dock came a shouted order:

"Silence!"

A buzz of excited words ceased. The men crowded into the narrow space between the two doors—the outer one partly jammed open by the spar—became silent.

"That's Eastman," said Corrigan. "Let's see what's new."

Outside in a Dantesque scene peopled by moving shadows:

"Launch just been signalled from the bridge," the invisible Eastman explained. "Are you held up there?"

"We were," Corrigan replied shortly. He turned to Nayland Smith. "What now?"

Nayland Smith, a parody of his normal self, wearing a shabby suit and a linen cap which had once been white pulled down over one eye, stood silent behind the speaker. He was tugging at the lobe of his left ear.

"A change of plan," he rapped. "This is something I had not foreseen. Get all the men under cover again, Corrigan, and run the launch out of sight downstream. Pick two good men to remain with us. Jump to it."

"D'you hear that, Eastman?" Corrigan shouted. "Everybody under cover, just like when we first came up. The launch to clear the dock, lay up and wait for signals. Get busy." He turned to two men who stood near to the spot where the spar projected into the partly open doorway. "You two," he said, "stand by. Everybody else up the ladder."

An ordered scuffling followed; three men tumbled into the launch and the others, some of whom had been crowded into the narrow space between the two doors, hurried up the ladder to the deck of the dock above. The launch went out astern, a phantom craft against the myriad lights reflected in the water, and disappeared from view.

"I want a small wedge fixed in that door; a clasp-knife would do, or anything that will bear pressure."

Smith ran inside, flashing the light of his torch ahead, and springing over the spar which crossed the tunnel. The iron door beyond was about two-thirds raised.

"All ready, Chief," came a voice. "I've got the door jammed."

"Good. Now Corrigan, join us. You two men get inside but hang on to the door."

There came further scuffling. The men, two black silhouettes, crossed the narrow opening.

"Are you ready?" rapped Nayland Smith.

"All ready, Chief."

"Pull. Now, Corrigan, we have to get the spar inside."

Pulling simultaneously, the thing was done and the spar laid down against one wall of the tunnel.

"Now," Nayland Smith directed breathlessly, "ease the door to. Don't let it bang if you can help it."

Slowly the door, propelled by a powerful spring, closed, almost dragging the two men with it; and as it closed, that second door which resembled a sluicegate rose, inch by inch. At last:

"Can't hang on any longer, Captain," one of the men reported; "we shall get our hands jammed."

"Let go," Smith ordered.

The door snapped to; there was a slight grinding sound as its edge came in contact with the obstacle which had been placed there to hold it. Nayland Smith flashed his light upward. . . .

Less than two inches of the drop-gate showed in the slot in the ceiling of the tunnel.

The exact working of this cunning mechanism was not clear, and the place in which they stood afforded no cover whatever.

"I get your idea," said Corrigan, "but short of shooting 'em down, we haven't a chance."

"No shooting without orders."

"I guess they'll see the door's phony, anyway," said one of the men.

"Once they're under the dock, Eastman will drop on 'em," Corrigan replied. "Get your guns out, boys. The moment that door comes open, the order is 'stick 'em up.' "

There was a moment of silence broken only by river sounds audible through the narrow opening made by the wedge.

"Just check up," said Corrigan. "I'm thinking, Chief, maybe the machinery won't work unless the door is tight closed. There's just time to see if we can haul it open. Go to it, boys!"

"I can just get a hold," came hoarsely.

"Pull—not far—just to see if she moves."

Another interval and then:

"Sure, we could haul it open right enough."

"Then stand by," rapped Nayland Smith; "haul if there's any hitch."

Up above, Eastman, peering through a gap in a row of barrels, saw the little motor craft stealing downstream, sometimes bathed in light, sometimes lost in darkness. One of the two Chinamen on board squatted in the bows, looking out sharply ahead, as the other drove the engine. A dim figure was seated astern; mist hovered over the water.

"This is some damned conjuring trick," Eastman muttered.

The man in the stern, as moving lights from a passing steamboat momentarily had revealed, wore black oilskins and a gleaming sou'wester beneath the brim of which his features were entirely hidden. His dress was identical with that of the other four who had preceded him as passengers in the launch!

The concealed party on the dock watched breathlessly as the little craft, rolling on an oily swell, was turned into the narrow opening all but invisible from mid-river and brought to the ladderway. The manoeuvre was performed smoothly; the man in the bows grasping the rail, extending one hand to the passenger in the stern. The engine had been shut off as they took the bend, and all lights doused.

Stepping cautiously, the passenger came forward and was assisted on to the ladder. There was an exchange of whispered words, indistinguishable to the men above. But Eastman, who had watched a previous arrival through binoculars from a police boat, guessed that the Chinaman who had been in the bows was leading the way. . . .

Inside, in utter darkness, four men waited tensely. Faintly to their ears came the sound of footsteps on the ladder.

"Stand by," said Corrigan in a low voice; "cover 'em."

The door opened—whether automatically or because it was pulled by the two men on duty was not at the moment apparent.

"Hands up!" rapped Nayland Smith.

He shot the ray of a torch fully into the face of the man who entered; a meaningless Mongolian face, which ever under these circumstances exhibited no change of expression whatever. The man raised his hands above his head. The figure immediately behind him clad in gleaming black made a similar movement.

From outside came a muffled shout, a clatter of footsteps—the sound of a splash in the river, and:

"Get that man!" Eastman was heard shouting. "He went in off the stern of the boat!"

Answering shouts responded, scurrying movements.

"Search the blackbird, Waygood," Corrigan directed. "You—search the Chink."

The man addressed as Waygood roughly snatched the sou'wester from the head of the traveller and peeled back his oilskin at the same moment that the other roughly overhauled the immobile Chinaman.

Nayland Smith stared eagerly into the face revealed. Recognition of an astounding fact had come to him. By one of those divine incidents which so rarely rallied to his aid, he had selected for this attempt on Fu Manchu's underground quarters a night when influential supporters of the movement were meeting in conference!

He had hoped to see the stoical features of General Li Wu Chang—but he was disappointed.

He saw a face Oriental in character, but rather of the Near then of the Far East; a proud, olive-skinned face with flashing dark eyes and supercilious lips. But the man was unknown to him.

The Chinaman was relieved of an automatic and a wicked-looking knife. The other was apparently unarmed, but a curious fact came to light when his oilskins were slipped off. Beneath them he wore a black robe, with a cowl!

Eastman burst in at the door.

"We've lost the second Chink," he reported. "I guess he swims like a shark. He must have swum under water for a long time, unless he knocked himself out! Anyway, there's no trace of him. And there's a sea mist coming up."

"Bad luck," snapped Nayland Smith, "but keep a sharp look-out," Turning to Corrigan: "Have this Chinaman taken outside," he directed. "I have some questions to put to the other."

A few moments later he stood before the dignified Oriental upon whose face Corrigan directed the light of a torch.

"Do you know the Chinaman, Corrigan?"

"No; but Finney, down on Mott Street, will know him when he sees him. He knows every Chink in the town."

Nayland Smith fixed his penetrating regard upon the features of the Egyptian: that the man was an Egyptian he had now determined.

"What is your name?" he demanded.

"By what authority do you ask?"

The man, who retained a remarkable composure, spoke easily, in perfect English and with a cultured voice.

"I am a government agent. What is your name?"

"Judging from the treatment received by my Chinese acquaintance," the Egyptian replied, "I have nothing but a man-handling to gain by silence. My name is Ahmed Fayume. Would you care to see my passport?"

"Hand it to Police Captain Corrigan."

The Egyptian, from beneath the curious robe which he wore, produced a passport which he handed to Corrigan, who glared at him in that intimidating manner cultivated by the police and opened the document savagely as though he hated it.

"When did you arrive in New York?"

"Last night by the *Ile de France*."

"And you are staying at . . ."

"The Grosvenor-Grand."

"What is your business in the States?"

"I am on a visit to Washington."

"Are you a diplomat?"

"I am attached to the personal suite of King Fuad of Egypt."

"That's right," growled Corrigan, looking up from the passport. "Something funny about this."

His expression became puzzled.

"Perhaps, Mr. Fayume," said Nayland Smith crisply, "you can explain what you are doing here to-night in the company of two suspected men."

The Egyptian smiled slightly.

"Naturally I was unaware that they are suspected men," he replied. "When the Egyptian consulate put me in touch with them, I was under the impression that I was being taken to a unique house of entertainment where hashish and other amusements were provided."

"Indeed! But why the fancy dress?"

"The black domino?" The Egyptian continued to smile. "This was provided by my guides, as visitors to the establishment to which I refer do not invariably wish to be recognized."

Nayland Smith continued to stare into the large velvety eyes of the speaker, and then:

"Your story requires investigation, Mr. Fayume," he said drily. "In the meantime, I must ask you to regard yourself as under arrest. Will you be good enough to empty your pockets?"

Ahmed Fayume shrugged his shoulders resignedly and obeyed the order.

"I fear," he said calmly, "that you are creating an international incident. . . ."

A report received out on the street as the party left Wu King's Bar, from the man whom Hepburn had dispatched to East River, was reassuring. The water-gate referred to by Nayland Smith had actually been discovered; two arrests had been made: operations on that front were proceeding in accordance with plan.

The life of Chinatown within the barricaded area carried on much along its usual lines. The stoicism of the Asiatics, like the fatalism of the Arab, makes for acceptance of things as they are. From a dry-goods store, when a customer entered or emerged, came mingled odours of joss stick and bombay duck; attractively lighted restaurants seemed to be well patronized; lobsters, crayfish and other crustacean delicacies dear to the Chinese palate were displayed in green herbal settings. John Chinaman blandly minded his own business, so that there seemed to be something quite grotesque about the guarded barrier at the end of the street.

Mark Hepburn was badly worried. Nayland Smith's unique experience had enabled him to postulate the existence of a Chinatown headquarters and of a river-gate. Right in this, it seemed improbable that he was wrong in his theory that there were exits and entrances somewhere on the streets surrounding this particular block.

He turned to Detective Inspector Finney, who silently walked beside him.

"You tell me there's nothing secret about Chinatown any more," he said slowly; "if that's true, there's a bad muddle here."

Inspector Finney, a short, thick-set man with a red, square-jawed face, wearing rainproofs and a hard black hat, turned and stared at Hepburn.

"There's no more iron doors," he declared defiantly. "An iron door couldn't get unloaded and set up without I knew about it. There used to be gambling joints and opium dens, but since the new regulations they've all moved over there—not so strict. All my boys can't be deaf and blind. When we get the word, we'll check up the block. If any strangers have arrived they'll have to show their birthmarks."

Mark Hepburn, inside one of the barriers beyond which stood a group of curious onlookers, pulled up sharply, and turning to Finney:

"There's just one part of this area," he said, "which I haven't explored—the roofs." He turned to one of a group behind him, and: "You're in charge, Johnson," he added. "I don't expect to be long."

Ten minutes later, followed by Inspector Finney and two men, Hepburn climbed the fire ladders at the back of a warehouse building which seemed to be deserted. No light showed from any of the windows. When at last they stepped upon the leads:

"Stick to the shadow," said Hepburn sharply. "There's a high point at the end of the block from which we might be seen."

"Sure," Finney replied; "that's the building where Wu King's Bar is located. He goes three floors up—the rest is a Chinese apartment house. I checked up on every apartment six o'clock this evening, and there's a man on the street entrance. Outside of this block we're overlooked plenty any way."

"There are lights in the top story of the Wu King building. Maybe you recall who lives there?"

"Wu King and his wife live up there," came the voice of one of the men, hidden in the shadows behind him. "He owns the whole building but rents part of it out. He's one of the wealthiest Chinks around here."

Mark Hepburn was becoming feverishly restless. He experienced an intense urge for action. These vague, rather aimless investigations failed to engross his mind. Even now, with the countless lights of the city around him, the curiously altered values of street noises rising to his ears, the taunting mystery which lay somewhere below, he found his thoughts, and not for the first time that night, leading him into a dream world inhabited by Moya Adair.

He wondered what she was doing at that moment—what duties had been imposed upon her by the sinister President. She had told him next to nothing. For all he knew to the contrary, her slavery might take her to the mysterious Chinatown base, that unimaginable den which in grotesque forms sometimes haunted his sleep. The awful idea presented itself that if Nayland Smith's raid should prove successful, Moya might be one of the prisoners!

A damp grey mist borne upon a fickle breeze was creeping insidiously through the streets of Chinatown.

"Is there any way of obtaining a glimpse of that apartment?" he asked.

"We could step right up and ring the bell," Finney answered. "Otherwise, not so easy. Looks to me as if the ladders from that point join up with the lower roof beyond the dip. And I don't know if we can get from this one down to the other."

"Stay in the shadows as much as possible," Hepburn directed.

He set out towards the upstanding storey of Wu King's building, which like a squat tower dominated the flat surface of the leads.

VII

"There's something wrong here," said Nayland Smith.

From the iron gallery upon which he stood he shone the light of his torch down upon slowly moving evil-smelling water.

"We've got into one of the main sewers," said Corrigan: "that's what's wrong. From the time it's taken us to make it I should say we're way up on Second; outside the suspected area, anyway."

He turned, looking back. It was an eerie spectacle. Moving lights dotted the tunnel—the torches of the raiding party. Sometimes out of whispering shadows a face would emerge smudgily as a straying beam impinged upon it. There were muffled voices and the rattle of feet on iron treads.

"Suppose we try back," came a muffled cry. "We might go on this way all night."

"Turn back," snapped Nayland Smith irritably. "This place is suffocating and we're obviously on the wrong track."

"There's a catch somewhere," Corrigan agreed. "All we can do is sit around the rat hole and wait for the rat to come out."

This was by no means what Nayland Smith had planned. He was savagely disappointed. Indeed the failure of his ambitious scheme would have left a sense of humiliation had it not been for the arrests made on the East River. Here at least was confirmation of his theory that the door under the dock belonging to the South Coast Trade Line undoubtedly was used by the group surrounding Dr. Fu Manchu.

It was infuriating to realize, as he had realized at the moment of the arrest of the Egyptian , that in all probability a meeting of the Council of Seven was actually taking place to-night!

The cowled robe was particularly significant. There were reasons why those summoned to be present did not wish to divulge their identity to the others: this was obvious. Ahmed Fayume was one of the Seven—a director of the Si-Fan. But it was improbable, owing to the man's diplomatic credentials, that they would ever succeed in convicting him of any offence against the government of the United States.

From experience he knew that all attempts to interrogate the Chinese prisoner must fail. He took it for granted that the captive was a servant of Fu Manchu: that such an admission could ever be forced from his lips was wildly improbable. The other Chinaman had escaped; by now, had probably given the alarm. . . .

Corrigan's words offered the only consolation. He recognized that it would be impracticable to sustain the siege of an area of Chinatown long enough to make it effective. He had been right, but he had failed. There was only one glimmer of hope. And suddenly he felt glad that the other Chinaman had escaped.

If, and he had little doubt upon the point, notable conspirators were present to-night, the raid on the secret water-gate might result in a desperate bid for freedom above!

But he was very silent as he brought up the rear of the party with Corrigan, groping back along the noisome tunnel. At points, vague booming noises echoed from above, the sound made by the heavy traffic. Always there was the echoing whisper of water. At a point where a lower inspection gallery crossed beneath that which they were following, he paused.

"Where do you estimate we stand, Corrigan?" he snapped.

"I should say about under Bayard and East Broadway. It's a guess—but I don't think I'm far out."

"Detail men to watch this junction."

"Stand on the foot of the ladder, Finney," Hepburn directed.
The detective inspector gingerly took his place.

"Now, you," indicating another man, "stand underneath and hold the rungs; and you," to a third, "hang on to the side so that it doesn't topple over. All set?"

The ladder, a short one, had been discovered in the warehouse yard and brought up on to the roof. Now, held by the three men, it perilously overhung a yawning gap, a gulley at the bottom of which, seen through a curtain of mist, were lights moving and stationary. Human voices distorted by the fog, muted sounds of movement were audible; but the characteristic hooting of taxicabs was missing, for this was one of the barricaded streets: the entrance to Wu King's Bar lay immediately beneath.

"All ready, Captain."

Mark Hepburn cautiously began to climb the ladder.

He moved in the shadow of the top storey of Wu King's apartment house. It was a dizzy proceeding: at the cold, starry sky which seemed to beckon to him from the right of the building he could not trust himself to look, nor downward into the misty chasm of the street. Rung by rung he mounted—his objective that lighted window still some six feet above. Upward he climbed.

And, presently, standing two rungs from the top, he could rest his hands upon the ledge and look into the room to which this window belonged.

He saw a sight so strange that at first he could not fathom its significance. . . .

An oddly appointed sitting-room was visible, its character and the character of the lamps striking a definite Oriental note. Brightly coloured rugs were strewn upon the floor, and he saw that there were divans against two of the walls. The predominant colour scheme of illumination seemed to be purple, so that he found great difficulty in making out what was taking place at the farther end.

A window there was widely opened, and two Chinamen seemed to be engaged in hauling upon a line. This in itself was singular, but the third and only other figure in the room struck an ultimate note of the bizarre.

It was that of a man wearing a black cowled robe. The cowl entirely covered his face, but was provided with two eyeholes, so that save for the colour of his dress he resembled one of the Misericordia Brethren!

He was standing quite still just behind the Chinamen, who, as Mark Hepburn watched, hauled in at the open window an equipment resembling a bosun's chair. Even now the significance of what was going on had not fully penetrated to his mind. The cowled man, clutching his robe about his legs and assisted by one of the Chinamen, took his place in the chair. Again they began hauling.

The black figure disappeared through the window. . . .

Now the truth burst upon him. Nayland Smith's raid of the water-gate had succeeded. . . . This was an emergency exit from the surrounded block!

How many had gone before? How many were yet to come? It was clear enough. A ropeway had been thrown across the street to some tall building on the opposite side, and above the very heads of the patrolling police the wanted men were being wound across to safety!

He moved his foot, urgent to descend. It was not too late to locate that other building. . . .

Then he paused.

As the two Chinamen bore upon the line, from a curtained opening left of the room another figure entered.

It was that of a tall man wearing a yellow robe; a man whose majestic features conveyed a sense of such power that Hepburn's movement was arrested. Tightly clutching the ledge, he watched—watched that high shouldered, imposing figure standing motionless in the curtained entrance. Perhaps his regard became so intense as to communicate a sense of his presence to the majestic newcomer.

Slowly the massive head was turned. Hepburn, through the glass of the window, met the regard of a pair of vivid green eyes which seemed to be looking directly into his own. . . . Never in his life had he seen such eyes. If, under the circumstances, he was actually visible from inside the room he could not be sure: but of one face, one astounding fact, he was certain:

This was Dr. Fu Manchu!

CHAPTER 25

SIEGE OF CHINATOWN (concluded)

MARK HEPBURN, keyed up by the immensity of the moment, ventured to the very top of the swaying ladder. He clutched a hook on one side of the window, placed there for the convenience of window-cleaners, and crashed his right heel through a pane of glass.

Stooping, he thrust his automatic through the opening, and: "Hands up, Fu Manchu!" he shouted, his voice rising from syllable to syllable upon notes of excitement.

The sea mist continued its insidious invasion of the streets below. One by one it blotted out the lights below. A voice spoke from the leads at the foot of the ladder:

"Go easy, Captain: we can't catch you if you fall!"

Hepburn scarcely heeded the cry: his entire interest was focussed upon the uncanny being who stood in the curtained opening. The two men straining on the rope were wonderfully trained servants; for at the glass crash and harsh words of command they had not started, had not turned, but had continued to perform mechanically the duty allotted to them!

Slowly, the perturbing regard of those green eyes never wavering, the tall Chinaman raised his hands. If he could not see the speaker, he could see the barrel of the automatic. From below:

"Bear left!" came urgently. "We can't hold the ladder."

During one irrevocable moment Hepburn tore his attention away. In that moment the room became plunged in darkness!

Clutching at the hook he fired in the direction of the curtained doorway. . . and the flash showed it to be empty. Further shots would be wasted. He craned downward.

"Pass the word there's a ropeway across the street. This damnable fog has helped them. Have the house opposite covered and searched."

Now came shouted orders, sounds of running, muffled cries from the police below. . . .

"Arrest everyone in Wu King's. Search the place from roof to cellar."

414

He fired again in the direction of the distant window, aiming over the heads of the Chinamen. Craning forward, he heard scurrying footsteps; then came silence. Perilously, but aided by a high exaltation which had come to him in the moment when he knew that he actually stood in the presence of the all but fabulous Dr. Fu Manchu, he found his foothold on the ladder and descended to the roof. Finney, one arm thrown out, hauled him back from the parapet upon which the ladder was poised, and:

"What's up there, Captain?" he demanded hoarsely. "I feel glued down here to the ladder."

"A getaway across the street. Get busy. We must hurry."

But already, delegating to a competent junior the matter of Wu King's and of those inside it, Lieutenant Johnson had entered the building indicated.

It consisted of a dry-goods store which had been closed half an hour before, and of apartments above. (Investigations were to prove that the landlord was none other than Wu King.) Employing those methods peculiar to the police responsible for the good conduct of Chinatown, entrance was forced to every apartment and every room right to the top. Here a hitch occurred.

On the top storey was a lodge of the Hip Sing Tong. No key was forthcoming, and the door defied united attack.

As a precautionary measure every man, woman and child found in the building had been arrested. Laden police wagons were taking them to the Tombs when Hepburn came racing up to the landing. The work of the demolition of the door of the Tong temple had commenced. It was proving a tough job when a cry came:

"Make way there!"

A grim-faced policeman appeared from below, holding an elderly Chinaman by the scruff of the neck.

"He's got the key," he explained laconically.

A moment later the door was thrown open. Light was searched for and found, and the garishly decorated place revealed.

It was permeated by a curious odour of stale incense wafted in their direction by a draught from a window overhanging the street. Tackle lay upon the floor; a pulley had been rigged to one of the beams which crossed the ceiling. It was to this spot that escape had been made from the top story of Wu King's building.

The Tong temple was empty from wall to wall. . . .

CHAPTER 26

THE SILVER BOX

IN HIS tower study Dr. Fu Manchu spoke softly. Two points of light glowed upon the switchboard on the table.

"It was well done, my friend, but the rest is merely a question of time. Base 3 must be vacated. It is regrettable that the representative from Egypt should have been arrested, but steps have been taken to ensure his release. Of Wu Chang's silence we are certain; other representatives are safe. You are short of helpers, therefore many splendid specimens must be sacrificed. But make good your own escape, leaving nothing behind that might act as a clue for the enemy,"

"I hear, Master," the voice of old Sam Pak replied as though he stood in the room. "I shall see to these matters."

"Instinct is greater than wit" the guttural voice of Dr. Fu Manchu continued. "By instinct Enemy Number One has smelled us out. I hear you hiss, my friend. We shall see. I have a plan."

"Do you desire, Marquis, that the way be made easy?"

"Such is my wish. Give them this hollow triumph: it will blind their eyes. Base 3 is of no further service: move in this matter, my friend."

Long fingers manipulated switches. Two lights became extinguished, but another appeared upon the board.

"Report," Dr. Fu Manchu directed, "of Number covering Base 3."

"Report to hand," the Teutonic tones of the Memory Man replied, "timed 11.36. Wu King's Bar was raided at 11.05 and everyone on the premises, including Wu King and members of his family, arrested by police. Emergency exit is also in their hands; many other arrests—some forty in all. The barricades have been raised, and everything is normal except that the area is being heavily patrolled. Government agent in charge of operations to-night identified as Captain Mark Hepburn, U.S.M.C. Captain Hepburn has left the area—covered. Report ends. From Number 37."

There was a moment of silence; the long fingers resting upon the lacquered table were so still that they might have been wrought of smoked ivory.

"Report," the voice directed, "of Number responsible for protection of representatives."

"Report of Protection Bureau to hand," the Memory Man replied, "timed 11.50. All are safely returned to their hotels or places of residence, with the exception of Egyptian representative. He was arrested at Entrance 4 together with one Wu Chang who was in his company. This arrest was the subject of an earlier report."

"Latest report of Number covering Exit 4."

"To hand, time 11.38. The raiding party believed to be in charge of Police Captain Corrigan has withdrawn, leaving men estimated at seven to nine covering the point. Report ends. This from Number 49."

"Prepare coast-to-coast reports. I shall require you to relay them in the order received, in one hour."

Amber light prevailed again in the domed room where the man of miraculous memory worked upon his endless task of fashioning that majestic Chinese head. And at the moment that the light reappeared, the long bony fingers of Dr. Fu Manchu reached out to the silver box. Raising the lid, he extracted the delicate equipment for opium smoking which this receptacle contained.

II

"What's the idea, Hepburn?" rapped Nayland Smith.

The New York *Times* propped up against a coffee-pot, he was sitting at a frugal breakfast as Hepburn came into the sitting-room. Save for a suggestion of shadows beneath his keen eyes, there was little in that bronzed face to show the state of sustained nervous tension in which Nayland Smith had been during the past forty-eight hours. Automatically filling his pipe, he stared at Hepburn.

The moustache and beard had vanished. Mark Hepburn was again his clean-shaven self. He smiled in his almost apologetic way.

418

"Wasn't it your friend Kipling who said that women and elephants never forget?" he asked. "I guess he might have included Dr. Fu Manchu. Anyway, I was shot at twice last night!"

Nayland Smith nodded.

"You're right," he said rapidly; "I had forgotten momentarily that he saw you at the window. Yes, the bearded newspaperman must disappear."

Fey entered from the kitchenette bearing silver-covered dishes upon a tray; an appetizing odour accompanied him. Fey's behaviour was that of a well-trained servant in a peaceful English home.

"I am making fresh coffee, sir," he said to Hepburn. "It will be ready in a moment."

He uncovered the dishes and withdrew.

"I am rapidly coming to the conclusion," said Nayland Smith while Hepburn explored under the covers, "that we have outstayed our welcome under the covers, "that we have outstayed our welcome here. It's only a question of time for one or both of us to be caught either going out or coming in."

Hepburn did not reply. Nayland Smith struck a match, lighted his pipe and continued:

"So far we have been immoderately lucky, although both of us have had narrow squeaks. But we know that this place is covered night and day. It would be wise, I think, if we made other arrangements."

"I am disposed to agree with you," said Mark Hepburn slowly.

"The papers"—Nayland Smith indicated a score of loose sheets upon the carpet beside him—"are reticent about our abortive raid. A washout, Hepburn! Impossible to hold either of the prisoners. We have no evidence against them."

"I know it."

Fey entered with coffee and then withdrew to his tiny sanctum.

"It is merely a question of time," Smith went on, unconsciously echoing the words of Dr. Fu Manchu, "for us to find this Chinese rabbit warren. I attended the line-up this morning but it's a waste of breath to interrogate a Chinaman. This fact undoubtedly accounts for the survival of torture in their own country. Wu King, as I anticipated, fell back on the story of Tong warfare. Centre Street is beginning to regard me as a tiresome fanatic. Yet"—he brought his palm sharply down upon the table—"I was right about the Chinatown base. It's there, but by the time we find it it will be deserted. An impasse, Hepburn, and our next move in doubt."

He pointed to the newspaper propped up against the coffee-pot.

"I begin to see the hand of Fu Manchu everywhere. Although I wore glasses and my clerical dress (upon which you have complimented me) I nearly came to grief on the corner right outside here this morning."

"What happened?"

"A heavy lorry, ignoring signals, drove at me hell-for-leather! Only the skill of my driver saved me. The man said his brakes had failed. . . . The lorry belonged to the Lotus Corporation."

"But Smith—"

"We must expect it. Our enemy is a man of genius. Our small subterfuges probably amuse him! Consider what's at stake! Have you glanced at the Abyssinian situation, for instance? Dr. Fu Manchu's triumph here would mean the end of Italy's ambition."

"You think so?"

Hepburn looked up sharply.

"I know it," Nayland Smith returned. "The map of the world is going to be altered, Hepburn, unless we can check what is going on in this country. Have you given due thought to the fact that almost overnight Paul Salvaletti has become a national figure?"

"Yes; I can't fit him into the picture."

"There is one very curious point . . . ."

"To what do you refer?"

"Lola Dumas is with Salvaletti. She is frequently in the news with him."

"Is that so strange? She has always been associated with the League of Good Americans."

"The League of Good Americans is merely another name for Dr. Fu Manchu," rapped Nayland Smith, standing up and beginning to pace the floor. "It is a point of very great interest:

it implies that Dr. Fu Manchu is backing Salvaletti; in other words, that Salvaletti is not an opportunist who has sprung into the breach——"

"Good heavens!" Hepburn laid down his fork, "the breach was *prepared* for him?"

"Exactly."

"Is it possible?"

"The pattern begins to become apparent. We have been looking too closely at one small piece of it. I have read the report upon Salvaletti. Even now it is far from complete but it would appear that his training throughout has tended inevitably in one direction. Thank heaven that Abbot Donegal is safe. I have said it before, I say it again: that priest's life is valuable. He may yet be called upon to stem the tide. Look at the papers. . . ."

In his restless promenade he stirred the loose sheets with his foot.

"The grave problems facing the Old World are allotted but little space. The nervous collapse (as such it is accepted) of Orwin Prescott merely occurs as a brief bulletin from Weaver's Farm. The several murders which have decorated the Doctor's visit to the United States are falling into the background. Even our Chinatown raid is granted scanty honours. No, Harvey Bragg, the Martyr, continues to dominate the news—his name now coupled with that of Paul Salvaletti. And—a significant fact, as I have said—Lola Dumas is creeping in."

There was a short silence interrupted only by the buzzing of the telephone, the subdued voice of Fey answering in an adjoining room. Evidently none of the messages was of sufficient importance to demand the presence of Nayland Smith or Hepburn. But Fey would be making careful notes. Smith, staring out of the window, saw that all traces of fog had disappeared; that icily clear visibility which sometimes characterizes New York City in the winter months was prevailing.

"Are you looking at the Stratton Building, Smith?" Hepburn asked.

"Yes," snapped Smith. "Why?"

"You remember what I told you about the strange man who lives up there at the top—as reported by Robbie Adair?"

"Yes."

"Perhaps—I admit maybe because it is associated with Mrs. Adair, I am very curious about this man. I put inquiries in hand late last night and I have a report this morning. There's rather a queer thing about the Stratton Building."

"What is it?"

Nayland Smith turned and looked at Hepburn.

"This—so far as the report goes; it's by no means complete: The whole of the building is occupied by offices of concerns in which the late Harvey Bragg was interested."

"What!"

"The New York headquarters of the League of Good Americans is there; the head offices of the Lotus Transport Corporation; even the South Coast Trade Line has an office in the building."

Nayland Smith came forward, resting his hands upon the table; bending down, he stared keenly into Mark Hepburn's eyes.

"This is interesting," he said slowly.

"I think so. It's odd, to say the least. Therefore I arranged early this morning to inspect the lightning conductors—by courtesy of the Midtown Electric Corporation. I may discover nothing, but at least it will give me access to a number of the rooms in the building."

"You interest me keenly," said Nayland Smith, returning to the window and staring up at the Stratton Building. "The League of Good Americans, eh? You must realize, Hepburn, that the great plot doesn't end with the control of the United States. It embraces Australia, the Philippines, and ultimately Canada! Middle Western farmers, crippled by mortgages, are being subsidized by the league and sent to Alaska, where unconsciously they are establishing a nucleus of Fu Manchu's future domination!"

"In heaven's name where does all the money come from?"

"From the Si-Fan, the oldest and most powerful secret society in the world. If the truth about the League of Good Americans—'America for every man and every man for America'—reached the public, I shudder to think what the reaction would be! But to return to personal matters—What are your plans in regard to Mrs. Adair?"

"I have none." Mark Hepburn spoke slowly, his usual voice sounding even more monotonous than usual. "I have told you everything I know about her, Smith. And I think you will agree that the situation is one of great danger."

"It is—for both. I assume that you are leaving it to Mrs. Adair to communicate with you?"

"I must."

Nayland Smith stared hard for a moment, and then:

"She may be a trump card, Hepburn," he said, "but frankly, I don't know how to play her."

III

"Saw my funny man last night, Goofy," said Robbie Adair, laying down his porridge spoon and staring up wide-eyed at Nurse Goff. "Funny man who makes heads."

"I believe he's just a dream of yours, child," Nurse Goff declared. "*I* have never seen him."

But Robbie was very earnest on the point, and was not to be checked. According to his account, the mysterious madman who hurled models of human heads from his lofty studio had appeared on the previous night. Robbie had awakened very late; he knew it had been very late " 'cause of the way the sky had looked." He had gone to the window and had seen the man hurl a plaster head far out over the dome.

"I never heard such a silly tale in my life," Nurse Goff declared. "God bless the child—he's dreaming!"

"Not dweaming," Robbie declared stoutly. "Please can I have some jam? Is Mum coming to-day?"

"I don't know, dear; I hope so."

"Are we going to the garden?"

"If it's fine, Robbie."

Robbie dealt with bread and jam for some time, and then:

"Will Uncle Mark be there?" he inquired.

"I don't think so, dear."

"Why not? I like Uncle Mark—all 'cept his whiskers. I like Yellow Uncle, too, but he never comes."

Nurse Goff suppressed a shudder. The man whom the boy had christened "Yellow Uncle" terrified her as her dour

Scottish nature had never been terrified before. His existence in the life of Mrs. Adair, whom she respected as well as liked, was a mystery beyond her understanding. Rare, though his visits were, that he was Mrs. Adair's protector she took for granted. But how Mrs. Adair, beautiful and delicately nurtured, ever could have begun this association with the dreadful Chinaman was something which Mary Goff simply could not understand. The affection of Robbie for this sinister being was to her mind even a greater problem.

"Give me an auto on my birfday," Robbie added reminiscently; "Yellow Uncle did."

"*Gave* you an auto, Robbie. God bless the boy! I don't know where you get these words. . . ."

When, an hour later, his "auto" packed behind in the big Rolls driven by Joe, the cheerful Negro chauffeur, lonely little Robbie accompanied by Nurse Goff set out for his Long Island playground, a "protection" party in a Z-car was following.

Far in the rear, keeping the Z-car in sight, a government car in charge of Lietenant Johnson brought up the rear of the queer procession.

CHAPTER 27

THE STRATTON BUILDING

MARK HEPBURN, in blue overalls and wearing a peaked cap, crept out from a window on to a dizzy parapet. Two men similarly attired followed him. One was an operative of Midtown Electric, the firm which had installed the lighting conductors; the other was a federal agent. They were on the forty-seventh floor of the Stratton Building. The leaded dome swept up above them; below the New York hive buzzed ceaselessly.

"This way," said Hepburn, and headed along the parapet.

He constantly looked down into a deep gutter which formed their path until at a point commanding an oblique view of the gulley which was Park Avenue, he pulled up sharply.

Storm clouds were gathering and sweeping over the city. To look upward was to derive an impression that the towering building swayed like a ship. Mark Hepburn was looking downward. He expressed an exclamation of satisfaction.

Fragments of clay littered the gutter; on some of the larger pieces might be seen the imprint of a modeller's work. The madman of the Stratton Building was no myth, but an actuality!

Hepburn glanced up for a moment. The effect of the racing clouds above the tower of the building was to make him dizzy. He felt himself lurching and closed his eyes quickly; but he had seen what he wanted to see.

Above the slope of the leaded dome was an iron gallery upon which two windows opened. . . . .

"Steady-oh, Captain!" said the government man, seeing him sway. "It's taken a long time to get up, but it wouldn't take long to fall down."

Hepburn, the moment of nausea past, stared again at the fragments at his feet.

"All right," he replied; "I was never a mountaineer."

He knelt down and examined the pieces of hard clay with keen curiosity. They surely formed part of a modelled head, possibly of more than one modelled head; but no one of them was big enough to give any indication of the character of the finished work. Over the shoulder:

"Gather all these pieces together," he directed, "and bring them away."

The man from the electric firm watched the two agents in respectful silence.

"Ha! What's this?" Hepburn exclaimed.

He had come upon a wired frame to which portions of crumbling clay still adhered. But what had provoked his words when he picked the thing up had been the presence upon the wooden frame, fixed by two drawing pins, of what resembled a tiny coloured miniature of a human face, framed around with white paper.

He detached this curious object from the wood and examined it more closely. Raising the mount he stared for a long time at that which lay beneath.

It was a three-cent Daniel Webster stamp, dated 1932, gummed upside down upon a piece of cardboard, then framed by the paper in which a pear-shaped opening had been cut. The effect, when the frame was dropped over the stamp, was singular to a degree. It produced a hideous Chinese face!

Mark Hepburn took out his notecase and carefully placed this queer discovery in it. As he returned the case to his pocket a memory came of hypnotic green eyes staring into his own—a memory of the unforgettable features of Dr. Fu Manchu as he had seen them through the broken window on the night of the Chinatown raid. . . .

Yes, the fact was unmistakable: inverted and framed in this way, the Daniel Webster stamp presented a caricature, but a recognizable caricature, of Dr. Fu Manchu!

A problem for Nayland Smith's consideration: no more false moves must be made. But here was a building occupied, so far as he knew, entirely by persons associated directly, or indirectly, with the activities of the League of Good Americans. At the top it seemed a madman resided; a madman who modelled clay heads, and who apparently had possessed and thrown away this queer miniature. Definitely there was a link here which must be tested, but tested cautiously.

Thus far he had every reason to believe that his investigation had been carried out without arousing suspicion. He had penetrated to a number of offices on many floors, craning out of windows in his quest of the supposed flaw in the lightning conductors. He had observed nothing abnormal anywhere, and had been civilly treated by a Mr. Schmidt in the office on the street floor, to whom, with his two companions, he had first applied. It remained to be seen if any obstruction would be offered to his penetrating the mysterious apartment which crowned the dome.

Five minutes later he climbed through the window into a room used apparently as a store by the firm leasing this suite of offices on the forty-seventh. He could not restrain a sigh of relief, as, quitting the swaying parapet, he reached the security of a rubber laid floor. Mr. Schmidt, representing the owners of the building, waited there as Hepburn's companions in turn climbed in through the low window.

"Everything seems to be in order up to this floor," said Hepburn. "How do we get to the top of the dome? The fault must be there."

Mr. Schmidt stared hard for a moment.

There's no way up," he replied curtly. The elevators don't go beyond this floor. There's a staircase to the flagstaff, but the door's been boarded up. Orders of the Fire Department, I guess. There's nothing up there; it's just ornamental."

"Then how do I carry out the inspection? It will cost plenty to rig ladders. Cheaper to break through to the staircase, wouldn't it be?"

"That doesn't rest with me," Mr. Schmidt replied hastily; "I shall have to ask you to give me time to consult directors on the point."

Mark Hepburn surreptitiously nudged the representative of Midtown Electric, and:

"When can you let us know, Mr. Schmidt?" the electrician inquired. "We have to make a report."

"I'll call you in the morning," Mr Schmidt replied.

Mark Hepburn experienced an inward glow of satisfaction. Apart from the testimony of Robbie Adair, he himself had seen lighted windows above the dome of the Stratton Building—and to-day they had found conclusive evidence to show that the rooms were occupied!

CHAPTER 28

PAUL SALVALETTI

LOLA DUMAS, concealed behind a partly-drawn curtain, looked down upon the crowded terraces. Palm trees were silhouetted against an evening sky; there was a distant prospect of steel-blue sea. The crowds below were so dense that she thought of a pot of caviare. Here was humanity, seemingly redundant, but pulsing with life so vigorous that its vibrations reached her on that high balcony.

They were cheering and shouting, and through all the excited uproar, like an oboe motif in an orchestral score, rose the name of Salvaletti.

Salvaletti!

This was merely the beginning of a triumphal progress which unavoidably should lead to the White House. Lola Dumas clutched the curtain nervously, her delicate fingers, on which she wore too many jewels, quivering with the tension of the moment. And they were still shouting and calling for Salvaletti when at the faint sound of an opening door Lola turned sharply.

Paul Salvaletti had entered the room.

Adulation, long awaited success had transformed the man into a god. His pale face was lighted up, inspired; the dark eyes reminded her of hot velvet. His habitual stoop was to-night discarded. He stood upright, commanding, triumphant. She looked now not upon the secretary of the late Harvey Bragg, but upon Caesar.

"Paul!" She took a step forward. "This is triumph. Nothing can stop you."

"Nothing," he replied; and even in speaking that one word the music of his voice thrilled her. "Nothing!"

"Salvaletti for the South!" A cry rose above the uproar below.

A wild outburst of cheering followed. Then came a series of concerted calls:

"Salvaletti! Salvaletti!"

The man plucked out of complete obscurity to be thrust upon a cloudy pinnacle, smiled.

"Lola," he said, "this was worth waiting for!"

She moved towards him, her graceful bare arms extended, and with a low cry of almost savage delight he clasped her. The world was at his feet—fame, riches, beauty. In silence he held her while, more and more insistent, the demand rose up from the terraces:

"Salvaletti! Salvaletti! America for every man. Every man for America!"

The phone bell rang.

"Answer, Lola," Salvaletti directed. "I shall speak to no one to-night but to you."

Lola Dumas glanced at him sharply. The heady wine of success had somewhat intoxicated him. He spoke with an arrogance the very existence of which hitherto he had successfully concealed. She crossed the room and took up the telephone.

A moment she listened; her attitude grew tense; and, ever increasing in volume, the cry "Salvaletti!" swelled up from below. Lola placed the receiver on the table and turned.

"The President," she said.

Those two words wrought a swift change in Salvaletti.

"What!" he whispered.

For a second he hesitated, then crossing with his characteristic catlike tread, he took up the phone.

"Paul Salvaletti here."

"I am watching you closely," came the imperious, guttural voice. "At this stage, you must not make one mistake. Listen now to my orders. Go out upon the balcony of the room in which you stand. Do not speak, but acknowledge the people. Then bring Lola Dumas out on to the balcony, that all may see her. Move in this matter."

The line was disconnected.

For three, five, ten seconds, as he hung up, Salvaletti's sensitive nostrils remained distended. He had heard the crack of the whip, had resented it.

"What?" Lola asked.

"An order," Salvaletti replied, smiling composedly, "which I must obey."

He crossed, drew the curtains widely apart, and stepped

429

out to the balcony. A roar of excited voices acclaimed him, and for a while he stood there, a pale, impressive figure in the moonlight. He bowed, raised his hand and, turning, beckoned to Lola Dumas.

"You are to join me," he said. "Please come."

He drew her on to the balcony beside him; and the woman associated for so long with Harvey Bragg, founder of the League of Good Americans, potential saviour of his country, received an almost hysterical ovation. . . .

Back in the room, the curtains drawn, Lola Dumas sank down on a cushioned settee, beckoning to Salvaletti with her eyes and with her lips. He stood beside her looking down.

"Paul," she said, "did the President give those orders?"

"He did."

"You see, Paul," she said very softly, "he has chosen for you. Are you content?"

CHAPTER 29

GREEN MIRAGE

MARK HEPBURN awoke; sat up. He found himself to be clammy with nervous perspiration, and the dream which had occasioned it was still vivid in his mind. It was this:

He had found himself in an apparently interminable tunnel (which he could trace to Nayland Smnith's account of the attempt to explore the East River water-gate). For a period which seemed to span many hours he walked along this tunnel. His only light was a fragment of thick, wax candle, resembling an altar candle. There were twists and turns in the tunnel, and always in his dream he had hoped to see daylight beyond. Always he had been disappointed.

Some great expediency drove him on. At all costs he must reach the end of this subterranean passage. A stake greater than his life was at hazard. And now, gaping blackly, crossways appeared in the tunnel; it became a labyrinth. Every passage revealed by the flickering light of the candle resembled another. In desperation he plunged into one which opened on his right. It proved to be interminable. An opening offered on the left. He entered it. Another endless tunnel stretched before him.

The candle was burning very low; his fingers were covered with hot grease. Unless he could win freedom before that fragment of wick and wax gave up the ghost and plunged him into darkness, he ws doomed to wander forever, a lost soul, in this place deep below the world of living men. . . .

Blind panic seized him. He began to run along tunnel after tunnel, turning right, turning left, crying out madly. His exertions reduced the fraction of candle almost to disappearing point. He ran on. In some way it came to him that the life of Nayland Smith was at stake. He must gain the upper air or disaster would come, not to Nayland Smith alone, but to all humanity. The candle now a tenuous disc, became crushed between his trembling fingers. . . .

It was at this moment that he awoke.

The apartment was very still. Save for the immutable voice of the city-which-never-sleeps, there was no sound.

Hepburn groped for his slippers. There were no cigarettes in the room. He decided to go into the sitting-room for a smoke and a drink. That ghastly dream of endless tunnels had shaken him.

The night was crystal clear; a nearly full moon poured its cold luminance into the rooms. Without turning on any of the lights—for he was anxious to avoid wakening Nayland Smith, a hair-trigger sleeper—he found his way to the sitting-room. There were cigarettes on the table by the telephone. He found one, but he had no means of lighting it.

As he paused, looking around, he saw through an open door the moon-bathed room beyond. It was the room which he had fitted up as a temporary laboratory; from its window he could just see the roof of the hotel where Moya Adair lived. He remembered that he had left matches there. He went in, crossed and stared out of the window.

His original intention was forgotten. He stood there, tense, watching. . . .

From a window of an out-jutting wing of the Regal-Athenian, one floor below and not twenty yards away, Dr. Fu Manchu was looking up at him!

Some primitive instinct warned him to reject the chimera—for that the man in person could be present he was not prepared to believe. This was a continuation, a part, of his uncanny dream. He was not awake. Brilliant green eyes gleamed in the moonlight like polished jade. He watched fascinatedly.

His impulse—to arouse Smith, to have the building surrounded—left him. Those wonderful eyes demanded all his attention. . . .

He found himself busy in the laboratory—of course he was still dreaming—preparing a strange prescription. It was contrary to all tradition, a thing outside his experience. But he prepared it with meticulous care—for it was indispensable to the life of Nayland Smith. . . .

At last it was ready. Now, he must charge a hypodermic syringe with it—an intravenous injection. It was vital that he should not awake Smith. . . .

Syringe in hand, he crept along the corridor to the second door. He listened. There was no sound.

Very quietly, he opened the door and went in.

Nayland Smith lay motionless in bed, his lean brown hands outside the coverlet. The conditions were ideal, it seemed to Mark Hepburn in his dream. Stealthily he stole across the room. He could not hope to complete the injection without arousing Smith, but at least he could give him some of the charge.

Lightly he raised the sleeve of his pyjama jacket. Smith did not stir. He pressed the needle point firmly home. . . .

II

Mark Hepburn felt himself seized from behind, jerked back and hurled upon the floor by unseen hands!

He fell heavily, striking his head upon the carpet. The syringe dropped from his fingers, and as Nayland Smith sprang upright in bed the predominant idea in Hepburn's mind was that he had failed; and so Smith must die.

He twisted over, rose to his knees. . . . and looked up into the barrel of a revolver held by Fey.

"Hepburn!" came sharply in Nayland Smith's inimitable voice. "What the devil's this?"

He sprang out of bed.

Fey, barefooted and wearing pyjamas, looked somewhat dishevelled in the glare of light as Nayland Smith switched on lamps: spiritually he was unruffled.

"It's a mystery, sir," he replied, while Hepburn slowly rising to his feet and clutching his head, endeavoured to regain composure. "It was the tinkling of the bottles that woke me."

"The bottles?"

Mark Hepburn dropped down into a chair.

"I was in the laboratory," he explained dully. "Frankly, I don't know what I was doing there."

Nayland Smith, seated on the side of the bed, was staring at him keenly.

"I got up and watched." Fey continued, "keeping very quiet. And I saw Captain Hepburn carefully measuring out drugs.

Then I saw him looking about as if he'd lost something, and then I saw him go to the window and stare out. He stayed there for a long time."

"In which direction was he staring?" snapped Nayland Smith.

Hepburn groaned, continuing to clutch his head. The memory of some strange, awful episode already was slipping from his mind.

"I thought, at a window down to the right and below, sir. And as he stood there so long, I slipped into the sitting-room and looked out from there." He paused and cleared his throat. "I was still looking when I heard Captain Hepburn come out. I shouldn't have behaved as I did, sir, but I had seen Captain Hepburn's eyes. . . ."

"What do you mean?"

"Well, sir, it might have been that he was walking in his sleep! And so, when I heard him coming, I ducked into a corner and watched him go by. I followed him right to your door. He opened it very quietly. I was close behind him when he crossed to the bed——"

Now, suddenly, in a stifled voice:

"The syringe!" Hepburn cried, "the syringe! My God! Did I *touch* you?"

He sprang up wildly, his glance questing about the floor.

"Is this what you mean, Hepburn?" Nayland Smith asked. He picked up a *fountain pen*, at the same time glancing down at his left arm. "My impression is that you jabbed the *nib* into me!"

Mark Hepburn stared at the fountain pen, fists clenched. It was a new one bought only that day, his old one had been smashed during operations in the Chinatown raid. So far as he could remember he had never filled it. The facts, the incredible facts, were coming back to him. . . . He had prepared a mixture: of what it was composed he hadn't at this moment the slightest idea. But he had imagined or had dreamed that he charged a hypodermic syringe with it. He must have charged the fountain pen, for he had no hypodermic syringe in his possession!

Nayland Smith's penetrating regard never left the troubled face, and then:

434

"Was I dreaming," Hepburn groaned, "or was I hypnotized? By heaven! I remember—I went to the window and saw his eyes! *He* was watching me."

"Who was watching you?" Smith asked quietly.

"I don't know who it was, sir," Fey interrupted with an apologetic cough, "but he had one of the most dreadful faces I have ever seen in my life. The moonlight was shining on him. I saw his green eyes."

"What!"

Nayland Smith sprang to his feet. From out of his varied experience an explanation of the strange incident, phantomesque, arose. He stared hard again at Mark Hepburn.

"Dr. Fu Manchu is the most accomplished hypnotist alive," he said harshly. "During those few moments that you watched him from the window above Wu King's he must have established partial control." He pulled on a dressing-gown which lay across the foot of the bed. "Quick, Fey, get Wyatt! He's on duty in the lobby."

Fey ran out.

Nayland Smith turned, threw up the window and craned forward. Over his shoulder:

"Which way, Hepburn?" he snapped.

Mark Hepburn, slowly recovering control of his normal self, leaned on the sill and pointed.

"The wing on the right, third window from the end, two floors below this."

"There's no one there, and the room is dark." The wail which tells that the Fire Department is out, a solo rarely absent from New York's symphony, rose, ghostly, through the night. "I have had an unpleasant narrow escape. Beyond doubt you were acting under hypnotic direction. Fey's evidence confirms it. A daring move! The Doctor must be desperate." He glanced down at the fountain pen which lay upon a little table. "I wonder what you charged it with," he murmured meditatively. "Dr. Fu Manchu assumed too much in thinking you had hypodermic syringes in your possession. You obeyed his instructions—but charged the fountain pen; thus probably saving my life."

It was only a few moments later that Wyatt, the government agent in charge below, found the night manager and accompanied by two detectives was borne up to the thirty-eighth floor of the hotel wing in which the suspected room was located.

"I can tell you there's no one there, Mr. Wyatt," the manager said, twirling a large key around his fore-finger. "It was vacated this morning by a Mr. Eckstein, a dark man, possibly Jewish. There's only one curious point about it——"

"What's that?" Wyatt asked.

"He took the door key away. . . ." Mr. Dougherty smiled grimly; his Tipperary brogue was very marked. "Unfortunately, it often happens. But in this case there may have been some ulterior motive."

The bedroom, when they entered, was deserted; the two beds were ready for occupation by incoming guests. Neither here nor in the bathroom was there evidence pointing to a recent intruder. . . .

The detectives were still prowling around and Nayland Smith on the fortieth floor of the tower was issuing telephone instructions when a tall man, muffled in a fur topcoat—a man who wore glasses and a wide-brimmed black hat—stepped into an elevator on the thirtieth floor and was taken down to street level. . . .

"No one is to leave this building," rapped Nayland Smith, until I get down. Don't concentrate on the tower; post men at every elevator and every exit."

Wyatt, the night manager, and the two detectives stepped out of the elevator at the end of the huge main foyer. The tall man in the fur coat was striding along its carpeted centre aisle. The place was only partially lighted at that late hour. There was a buzz of vacuum cleaners. He descended marble steps to the lower foyer. A night porter glanced up at him, curiously, as he passed his desk.

A man came hurrying along an arcade lined by flower shops, jewellers' shops and other features of a luxury bazaar, but actually contained within the great hotel, and presently appeared immediately facing the elevator by which Wyatt and his party had descended. Seeing them he hurried across, and:

"No one is to leave the building!" he cried. "Post men at all elevators and all entrances."

The tall visitor passed through the swing doors and descended the steps to the sidewalk. A Lotus cab which had been standing near by drew up; opening the door, he entered. The cab moved off. It was actually turning the Park Avenue corner when detectives, running from the westerly end of the building, reached the main entrance and went clattering up the steps. One, who seemed to be in charge, ran across to the night porter. Federal Agent Wyatt was racing along the foyer towards them.

"Who's gone out," the detective demanded, "in the last five minutes? Anybody?"

But even as the startled man began to answer, the Lotus cab was speeding along almost deserted streets, and Dr. Fu Manchu, lying back in the corner, relaxed after a dangerous and mentally intense effort which he had every reason to believe would result in the removal of Enemy Number One. Nayland Smith's activities were beginning seriously to interfere with his own. The abandonment of the Chinatown base was an inconvenience, and reports received from those responsible for covering the Stratton Building suggested that further intrusion might be looked for. . . .

CHAPTER 30

PLAN OF ATTACK

GREY MORNING light was creeping into the sitting-room.

"Last night's attempt," said Nayland Smith (he wore a dressing-gown over pyjamas), "is not uncharacteristic of the Doctor's methods."

"Poor consolation for me," Hepburn replied, speaking from the depths of an armchair in which, similarly attired, he was curled up.

"Don't let us worry unduly," said Nayland Smith. "I have known others to suffer from the insidious influence of Fu Manchu; indeed, I have suffered myself. Physical fear has no meaning for the Doctor. Undoubtedly he was here in person, here in the enemy's headquarters. He walked out under the very noses of the police officers I had dispatched to intercept him. He is a great man, Hepburn."

"He is."

"There is no evidence that you were drugged in any way last night, but we cannot be sure, for the Doctor's methods are subtle. That he influenced your brain while you were sleeping is beyond dispute. The dream of the interminable labyrinth, the conviction that my life depended upon your escape—all this was prompted by the will of Fu Manchu. You were dreaming, although even now you doubt it, when you thought you awoke. He only made one mistake, Hepburn. He postulated a hypodermic syringe which was not in your possession!"

"But I loaded a fountain pen with some pretty deadly drugs which now it is impossible to identify."

"You carried out your hypnotic instructions to the best of your ability. The power of Fu Manchu's mind is an awful thing. However, by an accident, a pure accident, or an oversight, he failed—thank God! Let us review the position."

Mark Hepburn reached out for a cigarette; his face was haggard, unshaven.

"We are beginning to harass the enemy." Nayland Smith, pipe fuming furiously, paced up and down the carpet. "That

438

there is a staircase below Wu King's with some unknown exit on the street is certain. At any moment I expect a report that the men have broken in there. It's construction has been carried out from the point that I call the water-gate; hence Finney's ignorance of its existence. Once we have reached it, with the equipment at our disposal we can break through. It doesn't matter how many iron doors obstruct us. The entrance from the sewers we have been unable to trace. But penetration to the Chinatown base is only a question of time."

He puffed furiously, but his overworked pipe had gone out. He laid it in an ash-tray and continued to walk up and down. Mark Hepburn, labouring under a load of undeserved guilt, watched him fascinatedly.

"What Mrs. Adair knows which would be of value to us is problematical. According to Lieutenant Johnson's report, it would seem to be perfectly feasible to obtain possession of the boy, Robbie, during one of his visits to Long Island."

"The owner of the house and his family are at the coast," Mark Hepburn said monotonously. "He is, as you will have noted, a co-director with the late Harvey Bragg of the Lotus Transport Corporation."

"I had noted it," Smith said drily; "but he may nevertheless be innocent of any knowledge of the existence of Dr. Fu Manchu. That's the devilish part of it, Hepburn. The other points are: (a) Can Mrs. Adair afford us any material assistance; (b) Is it safe to attempt it?"

"The negro chauffeur," Hepburn replied, "may have orders, for all we know to the contrary, to shoot the boy in the event of any such attempt. Frankly, I don't feel justified."

"Assuming we succeeded. . . ."

"Her complicity would be fairly evident—she would suffer?"

Nayland Smith paused in his promenade and, turning, stared at Hepburn.

"Unless we kidnapped *her* at the same time," he snapped.

Mark Hepburn stood up suddenly, dropping his recently lighted cigarette in a tray.

"By heavens, Smith," he said excitedly, "that may be the solution!"

"It's worth thinking about, but it would require a very careful plan. I am disposed at the moment—without imperilling the lives of Mrs. Adair and her son—to concentrate upon the Stratton Building. Your experience there was definitely illuminating."

He crossed to the big desk above which the maps were pinned, and looked down at a number of clay fragments which lay there.

"I feel disposed, Hepburn—if necessary with the backing of the Fire Department—to pursue your enquiry into the flaw in the lightning conductors. An examination could be arranged after office workers had left. But I think it would be unwise to give any warning to this Mr. Schmidt whom you have mentioned, of our intention. Do you agree with me?"

"Yes," Hepburn replied slowly; "that is what I had planned myself. But, Smith. . . ."

Smith turned and regarded him.

"Do you realize how I feel? In the first place you know—I haven't disguised it—that I am becoming really fond of Moya Adair. That's bad enough—she's one of the enemy. In the second place, it seems that I am such a poor weakling that this hellish Chinaman can use me as an instrument to bring about your murder! How can you ever trust me again?"

Nayland Smith stepped up to him, grasped both his shoulders and stared into his eyes.

"I would trust you, Hepburn," he said slowly, "as I would trust few men. You are human—so am I. Don't let the hypnotic episode disturb your self-respect. There is no man living immune from this particular power possessed by Dr. Fu Manchu. There's only one thing: Should you ever meet him again—avoid his eyes."

"Thank you," said Mark Hepburn; "it's kind of you to take it that way."

Smith grasped the outstretched hand, clapped Hepburn on the shoulder and resumed his restless promenade.

"In short," he continued, "we are beginning to make a certain amount of headway. But the campaign, as time goes on, grows more and more hectic. In my opinion our lives, as risks, are uninsurable. And I am seriously worried about the Abbot of Holy Thorn.

"In what way?"

"His life is not worth—that!"

He snapped his fingers.

"No." Mark Hepburn nodded, selecting a fresh cigarette and staring rather haggardly out of the window across the roofs of a grey New York. "He is not a man one can gag indefinitely. Dr. Fu Manchu must know it."

"Knowing it," snapped Nayland Smith, "I fear that he will act. If we had a clear case, I should be disposed to act first. The thing is so cunningly devised that our lines of attack are limited. Excluding an unknown inner group surrounding the mandarin, in my opinion not another soul working for the League of Good Americans has the remotest idea of the ultimate object of that League, or of the sources of its revenues! All the reports—and I have read hundreds—point in the same direction. Many thousands of previously workless men have been given employment. Glance at the map." He pointed. "Every red flag means a Fu Manchu advance! They are working honourably at the tasks alloted to them. But every one, when the hour comes, will cry out with the same voice: every one, north, south, east and west, is a unit in the vast army which, unknowingly, is building up the domination of this country by Dr. Fu Manchu, through his chosen nominee——"

"Salvaletti!"

"Salvaletti; it seems at last to become apparent. It is clear that this man has been trained for years for his task. I even begin to guess why Lola Dumas is being associated with him. In another fortnight, perhaps in a week, the following of Paul Salvaletti will be greater than that of Harvey Bragg ever was. Nothing can stop him, Hepburn, nothing short of a revelation— not a statement, but a *revelation*, of the real facts. . . ."

"Who can give it? Who would be listened to?"

Nayland Smith paused over by the door, turned, staring at the shadowy figure in the armchair.

"The Abbot of Holy Thorn," he replied. "But at the risk of his life. . . ."

CHAPTER 31

PROFESSOR MORGENSTAHL

THE MEMORY MAN worked industriously on his clay model.
Pinned to the base of the wooden frame was a photographic
enlargement of the three-cent stamp with the white paper
mask. He was engrossed in his task. The clay head was
assuming a grotesque semblance of the features of Dr. Fu
Manchu—a vicious caricature of that splendid, evil face.

Incoming messages indicated a feverish change of plan in
regard to the New York area. The names Nayland Smith and
Captain Hepburn figured frequently. These two apparently
were in charge of counter-operations. Reports from agents in
the South, identifiable only by their numbers, spoke of the triumphant progress of the man Salvaletti. Occasional reports
from far up in Alaska indicated that the movement there was
proceeding smoothly. The only discordant note came from the
Middle West, where Abbot Donegal, a mere name to the
Memory Man, seemed to be a focus of interest for many agents.

It all meant less than nothing to the prisoner who had
memorized every message received since the first hour of his
captivity. Sometimes, in the misery of this slavery which had
been imposed upon him, he remembered happier days in
Germany; remembered how at his club he had been challenged to read a page of the Berlin *Tageblatt*, and then to
recite its contents from memory; how, without difficulty, he
had succeeded and won his wager. But those were the days
before his exile. He knew now how happy they had been. In
the interval he had died. He was a living dead man. . . .
Busily, with delicate fingers, he modelled the clay. His faith in
a just God remained unshaken.

Without warning the door by which he gained access to his
private quarters opened. Wearing a dark coat with an
astrakhan collar, an astrakhan cap upon his head, a tall man
came in. The sculptor ceased to toil and sat motionless—
staring at the living face of Dr. Fu Manchu, which so long he
had sought to reproduce in clay!

442

"Good morning, Professor Morgenstahl!"

Dr. Fu Manchu spoke in German. Except that he over-stretched the gutturals, he spoke that language perfectly. Professor Morgenstahl, the mathematical genius who had upset every previous conviction respecting the relative distances of the planets, who had mapped space, who had proved that lunar eclipses were not produced by the shadow of the earth, and who now was subjugated to the dreadful task of a one-man telephone exchange, did not stir. His great brain was a file, the only file, of all the messages received at that secret headquarters from the whole of the United States. Motionless, he continued to stare at the man who wore the astrakhan cap.

That hour of which he had dreamed had come at last! He was face to face with his oppressor. . . .

Vividly before his eyes those last scenes arose: his expulsion from Germany almost penniless, for his great intellect which had won world-wide recognition had earned him little money; the journey to the United States, where no man had identified him as the famous author of "Interstellar Cycles," nor had he sought to make himself known. He could even remember his own death—for certainly he had been dead—in a cheap lodging in Brooklyn; his reawakening in the room below (with this man, the devil incarnate, standing over him!); his enslavement, his misery.

Yes, living or dead—for sometimes he thought that he was a discarnate spirit—he must at least perform this one good deed: the dreadful Chinaman must die.

"No doubt you weary of your duties, Professor" the guttural voice continued. "But better things are to come. A change of plan is necessitated. Other quarters have been found for you, with similar facilities."

Professor Morgenstahl, sitting behind the heavy table with its complicated mechanism, recognized that he must temporize.

"My books," he said, "my apparatus——"

"Have been removed. Your new quarters are prepared for you. Be good enough to follow me."

Slowly, Professor Morgenstahl stood up, watched by unflinching green eyes. He moved around the corner of the table, where the nearly completed model stood. He was estimating the weight of that tall, gaunt figure; and to ounces, his estimate was correct. But in the moment when, clear of the heavy table, he was preparing to strangle with his bare hands this yellow-faced horror who had rescued him from the grave, only to plunge him into a living hell, the watching eyes seemed to grow larger; inch by inch they increased—they merged—they became a green lake; he forgot his murderous intent. He lost identity. . . .

CHAPTER 32

BELOW WU KING'S

"LAY OFF there," shouted Inspector Finney.

The roar of the oxy-acetylene blowpipe ceased. They were working on the third door below Wu King's premises, from a tunnelled staircase of the existence of which Wu King blandly denied all knowledge. Turning upwards:

"What's new?" Finney shouted.

"We've got the street door open!"

Leaving the men with the blowpipe, Finney ran up. The air was stifling, laden with acrid fumes. An immensely heavy door, an iron framework to the outer side of which the appearance of a wall had been given by cementing half-bricks into the hollow of the frame, stood open. A group of men sweating from their toils examined it. Outside, on the street, two patrolmen were moving on the curious sightseers.

"So that was the game," Finney murmured.

"No wonder we couldn't find it," said one of the men, throwing back a clammy lock of hair from his damp forehead. It looks like a brick wall and it sounds like a brick wall!"

"It would," Finney commented drily: "it *is* a brick wall, except it opens. Easy to guess now how they got it fixed. They did their building from the other end, wherever the other end is. Now just where do we stand?"

He stepped out on to the street, looking right and left. The masked door occupied the back of a recess between one end of Wu King's premises and the beginning of a Chinese cigar merchant's. Its ostensible reason was to accommodate a manhole in the sidewalk. The manhole was authentic: it communicated with an electric main—Inspector Finney knew the spot well enough. Tilting back his hard black hat, he stared with a strange expression at the gaping opening where he had been accustomed for many years to see a brick wall.

"Well, I'll be damned!" he muttered.

"This lets Wu out, I guess," said one of the men. "If we didn't know the darned thing was here, he can claim he didn't."

"He'll do it," Finney replied. "And he'll probably get by with it. . . . There must be a bell some place: we traced the cable."

"We found it. Forced it out blowing through the iron. The brickwork's made to look kind of old, and there were posters stuck to it. I guess the push was under the posters; that's how it looks."

Inspector Finney went inside again, first glancing sharply right and left at the expressionless faces of a number of Chinamen who, from a respectful distance, were watching operations. There was an elaborate lock to this ingenious door, electrically controlled—but where from, remained to be discovered. . . .

Ten minutes later the third door was forced, and Inspector Finney found himself in a rectangular saloon curiously appointed but showing evidence of long neglect. The place, now, smelled like an iron foundry.

"This looks like an old dope joint to me," said one of the party, "but it's plain it hasn't been used for a long while."

"Strip all the walls," Finney ordered; "we're not through yet."

A scene of whole-hearted wrecking followed upon which the Fire Department could not have improved. Nevertheless, nearly an hour had elapsed before a cunningly hidden fourth door was discovered.

"Go to work, boys," said Finney.

The sweating workers got busy, bringing down the blow-pipe and rigging it for further operations. Finney stared speculatively at a patch of scarred wall. He did not know, indeed never learned, that beyond that very piece of wall upon which his gaze was fixed a spiral staircase led from a point below to the top floor of Wu King's building. Since only by measurements and never by sounding could the shaft in which it ran be discovered, it was not unnatural that Inspector Finney should concentrate the whole of his attention upon the fourth iron door recently discovered.

These iron doors made him savage. At the present moment he was recalling a recent conversation with the government agent Hepburn; he remembered boasting that no such door could be fitted in the Chinatown area without his becoming aware of the fact. It was a bitter pill, for here were four!

He reflected with satisfaction, however, that no man knows everything. At least he could congratulate himself upon the finding of this secret staircase. Between the eastern end of Wu King's premises and the western end of that adjoining, measurements had shown a space unaccounted for. Operating from inside Wu King's, floor boards had been torn up and a thick party wall brought to light. Through this Finney had caused a way to be broken; and they had found themselves on the first stair below street level.

That was good work! He resettled his hard hat upon his hard head and lighted a cigarette. . . .

Nevertheless, from the time that operations had commenced in early morning, up to the moment when the fourth door succumbed, many weary hours of toil had been spent by the party under Inspector Finney. He was up on the street wondering what all this secret subterranean building really meant when:

"We're through!" came a cry, hollow, from the acrid depths.

A minute later he stood on the lowest step, directing the ray of his torch upon oily, dirty-looking water.

"I guess that's tidal level," a voice said, "but sometimes these steps went deeper."

Inspector Finney flashed his light across the unwholesome-looking waters of the well. At the further end he saw a square opening two to three feet above the surface.

"There is or was another iron door," he growled, "but it's open. I wonder what's on the other side."

He was short and stocky himself. He turned to one of the men who had been working on the forcing of the doors.

"What's your height, Ruskin?" he asked.

"Six one-and-a-quarter, Inspector."

"You swim well, don't you?"

"Not so bad."

"If the stone steps carry on down below water level," Finney explained, "you won't have to swim. I figure you could keep your feet, hold a torch above your head and see what's beyond there. What do you say?"

"I'll try it."

Ruskin partly stripped for the endeavour and then, torch held in his right hand, he began, feeling his way with care, to descend the stone steps. The water, on top of which all sorts of fragments floated, ws just up to Ruskin's shoulders when he announced:

"I'm on the level now."

"Go easy," Finney warned. "If you loose foothold strike up to the surface and swim back."

Ruskin did not reply: he walked on, the torch held above his head. He passed under the square opening and stood there for a moment, then:

"Good God!" he screamed.

His torch disappeared—he had dropped it. There was a wild splashing and churning. Finney cast hat and coat aside and went plunging down the steps, another man behind him.

"Show those lights!" he shouted to the men who still remained upon the landing.

In the rays of the torches Ruskin's face showed above the surface. Finney grabbed him, and presently he was hauled up the steps. He lay there pointing down, shaking and gasping. . . .

"There's a great wide space of water back there," he panted—"and there's some awful thing lives in it—a monster! I saw its eyes shining!"

The temple of the seven-eyed goddess had been flooded by Sam Pak, but the head of its presiding deity remained just above the surface. . . .

CHAPTER 33

THE BALCONY

MR. SCHMIDT, representing the Stratton Estates, stepped out of the elevator on the top floor of the Stratton Building. Two men followed. One, wearing overalls and having a leather bag carried on a strap across his left shoulder, represented Midtown Electric. Mr. Schmidt recognized him as one of the pair who had been on the job before. The other, a tall, lean man wearing glasses and a brusque military moustache, came from the Falcon Imperial Insurance Corporation, which carried the fire risk of the Stratton Building.

A man in the uniform of the Fire Department, who was seated on a chair before a green baize-covered door, stood up as the party came out of the elevator.

It was really unnecessary, Mr. Englebert," said Schmidt, addressing the grey-moustached man, "to notify the Fire Department. The door which you see was formerly boarded up so that no door showed. The Fire Department has stripped it, in accordance, I suppose, with your instructions, and has seen fit to post a guard over it throughout the whole of the day. Quite unnecessary!"

Mr. Englebert nodded.

"My directors carry a heavy responsibility on this building, Mr. Schmidt," he replied, "and in view of the phenomenal electric storms recently experienced in the Midwest, we must assure ourselves of the efficiency of the lightning conductors."

"That's all agreed, Mr. Englebert. I have the keys of the staircase to the flagstaff, but you must have put us to quite some trouble."

Few of the hundreds of windows in the great building showed any light. The office workers engaged by firms occupying premises in the Stratton Building had departed for home. Only a few late toilers remained at their desks. In the three streets which embayed the tall structure, there was nothing to indicate that a cordon had been thrown around the building. Mr. Schmidt himself, who, indeed, was perfectly innocent of any complicity apart from the duties which he owed to the League of Good Americans, remained to this moment unaware of the fact that an office opening on the top floor, the staff of which had left at six o'clock, was now packed with police.

"All clear, sir," said the fireman.

Mr. Schmidt produced a bunch of keys, fumbled for a while, finally selected one, and not without difficulty opened the baize-covered door. He turned.

"I may say here and now," he remarked, "that I have never been in the dome: I have never known it to be opened during the time I have acted for the Stratton Estates. There are rooms up there, I know, which were formally occupied by the late Mr. Jerome Stratton. . . ." He shrugged his shoulders. "Of course, he was very eccentric. As there was no proper means of escape in the event of fire, they were closed some years ago. I'll lead the way. I have a torch. There are no lights."

He went in, shining the ray of his torch ahead. The man from Midtown Electric followed. Mr. Englebert paused at the threshold; and to the fireman:

"You have your orders," he snapped.

"Sure."

Nayland Smith, his facial disguise that which he employed for the Salvation Army officer, his dress that of a business man, followed Mark Hepburn—representing Midtown Electric—into the darkness illuminated only by Mr. Schmidt's torch. Hepburn supplemented it by the light of another.

They were in a curious, octagonal room in which, facing south, were three windows. There were indications that furniture at some time had stood against the walls. Now the room was bare.

"I guess we'll push right on to the top," said Hepburn.

Mr. Schmidt studied the rough plan which he carried.

"The door is on this side, I think," he said vaguely. "One of the late Mr. Stratton's eccentricities."

He walked to a point directly opposite the central window, stood fumbling there awhile, and then inserted a key in a lock and opened the hitherto invisible door.

"This way."

They went up an uncarpeted staircase at the top of which

another door was opened. They entered a second octagonal room appreciably smaller than that which they had just quitted, but also destitute of any scrap of furniture; there was an empty alcove on one side.

"You see," said Schmidt, flashing his light about, "there's a balcony to this room, outside the french windows there. . . ."

"I see," muttered Nayland Smith, staring keenly about him.

"From that gallery," said Mark Hepburn in his monotonous voice, "it is possible I could see the cable to the flagstaff."

"The window," Schmidt replied, "appears to be bolted only. I think you can get out there without any difficulty.

Nayland Smith turned suddenly to the speaker.

"There is still another floor above?"

Mark Hepburn had shot back a bolt and opened one of the heavy windows.

"Yes, so I understand. A small domed room immediately under the flagstaff. The door, I believe"—he hesitated—"is directly facing the windows, again. Let us see if I can open it."

He crossed as Hepburn stepped out on to the gallery—that gallery which Professor Morgenstahl had paced so often in the misery of his captivity. . . .

"Here we are!" Schmidt cried triumphantly.

"I see," said Nayland Smith, regarding the newly-opened door. "I should be obliged, while we complete our inspection, if you would step down and tell the fireman on duty that he is not to leave without my orders."

"Certainly, Mr. Englebert; then I'll come right back."

Mr. Schmidt crossed and might be heard descending the stair.

As he disappeared:

"Hepburn!" Nayland Smith called urgently.

Hepburn came in from the balcony.

"This place has been hurriedly stripped—and only a matter of hours ago! But, all the same, our last hope is the top floor!"

He led the way, shining light ahead. It was a short stair—and the door above was open. Small, domed, and surrounded by curious amber paned Gothic windows which did not appear to communicate with the outer air, it was stripped—empty!

451

"We are right under the flagstaff," said Hepburn quite tonelessly. "He's been too clever for us. I was marked on my first visit."

Nayland Smith's hands fell so that the ray from his torch shone down upon the floor at his feet.

"He wins again!" he said slowly. "That baize door has been covered all day. There's another way in—and another way out: the cunning, cunning devil." And now, his diction changed as that dauntless spirit recovered from the check: "Come on, Hepburn, downstairs again!" he snapped energetically.

But in the apartment below, with its bedroom alcove and tiny bathroom, formerly the quarters of the eccentric millionaire who had lived in semi-seclusion here, Nayland Smith stared about him in something like desperation.

"We have clear evidence," he said, "that this room certainly was occupied forty-eight hours ago. We are not defeated yet, Hepburn."

"I am anxious to study the view from the balcony," Hepburn replied.

"I know why you are anxious."

Undeterred by the note of raillery perceptible in Nayland Smith's voice, Mark Hepburn stepped out on to the iron-railed balcony: Smith followed.

"Where does the boy live, Hepburn?"

"I am trying to identify it. Wait a moment—I have seen these windows lighted from our own apartment. So first let's locate the Regal-Athenian."

"Easily done," rapped Nayland Smith, and pointed, "There's the Regal Tower, half-right."

"Then the penthouse lies somewhere west of where we stand. It must, because I know it isn't visible from our windows."

"That's a pity," said Nayland Smith drily.

"I'm not thinking the way you believe, Smith, at all. I'm trying to work out a totally different idea. It seems to me. . . ."

The sound which checked his words was a very slight sound, yet clearly audible up there where the Juggernaut hymn of New York was diminished to a humming croon, the song of a million fireflies dancing far below.

Nayland Smith turned as though propelled by a spring.

The open french window had been closed and bolted. Visible in the eerie light of a clouded moon, Dr. Fu Manchu stood inside watching them!

He wore a heavy coat with an astrakhan collar, an astrakhan cap upon his head. His only visible protection was the thickness of the glass. . . .

"Hepburn!" Nayland Smith reached for his automatic. *"Don't look into his eyes!"*

Those strange eyes glittered like emeralds through the panes of the window.

"A shot would be wasted, Sir Denis!" The cold, precise voice reached them out there upon the balcony as though no glass intervened. "The panes are bulletproof—an improvement of my own upon the excellent device invented by an Englishman."

Nayland Smith's finger faltered on the trigger. He had never known Dr. Fu Manchu to tell a lie. But this was a crisis in the Doctor's affairs. He took a step back and fired obliquely.

The bullet ricocheted as from armour plate, whistling out into space! Dr. Fu Manchu did not stir a muscle.

"My God!" (and it sounded like a groan) came from Mark Hepburn.

"You can hear me clearly through the ventilators above the window," the Asiatic voice continued. "I regret that I should have given you cause, Sir Denis, to doubt my word."

Hepburn turned aside; he was trying desperately to think coolly. He stared downward from the balcony. . . .

"You are one of the few men whom I have encountered in a long life," Dr. Fu Manchu continued, "of sufficient strength of character to look me in the eyes. For this I respect you. I know by what self-abnegation you have achieved this control, and I regret the necessity which you have thrust upon me. Our association, if at times tedious, has never been dishonourable."

He turned aside, placing a small globular lamp upon the bare floor of the room: within it a bright light sprang up. He took a step back towards the window.

"I am not prepared to suffer any human hindrance in this hour of destiny. I have chosen Paul Salvaletti to rule at the White House. Here, in the United States, I shall set up my empire. Time and time again you have checked me—but this time, Sir Denis, you arrive too late. You are correct in your surmise that there is another means of entrance to these apartments, formerly occupied by Professor Morgenstahl (whose name will be familiar to you) and myself."

"Smith," Hepburn whispered—"there's one chance . . ."

But Nayland Smith did not turn; he was watching Dr. Fu Manchu. The superhuman Chinaman was winding what appeared to be a watch. He placed it on the floor beside the lamp, turned, and spoke:

"I bid you good-bye, Sir Denis; and—I speak with sincerity—not without regret. Your powers of pure reasoning are limited: your gifts of intuition are remarkable. In this respect I place you among the seven first-class brains of your race. Captain Hepburn has excellent qualities. He is a man I should be glad to have in my service. However, he has chosen otherwise. The small apparatus which I have placed upon the floor (a hobby of the late Lord Southery, a talented engineer whom I believe you knew) contains a power which, expanding from so small a centre, will, I am convinced, astound you. I have timed it to explode in one hundred and twenty seconds. Its explosion will entirely obliterate the dome of the Stratton Building. I must leave you."

He turned, and in the glare of the globular light upon the floor crossed to the door and disappeared.

Nayland Smith, fists clenched, glared in through the bullet-proof glass.

"Hepburn," he said, "I have been blind and mad. Forgive me."

"Smith! Smith!" Hepburn grasped his arm. "I have been trying to tell you . . . ! You know what we're supposed to be here for?"

"The lightning conductor. What the hell does it matter now!"

"It matters everything. Look!"

Hepburn pointed downwards. Nayland Smith stared in the direction indicated.

The cable of a lightning conductor attached from point to point passed down immediately beside the balcony to a dim parapet below . . .

"God help us!" Smith whispered, "will it bear a man's weight?"

454

CHAPTER 34

"THE SEVEN"

"THE HISTORY of America," said the Abbot of Holy Thorn, "has acquired several surprising chapters since our last meeting, Sir Denis."

Nayland Smith, standing at the window of the abbot's high-set study staring out at a sun-bathed prospect, turned slightly and nodded. Every detail of his former visit had recurred in his memory. And at this hour, while the fate of the United States hung in the balance, he was really no nearer to success than on the night when first he had entered this room! His briar was fuming like a furnace. Abbot Donegal lighted another cigarette. . . .

The explosion at the Stratton Building in New York was already ancient history. Amid the feverish excitement now sweeping the country, a piece of news must be sensational indeed to survive for longer than forty-eight hours.

Fragments of the dome had fallen at almost incredible distances from the scene of the explosion. The huge building had rocked upon its foundations, great gaps appearing in the masonry. The firemen, faced with a number of problems unique in their experience, had worked like demons. The total loss was difficult to compute, but, miraculously, there had been few serious casualties.

Their descent of the dome by means of the lightning conductor was a thing to haunt a man's dreams, but Smith and Hepburn had accomplished it. Then had come that race along the narrow parapet to the window of the office occupied by the police party: finally, a wild dash down the stairs—for the elevator could not accommodate all. . . .

The mystery of the origin of the explosion had not been publicly explained to this day.

"Those amazing financial resources controlled by Salvaletti," said the abbot, "have enabled him to make heavy inroads. He has stolen many of my converts: the Brotherhood of National Equality has suffered. My poor friend Orwin

Prescott, as you know, has set out upon a world cruise. This most damnable campaign, this secret poisoning, unlike anything the world has known since the days of the Borgias, has wrecked that fine career. The other victims are countless: I doubt, Sir Denis, if even you know their number."

"On several occasions," Smith replied grimly, "I have narrowly escaped being added to their number. You also, I need not remind you. Your references on the radio last night to certain secret stirrings in the Asiatic colonies throughout the States created a profound sensation. It resulted in my presence here to-day. . . ." He rested his hands on the table, looking into the upraised eyes of the abbot. "Only because you have been silent have you remained immune so long."

That silence had to be broken," said the priest sternly.

"I should have preferred that you awaited the word from me," rapped Nayland Smith, standing upright and beginning to pace the floor. "I have insufficient men at my disposal for the work of protection they are called upon to do. Washington, you know as well as I, is an armed camp. The country is in a state of feverish unrest, unparalleled even in war time. Big names, now, are deserting to the enemy!"

"I am painfully aware of the fact, Sir Denis," the abbot replied sadly. "But I am informed that the circumstance under which some of these desertions took place have been peculiar."

He stared in an odd way at Nayland Smith.

"Your information is correct! Cruel forms of coercion have been employed in many instances. And the purpose of my visit is this"—he paused before the desk at which the abbot was seated. "You intimated that you intended to touch upon this phase of the campaign in your next address on Wednesday night. You implied that other revelations were to follow. As a result of those words, Dom Patrick Donegal, your life at this moment is in grave danger. I ask you as man to man: How much do you know? What do you intend to say?"

The abbot, his chin resting on an upraised hand, stared unseeingly before him. He resembled the figure of some medieval monk who out of the reluctant ether sought to conjure up the Great Secret. Nayland Smith watched him silently.

He had real respect for Patrick Donegal, and despite the slightness of their acquaintance something resembling friendship. His sincerity, if he had ever doubted it, he doubted no longer: he was deeply read, fearless, unshakable in his faith. And that the abbot had sources of information denied to the Department of Justice Nayland Smith knew quite well.

"I know," said the abbot, at last, speaking very slowly and with a studious distinctness, "the character of the man who, remorselessly and over many murdered bodies, has driven Paul Salvaletti forward to the place which he holds. I do not know his name. He is a member of a very old Chinese family, and a man of great culture. He controls, or at least he has a voice in the councils of a secret society based in Tibet, but represented in all parts of the world where Eastern nationals are to be found."

"Do you know the name of this society?" Nayland Smith asked.

"I do not. Our missionaries in the East, who sometimes refer to it as 'The Seven,' regard it as the power of Satan manifested in evil-minded men. The Mafia in Italy was for generations a thorn in the side of the Church. An old friend of mine working in Japan tells me that the Society of the Black Dragon exercises a firmer hold over the imagination of the people than any religion has ever secured. But . . . 'The Seven' . . ." He paused and glanced up.

Nayland Smith nodded.

"Their wealth is incalculable, I am told. Men in high places wielding great social and political influence, are among the members. And all their resources have been rallied to support this attack among the Constitution of the United States. You see, Sir Denis"—he smiled—"my inquiries have made great headway!"

"They have!" rapped Nayland Smith, and again paced the floor.

The Intelligence Department of Abbot Donegal's Church went up a notch higher. Never before this hour had he realized that the Rock of St. Peter was behind him in his fight against the powers of Dr. Fu Manchu.

"Satan in person is on earth," said the priest. His face bore the rapt look of the mystic—his voice rose upon a note of

457

inspiration. "His works are manifest. Ours are the humble hands chosen to cast him down!"

Abruptly his expression changed; he became again the practical man of the world.

"We are together in this," he said, smiling—"Federal Agent 56! Now I am prepared to listen to your advice: I do not undertake to accept it."

Nayland Smith stared out of the window. Far away to the right, through crystal-clear air, he could catch a glimpse of a wide river. He twitched at the lobe of his ear and turned.

"I never waste advice," he said rapidly. "You have set your course; I am powerless to alter it. But if, as you say, we work together, there are certain things upon which I must insist."

He rested his hands on the desk; steely eyes pierced into guarded recesses of the abbot's mind.

"I am responsible for your personal safety. You must help me. Your life from now onward is dedicated to our common cause. I shall make certain arrangements for your protection; the conditions will be onerous . . . but you must accept them. I will add to your knowledge of this cast conspiracy. You alone, can stem the tide. I will give you *names*. Upon the result our final success depends."

"Success or failure in human affairs invariably hangs upon a thread," the abbot replied. "The engagement of Paul Salvaletti and Lola Dumas has been given publicity greater than any royal wedding in the Old World ever obtained in America. In this the satanic genius who aims to secure control of the United States proves himself human—for it is human to err."

"I see!" snapped Nayland Smith; his eyes glittered with repressed excitement. "You have information touching the private life of Salvaletti?"

"Information, Sir Denis, which my conscience demands I should make public. . . ."

CHAPTER 35

THE LEAGUE OF GOOD AMERICANS

"IT IS ESSENTIAL, my friend, to our success, even at this hour," said Dr. Fu Manchu, "indeed essential to our safety, that we silence this pestilential priest."

The room in which he sat appeared to contain all those appointments which had characterized his former study at the top of the Stratton Building. The exotic tang of incense was in the air, but windows opened on to a veranda helped to sweeten the atmosphere. Beyond a patch of lawn, terminated by glass outbuildings, a natural barrier of woods rose steeply to a high skyline. The trees, at the call of Spring, were veiling themselves in transparent green garments, later magically to be transformed into the gorgeous vestments of Summer. The Doctor's ever-changing headquarters possessed the virtue of variety.

From the point of view of the forces controlled by Nayland Smith, he had completely disappeared following the explosion at the Stratton Building. The cave of the seven-eyed goddess had given up none of its secrets. Sam Pak, the much sought, remained invisible. A state-to-state search had failed to produce evidence to show that Dr. Fu Manchu was still in the country.

Only by his deeds was his presence made manifest.

Salvaletti was the idol of an enormous public. His forthcoming marriage to Lola Dumas promised to be a social event of international importance. An almost frenzied campaign on the part of those saner elements who recognized that the League of Good Americans was no more than a golden bubble, was handicapped at every turn. Men once hopeless and homeless who find themselves in profitable employment are not disposed to listen to criticisms of their employees. A policy of silence had been determined upon as a result of many anxious conferences in Washington. It was deemed unwise to give publicity to anything pointing to the existence of an Asiatic conspiracy behind the league. Substantial evidence in support of such a charge must first be obtained, and despite the feverish activity of thousands of agents all over the country, such evidence was still lacking. The finances of the league could not be challenged; they stood well with the Treasury: there were no evasions. Yet, as Sir Denis had proved to a group of financial experts, the League of Good Americans, at a rough estimate, must be losing two million dollars a week!

How were these losses made good?

He knew. But the explanation was so seemingly fantastic that he dared not advance it before these hard-headed business men whose imaginations had been neglected during the years that they concentrated upon solid facts.

Then, out of the blue, had come the Voice of the Holy Thorn. It had disturbed the country, keyed up to almost hysterical tension, as nothing else could have done. Long-awaited, the authoritative voice of the abbot had spoken at last. Millions of those who had awaited his call had anticipated that despite his known friendship for the old régime he would advocate acceptance of the new.

That Paul Salvaletti's programme amounted to something uncommonly like dictatorship Salvaletti had been at no pains to disguise. His policy of the readjustment of wealth, a policy which no honest man in the country professed to understand, nevertheless enjoyed the cordial support of all those who were benefited by it. The agricultural areas were becoming more and more thickly dotted with league farms. Their produce was collected and disposed of by league distributors: there were league stores in many towns. And this was no more than the skeleton of a monumental scheme which ultimately would give the league control of the key industries of the country.

Salvaletti had realized some of the promises of Harvey Bragg—promises which had been regarded as chimerical. . . .

Where a ray of sunlight touched his intricately wrinkled face, old Sam Pak crouched upon a stool just inside the windows, his mummy-like face grotesque against the green background of the woods.

"What has this priest learned, Master, which others had not learned before? Dr. Orwin Prescott knew of our arrival in the country. . . ."

"His source of information was traced—and removed. . . . Orwin Prescott served his purpose."

460

"True."

No man could have said Sam Pak's eyes were open or closed as the shrivelled head was turned in the direction of that majestic figure behind the table.

"Enemy Number One has been unable to obtain evidence which would justify his revealing the truth to the country." Dr. Fu Manchu seemed to be thinking aloud. "He has hindered us, harried us, but our great work has carried on and is nearing its triumphant conclusion. Should disaster come now—it would be his gods over ours. For this reason I fear the priest."

"The wise man fears only that which he knows," crooned old Sam Pak, "since against the unknown there can be no defence."

Dr. Fu Manchu, long ivory hands motionless upon the table before him, studied the wizened face.

"The priest has sources of information denied to the Secret Service," he said softly. "He has a following second only to our own. Salvaletti, whom I have tended as the gardener tends a delicate lily, must be guarded night and day."

"It is so, Marquis. He has a bodyguard five times as strong as that which formerly surrounded Harvey Bragg."

Silence fell for some moments. Dr. Fu Manchu, from his seat behind the lacquer table, seemed to be watching the woodland prospect through half-closed eyes.

Some reports indicate that he evades his guards." Fu Manchu spoke almost in a whisper. "These reports the woman, Lola Dumas, has confirmed. My Chicago agents are ignorant and obtuse. I await an explanation of these clandestine journeys."

Sam Pak slowly nodded his wrinkled head.

"I have taken sharp measures, Master, with the Number responsible. He was the Japanese physician, Shoshima."

"He *was?*"

"He honourably committed hara-kiri last night. . . ."

Silence fell again between these invisible weavers who wrought a strange pattern upon the loom of American history. This little farmstead in which, unsuspected, Dr. Fu Manchu pursued his strange studies, and from which he issued his momentous orders, stood remote from the nearest

461

main road upon property belonging to an ardent supporter of the League of Good Americans. He was unaware of the identity of his tenant, having placed the premises at the disposal of the league in all good faith.

Dr. Fu Manchu sat motionless in silence, his gaze fixed upon the distant woods. Sam Pak resembled an image: no man could have sworn that he lived. A squirrel ran up a branch of a tree which almost overhung the balcony, seemed to peer into the room, sprang lightly to a higher branch, and disappeared. The evensong of the birds proclaimed the coming of dusk. Nothing else stirred.

"I shall move to Base 6, Chicago,?" came the guttural voice at last. "The professor will accompany me; his memory holds all our secrets. It is essential that I be present in person on Saturday night."

"The plane is ready, Marquis, but it will be necessary for you to drive through New York to reach it."

"I shall leave in an hour, my friend. On my journey to Base 6 I may pay my respects to the Abbot Donegal," Dr. Fu Manchu spoke very softly. "Salvaletti's address on Saturday means the allegiance of those elements of the Middle West hitherto faithful to the old order. We must silence the priest. . . ."

CHAPTER 36

THE HUMAN EQUATION

MARK HEPBURN could not keep still: impatience and anxiety conspired to deny him repose. He stood up from the seat in Central Park overlooking the pond and began to walk in the direction of the Scholar's Gate.

Smith had started at dawn by air to reach the Abbot Donegal, whose veiled statements relative to the man and the movement attempting to remodel the Constitution of the country had electrified millions of hearers from coast to coast. A consciousness of defeat was beginning to overwhelm Hepburn. No charge, unless it could be substantiated to the hilt, could check the headlong progress of Paul Salvaletti to the White House. . . .

And now, for the first time in their friendship, Moya Adair had failed to keep an appointment. Deep in his heart Hepburn was terrified. Lieutenant Johnson had traced Robbie's Long Island playground, but Moya had begged that Mark would never again have the boy covered.

She had been subjected to interrogation on the subject by the President! Apparently her replies had satisfied him—but she was not sure.

And now, although a note in her own hand had been conveyed to him by Mary Goff, Moya was not here.

If he should be responsible for any tragedy occurring in her life he knew that he could never forgive himself. And always their meetings took place under the shadow of the dreadful, impending harm. He walked on until he could see the gate; but Moya was not visible. His restlessness grew by leaps and bounds. He turned and began to retrace his steps.

He had nearly reached the familiar seat which had become a landmark in his life when he saw her approaching from the opposite direction. He wanted to shout aloud, so great was his joy and relief. He began to hurry forward.

To his astonishment Moya, who must have seen him, did not hasten her step. She continued to stroll along looking about her as though he had not existed. His heart, which had leaped gladly at sight of her, leaped again, but painfully. What did it mean? What should he do? And now she was so near that he could clearly see her face . . . and he saw that she was very pale.

An almost imperceptible movement of her head, a quick lowering of her lashes, conveyed the message:

"Don't speak to me!"

His brow moist with perspiration, he passed her, looking straight ahead. Very faintly the words reached him:

"There's someone following. Keep him in sight."

Mark Hepburn walked on to where the path forked. A short thick-set man passed him at the bend but did not pay any attention to him. Hepburn carried on for some ten or twelve paces, then dodged through some bushes, skirted a boulder and began to retrace his steps.

The man who was covering Moya was now some twenty yards ahead. Hepburn kept him in view, and presently he bore right, following a path which skirted the pond. In the distance Moya Adair became visible.

A book resting on her knee, she was watching a group of children at play.

The man passed her, making no sign. And in due course Hepburn approached. As he did so, Moya bent down over her book. He went on, keeping the man in sight right to the gate of the park. When he saw him cross towards the plaza, Mark Hepburn returned.

Moya looked up. She was still very pale; her expression was troubled.

"Has he gone?" she asked rather wearily.

"Yes, he has left the park."

"He has gone to make his report." She closed her book and sighed as Mark Hepburn sat down beside her. "I seem to be under suspicion. I think the movements of everybody in the organization are checked from time to time. There has been some tremendous upset. Probably you know what it is? Frankly—I don't. But it has resulted in an enormous amount of mechanical work being piled up on my shoulders. I receive hundreds of messages, apparently quite meaningless, which I have to take down in shorthand and repeat if called upon."

"To whom do you repeat them, Moya?"

"To someone with a German accent. I have no idea of his identity." Her gloved fingers played nervously with the book. "Then there is the Salvaletti-Dumas wedding. Old Emmanuel Dumas and myself have been made responsible for all arrangements. Lola, as you know, is with Salvaletti. It's terribly hard work. Of course, it's sheer propaganda and we have plenty of assistance. Nothing is being neglected which might help Salvaletti forward to the Presidency."

"The murder of Harvey Bragg was a step in that direction," said Hepburn grimly; "but——"

He checked his words. A party operating under his direction had located Dr. Fu Manchu and the man known as Sam Pak in a farmhouse in Connecticut! Even now it was being surrounded. Lieutenant Johnson was in charge. . . .

Moya did not answer at once; she sat staring straight before her for a while and then:

"That may be true," she replied in a very quiet voice. "I give you my word that I don't know if it is true or not. And I'm sure you realize"—she turned to him, and he looked into her beautiful troubled eyes—"that if I had known I should not have admitted it."

He watched her for a while in silence.

"Yes, I do," he said at last, in his unmusical, monotonous voice. "You play the game, even though you play it for the most evil man in the world."

"The President!" Moya forced a wan smile. "I sometimes think he is above good or evil—he thinks on a plane which we simply can't understand. Has that ever occurred to you, Mark?"

"Yes." Mark Hepburn nodded. "It's Nayland Smith's idea, too. It simply means that he's doubly dangerous to the peace of the world. You are such a dead straight little soul, Moya, that I can't tell you what I have learned about the man you call the President. It's a compliment to you, because I think if you were asked what I had said, you would feel called upon to answer truthfully."

Moya glanced at him, then looked aside.

"Yes, she replied slowly, "I suppose I should. But"—she clenched her hands—"quite honestly, I don't care very much to-day who gets control of the country. In the end, all forms of government are much alike, I believe. I am frightfully, desperately worried about Robbie."

"What's the matter, Moya?"

Hepburn bent to her. She continued to look aside: there were tears on her lashes.

"He's very ill."

"My dear!" In the most natural way in the world his arm was around her shoulders; he held her to him. "Why didn't you tell me at first? What's wrong? Who is attending him?"

"Dr. Burnett. It's diphtheria! He contracted it on his last visit to the garden. I have heard, since, there's a slight epidemic over there."

"But diphtheria, in capable hands——"

"Something seems to have gone wrong. I want another opinion. I must hurry back now."

Mark Hepburn cursed himself for an obtuse fool, for Moya knew that he was a doctor of medicine.

"Let me see him!" he said eagerly. "I know that sounds egotistical; I mean, I'm a very ordinary physician. But at least I have a deep interest in the case."

"I wanted you to see him," Moya answered simply. "Really, that was why I came to-day. I only learned last night what was the matter. . . ."

II

Nayland Smith hurried down from the plane and ran across the floodlighted dusk of the flying ground to a waiting car. The door banged; the car moved off. To the other occupant:

"Who is it?" he snapped.

"Johnson."

"Ah Johnson, a recruit from the navy, I believe, as Hepburn is a recruit from the army? I have been notified that Dr. Fu Manchu and the man Sam Pak have been traced to a farmhouse in Connecticut. The latest news?"

"Dr. Fu Manchu left by road a few minutes ago, before I and my party could intercept him."

"Damnation!" Nayland Smith drove his right fist into the palm of his left hand. "Too late—always too late!"

466

"He was heading for New York. Every possible point en route is watched. I returned by air to meet you."

"However disguised," said Smith, "his height alone makes his a conspicuous figure. Tell me where to drop you. Keep in touch with Regal."

A police car preceded them on the lonely road and another brought up the rear. But a third car, showing no lights and travelling at sixty-five to seventy, passed.

A torrent of machine-gun bullets rained upon them! A violent explosion not five yards behind told of a wasted bomb!

The murder party roared away ahead—a Z-car, with Rolls engines built for two hundred miles per hour. . . .

The heavy windows had splintered in several places—but not one bullet had penetrated!

Johnson sprang out on to the roadside as they pulled up.

"Everything right in front?"

"O.K., sir."

Men were running to them from the leading car and jumping out of that which followed, when, leaning from the open door:

"Back to your places!" Nayland Smith shouted. "We stop for nothing. . . ."

In the covered car park of the Regal-Athenian Smith alighted and ran in. The door was still swinging when Wyatt, a government man, came out from the reception office.

"I have a message from Captain Hepburn," he said.

Nayland Smith, already on his way to the elevator, paused, turned.

"What is it?"

"He does not expect to be here at the time arranged, but asks you to wait until he calls you."

Upstairs, in their now familiar quarters, Fey prepared a whisky.

"What's detaining Captain Hepburn?" Nayland Smith demanded. "Do you know?"

"I don't, sir, but I think it's something to do with the lady."

"Mrs. Adair?"

"Yes, sir. Mary Goff—a very excellent woman who has called here before—brought a note for Captain Hepburn this morning, just after you left, sir. Captain Hepburn has been out all day, but he returned an hour ago, collected up some things from his laboratory, and went out again."

Nayland Smith set down his glass and irritably began to load his pipe.

This was a strange departure from routine. Smith did not understand. Admittedly he was ahead of time, but he had counted upon finding Hepburn here. In such an hour of crisis as this, the absence of his chief of staff was more than perturbing. Every minute, every second, had its value. Dr. Fu Manchu had thwarted them at point after point. Despite their sleepless activity that cold, inexorable genius was carrying his plans to fruition. . . .

The phone bell rang. Fey answered. A moment he listened, then, looking up:

"Captain Hepburn, sir," he said.

III

How is he, Dr. Burnett?"

Moya's voice was breathlessly anxious—her eyes were tragic. Dr. Burnett, a young man with charming manners and a fashionable practice, shook his head, frowning thoughtfully.

"There's really nothing to worry about, Mrs. Adair," he replied. "Nevertheless I am not entirely satisfied."

Moya turned as Mark Hepburn came into the sitting-room. His intractable hair was more than normally untidy. He was acutely conscious of the danger of the situation, for he knew now that his presence would be reported by those mysterious watchers whose eyes missed nothing. He had made a plan, however. If Moya should be in peril, he would declare himself as a Federal agent who had forced his way in to interrogate her.

"Dr. Burnett," said Moya, "this is"—for the fraction of a second she hesitated—"Dr. Purcell, an old friend. You don't mind if he sees Robbie?"

Dr. Burnett bowed somewhat frigidly.

"Not at all," he replied; "in fact, I was about to suggest another opinion—purely in the interests of your peace of mind, Mrs. Adair. I had thought of Dr. Detmold."

Dr. Detmold had the reputation of being the best consulting physician in New York, and Mark Hepburn, as honest with himself as with others, experienced a moment of embarrassment. But finally:

"The boy's asleep," said Dr. Burnett, "and I am anxious not to arouse him. But if you will come this way, Dr.—er—Purcell, I shall be glad to hear your views."

In the dimly-lighted bedroom, Nurse Goff sat beside the sleeping Robbie; her appearance indicated, correctly, that she had known no sleep for the past twenty-four hours. She looked up with a gleam of welcome in her tired, shrewd eyes as Hepburn entered.

He beckoned her across to the open window, and there in a whisper:

"He looks very white, nurse. How is his pulse?"

"He's failing sir! The poor bairn is dying under my eyes. He's choking—he can swallow nothing! How can we keep him alive?"

Mark Hepburn crossed to the bed. Gently he felt the angle of the boy's jaw: the glands were much enlarged. Slight though his touch had been, Robbie awoke. His big eyes were glassy. There was no recognition in them.

"Water," he whispered. "Froat . . .so sore!"

"Poor bonnie lad," murmured Mary Goff. "He's crying for water, and every time he tries to swallow it I expect him to suffocate. Oh, what will we do! He's going to die!"

Hepburn, who had hastily collected from the Regal those indispensable implements of his trade, a stethoscope, a thermometer and a laryngeal mirror, began to examine the little patient. It was a difficult examination, but at last it was completed. . . .

Although painfully aware of her danger, he hadn't the heart to deter Moya when, her face a mask of sorrow, she crossed to the boy's bed. He beckoned to Dr. Burnett, and outside in the sitting-room:

"I fear the larynx is affected," he said; "I am not equipped for a proper examination in this light. But what is your opinion?"

"My opinion is, Dr. Purcell, that the woman Goff, although she is a trained nurse, has a sentimental attachment to the patient and is unduly alarming Mrs. Adair. The action of the antitoxin, admittedly, has been delayed, but if normal measures are strictly carried out I can see no cause for alarm."

Mark Hepburn ran his fingers through his untidy hair.

"I wish I could share your optimism," he said. "Do you know Dr. Detmold's number? I should like to speak to him."

IV

"The human equation—forever incalculable," muttered Nayland Smith.

He hung up the telephone and crossing, stared out of the window.

The night had a million eyes: New York's lights were twinkling. . . Admittedly the situation was difficult; he put himself mentally in Hepburn's place and Hepburn had asked only to be allowed to remain until the famous consultant arrived.

Nayland Smith stared at the decapitated trunk of the Stratton Building. There were lighted rooms on the lower floors, but the upper were in darkness. The great explosion at the summit had wrought such havoc that even now it was possible the entire building would be condemned. That explosion had been the personal handiwork of Dr. Fu Manchu!

Their escape from the catastrophe prepared for them fell nearly within the province of miracles. Yet to this very hour Dr. Fu Manchu remained at large, his wonderful brain weaving schemes beyond the imagination of normal men. . . .

Could anything, short of the destruction of that apparently indestructible life, prevent the triumph of Paul Salvaletti? The Americans began frankly to assume the dimensions of a Fascisti movement, with the dazzling personality of Salvaletti at its head. On Wednesday next, at eight o'clock (if he lived), Abbot Donegal would tell the country the truth. What would the reaction be?

Dr. Fu Manchu was buying the United States with gold!

Once, in Nayland Smith's presence, he had said:

"Gold! I could drown mankind in gold!"

That secret, to the discovery of which so many alchemists had devoted their lives, was held by the Chinese Doctor. Smith had

470

known for a long time that gigantic operations in gold were being carried on. Indeed, although few had even suspected, it was these secret operations which had created the financial chaos from which every nation of the world suffered to this day.

To-night the end seemed to him inevitable. There, alone, staring out at the lights of New York, Nayland Smith fought a great fight.

Could he hope to check this superman who fought with weapons not available to others; who had the experience of unimaginable years ; who wielded forces which no other man had ever controlled? There was one certain way, and one only: that which Dr. Fu Manchu himself doubtless would have chosen.

The death of Paul Salvaletti would bring this mighty structure crashing to the earth. . . .

But, even though the fate of the country, perhaps of the Western world, hung in the scales, assassination was not a weapon which Nayland Smith could employ.

There was perhaps another way: the destruction of Dr. Fu Manchu. That subtle control removed, the gigantic but fragile machine would be lost; a rudderless ship in a hurricane.

A bell rang. Fey came in and crossed to the telephone.

"Lieutenant Johnson, sir."

Nayland Smith took up the receiver.

"Hullo, Johnson."

"Touch and go again!" came Johnson's voice on a note of excitement. "Dr. Fu Manchu was recognized by one of our patrols, but his car developed tremendous speed, and our men couldn't follow. They called through to the next point. The car was intercepted. It was empty—except for the driver! We've got the driver."

"Anything more?"

"Yes: a report that two men were seen to change cars in Greenwich. Descriptions tally. Second car sighted just over the line. But description now passed on to all patrols. Speaking from Times Building."

"Stand by. I'll join you."

Nayland Smith hung up.

"Fey!" he shouted.

Fey reappeared silently.

"Captain Hepburn is at the second address under the name

471

of Adair in the notebook on the telephone table. We have no number for this address. If I want him you will send a messenger."

"Very good, sir."

"I shall keep in touch. I am going out now."

"As you are, sir?"

"Yes," Nayland Smith smiled grimly. "My attempted change of residence was a fiasco, and I don't propose to give further amusement to the enemy by wearing funny disguises."

CHAPTER 37

THE GREAT PHYSICIAN

"I HAVE called Dr. Detmold," said Mark Hepburn, "and have told him to bring——" he hesitated—"the necessary remedies."

Moya clutched him convulsively. For the first time in their strange friendship he found her in his arms.

"Does that mean—" she was watching him with an expression which he was never to forget—"that——"

"Don't worry, Moya—my dear. It will be all right. But I'm glad I came."

"Mark," she whispered, "I never realized until now how I wanted—someone I could count on."

Mark Hepburn stroked her hair—as many times he had longed to do.

"You know you can count on *me?*"

"Yes—I know I can."

Hepburn tried to conquer the drumming in his ears, which was caused by the acceleration of his heart. When he spoke, his voice was even more toneless than normally.

"I'm not a very wonderful bargain, Moya; but when all these troubles are past—because it isn't fair to ask you now . . ."

Moya raise her eyes to his: they were bright with stifled tears. But in them he read that which made further, ineloquent words needless.

All the submerged poetry in his complex character expressed itself in that first ecstatic kiss. It was a passionate statement. As he released Moya he knew, deep in his buried self, that he had found his mate.

"Moya, darling."

Her head rested on his shoulder. . . .

"Mark, dear, messages from this apartment are tapped." She said. "It's quite possible that your conversation with Dr. Detmold will be reported elsewhere."

"It doesn't matter. If your—employers catch me here, I shall declare myself and put you all under arrest."

Moya gently freed herself and stepped away as Dr. Burnett joined them.

"In certain respects" said Burnett, "the patient's condition, admittedly, is not favourable. My dear Mrs. Adair"—he patted her shoulder—"he is in very good hands. Dr. Detmold is coming?"

"Yes," Hepburn replied.

"I am sure he will endorse my opinion. The symptoms are not inconsistent with the treatment which I have been following."

Mark Hepburn entirely agreed. Robbie's survival of the treatment was due to a splendid constitution.

"If you will excuse me for a moment," he muttered, "I should like to look at the patient."

In the silence of the sick room he bent over Robbie. There was agony now in the eyes of Nurse Goff. The boy had had a choking fit in which he had narrowly escaped suffocation. He was terribly exhausted. His fluttery pulse was alarming. Walking on tiptoe, Hepburn crossed to the open window, beckoning Nurse Goff to follow him.

There he held a whispered consultation. Presently the door opened and Dr. Burnett came in with Moya; the reassuring tone of his voice died away as he entered the room. He looked in a startled manner at his patient.

A change for the worse, which must have been apparent even to a layman, had taken place. Dr. Burnett crossed to the bed. There came a sound of three dull blows on the outer door, as if someone had struck it with a clenched hand. . . .

"Dr. Detmold!" Moya whispered brokenly, and ran out.

The two men were bending anxiously over the little sufferer when a suppressed cry from the vestibule, a sound of movement, bought Hepburn upright. He turned at the moment that a tall figure entered the bedroom.

It was that of a man in a long black overcoat having an astrakhan collar, who wore an astrakhan cap of a Russian pattern. Mark Hepburn's heart seemed to miss a beat—as he found himself transfixed by the glance of the green eyes of Dr. Fu Manchu!

For a moment only he was called upon to sustain it. The situation found him dumbfounded. Dr. Fu Manchu removed his cap and, throwing it upon a chair, turned to Dr. Burnett.

"Are you attending the patient?"

He spoke in a low voice, sibilant but imperative.

"I am. May I ask who you are, sir?"

Dr. Burnett glanced at a leather case which the speaker had placed upon the floor. Ignoring the inquiry, Dr. Fu Manchu bent over Robbie for a moment, then stood upright, and turned as Moya came in.

"Why was I not notified earlier?" he demanded harshly.

Moya clutched at her throat; she was fighting back hysteria.

"How could I know, President," she whispered, "that——"

"True," Dr. Fu Manchu nodded. "I have been much preoccupied. Perhaps I am unjust. I should have prohibited the boy's last visit. I was aware that there was diphtheria in that neighbourhood."

Something in his unmoving regard seemed to steady Moya.

"Your only crime is that you are a woman," said Dr. Fu Manchu quietly. "Even to the last you have done your duty by me. I must do mine. I guaranteed your boy's safety. I have never failed to redeem my word. From small failures great catastrophes grow."

"And I must protest," Dr. Burnett interposed, speaking indignantly but in a low voice. "At any moment we are expecting Dr. Detmold.

"Detmold is a dabbler," said Dr. Fu Manchu contemptuously, and crossing to the bed he seated himself in a chair, staring down intently at Robbie. "I have cancelled those instructions."

"This is preposterous," Burnett exclaimed. "I order you to leave my patient."

Dr. Fu Manchu moved a gaunt yellow hand in a fan-like movement over Robbie's forehead, then, stooping, parted his lips with the second finger and the thumb of his left hand, and bent yet lower.

"When did you administer the antitoxin?" he demanded.

Dr. Burnett clenched his teeth, but did not reply.

"I asked a question."

The green eyes became suddenly fixed upon Dr. Burnett, and Dr. Burnett replied:

"At eleven o'clock last night."

"Eight hours too late. The diphtheritic membrane has invaded the larynx."

"I am dispersing it."

Moya's hands closed convulsively upon Mark Hepburn's arm.

"God help me!" she whispered. "What am I to do?"

Her words had reached the ears of Dr. Fu Manchu.

"You are to have courage," he replied, "and to wait in the sitting-room with Mary Goff until I call you. Please go."

For one moment Moya glanced at Hepburn. Then Nurse Goff, her face haggard with anxiety, put an arm around her and the two women went out. Dr. Fu Manchu stood up.

"Surgical interference is unavoidable," he said.

"I disagree!" Burnett in his indignation lost control, raising his voice unduly. "Until I have conferred with Dr. Detmold I forbid you to interfere with the patient in any way. Even if you are qualified to do so—which I doubt—I refuse to permit it."

Dr. Burnett found himself transfixed by a glance which seemed to penetrate to his subconscious mind. He became aware of an abysmal incompetence which he had successfully concealed even from himself throughout a prosperous career. He had never experienced an identical sensation in the whole of his life.

"Leave us," said the guttural voice. "Captain Hepburn will assist me."

As Dr. Burnett, moving like an automaton, went out of the room, the fact crashed in upon Hepburn that Dr. Fu Manchu had addressed him by his proper name and rank!

And, as if he had read his thoughts:

"My presence here to-night," said Dr. Fu Manchu, "is due to your telephone message to Sir Denis Nayland Smith. It was intercepted and relayed to me on my journey. To this I am indebted for avoiding a number of patrols whose positions you described. Be good enough to open the case which you will find upon the carpet at your feet. Disconnect the table lamp and plug in the coil of white flex."

Automatically, Mark Hepburn obeyed the order. Dr. Fu Manchu took up a mask to which a lamp was attached.

"We shall operate through the cricoid cartilage," he said.

"But——"

"I must request you to accept my decisions. I could force them upon you but I prefer to appeal to your intelligence."

He moved his hands again over the boy's face; and slowly, feverish bright eyes opened, staring upward.

Something resembling a tortured grin appeared upon Robbie's lips.

"Hello . . . Yellow Uncle," came a faint, gasping whisper. "I's glad . . . you come . . . "

He choked, became contorted, but his eyes remained open, fixed upon those other strange eyes which looked down upon him. Gradually the convulsion passed.

"You are sleepy." Fu Manchu's voice was a crooning murmur. The boy's long lashes began to flicker. "You are sleepy . . ." His lids drooped. "You are very sleepy . . ." Robbie's eyes became quite closed. "You are fast asleep."

"A general anaesthetic?" Hepburn asked hoarsely.

"I never employ anaesthetics in surgery," the guttural voice replied. "They decrease the natural resistance of the patient."

II

Nayland Smith, seated in the bullet-proof car, a sheaf of forms and other papers upon his knee, looked up at Johnson, who stood outside the open door.

"What are we to make of it, Johnson? An impasse! Here is the mysterious message received by Fey half an hour after I left: a request from Hepburn that under no circumstances should we look for evidence at the apartment he had visited, as someone lay there critically ill. No hint regarding his own movement, but the cryptic statement: 'Keep in touch with Fey and have no fear about my personal safety. *I make myself responsible for Dr. Fu Manchu!*'

"Fey is sure it was Hepburn who called him," said Johnson. . . .

"But that was early last night," snapped Smith; "it is now 3.15 in the morning! And except for the fact that our latest reports enabled us to draw a ring on the map of Manhattan, where are we? Dr. Fu Manchu is almost certainly inside that ring. But since we cannot possibly barricade the most fashionable area of New York, how are we to find him?"

"It's deadlock sure enough," Johnson agreed. "One thing's certain: Hepburn hasn't come out since he went in! A mouse couldn't have got out of that building. There are lights in the top apartment. . . ."

And even as these words were being spoken, Mark Hepburn, in a darkened room, was watching the greatest menace to social order the world has known since Attila the Hun overran Europe, and wondering if Nayland Smith would respect his request.

He had witnessed a feat of surgery unique in his experience. Those long yellow fingers seemed to hold magic in their tips. Smith's assurance became superfluous. Dr. Fu Manchu, the supreme physician, was also the master surgeon. He was, as Hepburn believed (for Nayland Smith's computation he found himself unable to accept), a man of over seventy years of age. Yet with unfailing touch, exquisite dexterity, he had carried out an operation in a way which Hepburn's training told him to be wrong. It had proved to be right. Dr. Fu Manchu had performed a surgical miracle —under hypnosis!

But it had left the little patient in a dangerously weak condition.

The night wore on, and with every hour of anxiety, Moya came nearer and nearer to collapse. Except for the ceaseless, hoarse voice of New York the sick room was silent.

That strange, supercilious gesture of Fu Manchu before he began the operation was one Hepburn could never forget; it had a sort of ironic grandeur.

"Call your headquarters," the Chinese Doctor had directed, "at the Regal Tower. Ensure us against interference. Allay any doubts respecting your own safety: I shall require you here. Conceal the fact that I am present, but accept responsibility for handing me over to the law. I give you—personally— my parole. Instruct the exchange that no calls are to be put through to-night. . . ."

Nurse Goff was on duty again, although it was amazing how the weary woman kept awake. She sat by the open window, her hands clasped in her lap, her eyes fixed not upon the deathly face of Robbie, but on the gaunt profile of the man

478

who bent over him. Moya was past tears; she stood just inside the open door, supported by Hepburn.

For five hours Dr. Fu Manchu had sat beside the bed. Some of the restorative measures which he had adopted were those that any surgeon would have used; others were unfamiliar to Hepburn, who could not even guess what was contained in the phials which he opened. Once, in the first crisis, Fu Manchu had harshly directed him to charge a hypodermic syringe. Then, bending over the boy and resting his hands upon his head, he had waved him aside. Now, as Hepburn's training told him, the second, grand crisis, was approaching.

Moya had not spoken for more than an hour. Her lips were parched, her eyes burning: she quivered as he held her against him.

A new day drew near, and Hepburn, watching saw (and read the portent) beads of moisture appearing upon the high yellow brow of Dr. Fu Manchu. At four o'clock, that zero hour at which so many frightened souls have crossed the threshold to take their first hesitant steps upon the path beyond, Robbie opened his eyes, tried to grin at the intent face so near to his own, then closed them again.

It came to Mark Hepburn as a conviction that that lonely little spirit had wandered beyond recall even by the greatest physician in the world, who sat motionless at his bedside. . . .

CHAPTER 38

WESTWARD

DIM GREY light was touching the most lofty buildings, so that they seemed to emerge from sleeping New York like phantoms of lost Nineveh; later would come the high-flung spears of those temples of Mammon. As Blücher might have remarked, "What a city to loot!"

Nayland Smith rang a bell beside a glazed door with iron scrollwork. Park Avenue is never wholly deserted day or night, but at this hour its fashionable life was at lowest ebb, and every possible precaution had been taken to avoid attracting the attention of belated passers-by. It was necessary to ring the bell more than once before the door was opened.

A sleepy night porter, his hair tousled, confronted them. Nayland Smith stepped forward, but the man, an angry gleam coming into his eyes, barred the way. He was big and powerfully built.

"Where do you think you're going?" he demanded.

"Top floor," rapped Nayland Smith. "Don't argue."

The man had a glimpse of a gold badge, and over the speaker's shoulder saw that he was covered by an automatic held by Lieutenant Johnson.

"What's the fuss?" he growled. "I'm not arguing."

But actually, although he was only a very small cog in the wheel, he knew that the occupants of the penthouse apartment at the top of the building were closely protected. He had secured his appointment through the League of Good Americans, and he had had orders from the officers of the league, identifiable by their badges, scrupulously to note and report anyone who visited the apartment.

In silence he operated the elevator. At the top:

"Go down again," Nayland Smith ordered, "and report to the officer in charge in the vestibule."

As the elevator disappeared he looked about him: they were a party of four. Anxiety for Hepburn's safety had driven him to make this move. Belatedly he had remembered a letter once received from Orwin Prescott—and in Prescott's handwriting. He remembered that Hepburn quite recently had succumbed to that uncanny control which Dr. Fu Manchu possessed the power to exercise. . . . Hepburn's message to Fey might be no more than an emanation from that powerful, evil will!

"Be ready for anything," he warned sternly, "but make no move without orders from me."

He pressed the bell.

A moment of almost complete silence followed. He had been prepared to wait, perhaps to force the door. He was about to ring a second time when the door opened.

Mark Hepburn faced him!

Amazement, relief, doubt, alternately ruled Nayland Smith's mind. The situation was beyond analysis. He fixed a penetrating stare on Hepburn's haggard face: his hair was dishevelled, his expression wild, and with a queer note almost of resentment in his tone:

"Smith!" he exclaimed.

Nayland Smith nodded and stepped in, signalling to his party to remain outside.

Crossing a small vestibule, he found himself in a charmingly appointed sitting-room, essentially and peculiarly feminine in character. It was empty.

"I'm sorry about all this seeming mystery," said Hepburn in a low voice; "and I understand your anxiety. But when you know the facts you will agree, I think, there was no other way."

"You undertook a certain responsibility," Nayland Smith said grimly, "in a message to Fey—"

"Not so loud, Smith! I stand by it. . . . It's hard to explain"—he hesitated, his deep-set eyes watching Nayland Smith—"but with all his crimes, after to-night—I'm sorry. Moya—Mrs. Adair—collapsed when she heard the news—"

"What, that the boy is dead?"

"No—that he will live!"

"I am glad to hear it. Largely as a result of your discovery of the Connecticut farm," said Nayland Smith, continuing intently to watch Hepburn, "we have narrowed down our search to an area surrounding this building,. Your long, inexplicable absence following that message to Fey has checked us. I should be glad, Hepburn, if you would inform me where you believe Fu Manchu to be—"

The door opened, and Dr. Fu Manchu came in.

Smith's hand plunged to his automatic, but Fu Manchu, frowning slightly, shook his head, His usually brilliant eyes were dully filmed. He wore a black suit and beneath his coat a curious black woollen garment with a high collar. In some strange way he resembled a renegade priest who had abandoned Christianity in favour of devil worship.

"Melodrama is uncalled for, Sir Denis," he said, his guttural voice expressing no emotion whatever. "We are not in Hollywood. I shall be at your service in a moment." He turned to Hepburn. "My written instructions are on the table beside the bed: you will find there also the name of the physician I have selected to take charge of the case. He is a Jew practising in the Ghetto; a man of integrity, with a sound knowledge of his profession. I do not imply, Sir Denis, that he is in the class of our mutual friend, Dr. Petrie (to whom I beg you to convey my regards), but he is the best physician in New York. I desire, Captain Hepburn, to be arrested by Sir Denis Nayland Smith, who has a prior claim. Will you be good enough to hand me over to him?"

Hepburn spoke hoarsely.

"Yes. . . . Smith, this is your prisoner."

Fu Manchu bowed slightly. He took up a leather case which at the moment of entering he had placed upon the carpet beside him.

"I desire you, Captain Hepburn," he said, "to call Dr. Goldberg immediately, and to remain with the patient until he arrives. . . ."

All but imperturbable as he had trained himself to be, Nayland Smith at this moment almost lost contact with reality. At the eleventh hour, with counsels of desperation becoming attractive, Fate rather than his own wit had delivered this man into his hands. Swiftly he glanced at Hepburn and read in the haggard face mingled emotions of which he himself was conscious. He had never dreamed that triumph achieved after years of striving could be such a dead-sea fruit.

The dimmed green eyes were fixed upon him, but there was nothing hypnotic in their regard; rather they held an ironical question. He stepped aside, indicating with his hand the vestibule in which the three men waited.

"Precede me, Dr. Fu Manchu."

Fu Manchu, carrying the case, walked with his cat-like tread out into the vestibule, three keen glances fixed upon him, three barrels covering his every movement.

"Ring for the elevator," rapped Nayland Smith.

One of the men went out through the front door, which had been left open.

Dr. Fu Manchu set his case upon the floor beside a chair.

"I assume, Sir Denis," he said, his voice very sibilant, "I am permitted to take my coat and my cap?"

He opened a panelled cupboard and looked inside. Momentarily the opened door concealed him as a heavy black topcoat with an astrakhan collar was thrown out on to the back of the chair. Ensued an interval of not more than five seconds . . . then Nayland Smith sprang forward.

The leather case stood beside the chair, the black coat was draped across it; but the cupboard was empty!

Dr. Fu Manchu had disappeared.

II

"I am growing old, Hepburn," said Nayland Smith. "It is high time I retired."

Mark Hepburn, studying the crisp greying hair, bronzed features and clear eyes of the speaker, laughed shortly.

"No doubt Dr. Fu Manchu wishes you would," he said.

"Yet he fooled me with a paltry vanishing-cabinet trick, an illusion which was old when the late Harry Houdini was young! Definitely, Hepburn, my ideas have become fixed. I simply cannot get used to the fact that New York City is a former stronghold of the most highly organized and highly paid underworld group which Western civilization so far has produced. That penthouse apartment, as we know now, was once occupied by Barney Flynn, the last of the big men of boot-legging days. The ingenious door in the hat cupboard was his

483

private exit, opening into another building—a corresponding apartment which he also rented."

"Moya didn't know," said Hepburn.

"I grant you that. Nor was the apartment one of her own choosing. But she remembers (although in her disturbed state at the time she accepted the fact) that Fu Manchu appeared in the vestibule—although no one had opened the door! Had I realized that he had given you his parole, I might have foreseen an attempt to escape."

"Why?"

Nayland Smith turned to Hepburn; a faint smile crossed his lean features.

"He insisted that you should formally hand him over to me. You did so—and he promptly disappeared! Dr. Fu Manchu is a man of his word, Hepburn. . . ." He was silent awhile, then: "I am sorry for Mrs. Adair," he added, "and granting the circumstances, I think she has played fair. I hope the boy is out of danger."

Hepburn sat, pensive, looking down from the plane window at a darkling map of the agrarian Middle West.

"According to all I have ever learned," he said presently, "that boy should be dead. Even now, I can't believe that any human power could have saved him. But he's alive! And there's every chance he will recover and be none the worse. You know, Smith"—he turned, his deep-set, ingenuous eyes fixed upon his companion—"that's a miracle. . . . I saw surgery there, in that room, that I'll swear there isn't another man living could have performed. That incompetent fool, Burnett, had lost the life of his patient: Dr. Fu Manchu conjured it back again."

He paused, watching the grim profile of Nayland Smith.

Dr. Fu Manchu had successfully slipped out of New York. But the police and Federal agents urged to feverish activity by emergency orders from Washington, had made one discovery: Fu Manchu was headed West.

Outside higher police commands and the Secret Service, the intensive scrutiny of all travellers on Western highways by road or rail was a mystery to be discussed by those who came in contact with it for many years afterwards. Air liners received Federal orders to alight at points not scheduled;

private planes were forced down for identification; a rumour spread across half the country that foreign invasion was imminent.

Despite Nayland Smith's endeavours, a garbled version of the facts had found currency in certain quarters; Abbot Donegal's words had given colour to rumours. There had been riots in Asiatic sections: in one instance a lynching had been narrowly averted. The phantom of the Yellow Peril upreared its ugly head. But day by day, almost hour by hour, more and more adherents flocked to the standard of Paul Salvaletti; who represented, had they but known, the only real Yellow Peril to which the United States ever had been exposed.

"I'm still inclined to believe," Mark Hepburn said, "that I'm right about the object of the Doctor's journey. He's heading for Chicago. On Saturday night Salvaletti addresses a meeting on the result of which rests the final tipping of the scales."

Nayland Smith twitched the lobe of his left ear.

"The Tower of the Holy Thorn is not far off his route," he replied; "and Dom Patrick addresses the whole of the United States *to-night!* The situation is serious enough to justify the Doctor's taking personal charge of operations to check the voice of the abbot. . . ."

That the priest's vast audience even at this eleventh hour could split the Salvaletti camp was an admissible fact. Even now it was thought that the former Chief Executive would be returned to office; but the league faction would make that office uneasy.

"Salvaletti's magnificent showmanship," said Smith, "The sentimental appeal in his pending marriage, are the work of a master producer. The last act shows a brilliant adventurer assuming control of the United States! It is not impossible, nor without precedent. Napoleon Bonaparte, Mussolini, Kemal have played the part before. No, Hepburn! I doubt if Fu Manchu will passively permit Abbot Donegal to steal the limelight. . . ."

CHAPTER 39

THE VOICE FROM THE TOWER

ALL APPROACHES to the Tower of the Holy Thorn would have reminded a veteran of an occupied town in war time. They were held up four times by armed guards. . . .

When at last the headlamps of the road monster which had been waiting at the flood-lit flying ground shone upon the bronze door, so that that thorn-crowned Head seemed to come to meet them in the darkness, Nayland Smith sprang out.

"Is Garstin there?" Hepburn called.

A man came forward.

"Captain Hepburn?"

"Yes. Anything to report?"

"All clear, Captain. It would need a regiment with machine-guns to get through!"

Mark Hepburn stared upward. The tower was in darkness right to the top; the staff which dealt with the abbot's enormous mail had left. But from its crest light beaconed as from a pharos.

And as Mark Hepburn stood there looking up, Nayland Smith entered the study of Dom Patrick Donegal.

"Thank God I see you safe!" he said, and shot out a nervous brown hand.

Patrick Donegal grasped it, and stood for a moment staring into the eyes of the man who had burst into his room.

"Thank God indeed. You see before you a chastened man, Sir Denis." The abbot's ascetic features as well as his rich brogue told that he spoke from his heart. "Once I resented your peremptory orders. I have changed my mind; I know that they were meant for my protection and for the good of my country. You see"—he pointed—"the broadcasting corporation has equipped me with a microphone. To-night I speak in the safety of my own study."

"You have followed my instructions closely?"

Nayland Smith was watching the priest with almost feverish intentness.

"In every particular. You may take it"—he smiled—"that I have not been poisoned or tampered with in any way! My address for to-night I wrote with my own hand at that desk. None other has touched it."

"You have included the facts which I gave you—and the figures?"

"Everything! And I am happy to have you with me, Sir Denis; it gives me an added sense of security. At any moment now, the radio announcer will be here. I trust that you will stay?"

Nayland Smith did not reply. He was listening—listening keenly to a distant sound. Although he was barely aware of the fact, his gaze was set upon a reproduction of Carpaccio's St. Jerome which hung upon the plastered wall above a crowded bookcase.

And now the abbot was listening, too. Dim cries came from far below; shouted orders. . . .

A drone of aeroplane propellers drew rapidly nearer. Smith crossed to the window. A searchlight was sweeping the sky. A moment he watched, then turned, acted—and his actions were extraordinary.

Seizing the abbot bodily he hurled him in the direction of the door! Then, leaping forward, he threw the door open, extending a muscular arm, and dragged him out. On the landing, Dom Patrick staggered; Smith grasped his shoulder.

"Down!" he shouted, "down the stairs!"

But now the priest had appreciated the urgency of the case. Temporarily shaken by this swift danger, as a man of courage he quickly recovered himself. On the landing below:

"Lie flat!" cried Smith, "we must trust to luck!"

The noise of an aeroplane engine grew so loud that one could only assume the pilot deliberately to be steering for the tower. Came a volley of rifle fire. . . .

They were prone on the marble-paved floor when a deafening explosion shook the Tower of the Holy Thorn as an earthquake might have shaken it. Excited cries followed, crashing of fallen debris; an acrid smell reached their nostrils: the drone of propellers died away.

Abbot Donegal rose to his knees.

"Wait!" cried Smith breathlessly. "Not yet!"

The air was pervaded by a smell resembling iodine, he distrusted it, and stood there staring upward towards the top landing. The crown of the elevator shaft opposite the abbot's door was wrecked. He could detect no sign of fire. The abbot, head bowed, gave silent thanks.

"Smith!" came huskily, "Smith!"

An increasing clatter of footsteps arose from the stairs below, and presently, pale, breathless, Mark Hepburn appeared.

"All right, Hepburn!" said Nayland Smith. "No casualties!"

Hepburn leaned heavily against a handrail for a moment; he had outrun them all.

"Thank God for that!" he panted. "It was an aerial torpedo—we saw them launch it!"

"The plane?"

"Will almost certainly be driven down."

"What d'you make of this queer smell?"

Mark Hepburn sniffed suspiciously, and then:

"Oxygen," he replied. "Liquid ozone electrically discharged, maybe. For some reason" (he continued to breathe heavily) "the Doctor wanted to avoid fire. . . ."

Cautiously they mounted the stairs and looked into the dark wreckage which had been Dom Patrick's study. There were great holes in the roof through which one could see the stars, and two entire walls of the room had disappeared. All lights had gone out. Nayland Smith stared as a hand touched his shoulder.

He turned. Abbot Donegal stood beside him, pointing.

"Look!" he said.

One corner of the study remained unscathed by the explosion. In it stood the microphone installed that day, and from the plaster wall above, St. Jerome looked down undisturbed. . . .

"A sign, Sir Denis! God in His wisdom has ordained that I speak to-night!"

II

Lola Dumas lay curled up on a cushioned settee; she wore a rest gown and slippers, but no stockings. And in the dimly lighted room the curves of her slender, creamy legs created highlights too startling in their contrast against the blue velvet to have pleased a portrait painter. Stacks of crumpled newspapers lay upon the carpet beside her. Her elbows buried in the cushions, chin resting in cupped hands, her sombre eyes speculative, almost menacing.

On the front page of the journal which crowned the litter a large photograph of Lola appeared. It appeared in nearly all the others as well. She was the most talked-about woman in the United States. Drawings of the dresses to be worn by her bridesmaids had already been published in the fashion papers. It was to be a Louis XIII wedding: twenty tiny pages dressed as Black Musketeers, with Lola herself wearing the famous diamond broach upon the recovery of which Dumas' greatest romance is based. An archbishop would perform the ceremony, and not less than two bishops would be present. A cardinal would have been more decorative; but since the rites of the Church of Rome had been denied to Lola following her first divorce, she had necessarily abjured that faith.

Moya Adair in the Park Avenue apartment, assisted by extra typists called in for the occasion, had sent out thousands of polite refusals to more or less important people who had applied for seats in the church. None was left.

Lola was to be married from her father's Park Avenue home. Five hundred invitations had been accepted for the reception; the Moonray Room of the Regal-Athenian had been rented, together with the services of New York's smartest band.

So keen was the interest which the magnetic rise of Paul Salvaletti had created throughout the world that despite the disturbed state of Europe, war and the rumours of war, special commissioners were being sent to New York by many prominent European newspapers to report the Savaletti-Dumas wedding. In fact this wedding would be the master stroke of the master schemer, setting the seal of an international benediction upon the future President. Love always demands the front page.

But in the sombre eyes of Lola Dumas there was no happiness. She lived for what she called "love" and without admiration must die. In fact, after her second divorce, the circumstances of which had not reflected creditably upon her, she had proclaimed that she intended to renounce the vanities of the world and take the veil. Perhaps fortunately for her, she had failed to find any suitable convent prepared to accept her as a novice.

There came a discreet rap on the door.

"Come in," Lola called, her voice neither soft nor caressing.

She sat upright, slender jewelled fingers clutching the cushions as Marie, her maid, came in;.

"Well?"

Marie pursed her lips, shrugged and nodded vigorously.

"You are sure?"

"Yes, madame. He is there again! And to-night I have found the number of the apartment—it is Number 36."

Lola swung her slippered feet to the floor and clenching and unclenching her hands began to walk up and down. In the semi-darkness she all but upset a small table upon which a radio was standing. Marie, fearing one of the brainstorms for which Lola was notorious, stood just outside the door, watching fearfully. Of course, Lola argued, Paul's mysterious absences (which since they had been in Chicago had become so frequent) might be due to orders from the President. But if this were so, why was she not in Paul's confidence?

It was unlikely, too, for on many occasions before, and again to-night, he had slipped away from his bodyguard and had gone alone to this place. To-night, indeed, it was more than ever strange: the Abbot Donegal was broadcasting, and almost certainly his address would take the form of an attack.

Any man who admired her inspired Lola's friendship, but Paul Salvaletti had been the only real passion of her life. There were many who thought that she had been Harvey Bragg's mistress. It was not so; a circumstance for which Harvey Bragg deserved no blame. Given a knowledge of all the facts, his harshest critic must have admitted that Harvey had done his best. Always it had been Paul, right from the first hour of the meeting. She recognized him; had known what he was destined to become. Her other duties, many of them exacting and tedious, which the President compelled her to undertake, she had undertaken gladly with this goal in view.

The intrusion of the woman Adair had terrified her, followed as it had been by her own transfer to nurse's duties. (which she understood) in Chinatown. She hated the thought of this Titan blonde's close association with Paul. Mrs. Adair was cultured, too, the widow of a naval officer, a woman of good family . . . . and always the plans of the President were impenetrable.

Abruptly, long varnished nails pressed into her palms; she pulled up in that wildcat walk right in front of the radio.

"What's the time, Marie?" she demanded harshly.

"It is after eight o'clock, madame."

"Fool! Why didn't you tell me!"

Lola dropped down on to one knee; she tuned in the instrument. Nothing occurred but a dim buzzing. She knelt there manipulating the control, but could get no result. She looked up.

"If this thing has gone wrong," she said viciously, "I'll murder somebody in this hotel."

Suddenly came a voice.

"This is a National Broadcast . . . ." Formalities followed, and then: "I must apologize for the delay. It was caused by an accident to the special microphone, but this has been adjusted. You are now about to hear Dom Patrick Donegal, speaking from the Tower of the Holy Thorn."

Lola Dumas threw herself back upon the settee, curling her slim body up, serpentine, among the cushions. She was striving with all her will to regain composure. The beautiful voice of the priest helped to calm her; she hated it so intensely, for in her heart of hearts Lola knew that the Abbot of Holy Thorn was a finer orator than Paul Salvaletti. Then her attention was arrested:

"A torpedo of unusual design," the abbot was saying coldly, "fired from an aeroplane, wrecked my study and delayed this broadcast. I am now going to tell you, and I ask you to listen with particular attention, by whom that torpedo was fired into my study."

With the judgment of a practised speaker he paused for a moment after this sensational statement. Hourly, Lola had expected an attempt to be made to silence the abbot. It had been made—and failed! She began to listen intently. This man, this damnable priest, was going to wreck their fortunes!

When he resumed, Patrick Donegal with that unfailing art in which Cicero had been his master, struck another note:

"There are many of you I know, who, day after weary day, have returned from a tireless and honourable quest of work, to look into the sad eyes of a woman, to try to deafen your ears to that most dreadful of all cries coming from a child's lips: 'I am hungry.' The League of Good Americans, formerly associated with the name of Harvey Bragg, has—I don't deny the fact—remedied much of this. There are hundreds of thousands, it may be millions, of men, women and children in this country who to-day have won that need of happiness which every human being strives to earn, through the good offices of the league. But I am going to ask you to consider a few figures—figures are more eloquent than words."

In three minutes or less, the abbot proved (using Nayland Smith's statistics) that over the period with which he dealt, alone, some twenty million dollars had been expended in the country through various activities of the league which, even admitting the possibility of anonymous donations from wealthy supporters, could not have come out of national funds!

"You may say, and justly so: This is good: it means that unearned wealth is coming into the United States. I ask you to pause—to think . . . Is there such a thing as unearned wealth? Even a heritage carries its responsibilities. What are the responsibilities you are incurring by your acceptance of these mysterious benefits? I will tell you:

"You are being bought with alien money!" the abbot cried, "you are becoming slaves of a cruel master. You are being gagged with gold. The league and all its pretensions is a chimera, a hollow mockery, a travesty of administration. You are selling your country. Your hardships are being exploited in the interests of an alien financial genius who plans to control the United States. And do you know the nationality of that man? He is a *Chinaman!*"

Lola's jewelled fingers were twitching nervously upon the cushions, her big eyes were very widely opened. Marie, uninvited, had taken a seat upon a chair just inside the door. This was the most damning attack which anyone had delivered: its

492

horrible consequences outsped the imagination. . . .

"Who is this man who to-night attempted to murder me in my own room? This callous assassin, this ravisher of a nation's liberty? By the mercy of God my life was spared that I might speak, that I might tell you. He is an international criminal sought by the police of the civilized world; a criminal whose evil deeds dwarf those of any home-grown racketeer. His name will be known to many who listen: it is Dr. Fu Manchu. My friends, Dr. Fu Manchu is in America—Dr. Fu Manchu to-night attempted my assassination—Dr. Fu Manchu is the presiding genius of the League of Good Americans!"

A moment he paused, then:

"This is the invisible President whom you are being bribed to send to the White House!" he said in a low, tense voice, "not in his own person but in the person of his servant, his creature, his slave—Paul Salvaletti! Paul Salvaletti who stands upon the bloody corpse of Harvey Bragg . . . for I am going to tell you something else which you do not know: Harvey Bragg was assassinated to make way for Paul Salvaletti."

Even in the silence of that room where Lola Dumas crouched among the cushions it was possible to imagine the sensation which from coast to coast those words had created.

"The wedding of the man Salvaletti promises to be an international event, a thing for which distinguished people are assembling. I say it would be an offence for which this country would never be forgiven," he thundered, "to permit that sacrilegious marriage to take place! I say this for three reasons: first, that Paul Salvaletti is merely the shadow of his Chinese master; second, that Paul Salvaletti is an unfrocked priest; and third, that he is already married."

Lola Dumas sprang to the floor and stood rigidly upright.

"He married an Italian girl—she was just sixteen—Marianna Savini, in a London registry office on March the 25th, 1929. She accompanied him secretly when he came to the United States; she has been with him ever since—she is with him now. . . ."

"It was a good shot," said Captain Kingswell, "although at such close range that row of lighted windows offered a fine target. But it isn't the gunner, it's the pilot I want to meet. The way he dipped to the tower was pretty work."

"Very pretty," said Nayland Smith. "As I happened to be inside the tower, I fully appreciated its excellence. You were chasing this plane, I gather?"

Captain Kingswell, one of many army aviators on duty that night, nodded affirmatively.

"I should have caught him! It was the manoeuvre by the tower that tricked me. You see, I hadn't expected it."

The big armoured car sped through the night, its headlights whitening roads and hedges.

"It is certain that they were driven down?"

"Lieutenant Olson, who was covering me on the left, reports he forced the ship down near the river somewhere above Tonawanda."

"Is there any place around there," Mark Hepburn asked slowly, "where they might have landed?"

"I may as well say," the pilot replied, smiling, "it's a section I don't pretend to be familiar with. Landing at night is always touch and go, even if the territory is familiar. It's only halfway safe on a proper flying ground. Hullo! There's Gillingham!"

The headlights picked up a distant figure, arms outstretched, wearing army air uniform. This was an agricultural district where folks were early abed; the country roads were deserted. As the car pulled up the aviator ran to the door:

"What news, Gillingham," cried Captain Kingswell.

"We're shorthanded to surround the area where they crashed," replied Gillingham, a young fresh-faced man, immensely excited; "at least, it's ten to one they crashed. But I've done my best, and search parties are working right down to the river-bank."

"How far to the river?" jerked Nayland Smith.

"As the crow flies, from this spot a half mile."

Smith jumped out, followed by Hepburn. A crescent moon

swam in a starry sky. Directly above their heads as they stood beside the car outflung branches of two elms, one on either side of the narrow, straight road, met and embraced, to form a deep stripe of shadow.

"This is the frontier?"

"Yes, the opposite bank's in Canada."

Through the silence, from somewhere far off, came a sound like that of a ceaseless moan; at times, carried by a light breeze, it rose weirdly on the night, as though long-dead gods of the Red man, returning, lamented the conquest of the white.

Nayland Smith, his eyes bright in the ray of the headlamp, turned to Hepburn questioningly.

"The rapids," said Mark. "The wind's that way."

As the breeze died, the mournful sound faded into a sad whisper. . . .

"Hullo!" Smith muttered, "what are those lights moving over there?"

"One of our search parties," Gilligham replied. "We expect to locate the wreck pretty soon. . . ."

But half an hour had elapsed before the mystery plane was found. It lay at one end of a long, ploughed field: the under-carriage had been damaged, but the screw, wings and fuse-lage remained intact. Again the work of a clever pilot was made manifest. There was no sign of the occupants.

"This is a Japanese ship," said Captain Kingswell, on a note of astonishment. "Surely can't have crossed right to here in the air? Must have been reassembled somewhere. Looks like it carried four of a crew: a pilot, a reserve (maybe he was the gunner) and two others."

He had climbed up and was now inside.

"Here's a queer torpedo outfit," he cried, "with three reserve tubes. This is a fighting ship." He was prowling around enthusiastically, torch in hand. "We'll overhaul every inch of it. There may be very interesting evidence."

"The evidence I'm looking for," rapped Nayland Smith irri-tably, "is evidence to show which way the occupants went. But all these footprints"—he flashed his torch upon the ground—"have made it impossible to trace."

He turned and stared towards where a red glow in the sky

marked a distant town. Away to the east, half masked by trees, he could see outbuildings of what he took to be a farm.

"Tracks over here, mister!" came a hail from the northern end of the meadow. "Not made by the search party!"

Nayland Smith, his repressed excitement communicating itself to Hepburn, set out at a run.

The man who had made the discovery was shining a light down upon the ground. He was a small, stout, red-faced man wearing a very narrow brimmed hat with a very high crown.

"Looks like the tracks of three men," he said: "two walkin' ahead an' one followin' along."

"Three men," muttered Nayland Smith; Let me see . . ."

He examined the tracks, and:

"I must congratulate you," he said, addressing their discoverer. "Your powers of observation are excellent."

"That's all right, mister. In these per'lous times a man has to keep his eyes skinned—'specially me; I'm deputy sheriff around here: Jabez Siskin—Sheriff Siskin they call me."

"Glad to have you with us, Sheriff. My name is Smith— Federal agent."

Two sets of imprints there were which admittedly seemed to march side by side. The spacing indicated long strides; the depth of the impressions, considerable weight. The third track, although made by a substantial-sized shoe, was lighter; there was no evidence to show that the one who had made it had crossed the meadow at the same time as the other two.

"Move on!" snapped Nayland Smith. "Follow the tracks but don't disturb them."

From point to point the same conditions arose which had led the local officer to assume that the third traveller had been following the other two; that is, his lighter tracks were impressed upon the heavier ones. But never did either of the heavier tracks encroach upon another. Two men had been walking abreast followed by a third; at what interval it was impossible to determine.

Right to a five-barred gate the tracks led, and there Deputy Sheriff Siskin paused, pointing triumphantly.

The gate was open.

Nayland Smith stepped through on to a narrow wheel-rutted lane.

"Where does this lane lead to?" he inquired.

"To Farmer Clutterbuck's," Sheriff Siskin replied; "this is all part of his land. The league bought it back for him. The farm lays on the right. The river's beyond."

"Come on!"

It was a long, a tedious and a winding way, but at last they stood before the farm. Clutterbuck's Farm was an example of the work of those days when men built their own homesteads untrammelled by architectural laws, but built them well and truly: a rambling building over which some vine that threatened at any moment to burst into flower climbed lovingly above a porch jutting out from the western front.

Their advent had not been unnoticed. A fiery red head was protruded from an upper window above and to the right of the porch, preceded by the barrel of a shotgun, and:

"What in hell now?" a gruff voice inquired.

"It's me, Clutterbuck," Deputy Sheriff Siskin replied, "with Federals here, an' the army an' ev'rything!"

When Farmer Clutterbuck opened his front door he appeared in gum boots. He wore a topcoat apparently made of rabbit skin over a woollen nightshirt, and his temper corresponded to his fiery hair. He was a big, bearded, choleric character.

"Listen!" he shouted—"It's you I'm talkin' to, Sheriff! I've had more'n enough o' this for one night. Money ain't ev'rything when a man has to buy a new boat."

"But listen, Clutterbuck——"

Nayland Smith stepped forward.

"Mr. Clutterbuck," he said—"I gather that this is your name—we are government officers. We regret disturbing you, but we have our duty to perform."

"A boat's a boat, an' money ain't ev'rything."

"So you have already assured us. Explain what you mean."

Farmer Clutterbuck found himself to be strangely subdued by the cold authority of the speaker's voice.

"Well, it's this way," he said. (Two windows above were opened, and two heads peered out.) "I'm a league man, see? This is a league farm. Can't alter that, can I? An' I'm roused up to-night when I'm fast asleep—that's enough to annoy a man, ain't it? I think the war's started. Around these parts we

497

all figure on it. I take my gun an' I look out o' the window. What do I see? Listen to me, Sheriff—what do I see?"

"Forget the sheriff," said Nayland Smith irritably; "address you remarks to me. What did you see?"

"Oh, well! all right. I see three men standin' right here outside—right here where we stand now. One's old, with white whiskers an' white hair; another one, some kind of a coloured man, I couldn't just see prop'ly; but the third one—him that's lookin' up" he paused—"well . . ."

"Well?" rapped Nayland Smith.

"He's very tall, see? As tall as me, I guess; an' he wears a coat with a fur collar an' his eyes—listen to this, Sheriff—his eyes ain't brown, an' his eyes ain't blue, an' they ain't grey: they're green!"

"Quick, man!" Nayland Smith cried. "What happened. What did he want."

"He wants my motor-boat."

"Did he get it?"

"Listen, mister! I told you I'm a league man, didn't I? Well, this is a league official, see? Shows me his badge. He buys the boat. I didn't have no choice, anyway—but I'd been nuts to say no to the price. Trouble is, now I got no boat; an' money ain't ev'rything when a man loses his boat!"

"Fu Manchu knows the game's up. They had a radio in the plane!" said Smith to Hepburn in a low tone vibrant with excitement.

"Then God help Salvaletti!"

"Amen. We know he has agents in Chicago. But by heaven we must move, Hepburn: the Doctor is making for Canada!"

At roughly about this time, those who had listened to Patrick Donegal and who now were listening to radio topics received a further shock. . . .

"Tragic news has just come to hand from Chicago," they heard. "A woman known as Mrs. Valetti occupied Apartment 36 in the Doric Building on Lakeside. She was a beautiful brunette, and almost her only caller was a man believed to be her husband who frequently visited there. About 8.30 this evening, Miss Lola Dumas, whose marriage to Paul Salvaletti has been arranged to take place next month, came to the apartment. She had never been there before. She failed to get any reply to her ringing but was horrified to hear a woman's scream. At her urgent request the door was opened by the resident manager, and a dreadful discovery was made.

"Mrs. Valetti and the man lay side by side upon the day-bed in the sitting-room. On the woman's arms and on the man's neck there were a number of blood-red spots. They were both dead, and a window was wide open. Miss Dumas collapsed on recognizing the man as her fiancé, Paul Salvaletti. She is alleged to have uttered the words, 'The Scarlet Bride'—which the police engaged on the case believe to relate to the dead woman. But Miss Dumas to whom the sympathy of the entire country goes out in this hour of her unimaginable sorrow, is critically ill and cannot be questioned.

"The crisis which this tragedy will create in political circles it would be impossible to exaggerate. . . ."

CHAPTER 40

"THUNDER OF WATERS"

"THEY'RE JUST landing!" cried the man in the bows of the Customs launch—"at the old Indian Ferry."

"Guess those Canadian bums showed 'emselves," growled another voice. "We had 'em trapped, if they'd gone ashore where they planned."

Nayland Smith, standing up and peering through night-glasses, saw a tall, dark figure on the rock-cut steps. It was unmistakable. It was Fu Manchu! He saw him beckon to the second passenger on the little motor-boat; and the other, a man whose hair shone like silver in the moonlight, joined him on the steps. A third remained in the boat at the wheel . Dr. Fu Manchu, arms folded, stood for a moment looking out across the river. He did not seem to be watching the approaching Customs craft so swiftly bearing down upon him, but rather to be studying the shadowed American bank, the frontier of the United States.

It came to Nayland Smith, as they drew nearer and nearer to the motionless figure, that Dr. Fu Manchu was bidding a silent farewell to the empire he had so nearly won. . . .

Just as words of command trembled on Smith's lips Fu Manchu spoke to the occupant of the boat, turned, and with his white-haired companion strode up the steps—steps hewn by the Red man in days before any white traveller had seen or heard "The Thunder of Waters."

The motor-boat spluttered into sudden life and set off down-stream.

"Stop that man!" rapped Nayland Smith.

Dr. Fu Manchu and the other already were lost in the shadow.

"Heave to—Federal orders!" roared a loud voice.

Farmer Clutterbuck's motor-boat was kept on its course.

"Shall we let him have it?

"Yes—but head for the steps."

Three shots came almost together. Raising the glasses

again, Nayland Smith had a glimpse of a form crouching low over the wheel . . . then a bluff which protected the Indian Ferry obscured the boat from sight. As they swung in to the steps:

"What was that move?" somebody inquired. "I guess we missed him anyway."

But Nayland Smith was already running up the steps. He found himself in a narrow gorge on one side completely overhung by tangled branches. He flashed a light ahead. Three Federal agents came clattering up behind him.

"What I'm wondering," said one, "is, where's Captain Hepburn."

Nayland Smith wondered also. Hepburn, in another launch, had been put ashore higher up on the Canadian bank, armed with Smith's personal card upon which a message had been scribbled. . . .

Dr. Fu Manchu and his companion seemed to have disappeared.

But now, heralded by a roar of propellers, Captain Kingswell came swooping down out of the night, and the first Véry light burst directly overhead! Nayland Smith paused, raised his glasses and stared upward. Kingswell, flying very low, circled, dipped, and headed down river.

"He's seen them!" snapped Smith.

Came a dim shouting . . . Hepburn was heading in their direction. A second light broke.

"By God!" Nayland Smith cried savagely, "are we all blind? Look at Kingswell's signals. They have rejoined the motorboat at some place below!"

Two more army planes flew into view. . . .

"Back to the launch!" Smith shouted.

But when at last they set out again, the bat-like manoeuvres of the aviators and the points at which they threw out their flares indicated that the cunning quarry had a long start. It seemed to Nayland Smith, crouched in the bows, staring ahead, that time, elastic, had stretched out to infinity. Then he sighted the motor-boat. Kingswell, above, was flying just ahead of it. He threw out a light.

In the glare, while it prevailed, a grim scene was shown. The man at the wheel (probably the same who had piloted the plane) lay over it, if not dead, unconscious; and the silver-haired passenger was locked in a fierce struggle with Dr. Fu Manchu!

Professor Morgenstahl's hour had come! In the stress of that last fight for freedom the Doctor's control, for a matter of seconds only, had relaxed. But in those seconds Morgenstahl had acted. . . .

"This is where we check out!" came a cry. "Hard over, Jim!"

Absorbed in the drama being played before him—a drama the real significance of which he could only guess—Nayland Smith had remained deaf to the deepening roar of the river. Suddenly the launch rolled and swung about.

"What's this?" he shouted, turning.

"Twenty lengths more and we'd be in the rapids!"

The rapids!

He craned his head, looking astern. Somewhere, far back, a light broke. Three planes were flying low over the river . . . and now to his ears came the awesome song of Niagara, "The Thunder of Waters."

An icy hand seemed to touch Nayland Smith's heart. . . .

Dr. Fu Manchu had been caught in the rapids; no human power nor his own superlative genius could prevent his being carried over the great falls! The man who had dared to re-model nature's forces had been claimed at last by the gods he had outraged.

RE-ENTER DR. FU MANCHU

"HERE is *The Times* advertisement: 'Wanted, young man, American unattached. University graduate preferred, athletic and of good appearance. Work highly confidential. Business experience unnecessary. Must be prepared to travel. Apply Box, etc.' And here, Mr. Merrick"—Peter Wellingham looked down at a typed letter—"is your reply."

Brian nodded. "I imagine you had quite a big mail."

"You may be surprised to learn"—Wellingham lay back in his chair and pressed his finger-tips together—"that applicants were quite few."

"I'm certainly surprised."

"I refer, particularly, to suitable applicants. You, I may say, were quite easily the most promising. I need not tell you that I am acting for a third party. Now—let's see . . . You are a United States citizen, the son of Senator Merrick. You hold an American degree and have recently also graduated at Oxford. Your record in sports is good. Your degrees, if not outstanding, are respectable."

Brian picked up a brief-case from the carpet. "I have the credentials here."

Peter Wellingham waved a pale hand. He smiled a pale smile.

"I assure you, Mr. Merrick, applicants' qualifications have already been checked. My principal is highly efficient. Now— you are unattached?"

"Meaning unmarried?"

"Meaning unmarried and not engaged to marry."

"All clear," Brian grinned.

"And you are prepared to travel?"

"I'm eager. My father has given me six months' leave of absence before I go into the family business——"

"Which, I am told, is a very good business."

Brian experienced a return of that sense of resentment with which Peter Wellingham filled him. These F.B.I. methods offended him. He became more than ever certain that he had been subjected to close scrutiny whilst he had waited.

But, to be fair, what did this mean? Only that these people were looking for a man of exceptional qualities for what must be a highly important job.

"It's a good business all right," he admitted.

A rap on the door—and the willowy secretary he had seen before came in.

"Sir John is here, Mr. Wellingham. He is on his way to the House and is pressed for time."

Peter Wellingham stood up, smiled apologetically.

"I won't detain you many minutes, Mr. Merrick. My legal adviser is also a member of Parliament. Please excuse me." He crossed to the door; switched on indirect lighting, so that the crowded bookcase became illuminated. "You might like to look over my library."

He went out and closed the door.

Peter Wellingham was a slender man of uncertain age; pale, with scanty fair hair. He was faultlessly groomed and wore correct morning dress. His white hands were slender, and of effeminate beauty. His voice and speech were those of the cultured Englishman, and he wore the short, close-trimmed moustache which Brian associated with the British army.

But, somehow, he couldn't imagine Peter Wellingham as a soldier, and, try as he would, he couldn't like him. . . .

He looked around the small, but crowded room, trying to reconsider his first impression of the Honourable Peter Wellingham. The secretary who had received him was an attractive Eurasian, and many of the volumes on the shelves dealt with the Orient. There were antiques, too, placed here and there between the books, all of Eastern origin.

How strangely quiet this room seemed. Hard to believe that he was in the heart of fashionable Mayfair and less than fifty yards from Park Lane. Although his physical senses didn't support the idea, that uncanny suspicion overcame him again—a suspicion that he wasn't alone, that someone watched him. It had come to him when he first arrived, while he was waiting for the Honourable Peter.

Why? And from where?

There was only one point in the room from which an observer might be watching. This was a massive Burmese cabinet of dark wood with a number of fretwork cupboards. It seemed to be built into the wall, and there might be a space behind it.

But it was all too fantastic, although at one time his doubts had prompted him to decline the job if it were offered. Indications suggested it might involve exciting travel, and this prospect thrilled him. He crossed to a bookcase, and began to read some of the titles. Many dealt with the tangle in the Near East, and not all were in English.

There was one shelf with no books on it; only a bronze sphinx and several framed photographs.

Brian stood still, staring at one of them. It was of Senator McInnes, an old friend of his father's. At another he stared even longer; a lean-faced man with steady, keen eyes, his hair silvering at the temples.

He was still studying this, holding the frame in his hands, when the door opened and Peter Wellingham came back.

"Do you know Sir Denis?" Wellingham asked in evident surprise.

"Not intimately. But Sir Denis Nayland Smith was my father's house-guest in Washington two years back."

"Splendid! Sir Denis makes this his base when he is in London. If we come to terms, he will be your chief. . . ."

"It was Sir Denis's intention," Wellingham explained, "that this should be a six-month agreement. Renewable by mutual consent. This, I think would suit your plans?"

"Perfectly."

"Here is a form of agreement. Will you read it carefully, and if you find it acceptable sign all three copies."

Brian found himself walking on air. The terms of employment were generous, and he would receive two months' salary in advance. He must be ready to leave for Cairo at short notice and the cost of equipment he required would be defrayed by his employers.

He signed the three copies without hesitation; passed them across the desk. Peter Wellingham signed in turn and rang for his secretary who acted as witness. "Draw Mr. Brian Merrick's cheque," he directed.

The girl went out, and Brian's glance followed the graceful figure. As she opened the door, an oblique ray of sunshine touched the intricate carving of the Burmese cabinet—and Brian's glance was diverted, then held . . .

He suppressed a start. Through the delicately carved panel before one of the small cupboards he thought he saw two brilliant green eyes fixed upon him! He inhaled deeply; looked away. Peter Wellingham was scribbling notes on a pad.

With the closing of the door the apparition had vanished, and Brian tried to tell himself that he was the victim of an illusion. Some shiny object, such as a jade vase, probably stood in the cupboard. His slumbering distrust of Wellingham most not be allowed to upset his judgement. He knew Nayland Smith to be a high-up in the British Secret Service and a former Assistant Commissioner of Scotland Yard. Brian had longed to travel before settling down to serious work, but funds were short. Here was a golden opportunity!

Peter Wellingham looked up.

"I needn't warn you to observe great discretion concerning the nature of your employment, Mr. Merrick. Sir Denis is engaged upon a dangerous assignment and has entrusted me with the job of finding an additional assistant having certain qualifications. I think you are the man he's looking for."

The lissom secretary glided in again, laid a cheque on the desk, and glided out. Brian avoided glancing at the cabinet while Peter Wellingham signed the cheque.

Five minutes later Brian was striding along Park Lane. Wellingham, at parting, had walked to the doorstep, wished him good luck and shaken hands.

The slender white fingers were very cold. . .

As Peter Wellingham returned to the study, and before Brian had reached Park Lane, a section of the Burmese cabinet swung open, showing another room beyond.

A tall, gaunt man stepped out, a man with a phenomenally high brow, crowned with a black cap not unlike a biretta; a man whose strange emerald green eyes seemed to gaze, not *at* Wellingham but through his skull into his brain. He was unmistakably Chinese, unmistakably an aristocrat, and standing there, wearing a plain yellow robe, he radiated force.

He crossed and seated himself behind the desk. Peter Wellingham remained standing.

"For a moment, I feared"—he spoke pedantically exact English except that he stressed the sibilants—"that your peculiar personality had produced an unfortunate impression, Mr. Wellingham. This I should have regretted. I had Brian Merrick under close observation, and I am satisfied that he will admirably serve my purpose. But he inherits a streak of his father's obstinacy, and at one time he considered declining the offer. That was why I called you from the room—your cue to draw his attention to the photographs."

Peter Wellingham's white forehead was damp. He had detected a note of menace in that strange voice.

"I should have been sorry, Doctor——"

"But too late. With your succession to the title I cannot interfere. But the facts concerning your political views, if suspected by Lord Chevradale, would have disastrous results for you."

"I did my best, Doctor. I feel sure that he——"

"Be sure of no man. For the only man of whom you may be sure is yourself."

"Shall I take steps to have Merrick covered during the time he remains in London?"

The brilliant eyes were raised in a penetrating glance.

"Such steps have already been taken. I fly to Cairo tonight. Your instructions concerning Brian Merrick will reach you through the usual channels."

Brian hurried along Park Lane to his hotel. Lola was lunching with him, and he knew she would be pressed for time as usual. Lola Erskine was a designer for Michel, a famous Paris house which every season dictated to smart women the world over exactly what they must wear. Equally at home on Paris boulevard, Fifth Avenue, or Bond Street, he found her a fascinating companion.

He walked into the crowded lounge, looking eagerly around—and there was Lola, waving to him. He joined her, signalling to a waiter.

"Hello, Brian!" She greeted him with that half-amused and half-affectionate smile which he found so fascinating—although sometimes he vaguely suspected her of secretly laughing at him. "Don't order anything for me, yet. Look, I have one already."

"Have I kept you waiting?"

"Only five minutes. But I was dying for a drink. I had a desperately tough morning."

"You don't look like it! You look like a cover girl. Is that dress by Michel?"

"Why ask me! If I wore anything else I'd be fired on sight! Also, I get them at cost price."

"Lola!" He grasped her arm as a waiter came along. "Don't finish that martini or whatever it is. Share a bottle of champagne with me. It's a celebration. I have picked up a wonderful job!"

Lola stared. She had dark grey-blue eyes which never seemed to join in her smiles; abstract, mysterious eyes.

"Not that thing I showed you in *The Times*?"

He nodded. "Waiter, can I have a wine list?"

As the man went away:

"Is it something really good?" Lola asked. "I mean, worth a bottle of champagne?"

"It's worth a case! Listen—I know you'll have to rush right after lunch. There's so much I want to say to you. Are you free for dinner tonight?"

"I can be, Brian—if you're not being extravagant."

"Next, I have to leave London at short notice. And I hate that part of it now I've met you."

"That's sweet of you. It all depends where you're going. Michel has branches around the world and my job takes me to all of them."

"I'm going to Cairo."

"Cairo? No, we haven't opened in Cairo so far. What kind of a job is this, Brian? Commercial or political?"

The waiter brought the wine list, which Brian handed to Lola.

"I won't let you be extravagant," she told him, "and if I'm to eat any lunch it will have to be only a half bottle. Say, a half of Piper Heidsieck, '49."

As the waiter went away, Brian looked at Lola with frank admiration. She was unlike any woman he had ever known. Yet he felt that he had been looking for her all his life. He longed to know if his interest was returned; but those sombre eyes told him nothing.

"Lola, you're out of this world!" he declared. "By long odds you're the best-dressed and the prettiest girl in the lounge. You know all the answers, yet you're as sweet to me as if I meant something."

"Don't turn around!" Lola whispered. "But there's a queer-looking man sitting just behind us who seems to be interested in our conversation. This job of yours sounds rather hush-hush. Let's talk about Michel and frocks and me until we go in to lunch. Then you can tell me all about it. . . ."

Brian had reserved a cosy corner table in the grill-room, and when they were seated:

"Any sign of the spy?" he asked.

Lola smiled and shook her head. "I may have misjudged him. But he really did seem to be listening. He hasn't come in, anyway."

"I'm glad of it. There certainly seems to be something unusual about my new job. But as you put it in my way, Lola, you're entitled to know all about it. You had gone out when I got my mail this morning, and there was a very formal note which said something like 'The Honourable Peter Wellingham would be obliged if Mr. Brian Merrick would call at the above address at 11 a.m. in connection with his application dated the 15th instant.' You know all about that kind of people, Lola. Who is Peter Wellingham?"

Lola looked confused, almost alarmed; but quickly recovered composure.

"He's Lord Chevradale's son."

"Do you know him?" There was a note of suspicion in Brian's voice.

"Not personally. But I have heard that he's badly in debt."

"That's queer. Because he gave me a substantial advance on my salary. I hope it's not a rubber cheque! But let me tell you."

And so over lunch he told her all that had happened on this eventful morning, admitted that he had not taken to Peter Wellingham but that, because of the strong attractions of the job, he had overcome his prejudice, convinced that to work under Sir Denis Nayland Smith would be an education in itself.

Sitting there, facing a pretty girl and surrounded by normal, healthy people, many of them fellow Americans, with deft waiters moving from table to table, he dismissed the illusion of the green eyes behind the Burmese cabinet; decided not to mention it. . . .

"I really owe this chance to travel to you, Lola. You saw the advertisement in *The Times*, and if you hadn't encouraged me to do it, I don't believe I should have written."

"It read like a job created purposely for you, Brian." She smiled rather wistfully. "I know you wanted to see more of the world before going home, and I'm really glad you pulled it off."

"There's one fly in the ointment," Brian confessed. "Just as I get to know you I have to be dashed off to Egypt."

"But you told me the Near East fascinated you, that you'd always wanted to go there."

"That's true. And it would be perfect—if you were coming with me."

Lola took a cigarette from her case. "I never know where I'll be sent next. But I admit that Egypt's unlikely. I don't suppose you'll be there long. We're both world-wanderers, now, and certain to get together again somewhere. I must rush, Brian. Six-thirty at the Mirabelle. . . ."

IN AN OLD Cairo house not far from the Mosque of El-Ashraf, a house still untouched by Western "improvements", a tall, gaunt figure paced slowly up and down a room which once had been the saloon of the *harêm*.

High, and lighted by a lantern in the painted roof, it was brightly paved in the Arab manner, had elaborate panelled walls and two *mushrabîyeh* windows.

The man pacing the tiled floor wore the same yellow robe which he had worn during his brief interview with Peter Wellingham in London and a similar black cap on his massive skull. Although unmistakably Chinese, his finely lined features were those of a scholar who had never spared himself in the quest of knowledge. It was a wonderful face. It might have belonged to a saint—or to the Fallen Angel in person.

His walk was feline, silent. He seemed to be listening for some expected sound. And, suddenly, it came . . . a strange, muffled, animal sound.

He crossed in three strides to a screen set before one of the recessed windows, and drew it aside.

Two glass boxes stood on a narrow table. In one was a rat, in the other a rabbit. It was the rabbit which had made the queer sound. The little creature thrashed around there in convulsions, and even as the screen was moved aside became still. The rat already lay rigid.

The man in the yellow robe walked in his catlike way through an arched opening into an adjoining room equipped as a laboratory. Some of the apparatus in this singular room would have puzzled any living scientist to name its purpose or application. From a wall-safe which he unlocked he took out a small phial. He seated himself at a glass-topped table, removed the stopper from the phial and inserted a dipper. The delicacy of touch in those long-nailed fingers was amazing.

Smearing a spot from the dipper on to a slide, he set the slide in place in a large microscope and, stooping, stared through the lens, which he slightly adjusted.

Presently he stood up and, using a lancet, took a spot of his own blood and dropped it on to the smeared plate, which he immediately replaced and again bent over the microscope. When he stood up a second time his expression was the expression of a demon.

He composed himself and pressed a stud on a panel. A door opened and a young Japanese came in. He wore a white tunic.

"Bring Josef Gorodin here, Matsukata. Then wait in the saloon with two of my Burmese until you hear the gong."

Matsukata bowed and went out. He returned shortly with a thick-set man, also in white, whose heavy Slavonic features were set in what might have been a permanent scowl. He tried to meet the gaze of emerald-green eyes, but had to look aside. He spoke.

"You wished to see me, Comrade Fu Manchu?"

Dr. Fu Manchu continued to watch him. "You may address me either as Excellency, or as Doctor. Comrade—no! I have offered my services—at my own price—to your masters. This does not mean that I kneel at the shrine of Karl Marx. I have something to say. Sit down."

It was not an invitation; it was a command. Josef Gorodin sat down.

"On the evening I returned here from London," Fu Manchu went on, "you were at work here upon some experiments which I wished you to carry out in my absence. They had no practical importance. They were designed to test your ability. Your results convinced me that you were not untalented."

"Thank you," Gorodin muttered sarcastically.

"I showed you this phial." Fu Manchu held it up. "I told you that many years ago I had completed my long experiments— those experiments so vainly attempted by the old alchemists—that I had discovered what they termed the *Elixir Vitae*, the Elixir of Life. I said, 'The small quantity of the elixir in this phial contains three additional decades of life for any person who knows how to use it.' You remember?"

"I remember."

"I told you that by certain familiar symptoms I had been warned that the time had come for me to renew the treatment; that otherwise death might claim me at any hour. You remember?"

Gorodin bowed his head.

"You returned later, Josef Gorodin, and begged me to give you a drop of the preparation for analysis. I consented—for I knew it would defy your analysis. I told you to return the phial to the safe. You remember?"

Gorodin moistened his heavy lips, glanced up, then down again. "I remember."

Dr. Fu Manchu reached along the table and struck a small silver gong which stood there. Matsukata, silently as an apparition, appeared in the archway, followed by two stocky Asiatics. Gorodin sprang up, fists clenched, but was instantly seized by the experienced man-handlers of the Chinese doctor's bodyguard. And when Fu Manchu, watching without expression, spoke again, his voice came as a sibilant whisper.

"I am sure your analysis had no result, Josef Gorodin. But I am about to give you conclusive evidence of the nature of this elixir. Seat him there, Matsukata. Slit his sleeve up to the shoulder."

Gorodin had turned purple with passion. He was a powerful man, but had quickly given up struggling as every movement resulted in violent pain.

"You misjudge your position, and mine!" he shouted. "I am senior aide to the Minister of Scientific Research!"

Dr. Fu Manchu was charging a hypodermic syringe from the phial.

"This one injection will arrest both mental and physical decline, and give you ten more years at your present robust age to pursue your researches for the Ministry."

"If you dare to harm me you will sign your own death sentence!"

"Hold his arm still, Matsukata." Fu Manchu spoke softly, holding the syringe in a steady hand. "Were you attached to my staff merely to watch me—or to destroy me? Answer."

Gorodin avoided those green eyes, but he began to tremble. He clenched his teeth.

"You daren't do it!" he muttered.

"You mean *Doctor* Gorodin, that you fear to have your useful life extended for ten years beyond its normal span?"

The needle point touched Gorodin's skin.

"Stop!" It was a scream. "What do you want to know?"

The needle point was removed an inch or so. "You heard my question. Answer it."

Gorodin swallowed noisily. "There are those who believe that to give you control of all our resources was a dangerous price to pay for your services—that the power once held by Stalin would be seized by you."

"My poor Gorodin! The power *I* shall possess will exceed his wildest dreams." The gaunt face became transfigured. Fu Manchu's brilliant eyes blazed with the light of fanaticism. "But—no matter. And you, no doubt, are one of those who believe this?"

"Yes."

"And so you attempted to—what do you term it?—*liquidate* me? Where is the phial of elixir?"

"There beside you."

"I shall repeat my question—*once*. Where is the phial of elixir?"

"There beside you."

"Then you must welcome these ten additional years of life."

And Dr. Fu Manchu injected the contents of the syringe into Gorodin's arm.

A scream more animal than human came from the man's lips. He fought like a captive tiger, ignoring the agony which every movement produced. But his bare arm he could not move. Matsukata held it in a grip of steel. Gorodin's veins bulged like blue cords on his forehead. Then, he relaxed, panting.

"You have murdered me." He spoke breathlessly. "You will pay with your own life for this."

"You have courage." Dr. Fu Manchu studied the inflamed face with scientific curiosity. "From the shape of your head I had not expected it. Until I have leisure to examine the contents of this phial which you ingeniously substituted for my own, I cannot say if there is any antidote to the poison. Could you enlighten me?"

Gorodin's lips were turning blue. "There is none."

"Then you will have the honour to die as you planned *I* should die. Recently I watched a rat in its last agonies from this treatment. I have no desire to watch another rat die in the same way." He dropped the syringe in a glass bowl and glanced at Matsukata. "Sterilize. Incinerate the body."

Dr. Fu Manchu turned and walked slowly out of the laboratory. . . .

For Brian Merrick the days that followed in London seemed more like a dream than a reality when, later, he looked back on them. Mr Wellingham, always operating in the background, made all the necessary passport and medical arrangements, fixing appointments at times to suit Brian's convenience. The organization for which he acted was undeniably efficient. Lola took charge of his shopping list and, whenever possible, went with him to a famous store at which an account had been opened in his name. She sternly checked some of his wilder impulses—such as the purchase of a sun helmet.

"You'd look a fool in Cairo wearing such a thing! If they send you up to the Sudan there are plenty of stores in Cairo where you can buy all you want."

They lunched, dined and danced together. The sun shone and Brian was ridiculously happy. One afternoon sitting in Hyde Park with Lola he said: "Today I felt as though we were shopping for a honeymoon abroad! Oh, Lola! If only it had been true!"

He saw her flush, lower her lashes and glance away, then:

"We come from a country of hasty marriages," she told him, softly, her usual composure restored. "Such a marriage, as often as not, is just the first of several more. We enjoy being together. Why get serious about it?"

"Lola, I hate leaving you."

"I know I shall miss you, too, Brian. But we both have jobs to do and our jobs are interesting. All you know about me is what I've told you. But you find me good company and physically attractive. The same applies to you."

Brian watched the piquant face. "But you won't drop out of sight? You'll write to me?"

"Of course I shall—if I know where to find you."

"Sure! I hadn't thought of that! But this is what I'll do. Directly I reach Cairo I'll radio my address to you at Michel's in London."

"No, Brian dear! Don't do that. Michel won't deal with private correspondence. And I might be anywhere. I'll tell you

517

what, Brian. When I get my sailing orders I'll leave a forwarding address at the hotel if I haven't heard from you by then."

"It might take weeks to reach you!"

"I'll tip the hall porter to send it airmail. . . ."

That night they were out together later than usual, Lola lovely to look upon in her cunningly simple dance dress, Brian drunk with longing but kept in check by those sudden moods of aloofness which sometimes came over Lola, like a mysterious cloak, changing her entire personality. At one moment all sweet surrender, in the next she became the unattainable woman.

But in the taxi going back to the hotel he took her in his arms and kissed her, passionately. . . . "Lola," he murmured, "I love you . . ."

She returned his kiss, which set him on fire, but gently pushed him away.

"Don't make love to me now, Brian—when I know we're parting so soon. I'm very fond of you. But please wait. I feel we shan't be parted for long."

He detained her in the dark lounge of the hotel for an unreasonable time; and in the lift when, very tired, she stepped off (Lola lived on the floor below Brian) he felt that he had lost her for ever. A sense of desolation swept over him. . . .

It was approximately at the same hour that an event occurred in the old Arab mansion near the Mosque of El-Ashraf which would have a great influence upon Brian Merrick's life.

The lofty saloon was dimly lighted by hanging lamps of perforated brass. On a cushioned seat in one of the *mushrabîyeh* windows Dr. Fu Manchu lay, so that what little breeze there was could reach him from the courtyard outside.

His normally gaunt features were so grey and sunken that now they resembled a death's head. His eyes were dim. It seemed to Matsukata, the Japanese physician who sat watching him, that only the man's unquenchable spirit remained alive. When he spoke, the once imperious voice was a mere croak.

"You have never . . . seen me . . . in this pitiable condition

. . . before. I knew I had . . . little time. But the . . . dreadful change has . . . come so suddenly." Fu Manchu panted for some moments. "Gorodin's treachery . . . has destroyed me. . . . . You have searched . . . every inch . . . of his rooms . . . for the stolen . . . phial?"

Matsukata bowed his head. "Every fraction of an inch, Excellency. But the Sherif Mohammed has been at work near- ly twenty-four hours without sleep or rest on the material."

Dr. Fu Manchu's eyes closed. "If I die . . . tonight," he whis- pered, "mankind will . . . not long . . . survive me."

He became silent. Matsukata bent over him in sudden anx- iety. A door opened in the other end of the saloon and a man entered quietly, an old, white-bearded man who wore Arab dress. A change crept over Fu Manchu's grey face. Without opening his eyes:

"You have it, *Hakim?*" he whispered, speaking in Arabic.

"I have it, Excellency, at last."

From under his black robe, the old physician took out a small phial, half filled with a nearly colourless fluid.

"You are . . . sure . . . of the antacoid?" The words were bare- ly audible.

"Positive."

"Pro . . . ceed . . . quickly . . ."

"His heart"—Matsukata spoke close to the Arab doctor's ear—"is dangerously weakened."

"I understand. We have no choice. The convulsions which follow the administration of the elixir are frightful. Be pre- pared for this. But any attempt to check them would be instantly fatal. . . ."

Brian had a restless night, not falling asleep until dawn was peering in at the window. He was wakened by the buzzing of his bedside phone. As he took up the receiver, he noted vaguely that it was ten o'clock.

"Is that Mr. Merrick?" a woman's voice inquired.

A hope that the caller was Lola died. "Brian Merrick here."

"Hold the line for Mr. Wellingham."

Peter Wellingham came on. Even without seeing the pale face, those tones of false geniality chilled him.

"Good morning, Merrick. Hope I haven't wakened you up.

519

Your instructions are just to hand, in the form of a reservation for a BOAC flight to Cairo, leaving at the uncomfortable hour of 5.30 a.m. tomorrow morning. You'll be picked up at your hotel at 4, so I thought I'd give you time to pack!"

"Very thoughtful," Brian murmured.

"A member of Sir Denis's staff, a Mr. Ahmad, will contact you when you arrive in Cairo. You'll like him. I'll send all papers along right away. Everything else is in order?"

"Everything."

"I'm off to Paris in an hour, or I should have loved to have you to lunch with me. But I expect you'll be well occupied with your own affairs. I saw you in Pall Mall one afternoon with an uncommonly pretty girl. You Americans seem to be damned popular!"

When Wellingham hung up, Brian lay back on his ruffled pillow and tried to figure out just where he stood and how he felt about it.

He had sent a long airmail letter to his father, telling him that a chance to travel had some his way in the form of a job as assistant to no one less than Sir Denis Nayland Smith. The senator had replied, offering good advice and assuring Brian of his support if ever it should be needed. Then had followed some disturbing facts about the situation in the Near East.

"The public," his father wrote, "don't appreciate the seriousness of the situation out there. Here at home they think it doesn't concern them as the trouble is so far away. But I can assure you that the President is deeply disturbed. The U.S.A. is the only partner in the Western bloc with any cash in the bank. This piles a terrible responsibility on to us. I'm sure you know how to take care of yourself, my boy, but be very careful when you get to Egypt. You couldn't have a better man beside you than Nayland Smith. . . ."

But now that the moment of departure was near it all seemed unreal. A dream had been realized. He had knocked, and the gate of adventure had opened.

And it meant that he had only one more day with Lola!

He snatched up the phone; asked to be put through to her room.

There was no reply. But she had probably slept late as he had done, and was now in her bath. He hung up, waited impatiently for ten minutes, and then called again.

No reply.

He jumped out of bed, called room service, ordered coffee, and went into the bathroom. The waiter came while Brian was in there. He rapped on the door.

"Your coffee, sir—and a note for you."

Brian came out wrapped in a towel before the man had left the room. On the tray he saw a hotel envelope addressed to him . . . in Lola's handwriting!

He tore it open impatiently and read:

> Brian dear: I found instructions when I got in last night to take a 9.35 a.m. train to Nottingham where there's a sale of old lace. Which means I can't get back until tomorrow! This drove me crazy. But I called the office this morning and asked for tomorrow off. I had to leave at 8.30 and didn't like to wake you. But we can spend the whole day together.
>
> Love, Brian dear.   Lola.

Native Cairo slept. No sound came from the narrow street upon which the gate of a tree-shadowed courtyard opened. Inside the house there was unbroken silence. . . . And Matsukata and the old Arab physician never stirred.

They had witnessed the appalling convulsions brought about by the injection of the secret elixir. In intervals of exhaustion, the Japanese surgeon had anxiously tested Dr. Fu Manchu's heart, and had shaken his head. Even his wonderful composure had almost deserted him. But:

"It is always so," the old Arab had murmured. "Only, his heart is ten years older than the last time."

For four hours they had been watching there, tirelessly. The convulsive struggles had subsided long before. Dr. Fu Manchu lay still as a dead man, so that his resemblance to the mummy of the long dead Pharaoh Seti I was uncannily increased.

The great change came slowly. First, the grey tinge faded from the face of the apparently dead man. Then, hollow cheeks seemed to fill out. Faintly, and soon more clearly, Fu Manchu's breath became audible. The two doctors exchanged glances. The old Arab drew a handkerchief from the sleeve of his robe and dried his forehead.

And, at last, Dr. Fu Manchu awoke—a dead man snatched from the tomb by his own superhuman knowledge.

He opened his eyes. They were clouded no longer. They were brilliantly green. He looked from face to face.

"Mankind is spared." His voice had all its old authority. "My star rises in the East. . . ."

Brian spent a most unhappy morning. He decided that he needed company, and called up everybody he could think of to join him for lunch. But everybody either was away or had a prior engagement.

His packing was done in half an hour, for he travelled light, and he lunched alone in the hotel grill-room, wondering if he would ever lunch there again with Lola. Now that separation had come, swift as a sword stroke, he realized acutely how much she meant to him. He thought of the wildest plans, such as chartering a plane to Nottingham, but common sense rejected them. It was Fate. He must bow to it. He wouldn't see her any more before he left for Cairo. . . .

After a miserable lunch he walked across to Hyde Park, a hotel writing-pad in his pocket, and took a chair at a spot where he could see the boats on the Serpentine. Lola and he had often sat there. He settled down to write her a long letter. It proved to be even a longer letter than he had intended it to be, and he decided to read it through and see if he had repeated himself.

It was at this point that he became aware of a voice. This voice was in some way familiar. The speaker seemed to be seated somewhere behind him, but too far away for Brian to make out what he was saying. Yet he seemed to recognize the voice, its curious intonations.

He tried to tune in to this voice; to blot out other sounds: oars in rowlocks, shouts of young oarsmen, splashing; to pick out words. And, up to a point, he succeeded.

". . . no choice . . . instructions are . . . break off . . . association . . . Sorry . . . all that . . ."

And now, Brian's curiosity had to be satisfied. Taking out a cigarette, he sparked his lighter and turned aside as if to guard the flame from a trifling breeze, but really so that he could glance over his shoulder.

His curiosity was satisfied.

The Honourable Peter Wellingham sat in the shade of a fine old oak tree talking animatedly to a girl whose face was shadowed by a large wide-brimmed hat but who almost certainly was Lola!

Brian turned his head quickly. He had a sudden sensation almost of nausea. Desperately he clung to the fact that he couldn't be sure the girl was Lola; but . . . Although Wellingham had called him on several occasions this was the first time he had seen him since that fateful morning when the agreement had been signed. And Wellingham had told him only a few hours ago that he was leaving for Paris almost immediately!

His world was turning topsy-turvy. Wellingham had lied to him—unless he had missed his plane—and, unless he had made a stupid mistake, Lola was not in Nottingham!

Brian put his pen back in his pocket, stared at the long, unfinished letter. First, he must regain control of himself, then make sure that he hadn't been mistaken about the identity of the girl with Wellingham. He must be cautious. If he had been lured into some kind of trap, if Wellingham and Lola (his heart seemed to miss a beat or two), were in league, what was their purpose?

He became calmer; listened again. He could no longer hear Wellingham's voice. He turned cautiously and looked back.

They were walking away!

Brian jumped up and followed. Already they had a long start and were headed for the highway parallel to Rotten Row where cars could be parked. He began to run.

The graceful carriage of the girl, her figure, even the dress she wore, told him that she was Lola. The big flop hat he had never seen. But it might be worn to shade her face if they chanced to meet him.

He was still yards behind when Wellingham opened the door of a smart convertible for the girl, walked around and got into the driving seat. The car glided off. . . .

Brian called Peter Wellingham's number, but was told by a soothing female voice which he seemed to recognize as that of the Eurasian secretary, that Mr. Wellingham was not at home. He gave his name and asked where Mr. Wellingham had gone. She was so sorry, but she didn't know. Was there any message?

His next impulse was to call Michel's. But Lola had been so insistent on this point all along that he hesitated. After all, even now he wasn't *sure* that the girl with Wellingham had been Lola. And Lola had told him that "Madame" simply wouldn't tolerate personal calls to members of her staff.

All his old distrust of Wellingham had swept over him again like an avalanche. Of Lola he hardly dared to think, except that he flogged his memory of the girl in the Park in search of something different about her to prove that she was *not* Lola.

In any case, he was committed to go to Egypt. He couldn't allow his personal doubts and frustrations to make him break faith with Sir Denis. . . .

An Oxford friend invited Brian to dine with him, which revived his drooping spirits. He managed that evening to forget his problems for an hour of two, had a few drinks and felt better. He returned fairly early, remembering his four o'clock appointment and tried to hypnotize himself to sleep by conjuring up mental pictures of Cairo. But, somehow, Lola always got into the pictures. . . .

CAIRO, from the air, whilst not so breath-taking as Damascus seen from above, proved exciting enough all the same to Brian. His urge to visit the Near East had been gratified. But every human blessing has a string to it. The string in this case was one he had knotted himself—Lola.

He had left a letter at the reception desk for her, but not the letter he had been writing in the Park. The second one had been even harder to write than the first; for although he had no positive proof that it was she he had seen with Wellingham, he remained obstinately convinced that it had been no one else.

The terms of *The Times* advertisement, the fact that Lola had drawn his attention to it, her words—"It read like a job created purposely for you"—added up to a dark, a horrible suspicion. *Had* it been created purposely for him? Was it a new variety of the old confidence trick? Until he actually met Nayland Smith he couldn't be sure that it wasn't.

But its purpose? The money in his wallet was real enough. His fare had been paid to Cairo. Why? Could it be a case of abduction—a plot to bring about his disappearance? His father was a wealthy man. . . But the idea was too preposterous. He had to laugh it off.

In fact, he was really trying all the time to convince himself that there was nothing wrong in the business. If Lola was really Peter Wellingham's girl friend and had merely been fooling with him, well—she wasn't the only pretty girl who enjoyed the attentions of more than one man.

He would get over it. Anyway, he must wait and see. . . .

Accommodation had been reserved for him, and an Egyptian wearing hotel uniform was standing by when the plane taxied to a stop on the runway. This experienced courier brushed him through the Customs as if by magic, and in no time Brian found himself speeding along a *lebbekh*-lined avenue into the ancient city. The colourful crowds, the palm trees, the unfamiliar buildings, and the queer smell which peculiarly belongs to Cairo all came up to expectations.

His apartment had a balcony overlooking a busy street and the Esbekîyeh Gardens. The ruins of Shepheard's Hotel, near by, which the driver pointed out, struck a warning note, recalling his father's advice, but it wasn't sufficient to depress him. Whilst he was having a shower and brush-up, a boy brought him a message. It was neatly typed on paper headed with an address in Sharîa Abdîn and a phone number. It said:

> Dear Mr. Merrick: I shall give myself the pleasure of calling upon you in the morning. Probably you are tired after your long journey; but if you want to do any sightseeing, please don't go out without a reliable dragoman. Sir Denis is expected to arrive at any moment.
>
> Yours obediently,
A.J. Ahmad.

This suited Brian well enough. He was certainly tired, and beyond perhaps a stroll in the surrounding streets he had no wish to go sightseeing. He planned to hit the hay soon after dinner; which programme he carried out and turned in by ten o'clock. . . .

He was at breakfast when Mr. Ahmad arrived.

Mr. Ahmad, correctly dressed in European clothes, proved to be a good-looking Egyptian with a marked resemblance to Egypt's Prime Minister. He spoke perfect English, but his phrasing was French.

"The cause of Sir Denis's delay," he told Brian, "is unknown. But his movements are always unpredictable. We expect him hourly. He appears like the *djinn*. There is a draught of air. A door opens. And Sir Denis Nayland Smith is with us!"

"That's good fun for the staff!" Brian grinned. "I suppose the moment he appears I'm expected to report?"

Mr. Ahmad shrugged slightly. "Of course as soon as possible."

"Of course. I mean he wouldn't want me to hang around the hotel?"

"Most certainly not. You know him. Judge for yourself.

Provided you don't leave Cairo, so that I can find you at short notice—it is sufficient. But, a word of warning. If you are disposed to wander in the older parts of the city——"

"Take a dragoman? Now listen, Mr Ahmad: Is that an order from Sir Denis?"

"But certainly not! It is merely a suggestion."

"Meaning I can do as I like? You see, I don't favour the idea of being taken in tow by a guide. I like to find my own way, go where I please and stay as long as I want to."

Mr Ahmad smiled a dazzling smile.

"The true sentiments of your freedom-loving country! Please yourself."

"Thank you."

"But take care. European and American travellers are not too popular in certain districts. If any trouble should start, take cover. . . ."

When, later, Brian set out, brushing off the beggars, the guides, and the vendors of scarabs and amulets, and trying to brush off the flies, he looked up to a fleckless sky and found, paradoxically, that he was no longer unhappy.

He wondered if the atmosphere of Cairo had some magical soothing quality; for he seemed, now, to be prepared for whatever lay in store for him. He had suddenly become a fatalist. If he had been made the victim of some mysterious plot it didn't matter. The plotters had gained nothing so far, and he was living in luxury. If Lola didn't answer his letter, never mind. He had had a good time with her in London. He wondered if the mood would last, or if later there would be a sharp reaction.

Sauntering across the Esbekîyeh, he was deeply interested in all he saw, and went on into a street bisected by a maze of narrower streets, all teeming with noisy humanity. He was in the Mûski, artery of many bazaars. Beggars, sellers of bead necklaces, scarabs and what-not buzzed around him like flies around a honey-pot. But he smilingly ignored them, which the head hall-porter had told him was the best method. From passers-by who wore European dress and therefore might speak English, he inquired the way to the Khân Khalîl where (the same authority had informed him) swords, daggers, silk robes, amber mouthpieces and other colourful native products were on view.

And presently he found it. The hall-porter had advised him, if he wished to make any purchases, to consult a certain Achmed es-Salah whose shop anyone would point out. ("He sells very good cigarettes.") It proved to resemble nothing so much as an artificial cave. The venerable Achmed sat in the entrance smoking, and at sight of a card which Brian had brought along, waved him to a chair and offered coffee and cigarettes.

Brian had a low opinion of the syrupy Arab coffee, but found the Egyptian cigarettes, with their unfamiliar aroma, a pleasant change from the American variety. He asked if he could buy some.

Achmed reached behind him, opened a drawer and produced a flat tin box containing a hundred. Smilingly he began to explain that only from him could these cigarettes be obtained. But Achmed had lost his customer's attention. Farther back in the shadows of the shop a female figure was vaguely visible to Brian—a girl who held a veil around the lower part of her face. She appeared to be watching him. He glanced away again. Dimly understanding what Achmed had been saying:

"I'll take the cigarettes," he told him. "If I want more I'll write and send dollars as you suggest."

"I supply them to many American gentlemen," Achmed declared, accepting the ten dollars which he claimed to be their price.

Brian concluded that many American gentlemen who visited Cairo must be wealthy gentlemen. Achmed, indicating those shops which were in sight, told him where amber goods, silk robes, authentic antique pieces, might be bought cheaply. Brian thanked him and stood up to go.

Glancing once more into the shadows, he saw that the girl's remarkable eyes—they were amber eyes—seemed to be fixed upon him . . .

He looked in briefly to some of the shops Achmed had recommended, but bought nothing. Coming out of the last one (which stocked scimitars, Saracen daggers and other queer Oriental weapons) he found himself staring into a shady alley nearly opposite.

He had caught a glimpse of lustrous amber eyes!

The girl from Achmed's had followed him! Why? Was she a Lady-of-the-Town, or had she some other purpose? Perhaps she was a member of Achmed's household, instructed to find out if he did any business upon which Achmed could claim a commission.

He strode off at a pace which gave many of the leisurely natives a jolt and called down on him dreadful curses which, fortunately, he didn't understand. He recovered his good humour in a street which seemed to lead to a city gate, turned right, into another, now hopelessly lost, and saw the minaret of a mosque right ahead. He glanced back quickly. There was no sign of the Arab girl.

But from behind came shouts and a sound of many running feet. This sound drew nearer. Brian wondered if he had started a riot. The word *"Inglizi"* sometimes rose above the roar of voices. *He* might be the person referred to!

He put on a spurt, passed the mosque, and looking back saw the head of what was evidently an excited mob pouring around the corner.

Just as he was clear of the mosque, out from its courtyard spurted a party of Egyptian police. He noticed an open doorway almost beside him, darted in and found it led to nowhere but a rickety staircase. Outside, came a clash. Wild shouting—fighting. Then a shot.

Brian started upstairs, as the tumult suggested that the police were being pushed back. On the first dark landing he nearly knocked over a water jar which stood near the stairhead. But the house seemed to be inhabited only by a variety of stenches. He mounted higher. The battle, now, was raging immediately outside the door below. Went up another flight—and found himself on the flat roof!

He saw all sorts of pans, jars and indescribable litter lying about, but nobody was up there. Brian crouched and looked over the low parapet down into the street.

The rioters had been rounded up by the armed police. They were all young, wild-eyed, typical tinder for the rabble-rouser. They were falling back, three of them carrying a wounded comrade. Brian could see a second police party extended in line before the mosque. The rioters were trapped.

He sighed with relief. Slightly raising his head, he looked

across the street to find out if he had been observed from there. He saw something which staggered him.

A heavy iron gate in a high wall which he remembered having noticed as he ran into the doorway below opened on the tree-shaded courtyard of a fine old Arab house. *Mushrabîyeh* windows overhung the courtyard on one side, but directly facing Brian were two large barred windows. Evidently there must be another which he couldn't see; for the room was well lighted.

And in this room, pacing restlessly about, he saw a tall, lean man who smoked a pipe, and who seemed to be talking angrily to someone else who wasn't visible from Brian's viewpoint.

For some time he lay there on the dirty roof, enthralled, unwilling to credit what he saw, but anxious to make sure that he wasn't suffering from a strange delusion. The shouts below had merged into sullen murmurs as the young rowdies were taken in charge by the police and marched off.

Brian scarcely noticed them, now. He was watching—watching.

And at last he was sure.

The man in the barred room was *Nayland Smith*!

Dr. Fu Manchu sat on a divan in the saloon of the old house near the Mosque of El-Ashraf. Beside him on an ivory and mother-o'-pearl coffee table a long-stemmed pipe with a tiny jade bowl lay beside the other equipment of an opium smoker. Before him a girl was kneeling on a rug, her long, lustrous amber eyes raised anxiously to the wonderful but evil face. She wore native dress, but no longer concealed her features with a veil.

"It was the disturbance made by the students from El-Azhar, Master. I lost sight of him and could not get through."

"I heard the young fools. Shouting phrases coined by aliens who are planning their destruction. Such half-moulded brains are fertile soil for the seeds of violence. All the same, you have failed me. The point at which he disappeared is one dangerously near us."

"Master, I——"

"You shall have one more opportunity. Change into

530

European dress. Go to Brian Merrick's hotel and make his acquaintance. He will be lonely. Attach yourself to him . . ."

He said no more, but watched her go out, then stood up slowly and walked along the saloon to a door, opened it, and went into another lofty room furnished as a studio.

No one was at work there.

On a wooden pedestal was a life-sized head of a man modelled in clay—the most conspicuous object in the studio. A number of sketches and photographs of the same subject were pinned to the walls. It would appear that the sculptor had worked from these and not from the living model.

It was a fine, virile portrait of a masterful character; but Dr. Fu Manchu appeared to be particularly interested in the shape of the moulded nose. He surveyed it from every side, the all-seeing gaze of green eyes absorbed in the finer lines of the nostrils, the straight bridge. He compared the clay model with the photographs, and at last seemed to be satisfied.

He passed on. He went down a short stair and entered a fully-equipped surgery filled with a nauseating odour of anaesthetics.

A patient lay on an operating table, two surgeons bending over him. They sprang upright as Fu Manchu appeared. He ignored them, stooped, studied the face of the man who lay there, and then turned blazing eyes upon the surgeons, one of whom was Matsukata.

"Who operated?" he demanded.

The taller surgeon turned a white, nervous face to Dr. Fu Manchu.

"I operated, Master." He spoke in French and used the word *maître*.

"I thought better of Paris surgery," Fu Manchu told him, speaking the same language sibilantly, "There will be a scar!"

"I assure you——"

"There will be a scar were my words—and no time to rectify the error. The consequences of this may be grave, for me—and also for you. . . ."

THE MOMENT the narrow street was cleared of police and rioters, Brian crept downstairs, unobserved, looked cautiously left and right and then started out to try to retrace his route. At the courtyard gate of the old house in which he had seen Nayland Smith he hesitated for a moment, but then hurried on. He considered it a stroke of luck that the inhabitants of the ramshackle tenement in which he had sheltered were apparently otherwise engaged.

More by luck than good navigation he presently found himself once more in the street leading to the Khân Khalîl. He looked around for a stray cab, for he was wildly impatient to solve the mystery of Sir Denis's presence in Cairo, and in a house in the heart of the native quarter. What in the name of sanity did it mean?

He could not very well be wrong about the identity of the man in the room with barred windows. Nayland Smith's personality was unmistakable, although Brian hadn't seen him for two years. He had recognized some of his curious mannerisms: the way he held his briar pipe clenched between his teeth; a trick of twitching at the lobe of his ear as he talked.

No—he had made no mistake, Sir Denis was in that strange old house hidden in the heart of the Oriental city.

Why?

Getting back at last, hot, tired and dusty, he paused in the lobby of the hotel, to talk to the all-knowing hall-porter. He had consulted him on many matters and tipped him liberally. He described his unpleasant experience with the rioters.

The uniformed Egyptian smiled.

"You should take a good dragoman with you, sir. He would see to it that you avoided such things."

"Very likely," Brian agree. "Maybe I'm too independent. But perhaps you can tell me something. I got lost, and wandered on into another quarter, 'way beyond the Khân Khalîl. It wasn't far from a city gate—and there was a mosque."

"There are many!"

"It was near a street where they sold cotton goods, pottery and that sort of thing."

"The Ghurîyeh! But I understand, sir."

"Well, in a narrow street leading to what you call the Ghurîyeh there's a fine old mansion with a high wall around it. Most unlikely spot for such a house. There's a courtyard, and——"

"I know what you have seen, sir. It is the house of the Sherîf Mohammed Ibn el-Ashraf."

"And who is he?"

"A very holy man, sir. A descendant of the Prophet—and the greatest physician in Cairo. . . ."

Brian was more hopelessly mystified than ever. What possible connection could there be between Sir Denis and the Sherîf Mohammed?

He called Mr Ahmad's number, but failed to get a reply.

What to do next was the problem. But the more he thought about it the more completely it baffled him . . .

He went into the cocktail bar fairly early in the evening, and saw that he had it to himself. He had made several further attempts to call Mr. Ahmad, but could get no reply. He ordered Scotch-on-the-rocks and sat there sipping his drink and feeling very puzzled and very lonely.

It was a perfect night, a half-moon sailing in a jewelled sky, and he would have liked to go somewhere, do something; get away from himself.

He smoked two cigarettes and then ordered another drink. He had made up his mind to take it out on to the terrace. When the bartender served it, Brian picked up the glass, slipped down from the high stool and turned to go.

How it happened he could never quite make out. He had heard no sound, had no idea anybody was there. But a girl wearing a strapless gown which displayed her creamy arms and shoulders had apparently been standing just behind him.

She raised her hand too late. He had spilled most of the whisky (and some of the ice) all over her!

She stifled a squeal. Reproachful eyes were raised to him. Brian grew hot all over. He called to the bartender:

"Quick! A napkin or something!"

A napkin was produced. The girl took it from his hand, looking aside, and began to try to dry her frock and her bare shoulders.

"What can I say?" he fumbled. "Of course I shall replace your dress, which is ruined. But there's no excuse for my clumsiness!"

She glanced at him. "You are right about my dress." She had a quaint, fascinating accent. "But truly I think I was to blame. I was looking for someone, and how could you know I was right behind you."

"I *should* have known! I shall never forgive myself, but say that *you* forgive me. You must let me drive you to wherever you live, so that you can change." He detected the dawning of a smile stealing across her face. "Then, as I guess you have a dinner date, just allow me to see you tomorrow and fix up everything for a new dress."

"I live in this hotel. I arrive only today. I can go to my room and change my dress. It will clean quite well. But it is very sweet of you to offer to buy another."

"That isn't an offer. It's a promise!"

She really smiled now. And Brian realized with a sort of shock that she was a very pretty girl indeed.

"Perhaps I won't hold you to it." She spoke softly. "It would not be fair."

"We'll leave that for the moment. Maybe, when you're changed, you'll find time to have a cocktail with me before you go?"

"Thank you. I am going nowhere. I meant to dine here, in the hotel."

"Then you'll dine with me?"

"Yes—if you really want it so."

When she had gone, Brian had his glass refilled.

"Do you know that lady's name?" he asked the Egyptian barman.

"No, sir. I never see her before." He displayed rows of perfect white teeth. "She is a beautiful young lady."

Brian sipped his whisky; lighted another cigarette. He was trying to figure out why her wonderful eyes seemed to awaken a memory.

She returned much sooner than he had expected. She wore,

now, a green dress which sheathed her lithe figure to the hips like a second skin. . . .

They dined in the terrace of an hotel overlooking the Nile. Brian's friend said her name was Zoe Montéro, that her family lived in Spanish Morocco. She was on a visit to an aunt and uncle who had a business in Luxor but who had arranged to meet her in Cairo. She had just received a message to say that her aunt had been taken ill and so they were detained.

"I shall know tomorrow if they can come or if they want me to go up to Luxor," she told Brian.

They danced in the moonlight, and the dark beauty of his graceful partner stirred Brian's pulses dangerously. He had decided that she was partly of Arab blood. Zoe's voice, her quaint accent, her natural gaiety, fascinated him. Sometimes, when he looked into her eyes, that dormant memory awoke. He tried to grab it—and it was gone.

But he enjoyed the evening. There was no word from Lola. . . .

It was quite early next morning when Mr. Ahmad called and found Brian having a smoke on the terrace.

"I have good news," he announced. "Sir Denis expects to reach Cairo late this afternoon."

Mr. Ahmad turned at that moment to bow to a passing acquaintance, or he could hardly have failed to note Brian's change of expression. All his suspicions had been justified. He had become enmeshed in a cunning plot, a most mysterious plot. If Lola had any part in it he couldn't be sure. But Peter Wellingham was one of the conspirators—and Mr. Ahmad was another! He was no diplomat and he spoke impetuously:

"But I saw Sir Denis right here in Cairo yesterday."

The effect of those few words upon Mr. Ahmad was miraculous. He changed colour alarmingly, clutched at the edge of the table and stared like a man who has been struck a body blow.

"You saw . . . him . . . in Cairo . . ."

Words failed Mr. Ahmad, and Brian could have kicked himself; knew he had played the fool. He had had the game in his hands and had thrown his chance away. If, as he now had fresh reason to believe, Wellingham and Ahmad were conspiring against Nayland Smith, were no more than spies of the enemy (whoever the enemy might be), he could perhaps have exposed their game by the use of a little tact.

Brian wondered if he had left it too late. He could try.

"Yes." He spoke easily. "Coming back here last night with a friend, our taxi passed a smart English sports car. (I think it was a Jaguar.) There were two men in it. And one of them was Sir Denis."

Mr. Ahmad moistened his lips with his tongue.

"Where was this?"

"I asked the driver as it happens, and he told me we had just passed the British Consulate."

"The British Consulate," Mr. Ahmad echoed mechanically, his expression ghastly. "You alarm me, Mr. Merrick. I must make immediate inquiries. Sir Denis's mission is a vital and a dangerous one. He has powerful enemies. It is possible that he has returned secretly for some reason of his own."

He left soon afterwards, a man badly confused; and Brian settled down to try to puzzle out the truth. Mr. Ahmad had behaved like a crook unmasked, but on the other hand there could be a different explanation.

If Ahmad was on the level, he had done the wrong thing . . .

Dr. Fu Manchu was writing at a large desk of Arab manufacture, most cunningly inlaid with ivory, mother-of-pearl and semi-precious stones. It was loaded with books, racks of test tubes, manuscripts and certain queer objects not easy to define. Peko, the tiny marmoset, a companion of Fu Manchu's travels, crouched on the doctor's shoulder, beady eyes moving from point to point restlessly.

There was a faint buzzing. A voice spoke.

"Abdûl Ahmad is here."

"I will see him."

Dr. Fu Manchu continued to make notes in small, neat characters in the margin of a bulky, faded volume until a door opened and Mr. Ahmad came in. He bowed obsequiously, then stood still. Fu Manchu glanced up.

"Yes? You wish to report something?"

"Excellency!" Ahmad stammered. "It is that Brian Merrick claims to have seen Nayland Smith last night!"

Dr. Fu Manchu closed the large volume and fixed a glance

upon Mr. Ahmad which seemed to freeze that gentleman to the floor.

"Tell me what he said, exactly—exactly—and also what *you* said."

Mr. Ahmad evidently had a phenomenal memory, for he repeated the conversation practically word for word under the barely endurable gaze of those strange green eyes.

Dr. Fu Manchu looked down at the emerald signet ring he wore and there was silence. The marmoset broke this silence by uttering one of his whistling cries and leaping to the top of a tall cabinet behind the Chinese doctor, where he sat chattering wickedly at Mr. Ahmad. Fu Manchu spoke.

"Merrick is lying for some reason of his own. There has been bungling. He suspects something. He did not see Nayland Smith where he claims to have seen him. But he may have seen him—elsewhere. This we must learn. Vast issues are at stake. Order Zobeida to report to me, here, immediately."

Mr. Ahmad went out, and shortly afterwards Zobeida came in. Brian would have recognized Zobeida as Zoe Montéro . . .

The memory which had been dodging Brian like a will-o'-the-wisp, came out into the open that evening. He was waiting on the hotel terrace for Zoe. He stood up when he saw her coming. Dusk had fallen and she moved gracefully through shadows, into the light of the moon, and out again. Once, when she was quite near, in shadow, a stray moonbeam touched her, briefly, lighted up her eyes.

And he knew where he had seen those beautiful eyes before . . . She had been in the shop of old Achmed es-Salah, wearing native dress and veiling her face! She had followed him when he left!

He was entangled in an invisible web! Every move he made was covered. Someone who had known he was going to Achmed's shop had planted the girl there. She was infernally clever, too. That trick in the cocktail bar had been done beautifully!

And he could no longer doubt that Lola also was in the plot. . . .

What did it all mean?

Why had no word come from Sir Denis? And why was he hiding in that old house in the native quarter?

Zoe smiled and gave him both her hands. She looked very lovely tonight.

"If I keep you waiting I am sorry, Brian. But an old friend of my father's, an Englishman, hears I am in Cairo and calls me. He talks for so long. Yes. I am thirsty with talking. Please get me a big, cool drink."

Brian clapped his hands for a waiter and gave the necessary orders.

"Does this old friend of yours live here in Cairo?" he ventured cautiously.

"Oh, no! He comes only yesterday and from my uncle in Luxor he finds I am here. He is very quick to find things out. He was for many years of the English police."

"Is that right? I guess he's here on some investigation?"

Zoe shook her head. A waiter brought two tall glasses.

"I don't know. He doesn't tell me. But I know from my father that Sir Denis now belongs to the British Secret Service."

She took a long drink; sighed contentedly. Brian tried to tell himself that her remark hadn't stupefied him.

"What's the rest of his name?"

"Sir Denis Nayland Smith."

"Well I'll be damned!" Brian breathed; and met the regard of wide-open amber eyes.

"What so much surprise you, Brian?" And even now the way she said "Brian" fascinated him. But he knew he must step warily.

"Just that I happen to know him, too."

Zoe smiled delightedly.

"That is wonderful! And you don't know he is here?"

"Well"—he spoke very slowly—"maybe he doesn't know *I'm* here."

He was doing some hard thinking. In that first startling moment of revelation, when he became suddenly convinced that Zoe and the girl in the bazaar were one and the same, which seemed to reveal this bewitching little tramp for an impostor, a spy set to watch him, he had decided what he would do. But this new development threw the whole plan out of gear.

Could he possibly have been wrong all along? Prejudiced by his dislike for Peter Wellingham, he might have jumped to the conclusion that the girl he had seen with him in Hyde Park was Lola—for he had never actually caught even a glimpse of her face. Still hag-ridden by his suspicions, he might also have assumed, wrongly, that Zoe and the veiled lady of the bazaar were identical, for no better reason than that both had amber eyes! Amber eyes were not uncommon in the East.

Zoe's claim that she knew Nayland Smith couldn't very well be bogus, or she would have reacted very differently when he told her that he, too, knew Sir Denis.

Where did he stand? Had he misjudged Mr. Ahmad as well?

"You are very thoughtful," Zoe whispered softly. "Don't you like me tonight?"

"My dear Zoe!" They sat side by side on a cushioned cane divan. "I was so surprised that I forgot to tell you how lovely you are."

He put his arm around her shoulders and drew her to him. She smiled, raising pouting lips. And Brian didn't even try to resist the sweet temptation. . . .

Dawn was not so far away when Brian finally turned in that night, and he slept late into the morning. He sent for his mail when he ordered coffee, but again there was nothing from Lola.

He was a man who once his suspicion had been aroused could never let the matter rest, but must leave no stone unturned to prove or disprove his doubts. If indeed he had become involved in a conspiracy against Nayland Smith, a conspiracy in which Wellingham, Lola, Ahmed, and Zoe were concerned, a love affair with Zoe was the best, and by far the most pleasant, way to find it out. So he argued.

And he had wasted no time.

Zoe, who, for all her youth, he suspected to be far from unsophisticated in love and the ways of lovers, had responded to the point of unconditional surrender. And it was then that Brian began to distrust himself. Never once, even while he caressed her, mingling kisses with what he believed to be artful leading questions, had she breathed one word that he wanted to hear. He had been equally reticent.

She didn't know if she would see Nayland Smith. She hadn't seen him since she was a child. He hadn't told her where he was staying in Cairo. Sir Denis had met her uncle when he was in Egypt with Sir Lionel Barton, the famous archaeologist, many years ago. Sir Lionel had been excavating a tomb in the Valley of the Kings.

And Brian remembered that Nayland Smith had spoken of this very expedition when he had visited their home in Washington!

Brian, being no roué, began to reproach himself. If Zoe was really not a conspirator sent to trap him, he was behaving rather like a cad. He must not pretend to himself that the zeal of the investigator and not the fact that Zoe was very desirable inspired his love-making. It wouldn't be true. If he had known, beyond all doubt, that she was a spy of the enemy he might have scrapped his scruples. But he didn't know.

He pondered the situation over his morning coffee and smoked a number of Achmed es-Salah's cigarettes. Then he called Mr. Ahmad's number, but failed, as usual, to get a reply. He began to feel like a man lost in a maze.

Two things he made up his mind to do. First, he would call at the address which appeared on top of Ahmad's letter. Second, he would return to the house hidden away in the native town, ring the bell (if there was one) and ask for Sir Denis Nayland Smith.

This prospect of even a little action cheered him while he took his bath; and going down to the dining-room he made a good, if late, breakfast.

He took a cab to the address in Sharîa Abdîn, which he saw to be a modern office building only a few minutes' walk from the hotel. This made him feel a fool, and he asked the man to wait; went in. He found a list of tenants just inside the door and read all the names carefully.

But Mr. Ahmad's was not one of them.

More mystery! Until it occurred to him that Ahmad might be a member of a firm which didn't bear his name at all. As there seemed to be no hall porter, he stepped into the nearest office ("The Loofah Product Coy") and found a smart young Jewess seated before a typewriter.

She greeted him with a brilliant smile. Many women greeted Brian in that way.

"Excuse me," Brian began, "but I'm looking for someone called Mr. Ahmad——"

The smile was wiped out. Dark eyes challenged him.

"I'm sorry. There's no one of that name here." It was final; a plain rebuff.

"I'm sorry, too, for troubling you. But, you see, I have a letter from him here"—he produced Ahmad's letter—"and it has this address on it."

The dark eyes melted a little. "There are many offices in the building. Perhaps someone else could help you."

"I'll try." He turned to go; when the girl said, more softly: "Try the Aziza Cigarette Corporation, third floor. They have been here longer than we have. They may know. But don't say I sent you."

Brian swung around, and met the brilliant smile again.

"Thanks a million!" He gave her a happy grin.

He was really getting somewhere. The cigarettes he had bought from old Achmed es-Salah were called "Aziza"! This was becoming exciting. But it revived all his half-discarded doubts. If, as he had at some time suspected, it was Zoe he had seen in Achmed's shop and Zoe who had followed him when he left, than Achmed was back in the picture. And if Mr. Ahmad belonged to the Aziza Cigarette Coproration, then the chain was complete. And he had good reason to believe that he did.

The reason was this: The girl in the Loofah office (who evidently disliked Mr. Ahmad) had warned him: "Don't say I sent you. . . ."

THE OFFICE of the Aziza Cigarette Corporation was, if any-thing, even smaller than the one he had just left. An Egyptian youth, incredibly cross-eyed, looked out through a little win-dow. What Brian could see of the room behind this window seemed to indicate that it was totally unfurnished.

"Can I see Mr. Ahmad?" he inquired.

The young Egyptian looked blank. "Nobody here."

"Are you expecting Mr Ahmad?"

"Don't know him, sir. Don't know any of the gentlemen."

Brian frowned irritably. "What do you mean? You must know who employs you."

"Why, for sure, sir. Mr. Quintero pays me to come here every morning and collect the letters. This business it has moved to Alex. This office is for renting."

He looked proud of having given so much information. His mouth expanded in a huge grin which seemed to split his face in half and also to increase his squint.

"Who's Mr. Quintero?"

"The landlord, sir."

"Is he in the building?"

"No, sir. He lives in Gezira. I go there now."

Brian turned abruptly and walked out. This game of blind man's buff was beginning to get on his nerves. He couldn't very well call at every office in the building and inquire for Mr. Ahmad; and the unbroken silence of that gentleman's phone made it difficult to get in touch.

When he came out on to the street he nearly fell over the dirty person of an old beggar seated on the ground right beside the doorway. This ragged object stood up. "*Bakshîsh*," he whined, his hand stretched out.

Brian walked across to the waiting *arabîyeh*.

"Do you know the house of the Sherîf Mohammed Ibn el-Ashraf?" he asked the driver.

The man looked startled. "Yes, sir. But this house not open to visitors."

"Never mind. I want to go there."

Brian turned to open the door. But the old mendicant had it open already. "*Bakshîsh*, my gentleman."

Again the eager hand was extended, and Brian threw him a coin as the cab was driven away, and thought no more of the incident.

And so before long he found himself once more in the odorous, noisy, narrow streets of the Oriental city. Here were the hawkers of fruit, vegetables, lemon water and what not, intoning their timeworn cries, descendants of those who had hawked the same wares and cried the same calls when Harûn al Raschîd ruled Egypt from Baghdad.

Before the iron gate his driver pulled up. "This is house of Seyyîd Mohammed."

Brian got out and tried the gate. It was locked. He could see nothing resembling a bell-push and was wondering what to do next when he realized that a man had come out of the house and was ponderously approaching.

This was a fat fellow with a large, shiny face expressionless as a side of bacon. He wore native dress and a large white turban. Standing close to the locked gate, he said something in a fluty voice which Brian didn't understand.

"I want to see the Sherîf Mohammed," Brian told him.

The fat man shook his head, turned and slowly walked back again.

Brian rattled the bars angrily. "Did you hear me?" he shouted.

The fat man went in, but came out almost at once with another man, and pointed to the gate. The second man, dressed in black and wearing a red *tarbûsh*, was slight and intelligent-looking. He hurried forward.

"You wish to see the Seyyîd Mohammed, sir?" He spoke in English.

"Urgently. My name is Merrick, Brian Merrick. I am a friend of Sir Denis Nayland Smith."

The man unlocked the gate and stood aside for Brian to go in. Then he locked it again. And Brian experienced a pang of apprehension, almost a physical chill, when he recognized the fact that he was fastened into this mystery house. He turned and called to the driver:

"Wait for me!"

"Will you come this way, please."

Brian followed on into the house, which was evidently very old. From a tiled apartment in which a small fountain tinkled he was led upstairs to a lofty room lighted partly by an opening in the painted ceiling and partly by sunshine filtering through the lattices of two recessed windows. The floor was tiled, but several rugs were strewn about on it. His guide pointed to a divan.

"Please wait a few moments, Mr. Merrick. I will inform the Seyyîd that you are here."

He walked out, closing the door behind him.

Brian began to examine the room more carefully. Glancing behind him, he saw a window fitted with bars. He crossed to it; looked out. Then he knew.

He was in the room in which he had seen Nayland Smith!

It was easy, now, to recognize the two *mushrabîyeh* windows. But something else he saw puzzled him. High up in a wall was an opening like a small window covered with a grille of ornamental wrought iron. He couldn't imagine what purpose it served, but it had an ominous look. There seemed to be only one door to the room, and this door, for he tried it, had been quietly locked by the man in the red *tarbûsh* when he went out!

That sensation of physical chill stole over Brian again.

Perhaps Sir Denis was a prisoner in this strange, silent house, and he, Brian, had been cunningly lured into the same trap!

He was still staring up at the iron grille, his brain feverishly active and bubbling with wild theories, when the door opened very quietly and a man came in. Brian turned to face him.

He saw a venerable and arresting figure: a tall man, with heavy brows overhanging piercing dark eyes, a pure white beard and the bearing of one used to respect. He wore native dress and a closely-wound green turban.

"I am Mohammed Ibn el-Ashraf. You wished to see me?" The words were spoken in perfect English.

"I certainly did!"

"Please be seated, and tell me how I may serve you."

Brian returned to the divan, and the Sherîf (evidently known here as "The Seyyîd") seated himself cross-legged on a large ottoman facing him. His unwavering regard Brian found very disconcerting.

"My name is Merrick——"

"So I am told, Mr Merrick."

"I'm a friend of Sir Denis Nayland Smith, and I'm here to ask you to be good enough to let me see him."

The gaze of the dark eyes never left his face. "Did Sir Denis notify you that he was here, Mr. Merrick?"

"No. I *saw* him, right in this room!"

"A singular accident. Where were you at the time?"

"On the roof of a house right opposite."

"Indeed? It was fortunate that you, and no one else, observed him. But the ways of the All Knowing are inscrutable." He touched his brow, his lips and his breast in a gesture which reminded Brian of a Roman Catholic making the sign-of-the-cross. "Sir Denis is in great danger, Mr. Merrick; and his health is impaired. He sought sanctuary in my house, for he knows me well."

Brian felt like someone drowning who finds himself dragged to the surface. Here was a clear explanation at last of the mystery which had baffled him. For it was impossible to doubt the assurance of this dignified old man.

"I am sorry to hear this. Can I see him?"

"Not this morning, I regret to tell you. I am, as I presume you know, a physician. Sir Denis has placed himself under my care and the course of treatment I have prescribed will not be completed until this evening. If I think it wise, I will allow him to call upon you tonight. No doubt he knows where you are lodged?"

"He does. I may count on that, sir?"

"Absolutely, Mr. Merrick. He is sleeping at the moment. I am treating him for nervous exhaustion. Directly he awakes, I shall inform him of your call. . . ."

As the courtyard gate closed with a slight metallic clang upon the visitor's departure, Dr. Fu Manchu opened the door of a closet and came out. The back of it accommodated the grille which, from below, on the other side, had so badly intrigued Brian. The doctor walked down a short flight of stairs and into a room part laboratory and part study. A tall cabinet with a rounded top swung inward at his touch and where it had been an arched opening appeared.

He stepped through, with his silent, curiously catlike step, and glanced around the lofty apartment in which Brian had interviewed the Sherîf Mohammed. That dignified descendant of the Prophet was waiting for him and bowed as he came in. Fu Manchu, his crossed hands hidden in the sleeves of his robe, watched him.

"It was well done, Mohammed." He spoke softly, in English; "and even better that we were prepared for such an emergency. Brian Merrick is an almost irreplaceable unit in my plan, but had you stumbled or faltered, I fear we should, nevertheless, have been forced to dispense with him. His life hung in the balance."

The Sherîf Mohammed hesitated, and then, "His transparent honesty is a great asset to us," he declared. "He would be hard to replace. If he had insisted upon seeing Nayland Smith I should have lost my control of him. the promise I made was the only alternative."

"And it shall be carried out. Matsukata is not ready; but the risk must be taken."

The Sherîf bowed. "The urgency is great, Excellency. Inquiries reached me only an hour ago from Moscow concerning the lack of a report from Gorodin. If we lose Soviet confidence it might mean the abandonment of our plan."

Dr. Fu Manchu laughed. It was strange, chilling laughter.

"Soviet confidence!" He spoke softly, almost hissing the sibilants. "We have had one instance of their *confidence*! How little they suspect, Mohammed, that we and not they, hold the East in our hands! How many times have I offered them my co-operation? How many times have they wisely declined it? But at last they have accepted . . . their ruin!"

The Sherîf inclined his head. "Doubtless Excellency will deal with the inquiry himself?"

"It may be left to me. But tonight Sir Denis Nayland Smith must pay a brief visit to Mr. Brian Merrick. Cancel my instructions to Zobeida. . . ."

Brian was smoking on the terrace of the hotel after lunch when he was joined by Mr. Ahmad.

"My dear sir!" Ahmad sat down beside him. "How you startled me with your story of having seen Sir Denis in an English car! You must be psychic!"

"How do you mean?"

"Because, although I cannot learn if he uses such a car, it is beyond dispute that he was in Cairo at that time! I have traced him to the house of the Seyyîd Mohammed Ibn el-Ashraf, an old friend of Sir Denis. He is living there, *inconnu*, from motives of safety."

"I know," Brian answered shortly. "You might have told me so earlier if I had been able to find you. Listen. Where is your office located? And why can I never get any reply when I call your number?"

Mr. Ahmad spread his palms apologetically. "You have been looking for me?"

"Certainly. I could find nobody in the place who knew you!"

"I am so sorry. I have no office there. It is an accommodation address which I use when business brings me to Cairo. The number you have is that of a friend who lives in a small flat on top of the building."

"And who's never home!"

Ahmad laughed. "You have perhaps been unlucky, Mr. Merrick. Entirely my fault. Please excuse me. You have already talked to Sir Denis?"

"No. But I shall expect to meet him this evening."

"So I came to tell you. But it seems you anticipated me. You will, of course, make a point of not leaving the hotel until you have seen him?"

"Of course."

"Then I must leave you. I have urgent business to deal with, concerning Sir Denis's future plans. Concerning your own duties, no doubt he will inform you."

Brian wasn't sorry when Mr. Ahmad went. Whatever might be the position Ahmad held in Nayland Smith's organization, he couldn't shake off a feeling of distrust of the man. He took a book out into a shady corner of the garden and settled down to do nothing until cocktail time. He had little exercise these days, apart from a morning swim, and so far had found no time to do any sight-seeing. He wondered how much longer he would be in Cairo. There were so many things he wanted to do.

He was half dozing over his book when a boy came to look for him. He was wanted on the phone.

It was Zoe. "Oh, Brian! I am so sorry. My uncle from Luxor will be here this evening and I cannot see you! It is perhaps that I have to go back with him. I don't know."

"I hope you don't, Zoe. I doubt if I could find time to get up to Luxor, much as I'd like to. But as it happens I'm tied up this evening, too. I have to wait in for Sir Denis."

"So, he finds you! I know he will. You may give him my love, but don't tell him how much love I give *you*!"

Brian heard her musical laugh. "When shall I know if you're going to Luxor?"

"As soon as I find out. Perhaps tonight." She wafted a kiss over the wire.

Brian returned to his seat in the garden; thought about Zoe, tried to read, tried to keep himself awake by watching other visitors who strolled about there from time to time. But at last the restful, warm air, the drone of insects, conquered, and he fell asleep. He dreamed he was being bitten by thousands of mosquitoes and woke up to find that the dream was based on fact.

A boy was shaking him by the shoulder. "Wanted on the phone, sir."

And when he got there and said, "Hullo!" a snappy voice replied, "Brian Merrick, Junior?"

"I am Brian Merrick."

"Nayland Smith here. How are you, Merrick? Don't bother to tell me. Listen. I'm in a hell of a position. You're in it with me. At eight o'clock—*exactly eight o'clock*—wait in your room. Leave the door ajar. Don't tell me the number. I know it. At eight o'clock—with the door ajar. Good-bye. . . ."

After an early dinner, Brian went up to his room. A bottle of Scotch and a supply of soda water in an ice-bucket were there by his orders. And feeling oddly strung-up, excited, he sampled the whisky while waiting, constantly looking at his watch.

At last he was to learn the whole truth.

He would know tonight what he had committed himself to do; what his duties were to be. All the minor mysteries and misunderstandings would be cleared up. The grand mystery—the nature of the project in which Nayland Smith was engaged—would be unfolded.

It was such an adventure as he had often dreamed of. And even before this strange appointment with Nayland Smith it had brought events into his life more unusual than any he had known before. His meeting with Lola in London. Her drawing his notice to the advertisement in *The Times*. The strange interview with the Honourable Peter Wellingham and his appointment to what looked like a fabulous job.

Then, the journey to Cairo. The silence of Lola. Zoe! That unforgettable interview with the Sherîf Mohammed in the house in the Oriental city. And now—this strangest incident of all: "At eight o'clock—with the door ajar"!

What could be Sir Denis's object? Unless he was in actual physical danger and feared an attack upon him somewhere in the corridor leading to this room. Brian could think of none. Of course he might be hoping to avoid observation altogether; suspect that there were spies in the hotel. But how could he hope to escape detection in the lobby?

It was a puzzle. Brian looked again at his watch.

Three minutes to eight . . .

Excitement mounted second by second, now. He listened, intently, watching the slit of light from the corridor.

He heard the lift stop at his floor, the clang of the opening gate. Someone stepped out, walked briskly along towards his door . . . and passed it!

One minute to eight . . .

Another door was unlocked some distance away, and closed. That was the person who had just come up.

Silence.

And this almost unbearable silence remained unbroken until a very slight creaking disturbed it—and the slit of light began to grow wider!

Brian shot up from his chair. "Who's there?" he challenged.

A man came in—and closed the door.

It was Nayland Smith!

He wore a light topcoat with the collar turned up and a soft-brimmed hat, the brim pulled down. Brian sprang to meet him.

"Sir Denis! At last!"

"One moment, Merrick. Wait till I get to the window and then switch everything off." He crossed the room. "Lights out!"

Brian, utterly confused, obeyed the snappy order. Complete darkness came, until it was dispersed by faint streaks of light as Nayland Smith moved the slats of a Venetian blind.

"What's the idea?" Brian asked.

"Lights up! Wanted to know if you're overlooked." The room became illuminated again. "We're dealing with clever people who mean to stop us. And I'm Target Number One! Ha! Whisky and soda! What I need!"

He dropped his coat and hat on the carpet beside a cane rest-chair and was about to sit down. Then, as an afterthought, he stretched out his hand.

"Glad to see you, Merrick. How's your father?"

Brian grinned as he grasped the extended hand. This was the Nayland Smith he remembered, and yet, in some way, a changed Nayland Smith. His snappy, erratic style of speech, sometimes so disconcerting, remained the same as ever. The change was in his expression. He had the kind of tan which never wears off, but through it Brian seemed to see that he had become unhealthily pale. His features, too, were almost haggard, and he wore a thin strip of surgical plaster across the bridge of his nose.

As he mixed two stiff drinks: "My father is well, thank you, and sends his best wishes," he said. "But I'm told you have been a sick man, Sir Denis."

"Right. Do I look it?"

"You look fit enough now, but I can see you've been through a tough time."

"I owe my life, Merrick, to the Seyyîd Mohammed. The man's a master physician. Lucky for me I knew him. Those devils were hard on my heels when I got to his house. They'd penetrated my disguise, you see."

Brian passed a drink; sat down facing him.

"I'm afraid I *don't* see, Sir Denis! I have been walking in circles ever since I was selected for this job. I don't know what I have to do. I don't know what you're up against. I'm honoured and delighted to be with you, whatever the game may be. But I do want very much to know what it is."

Nayland Smith, who wore grey flannel trousers and an old shooting jacket, pulled out from one of the large pockets an outsize tobacco pouch and began to stuff some rough-cut mixture into the bowl of a very charred briar pipe.

"Naturally," he snapped. "I'm here to tell you. First, you might like to know how I got in? Service entrance. Walked up the stairs."

"Why?"

"*He* knows you're here to join me, Merrick!"

"He? Who's he?"

"Doctor Fu Manchu! You heard me talk to your father about him. He's the biggest menace the Western world has ever had to cope with. He has the brain of a genius and the soul of Satan! He's stronger today than ever he was. His agents are everywhere, in every corner of the world. This building is certainly covered. So are you. Either one of us might disappear tonight!"

"Good God!"

"It's a fact. Not until I have got in touch with the British authorities (who so far don't know I'm here) can I show myself in Cairo! After that, we'll both have official protection.

Abdûl Ahmad is an old worker of mine. He's sworn to secrecy. So is the Seyyîd Mohammed."

He dropped the pouch back in his pocket and lighted his pipe. Brian stared.

"This is a deeper mystery than ever, Sir Denis! You were on your way back from the Far East, I guess——"

Nayland Smith shook his head. "East Berlin."

"Berlin! Then whatever brought you to Cairo?"

"I wasn't alone, Merrick. The man I had rescued from behind the Iron Curtain was with me! My mission was financed by Washington. United States agents had reported that Dr. Otto Hessian, the world-famous physicist, was held a prisoner, working under compulsion on an invention calculated to end nuclear warfare."

"Didn't England want him?"

"His results will be shared by both governments. We got into France. I planned to cross by sea from Havre to New York. In fact we were on our way to the *Liberté*'s dock when a car passed our cab going the same way."

Nayland Smith's pipe went out. He stopped to re-light it.

"Yes?" Brian spoke excitedly.

"There was only one passenger in the car. . . . But it was *Dr. Fu Manchu!*"

CHAPTER 6

ENTHRALLED by all he had heard, and awed by the mighty responsibility which he had been chosen to share with Sir Denis, Brian was about to speak when Nayland Smith raised his hand.

"*Ssh*! Listen!"

He seemed to be watching the closed door. Brian watched it too. But he saw, and heard, nothing.

"What?"

"Wait a moment. I may be wrong, but——"

Nayland Smith moved quietly across the room until he could press his ear to a panel of the door. Then, very gently, he opened it—looked out. He closed it again silently and came back.

"Too late. There was certainly someone there. Let's hope they don't know I'm in here! I must be brief. But I want to bring you up to date. . . . We doubled back to Paris and flew here to Cairo. Dr. Hessian needed rest, facilities, and safety, to complete his plans for a laboratory demonstration. I knew he could find all this with the Seyyîd Mohammed. Also, I was rather shaken, and as you see"—he touched his nose—"had had a spot of trouble in Berlin!"

The phone bell rang.

"Be careful!" Nayland Smith warned as Brian took the call. It was Zoe.

"Oh, Brian dear, I can only speak for a moment. But I do not have to leave Cairo for another week! Are you glad?"

"Very glad indeed."

"I will call you in the morning."

The sound of a kiss. Zoe hung up. Brian turned, and met a quizzical stare from Nayland Smith.

"Evidently a lady," he snapped in his dry fashion.

Brian grinned rather guiltily. "As a matter of fact, Sir Denis, it was someone you know. Zoe Montéro."

Nayland Smith smiled. It wasn't quite the boyish smile which Brian seemed to remember, but he had to allow for the fact that Sir Denis had obviously been through hell, although he treated his troubles lightly.

"Little Zoe? Her uncle and I became close friends some years ago when I was in Luxor. She's a sweet little girl, and I know she's safe with you. And now I must be off." He stooped, picked up his coat and hat and put them on. "Never go out alone, Merrick. And lock your door at night."

"I must come down with you, Sir Denis!"

"Not on your life! You're the last man in Cairo I want to be seen with! Look—walk along to the lift, and when you get there, just open the door opposite—the one with a red light above it—and make sure there's nobody on the stair it leads to. If all's clear, pretend to press the bell for the lift, and don't attempt to contact me. Enjoy Zoe's company! She doesn't know you're working with *me*?"

"I never told her so."

"Never do!" Good night!"

But when Nayland Smith had gone in his mysterious way, Brian sat down to try to get these new developments into focus.

One thing was crystal clear. He had let himself in for a devil of a job! He was up to his ears in an international intrigue which obviously involved the safety of the United States—perhaps of the whole Western world. He thrilled to the prospect, but asked himself, in cold blood, if he felt competent to go through with it. Something more than mere physical courage was called for.

Did he possess those extra qualities? And was he justified in taking it for granted that he did when nothing in his life to date had given him an opportunity to find out?

He believed he had a fairly good brain, but he wasn't vain enough to pretend that it was a first-class brain. Yet, according to Nayland Smith he was soon to find himself in the ring against an opponent who had the brain of a criminal genius! In such a contest, of what use could he be to Sir Denis?

Evidently Peter Wellingham had decided that he was the very man Sir Denis was looking for, so that, although he didn't recognize the fact, he must possess some qualification which was necessary.

What could it be?

So far he had been asked to do nothing. He wondered how long that state of affairs would have lasted if he hadn't blundered upon Sir Denis's hiding-place.

And now it appeared he had *carte blanche* to do as he pleased for the next few days.

Yet Nayland Smith had warned him that his every move was covered!

Brian took another drink.

He decided that if he were to prove a success as a secret agent he must learn to control his hasty judgements. Men engaged in such perilous work were sure to move in an aura of mystery, for mystery, danger surrounded them. He, himself, had become aware of this fact. Making bad beginnings by distrusting Peter Wellingham, he had transferred his doubts to Lola (who had nothing to do with the matter); then to Ahmad, and finally to little Zoe!

Thinking of Zoe reminded him of the fact that he owed her a new frock. He would take her out shopping in the morning. Then they would lunch at Mena House and visit the Great Pyramid, an old ambition of Brian's.

He hoped she would call him when she got back, and be in time for a drink and a smoke before parting for the night. Brian had made few acquaintances since his arrival in Cairo, and none, except Zoe, whom he cared to cultivate. He settled down to write a report to his father of his first meeting here with Sir Denis Nayland Smith and his impressions of that remarkable man. . . .

Midnight drew near before the long letter was finished, and Brian felt very sleepy. Zoe hadn't called, and he settled for a final drink and bed. He fell asleep almost immediately.

Perhaps (as he thought afterwards) it was an aftermath of his concentration on the character and strange life of Sir Denis which had gone into the writing of the letter, but he had a singular and very disturbing dream. . . .

He found himself in a state of unaccountable and helpless panic, incapable of movement or speech. It was a condition he had never experienced in reality, and for that reason was all the more horrible. . . . Nayland Smith was pacing up and down the room in which he, Brian, had interviewed the Sherîf Mohammed—exactly as he had seen him from the roof of the neighbouring building. But, in the dream, Brian was in the room; could hear as well as see. And the first sound he heard came from behind the iron grille high in one wall. It was a strange, harsh, but dreadfully compelling voice:

"You have crossed my path once too often, Sir Denis . . .The time has come for me to order, for you to obey . . ."

The vision faded. . . . Brian was in Zoe's arms. "Brian!" she whispered, trembling—"Brian, listen to me! Leave here at once. . . . I love you, but you must go. Promise me you will go!" But he couldn't utter a word. He was dumb with fright. . . . Then the harsh voice came again. "Do you dare to forget who is your master?" Some unseen force dragged Zoe away. "Brian!" he heard. "Brian! Answer me . . ."

And Nayland Smith was there again, not in the lofty saloon but in a small room, stone-paved like a dungeon. He was chained by his ankle to a staple in the stone wall. Haggard eyes watched Brian.

"Don't do it, Merrick! Give me your word!"

And Brian could only gasp, mumble. Not one word could he utter. . . .

A sound of banging reached him. He couldn't move. He was no longer in the stone cell. He was lying in darkness so complete that a ghastly idea crossed his mind. . . . He had been buried alive!

The banging went on. Someone was trying to break into his tomb! A voice came faintly, from a long way off:

"Brian! Brian! Are you there? Answer me. . . ."

It was Zoe!

He was unable to make a sound!

But still he could hear the banging—only it grew less and less audible. . . .

That frightful oppression seemed to be lifting. He found he could move; stretched out his arm. And in doing so he nearly upset the reading-lamp! He was in bed!

Gladly, he switched on the light; got out and ran to the door (which he had forgotten to lock). That banging sound, and Zoe's voice, still echoed in his ears. He opened the door and looked out. . . . There was no one there.

His wristwatch recorded 3 a.m. His pyjama jacket was damp with cold perspiration. . . .

He fell asleep analysing this strange nightmare while it was still fresh in his memory. And finally he read it to be a sort of panorama of the half-submerged doubts and fears which had haunted him so long. He saw them now as myths of his imagination, but while they had been present in his mind they were as real as the horrors of the dream.

The next time he woke up blazing Egyptian sunshine was peering in through the slats of the window blinds and he could hear the familiar noises of the busy street below his balcony. The terrors of the night were finally dispersed by a cold shower.

Whilst he drank his coffee and enjoyed the first cigarette (there was no news from London), he called Zoe. She was often out in the morning unless they had an early date, and he had never discovered where she went. But he knew that she rarely left before ten o'clock. She answered at once, and he thought her voice sounded rather listless.

"I believe you were out disgracefully late," he told her with mock severity. "Admit that I'm right."

He heard her laugh. "It is true, Brian. But it is not the gay time you think! There is so much family trouble to talk about. My poor Aunt Isobel, who is my father's sister, has been so ill. She cannot put up with me yet at Luxor, although she is getting better. I told you last night that I am to stay here awhile. Are you glad?"

"Of course I'm glad, dear! Very, very glad. Listen. Are you free for lunch? Because I want you to lunch with me at Mena House and then go and explore the Great Pyramid. Is it okay?"

"Quite very much okay, Brian! When shall I be ready?"

"Is eleven-thirty too early?"

"No. Downstairs at eleven-thirty."

And at eleven-thirty Zoe came down to the lounge wearing a cream dress which left her arms and shoulders bare. They were slightly sun-tanned to the hue of *café-au-lait*. A large sunhat shaded her face, and Brian decided that she looked even more lovely than usual.

557

The drive out to Gîzah was all too short. He held her close in the near privacy of the cab, and this morning, for some mysterious reason, Zoe thrilled him in a new way.

They had some drinks in the Mena House bar and then went in to a cold luncheon. Afterwards they took their coffee out in the garden, choosing a shady table near the flower-draped wall overlooking the road.

Zoe became strangely pensive. Several times Brian caught her glancing at him furtively, as if wanting to tell him something which she hesitated to put into words. And so at last:

"Zoe," he began uneasily. "Something is bothering you. Tell me what it is. I must know."

Still she hesitated, glancing around as if she feared to be overheard. Brian reached across and took both her hands. "Tell me, Zoe. What is it?"

"It is something very, very hard to say, Brian."

He had an uneasy moment. "You don't mean—you are to see me no more?"

She shook her head, helplessly. "It is not as you think, Brian. I want to see you always. It is that I have to ask you something which, even if it break my heart, for *your* sake I must ask."

Brian became really alarmed by her earnestness. Her wonderful eyes were so bright that he knew tears were not far away. "Whatever do you mean, dear?"

"I mean"—she paused, as if seeking the right words—"I mean that, although it will be terrible for me if—someone—find out what I do, I *must* warn you, Brian . . . You are in very, very great danger. Soon, it will be too late. I hate—how I hate!—to say it. But please, oh please! Whatever else it mean to you, to me, leave Cairo at once—tonight if you can!"

This incomprehensible request so completely baffled Brian that for some moments he could think of no reply. Part of his dream had come true! Zoe had turned her eyes aside, but tears were gathering on her long, dark lashes; her hands, which he held tightly, were shaking.

He wondered if she had seen Nayland Smith since he had seen him, if it could be something Sir Denis had told her which accounted for her present state of mind. Then it occurred to him that it was odd she hadn't asked him about

Sir Denis's visit, for he remembered telling her he expected him. He wasn't dreaming now, yet all this had happened before.

"This would mean—if I did it—that we shouldn't see each other again?" He spoke in a toneless voice, trying to think.

Zoe didn't answer. She suddenly dragged her hands away. He saw her eyes—wide with terror. She pointed to the low wall beside which they sat.

"Brian!"—a whisper—"Brian! Down there—I heard someone move!"

Brian sprang up; craned over the wall and looked down . . . Zoe was right.

A ragged old mendicant sat on the dusty road, his back propped against the wall, immediately below their table!

"Hi, you! What are you doing down there?" Brian shouted.

A skinny, dirty hand was stretched out. *"Bakshîsh—bakshîsh!"*

Brian caught his breath. He leaned farther over.

"Let me have a look at you!"

The old beggar looked up. One glance was enough.

He was the man who had been seated beside the door of the office building in Sharîa Abdîn when Brian came out after his useless search for Mr. Ahmad—the man who had been holding open the cab door when he directed the driver to take him to the house of the Sherîf Mohammed!

This discovery shook him badly. He could doubt no longer that he was closely covered; had been in all probability from the moment of his arrival in Cairo. He had been right about this all along, but had suspected the wrong persons.

Nayland Smith knew, for Nayland Smith had warned him. Long ago, returning from Washington to renew his Oxford studies, Brian had forgotten the discussion between his father and Sir Denis concerning (as he thought at the time) the possibly mythical creature called Dr. Fu Manchu. But now——

This fabulous Oriental genius had cast his net around him . . . and Nayland Smith himself was fighting to escape from it!

What was he to make of Zoe's warning?

Clearly, she knew of his danger. Perhaps she had learned it

at that very moment when the dream had appeared to him. How she had come to know he couldn't imagine. But she was evidently aware of the fact that in urging him to run for it she herself might become enmeshed.

Here were very troubled waters; for whatever might be the source of her information, whatever underlay her queer reticence, that Zoe's warning had been desperately sincere he couldn't doubt. She was in a state of terror, and first he must do his best to reassure her about the eavesdropper.

He dismissed the old beggar, then sat down again and forced what he feared might be a parody of his usual happy grin.

"There is someone there. Who is it?" He saw how pale she had become.

"Nobody to worry about, dear. Just a dirty old beggar man. I dropped him an English shilling and told him to go take a long walk."

"He was listening," she whispered. "He heard me."

"I don't believe he has a word of English."

"But I heard you say, 'Let me look at you!' Does he look?"

"He just knew I was mad at him and looked up. It doesn't mean he knows English."

Zoe's amber eyes blazed. "He was listening. You *know* he was listening!"

Brian tried to think clearly. "Suppose he was, Zoe. And suppose he does know English. What have you to worry about?"

She turned her head aside, so that the brim of her hat quite shadowed her face.

"I cannot explain to you, Brian. What was told to me was told—in confidence. For your sake I speak. If it is found out——"

"Well, Zoe dear, what then?"

"It could be terrible. But you can do nothing about it. Only one thing, to give me peace of mind about you . . . Do as I ask. Do not stay here one hour longer than you can help!"

"But, Zoe. I don't know, and I'm not going to worry you to tell me, where you got hold of the idea that I'm in danger, but isn't it possible you're letting yourself get all het up for nothing?"

She turned, and her eyes challenged him. "It is *not* for nothing! Could it be for nothing that I beg you to go away when I want you to stay with me? How can you think this!"

Brian realized, at last, that Zoe was in a state of tremendous nervous tension. His well-meant but perhaps clumsy attempt to soothe her fears had only increased this. He must change his tactics. The situation was utterly fantastic. But he knew that the danger was real enough.

"I guess you'd like to get back." He spoke uneasily. "I'll try to contact Sir Denis."

"It will be no use," Zoe whispered. "But—yes—let us go, Brian."

There was a note of such black despair in her voice that he felt chilled. A cloud seemed to darken the Egyptian sunshine. He stood up, walked around and rested his hands on Zoe's bowed shoulders.

"Don't let it get you down, Zoe. I'll go in and order a car right away to take us back to Cairo."

She reached up and held both his hands. "Not to Cairo, Brian—to Port Said where we can find a ship! Do this and I will come with you. Leave all you have. It will be better—for you and for me. I am not mad. I know what I say. Do it—do it, Brian!"

"But, Zoe, dear, tonight——"

"Tonight is too late. It is now or never! . . . Oh! It is hopeless!" She thrust his hands away. "I can never make you understand! Go, then. I will wait here."

His brain behaving like a carousel, Brian went into the hotel and arranged for a car. He could no longer delude himself. The ragged old ruffian he had found seated in the road was a spy. And he was there to listen to their conversation. Zoe knew this, and her pitiable panic was clear enough evidence of the menace overhanging them.

He toyed longingly with the temptation to accept her warning. She had become more than ever desirable. She was beautiful, and a delightful companion, responding to all his moods, equally prepared to dance, to swim or to ride as the humour moved him. And in all they did together she was graceful and efficient.

But it was morally unthinkable that he should break his contract with Sir Denis—particularly now, when Nayland Smith needed him.

561

He walked slowly back to the garden and along to their table.

But Zoe wasn't there!

Brian felt his heart jump and then seem to stop for a moment. He sat down, looking at the empty chair. And by degrees he recovered himself. He, too, was giving way to panic. No doubt she had merely gone into the hotel to prepare herself for the drive.

This theory kept him quiet for five, ten, fifteen minutes. Then he decided that it was wrong.

He went in to make inquiries. But no one had seen her. He went back to the deserted table . . . and it was still deserted.

A boy walked down the path, and Brian jumped up expectantly.

"Your car is waiting, sir. . . ."

CHAPTER 7

DR. FU MANCHU, seated on a divan in the saloon of the old house near the Mosque of El-Ashraf, gazed straight before him as a man in a trance. A sickly smell of opium hung in the still air. The long, hypnotic eyes were narrowed. Sometimes a sort of film seemed to pass across them and was gone, leaving them brilliantly green.

He aroused himself; struck a small gong which stood on a table beside him. And immediately, like a *djinn* answering a magic summons, a stocky Burmese with a caste-mark on his forehead, came in and saluted deeply. Fu Manchu spoke to him in his own language:

"Is Zobeida here?"

"She is here, Master."

"Send her in to me."

So soon after the man went out as to suggest that the girl had been waiting in some adjoining room, Zoe came in. She was dressed as she had been dressed at Mena House, except that she no longer wore her sun-hat. Although pale, she was quite composed. It was the composure of resignation.

Without attempting to meet the glance which Fu Manchu fixed upon her, she dropped to her knees and lowered her head. There was a long silence in the saloon. Sounds from the street outside sometimes penetrated dimly, but no word was spoken, until:

"Look up," Dr. Fu Manchu commanded harshly, now using Arabic. "Look up! Speak!"

Zoe, known here as Zobeida, looked up.

"I have nothing to say, Master." She lowered her head again.

"To *me* you mean, little serpent! But Abdûl al-Taleb ('Abdûl the Fox') reports that you had much, too much, to say to Mr. Brian Merrick. Be so good as to tell me with what object you tried deliberately to disturb my plans."

"I was sorry for him."

Dr. Fu Manchu took a pinch of snuff from a little silver box, but never once ceased to watch the kneeling girl.

"There is no room for these moods of compassion in those who work for the Si-Fan. I bought you in an Arabian slave-market. I bought you for your beauty. A beautiful woman is a valuable weapon. But the blade must be true. You were trained to take your place in any walk of society. You have all the necessary accomplishments. Neither time nor money was spared in perfecting you for my purpose. Yet, like another I trained and trusted, your Arab blood betrayed you—and betrayed *me*!"

Fu Manchu's strange voice rose to a hissing falsetto on the last word. Zoe raised her hands to her face, and seemed to droop like a fading flower.

"Whispered words," the remorseless voice went on, "a man's caresses, and those years of patient training became wasted years in as many minutes. Yet, Zobeida, this was not by any means the first assignment you have carried out. You have passed through those fires unscathed—as you were taught to do. Tell me, Zobeida, are you afflicted by the delusion miscalled *love*?"

He gave to "love" so scornful an intonation that Zoe shrank even lower. She was trembling, now. Her answer was a whisper:

"This one is young, and without experience, Master. He is not like—those others."

Dr. Fu Manchu considered her silently for a moment.

"Had you spoken the unforgivable words, 'I *love* him', I should have sent for whips. It would have meant that you were of no future use, and therefore lash marks on your smooth skin would no longer have concerned me. But—you have betrayed the plans of the Si-Fan."

Zoe looked up. "I have not! He knows nothing of your plans, for even had I wanted to, I could have told him nothing. He knows that I think he is in danger, that he should go away——"

"With *you*, unless I misunderstood Abdûl, who was listening."

Zoe dropped her head again. "I would not have gone, Master, farther than Port Said. I dare not have gone. I thought, if I said this, he might be tempted to listen to me."

Another silence fell—a long silence, and then:

"Your desire to guide this attractive young man into the straight and narrow path is most touchng. Fortunately, I was able to take instant steps to check further confidences." Fu Manchu spoke softly. "Go to your room. You will not be returning to the hotel. . . ."

A faint hope that Zoe, piqued by his refusal to take her strange advice, might have found an empty cab at Mena House and returned alone to Cairo was disappointed when he got back to his hotel. She had not come in.

He had exhausted every probability before leaving Mena House. There was no doubt that she had gone. . . . But no one had seen her go!

Frantically, he tried to think of possible sources of information. Apart from Nayland Smith, he knew none of her friends. In fact, as he realized now, he knew next to nothing about her except what she had told him. And Nayland Smith had impressed upon him, "Don't attempt to contact me . . ."

Who was this uncle by marriage, possibly still in Cairo, with whom Zoe had discussed those family matters on the previous night? Where was he staying? What was his name?

He didn't know!

Once, as his widely travelled father had told him, when the British controlled Egypt, the Cairo police had been a highly efficient force. But now, when neither Britons nor Americans were too popular, what hope had he of co-operation?

The mystery of the thing appalled him . . . Had Zoe been abducted?

Clearly enough, she had picked up information somewhere concerning the existence of Fu Manchu—information which had terrified her. It was folly to try to pretend to himself that the dirty old vagabond sitting on the road at Gîzeh in hearing of their conversation was not a spy; that his previous appearance in Sharîa Abdîn had been a coincidence.

Brian went up to his room and paced about there like a madman.

He had not dreamed. He had seen a vision. Could it be that the rest of it was true? Had Nayland Smith fallen into a trap? He smoked countless cigarettes; had several drinks. In desperation, he called Mr. Ahmad's number . . . No reply.

He was wondering what to do next when his phone buzzed. He grabbed it.

"Oh, Brian dear!"—*Zoe*!—"I cannot tell you how unhappy I am. My uncle finds out from the hotel porter where we are gone and comes out by car to Mena House to get me. There is not one moment to lose. My poor Aunt Isobel is dying. She asks for me. So we rush for the train. I am at the station now . . . The train just comes in! I must run." The sound of a kiss. "Good-bye, Brian . . ."

"But, Zoe——"

She had gone . . .

Mr. Ahmad called early in the morning. He found Brian on the terrace, looking wretched, toying with biscuits and cheese and a cup of coffee—apparently his breakfast. Mr. Ahmad sat down in a cane chair.

"You are not feeling so well, Mr. Merrick?"

"Thank you. I feel fine."

"You looked, or so I thought, unhappy. Yes?"

Brian stared hard at Mr. Ahmad. And Mr. Ahmad forced a smile of sympathy.

"Shall I tell you something?" Brian asked. "I'm sick to death of all this mystery business. I'm told there's a serious danger threatening the Western World. I'm told that I'm a marked man. Queer things happen. And I'm left alone to think it all out. What kind of game is this? I can never get in touch with *you*—and Sir Denis orders me not to contact *him*!"

Ahmad shrugged. "Forgive me if I fail to follow you. I cannot know what took place between Sir Denis and yourself. I was not there. If your personal expenses have embarrassed you, I think I can promise that this can be arranged——"

"They haven't! It's not a question of money."

"Then of what?"

"Of self-respect, I guess! I find out I have a spy on my trail. I should like to report it. There's no one to report to! I'm supposed to be in on this thing. But I'm left sitting right outside."

Even as he spoke so bitterly he was well aware that the real cause of his bitterness was the strange disappearance of Zoe. Her words, when she had called him, had sounded false, unreal. Either she had been playing a double game all along, and had now gone off with some unknown man she really loved, or she had been abducted, had been forced to speak to him in order to put him off the scent.

But he didn't want to talk to Ahmad about Zoe, and:

"Could you deliver a message from me to Sir Denis?" he asked.

"But certainly. With pleasure."

But Mr. Ahmad spoke in a curiously uneasy way.

"If you can see him, why not I?"

Mr. Ahmad now looked unmistakably embarrassed. Brian could see that he was trying hard to think up an answer to that one. But at last:

"I can only obey Sir Denis's orders, Mr. Merrick," he explained. "Surely you know that he thinks it important, until his plans are complete, that no connection between you should be suspected?"

"Yes, I know that. But unless my hotel phone is tapped, why can't I call him?"

Mr. Ahmad leaned forward, his expression very earnest.

"Has Sir Denis told you where he is?"

"Yes. I knew, anyway. I didn't tell you at the time, because I thought maybe he didn't want me to know yet."

Ahmad forced a smile. "It was discreet—for I, too, was in ignorance of his presence in Cairo at that time. But, now that you know, Mr. Merrick, I ask you: Is it likely that such a household would be on the telephone?"

Brian thought a while, and then, "No," he agreed. "I guess not. But if I step in to a desk for a minute and write a note, can you undertake that he'll get it?"

He stumped out the butt of his cigarette in an ash-tray.

"Most certainly. May I offer you one of mine?" Ahmad held out a gold case. "They are different from yours. Unusual. But you may like them."

"Thanks."

Brian took one. It was an "*Aziza*"! He accepted the offer of Mr. Ahmad's lighter and went in to write his note. But he sat at the desk a long time, pen in hand, before beginning to do so. Was it another coincidence that the girl in the Loofah office had advised him to inquire for Mr. Ahmad from the Aziza Cigarette Company? And was it a still further coincidence that a spy whom he had mistaken for Zoe had followed him from the shop of the merchant in the Mûski who claimed to be the sole Cairo agent for the sale of those cigarettes?

He sighed, looked once more at the name on the cigarette, and then went on smoking. He began to write. Above all things he mustn't let his imagination run away with him again. . . .

When he came back to the terrace and handed the note to Mr. Ahmad: "I shall see that this is placed in Sir Denis's hands not later than noon," Ahmad promised.

"Fine. Now, what about a drink?"

"Many thanks. But it is much too early for me! What I really came to tell you is that Sir Denis expects to be ready to start tomorrow or the next day."

"Start for where?" Brian wanted to know.

"This I cannot tell you, because I have not been told myself."

"I see. Well, I'm ready at short notice."

"Good. And now I must go. My time is not my own. . . ."

Brian had a poor appetite for lunch, and was already finished when he was called to the phone. When he said, "Hullo," a voice snapped, "Is that Brian Merrick?"

"Here, Sir Denis!"

"Didn't recognize you for a moment. What's up? Something gone wrong?"

"Not exactly. That is, nothing that concerns you, personally. But Zoe Montéro left in a tremendous hurry yesterday. Called me from the railroad station (or so she said) and seemed very agitated. Told me her aunt in Luxor was dying. I'm rather worried, Sir Denis. I have a hunch something queer may be going on. We were covered by a man I'm almost sure was a spy while lunching at Mena House. Could you give me her uncle's address and phone number?"

"Oh! I hope your hunch is wrong, Merrick. Don't want that poor kid dragged into our troubles. Situation rather complicated. Friend of the Sherîf Mohammed happened to be leaving for Luxor day I got in. Asked him to let Zoe's uncle know I was in Cairo. Safe man, Merrick; name of Jansen, Swedish artist. Jansen wired me Zoe was here."

"But what's his phone number?"

"That's the snag, Merrick. Doubt if he has one. Runs a sort of art shop near the Palace Hotel, Never knew the address. Does reproductions of murals from the old temples, statuettes of gods and so on. Sir Lionel Barton employed him when he was excavating a tomb up there."

"Well, how am I to contact him? Would a radiogram to the Palace Hotel find him?"

"It might, Merrick—in time. I can suggest nothing better. Shall be sorry if anything happens to Isobel Jansen. I know Jansen was devoted to her. By the way, stand by tomorrow. I'm breaking cover. Look out for me!"

Nayland Smith hung up. Brian rather resented the light dismissal of his concern for Zoe, but reflected that Sir Denis had affairs more serious on his mind than the erratic movements of a girl he evidently thought of as a child. He wrote out a careful message addressed to Jansen (he didn't know his first name) at the Luxor Palace, and gave it to the operator for transmission.

But, try how he would to fight it off, a mood of black depression swept down upon him. . . .

CHAPTER 8

DR. FU MANCHU sat behind his desk, his disconcerting eyes focused upon Mr. Ahmad.

"You have instructed our agent at Luxor?"

"In detail, Excellency. The situation is under control."

"Good. Return to your duties." He resumed his reading of a closely written manuscript.

And Ahmad had not long gone out by one door when the Sherîf Mohammed came in at another. "A messenger from China has just arrived, Excellency."

Dr. Fu Manchu glanced up. "What has he to report?"

"There have been serious disturbances in three provinces. The Communist authorities have been compelled to send military reinforcements to——"

Fu Manchu suddenly stood up. His eyes blazed as though fires burned behind their greenness.

"What folly is this!" The words were rather hissed than spoken. "Are our Si-Fan directives no longer obeyed? My orders were clear: Accept whatever conditions, however harsh are imposed upon you. Lull the enemy into a state of false security. Wait! Wait for my word! Then—but not until then—strike, all my millions together. And at last China, our China, will lie like a choice pearl in my hand!"

Fu Manchu spoke as a man inspired—or possessed. The Sherîf Mohammed lowered his head and muttered a Moslem prayer.

"It is true, Excellency. But agents of our enemy are sent amongst them to stir up rebellion, as an excuse for massacre. Here in Egypt I have great difficulty in preventing premature action, also."

Dr. Fu Manchu clenched long, slender hands and sat down again. From some spot high above his head, Peko, his pet marmoset, sprang down on to his shoulder, giving his curious cry, which sounded like a short whistle. Fu Manchu reached up and stroked the little creature.

"Ah, Peko! You come to soothe me, my tiny friend."

"No doubt," Mohammed murmured, "Excellency will wish to send further orders back to General Huan Tsung Chao?"

Fu Manchu nodded. "Let the messenger wait. The fate of all the world hangs now upon a silk thread. Communism is not ready for war, and has nothing to gain by it. Washington fails to see how one step in the wrong direction may force the hazard. I have been selected to prevent this catastrophe, since I alone could hope to carry out the plan. Upon my success everything depends. Be good enough, my friend, to ask Dr. Matsukata to come in."

The Sherîf Mohammed salaamed and went out, leaving Dr. Fu Manchu playfully teasing the marmoset, which sometimes tried to bite him, whistling with fury, and sometimes snuggled up against his silk robe affectionately.

Matsukata came in; bowed ceremoniously. "Excellency wished to see me?"

Fu Manchu fixed his strange gaze upon the Japanese surgeon.

"No later than forty-eight hours from now, Matsukata, we must be on our way. You are ready?"

"I am ready."

"And your last patient?"

"Is ready also."

"You are satisfied?"

"He is sleeping. But Excellency might wish to see him."

Fu Manchu slightly shook his head. "It is unnecessary. He must make the journey."

Matsukata bowed again. The marmoset sprang across the desk and whistled at him angrily . . .

Brian spent a wretched day. He remained extremely uneasy about Zoe. Whatever the urgency, he couldn't understand why she had gone with never a word to him. He had found out from the management that she had left all her luggage behind, and all her expensive dresses!

They had never seen her before and could give him no information about her. They hoped nothing unpleasant had happened. But as the value of her abandoned property was apparently greater than the amount of her unpaid bill, they weren't so deeply concerned as otherwise they might have been.

It was late in the afternoon when a boy handed him a telegram. It was signed "J. Jansen." The message was brief, merely stating that Zoe had hurried back to Luxor with the writer and that there were hopes for her aunt's recovery. She sent her love to Brian and Sir Denis.

Brian gave a great sigh of relief.

He had built up a pyramid of doubts based upon her disappearance. These included the theory that Mr. Ahmad was a traitor in Sir Denis's camp; that Sir Denis was losing his grip and didn't recognize friend from enemy.

This telegram shattered these delusions, lifting a dreadful load from his mind.

Perhaps he would never see Zoe again, but she had given him many hours of happiness and, after all, he wasn't in Cairo to enjoy himself!

During the remainder of the evening he wrote a long letter to her, addressed c/o J. Jansen, but never wandered far from the hotel, expecting Nayland Smith to walk in at any moment.

But up to the time that he went in to dinner Sir Denis hadn't appeared.

He was about to stand up and go out on to the terrace for coffee when he saw him hurrying in his direction and accompanied by another man quite unmistakably English. Both wore evening dress.

"Ah, there you are, Merrick!" Sir Denis snapped. "Want you to meet Sir Nigel Richardson from the Embassy!"

"How do you do, Mr. Merrick!" Sir Nigel shook hands cordially. "Devil of a game you fellows have taken on! Smith's been telling me all about it."

Brian felt quite confused. "Will you join me for coffee?"

"Came to fetch you," Sir Nigel explained. "You're coming back to the Embassy for your coffee and so forth. Business to be done! Lots of work. Very little time."

Brian found an Embassy car waiting outside, and a few minutes later found himself in Sir Nigel Richardson's study. Coffee was passed around and an assortment of liqueurs offered by a butler who would have delighted P.G. Wodehouse; also excellent cigars. A young attaché, Captain Arkwright, joined the party and made notes from time to time. He was earnest, efficient, and highly excited.

"Please give my regards to your father, Mr. Merrick." Sir Nigel raised his glass to Brian. "He was with the American Legation in Madrid some years ago when I also was posted to Spain. We were much younger!" He smiled, glanced at Nayland Smith, "You were a policeman in Burma in those days, Smith!"

"Where I first crossed the path of Dr. Fu Manchu!" Sir Denis stood up, and began to move about restlessly, filling his pipe, which he rarely forgot to bring along, as Brian recalled. "And he's a bigger menace today than he was then."

Sir Nigel Richardson frowned thoughtfully, drawing together his heavy eyebrows, black in contrast with his silvered hair.

"Your sudden appearance, Smith, has set me thinking. Rumours of this man's doings, nothing further, have come my way in spots as far apart as Teheran and Paris. What should you guess his age to have been the first time you saw him?"

"I should have taken him for seventy—well preserved, but seventy."

Sir Nigel stared, watching Nayland Smith light his pipe.

"Then, for heaven's sake, if he's really still alive——"

"I know!" Smith snapped. "He's over a hundred! I have believed for a long time that he has mastered the secret of prolonged life. He's a scientific genius. But unless he's also a Chinese edition of the Wandering Jew I'll finish him one day!"

"He has certainly proved hard to finish," Sir Nigel commented dryly.

And as Nayland Smith grinned in rather a grim way, Brian noted a faint mark like a wrinkle appear on the bridge of his nose and realized for the first time that the plaster had been removed.

"If I fail to get him this time, Richardson, it'll be because he's finished me! And now, to the job . . . As you know, my passport, as well as everything else I had with me, is lost——"

"A new diplomatic passport is ready, Smith." He glanced at the attaché. "You have it there, Arkwright?"

"Here, sir." The passport was laid on a coffee-table.

"Transport?" Sir Denis snapped.

"A plane manned by Royal Air Force personnel will be at your disposal."

"And Mr. Merrick?"

"I have made an appointment for him to meet Mr. Lyman Bostock, my United States opposite-number, at ten o'clock tomorrow morning. Take your own passport along, Mr. Merrick. It will be exchanged for one giving you diplomatic privilege."

Brian's head began to swim. He didn't know if this was due to Sir Nigel's old Napoleon brandy or to the miraculous speed with which Nayland Smith got things done.

"And the third passenger?"

Sir Nigel lighted another cigar. "That matter, Smith, I had to pass to Bostock. He has promised me that a passport with a suitable visa will be issued by the United States Consulate and ready for Mr. Merrick to pick up in the morning when he calls for his own. . . ."

When the Embassy car took them back, Nayland Smith got out at the hotel entrance and dismissed the chauffeur.

"To take that official chariot through the Mûski tonight, Merrick, would be calculated to start a riot! The bar's still open. I'm thirsty. So let's have a drink and then I'll get a cab."

Brian thought, as they sat down at a corner table, that Sir Denis looked oddly drawn and very tired. "I'd say you'd had one hell of a time," he told him, sympathetically.

"Why?" came with almost a fierce snap. "Do I look chewed up?"

"Not at all, Sir Denis! In fact, though I don't know the details, I consider you have made an amazing come-back."

Nayland Smith smiled. But even now it wasn't the happy smile which Brian seemed to remember. Undoubtedly, he had suffered more than he cared to admit.

"I suppose I look as well as I can expect to look." He took a long drink. "By the way, Merrick, have you had any news from Luxor?"

Brian told him about the message from Mr. Jansen.

"That's good." Nayland Smith glanced at his watch. "Time I was moving. Don't waste regrets on Zoe, Merrick. She's a charming girl, but her mother was an Arab. These people are unpredictable, you know. Like snow upon the desert and so forth . . . Don't be late in the morning." He jumped up. "We must be ready to leave at any hour tomorrow."

Brian stood up, too. "But where are we going?"

"New York . . . Good night, Merrick!"

Mr. Lyman Bostock turned out to be another friend of Senator Merrick, as Brian discovered when he presented himself in that gentleman's office at ten o'clock.

"You might be your father as I remember him at Harvard!" Mr. Bostock declared. "I suppose he got you this appointment as aide to Sir Denis Nayland Smith?"

"Not at all, sir. I got it myself—just by accident!"

"Is that so?" Mr. Bostock, with his smooth white hair and fresh complexion, his soft, Southern voice, had a gentle manner which made Brian wonder what he was doing in such a smouldering volcano as Cairo. "I naturally supposed, as Sir Denis is acting for Washington, by arrangement with London, that your father had proposed you. You will find your duties exciting."

"I have found them exciting already!" Brian laid his passport on the desk.

"This is your new passport." Mr. Bostock passed it across. "When your present employment ends you may be asked to return it: when you will receive your old one—which I am sending to Washington. And now"—he opened an envelope—"here are Dr. Hessian's papers." He looked up. His mild, blue eyes twinkled. "Rather irregularly, I confess, he is being admitted to the United States under the quota system! And here is Dr. Hessian's passport. . . ."

When Brian, back in his room, had put the neat little diplomatic passport in an inside pocket and locked the other documents in a suit-case, he went downstairs and out into the garden.

And he was still lingering over it, wondering how soon they were to start for New York, when a boy came up with a radiogram. Brian tore it open—and felt his heart give a queer little jump.

It was from *Lola*!

Brian, I wonder if you realize that you left no address. I have only just found out through Thomas Cook agency where you are. Please reply how long staying in Cairo. Love. Lola.

Brian felt suddenly on top of the rainbow. What a multiple idiot he had been! Waiting, day after day, for a word from Lola—and except that he had told her he was flying to Cairo, leaving her no means of reaching him! But she had found a way. He seemed to be looking again into those grey eyes with their hint of hidden laughter, to hear her voice. And he knew, in this moment, that Zoe had been a distraction; no more. He hoped, as Nayland Smith had encouraged him to believe, that Zoe felt the same way about it.

He suddenly decided to make a dash to the Mûski and order five hundred Aziza cigarettes to be sent by air to Lola in London. He knew that she liked Egyptian cigarettes.

Without allowing himself time to change his mind, he went out, jumped in a cab and told the driver to take him to the shop of Achmed es-Salah in the Khân Khalîb. He had good reason to distrust Achmed, but he sold excellent cigarettes. This done, he would at least have time to send a radiogram to Lola before he left Cairo.

And so presently he found himself again passing through those crowded, colourful, dusty streets, listening to cries musical and discordant, the vehicle sometimes nearly running over a tiny donkey and always meeting with some sort of obstruction. Brian found the scene entirely fascinating; ignored frowning faces, returning their frowns with smiles. He wished he could have made these people understand that he was a friend, that he regretted having to leave so soon a city which he had longed to see. . . .

Achmed sat smoking in the entrance to his cavernous shop.

Brian looked hard into the shadows beyond. But, today, he found no amber eyes watching him.

"Ah, my gentleman!" Achmed greeted him. "You come for my cigarettes. Is it so?"

"It is so. You can mail some to London?"

"Of course. I send many to England, and also to America."

Brian ordered five hundred Azizas to be sent to Lola, writing the address on a little card which Achmed gave him. He paid the price demanded (which he knew was exorbitant), and a small sum for postage; hurried away. He had kept the cab.

The driver had gone no more than a few hundred yards when he was held up. He had upset and narrowly avoided running over, a very large man riding a very small donkey. The language of the fallen rider, which Brian didn't understand, was evidently so ornamental, even for an Arab, that a laughing crowd gathered around him. They ignored the driver's warnings and encouraged the furious victim to further abuse.

A car going in the opposite direction, its Nubian chauffeur tooting remorselessly, forced a way through the outskirts of the audience and passed on. Brian had a glimpse of the solitary passenger.

It was Mr. Ahmad!

Those suspicions concerning this man, never far from his mind, awoke again. Was Ahmad going to the shop which he, himself, had just left? Even so, he might be going only to buy cigarettes. But Brian reviewed the chain of events which linked old Achmed with the girl who had followed him, and joined up with that ragged beggarman who had undoubtedly been waiting for him outside the building which accommodated the Aziza Cigarette Company.

He wondered if he should speak to Nayland Smith about it, but he hesitated for fear of giving Sir Denis the impression that he was inclined to form wild theories which lacked any basis in proven fact.

A time was to come when he would regain confidence in his instincts. But that time was not yet. . . .

The call came just after two o'clock. Brian had dispatched a radiogram to Lola and was crossing the lobby when Nayland Smith burst in.

"Baggage down, Merrick? Got the passports and entry papers? Good. Everything will be settled up here. We're off!"

Sir Nigel Richardson's chauffeur was standing outside to dispose of Brian's luggage in the big Embassy car. Four motorcycle police were lined alongside and a number of spectators had gathered, curious to get a glimpse of the distinguished visitor. They probably expected to see a Hollywood celebrity, and were plainly disappointed when Brian and Sir Denis came out and got into the car. Brian found another passenger inside, a tall, stooping man wearing a wide-brimmed hat and dark sun-glasses, his chin buried in the upturned collar of his light topcoat.

As the car swept smoothly away with its escort:

"Oh, Merrick," Nayland Smith said in his jerky fashion. "I want you to meet our fellow traveller, Dr. Otto Hessian. This is Mr. Brian Merrick, Junior, Doctor."

The doctor acknowledged this introduction by nodding slightly.

During the drive out to the airport, Dr. Hessian never spoke a word, and rarely moved. Sir Denis, in a low voice, explained the situation to Brian:

"Dr. Hessian has been under medical care since I smuggled him into Cairo. He was in even worse shape than I was. But he went ahead with his work. We had to leave all his apparatus behind of course. Smashed it. But the man has a majestic brain. Memorized every detail. The whole thing is ready again, in blueprint, for setting up directly we reach New York."

"That's a wonderful job, Sir Denis."

"He's a wonderful man. Hasn't much English, but loads of science. We're not sure if the enemy has traced him here. Hence the precautions. Once we're airborne our troubles are over. Detailed instructions have been sent ahead in code. Hessian expects to find all the necessary equipment on hand when we get there."

And so for the second time Brian found himself speeding along the tree-lined road to the airport—and this time leaving Cairo behind.

He would dearly have loved to stay longer, for he had seen little more of the ancient Oriental city than is seen by a cruise passenger. He wondered if he would have a chance to return one day—and he wondered if he had treated Zoe badly. . . .

A surprise awaited him when they came to the airport.

Sir Nigel Richardson and Captain Arkwright were waiting to see them off . . . and they were talking to Mr. Ahmad!

Mr. Bostock came up while Dr. Hessian was being presented. He shook hands with the doctor and made some complimentary remarks in German. Dr. Hessian nodded and hurried aboard the plane. He was clearly a man so completely wrapped up in his studies that he had neither time nor inclination for the social amenities. Nayland Smith drew Brian aside with Ahmad.

"I thought, Merrick, there might be some last-minute commissions to carry out. Mr. Ahmad is at your service. He will see to it that any correspondence which may arrive for you after we leave will be air-mailed to New York."

"Thanks a lot." Brian found himself forced once more to reconsider his views of Mr. Ahmad. "Although I don't expect anything. And I can think of nothing else."

"If you do, Mr. Merrick"—Ahmad gave his glittering smile—"don't hesitate to notify me, at any time."

Five minutes later the plane took off on the first leg of its long journey. . . .

BRIAN stared from a window of the suite in the Babylon-Lido Hotel which he shared with Nayland Smith. Sir Denis, he knew, had been retained by Washington, and certainly they had done him royally in the matter of accommodation. Their suite was on the top floor, and from where he stood the view stretched right out to the Statue of Liberty. There was a penthouse apartment on the roof above them, occupied by Dr. Hessian. One room, he understood, was equipped as a laboratory.

Throughout the journey from Cairo he had never succeeded in getting a single word out of that distinguished but silent physicist; nor had the doctor once removed the dark glasses in his presence.

Brian had no excuse to complain about his living quarters, and his salary was princely. All the same, he wasn't happy. From the hour when he had signed on in London for this strange job up to the present moment he had been called upon to do exactly nothing, had been left entirely to his own devices!

Only that morning he had tackled Nayland Smith on the subject.

And Nayland Smith had replied, "Cultivate patience, Merrick. There are long spells of idleness in a soldier's life, too. But when war starts he has his hands full. We're in just that position. I might have had desperate need of you in Cairo. As it chanced, I didn't. We got Hessian away without a hitch. But Dr. Fu Manchu's forces are here, in Manhattan!"

"What!"

"They are here—a group of thugs pledged to stop Hessian's work! How they'll operate I don't know. I can't tell you if I'll need your brawn or your brain. But I can assure you that you'll be an essential figure in the picture. This is by far the biggest thing I ever took on, and if it breaks me and Fu Manchu wins, it means the end of all we stand for."

Before he went out that morning, Sir Denis drew Brian's

attention to a portable phone in the living-room. It was connected with the penthouse above.

"By arrangement with the management, Merrick, the elevator goes no higher than this floor. Visitors to the penthouse must use the stair. But the door is locked from the inside. You'll see a typed notice on it which says: 'Apply No. 420 B.'

That's this apartment. If anyone applies, take particulars and call Dr. Hessian. His secretary will answer. She's a young lady supplied by the F.B.I."

And so Brian realized that whenever Nayland Smith was out, *he* had to stay in. He was on a kind of sentry duty.

Many hours had passed since then. But no one had applied for permission to visit Dr. Hessian. He had ordered his lunch from Room Service and written a long letter to Senator Merrick, walked along a corridor and dropped it in the letter chute.

As he returned, he had an odd impression that the door to the penthouse stair had been slightly opened, that someone had looked out and then quickly drawn back. Before going in to the suite, he stood for a moment looking at the mysterious door. He could see a sheet of paper pinned to it, and beyond doubt the door was closed. He concluded that he had been mistaken.

And now he had nothing to do but to stare out of a window.

He was watching smoke from a distant steamer, hull-down on the skyline, when the penthouse phone buzzed. This was so unexpected that it startled him. He took it up.

"Hullo!"

"Nayland Smith here," came the snappy voice. "Any visitors?"

"No."

"Callers?"

"No one called."

"Boring for you, Merrick. Relax for a couple of hours. I'll take over. Cut downstairs and try a champagne cocktail in the Paris Bar. They used to be good when I was here before. Then dine in the Silver Grill. I shall know where to find you if you're wanted."

"Thanks, Sir Denis. I'll take your advice."

He looked at his watch, surprised to find how the afternoon

had passed, how late it was. He spruced up and went downstairs. Although he wasn't familiar with the Babylon-Lido he had no difficulty in finding the Paris Bar. It was equipped in Montmartre style, with coloured advertisements for French drinks on the walls, and framed Lautrec reproductions. There were red and white check cloths on the little tables, French waiters and a French bartender.

The bar was already well patronized, but he saw no one he knew. He sat down at a vacant table and ordered a champagne cocktail. He supposed he should be grateful to find himself back in his native land, but all the same a voice within kept asking, "Why New York? Why couldn't it be London?" When his drink came and he had sampled it and lighted a cigarette he began to feel better. He recalled what someone had told him once, that Secret Service routine can be as dull as banking.

This thought consoled him, and he had just ordered a second cocktail when soft hands were pressed over his eyes from behind and a soft voice said, "Guess, Brian! Who is it?"

He grasped the slender hands, twisted in his chair . . . and found himself looking up into eyes which smiled while they seemed to mock him.

"*Lola!*" He almost failed to recognize his own voice, "Lola! But—but—you ought to be in London!"

Lola freed her hands, came around and sat down in the chair facing him. "You mean I shouldn't be in New York?"

"My dear!" Brian partly recovered from the glad shock, wondered about the way his heart was thumping. "Your being here is the answer to a prayer. It's impossible but true."

"Did you get my radiogram?"

"I did. But did you get my reply?"

Lola shook her head. A waiter was standing beside her. Brian ordered two champagne cocktails. As the waiter moved away:

"How could I?" Lola asked him. "I had to leave London an hour after I sent my message to you in Cairo. Madame had booked me for a flight leaving the same afternoon. I told you, Brian, we should meet again before long."

Brian's eyes devoured her. Lola, as always, was perfectly dressed, with that deceptive simplicity which only much money can buy. He was so overpowered by her appeal—her sudden presence—that he became almost tongue-tied.

"It will be sent on?"

"Of course. Everything that comes will be air-mailed to me here."

"You are staying here—in the Babylon-Lido?"

"I am! Madame believes in Michel representatives being seen in smart places."

"Lola—it's a miracle!"

Lola, watching him, smiled that odd smile which at once irritated and infatuated him. "There are men even today, Brian, who can perform miracles."

Her words were puzzling; but as the waiter brought the cocktails, he forgot them, clinked glasses, and was glad to be alive.

"You didn't know I was here, Lola?"

"How could I? I saw you as I came in."

"Are you free for dinner?"

"Of course, Brian dear, I only just arrived. . . ."

Dr. Fu Manchu sat in a small room which apparently had no windows. A single bright light shone down on to a large-scale plan pinned to a board, so that sometimes a shadow of his head or hand would appear on the plan as he bent forward to study it. The room was profoundly silent.

The plan represented a number of suites of apartments, some adjoining one another, but roughly half of them separated from the others by a wide corridor. An elevator door and a descending stair were marked opening off a square landing; an ascending stair appeared at the other end of the corridor.

It was a plan of the top floor of a wing of the Babylon-Lido.

Of the three suites shown on the east side of the corridor that in the centre was marked 420B. 420A was on the north of it and 420C on the south. There were four smaller apartments on the west side, numbered from 421 to 424.

Dr. Fu Manchu took a pinch of snuff from a silver box, then turned his shadowed face towards a cabinet which stood near. He pressed a switch.

"Connect 420A."

An interval, and then a man's voice speaking English with

a pronounced accent: "Four-twentyA."

"You are unpacked and established?"

"Yes, Master."

"Your transmitter is well concealed?"

"Yes, Master."

"You may not be wanted tonight, but remain in the hotel."

A faint click and the order: "Connect 420C."

There was an almost instant answer in such bad English as to be nearly unintelligible.

"Speak in your own language. You are ready?"

The reply came in a Burmese dialect: "I am ready, Master."

"Remain where you are until further orders."

The four apartments on the west side were connected one after another; orders given and accepted in a variety of tongues. Dr. Fu Manchu was a phenomenal linguist. At last he was satisfied, leaning back in his chair and hissing softly between his teeth.

Suite 420B, occupied by Sir Denis Nayland Smith, was entirely surrounded by agents of Fu Manchu!

While Brian, having booked a table, waited for Lola to join him in the Silver Grill, his reflections took an odd turn. There was a queer similarity between this meeting with Lola in New York and his meeting with Zoe in Cairo. They might have been planned by a producer too lazy to alter the routine. Brian laughed silently, and wondered why so grotesque an idea had occurred to him as he saw Lola coming.

She had changed into an unpretentious but charming dinner dress. It might have—and had—been designed expressly to set off her particular type of beauty. She looked radiant and attracted the tribute of many frowns from the women present.

When they had ordered their dinner, and Lola had selected the right Bordeaux to go with it:

"I'm simply dying to hear what you're doing in Manhattan, Brian," she declared. "I thought your mysterious affairs were connected with the East, not the West."

"So did I," Brian admitted, then stopped.

How much was he entitled to tell Lola? She knew some of the facts, already, but only as little as he had known, himself, up to the time of his leaving London.

"New York was the last place in which I expected to find myself." Lola delicately nibbled an olive. "You were the last person I expected to meet."

Brian went through the pangs of an inward struggle. He longed to confide in *somebody*. He was made that way. And if he couldn't trust Lola, in whom could he put his trust? After all, she knew already that he was employed by Nayland Smith, and even if he told her all he knew of Sir Denis's plans it didn't add up to much. For he recognized, with a return of his sense of frustration, that he had been kept in the dark all along. He imposed only one condition upon himself: he must say nothing about either Hessian or Dr. Fu Manchu.

"If I could make you understand, Lola, how mad I was to learn that we were coming to New York when where I wanted to be was London you'd know how I longed to be with you again. To find you right here made me think I had Aladdin's lamp in my pocket and didn't know it!"

"I was just as delighted to see you, Brian. Your last letter—the one you left for me—made me rather sad. Perhaps you were just mad at having to leave so suddenly. But it was a very chilly letter, Brian!"

Brian's sense of guilt dried up speech for a moment. Then he forced a grin, reached across and squeezed Lola's hand.

"I'm no good at writing that kind of letter," he told her, lamely. "I can say what I want to say, but I can't write it!"

"You can't!" she agreed; but the grey eyes were dancing with mischief. "Maybe it's just as well. You might be prosecuted for libel! But tell me all about what you're doing, Brian. Is Sir Denis all you expected him to be? Does he match up to your memories of him?"

"Well——" He frowned thoughtfully. "He looks older. That's to be expected, I guess. And of course he's been through hell since I saw him in Washington. I have a hunch he's lost some of his pep. But I'll tell you he can still get things done. He's great alright."

A waiter came to serve the first course, and when he had gone:

"What did you do in Cairo?" Lola wanted to know. "Any perilous adventures? I mean—male or female?"

"Nothing much." Brian spoke hastily. "Except that I was tailed everywhere I went."

"Tailed? By whom? What for?"

"Because they knew I was with Nayland Smith, I suppose."

Lola buttered a roll. "Who are *they*, Brian? I don't understand."

"Well . . . from all I can make out, Lola, it's a Communist plot Sir Denis is up against."

"How exciting! What's the plot?"

"Even if I knew—and I don't—I couldn't tell you, Lola."

"It must be something to do with this country, Brian. Is Sir Denis with you?"

"Sure. He's right here, in the Babylon-Lido."

"But Brian, dear, you must know what for. Is he looking for somebody?"

Brian realized that he was on perilously thin ice. Secret agents were expected to keep their secrets from *everybody*.

"Let me make one thing plain, Lola. I'm not in on the master plan. I get my orders from the chief and ask no questions. All I know is that it's something very big. . . ."

During the rest of dinner they talked about London and the happy days they had spent there. Every minute Brian knew more and more how much Lola meant to him. She was in a category widely different from that of the alluring Arab girl, Zoe. He had always known it, but tonight his last doubt left him. . . . He was sincerely in love with Lola.

A page appeared at his elbow. "Mr. Brian Merrick?"

"Yes."

"Wanted on the phone."

He excused himself and went to a box at the end of the grill-room. Even before he heard the voice he knew that this delightful interlude with Lola had come to an end.

"Thought I'd find you there, Merrick," Sir Denis snapped. "Don't bolt your dinner, but come up when you finish."

Lola knew before he spoke. "Wanted by the chief?"

She smiled—that slightly one-sided smile which made him want to kiss her, because it was part invitation and part mockery.

"You've guessed it, dear. But he was good enough to tell me not to hurry."

"In the case of Madame Baudin—that's Mrs. Michel—this would mean twenty minutes. But never mind. There's all my packing to do, and we have lots of time ahead. . . ."

Brian found Nayland Smith pacing up and down their large living-room. The air was foggy with tobacco smoke. He turned as Brian came in; spoke without taking his pipe out of his mouth.

"News for you, Merrick. Your father's coming tomorrow."

"That's fine! I mailed a letter to him only this afternoon."

"The Senator is bringing some brass-hat from the Air Service. But they'll both be disappointed if they expect to see Dr. Hessian. He declines to receive any visitors until his model is ready for a demonstration."

"Why is the Air Service interested?" Brian wanted to know.

"Because Hessian claims that his invention will put 'em out of business!"

"What! That doesn't make sense, Sir Denis."

"Think not?" Nayland Smith shot a quick glance at him. "You're going to be surprised."

"What is it? A guided missile?"

"No. Something to make guided missiles a waste of time. I'm not a physicist, Merrick, so I can't explain the thing. But it means immunity from every from of air attack—including H bombs!"

"Good Lord! But can he really do it?"

Nayland Smith stared at Brian with a grim smile.

"Why do you suppose I risked my neck to get him here?"

It was a sound argument in its way; and, "I begin to see," Brian admitted, "some reason for all the precaution."

"Particularly now that Dr. Fu Manchu has traced him!"

"I still don't understand where Dr. Fu Manchu comes in."

"Then I'll explain. I was retained by the United States government to get Hessian out of the hands of the Communists, to enable him to use his phenomenal brain for the side he belongs to. Dr. Fu Manchu has been retained by the Communists to see that he doesn't do it!"

Brian was reduced to stupefied silence for a moment. He remembered saying to Lola, "All I know is that it's something very big." How big he hadn't dreamed! Nayland Smith went on pacing about like a caged animal.

"Can you tell me one thing more, Sir Denis?" Brian ventured. "If you're sure that agents of Dr. Fu Manchu are actually in New York, why don't you have them arrested?"

Sir Denis turned, fixed him with a penetrating stare.

"Have you any idea, Merrick, how long I tried to trap Fu Manchu himself during the time I knew, as all Scotland Yard knew, that he was in London? Six years! And he's still free! As for his unidentified agents, New York is an even tougher problem than London." He knocked ashes from his pipe into a tray. "Dr. Fu Manchu is president of an organization known as the Si-Fan. It has members throughout the East, Near and Far. It has agents in every city in Europe and every city in the United States. Its power is second only to that of Communism if not equal."

He began to stuff some sort of coarse-cut mixture into the hot bowl of his pipe. Brian said nothing.

"Its greatest strength, Merrick, is in its secrecy. Few people have even heard of the Si-Fan. As a result, there's never been any concerted action against it. If they can't have Hessian's invention themselves, the Reds don't intend to let anyone else have it. Heaven knows what they'll try. But it's our job to guard Hessian until he passes his plans over to the United States. . . ."

CHAPTER 10

IN EGYPT, not long afterwards, on a night when there was no moon in Cairo, something happened designed to have an important bearing upon affairs in New York.

A small, lean man, very dark-skinned, was discarding his cloak upon the doorstep of the house in which Brian had once taken shelter from the student rioters. When he stepped out on to the narrow street he wore only a black loin-cloth and a small, tightly-wound black turban.

The quarter had sunk into silence. Except for the distant sound of a pipe and the barely audible thud of a drum, nothing disturbed its stillness. The little man glanced once to right and left, then crossed the narrow street to the gate of the courtyard opposite. He peered through the bars. He could see the house opposite. He peered through the bars. He could see the house of the Sherîf Mohammed, its projecting windows outlined against starlight. The windows were dark. Nothing stirred.

He clasped the metal bars, bare toes and fingers, and with the agility of a monkey climbed to the top. He dropped lightly on the other side, moved across the courtyard and surveyed the front of the building. Hesitating for a moment, he ran to the end and looking up, saw what he wanted.

A sturdy bougainvillaea covered the south wall. On the floor above were several windows. He mounted to the first of these at incredible speed, but found it securely fastened. He swung to another. It was slightly open. He held his ear against the narrow opening, listening intently. Then, inch by inch, he raised the window and dropped noiselessly inside the room.

Motionless, he lay where he had dropped. But there was no sound. From his loin-cloth he pulled out a small flash-lamp; lighted it for a moment. His acute hearing had told him there was no one in the room. He was looking for the door. He found it.

In a matter of seconds he was out on a tiled corridor. Again he stood still, listening. He moved to the left, attracted by a sound of snoring; peered into an ante-room richly furnished, for it had a large window and the starlight was enough to enable this strangely endowed visitor to see all he wanted to see.

A fat man lay asleep on a cushioned divan—the man who had first come to the gate when Brian called to demand an interview with the Sherîf Mohammed.

It was the ante-room of the women's quarter, the *harêm*.

The keen eyes of the little dark man detected a doorway on the right of this ante-room. He crossed to it, went through, and found a descending stair. It led to another corridor.

Here, for the first time, he was at fault. But after cautiously opening several doors again, he found what he was looking for: another stair. He went down at extraordinary speed for one running in the dark—and found himself in the paved entrance hall of the house.

Now that his eyes were accustomed to the dim light he could evidently see as clearly as a cat. And he seemed to know just what he was looking for.

With complete assurance, and making no sound, he moved around the walls of the large and lofty apartment, and presently, near the entrance door which opened on the courtyard, he found what he sought. At the back of a small room intended for a porter's lodge there was a strong teak door, iron-studded, the woodwork bleached with age. A bunch of old-fashioned Arab keys hung on a hook beside it.

And the largest of these fitted the ancient lock.

A stone stair led the midnight intruder to the cellars. Here he used his flash-lamp without hesitation. He found stores of various kinds, including casks of wine which no True Believer would expect to find in the cellars of a descendant of the Prophet.

Pressing on farther he came to a smaller cellar, long and narrow. There was nothing in it. But on one side were two more of the heavy teak iron-studded doors. They differed from that at the top of the stair in one respect. Each had an iron grille in it. He had thrust the bunch of keys in his accommodating loin-cloth; was about to pull them out, then stopped dead, as if stricken motionless—a trick of many wild animals when surprised.

Quite still he stood, and listened.

The sound was very faint, but this man's senses were super-normal.

Someone was sleeping behind one of the doors!

He remained still for nearly a minute, debating what he should do. Then he crossed to the grille from behind which the sound came, peered in, could see nothing, and so shone a momentary ray from his lamp into the blackness.

"Who's there?" came an instant challenge.

The little man switched the light off and glided from the cellar, silent as a phantom. He fled up to the porter's lodge, relocked the door as he had found it, making more noise than he cared about, and came out into the entrance hall.

Here he stood still again to listen.

No sound.

In niches of the mosaic-covered wall were many rare porcelain pots and other beautiful objects. On some of those the little man shone brief flashes from his lamp . . .

He began to examine several windows facing on to the courtyard, selected one of them, opened it slightly, and slipped through like a lizard. Once outside, he succeeded in partly closing it again.

He was over the gate and across the street to the doorway where he had left his cloak with a silent agility more like that of some nocturnal animal than of any human being. . . .

Mr. Lyman Bostock, United States representative in Cairo, twirled a cigar between his finger and thumb and stared reflectively across at Sir Nigel Richardson, his British confrère, who lay in a split-cane lounge chair with an iced drink beside him in the hollow of the chair-arm provided for that purpose. Mr. Bostock's study opened on to a balcony and the balcony over-hung a pleasant garden, shadowy on this moonless night.

"I'm only just finding it out," Mr. Bostock remarked, with his soothing drawl; "but you're a queer bunch, you Englishmen."

"I happen to be Scotch."

"Maybe that's worse. But what I'm coming to is this: I hand it to you that there's not much about this country you don't seem to know—including all the crooks in Cairo!"

591

"That's base ingratitude, Bostock! I'll let you into a secret, Murdoch, whom you've met with me (he has confidential employment in our Embassy), is an ex-officer of Egyptian Police. That was in the days when *we* ran the show. And what Murdoch doesn't know about the Cairo underworld could be put in a thimble. You asked me to find the right man. I found him."

Mr. Bostock glanced at his watch, took a drink, and put his cigar back in his mouth.

"Agreed. I accept the responsibility."

"You don't have to. We're in this thing together. If your F.B.I. has unearthed a mare's nest—and that's my private opinion—there was no alternative so far as I can see. Course of action was left to you. What could you do? Neither you nor I could get a search warrant on a mere suspicion, particularly in the case of so highly respected a citizen as the Sherîf Mohammed Ibn-el-Ashraf."

"True enough. I could see no alternative to your suggestion—short of declining to act in the matter. But, with apologies to your British gift of understatement, it's slightly unconstitutional!"

"Unconstitutional be damned! What do we stand to lose? Let's examine the facts. Who knows you were asked to make this investigation?"

"Except yourself——"

"And Murdoch. I had to let him in."

"Nobody but myself and Arkwright, who decoded the message."

"Good. Let's look at possible consequences. Suppose Ali gets pinched. It's unlikely, but he might. He has a record, not only as a cat-burglar but also for jail-breaking. He's escaped twice, and they're still looking for him. To lock up Ali Yahya is about as useful as to try to hold an eel by the tail. He can climb up or down almost anything, slip in and out of incredibly narrow openings. He's a living legend with the natives, who claim he can make himself invisible. They call him Ali al-Sehlîya—Ali the Lizard."

"I trust he lives up to it," Bostock drawled. "But, all the same, suppose he gets . . . 'pinched,' I think you said?"

"Pinched was the word. You don't seriously suggest he

would tell the police that he was acting under instructions from the United States Embassy?"

Mr. Bostock stood up and refreshed their two glasses. Sir Nigel watched him, grinning mischievously, until he sat down again.

"No," Bostock admitted. "He would probably choose to escape a third time and collect the price of his crime which you and I promised to pay!"

"That's the answer!" Sir Nigel took a long drink. "Nobody knows we have seen him——"

"Except Murdoch!"

"Except Murdoch. And Murdoch provided him with a complete plan (which Ali memorized), of the house of the Sherîf Mohammed."

"Useful man, Murdoch," Mr. Bostock murmured, looking again at his watch. "Also Scotch, no doubt?"

"Also Scotch." Then Sir Nigel, too, consulted his wristwatch. "Ali is about due back."

"Pinched!" Mr. Bostock muttered. "He's *over*due."

Sir Nigel shook his head, smiling. "Our reputations are in safe hands, Bostock! Think of how far he has to travel."

"Isn't Murdoch giving him a lift?"

Sir Nigel raised his black brows. "Really, my dear fellow! Do you want Murdoch pinched as well?"

"Meaning that Ali will have to walk here from the Mûski?"

"Ali's methods of transport are his own secret."

They fell into silence, each thinking his own thoughts. A faint breeze arose, rustling the palm fronds outside and making a noise like the crackling of stiff paper. A faint perfume from some night-scented flower in the garden was wafted into the study. A large bat flew past the window.

So they sat when, unheralded by any sound, a small dark figure materialized on the balcony, glided into the room and performed humble *salaam*.

Mr. Bostock nearly dropped a cone of cigar ash on the carpet, but recovered himself in the nick of time. Sir Nigel, though equally startled, hailed the apparition in Arabic.

"Good evening, Ali Yahya."

"Good evening, Richardson Pasha."

"What have you to report, Ali?"

"It is true—what I was told. Someone is there!"

Mr. Bostock sprang up. "You say someone is there?"

But in his excitement he used English instead of Arabic, a language which he understood better than he spoke. Ali Yahya stared blankly. He had discarded his cloak and presented a queer figure in that sedately appointed room in his black loin-cloth and turban. Mr. Bostock corrected himself hastily, and Ali said again:

"Someone is there, *effendi*."

Bostock glanced at Sir Nigel. "We must get the exact facts, Richardson. You ask the questions. You're more fluent than I. Let him sit down. The man must be tired."

Ali accepted the invitation and dropped down, cross-legged, on the carpet. Then, speaking impassively in simple words, he described what he had found in the Sherîf's cellar.

"You didn't see the face of this man?" Sir Nigel asked.

"No. He slept, it seems, like a desert fox, with one eye open. I obeyed my orders and came away quickly."

"That was wise, Ali. You did well. You relocked all doors?"

"And replaced the keys where I found them."

"No one saw you leave?"

"No one ever sees me, Richardson Pasha, when I do not wish to be seen."

From the drawer of a coffee-table Sir Nigel took out a wad of notes fastened with an elastic band and tossed it across to Ali, who caught it deftly.

Ali Yahya *salaamed* so deeply that his forehead touched the carpet. "O, well of Justice!"

He tried to thrust the bundle of money into his loin-cloth, but had some difficulty in doing so. The "well of justice" was watching him.

"There must be many treasures in the house of the Sherîf Mohammed, Ali?"

"It is true. The Seyyîd Mohammed is very wealthy, Richardson Pasha."

"So I believe. Tell me, O Ali, what is that you have concealed?" Ali Yahya produced a flash-lamp. "No, no! Something more bulky."

Ali hesitated for one tremendous moment, his bright eyes flashing sideways to the balcony, then back again to meet the inflexible stare of Sir Nigel.

"I feared you might misjudge my motive, Richardson Pasha. For this reason I said nothing. But it seemed to me, O wise one, that in case a window which I was unable to close properly might arouse suspicion, it would be provident to leave evidence to show that a common sneak-thief had entered the house."

"I see. Show us the evidence."

With great reluctance Ali the Lizard drew out from his loin-cloth an object wrapped in a piece of faded silk. He opened the wrapping and held up a small *mibkharah*, or incense-burner, most delicately chiselled in pure gold, a relic of some sultan's *harêm*, a museum piece, for which collectors would pay a fabulous price!

"Good heavens, Richardson!" Mr. Bostock gasped. "We can't stand for this! He must hand it over!"

Ali Yahya was rewrapping the treasure. Sir Nigel tried to hide a grin.

"Do you prefer it to be found in Ali's possession, or in the United States Embassy?"

Mr. Bostock dropped back in his chair with a groan. Ali, obeying a silent signal from Sir Nigel, faded away, disappearing silently over the wall of the balcony. A whispered farewell came out of the darkness.

"May your night be a glad one, O Fountain of Wisdom . . ."

"We know what we wanted to know," Mr. Bostock admitted. "But what a price to pay!"

"Forget that, Bostock. Our problem is: What are we going to do now?"

"WELL, MY BOY!" Senator Merrick held Brian at arms' length, sizing him up with shrewd hazel eyes. "You look fighting fit. If official despatches from Cairo and the word of Sir Denis are to be credited, you have helped to pull off something that may well prove to be a turning point in military history."

Brian felt his cheeks flush. "I had next to nothing to do with it, Father. All the credit belongs to Sir Denis."

"So you say, Junior. And I like you none the less for it. But Sir Denis Nayland Smith is a brilliant man, and he wouldn't have wanted you if he hadn't had use for you. Dr. Hessian arrives at the psychological moment. If he can prove what he claims, it may be a means of stopping the President, my very good friend, from plunging us into war."

"Just what does that mean, Father?"

"Well, it is a top secret—but there's an order to the Chief of Staff, already drawn up, which only requires his signature. His military advisers favour it. I don't, and I'm not alone in my opposition. This country, Brian, is dangerously open to air attack with modern missiles. We should step warily."

Nayland Smith was talking to General Rawlins and another Air Force official, and at this moment he brought them across. Brian had already met both that morning.

"I'm getting into hot water!" Sir Denis declared. "These fighting men tell me they expect orders by this week-end which seem to me to mean a shooting war."

"And to me," Senator Merrick agreed. "But nothing's signed yet."

"It will be signed not later than three days from now." General Rawlins spoke with calm confidence. "For my part, I doubt the claims of this German scientist, in spite of all we've heard—and that's not much. In the first place, I don't expect open hostilities to start. In the second place, if they do, the Air Force hasn't been asleep."

"The trouble about democracy," Brian Merrick Senior growled, "is that it speaks with too many voices all at the same time."

"It's no good flying off the handle, General," Nayland Smith snapped, "because Dr. Hessian refuses to see you until his plans are complete. I warned you of this before you left Washington, so don't blame *me*. He's a genius, and he's been through hell. He doesn't give a damn for you or anybody else. He cursed me in German when I told him you were coming. Fortunately, I don't know much German."

"But when," General Rawlins demanded, "will these plans of his be complete?"

"So far as I can make out, in the next two days."

"When he'll graciously consent to see us?"

"His proposal is this: As soon as he's ready to give a demonstration, he will receive a committee of responsible Service officers, scientists and policy makers, to be selected by Senator Merrick as acting for the President. To me this seems fair and reasonable."

"And the President will agree with you," Senator Merrick declared. "World tension is reaching a peak; and I can assure you of the President's keen interest . . . . Have I your permission, Sir Denis, to take my son to lunch at my club?"

Out of darkness complete except for one point of green light which might have been the eye of some nocturnal animal, Fu Manchu's voice spoke:

"It is certain that Brian Merrick Junior is ignorant of my purpose?"

A dull, mechanical voice replied: "There is no evidence to the contrary."

"You have not answered my question."

"His behaviour gives cause for confidence, Excellency."

"Explain your meaning."

"He lunched at Senator Merrick's club."

"He was closely covered?"

"It was difficult. But an agent of The Order waited upon their table. He was, of course, very attentive."

"Their conversation?"

"Chiefly concerned Sir Denis Nayland Smith."

"It was satisfactory?"

"Entirely."

"And after lunch?"

"Brian Merrick Junior saw his father off. The Senator was joined by two Air Force officers, who had lunched with Sir Denis at the Babylon-Lido."

"Retain all contacts. Report hourly."

The Si-Fan was watching . . .

When Brian returned to the suite in the Babylon-Lido (of which he had a key) he was in a queer frame of mind. Sir Denis sat writing; looking up, nodded.

"Decent lunch, Merrick? Don't think too well of the catering at these University clubs, myself."

"The lunch was all right. But I didn't like the waiter."

Nayland Smith laid his pen down. "Why not? Did he upset your soup?"

Brian grinned, but not happily. "No. He listened to everything I said to my father!"

"Hullo!" Sir Denis stood up quickly. "So the Reds have agents in the best clubs! I warned you, Merrick. What were you talking about?"

"Well—I tried to keep my father off the topic of Dr. Hessian's invention. But, of course, he never seemed to suspect that a club servant might be a spy."

"No. I see the difficulty. You're pretty sure the man was listening?"

"Dead sure!"

Nayland Smith began to walk about in his restless way.

"The climax is so near. And we have two enemies, not one: the Reds and the Si-Fan! It's a formidable combination, Merrick. I'm backed by two governments, but I doubt if my double backing's as good as Dr. Fu Manchu's! We have worked like beavers to keep Hessian's presence here a secret. We have failed."

Brian thought for a minute. "It seems to me that it wasn't to be expected we could do that, Sir Denis. As I see it, all we have to do is to make sure he's safe. And on that point I have something to say."

Nayland Smith checked in his promenade, darted one of his swift glances at Brian.

"What is it?" he snapped.

"Just this. Sometimes, when I've been alone here, I have

heard someone being admitted through the penthouse door. I'm sure of it. And I hear all sorts of footsteps above. If this suite is supposed to be a sort of guard-room, and we're responsible for Dr. Hessian's safety, shouldn't we be advised of who is being allowed to go up?"

Nayland Smith knocked out his pipe, then produced the old pouch. He began to stuff tobacco into the cracked briar bowl.

"Point a good one," he snapped. "*We* are responsible. But the F.B.I. operative attached to Hessian has authority to admit visitors whose identity we don't know. I'm not disputing his integrity. Fact remains, responsibility is ours. I'll see to this, Merrick. You're right."

Sir Denis lighted his pipe and walked out.

But, when he had gone, Brian remained uncomfortably ill at ease. Up to the time of their arrival at the Babylon-Lido, Nayland Smith had seemed to be so firmly in charge of operations. Now, something was lacking.

Had his phenomenal success in smuggling the German scientist through the Iron Curtain, in getting him from Cairo to New York, induced Sir Denis to relax—too soon? It didn't seem to fit in with the man's dynamic character. Surely, now was the crucial hour—in fact, he had said so. What was wrong?

In his very bones, Brian had a foreboding that something pended which he didn't understand. He was conscious of a longing to talk it all over with some reliable and sympathetic friend, someone he could trust.

Lola was both reliable and sympathetic . . . But he was bound to secrecy!

Brian walked about for some time in an unhappy frame of mind; smoked countless cigarettes. Once, hearing faint footsteps in the corridor, which seemed to pause at the far end, he crossed the lobby and quietly opened the door; looked out.

He was just in time to see the door to the penthouse stair closing!

"Damn!" he muttered—for he had caught not even a glimpse of the person who had gone in.

Listening intently, he detected the unmistakable click of a key being turned in a lock.

This irritated him unreasonably. His job, so far as he could see, remained that of an attendant; a sort of paid companion for Nayland Smith. Plots and counter-plots involving the security of the United States seethed around him, but he had no part to play.

Never once had he entered the penthouse since Dr. Hessian had taken up residence there; nor once set eyes upon him from the time of their arrival to the present moment.

It was a humiliating position—or so it seemed to him, now. The phone on the big desk buzzed.

"Hullo!" he called.

"Oh, Brian, I'm so glad I caught you!" . . . *Lola*! "When do you expect to be free? I can be in the Paris Bar around cocktail time. Any hope?"

"Where are you now, Lola?"

"At Michel's. But for mercy's sake don't call me back, here! I'll wait downstairs until seven, Brian. Do try!"

And she hung up.

Brian glanced at his watch. Five o'clock. Then he stood quite still, listening. French windows opened on a balcony were partly open. . . . and he could hear voices from above. Someone was talking on the terrace of the penthouse.

He opened the windows fully, but silently, and stepped out.

A strange voice, alternately guttural and sibilant, spoke slowly, with impressive pauses. Something in this voice touched a chord of memory, but so faintly that no idea of the speaker's identity was conjured up. It bore a vague resemblance to the rarely-heard speech of Dr. Hessian. But the language was neither German nor English. It was a language which Brian knew he had never heard before.

There were occasional replies; monosyllables in the same tongue.

Once, Brian was almost sure, the name "Nayland Smith" was introduced into the otherwise unintelligible jargon. But he knew he might be mistaken, for if it had in fact been that name, it was so mispronounced as to be barely recognizable.

The conversation ended abruptly. He heard a shuffle of footsteps, and knew that the speakers had gone in. . . .

"You made it, Brian!" Lola stood up to greet him as he hurried into the Paris Bar. "I nearly gave up hope. This is my second cocktail! Did the Big Chief have a heart, after all?"

Brian dropped into a chair facing her. He longed to have her in his arms; but this was not the time. And he felt oddly dispirited.

"When at last he came in, I told him about one or two queer things that had happened, and he said boredom was getting on my nerves and ordered me to forget the job and play a while."

He looked up at a waiter who had just appeared and ordered two more cocktails.

Lola checked him. "Not another for me, Brian. I'll finish on this one."

Brian didn't argue. He knew Lola. And when the waiter went off:

"Surely you're through for the day, Lola?" he asked.

"Yes." She was watching him, smiling. "But I like to stay sober all the same. What were these queer things that happened, Brian?"

"Oh!" He lighted a cigarette. Lola already was smoking. "We seem to have some curious neighbours up above us in the penthouse. I overheard somebody talking in a queer sort of jargon and mentioned it to Sir Denis."

"He probably said that representatives of United Nations lived there?"

"No. He didn't say that." Brian tried to draw a cloak of secrecy about himself, but wasn't quite successful. "For a man on a dangerous mission—or so I understand—he brushed it off very lightly. Between ourselves, there are times when I wonder if Sir Denis is really up to his old form."

"Please, Brian!" Lola smiled her one-sided smile. "Don't talk Oxford. After all, you're still an American."

Brian grinned almost happily. Lola's impudent criticism of his occasional traces of English idiom and speech, far from annoying, delighted him. It proved her interest, or so he argued. His cocktail arrived; he sampled it.

"Maybe I mean he's getting too old for his job."

Lola frowned thoughtfully, twirling her glass between sensitive fingers.

"As I haven't met him I can't judge, Brian. But there's just one thing I'd like to know. The first time you saw him in Cairo did you think he had changed?"

Brian considered the question; decided that no harm could be done by telling Lola the facts.

"That makes me think, Lola. The first time I saw him in Cairo was under very peculiar circumstances. It's quite a story."

And he outlined the incident which had led him to take refuge on the roof of a house overlooking that of Sheríf Mohammed, and told her what he had seen from there. . . .

"There was no mistake about it, dear. The way he gripped his pipe, the trick of twitching the lobe of his ear. I knew I was looking at Nayland Smith.

"How excited you must have been! And after that?"

Now well in his stride, and delighted to have Lola for an audience, Brian related how he had demanded an interview with the Sheríf and what had happened there.

"So you didn't see him," Lola murmured. "When *did* you see him again?"

Brian gave her an account of Sir Denis's secret entrance to his hotel apartment, and equally secret exit.

"Was it then, Brian, when you actually talked to him, that you began to wonder if he had outlived what you call 'his old form'?"

"Not exactly right then, Lola——"

Brian paused, finished his cocktail. He had thought of something; and the thing, though perhaps trivial, had staggered him, chiefly because he had never thought of it before.

"Then when, dear?"

"Later, I guess. But—when Sir Denis came to see me he had a strip of surgical plaster on the bridge of his nose."

"Had he been in a fight?"

Lola asked the question jokingly. But her grey eyes weren't smiling.

"He'd had one hell of a time getting out of the hands of the Reds. But that's not the point. Something which he didn't tell me must have happened right there in Cairo. Because, when I saw him pacing around that room, and I saw him clearly, there was no plaster on his nose!"

One of the hourly reports ordered by Dr. Fu Manchu was just coming in. That solitary spark of green light glowed in the darkness. . . .

"Brian Merrick's complete ignorance of Operation Zero confirmed."

"He has served his purpose, and could be dispensed with. Henceforward he becomes a possible source of danger. . . . Where is he now?"

"In the Sunset Room."

"He is covered?"

"Closely, Excellency."

"What Federal operatives are on duty there?"

"Two F.B.I. agents."

The green light disappeared. And, invisible in the darkness, Dr. Fu Manchu laughed. . . .

In the popular but expensive Sunset Room high up in the Babylon-Lido, with its celebrated dance band and star-spangled floor show, Brian found himself transported to Paradise. With Lola in his arms, wearing an alluring dance frock, he was lost to the world, lifted above all its petty troubles—a man rapturously in love.

His frustrations, doubts and fears had dispersed like mist under the morning sun.

"Are you happy, dearest?" he whispered.

"Very happy, Brian."

He was silent for a long time, living in a dream.

"I often wonder, Lola, in your wanderings about the world, if you ever met someone else who meant more to you than I do."

"There's no one who means more to me than you, Brian. But, like you, dear, I have a job to do. We're both young enough to enjoy ourselves without spoiling it by getting serious, yet awhile."

Brian drew a long breath, made fragrant by the perfume of her hair.

"You mean you'd rather stay with Michel than cut it out to marry me?"

Lola sighed. "I told you once before, Brian dear, that early marriages, so popular in our country, are often failures."

"But not always."

"Brian, we're happy! Maybe we'll never capture this wonderful thing again. *Please* don't get serious—tonight!"

He swallowed, but found enough discretion to respect her

603

wishes, to surrender himself to the spirit of the dance. As always, Lola was elusive—and all the more maddeningly desirable. He was silent for some time, until:

"There's a man standing over by the door," he said, "who seems to be watching us. Do you know him?"

"Which one do you mean, Brian?"

"The tall, dark fellow just lighting a cigarette."

Lola laughed. "No, I don't know him, Brian. But I'm willing to bet he's the house detective!"

BRIAN returned to the suite earlier than he had intended. Lola had been paged just before the star entertainer appeared, and returned, looking very wretched, to tell him that Madame Michel had taken up residence in the Babylon-Lido that night and would remain until her forthcoming dress show there took place. Madame insisted upon an immediate conference in her apartment. . . .

He found Nayland Smith at the desk reading what looked like an official document, and smoking as usual, like a fact-ory chimney. The suite was luxuriously furnished, in Babylon-Lido style, and a tall, painted Italian screen enclosed the desk, so that the limited space around it had the quality of a fog. Sir Denis looked up when Brian came in.

"Hullo, Merrick! A rumour reaches me that you were seen in the Sunset Room with a very pretty girl. Don't apologize! You have had a dull time, I know. Glad you can find agreeable company."

"Thanks, Dir Denis—though I can't imagine who told you."

Nayland Smith smiled. But, again, it wasn't the happy smile which Brian remembered—a smile which had seemed to sweep the years aside and reveal an eager boy.

"One of the F.B.I. men detailed to keep an eye on you!"

"On *me*? Why?"

Sir Denis tossed the typescript aside; stood up.

"Merrick, we're marked men!" The smile vanished. His face became grim. "If Fu Manchu could trap either of us it would give him a lever with Washington—that he'd know how to use. I have warned you before. Trust nobody—not even a taxi driver you may pick up outside the hotel."

"But——" A hot protest burned on Brian's tongue, for he detected an implication that Lola was suspect; checked the words. "You suggest that this man would try to hold us?"

"And could succeed, Merrick. Remember how long I was held! He has not only the Si-Fan behind him, but the Reds as well!" He began to pace up and down. "Dr. Fu Manchu has little time left. Tomorrow night Dr. Hessian has agreed to give a demonstration!"

"Tomorrow night!"

"A committee formed by your father, and approved by the President, will be here. Not one word of this must leak out. Their visit is a top secret. . . . And Fu Manchu would stop at nothing to prevent it!"

Sleep didn't come easily to Brian that night. Between uneasy dozes, he found himself trying to figure out if Lola really had been called to attend upon "Madame", or if she was avoiding being left alone with him, and trying to convince himself that Dr. Hessian's invention was not a mirage, the dream of a mad scientist, but all that Nayland Smith believed it to be. He drove himself near to a mental frenzy.

That Sir Denis deliberately kept him in the dark concerning certain vital facts of the business was beyond dispute. Why? Didn't he trust him?

Crowning mystery—which he had never been able to fathom—for what possible reason had he been employed? Those qualifications stipulated in *The Times* advertisement, all of which he possessed, had never been called upon. For all that had happened to date, almost anybody, graduate or coal miner, athlete or cripple, would have done as well!

He switched on the bedside lamp, saw that the time was 2 a.m., and got up to get a drink. He didn't want whisky; he was really thirsty; and there was beer in the icebox. He made his way to the kitchenette and opened a can.

As he poured out the cold beer, he wondered if Nayland Smith had gone to sleep, and, carrying the glass in his hand, walked bare-footed to Sir Denis's door to find out.

His door was open—and even in the dim light Brian could see that the bed was unoccupied. There was no light in the living-room.

He stood for a moment, hesitating. Then went out to the lobby.

The door of the suite was unlocked!

In view of what Nayland Smith had told him earlier that night, and of Sir Denis's insistence that the door must always be locked and bolted at night, this was more than puzzling. . . .

"We're marked men! If Fu Manchu could trap either of us——"

He remembered the very words.

What was he to think?

Brian knew that he had dozed more than once, but if there had been any struggle it couldn't have failed to arouse him.

And while he stood there in a state of hopeless indecision a sound came which confirmed all his fears. It came from the penthouse.

A pistol shot! . . . A second . . . a third! Then—a muffled explosion, which shook the apartment!

Brian ran back to the living-room, spilling beer as he went.

He switched the light on, set the glass down and crossed to the penthouse phone. . . . Before his hand touched it the instrument began to buzz!

As he took it up: "That you, Merrick?" came Nayland Smith's snappy voice.

"Yes. What's happened? Shall I come up?"

"No. Stay where you are. Dr. Hessian called me an hour ago. He had decided upon a test experiment. It was successful. Probably have most of the residents of the Babylon-Lido phoning like mad! Turn in. All's well."

And Sir Denis hung up.

Brian wondered if he should obey orders and lock the outer door; decided against it, and went back to bed. . . .

He woke early in the morning, vaguely aware of disturbed dreams in which Nayland Smith had become transformed into a sort of prehistoric monster about to devour him and had then vanished in a cloud of smoke.

Wondering why he felt so jaded, he gave an order for coffee and went into the bathroom. If Sir Denis had returned or not he didn't know, and for some reason didn't care. There was no sound in the suite. He was finishing up with an ice-cold shower when the waiter came into the living-room.

Brian called out, "Leave my coffee in there, waiter."

"All ready." But the man lingered, drew nearer to the open bathroom door. . . . "Explosion upstairs last night, I hear. Did it wake you?"

Brian hesitated, towel in hand. He must be cautious.

"Yes, it did. Any damage?"

"Not that I've heard. One of those pressure cookers blew up, I'm told. But nobody hurt."

"Lucky. I wondered what had happened. . . ."

He was drinking coffee and glancing over the morning newspapers which the man had brought up when Sir Denis burst in. He was dressed in one of his well-cut and well-worn tweed suits, so that evidently he, too, had been an early riser.

"Good morning, Merrick. Sorry about last night. Started a lot of rumours. Not good for us. One thing certain. Hessian is a genius compared with whom Einstein was a beginner! I want you with me up there tonight—and you're going to see a miracle. . . ."

When, soon afterwards, Nayland Smith dashed out again, saying that he had an important conference at police headquarters, Brian was left as much in the dark as he had been before Sir Denis dashed in. Mingled with the promised excitement of what the night had in store was a growing resentment at being treated like a figure of no consequence where the big issues at stake were concerned.

Irritably, Brian looked at his watch, and decided that it wasn't too early to call Lola. He asked to be put through to her apartment. She answered almost at once.

"Did I wake you, dear?"

"No, Brian. I'm all ready to go out. A long day ahead at Michel's, and I was up so late last night. Heaven only knows when I'll be through. This was the job I was brought here to do. I have to pass all the models who'll display Michel's creations at the show!"

"Poor darling! Any hope for lunch?"

"Not a shadow. It will be sandwiches and coffee on Fifth Avenue. If I can make it between seven and eight for a quick drink I'll call you."

Brian's spirits sank to zero. The Washington committee, headed by his father, was due at eight o'clock.

"I'm afraid I may be tied up by then, Lola. But call all the same. We might fix something later. . . ."

It was a seemingly interminable morning. Around one o'clock Sir Denis called to say that Brian could leave the suite for his lunch provided he didn't leave the building. . . . "Acting on your advice, I have made other arrangements to safeguard the penthouse. But in case I'm delayed, stand by to receive your father's party from seven on."

Brian lingered over his lunch and then wandered about the huge hotel hoping to find somebody he knew; but, as happens on such occasions, without success. Merely to kill time, he dropped into a lounge in one of the public rooms and ordered coffee.

A strange-looking man sauntered by. He was young, dark-complexioned and handsome in a sinister way, with large, black and brilliant eyes. Otherwise conventionally dressed in European fashion, he wore a blue turban. He seemed to take an unwholesome interest in the younger women present.

Just then, the waiter brought Brian's coffee, and:

"Is the character in the blue turban staying here, waiter?" Brian asked.

The waiter nodded. "Sure he is, sir. They tell me he's an Indian prince. All I know is he has a servant with him that looks like a gorilla. I've taken orders to their apartment."

Finally, Brian bought a bundle of newspapers and magazines and went upstairs to try to amuse himself until the committee arrived. It was important that he should distract his thoughts from hazy doubts and misgivings that crowded upon him. . . .

Almost on the stroke of seven, his father arrived—alone.

"This is a very wonderful occasion, my boy," he declared; "and you're entitled to be proud that you've been chosen to take part in it. The Secretary for Foreign Affairs is coming, General Jenner, General Dowson of the Air Force, and Admiral Druce, representing the Navy. Last, but not least, Dr. Jurgonsen, the physicist and the President's personal adviser on development of atomic projects. Where is Sir Denis? With Dr. Hessian, I suppose?"

"I don't know, Father," Brian confessed. "But he warned me that he might be detained."

Brian Merrick Senior nodded. "A man carrying a heavy load of responsibility on his shoulders."

The party assembled in ones and twos, Nayland Smith last except for Dr. Jurgonsen. Sir Denis looked physically exhausted—or so Brian thought. The three Service officers (all of them in mufti) were so typical of their services as to be

609

without individual characteristics. They showed one trait in common; a reserved but unmistakable hostility for each other.

At three minutes after eight the physicist arrived, a spare grey man in powerful spectacles and a bad temper. He looked around irritably.

"To the devil with New York taxi drivers," he remarked. "The one I hired didn't know the way to the Babylon-Lido!"

The three officers transferred their mutual hostility to the civilian. But Senator Merrick tried to pour oil on troubled waters, as Nayland Smith said:

"If you will be good enough to follow me, gentleman, we will now proceed to the demonstration."

They filed out and long the corridor to the penthouse door, which proved to be open. Brian's curiosity rose to fever pitch. This was his first visit to Dr. Hessian's hideaway. There was another door at the top of the stair which was opened by an expressionless Japanese who wore a white tunic.

He led them through a lobby crowded with oversized trunks and cases and into what was evidently the main room of the penthouse. Although french windows were opened, so that the light-studded panorama of Manhattan could be seen stretched out below the terrace, the air was heavy with some pungent chemical odour.

The Japanese, apparently Dr. Hessian's assistant, closed the door as the last of the party came in.

"Here, gentlemen, as you see, we shall witness a demonstration of Dr. Hessian's supreme achievement."

All eyes became focussed on a long, narrow table in the middle of the room. It was entirely covered by a large-scale plan of Manhattan from the Battery to the Bronx. Roughly midway on the plan a miniature radio mast stood.

Three large metal balls of some dull metal that looked like lead were suspended above the table from the lofty ceiling. Hanging down lower than these was a small box.

Ten chairs were placed around, four on either side and one at each end.

"Your places are marked, gentlemen," the Japanese receptionist told them in perfect English. "Writing materials are provided."

They sorted themselves out, and Brian found himself

beside Nayland Smith. Senator Merrick had been placed at one end of the long table.

"Stand by to make notes of anything worth remembering, Merrick," Sir Denis rapped in his staccato fashion.

He seemed to be highly strung, or so Brian thought. Nor was he the only one. When everybody was seated, only two chairs remained vacant. That to the left of Dr. Jurgonsen and that facing Senator Merrick at the other end of the table. A hum of conversation arose, and Brian detected a theme of incredulity running through it.

"Looks like a new gambling game," Admiral Druce growled. "Where do we put our chips?"

But silence fell suddenly when a strange figure appeared in an inner doorway. A tall man, stooping slightly, he, also, wore a white tunic, as well as tinted glasses, a small skull cap, and gloves which appeared to be made of black rubber.

"Gentlemen," the Japanese assistant announced in his toneless English: "Dr. Otto Hessian." Dr. Hessian rested one hand on the back of his chair and nodded. "Allow me, Doctor, to introduce your visitors."

And beginning with Senator Merrick, as chairman of the committee, he named them one by one, finishing with "Mr. Brian Merrick Junior."

Dr. Hessian nodded to all and then sat down. He put some typed pages before him, so that they partly hid the Bronx.

"If you please," he began in a guttural voice and a very marked German accent, "of English I have not enough properly to explain myself. So these notes I have had translated from German more clear to make it—what I have to say."

There was a faint murmur of sympathy. Evidently Dr. Hessian could see quite well through his dark glasses, for he now consulted his notes and went on, speaking better English but with no better accent:

"Sound vibrations, like all others of which we have knowledge, move neither straight up nor straight along, but, so—" One black-gloved hand described an arc. "They conform to the shape of the envelope in which the earth is enclosed: our atmosphere. Very well. There are sound vibrations, many of them inaudible to our ears, which can shatter a glass goblet. There are others, fortunately rare under normal conditions, which are even more destructive. Such a vibration I have succeeded in producing."

He raised his head, looked around. But although one or two of his audience stirred restlessly, no one spoke.

"It is not only inaudible, but no receiver yet invented (except mine) can transmit it. So. It is as simple as this. Very well. Above my target area, in this case"—he laid a hand on the plan—"Manhattan, a plane flies at a given elevation. The antenna projecting above this plane carries a special receiver from which this vibration inaudible to human ears is cast upon the atmosphere. The plane, although in fact below the denser sound-belt, is immunized."

Another voice broke in. "Dr. Hessian! Your words, so far, leave me more completely mystified than ever. What do you mean by 'the denser sound-belt'?"

Dr. Hessian looked up from his notes, and stared at the questioner.

"It is Dr. Jurgonsen who speaks? I thought this. No doubt you speak also German? Be so good, Doctor, as you question to repeat in German."

And then began a heated exchange in that language, which rose to a pitch of violence. At this point Senator Merrick banged his hand on the table.

"Gentlemen! In the first place, many of the committee don't know what you're talking about. In the second place, you are delaying the demonstration which we are here to see."

Dr. Hessian nodded and looked down again at his notes.

"I am far from being satisfied," Dr. Jurgonsen muttered.

"The demonstration will explain my words," Hessian's guttural voice continued. "My assistant will now lower the objects which you see suspended there."

These "objects", which had excited so much interest, were attached to hooks in the ceiling by slender metallic cords, the ends of which had small rings. These hung down over the table. The Japanese assistant lowered the one suspended above the Battery.

"Open please the container," Dr. Hessian directed.

The halves of the dull metal ball opened on a hinge.

And the ball contained a large coconut!

Everybody laughed, except Dr. Jurgonsen. "Preposterous!"

he choked. But Dr. Hessian, quite unmoved, went on to explain:

"This nut, although out of proportion to the scale of the plan, represents an enemy dive bomber which has penetrated the air defences and will presently swoop down upon lower Manhattan to discharge its load of destruction. These containers are immunized against any sound vibration. Close and return, please."

The metal ball was re-closed and hoisted back to its place.

"Each of these has a trigger on the top which releases the contents when a ball is raised to touch the ceiling," the guttural voice explained. "And now, the guided missile which could destroy the whole city."

A second metal ball, hanging over mid-town New York, was lowered. It was evidently very heavy. The Japanese, leaning over between Admiral Druce and General Rawlins, opened the container. In it, point downward, and carefully held in place by the Japanese, lay what looked like a miniature torpedo.

"Here is a scale model of the latest guided missile, with an atomic warhead—as it would reach our atmosphere with what I may term its outer garments discarded."

Those further removed from the centre of the table stood up and eagerly grouped behind Admiral Druce and General Rawlins for a close view of the model.

"I completed it in Cairo," Dr. Hessian told them. "Only externally is it true to type. It weighs nearly eight pounds and has a small charge of high explosive for the purpose of this demonstration. It is so weighted that it will fall nose downward. Close and return, please."

Looking puzzled and excited, everybody went back to his place as the metal ball was swung up again to the ceiling. Dr. Jurgonsen shrugged his shoulders contemptuously.

"Exhibits A and B I have shown you," Dr. Hessian carried on his guttural monotone—due, perhaps to the fact that he was reading his English transcription. "Exhibit C, just above me, represents a sneak raid" (he had difficulty with the words) "on the Bronx."

The metal ball nearly above his head was lowered. He opened it himself, and displayed a Service revolver!

"I shall detach the weapon from its container." He did so. "Because, in this case, it remains there throughout the experiment. It is set at safety. But, before I return it, the revolver will be ready to fire. I shall request General Rawlins to confirm the fact that the cartridges are live."

It was passed to that officer, who took out several shells and nodded, replaced them and handed the weapon back to the doctor. He adjusted it and the metal ball was raised to its place.

"This exhibit is so adjusted," Dr. Hessian explained, "that whenever the trigger of the receiver is brought in contact with the ceiling the revolver fires a shot at the Bronx. And now, my final exhibit: the small box which you see suspended roughly above the centre of Manhattan. Time prohibited the preparation of a model of an aeroplane resembling the one I have described. Therefore, if you please, imagine that this is such a plane. Its height above the city is out of proportion with the scale. An altitude of three miles would be enough. But I have set it much higher purely in the interest of your safety. I beg, from the moment contact is made—watch for the red light—that you will all remain *seated*. On no account stand up."

Brian experienced a wave of almost uncontrollable excitement. He noted that Nayland Smith's hands were clenched below the table. Every face he looked at registered high nervous tension.

The Japanese moved to a small side table and opened a cabinet which stood there.

"A very ordinary transmitter, gentlemen," came the guttural tones. "Such as any amateur can make. But a mechanism is attached which no one but myself could make. It transmits the lethal note which can throw a protective umbrella over the whole of the New York City! Proceed . . ."

Brian held his breath, and looking upward saw a speck of red light glow in the suspended "receiver". There was no sound.

"Contact is established," Dr. Hessian declared. "The enemy approaches."

The unemotional Japanese returned to the centre table.

"Hold out your hands, Senator Merrick," the new commanding voice ordered. "Prepare to catch the débris of the dive bomber."

Brian saw his father's colour change slightly; but he stretched out his hands, looking up.

The metal ball opened. The big coconut fell . . .

But well above the heads of the seated committee it was shattered to bits!

Fragments of shell and pulp shot miraculously across space to be piled against the walls!

An almost hysterical, concerted gasp told of the reactions of the committee.

"And now, if you please, the guided missile." Dr. Hessian looked up from his notes. "You will note, Dr. Jurgonsen, that any hollow object it is burst instantly on contact with my sound belt. Had you so indiscreet been as to stand up, imagine what happens to your head!"

Before Dr. Jurgonsen could think of a suitable reply, the second metal ball was opened.

The miniature projectile fell swiftly. Several heads were ducked, protective arms raised.

There was a shattering explosion. Fragments of metal spurted across the room as the shell of the coconut had done. Plaster fell from walls as they became spattered with this shrapnel. But not one particle fell on the table or on the surrounding carpet:

"The guided missile is dispersed." Dr. Hessian spoke calmly. "In practice the inaudible sound would be greatly amplified. There would be a thunderstorm far above New York of a violence which no man has ever heard. But nothing more. The protective belt would also be relayed to outlying points. I could throw up a ceiling of sound over the whole of New York City at a cost below that of maintaining a fighter squadron for a month. And now, gentlemen, the sneak raid on the Bronx."

As Dr. Hessian laid his hand on that section of the plan, the Japanese, standing beside him, head carefully lowered, stretched forward and grasped the suspended ring.

"Proceed."

The ring was jerked sharply. A spurt of flame spat down out of the opening in the container. A dull impact . . . a cloud of grey matter spread like smoke across the air, and a flattened bullet rebounded nearly to the ceiling in a ricochet and finally came to rest against a gap in the wall made by shrapnel from the "guided missile."

Two more shots were fired, with similar results. The spectacle was bewildering, for the effect, looking upward, was as though a sheet of miraculously impenetrable glass extended across the room.

But there was nothing—nothing visible . . .

"Let no one stir," Dr. Hessian warned. "Cover everything up."

The Japanese went out and returned with several large sheets. One he spread over the table. Others were laid on the surrounding carpet.

"Disconnect."

A switch was moved in the near-by cabinet . . . and as if a palpable obstacle had been drawn aside, down showered débris of all the experiments!

CHAPTER 13

AT THE CONCLUSION of that amazing demonstration in the penthouse, Dr. Hessian had excused himself and retired. He had been at work day and night, he explained, ever since his arrival, and was far too weary for debate. He referred members of the committee to his assistant, Dr. Yukio Yono, who was qualified to answer all their questions.

Dr. Jurgonsen had tried to detain him, but Hessian had merely nodded and gone out.

Then the imperturbable Japanese scientist had been made the target of a verbal bombardment. But he had never faltered, never changed the tone of his voice, even when others were shouting. Nayland Smith had tapped Brian on the shoulder and nodded towards the door. Back again in their own quarters:

"We're out of our depth, Merrick," he told Brian, "up there. But words can't alter facts." He poured out two liberal shots of whisky. "Otto Hessian had solved the problem of protection from all form of aerial attack. You agree?"

"I can't doubt it. The thing's a miracle. It's magic."

"There's no difficulty whatever in throwing up this sound ceiling over a wide area. Strong feature is the low cost. Everybody's convinced, of course. But old Jurgonsen is boiling with professional jealousy. Your father has tried to persuade the Japanese to get Hessian to set up his apparatus in Washington for the President's okay. But Hessian blankly declines. Genius has its privileges. It's a case of Mohammed and the mountain. The President will come."

"Here?" Brian jerked, startled by such a proposal.

"Here, Merrick, and soon. You saw the vacant chair at the table? That's for your father. The place occupied by Senator Merrick tonight will be reserved for the President."

When presently the members of the committee re-assembled it was clear that their opinion was unanimous. Even Dr. Jurgonsen was forced to admit that Otto Hessian had broken new ground in the aerial defence problem, opening up a

617

prospect of entire immunity on a remarkably low budget.

"Secrecy and speed are vital," he declared. "Dr. Hessian, whom I knew only by name, had vilely bad manners but clearly knows his subject."

"I'll see the President tonight," Senator Merrick promised. "It was arranged I should do so, however late I got back. Dr. Hessian is certainly a most irascible character, and I must persuade the President to come here, incognito, without delay, not later than tomorrow or Friday. Not a word of this must leak out. There will be no press conferences, gentlemen!"

"Every conceivable precaution has been taken," Nayland Smith assured him. "You all entered the hotel by a door not normally in use and came up in a reserved elevator."

"I thought the man on duty looked hard at me," Dr. Jurgonsen complained.

"Quite likely. He's an F.B.I. operative!"

In a hotel bedroom a stockily-built Asiatic, with thick, sensual features and fierce eyes, was listening to a voice which came out of an open suit-case standing on a trestle. It was a sinister, sibilant voice, its curious quality enhanced by the language in which it spoke—Hindustani.

"You understand that this is the emergency called Project Zero?"

"I understand, Master."

"Is Nogai with you?"

"He is downstairs, Master."

"Order him to avoid the public rooms. He has attracted attention. Because he is registered as a Rajah's son he must not act like one. Both remain in your apartment until further orders. Take your meals there. Now, repeat your emergency instructions."

"Yes, Master. At the signal——"

"Repeat the signal."

"Three raps on the door . . . ."

"Continue."

"The door will be unlocked on the other side and I unlock it on this side. I put all lights out. I open the door enough to see in, and wait for the man to come. The first time he has his back to me, I act."

"You must make no mistake."

"I never make mistakes, Master. Nogai and I open the big box and drag him in. We close the door; and wait for further orders."

"And if he is not alone?"

"Nogai goes to the front door and rings. Whichever one answers I deal with the other. Nogai deals with the man at the door."

"Silently!"

"Nogai's method is as silent as mine, Master . . ."

A few minutes later, a woman seated manicuring her fingernails was addressed by the same strange voice, speaking in French, from a cream leather toilet case on the table beside her. She started nervously, staring across the empty room with a haunted look in her eyes.

"I am here, Excellency," she replied, also in French—apparently her native tongue.

"A general emergency has arisen. You have maintained your contact with personnel at the airport?"

"I have."

"Make your own plans, provided I have no occasion to direct otherwise. You know already the information I must have. It is vital that this reaches me *at once*. When you notify me of the expected arrival you will be directed how to proceed. You understand?"

"I understand, Excellency."

"No orders, other than those preceded by the code-word Si-Fan, are to be accepted. You understand?"

"I understand perfectly."

"I count upon unremitting vigilance. Keep in constant touch wherever you are. Report hourly from the time you set out. . . ."

Dr. Fu Manchu leaned back in his chair, his ascetic face lined with anxiety. For more than an hour he had been assembling his forces for some secret purpose which might mean world chaos. He stood up wearily and crossed the small room without a window which he seemed to use as a remote control base. Even now it was only dimly lighted by a lamp on a buffet where there were no homely decanters but only an array of chemical equipment and a large medicine chest containing many bottles and phials.

He took a measuring glass and prepared a draught composed of one part of a greenish liquid, two of amber and one of red. This he emptied carefully into a larger glass and filled it with distilled water. The contents bubbled slightly, became cloudy and then still. Dr. Fu Manchu began to drink, when a faint ring sounded. He turned. A speck of blue light had sprung up in the radio cabinet.

Returning to his chair, he moved a switch and spoke:

"What have you to report?"

A woman's voice answered. "Earlier information of the disaster in Cairo is confirmed, Doctor. The person responsible for it I have been unable to trace, for all have left."

"The absence of any publicity, of any official reaction, is disturbing."

"But understandable. The President is expected tonight."

"I am aware of this, and have spread my net; for the hour of danger is earlier. I am staking everything upon my knowledge of the *man*. He never does the obvious."

"You judge wisely, Doctor. I have information from a reliable source that 'the obvious' was proposed, but rejected. What you have foreseen will happen."

"If I could be as sure of one other thing I would trust to Routine 5 and cancel all other orders."

"What is this one other thing, Doctor?" The woman's voice remained soft but revealed tension.

Dr. Fu Manchu clenched his hands; his features became convulsed, and then calm again.

"His being alone at the crucial moment."

"If I undertake to arrange this one thing, Doctor, will you give me *carte blanche* to deal with it?"

"You never yet failed me, once. And no one ever failed me twice. It is a gambler's choice—but I have always been a gambler. . . ."

Brian had great difficulty getting to sleep that night. The astounding experiment in the penthouse had left him in a state of high excitement. He would seriously have doubted the evidence of his senses if the wonders he had seen hadn't been confirmed by other competent witnesses.

Then, at some remote hour, just as he was dozing off at last, the phone in the living-room buzzed and he heard Nayland Smith's voice. The conversation was a brief one and a moment later Sir Denis burst in.

"Your father, Merrick! We're to expect the President at ten o'clock tonight!"

This made sleep a hundred per cent more difficult. He simply could not stop thinking. For some reason which his mental powers were incapable of grasping he had been dragged into the heart of a top secret which might very well involve the survival of civilization.

Why? He kept asking himself—*Why*?

But he could find no answer.

Nature conquered at last, and he forgot his problems. It was after nine o'clock when he woke, and he went into the living-room to see if Nayland Smith was there. He found a note on the desk—which, enclosed in the painted screen, sometimes reminded him of a pulpit—pencilled in block letters (presumably because Sir Denis's handwriting was illegible).

It said: "Don't go out until I come back. D.N.S."

Brian took up the phone and asked to be put through to Lola's apartment.

She answered at once.

"Listen, Lola honey—did you call me last night? I had to go out."

"No, Brian. I couldn't make it."

"How are you fixed today? I'm uncertain about lunch, but——"

"I'm quite certain about it, Brian. I don't get any! There's only one possible spot, maybe an hour, about four o'clock. Will you be free, if I am?"

"I'll see that I'm free! I'll wait in the Paris Bar. We can't miss each other there."

When presently he hung up, Brian had become uneasily aware of the fact that Lola was preoccupied, tensed up in a new way. He wondered if Madame Michel had been overtaxing her and he wondered, not for the first time, if Lola was changing, slipping away from him . . .

When Nayland Smith came in, around noon, he showed such signs of agitation that Brian felt alarmed. The state of nerves in which Sir Denis had been on his first, clandestine, visit was mild compared to his present condition.

"Sir Denis! Something has upset you. Whatever has happened?"

Nayland Smith turned aside irritably, crossed to the buffet and mixed himself a stiff drink. He dropped down in a chair, took a long draught, and then raised haggard eyes.

"The worst that *could* happen, in the circumstances. Dr. Fu Manchu is here!"

"Here! You mean in New York?"

"Right here in Manhattan." He emptied his glass. "In just a few hours the President will leave Washington. I shall find myself up against the master mind—and Fu Manchu will stick at nothing——"

He stood up and refilled his glass.

This was so unlike the abstemious, cool-brained Nayland Smith Brian had known that he was gripped by a swift and dismal foreboding. Sir Denis was *afraid*!

The idea chilled him. It was unthinkable—like something blasphemous. But many incidents passed in lightning parade across his mind, incidents which, individually, had shaken his faith at the time, but which collectively threatened to shatter it.

Suffering had broken this man of iron. It was a tragedy.

"You don't suggest, Sir Denis, that the President may be in personal danger?"

"Now that Fu Manchu is here we are all in personal danger. Look, Merrick—I'm going up to see Dr. Hessian. It's vital he should know. Go out and get some lunch. When you come back—and don't hurry—I may be asleep. I had no sleep last night, so don't disturb me. . . ."

Lingering over his lunch, feeling miserable and about as useful as a stray dog, Brian tried to muster his wandering ideas, to form some sort of positive picture.

Fu Manchu was in New York. And Nayland Smith had gone to pieces.

These two facts he must accept, for they stood for cause and effect. For the first he had been prepared; for the second he had not. As aide to Sir Denis (hitherto unemployed), the duty clearly fell upon him of taking over if his chief failed!

The responsibility thrilled, and at the same time chilled.

He lacked almost every essential facility. Sir Denis hadn't troubled to put him in touch with the F.B.I. operatives associated with them. He didn't know one by sight. He had no more than a nodding acquaintance with Dr. Hessian; and, for all that scientist's undoubted genius, found his personality strangely repellent.

Brian seriously considered calling his father, laying all the circumstances before that man of wide experience, and abiding by his advice. But the difficulty of doing so on a long-distance call, and an implied betrayal of the trust imposed upon him by Sir Denis, ruled this plan out.

The decision—what to do—rested squarely on himself.

It was close on three o'clock when he went up to the suite. He found a "Do Not Disturb" card outside, but opened quietly and went in. A similar card hung on Nayland Smith's bedroom door. There was a note, in block letters, on the desk. It said:

Do what you like until seven o'clock. But stay out of the Babylon-Lido until that hour. Don't enter on any account. Then wait in the Paris Bar until I page you. Please regard this as an unavoidable order. D.N.S.

WHEN Brian went into the Paris Bar he found it empty, as he might have expected it to be at that hour. Conscientious by nature, he wasn't sure that his being there didn't amount to disobeying the orders of a senior officer.

He was still studying the problem when Lola came in.

"Lola!" There was no one in the place, not even a bartender, and he took her in his arms. "How very glad I am to see you!"

It was an impulse quite irresistible. He held her close and gave her a lingering kiss. Then he recovered himself as she drew back and looked up at him with that quizzical smile.

"So it seems, dear!" But her grey eyes didn't register resentment; they invited. So did the tempting lips.

Their second kiss was so like one of mutual passion that Brian's heart leapt. Lingering doubts were dispelled. Lola loved him!

"Let's get out of here, dearest." He spoke hoarsely. "I want to talk to you, quietly. Queer things are happening." His arm was around Lola's waist. "Where can we be alone—if only for half an hour?"

"Well"— Lola hesitated—"I have one of the tiniest apartments in the Babylon-Lido. Madame doesn't squander dollars. We could go there, but—"

She glanced up at him.

"I promise to behave. I admit I'm mad about you, but I won't break out again."

The apartment was on the eighth floor; its windows commanded an excellent view of a brick wall. The living-room wasn't much larger than either of the bathrooms in the lordly suite reserved for Sir Denis. Lola boiled water in an electric kettle to make tea, which she prepared with the manner of an experienced traveller. . . . "You can imagine you're back at Oxford, Brian."

It was all delightfully intimate, and Brian's mood of depression magically dispersed. When, seated in an easy chair nursing a cup of tea, Lola offered him a cigarette, he felt that this was a foretaste of bliss.

He sparked his lighter; glanced at the cigarette—and paused.

"Please light mine," Lola said sweetly. "They arrived this morning—enough to last me for two months! Your extravagant tastes need watching, Brian."

The cigarettes were "Azizas"—those he had ordered in Cairo!

"Did you get my letter, Lola?"

"Yes. I got your letter. Thank you for everything, Brian. And now, what is it you want to talk about? I warned you, dear. I hadn't much time. On the stroke of five I have to be off."

"Then I'd better begin. What I want to say is strictly confidential. But I just have to say it to somebody—and there's nobody else but you I can say it to. I'm worried about Sir Denis."

"Why, Brian?" Lola drew her brows together in a frown of concentration. "Is he ill?"

"Yes." Brian nodded, "Mentally ill, I'm afraid. His sufferings have shaken him badly. I think he's losing his nerve."

"From your account of Sir Denis, I supposed he had no nerves."

"So did I. But today he seemed to fold up."

"Why, Brian? Has something happened?"

Brian began to remember that it was his duty to keep his mouth shut. He must put a curb on his confidences. But he believed in Lola's worldly wisdom, and desperately needed her advice.

He glanced at her. It had occurred to him almost from the moment of their meeting that she kept up her usual air of easy self-possession only by means of a sustained effort. Perhaps his passionate greeting had shaken her. But certainly, although she masked the fact, she was queerly keyed up; kept glancing at her watch.

"Sir Denis seems to think some new danger has developed," he told her.

"Danger? To whom?"

"To all of us, I guess." He began to grope for words. "My father's expected tonight, and some other important visitors. If this danger is real, I'm wondering if I should stop them."

625

"Surely Sir Denis would have done so, if he couldn't guarantee their safety."

"You don't know," Brian assured her, "how completely he's gone to pieces."

"As your father is involved, surely you could at least discuss it with him."

Brian shook his head wearily. "He's asleep up there! And I have his written order. Look at this." From his pocket he took out the note he had found on the desk. "They'll be on their way before seven o'clock!"

Lola read the note, but made no comment; passed it back; glanced at her wrist-watch.

"What would you advise me to do, Lola?"

She stood up. "In the first place, get a move on. I have to go. As for Sir Denis's order, I advise you to do nothing—except obey it to the letter. . . ."

Brian watched Lola's taxi weaving its way into the traffic torrent and finally becoming lost to view, with a sense of desolation. She had her troubles, too, he knew, although they didn't involve millions of human destinies but only the vanity of a few wealthy women who bought their dresses at Michel's.

He started away at a brisk pace towards Central Park. An hour's walk in fresh air might help him to shake off that appalling sense of gloom, which Huckleberry Finn called then fantods.

From the moment that he entered the Park he hardly noticed where he was going, but evening was drawing in when he found himself passing behind the Museum and pulled up to check the time. He decided to turn back, swung around, and saw that the only other pedestrian in sight, a man walking twenty yards behind him, had done the same.

He thought nothing of this at the moment. Returning along the same path, he saw the man ahead turn to the left for a gate on Fifth Avenue. Brian passed on, nervously considering the night's programme, wondering why the mere approach of Dr. Fu Manchu had so shattered Nayland Smith's courage and what it could be that Sir Denis feared. . . . Did he seriously believe the President's life to be in danger? And did he doubt his own ability to protect him?

Something—perhaps a subconscious urge—prompted Brian to pause and look behind. . . .

The man he supposed to have left the Park was following him again!

Anger came first; then, an unpleasant chill.

His follower might be an agent of Dr. Fu Manchu, or he might be one of the F.B.I. men detailed, according to Sir Denis, to keep him under observation. In any case, it was getting dark, the Park seemed deserted, and Brian went out by the 72nd Street gate and hailed a taxi.

In the main entrance to the Babylon-Lido he looked at his watch.

Twenty minutes to seven.

He turned away and walked around the corner. He had noticed a little bar almost directly facing the trade entrance to the hotel and decided that he could pass the time there over a drink and a smoke. It was better than walking about; he was tired of walking, now, and feeling thirsty.

Taking a corner stool just inside the door, he ordered a drink, lighted a cigarette; settled down to wait for seven o'clock.

For what possible reason had Nayland Smith banished him from the Babylon-Lido until that hour? It was incomprehensible. Unless, which seemed probable, he was followed by a Federal agent wherever he went, why was Sir Denis's warning "never to go out alone" apparently forgotten?

Either he had become a mere cipher in the game, or Nayland Smith had thrown his hand in and didn't care what happened.

Brian started a fresh cigarette, looked at his watch. Ten minutes to wait.

With some unknown menace, embodied in the name Dr. Fu Manchu, hanging over the party assembling—a party to include the President tonight—this enforced inertia was almost unendurable. Brian found it nearly impossible to remain still. Although he did his best to retain control, he saw the bartender glancing in his direction suspiciously.

Brian stared out of the window—and became very still indeed; so still that he might have been suddenly frozen to his seat. . . .

Lola was standing in the trade entrance to the Babylon-Lido talking to Nayland Smith!

Her face was in shadow, but she was dressed as he had left her at five o'clock. This time there could be no room for doubt. Nor could he be wrong about the man. It was Sir Denis. The coat, the soft-brimmed hat, his poise—all were unmistakable. He saw them go in.

In half a minute he had paid for his drink, and dashed recklessly across the street, ignoring traffic lights.

He had never been in this warren of stores-cellars and kitchens before, but somehow made his way through and at last penetrated to the vast but now familiar lobby. His heart was beating fast; for his world had turned topsy-turvy. What had Lola to do with Nayland Smith? She had told him only that afternoon that she had never met Sir Denis!

The clock over the reception desk recorded five minutes to seven.

People buzzed about in a state of perpetual motion. They all appeared to be in a hurry. Smart women in gay evening gowns who couldn't find their men. Eager-eyed young men rushing around looking for their girl friends. Pages carrying flowers. The scene seemed to swim before Brian like a colour film out of focus. It was a ballet inspired by a mad director.

But the two figures he was looking for were not to be seen.

He debated with himself, looking again at the clock. He could endure this suspense no longer. He must know the truth, orders or no orders. To wait to be paged in his present frame of mind was out of the question. He turned and hurried off to the corridor where the express elevators were situated. The man on duty knew him and smiled a greeting as Brian stepped in.

"Sir Denis has just gone up, sir," he reported.

Brian experienced a fluttering sensation in the pit of his stomach.

"Was he alone?"

"Yes, sir."

The elevator began its dizzy ascent. Nayland Smith, Brian reflected, must have gone out to meet Lola. They had evidently parted on entering the hotel. But why had they come in by the trade entrance? He could only conclude that the meeting had been a clandestine one.

When he arrived at the top floor he stood for a moment to get a grip on himself.

Then, he walked along to the door of Suite 420B. The "Do Not Disturb" card had gone; and he pulled up, trying further to compose his ruffled nerves.

At last he quietly slipped the key into the lock and opened the door.

Dusk had fallen now and he saw that lights were on in the living-room. There was no sound.

He walked in quietly. . . . Then gulped, and stood quite still.

Flat on his back on the floor, his knees drawn up, his fists clenched, Nayland Smith lay. His face was purple, his teeth were bare, and his eyes bulged from his head. . . .

He had been strangled!

THE HORROR of his discovery quite literally paralysed Brian. His senses were numbed. He stood speechless, incapable of movement, of thought; aghast.

A slight sound in the room roused him, bringing swift realization of his own danger. He turned to the big desk, for from there the sound had come, and . . . his brain reeled. He was gripped by the agonizing certainty that the murder of Nayland Smith had disturbed his reason—had driven him mad.

Standing beside the tall, painted screen, a finger on his lips, urgent command in his eyes, and beckoning Brian to join him, he saw *Nayland Smith*!

Brian clenched his fists, glancing from the dead man to this phantom of the living.

And the living Sir Denis was beside him in three strides; gripped his arm, speaking softly into his ear:

"Not a word! Behind the screen, Merrick—for your life—and for mine!"

There was nothing ghostly in the grip of those sinewy fingers, nothing but vital necessity in the whispered orders.

Brian found himself in shadow behind the screen. One spear of light shone through a hole in the parchment, and still half stupefied in this gruesome and almost incredible situation, he saw Nayland Smith jab his thumb through another panel in the screen and make a second hole.

"Look!" came a whisper in his ear. "Do nothing. Say nothing. . . ."

Silence.

Peering through the slot in the parchment, Brian's gaze automatically became focussed on the dead man. For all that agonized expression, swollen features, protruding eyes, he was prepared to take oath and swear that it was Sir Denis who lay there.

But another Sir Denis—very much alive—stood beside him, and continued to grip his arm!

He felt suddenly sick, wondered if he was going to make a

fool of himself—and then noticed something he hadn't noticed before . . . . A door which communicated with the next suite, normally locked, stood partly open. The room beyond was in darkness.

Muttered words—and two men came in!

The first was a thick-set Oriental whose coarse, brutal features and abnormally long arms were simian rather than human. The second Brian recognized; a slender, elegant man wearing a blue turban—in fact the man whom a waiter had reported to be an Indian prince!

They lifted the body and carried it out. The communicating door was closed, and Brian heard the click of a lock.

"Don't speak!" The words were hissed in his ear. "This room is wired!"

The new Sir Denis crossed to the recently closed door and locked it. He turned and beckoned Brian to follow him. In the lobby: "Say nothing," he whispered, "but take your cue from me." Brian nodded. Nayland Smith opened the outer door; shut it again noisily. "Hullo, Merrick! Before your time." He spoke, now, in a loud tone. "Anything wrong? You look under the weather. Go and lie down. I'll bring a drink to your room."

Brian crossed, rather unsteadily, to his own room and went in. Sir Denis's extemporized "cue" wasn't far from the truth. This experience had shaken him severely. Even now he couldn't get the facts into focus.

Nayland Smith rejoined him, carrying two drinks on a tray. He quietly closed the bedroom door behind him.

"I need one, too, Merrick," he confessed. "That premature entrance nearly resulted in a second murder—*yours!*"

"But——"

"Wait a minute." Sir Denis held up his hand. "Let's get the important thing settled first, because there's a lot to say and not much time to say it. You wouldn't be human if you didn't wonder which of us is the real Nayland Smith. I had a fair chance to study my double—and I felt like a man looking in a mirror. Hark back to the time I stayed in Washington. Ask me something about your home life that nobody could know who hadn't lived with you."

Brian tried to force his bewildered brain to think clearly, and presently an idea came.

"Do you remember Father's dog?" he asked.

"Do I remember Rufus!" Nayland Smith smiled—and it was the smile Brian had known, the boyish smile which lifted a curtain of years. "Good reason to remember him, Merrrick." He pulled up his left trouser leg. "There's the souvenir Rufus left me when I tried to break up a scrap he was having with a Boston terrier. Rufus thought my interference unsporting! It was you yourself who phoned the doctor, and damn it! He wanted to give me Pasteur injections!"

And, in that moment, all doubt was washed out. Brian knew that this was the real Nayland Smith, that the man he had been employed to work with was an impostor—and a miraculous double!

He held out his hand. "Thank God it's *you* that's alive!"

"I have done so already, Merrick, devoutly. I have passed through the unique experience of witnessing my own execution. I was desperately tempted to rush to the aid of my second self. But to do so could only have meant that the super-criminal, the most dangerous man in the world today, would have slipped again through my fingers. So I clenched my teeth when the thug sprang out on him and said to myself, 'There, but for the grace of God, goes Nayland Smith'!"

"Who is—who was—the man impersonating you? It was a star performance. Even the British Embassy in Cairo fell for him! So did my father."

Nayland Smith pulled out the familiar pipe and began to load it.

"So would my own mother, if she had been alive. . . . You're staring at my pipe? Fortunately I had a spare one with me. The poor devil who was strangled probably has the other in his pocket. I don't know who he was, Merrick. But he must have been a talented actor, with a nerve of iron."

"His nerve began to fail."

"I don't wonder. They had news of my escape. There wasn't room in New York for two Nayland Smiths!"

He rapped out the words like so many drum-taps, and at a speed which Brian realized that his impersonator had never acquired.

"He had every intonation of your voice, Sir Denis! All your gestures, every mannerism. Even that trick of twitching at the lobe of your ear! And I believe he smoked more than you do."

Nayland Smith smiled. "Sounds like overacting! Poor devil. He probably played for big stakes. He had several weeks to study me, Merrick, while I was a prisoner in that damned house in Cairo."

"In Cairo! Then it must have been you, yourself, I saw in a room with barred windows—the house of the Sherîf Mohammed!"

Sir Denis stared for a moment, and then: "This is news," he admitted, "but probably right. You can tell me later. We have little time, and you're entitled to know the truth."

He lighted his pipe, stood up and began to walk about.

"I had been on a mission behind the Bamboo Curtain. We had information that Dr. Fu Manchu was operating with the Red Chinese. Knowing the Doctor intimately, I doubted this. He controls a world-wide organization of his own, the Si-Fan. And if anyone succeeds in taking over China it won't be the Communists!"

This was so like what the false Nayland Smith had told him, that Brian listened in growing wonder . . .

"On my way back, by sea (secretly, as I thought) I walked into a trap in Suez which I should have expected an intelligent schoolboy to avoid, and a few hours later found myself a prisoner in the house of the Sherîf Mohammed. The Si-Fan had traced me. I was in the hands of Dr. Fu Manchu!"

"How long ago was that?"

"Roughly, two months. I had secured evidence that Fu Manchu had recently been in China, for his chief-of-staff, a brilliant old strategist, General Huan Tsung, was operating under cover right in Peiping. Some highly important scheme was brewing, and I scented that it would be carried out, not in the East, but in the West. I was right!

"It became clear from the beginning of my imprisonment that Fu Manchu hadn't planned to kill me. For some reason, he wanted me *alive*! My ancient enemy was there in person, in the house of the Sherîf Mohammed; and at first I had easy treatment. I was well fed and allowed to exercise in a walled courtyard. But for several hours every day I was brought to a room, two windows of which were barred, as you state, and put through a sort of brain-washing by Dr. Fu Manchu. He spoke to me from behind an iron grille high up in one wall——"

"I have seen it!"

"Remarkable. Details later. He argued on ideological grounds, tried to convert me to the theories of the Si-Fan. Sometimes, he taunted me. He worked over me, Merrick, like a skilled performer playing on a stringed instrument. And not for a long time did the fact dawn that every move I made, every word I spoke, some *other person*, hidden behind the grille, studied, watched, listened to!

"He betrayed himself once only, but from that moment I knew he was always there—and a hazy idea of the plot began to appear. Someone was being trained to impersonate me! The scheme wasn't a new one. I believe Fu Manchu had had it in mind for several years; probably searched the world for my near-double. I suspect, but may be wrong, that tape recordings of these conversations were made on a hidden microphone, to help my understudy to perfect his impersonation at leisure."

"It beats everything I ever heard! Of course you tried to make a getaway?"

Nayland Smith checked his restless steps and stared grimly at Brian.

"During the day relays of Fu Manchu's professional stranglers had me covered. You saw two of them just now. At night there was a hidden microphone in my room. It not only recorded my slightest movements, but could also be used to transmit a note inaudible to human ears. Its production is Fu Manchu's secret, as he was good enough to tell me. Its effect would be to kill me instantly by inducing haemorrhage of the brain!"

"But that's Dr. Hessian's invention!" Brian broke in.

Nayland Smith relighted his pipe. It had gone out while he was talking.

"Unless my deductions are wide of the mark, Merrick, the man you know as Otto Hessian is *Dr. Fu Manchu!*"

A faint buzzing reached them from the living-room.

"That's the penthouse!" Brian spoke breathlessly.

"Then I had better answer."

"But what are you going to do?"

Nayland Smith turned in the act of opening the door. "Whatever the late Nayland Smith the Second was expected to do. . . ."

As the door was left open, Brian could overhear Nayland Smith when he spoke on the penthouse line. The conversation was a short one. He came back, his expression grim; reclosed the door.

"Tell me, Merrick—is there anything, any trifle, about my appearance which strikes you as different from—his?"

Brian studied the clean-cut features, thinking hard.

"His skin maybe was artificially sunburned. It didn't look quite natural."

"Nothing to be done about that. What else?"

"Well, something had happened to the bridge of his nose. He wore plaster the first time I saw him. There was no scar, except when he smiled. Then, there was a faint wrinkle where the plaster had been."

"That may explain what was found in a sort of studio in the Sherîf's house: a wonderful clay model of my head! These people must have got out in a desperate hurry. The studio adjoined a small operating theatre. It seems likely that my double had undergone plastic surgery . . . H'm! Avoid smiling!"

"What was the phone message, Sir Denis?"

"In thirty minutes, I'm bidden to a conference with Dr. Fu Manchu, and probably my life hangs on not arousing his suspicion. The odds are in my favour. But my opponent——"

"Where are you to meet?"

"Up in the penthouse."

"You mean Fu Manchu really *lives* there?"

"It's his base of operations. I don't wonder it staggers you. But let me bring you up to date. One day, in Cairo, there was considerable disturbance in the Sherîf's household. I sensed that something unusual was going on. Of course, it was the departure of Fu Manchu and most of his unsavoury crew for the United States. Don't ask me how he travels, unless he has a magic carpet, or avoids being identified, because I don't know."

"That time, Sir Denis, if I'm not wrong, he travelled with me (and your double), posing as Dr. Hessian, in a plane provided by the British government!"

Nayland Smith laughed out loud. "You're not wrong, Merrick. Thanks for the information. You see, I know his impersonation of an eccentric German scientist. He has worked it before. He's a master of numberless languages and dialects. To the Western idea, he isn't typically Chinese. He's at least as tall as I am, has fine, ascetic features and a splendid head. His eyes, alone, and his hands, betray the Asiatic."

"But the real Dr. Hessian?"

"If he's alive—which I doubt—Otto Hessian is probably in Siberia. He disappeared behind the Iron Curtain three years ago. Well, as I said, there was a disturbance in the household—and an unpleasant change for me. I was transferred to a room in the cellar. Unmistakably a dungeon, belonging to the days when the old house had been the palace of some wealthy pasha!

"Merrick! I all but lost hope! Two of Fu Manchu's thugs had been left behind to guard me, and I expected from hour to hour they would get word to finish me off! My only exercise was walking about the cellar. And the nights were dreadful. I suspected, but couldn't confirm the suspicion, that some kind of murder machine was installed in my cell.

"Then, one night a queer thing happened. I was roused by a faint noise outside my locked door. I thought my time had come! A light shone through the grille, and I called out, 'Who's there?' The light vanished. Complete silence. Nothing happened . . . until the next day.

"Neither of the assassins brought me my breakfast. There wasn't a sound to be heard. Hours passed. No one came. I asked myself was I doomed to starve to death! But early next morning a party of Egyptian police, accompanied by Nigel Richardson of the British Embassy, and Lyman Bostock, his American opposite number, burst into the cellar."

"How had they traced you?" Brian demanded excitedly.

"Top marks to your F.B.I., Merrick. My understudy (then arrived in New York), had excited the suspicion of one of their brightest under-cover agents. A code message reached Bostock. It asked for a secret examination to be made of the house of the Sherif—not neglecting the cellars! A tall order. How the devil they arranged it I don't know; and they both laughed when I asked them. But I remembered the light through the grille of my cell. Anyway, they succeeded in getting a search warrant. And I can assure you that getting that warrant must have taken a lot of doing! . . . The place was deserted. Not a soul in the building . . . except myself! The Sherif had got wind of the thing and pushed off in a hurry with his entire household, including, I was told, several ladies and a fat eunuch. When I heard of the astonishing deception to which Richardson and Bostock had been made parties I knew that not another hour must be wasted. Both wanted the impostor arrested by the New York police at once. I disagreed.

"I made them see that the arch-conspirator would slip through our fingers. We must find out first the purpose of this amazing plot—which was what the F.B.I. wanted to know, too. Then, we'd have the whole gang in the bag."

"What I don't understand," Brian declared, "is why they left you alive."

Nayland Smith smiled grimly. "Because somebody blundered—or got cold feet. My cell (as I suspected) was fitted with the brain-blasting equipment, and for purposes of concealing evidence, there was a man-sized bath of curious construction in another room which was intended to contain acid: something had thrown the gang into a panic, and these little arrangements, by the mercy of Providence, were overlooked at the last moment."

"Tell me one thing, Sir Denis. By what accident did I get into the picture and why?"

"Not by accident, I assure you! Fu Manchu already had me in his hands, and no doubt his agents were combing likely spots for a young, unemployed American with an influential background, to make doubly sure of my understudy's acceptance. You were the very man. The F.B.I. had operatives in London (I don't know why), and they found out that you had been employed by a Communist group, but were ordered not to interfere. Washington had no idea what was brewing, but thought that you, as an innocent accomplice, might come up later with some useful information."

"You mean"—Brian flushed indignantly—"that I was allowed to walk blindfolded into this thing?"

"I mean that, yes. And don't glare at me! *I* had nothing to do with it. What's more, it's been done before. You see,

Merrick, if you had known, you'd have betrayed yourself. Under-cover espionage isn't your *métier*. How well it has worked out you can see for yourself. They are quite sure of you, and so we have the game in our hands."

Brian lighted a cigarette, but said nothing.

"Well," Nayland Smith went on, 'I got my own way and was smuggled out of Cairo. I travelled as Major S. D. Smith, wore a toothbrush moustache and a monocle. Not a word was allowed to leak out about the raid on the Sherif's house. All the same, the Si-Fan got the news. When I arrived at Idlewild, at five-thirty this afternoon, I was met by the F.B.I. Their star operative, already a member of the Communist party, had managed, by what I can only call a stroke of genius, to become a top executive of the Si-Fan! Every detail of my projected execution was known!

"First, you had to be kept away until it was all over. Second, as it was assumed that I should apply for a spare key and walk right up to the suite reserved in my name (exactly what I had planned to do), my double had orders to go out."

"Yes?" Brian was getting excited. "What happened?"

"A tactical move by the F.B.I. worthy of Napoleon. My double's orders were to slip around to a back entrance, go up in the service elevator and return to the suite. He had to unlock the communicating door and then take cover until I came in and had been liquidated. They managed to detain him long enough for me to come up first, open the door and lie low. When my wretched double appeared he got what was coming to *me*!"

"Do you mean to say the police and the F.B.I.suspected nothing right up to the time you were found in Cairo?"

"They accepted Nayland Smith the Second and Dr. Hessian as authentic. They still think Hessian is. They didn't know where *you* fitted in. In other words, it was the discovery by their operative in London that you had been employed by a Red agent which sparked the inquiry!" Sir Denis glanced at his watch. "And now I must be off. . . . Don't look so desperate, Merrick! I'm well briefed, and"—he tapped a coat pocket— "prepared for anything. Stand by. . . ."

DR. FU MANCHU sat at the long table in the room without windows when Nayland Smith came in. "Sit down," he ordered. "I have much to say to you."

Nayland Smith sat down in a chair on the other side of the table. He found that whilst Fu Manchu's face remained in shadow, his own was brightly lighted. As of old, he experienced a tingling of the scalp whenever he came into contact with the *force* which seemed to proceed from this evil superman. He recalled the form of address which he had been told to use.

"At your service, Excellency."

Fu Manchu watched him. A stray beam of light touched the green eyes. Their regard was hard to sustain.

"You had done well, William Hailsham," the sibilant voice continued, "until I had to warn you that your prototype had escaped death and was on his way. Your behaviour in face of danger disappointed me. I asked myself if I had rescued a cur from a Soviet labour camp for this!" The strange voice hissed the last word. "Your political views terminated your career as an actor. Your arrogance offended even your Communist employers. I, alone, offered you a way to speedy fortune, security."

Nayland Smith remained silent. Dr. Fu Manchu took a pinch of snuff.

"I am too closely tied to this project. I had hoped to bring with me what you would term a 'stand-in' for Dr. Hessian as you are 'stand-in' for Nayland Smith. Unfortunately, certain surgical treatment proved unsatisfactory at the last moment. Therefore, my personal presence, although necessary, is dangerous."

He closed the lid of the silver snuff-box.

"The first crisis is over. Those responsible shall pay a heavy price. There is only one Nayland Smith—yourself. But, falter tonight . . . and there will be *no* Nayland Smith." He passed his hand over his high brow. "I regret the necessity.

Physically, you might have been twins. But there the likeness ends. Had the real Nayland Smith been not my enemy but my ally, I should sit today on the throne of an empire greater than Rome ever knew. . . . Listen."

And Nayland Smith listened intently.

"The entire routine for tonight is changed. You handled the premature appearance of that impetuous fool, Merrick, very well. You seemed to have recovered your nerve—for you had no more than locked the communicating door when he arrived. I have not lost hope that you may carry off the situation tonight."

Dr. Fu Manchu paused, and his eyes seemed to film over; but soon he went on:

"The plan of the Reds was to ensure that a certain order to the Chiefs of Staff should not be authorized. This you know. It was a desperate plan, and a bad one. I had never intended to carry it out. This also you know. My own plan would have served the same purpose—but gone further. For, with the acceptance of the so-called 'Hessian Sound Zone' I should have had access to every important air base, every military objective, from coast to coast. I should have made them invulnerable!" His voice quivered with the enthusiasm of the fanatic. "Then—at last—I could have challenged the power of Communism . . . and broken it!"

Fu Manchu raised clenched hands above his head, then lowered them; spoke softly.

"These are your new orders. . . ."

Brian paced the living-room like a man possessed.

He had been allowed to become party to a conspiracy directed against the United States government by the very people sworn to defend it; used as a tool! He grew hot with indignation. The mystery which had puzzled him all along was a mystery no more. He had been employed solely as a link with his father, and, through his father, with the President.

But it was the part played by Lola which crowned his misery. Peter Wellingham, he knew now, was a Red agent. Beyond doubt he had been right when he thought it was Lola he had seen with Wellingham in Hyde Park. Lola had drawn his attention to *The Times* advertisement. If any room for doubt had remained, seeing her in the company of the false Nayland Smith would have swept it away. How little either of them could have suspected that their murder plot was known!

Brian groaned in his misery. From first to last he had been in the hands of creatures of Dr. Fu Manchu.

Zoe Montéro—Ahmad—all had played him like a hooked fish!

He remembered, bitterly, Lola saying about *The Times* advertisement, "It read like a job created purposely for you." It *had* been created purposely for him, and she knew it!

Fu Manchu or the Reds, whichever of them she worked for, had sent her off to New York to take him over as soon as he arrived. They were naturally anxious to know if he suspected anything. Many of her questions about Nayland Smith recurred to him, and he could see their purpose, now. . . . Perhaps little Zoe—alone—had really weakened and tried to help him.

He would have loved to think so.

But Lola . . .

This mood of self-contempt so burned him up that he wanted to curse aloud. It called for a mighty effort to put his own petty troubles aside, to get back to the concrete inescapable fact that he was still involved in a giant conspiracy which might change world history.

He looked at the time. Surely Sir Denis should be back?

And, as he arrived at this conclusion, Sir Denis did come back. He entered quietly, put one finger to his lips, and pointed to the open door of Brian's room.

They went in, and Nayland Smith closed the door.

"Lucky I was warned that our living-room is wired," he remarked. "Well—I think I have passed, Merrick. At least, I'm still alive! But those X-ray eyes may have seen more than Fu Manchu thought it diplomatic to give away. He was employed by the Reds—rather reluctantly, I gather—to carry out a certain scheme."

"He—your double—told me the same thing! That Fu Manchu had been employed to prevent Dr. Hessian's invention falling into the hands of the United States!"

"That was the story my double sold to the authorities. Remember, he was accepted for myself. Hessian wasn't doubted. The only dark horse in the stable was *you*! The F.B.I. rarely let you out of their sight!"

"You mean they suspected me of being a Red spy?" Brian blazed angrily.

"They didn't know what or whom to suspect, Merrick, until I came on the scene. By the way, they'll be expecting me to report. But I'm in rather a quandary."

"If Fu Manchu already knows the secret of this sound cover, what on earth is he doing here?"

Nayland Smith laughed dryly. "What Fu Manchu, himself, described to me as the 'so-called Hessian Sound Zone' he really meant to place in the hands of the United States! He had no intention of following his Red instructions. These were designed simply to prevent the President signing an order to Chiefs of Staff which would have upset certain of their plans. It involved an urgent telephone call from the White House, a mouthpiece which ejected an odourless gas, and some other details which Fu Manchu could undoubtedly have provided."

"But why such an elaborate set-up?"

Nayland Smith began to fill his pipe, glancing aside at Merrick.

"Have you ever thought how hard it would be to get the President of the United States *alone*? Had the Red plan been carried out, he would have been struck down by what any physician would have diagnosed as a heart attack, and been incapable of transacting any business for a long time!"

"Good God! What a villainous plot!"

"But child's play for Dr. Fu Manchu. That's why he was employed."

"Then the Hessian Sound Zone is just an illusion—a hoax?"

Nayland Smith dropped his pouch back into his pocket; struck a wooden match.

"Not a bit of it. The Sound Zone is Dr. Fu Manchu's invention. He's a scientific genius. The thing is an astounding reality!"

"Astounding's an understatement."

"It would give complete immunity from blast. No projectile could penetrate it. The nuclear fall-out would be dispersed over a wide area of the upper atmosphere. This, if such horrible weapons are ever used, is unavoidable. The consequences would depend upon the direction of the wind over which no man, not even Dr. Fu Manchu, has control."

"Then why not let bygones be bygones, if Fu Manchu has really come clean?"

"Because, to mention one reason, its adoption, whilst making America, and I suppose the other Western allies, immune to direct air attack, would also give the Si-Fan absolute control of the Near and Far East."

"But if it's real——"

"Just so, Merrick." Sir Denis lighted his pipe. "That's why we have to hold the candle to the devil. That's why we can't arrest the two assassins next door, and produce the body which, I suppose, is hidden there. That's why I don't know what to report."

Brian was dumbfounded. "You mean that, after what happened tonight, Fu Manchu will still go ahead with his project?"

Nayland Smith nodded; dropped the match-end in a tray.

"It's his master-plot. He won't resign it easily."

The smell of tobacco-smoke spurred Brian to light a cigarette; to put himself in the background; concentrate on these vast issues at stake.

"This master-plot may be clear to you, Sir Denis, but I can't get it. Why would the fact (and I accept your word it *is* a fact), that the West was safe from air attack, help this amazing man to take over the East?"

"Because the Reds, helpless to retaliate, could be blasted into submission, or unconditional surrender. And the vast underground movement throughout the East, which he has developed, would seize power. There'd be no holding him! I assure you, Merrick, that Hitler and Stalin were babes and sucklings compared to Dr. Fu Manchu!"

Nayland Smith continued his usual promenade. Brian was deep in thought.

"His cutting-in with a double for yourself," he admitted, "wasn't far short of criminal genius. His preparations to handle the thing if you happened to be alive were masterly."

"Dragging the son of a prominent Senator and friend of the President into his programme also had elements of talent," Sir Denis remarked dryly. "Never underestimate Dr. Fu Manchu. If he hadn't been bitten by the bug called Power he would be honoured today as one of the world's greatest

643

intellects. Fortunately (in this case) like many men of genius, he's more than slightly mad."

"But what are you going to do?" Brian demanded. "The F.B.I. know, now, that Dr. Hessian isn't the real man——"

"They don't!" Nayland Smith rapped. "I haven't told them. They accepted my double and Hessian as authentic. They began to worry about Nayland Smith the Second. Thought I had been brain-washed or something; but, all through, never doubted Hessian. They know now that my understudy wasn't Nayland Smith; but they believe that Hessian is Hessian and that the purpose of the plot is to steal his invention."

"Then why keep them in the dark?"

"Because, as he believes that I am his own man (I hope), Fu Manchu still plans to meet the President tonight and to hand over his system to the United States! The late Nayland Smith the Second was an actor called William Hailsham, an active member of the Communist Party. My orders are to tell the committee that the impostor attempted to kill me and that in self-defence I strangled him!"

"But are you really going to do it?"

Nayland Smith twitched the lobe of his ear. "I don't know. I'm thinking hard. . . ."

This remarkable conversation was still going on in Brian's room in Suite 420B when a tall, spare figure wearing a long black coat and a wide-brimmed black hat rapped in a peculiar manner on the door of Suite 420C.

The door was opened immediately by the slender man who wore a blue turban.

He salaamed deeply. "Master!"

Dr. Fu Manchu walked in with his majestic yet curiously feline step, and in the main room, which, although richly furnished, was smaller than that in the adjoining suite, faced the second occupier—whose apelike ugliness had so appalled Brian when he had seen him through a hole in the screen.

He, too, saluted the doctor as one doing reverence to a pagan god.

"Everything found in his possession," Fu Manchu demanded, speaking Hindustani. "Quickly. Show me."

The thickset man ran to an open suit-case, took out a parcel and spread all it contained on a table. "Here is everything, Master."

Fu Manchu examined the exhibits found on the person of the dead man, one by one. A silver disk stamped with a number and a curious design seemed to excite him strangely. His eyes, when he raised them, gleamed with a light of madness.

He turned, pointed to an outsize wardrobe trunk standing against the wall. On it was painted "Prince Ranji Bhutani."

"Unlock it!" he commanded.

His voice, which ranged at times from the guttural to a sort of menacing hiss, was no more than audible.

The younger man, his handsome but sinister features registering intense alarm, produced a bunch of keys and, not without difficulty, unlocked the big trunk.

Upright inside, and secured with leather straps, the double of Nayland Smith stood, his head drooping so that the swollen features were in shadow. Dr. Hu Manchu stepped forward and tilted the head upward—no easy matter, for the neck muscles were already stiff.

From a pocket of his black coat he took out a lens and, peering closely, examined the nose of the victim.

He replaced the lens, turned, and struck the long-armed thug a flat-handed blow across his face. The younger killer fell to his knees, clasping his hands.

"Master!"

"Fools!" Fu Manchu's features were contorted; his expression was that of a dangerous maniac. "You have killed the wrong man!" . . . By a stupendous effort of will, he recovered his usual calm. "Relock the trunk. Remain here until further orders reach you."

With his silent, catlike walk, Dr. Fu Manchu turned away, opened the door, and went out. He passed the suite occupied by Nayland Smith, and went up to the penthouse. In the dark room which adjoined that equipped for the demonstration he seated himself at the radio switchboard and made an adjustment.

A point of blue light appeared. A woman spoke. "Yes, Doctor?"

"Tonight's plans changed. Report to me—immediately. . . ."

At about this time, Brian, chain-smoking in his agitation, was watching Nayland Smith pacing the floor of the room like an English Guardsman on sentry duty. At last, Sir Denis broke his long silence.

"I have chosen my course, Merrick. Heaven grant it's the right one. Bearing in mind what I mean to do tonight—*must* do—I doubt if Fu Manchu' s secret device would be handed over. He has the cunning of the serpent. He takes fantastic risks; but always assures himself of a way out. My explanation to the committee, which I am supposed to give verbatim (the deceased actor was evidently a quick study), would certainly break up the conference."

"Sure! Just what I was thinking! The meeting tonight——"

"I can't believe that a man so astute as Dr. Fu Manchu ever intended it to take place. He has changed his plans. He may be laying another trap—he may be preparing to make a getaway! This could only mean that the cunning devil recognized me!"

"Then why didn't he bump you off when he had you up there in the penthouse?"

"Think again, Merrick," Sir Denis rapped. "Consider *two* dead Nayland Smiths on his hands in the Babylon-Lido! No. There hasn't been time to move the other one. We may lose the secret of the Sound Zone, but, at last, we have Dr. Fu Manchu!"

"What are we going to do?"

Nayland Smith knocked ash from the hot bowl of his pipe.

"I can't stop the others. That doesn't matter. But I shall signal the plane bringing your father and the President, and their course will be changed. We don't know what new devilry may be brewing, and I daren't risk it. Our best defence is attack."

He headed for the door.

"What's my job?" Brian wanted to know.

"We'll slip down and talk to Ray Harkness. He's in charge of the F.B.I. engaged on this job. We have worked together before. This double business has shaken him badly. Before I went up tonight we arranged a password—in case the wrong man had survived!"

BRIAN saw a smallish, dapper man who might have been an accountant or a bank manager, but couldn't possibly be a detective, except that it happened he was.

He jumped up as they came in.

"Bamboo!" Nayland Smith greeted (presumably the arranged password). "Virtue triumphed for once in a while, Harkness!"

Raymond Harkness sat down again. "Thank God I see you alive! It was a crazy, and, in my opinion, an unnecessary risk."

Nayland Smith rested his head on Harkness's shoulder.

"Your staff work was excellent. Merrick, here, threatened to disturb the plan at a critical moment. But our luck held, and I held on to Merrick. By the way, you haven't met."

"No." Harkness shook hands with Brian, smiling. "But we have wasted a lot of time covering you, Mr. Merrick! For heaven's sake what happened? Where's . . . the other one? We knew all the details of the trap, but not what it was planned to do when you walked into it."

"An expert job of strangling! He never uttered a sound."

"Good God! They have murdered their own man?" Sir Denis nodded. "What have they done with his body?"

"Still in the room next to ours, I suppose. But if we're to get the whole gang in the bag I want quick action. You have the list of tenants occupying apartments on our floor?"

Harkness held up a typed sheet. "It's been impossible, at short notice, to check all of them. But speaking of the room next to yours——"

"No time, now. Look—I'll tell you what we must do. Hold the elevators on this floor. Instruct operators to tell upcoming passengers to use stairs. There are two elevators but only one stair. Post a good man at the foot of the stair. Order him to direct such passengers to this room. Keep your door open. Tell 'em what you like, but hold 'em."

Harkness raised his eyebrows, but took up the phone and

gave these unwelcome instructions to the hotel office, adding, "To go into force as from now." He hung up, glanced at Nayland Smith. "Well—what about anyone coming *down*?"

"They must be told to go up again until further notified. Police Department orders. An experienced patrolman in uniform best for stair job."

Harkness nodded and spoke again on the phone. Then:

"You're in charge tonight, Sir Denis," he acknowledged, "but we've worked together before and I like to know what to expect. Do you think it's a plot against the President?"

"Not against his life, Harkness," Nayland Smith rapped. "At least, I don't think so. But in any event he won't be here. I gave orders a few minutes ago to have his course diverted."

Raymond Harkness watched Sir Denis with steady eyes.

"Then you believe Fu Manchu is still in Manhattan?"

"I know it."

"Where?"

"In the penthouse!"

"What!" Harkness sprang up. "Then he's holding Dr. Hessian! He's in our hands! What are we waiting for?"

"Go easy!" Nayland Smith smiled his grim smile. "And don't worry about Dr. Hessian. *I'm* looking after him!"

Harkness sat down again. "You know, now that I hear you, and see you, I wonder I ever fell for your double! But at the time I was completely sold."

"So was everybody else. Who but Dr. Fu Manchu could have pulled off such a thing?"

There was a rap on the room door, and a smart-looking police sergeant came in and saluted. Harkness looked up.

"Ah! It's Sergeant Ruppert. I knew you were detailed for duty here tonight. I want you to mount guard at the foot of the stair to the floor above. Stand on the other side of the door. No need to alarm residents on this floor. Anyone wanting to go up to be directed to this apartment. Make sure they come here, but don't lose sight of the staircase exit. Anyone coming down to be sent back—*anyone*. All clear?"

"All ready, sir. But what about the elevators?"

"They've been stopped from this floor upward." Harkness glanced at Nayland Smith. "Anything else?"

"One thing," Sir Denis rapped. "Jump to it, Sergeant! Every minute counts!" Sergeant Ruppert saluted and ran out. "Any news from Number One, Harkness?"

Raymond Harkness shook his head. "No. Can't figure it out. She expected to have something to report on the latest move. It could be useful. But not a word. And I can't locate her. I hope——"

"So do I." There was a deep sincerity in Nayland Smith's voice. "She takes risks few men would take—and Fu Manchu is merciless . . . ."

"How many have you on duty tonight, Harkness?" Nayland Smith asked. "Without Merrick and myself?"

"Eleven. Four F.B.I.s and, on the present occasion, nine police. Four in uniform, including the sergeant, and five plain-clothes men. If I can count Number One, twelve."

"Assemble them all here. There are seven apartments upstairs, including mine. I want them all searched. You have keys from the management?"

"Here."

"I'll take the key of the stair door to the penthouse and the key of the inside door."

Harkness passed over three keys. "There are two doors to the penthouse," he explained. "The second I believe opens into a kitchen."

"And now, can you lend Merrick a gun?"

"Sure." Harkness pulled a drawer open and took out a regulation police revolver. "It isn't easy to carry, Mr. Merrick, but it's practical."

"Thanks."

Brian put the heavy weapon in a coat pocket. He didn't know what was going to happen, but the more exciting it turned out to be the better he would like it. He needed an antidote to his mood of angry self-contempt.

"Let the whole party stand by, Harkness," Sir Denis went on in his quick-fire way, "until I give the word. Merrick and I are going to do a spot of reconnaissance. If a trap is being laid we don't want to walk into it."

They met no one in the long corridor as they headed towards the elevators. The door to the stair, with a red light

649

above it, was in a side passage a few paces beyond. It was that hour which comes in every big hotel when nearly all the guests are out for the evening.

Suddenly, Nayland Smith said something which brought Brian to a stop as though he had hit a wall.

"I pray no harm has come to Lola Erskine," he rapped.

Brian made a gasping sound; stood stock still. Sir Denis paused, looked back, and then stared, amazed, at the suddenly pale face he saw behind him.

"Merrick! What's wrong? Are you ill?"

Brian tried hard to recover poise. It wasn't easy.

"I'm sorry—behaving like a fool. But you *did* say Lola Erskine?"

"I did. What about it?"

"Is she the woman you called Number One, who was expected to report to Mr. Harkness?"

"She is." Nayland Smith stared hard. "She's the star operative I mentioned to you, who had worked her way into the Reds' confidence, and from there (an even more astonishing undercover feat) into the Secret Order of the Si-Fan. Have you met her?"

"Yes." Brian spoke hoarsely, but had himself in hand again. "In London."

"In London? Then it was she who sent the information that you had been employed by Red agents. Wonderful girl! She was the first person to suspect my double. You see, Merrick she was working close to Dr. Fu Manchu! Just think of that! A mere girl—and a very pretty one; she met me at Idlewild—getting away with such a thing!"

"I *am* thinking, Sir Denis, and I'm frightened stiff. Because, you see, I'm very fond of Lola."

Nayland Smith smiled—the smile Brian remembered.

"Ho, ho! That's how the wind blows! I'm frightened, too. First, I owe my freedom to her. She was responsible for the search of the house in Cairo. Second, I owe her my life. She learned all about the trap set for me here, briefing me (I knew all the routine), and was instrumental in getting my double's instructions mixed up."

Brian clenched his fists. "If Dr. Fu Manchu knows the truth, Sir Denis, he must know——"

"That Lola Erskine has double-crossed him? . . . That's why I'm frightened."

They had been standing still in the long passage, talking in hushed voices; and now:

"Come on!" Nayland Smith rapped. "We must act."

He set off at a run. As they passed the elevators and turned into the passage where a red light shone above the stair door, Brian found himself wondering if a girl like Lola could possibly give a damn for such a despicable, distrustful creature as himself. . . .

Nayland Smith pulled the heavy door open.

"Hullo! What's this?"

There was no one there!

"Where's Sergeant Ruppert?" Brian cried out.

Sir Denis raised his hand. "Ssh! We don't know who may be listening. But I don't like it. Come on—and be ready for anything."

He started up the stair, walking softly, one hand in a pocket of his tweed jacket. At the top he peered out cautiously along the corridor. It was empty from end to end. He banged his fist into the palm of his left hand.

"I should have known better than to rely on one man in dealing with Fu Manchu!"

"What do you figure happened? He didn't call out. We'd have heard him!"

"*When* it happened is what worries me. How long has this stair been open? Stand by, Merrick. Have your gun handy. If anyone comes near you, cover him and make him stand still, hands up, until I return."

And Nayland Smith darted back down the stairs. . .

"When it had happened" was fully twenty minutes earlier.

Apartment 421 was across the passage and not far from Nayland Smith's suite. A smartly-dressed woman, her beauty hall-marked with the stamp of sophistication which some men (particularly young ones) find irresistible, had just come in. She had not long returned from Idlewild where Dr. Fu Manchu had ordered her to go to report the instant of Sir Denis's arrival. She had means of learning such things, for beauty is a key which opens many doors.

651

Wearily she tossed an expensive hat on to the bed and sat down in front of her mirror. She opened a cream leather jewel case, unstrapped a conspicuous, diamond-studded wrist-watch and was about to put it away when a voice spoke—apparently coming from the watch.

"Where are you now?"

She started, stooped forward, and answered, "Back in my room, Doctor."

"No one obstructed you?"

"No one."

"You have done well. You were only just in time. But there is more to do. Put the amethyst ring on your finger. It is live. Be careful not to turn the bezel until needed. Remember the volume is low. Direct contact is necessary. Wear the diamond watch also. You understand?"

"I understand."

"Your freedom is in your hands tonight."

The woman's eyes opened widely. They were of the colour of the ring which Dr. Fu Manchu had ordered her to wear—amethyst—and, with her auburn hair, gave her an exotic beauty. Her delicate colour paled as she spoke:

"You mean—my complete freedom?"

"Your absolute freedom. The task I am giving you shall be your last. So you cannot afford to fail. These are your orders. . . ."

As an immediate result of those orders, Sergeant Mike Ruppert, taking up his station at the foot of the stairs, a post which he expected to find very dull, had just ventured to start a cigarette when he heard light footsteps descending.

He dropped he cigarette and put his foot on it, turned—and saw a vision.

A disturbingly attractive woman was coming down. From her slender foot, her arched instep, to the flaming crown of her wonderful hair, Sergeant Ruppert found no flaw in her beauty. He began to rack his memory, convinced that she must be a film star. For he suffered from a fixed idea that Hollywood had a corner in such feminine perfection.

She smiled alluringly, and made to pass him.

Sergeant Ruppert intruded his bulk. "Sorry, lady. No one allowed down this way."

"What do you mean, Sergeant?" She had an enchanting accent. "I live here. You can't keep a guest a prisoner!"

The sergeant wasn't enjoying his job. "Department orders, miss. There's—er—some inquiry going on. It'll be all clear soon."

"Soon! But my friend is waiting."

"He'll wait!" Sergeant Ruppert grinned.

A ghost of the smile stole back to the lovely face.

"*He* is a *she*, my sergeant! But please let me go. It is bad enough that the elevators are out of order, that I have to walk up and down. But this!"

"That's right." The sergeant was sympathetic. "But it's not my fault, miss. All I can do is obey orders,"

"It is so stupid!" she pouted. "Never again do I stay at the Babylon-Lido! I shall go up and call the manager. Come with me. You shall hear that I am to be allowed to go out."

"Sorry, miss. I'd like nothing better——"

"I can give you a nice cool drink while I phone."

Sergeant Ruppert had never heard of St. Anthony, but he was going through similar fires. Years of discipline won. Dizzy but unconquered:

"I can't leave my post, miss," he told her.

"*Ah, parbleu!*" she sighed. ("French," the sergeant decided!) "So I am imprisoned—yes?"

"It's not as bad as that, lady. I'll tell you what you do. I don't think it's meant for a young lady like you to be inconvenienced. So go back to your apartment and call the manager like you said. Ask him to speak to the officer in charge, and——"

She turned away impulsively. "It is preposterous! All this trouble! . . . Ah! *mon Dieu!*" She stumbled, turned back, clutched Sergeant Ruppert. "I twist my ankle!"

Her slender hands—he noted a great violet ring (the colour of her eyes!) on one white finger—slipped around his neck. Her touch made him tremble. And this moment of emotion was the last thing he remembered. . . . She had turned the bezel.

He experienced a sensation as though he had been clubbed on the back of his head—and knew no more.

She had carried out her last task—for she couldn't afford to

653

fail. In a fractional moment she reversed the bezel—a miniature receiver, tuned to pick up the lethal note from the transmitter in the penthouse. But as the big, good-looking policeman pitched forward and fell on his face, tears dimmed her eyes. She raised the jewelled wrist-watch. Her hands trembled when she adjusted the cunning radio mechanism.

"It is done!" she whispered.

"Good. Do not return to your apartment. Whatever you leave behind there shall be recovered or replaced. Walk down one more floor. Then use the elevator. You have money with you?"

"As you ordered, Doctor."

"Avoid observation going out. Use a side entrance. Take a taxi to East 74th Street at Park Avenue. A man will be standing outside the drug store on the corner. He will wear evening dress and a red rose in his buttonhole. Say 'Si-Fan' and he will make all arrangements. Your life is your own. . . ."

BRIAN'S VIGIL at the stair-head proved something of a tax on his nerves.

If the strange and oddly sinister figure who had dominated the meeting in the penthouse was none other than Dr. Fu Manchu then his uneasy feeling in the presence of the man he had accepted as Otto Hessian called for no further explanation. During the journey from Egypt he had had a strong inclination to avoid him, and, as he now recalled clearly, the bogus Nayland Smith had encouraged him to do so, saying, "He has the brains of a genius but the manners of a gorilla. . . ."

And now, the fabulous Dr. Fu Manchu was near, on the defensive, at bay!

Already he had spirited away a physically powerful police officer, armed and keenly alert to danger. . . .

In the long, lighted corridor there was unbroken silence. Guests occupying the several apartments were probably away for the evening, he assumed—unless (a disturbing thought) there were other apartments as well as that adjoining their own which harboured servants of the Chinese doctor. He saw again, mentally, the two Asiatic assassins dragging away the body of the unfortunate double.

Perhaps they had strangled Sergeant Ruppert!

He changed his position slightly, so that he had his back to a wall; tried to blot out a ghastly memory of the dead man's face, and to call up the image of Lola.

What had happened to her? He seemed to have lived through another life since that wonderful hour in her room. In fact, during this one day he had experienced every emotion of which humanity is capable. Love, when he held Lola in his arms; horror, and a great fear, when he saw Nayland Smith lying dead on the floor. And fear had come again—fear that he was insane—when *another* Nayland Smith had appeared.

The belief, the conviction, that Lola was nothing more than a decoy of Dr. Fu Manchu's had brought a sorrow such as he had never known. . . . And now when he knew the truth—she had gone!

A faint sound broke the silence of the corridor.

Brian stood, tense, almost holding his breath, listening.

The sound came from the stair.

He pulled out the big revolver, readied it for action, and slightly turned his head, looking down. Soft footsteps were mounting the stair. He raised the barrel, sighting it on the bend at which the person coming up would appear.

No one appeared. But a snappy voice came:

"Don't shoot, Merrick!"

It was Nayland Smith. A moment later he stood beside Brian. "Phew!" Brian felt hot all over. "Glad you spoke!"

"So I see," Sir Denis commented dryly. "But don't relax your vigilance. We have the situation in hand, if——"

"If what?"

"If we're not too late." Nayland Smith spoke in a low tone. "First, we go to our own apartment. Don't open your mouth while I try to call the penthouse. Remember, the room has been wired."

Brian nodded, and they walked along to 420B. Nayland Smith unlocked the door, stood for a moment listening, and then went in. He crossed straight to the penthouse phone, lifted the receiver, held it to his ear awhile and then put it back. He frowned grimly; beckoned Brian to follow and went out of the apartment.

"Step as nearly like a cat as you can," he whispered. "I'm going up to listen at the door. If I hear anything we won't go in alone. We'll wait for reinforcements."

Fighting down a growing excitement (for Lola might be a prisoner there!), Brian watched while Sir Denis quietly unlocked the door to the penthouse stair.

They stole up.

The stair opened on a landing, and the door was nearly opposite, as Brian remembered. To their right was the elevator which normally served the penthouse, and beyond, a second door.

Nayland Smith tiptoed forward, apparently with the intention of pressing his hear to a panel—then paused. Closer contact was unnecessary.

A voice was speaking, muffled by the intervening door, but still audible—a strident, sibilant voice:

"Do you imagine," it said scornfully, "that your puny interference can check the wheels of the Inevitable? The dusk of the West has fallen. The dawn of the East has come. . . ."

Nayland Smith turned, a triumphant grin on his lean face; pointed to the stair. Brian followed him down. Sir Denis partly closed the door below.

"You heard him, Merrick—you heard him?" he whispered. "One of his favourite slogans. How often have I listened to it! That's *Dr. Fu Manchu!*"

Brian's heart jumped uncomfortably.

"Who is he talking to?"

"I fear—to Lola Erskine. . . ."

Brian went through hours of torture in the few minutes that it took to muster the party. Harkness had a search-warrant, and two of the plain-clothes men came from Homicide; for there was evidence to show that a murder had been committed on the top floor of the towering wing of the Babylon-Lido.

When duties had been allotted, Harkness and another F.B.I. man joined Brian and Nayland Smith, and all four went up to the penthouse. Harkness and his assistant—his name was Dakin—were to deal with the kitchen entrance; Brian and Sir Denis concentrated on the other door.

They stood for a moment, listening.

Complete silence.

"Get the door open!" Brian gasped, quivering with suspense. "For God's sake, open it!"

Nayland Smith, very grim-faced, put the key in the lock—but never turned it.

"*No, no!*" A stifled scream came from inside. "Don't open that door! It's the end of all of us if you do! Break in at the other end. But don't open that door!"

Lola!

Sir Denis grasped Brian's arm in a grip that hurt. He withdrew the key.

"I don't know what this means, Merrick, but we must do as she directs. Come on!" They ran to join Harkness. "In through the kitchen!"

Harkness unlocked the door. The door swung open.

Brian tried to hurl himself in. Nayland smith grabbed him. "Go easy, Merrick! We can't be sure. This is *my* pidgin."

An automatic in his hand, Sir Denis stepped warily into a well-equipped kitchenette. Brian followed. There were traces of that peculiar chemical smell which he had noted before, on the night of the demonstration.

They pushed on into what was evidently a dining-room. But it didn't appear to have been used for one. The only window was blacked out with heavy velvet drapes. On the buffet odd pieces of chemical apparatus stood, as well as a number of bottles and phials. There was very little furniture except a narrow table covered with green baize and a large chair. A green-shaded lamp stood on the table—the only light in the room.

Near the lamp was a cabinet the front of which consisted of a small switchboard.

"Some kind of radio control," Nayland Smith commented.

"In here! Oh! Be quick!"

Brian, at that wild appeal, pushed past Sir Denis and burst in ahead of everybody.

He stopped so suddenly that he was nearly floored by the rush from behind.

The room in which he had witnessed the extraordinary experiment carried out by the man calling himself Dr. Hessian seemed to swim before his eye. A plan of Manhattan still covered the whole of the top of the long table; but the rows of chairs had been removed. The metal containers which had hung from the ceiling were there no longer. The radio set which produced the "inaudible note" remained in its place on a bureau. A small box, which might have been the one used at the demonstration to represent a specially-equipped plane, stood on one end of the table.

Near by, in a heavy armchair, Lola was seated, white and wild-eyed. Her ankles were lashed to the front legs. Both wrists had been tied to the arms of the chair, but she had managed to free her right hand and to tear off the adhesive tape strapped to her mouth.

It had been done in frantic haste, for her lip was red and swollen.

Brian sprang to her side and began to unfasten her other wrist, but:

"Smash that thing!" she said, in a shrill, unnatural voice, pointing to the little box. "The *Sound* comes from there! Smash it!"

Brian stood upright, and ignoring Nayland Smith who had a hand on his shoulder, pulled out the police revolver and fired two shots into the flimsy framework.

There came a loud explosion, a crash of glass, splinters flew, and one bullet rebounded to be buried in the wall beyond. Then—the box burst into flames!

Dakin acted promptly. Dashing out to the kitchen, he was back in quick time carrying a big pitcher of water. With this, he dowsed the flaming fragments on the table.

When Brian turned—Lola had fainted. . . .

Brian carried Lola downstairs, using the kitchen entrance. Dakin came with him to unlock the door of the suite. All the other doors along the corridor were wide open, and sounds indicated that the search-parties were at work—apparently without success. As Brian laid Lola on the big couch:

"She'll soon pull out of it," Dakin assured him. "Number One has the heart of a lion. If you have any brandy, I think"— he smiled—"I can leave the patient in your hands. I'll leave the key, too."

Dakin retired, closing the outer door. Brian ran to the buffet and was looking for the brandy when he heard Lola's voice:

"I don't think I ever fainted in my life before——"

He turned, ran to her. She was sitting up.

"Lola, my dearest!"

"But I do believe a small glass of brandy would do me good!"

Brian ran back, found the brandy, and poured out a liberal shot.

He knelt beside her, his arm around her shoulders as she took the glass. Lola smiled, that fascinating, mocking smile.

"If I drank all this, Brian, I should faint a second time!"

She took a sip of the brandy, and he drew her to him.

"Lola!" he whispered.

"My lips are sticky from that beastly tape," she protested.

Brian held her very close, but kissed her gently.

"I nearly went crazy when I heard you were missing."

Lola took another sip and then set the glass down. "So you have found me out." She spoke softly. "You know what a little liar I am!"

"I know you have more grit in your little finger than I have in all my hulking carcass!"

"You mean you forgive me for what I had to do?"

"Forgive you!" She raised her hand; checked him.

"Brian, dear, go back now, and let me lie here for five minutes. I shall be quite all right, when I have rested—and cleaned the gum off my face! Then I'll join you."

"Leave you here alone! And Fu Manchu——"

"Fu Manchu is too far away to harm me."

"But we heard his voice!"

"I know you did. He intended you to hear it. But he isn't there! Go up and see for yourself. I'll be with you in a few minutes. . . ."

And when Brian, torn between his desire to stay with Lola and a burning curiosity, returned to the penthouse, he found the proper entrance door open. Harkness was bending over the cabinet which looked like a radio set, the back of which had been removed. Nayland Smith was pacing the room and twitching the lobe of his ear.

"How is she?" he rapped.

"Fine. She's coming up after a little rest. But where's . . . Dr. Fu Manchu?"

Sir Denis pointed to an open drawer of the bureau.

"There—all we have of him! A tape-recorder playing back our conversations in Cairo! If you and I had listened a while longer we should have heard my voice as well! Brought over for the benefit of my successor. The machine had played right through the records. The cunning devil!"

Brian stared about the room incredulously, still half expecting to see the dark spectacles of Dr. Hessian (the only picture he had of the dreaded Fu Manchu) peering out from some shadowy corner.

"But the door! What was the danger of opening the door?"

"The danger's on the table there," Harkness called out. "Three ordinary bell-pushes which were under the carpet where anybody coming in couldn't miss stepping on one of them!"

"Wired to the receiver you shot to pieces!" Sir Denis added

grimly. "If Lola hadn't lost her head (although God knows I don't blame her) we might have disconnected them, and so had the secret of the Sound Zone in our hands!"

"Then the other thing"—Brian nodded towards the cabinet—"was connected all the time?"

"It was. One step, and Lola, as well as everyone else and everything breakable in the penthouse, would have gone West! Which reminds me of something you may be able to tell me. . . . The french windows. You saw the demonstration. Why weren't the windows blown out?"

Brian thought hard; tried to picture this room as he had seen it then—and a memory came.

"I think I can tell you. I remember now that just before Dr. Hessian began to talk, the Japanese lowered what looked like metal shutters over the windows, and then drew those drapes over them."

"Shutters still there," Sir Denis told him. "Couldn't make out if they were a hotel fixture. Now I know, they should be examined. Evidently made of some material non-conductive of the fatal sound."

Harkness stood up from his examination of the cabinet, and lighted a cigarette.

"Fu Manchu planned to leave no evidence, Mr. Merrick," he remarked. "We found a small, but I guess effective, time-bomb inside this thing! Dakin worked with a bomb-disposal squad in England in the war. He's an expert. He's out in the kitchen fixing it."

"You see, Merrick?" Nayland Smith rapped. "I'm naturally proud of Scotland Yard, but your F.B.I. isn't without merit. What d'you make of that set, Harkness?"

"This is by no means an ordinary radio set, Sir Denis. It's some kind of transmitter. Though what it transmits and where it gets it from are mysteries. We haven't tinkered with it. That's a laboratory job. But Dakin thinks it can convert all sorts of sounds into that one, high, inaudible note on which we had a report from Number One. Evidently this note doesn't become dangerous until it has passed through the special receiver——"

"It's the *receiver* that converts the sound," a clear voice explained.

661

All three turned in a flash. Lola stood there smiling at them. Sir Denis was first with a chair. Lola thanked him and sat down.

"If you feel up to it, Miss Erskine," he said quietly, "perhaps you would explain in more detail."

"I feel up to anything. Particularly, I feel like an idiot for getting hysterical and then passing out! You see, Sir Denis, *he*" (she seemed to avoid naming Dr. Fu Manchu, as Nayland Smith had known others to do), "was good enough to give me all particulars before leaving me to be shattered. The transmitter, he informed me, is really a sort of selector, or filter. It picks up only certain high notes, vocal or instrumental. On an ordinary receiving set this would come through as atmospheric interference. It was the thing that Brian blew up which converted the sound to what *he* called 'the super-aural key' which shatters everything within range."

She glanced up as Dakin returned from the kitchen quarters.

"It's harmless now, sir," he reported to Nayland Smith. "We have saved *some* evidence."

Another member of Harkness's party appeared in the doorway.

"What now?" Harkness demanded.

"Doc Alex reports that he's suffering from thundering concussion . . . but there isn't a single bruise on his head!"

"Who's this?" Brian asked excitedly.

"Sergeant Ruppert."

"Sergeant Ruppert! Where did you find him?"

"In 420C, the apartment of our next-door neighbours," Nayland Smith told him dryly, "while you were taking care of Miss Erskine." He turned to the man at the door. "Does the doctor think he will recover?"

"He does, sir—and hopes there'll be no complications."

"They found a dead man in there, too, Mr. Merrick," Harkness broke in. "You mightn't recognize him, the way he looks now. But up till today we all mistook him for Sir Denis!"

"I know! But the man in a blue turban?"

"Prince Ranji Bhutani?" Harkness laughed. "He and his horrible-looking servant have vanished, of course. I don't imagine the 'prince' was wearing his blue turban! They must have got away soon after strangling your double, Sir Denis. We had that pair under observation already and there's a fifty-fifty chance we pick them up."

"If Sergeant Ruppert was found there, they evidently got him, too!"

Ray Harkness shook his head. "Four guests on your floor, Mr. Merrick, checked out earlier today. We don't know if any of them belonged to the gang. Only one, Mrs. Nadia Narovska, has disappeared like the 'prince' and left her luggage behind: Number 421. Said to be a very good-looker."

"But she may be coming back," Brian pointed out.

"The management report she came in only a few minutes before the elevator was stopped and the sergeant went on duty at the stair door. How did she get out?"

"But it would be impossible for her to have overpowered a big fellow like that!"

"If she belonged to Fu Manchu," Nayland Smith said bitterly, "and she sounds like one of his women, nothing is impossible! I haven't settled down yet to the fact that that cunning fiend has escaped me again. In my crazy over-confidence I missed my chance. It was my duty to the world when I stood before him to shoot him dead."

He banged his fist into the palm of his left hand.

"They all slipped away in whatever time they had from the attack on Ruppert until Merrick and I came upstairs," Sir Denis went on. "Once on street level, Manhattan was open to them. Our hush-hush policy has defeated its own ends."

"It's not so black as you paint it," Harkness insisted. "We may have lost the secret of this wonderful air-cover, but if the price Uncle Sam had to pay for it was putting our defences in the hands of Dr. Fu Manchu, we gain more than we lose."

Nayland Smith forced a smile.

"You may be right. Dr. Fu Manchu has still to get out of the country. . . . Oh, Merrick, Miss Erskine has passed through a frightful ordeal. I suggest you take her along for a champagne cocktail and a good dinner. Dine downstairs. I'll page you when your father arrives. . . . We shall all have many things to talk about. . . . And I can see that you have a lot of things to say to Lola. . . ."

ALLISON & BUSBY CRIME

Jo Bannister
A Bleeding of Innocents
Sins of the Heart
Burning Desires

Brian Battison
The Witch's Familiar

Simon Beckett
Fine Lines
Animals

Ann Cleeves
A Day in the Death of
Dorothea Cassidy
Killjoy

Denise Danks
Frame Grabber
Wink a Hopeful Eye
The Pizza House Crash

John Dunning
Booked to Die

John Gano
Inspector Proby's Christmas

T.G. Gilpin
Missing Daisy

Bob George
Main Bitch

Russell James
Slaughter Music

J. Robert Janes
Sandman

H. R. F. Keating
A Remarkable Case of
Burglary

Ted Lewis
Billy Rags
Get Carter
GBH
Jack Carter's Law
Jack Carter and the
Mafia Pigeon

Ross Macdonald
Blue City
The Barbarous Coast
The Blue Hammer
The Far Side of the Dollar
Find a Victim
The Galton Case
The Goodbye Look
The Instant Enemy
The Ivory Grin
The Lew Archer Omnibus
Vol 1

The Lew Archer Omnibus
Vol 2
The Lew Archer Omnibus
Vol 3
Meet Me at the Morgue
The Moving Target
Sleeping Beauty
The Underground Man
The Way Some People Die
The Wycherly Woman
The Zebra-Striped Hearse

Priscilla Masters
Winding Up The Serpent

Margaret Millar
Ask for Me Tomorrow
Mermaid
Rose's Last Summer
Banshee
How Like An Angel
The Murder of Miranda
A Stranger in My Grave
The Soft Talkers

Jennie Melville
The Woman Who Was Not There

Frank Palmer
Dark Forest

Sax Rohmer
The Fu Manchu Omnibus
Volume I
The Fu Manchu Omnibus
Volume II

Frank Smith
Fatal Flaw

Richard Stark
The Green Eagle Score
The Handle
Point Blank
The Rare Coin Score
Slayground
The Sour Lemon Score
The Parker Omnibus
Volume 1

Donald Thomas
Dancing in the Dark

I. K. Watson
Manor
Wolves Aren't White

Donald Westlake
Sacred Monsters
The Mercenaries
The Donald Westlake Omnibus